# TRANSIT
## TALES OF MYSTERY, HISTORY, AND CRIME

*Portrait, E.M. Schorb*
*Sculpture by Natale de la Padura, "The Writer"*

# TRANSIT
## TALES OF MYSTERY, HISTORY, AND CRIME

### E.M. SCHORB

**HILL HOUSE**          **NEW YORK**

ISBN: 978-0-578-77900-3

Cover Design: Selah Bunzey
Cover Painting "Mister Mask" by the Author

ACKNOWLEDGEMENTS

The two novels, *Paradise Square* and *Needleneck* (originally titled *Scenario for Scorsese*) were published by Denlinger's Publishers Ltd. *Paradise Square* won the Grand Prize for Fiction at the Frankfurt Book Fair and was later re-printed by the Authors Guild and subsequently re-printed, as was Needleneck, by Hill House. "Murder in the Family" is an abbreviated version of the Cherokee McGhee-published novel *Fortune Island*. "Murder on the Road," under the title "Bad Trip" appeared in the Hopewell Publications anthology, *Best New Writing 2015*. Other stories included in this collection originally appeared in: Mystery Weekly Magazine, OffCourse Literary Journal, Blue Ridge Literary Services, Ginosko Literary Journal, The Roanoke Review, Salzburg Review (Austria), and Mike Shayne Mystery Magazine.

# INTRODUCTION

*TRANSIT*, as its subtitle says, is a passage through *tales of mystery, history, and crime*. You must embark on that journey yourself. I will tell you about some of my experiences at stops along the way.

*Paradise Square* is the novel that introduced me to E M Schorb. As I said at that time, it deserves to be read simply because of the use of the English language. Schorb writes in a style that aligns the book with contemporary literature of the period that he writes about. That is not an easy feat. If you're a fan of Poe you should read it too. And if you've seen (or plan to see) Scorsese's 'Gangs of New York' (Schorb's novel preceded Scorsese's film), then come and visit the Five Points district of New York, so capably brought to life here.

As a writer, *Pour Les Oiseaux* captures my soul. And I hope, as a reader, it will do the same for you. It's short, humorous, and quirky. Each sentence is pecked out, just like a bird. As it should be. And I should be honest: birds do capture me. Our swallows have just left for Africa after spending the summer with us and teaching their young to fly. It brings to mind Colm McCann's novel, *Apeirogon*, set in Israel and Palestine. It starts, disarmingly, describing the hills as the birds' migratory highway; five hundred species of birds torrent through, riding different levels in the sky. And I cannot forget Dickey's fascination with human reincarnation as birds. In his poem *Reincarnation II*, he describes a man, reincarnated as a bird, on his long flight towards the Southern Cross, always dreaming of his life as a man. So, in his own way, Schorb has incarnated man as bird in *Pour Les Oiseaux*.

*A Man of Conscience* explores torture, terrorism, fascism, and conscience. Forgiveness is considered but the pain of loss and the unintended act of retribution are a mirror into the wars and disputes on our planet today. But wars are always here and forgiveness is rare. One rare example of forgiveness is found in Michael Longley's poem *Ceasefire :..... Achilles took him by the hand and pushed the old king gently away, but Priam curled up at his feet and wept with him until their sadness filled the building......Priam good-looking still and full of conversation, who earlier had sighed: I go down on my knees and do what must be done and kiss Achilles' hand, the killer of my son.*

*Murder in the Family* is the heart of Schorb's novel, *Fortune Island.* In his skilled hands, *Fortune Island* becomes a laboratory where he explores the depths and the heights of the human condition. On one level, it's a story of man's struggle to make a living and brave the elements on this isolated island. On a deeper level, it's a tale of childhood abuse, the exploitation of women, and the failure of men. Schorb takes us into the dark soul of the Carolinas, from the mountains to the sea to the Outer Bank. It's an isolated place, home to only a few. But his story lifts the people of the island out of their isolation and shows their roots in a larger diaspora; the background of all Americans, even those who live in the most remote places. We meet Jessie Judas, a marine biologist and author, basking in international fame, as she faces an early death from a terminal illness. We also meet her as a young girl, daughter of a mountain girl turned hooker and a seafaring hillbilly turned jailbird. Jessie commands center stage in this saga. It's her story, a tale of her achievement, an achievement of the mind despite her lack of an early education. A fine poet, Schorb weaves Jessie's past and present into a seamless saga. The power of unselfish love is demonstrated through Jessie's father, whom she does not know. In Ruth, a writer who adopts

Jessie, Schorb has created a person of character, a lady who chooses the value of life's work over the value of great wealth, and who lives life with passion.

*Needleneck*: This great story begins in a bar called The Saints and Sinners Club. You've been in bars like The Saints and Sinners Club. I know you have. I certainly have. And I'm sure you have met a Father Michael Din, a young priest who never had a vocation. So easy to be groomed as an altar boy, promised to God by his father, and committed to the life by a politically powerful Bishop. You will meet Father Din in this bar and you'll be there when he meets Toddy Muir, an unusual young lady. And so commences a journey for him in the Needleneck neighborhood. A journey that lets you explore the humanity that crosses his path: Christians, Muslims, Atheists, non-believers, white, black, Palestinian, Asian, drug dealers, drug addicts. A true American melting pot. A neighborhood of junkies, muggings and robberies, but one gentrifying with lots of artists and galleries moving in. The story is presented in six parts, six acts of a grand play. It's a drama of passion and pain, love and loss. But always driven by dialogue that lets you enter the hearts, minds, and souls of the diverse characters that populate Needleneck.

Read *TRANSIT* to be captured by characters who are brought to life more vividly than any you've encountered before. Read it to be enthralled by dialogue so real that you are taken inside the life of each. Read it to feel the poetic resonance of the language. Read it to experience E M Schorb, a writer who will, from now on, stand at the top of your reading list.

*—Pat Mullan, poet, essayist,*
*member, International Thriller Writers*

*for Patricia*

*I wish to prove . . . that nothing is explained
in the mysteries which surround us.*

*—Jois-Karl Huysmans*

# CONTENTS

# PARADISE SQUARE

*About what happened during the days of which we have no record we can believe anything we choose, including either that Poe had spent his time in a drunken debauch or that he did not drink anything at all. Extant testimonials simply cancel each other out, and there is no way, at this date, to determine who is telling the truth.*

> —Edward Wagenknecht
> *Edgar Allan Poe*
> *The Man Behind the Legend*

## Chapter 1

### I FIND POE

I found Edgar Poe at the Old Brewery, seated at a table in a taper-lit, basement room, his large head resting on his folded arms, in a drunken, obviously troubled sleep.

It had not been difficult to find him. I had simply followed the trail of the "reciting poet" from diving bell to diving bell, as these basement rum-parlors are called, at the last of which it had been overheard that he, in company with "some other Irishmen," was going to the Old Brewery to pass the night. The "other Irishmen" may have been those who slept noisily at the table with Poe.

Apparently, he had not been robbed or brutalized, probably because he did not look like a man who had any money. He was unshaven and dirty, his suit threadbare and his linen

soiled. An unpromising picture of a man in whom Peter Van-
Brunt, and, to a lesser degree, I myself, had placed hope.

Chapter 2

THE FIVE POINTS

The intersection of Anthony, Little Water, Cross,
Orange, and Mulberry Streets gave the name Five Points to
New York's most infamous slum. At the center of this intersection was Paradise Square, a fenced-in plot of sparse grass
and caked mud serving the purpose of a small park. If Paradise Square was the geographical center of the Five Points,
the Old Brewery was its dark heart. One block north of Paradise Square, it was built as Coulter's Brewery in 1792, and
became famous in the eastern states for its brew. By 1837, it
was abandoned, and claimed by squatters, eventually housing
over a thousand men, women, and children, black and white,
a large proportion of whom had no other means to earn their
sparse living but by gambling, harlotry, thievery and violence. It averaged a murder a night. Seldom were the murderers brought to book. The police did not have the numbers required for an invasion of such a thug-infested tenement.

The Municipal Police, even patrolmen, wore no uni-
forms at this time, a policy I was to play a part in changing,
but that served the purpose of anonymity at the moment. I had
pocketed my copper star, which I sometimes wore pinned to
my breast pocket, even though I had lately been assigned as a
detective, and had no need to wear it, and had been as careful
as possible to be inconspicuous. A copper caught in the Old
Brewery had little chance of leaving it alive. I reached across
the table and tapped Poe on the shoulder. He jerked awake
like a man to whom healthy sleep is unknown. I spoke in a
whisper.

"Mr. Poe?"

"Yes, I think so," he said, rubbing his eyes. "In any case, his remains."

"I am Sergeant Jonathan Goode of the Municipal Police," I said, and quickly stated my business. When Poe had heard enough, he gathered himself and followed me out through the catacomb-like passages of the Old Brewery.

Outside, I could see the damage Poe had done himself.

I knew him to be between thirty-five and forty years of age; but, at the moment, he looked much older. He was ashen, his gray restless eyes shot with a web of hemorrhaged veins. He was a bit below middle height, but carried his sturdy physique in a military manner, and could not be described as a small man. His temples and forehead were remarkably prominent; his mouth and jaw determined, decisive. He wore black from hat to heel. Hat, frockcoat, gloves, and boots had seen better days, but "gentleman" was written all over him.

I knew he must be attended before we could proceed to our business.

"We'll get you a room at Red Kate's Emerald Isle. Mr. VanBrunt stays there. You can get a meal, a bath, and a change of linen. Unless, of course, you have a place."

"I believe I had one, but I can't remember where. In any case, I doubt if I should be welcomed back."

"If I may ask, sir, where have you been sleeping?"

"On tables, I should think—or under them. I have no money, I'm afraid."

"I'll tend to everything, Mr. Poe, and you can repay me when you're able."

"That's very good of you, Sergeant. Yes, I shall go to my publisher. He'll have royalties for me." He did not seem very positive about this.

I liked his voice. It was of middle range, and possessed of a soft Southern accent.

This was Wednesday, just before noon, November 15th, 1847, a cold, drizzling day, and one that I shall never forget.

I was wearing my mackintosh. Poe did not seem to notice the rain any more than did the swarming rats, cats, dogs, pigs, horses, or suffering humanity of the Five Points.

Chapter 3

THE EMERALD ISLE

There were scores of dance houses in the Five Points, but Red Kate's Emerald Isle was unusual, if not unique, in being a hotel-boarding house on its upper stories and a dance hall-saloon at street level. It was an emerald-green clapboard building, with windows ornamented in red bombazine. From the saloon ceiling hung hoop chandeliers filled with candles. Sand was liberally distributed on the dance floor to afford better footing for heavy boots. Time had no meaning in the Five Points, for regularity of employment did not exist for the great mass of its denizens, and the music never stopped in the dance houses. Morning, noon, and night, the hornpipe and fiddle bit at drunken ears and gave rhythm to the staggering. As we approached, the lively fiddle strains of "The Land of the Potato O" could be heard emanating from within.

"I know this place," said Poe. "I've been here. In fact, it was here that I ran into VanBrunt. I remember now that he said something about getting married. Was he speaking of the murdered girl?"

"Yes, sir, I believe he must have been."

Poe took the lead and made his way through the crowd to the oaken bar.

Red Kate was a plump, pretty woman in her late thirties, henna-haired, with a wide-eyed, bow-lipped face, and rough voice, who had started out as something under a cab moll, or madam, and worked her way up to something like legitimacy. It was said that she could be violent to the point of ferocity when crossed. Behind her was a large glass jar, on hideous

4

display, containing ears which, it was said, Kate had bitten from the heads of difficult customers. She was busy with a customer up the bar.

I gave Poe the chance to down a beer and a few free black sturgeon caviar sandwiches, and called Kate over.

"'Lo, copper!"

"Hello, Kate. I'd like you to meet Mr. Edgar Allan Poe, the writer. He's a friend of Mr. VanBrunt's. He's going to try to help him."

"I met Mr. Poe, but he probably don't remember. He was with Peter on Saturday night, and something the worse for wear."

"Madam." Poe attempted to click his rundown heels, and nodded his head in a courtly bow.

"Mr. Poe needs a room—and some tending."

"*No-Nose!*" Red Kate boomed over the dance-house din, "*No-Nose Mullins!*" In a moment, a long haired, black-bearded giant emerged from the dancers on the floor.

Poe was self-possessed in not showing the shock everyone felt when first confronted with No-Nose Mullins. In place of the missing feature, the huge bouncer wore a scrimshanked ivory nose, held in place by two cat-gut thongs tied behind his neck and head. He was Kate's bodyguard and general factotum.

"Yes, ma'am," he said, presenting himself.

"Take Mr. Poe here to a room, get him a tub of hot water, let him bathe, shave, give him a massage, and when he's ready, I'll send up some food. Take a bottle of good rum and some glasses along."

I saw rebellion flicker in Poe's eyes, and his firm jaw set; but Kate knew her men. The "bottle of good rum" mollified him.

"I am in your debt, madam." Poe bowed and followed Mullins into the upper regions of the place.

"Can he help?" Kate asked doubtfully.

"You can't judge a poet by his boots, Kate."

Kate and I had a lunch of pigs' feet, boiled potatoes, bread, and beer. The food at the Emerald Isle was very bad, but for me that day it was on the house, so I didn't complain, and contented myself while eating with listening to Red Kate sing—

> *Faith, if such was my lot,*
> *Little Ireland's the spot*
> *Where I'd build my snug cot,*
> *With a bit of garden to it O!*
>
> *And I'd ne'er places come,*
> *Nor abroad ever roam*
> *But enjoy my sweet home*
> *In the land of the potato O . . .*

Within the hour we joined Poe in his room. A bath had put some color in his face, and the rum had animated him.

Kate seemed to find his rugged, Celtic good looks, and courtly, Southern manner attractive. In a half-hour, she told him to call her Kate and asked if she could call him Eddie.

"Indeed, Kate," he said, "all my friends call me Eddie."

"Sir, are you prepared to hear more of the circumstances of the murder?"

Poe drew on a slim green cheroot. Smoke swirling about his head, he said:

"Fire away, Sergeant!"

Chapter 4

THE HIDEOUS MURDER OF THE HOT CORN GIRL

"The details are as follows, sir. The victim was a Hot Corn Girl. Perhaps you've seen them, vending corn on the cob. They appear around dusk, and mingle with the crowds on the sidewalks and in the dance houses. They're on the streets until late November, the end of harvest season. Some of the girls are followed by young bloods who hurl brickbats at any cove who dares to flirt with them. Mary Hart, the victim, apparently had no such champion. She entered Paradise Square, and, in a matter of seconds, a scream was heard. Mr. VanBrunt was discovered kneeling over her body, holding a cleaver. A short time before, he was at the bar downstairs, drunk, and saying that he intended to propose to her. He had been seeing her for some time. *He* says, that, after leaving here, he made his way, with a few stops at diving bells, to Paradise Square. The Square has a fence around it and, as you may have noticed, sir, the women in the neighborhood use it as a clothes-line, thus generally blocking any view of the interior. There are two entrances to the park, one to the east and one to the west. He says that as he approached the east gate he heard a scream, and ran the remaining few yards into the Square, where he found Mary Hart, in a butchered condition, the cleaver by her side.

"There was a gang of street urchins at the east entrance. They gather there constantly and collect a bit of change from the women for guarding the laundry, and spend their time dicing and fighting over the spoils. The only witness to come forward is a clubfooted boy who seems to have no other name than the 'Gimp.' He's a hardcase of about sixteen. Most of the boys are much younger. I imagine the Gimp hangs about to take advantage of the younger boys. He's a cruel little brute who tortures animals. As a patrolman, I've had occasion to caution him on that. In any case, the others ran off at the first stir of trouble. Apparently, the Gimp's deformed foot prevented him from taking a similar flight. He says that he heard a scream, looked in at the west gate, where he alone had been posted, and saw Mr. VanBrunt."

Poe mused for a moment, then said: "What exactly is it that you wish me to do, Sergeant?"

I asked to speak with Poe in private. When Red Kate and Mullins had gone downstairs, I said:

"It was Mr. VanBrunt who suggested that I enlist your aid, sir. He said you would help him—and me."

"I owe Peter VanBrunt a great debt. He and I were classmates at West Point."

"He told me that, sir."

"Did he tell you the circumstances?"

"No, sir."

"I was forced to leave West Point under a cloud. There were social obligations at the Point, and I was unable to meet them because my stepfather did not give me an adequate allowance. I refused to attend classes until my allowance was increased. He refused to increase it, though it was clearly inadequate, and I was expelled. I had bills, and had had to borrow from other cadets. Peter pressed a sum upon me, so that I could pay back the others, and not leave feeling that I'd abused anyone's friendship. I regret to say, I've never been in a position to repay him. Yes, Sergeant, I'm certainly willing to help Peter VanBrunt. But why do *you* need my help?"

"Well, sir, it requires a bit of an explanation. Would you do me the honor of hearing me out?"

"Please proceed."

I hesitated as to how to proceed, then plunged on as best I could. "One day I was hunting quail in New Jersey with my cousin, and he asked me if I'd like to take his place as a leatherhead—"

"A leatherhead?"

"A patrolman. Down here in the Five Points we wear leather helmets, our only uniform. Somebody's always throwing a brickbat at you. My cousin was going to quit, having come upon a profitable venture, and 'Boss' Meade, the alderman of this ward, the Sixth, fondly known as 'the Butcher' because he began his career as one, had given him the chance to name his successor. Aldermen nominate men from their districts. Well, I had no work, and thought I might as well carry a club until something better came along. When my cousin resigned, I was sworn in. Then I learned that my cousin had paid Meade a hundred dollars to set me up, and that such bribes are common practice. Furthermore, my cousin had paid double the usual rate of fifty dollars to by-pass the residency laws, which state that a police candidate has to have resided in the area where he is to work for at least five years, and has to remain in that district after appointment. I had never set foot in the Five Points, and still live in Green-wich Village. Though nowhere near of your caliber, sir, I am a literate man, and harbor a hope yet of someday writing something worth while."

"The writing life is a harder one than you may imagine," said Poe. "But carry on."

"I've paid my cousin back, but I feel as if I've paid a bribe at second hand."

Poe said: "But Sergeant, you still haven't answered my question."

"I am by way of answering it, sir. If you'll bear with me."

Poe nodded, puffing thoughtfully at his cheroot.

"I was thrown on to patrol without any instructions as to my duties, merely ordered to report to Captain Henchard of the Sixth Ward Station on Anthony Street. Until yesterday morning I was a patrol sergeant. All this is by way of saying, sir, that there are no examinations required to be a Municipal Policeman, no attention whatever paid to the physique or mental qualities of the applicant. Service is for a term of two years, of which I've barely completed one. As for detailment for detective work, which is more healthy than pounding a beat in all kinds of weather, that comes at the whim of the captains, who usually select their favorites for it. In sum, sir, I suspect that I've been put on this case for the very reason that I am *not* qualified, and I resent it. I don't like being used.

More, I've seen Mr. VanBrunt around, on the streets and here at Red Kate's, and I cannot believe he's guilty. The idea of such a man using a cleaver on a young woman is not to be believed. He's a gentleman." I didn't know quite how to put the next bit, so I just blundered ahead. "I've always believed your analysis of the murder of Mary Rogers, in 'The Mystery of Marie Roget,' to be correct. Naturally, when Mr. VanBrunt suggested that I seek your help, I leaped at the opportunity."

"Let me ask you this, Sergeant. Is there no more experienced detective at your station who could help you?"

"As I say, sir, I believe I've been chosen because I am *not* experienced, and so can expect no help from anyone at the station."

"Would you care to explain more fully?"

"There are political implications, sir. Mr. VanBrunt is a friend of Miss Kate's and Miss Kate is no friend of Boss Meade."

"Ah. What about a lawyer? Does VanBrunt have one?"

I laughed. "Kate sent hers to Anthony Street, and Captain Henchard locked him up, saying he was drunk. Now he's in the cell next to Mr. VanBrunt's. I've been told they can't wake him up. He may have been beaten."

Poe said, "Let's beard the lion," and rose to his feet.

Downstairs, at the bar, we stopped to speak with Kate.

"Have you been to see Peter?" Poe asked her.

"Captain Henchard wouldn't let me see him."

Poe shook his head and dropped his cheroot in a spittoon.

Red Kate said: "Peter didn't kill that girl, Eddie. He's just a party balloon filled with a wind of blarney. It was the drink that made him think he was young again, and in love with a girl half his age."

"I understand," said Poe, but there was a cast of doubt in his gray eyes.

"Wait now," said Kate. "I think you should take my man

Mullins along. The Sergeant's a greenhorn in the Five Points. If you mean to go on with this, Mullins'll be useful. He can get you in where you wouldn't be let, and get people to talk to you as would develop a case of lockjaw if they thought they was talking to coppers."

Chapter 5

WEST POINT TIES

At the Anthony Street station, VanBrunt sat dejectedly on the plank bunk of his damp, basement cell. He was a long thin grizzled blond with watery pale eyes, aquiline nose, and a parted goatee. He was also a former army officer, and at one time a promising magazine illustrator, who had gone to seed, abetted by personal demons. Greeting him, Poe gave his shoulder a push. "Look, I've come to help, as you requested. Try to lift your spirits. Think of our times at Benny Havens' tavern in Highland Falls. He said to me, "I used to call Benny the sole congenial soul at West Point. Of course, that was before Peter befriended me." He gave VanBrunt a wink. "You remember: *We'll sing our reminiscences of Benny Havens, Oh!* You know," he said, turning to me again, "it is the custom for each class to add a stanza to the song before graduation. It must be getting interminable. *Oh, we'll sing our reminiscences of Benny Havens, Oh!* Now, I promise you, Peter, you are not going to die for a murder you did not commit. In the spirit of Benny Havens I have brought you a gift." Poe took the bottle of rum from his coat and gave it to him. VanBrunt seized upon it, taking several breathless drafts. I had not known about the rum. It was strictly forbidden; but I said nothing. Poe was right. VanBrunt needed it.

"Why hasn't Kate come to see me?" he asked, wiping his mouth.

"She tried," I said. "Captain Henchard wouldn't allow

11

it. But I think if she were to try again—now—he'd relent. He knows your background by now."

"Well," VanBrunt persisted, not fully taking in what I had said, "why hasn't she sent a lawyer?"

"She did send her lawyer. He came in drunk, and Captain Henchard locked him up. But I believe he may be willing to release him now. You see, sir, a journalist named McNeil wrote the murder up. He described you as being from an influential family. That changed things. Boss Meade probably would have let you rot otherwise. Captain Henchard told me that your case should be handled gingerly."

"In other words," said Poe, "Meade and Henchard became willing to put an inexperienced detective on the case, to show that something was being done."

"Yes, sir. You see my position. Fortunately," I directed to VanBrunt, "the officer who arrested you only brought you in on suspicion, and that's all you're being held on."

"What about bail?" asked Poe.

"We have no station house bail, as they do in London, sir—a policy we should emulate. Besides, it wouldn't apply in the case of suspicion, particularly suspicion of murder. But we can only hold a suspect for five days without charging him."

VanBrunt downed another draft of rum. Letting the bottle drop into his lap, he said:

"But, Eddie, you haven't asked me if I'm guilty."

"I know you and therefore know that you are not. But say it, if you wish."

"I am innocent."

"You loved her?"

"To know her was to love her, Eddie. She came from a decent shopkeeper's family, but she was too young to have enjoyed its value when misfortune struck. Her father lost his business, and died soon after. Her mother, a blind woman, came upon unimaginable hard times with widowhood. Mary was reared, along with a sister, in poverty. But she never lost her fineness. You *must* find her murderer, Eddie, not just to free me, nor even to clear my name, but to punish the fiend that could harm so dear and lovely a girl."

"Where—*how* did you meet her?"

He shrugged. "It's lost to me now. For years I've been soaking my mind in rum for the express purpose of forgetting. Perhaps I talked to her first in Red Kate's, when she was vending—perhaps it was on the street. I don't remember."

"What is it you are trying to forget?"

"Ah, Eddie. . . everything! You should have had the money, you had the talent. But the money's tainted. My ancestors were cruel, greedy, and stupid, and my guilt at being descended from such men has plagued my life. They killed the red man for his land and scalped him to sell his hair in Europe. It was Dutch trappers who taught the Indian to take scalps. They sold Indian scalps to the Europeans like a kind of novelty fur. And then these sons and grandsons of scalpers, these rich and respectable murderers, disowned me because I left the military to be an artist. I have an artist's sensitive temperament. I drank to forget. And now what character I do have has been weakened by my aimless bohemian life.

"As for Mary, at first I entertained thoughts of seduction with regard to her, but she soon made clear to me that, though not of my so-called exalted origins, she was nevertheless of that natural nobility which would not enter into a dishonorable intrigue. She avowed her love for me, but held that love must prove itself elevating of its object, or be proven false to itself. In short, she challenged me to rise to the lofty, to abjure drink, and to consider marriage. I told you, though you may not remember, as I told everyone at Red Kate's, that I intended to propose marriage. But was that Saturday, or was it Sunday, or Monday?"

"You may have told me on Saturday," said Poe. "I'm not too clear on that myself."

"It was Monday evening," said Mullins, who was standing by. "I was there."

"Monday? The thing is, I was trying—trying to convince myself, perhaps—that I could live up to her idea of my ultimate decency. That's right. We had an appointment to meet in Paradise Square on Monday evening."

I said, "Theory has it that you kept your appointment, made your proposal, which she refused, and murdered her while in a drunken rage."

"No, *no!* I made my announcement, left Red Kate's, stopped at a few diving bells to strengthen my resolve, and went to meet her. As I approached that verminous little plot, I heard a scream. You can't see into the place, Eddie, for all the laundry on the fence, and it was dark. I ran and found her, an angel, butchered like an animal. Oh, God! But we've gone through this before, Sergeant. Don't you believe me?"

"Were there others who saw this," asked Poe—"Heard her *scream* before *you* entered?"

"There was a group of little toughs, dicing." He looked at me. "Have you questioned them?"

"By the time the officer came," I said, "they were part of a crowd. We don't know which boys were there at the time of the murder. We only have the Gimp for witness."

"Is there no way," Poe asked me, "to get Peter out of this dungeon?"

"Oh, yes, sir. Under the Municipal Code, an alderman, who is, ex-officio, a magistrate, can discharge a prisoner. But, to be frank, sir, aldermen generally only release their political supporters without an investigation. And, as I've said, Boss Meade doesn't look with favor on Red Kate—or any friend of hers."

"What is the nature of the animosity between Boss Meade and Red Kate?"

I don't know, sir. It appears to go back a long way. But the police have considerable discretionary power. Had I one statement, one witness, one instance, in contradiction of Mr. VanBrunt's guilt, I should certainly deliver him from this place. I have the authority to release him, or can come by it, but I must have the justification."

"Then let us get justification," said Poe. "Let us go and speak with our only witness. It should not be difficult to locate a boy who has the misfortune to have a clubfoot."


Chapter 6


A WITNESS SPEAKS


It was nearing dusk as we approached Paradise Square. It had been raining a cold rain on and off all day. For the moment it had let up, but the ground was spongy and the morning's laundry, hanging about the fence of Paradise Square and creating the mirage of an Arabian tent from a distance and in the weak shadowed light, was still wet, and, on closer inspection, covered with a film of black soot from nearby stacks and street fires. The washerwomen would wait for it to dry in the first sun and simply shake what soot they could out of it. Especially in winter, the locals often looked smeared and streaked.

"There's the boy," I said, needlessly pointing him out. Older than the other boys, bigger, and clubfooted, he was not easy to miss.

"I know that boy," said Poe. "He was at the Old Brewery—sleeping in the room where you found me. I didn't notice his foot. Introduce us, Sergeant. Give me official color, if you will, so that I can ask my questions freely, with apparent authority."

Poe and Mullins hung back a few yards while I stepped up to the Gimp. I told the boy that Poe was a police inspector and that he must answer his questions with great honesty or fear for the consequences.

"He ain't no copper," said the boy, sneeringly. "I seed him drunk last night at the Brewery."

"He was engaged in dangerous secret work, you little rogue. Come along now."

The clubfooted boy and the noseless man eyed each other with distaste. Poe took the boy's shoulder in his hand to shift his attention from the ivory nose. For his part, Mullins had eyed the boy as if he were looking at a grotesque. I had observed before that these toughs were sensitive enough about themselves but insensitive to the point of brutality about one another.

The Gimp was dressed in ragged garments and mud-spattered boots. One boot, built up in the sole and heel was twisted nearly backwards. He had shrewd, evasive eyes, but spoke directly when asked what he had seen and heard on the evening of the murder. I was struck by his alacrity. These boys did not rap with "coppers."

"We was guardin' the laundry," he said, hefting an omnipresent brick-bat. "Then we got into a game of craps. It was gettin' dark. We was gaddered by the east gate, so we would take turns to stand guard by the west gate, and that's where I was when I seed this Hot Corn Goil go into the park. In a minute she screamt. I looks in the gate. This gent is bent down over her and he's got this meat cleaver in his hand. He's kilt her. Then comes a crowd, and the cove can't get away. But he don't even try. He just stares around at everybody like he's crazy or sumpin'."

"What then?" said Poe.

"Well, the leadderhead comes."

"And then?" prompted Poe.

"And then you ast me the same questions that the leadderhead who stayed in the park ast me—and now I gotter answer the same questions again. Maybe I shouldn't have squealt."

"Why did you?" asked Poe.

16

"Cuz I couldn't run. Lookit me foot."

"You could have stayed and said nothing. Everyone else did."

"They'd of beat it outter me."

"How did the patrolman know you knew anything until you volunteered it?"

The boy shrugged. "Just the same," he said.

"No, not just the same," said Poe. "But no matter. Let's have a look inside the fence."

We stepped into the park by the west gate.

"It's only a few square yards of mud," said Poe. "No need to ask where the body was found. Where is the body now?"

"The pauper's graveyard, I should think, sir."

"Sergeant, it's been a long afternoon. I feel the need of some refreshment. Let's get off the streets for a bit and do some thinking. There's a diving bell across the way. I suggest we adjourn to it. But first, would you please spread the word among the boys now guarding the laundry that I will give a substantial reward for any information about the murder. They can call on me at my table in the aforementioned establishment at their leisure for the next hour. I'm sure that such clever young coves will be able to find an anonymous method of approach."

It occurred to me that I should have to pay any reward. "What good will it do, Mr. Poe?" I asked. "They're a bunch of little liars and will say anything for money—anything but the truth. You might interview one who was not even there Monday night, and yet he'll tell you that he saw everything."

"Let's try it, shall we?" said Poe, and walked off toward the rum parlor. Mullins stood in doubt for a moment, then followed in Poe's wake leaving the clubfooted boy with a last vision of the "bloke with no boke," as he would undoubtedly later describe the mutilated Mullins.

"Is that all?" he asked.

"For now," I said, and went about my business among the other boys, who had hung back, apparently in fear and deference to the Gimp, but whose curious eyes, buried in uncut hair, so that they almost seemed in the backs of their heads, had never left us.

Chapter 7

## DIVIDED JUDGMENT

In a quarter of an hour I found Poe and Mullins in the diving bell. They were drinking rum in silence. The place smelled of sooty air and rising damp, of wet, dirty clothing, alcohol and tobacco fumes. Poe appeared oblivious of this rank olla podrida. He sipped a rum, his dark eyebrows down in a V, deep in thought. I wasn't certain that he was aware of me.

"You did not like the Gimp," I said to Mullins as I sat down.

"Didn't like, didn't dislike," said Mullins. "His foot was ugly."

"Mr. Mullins has a sense of beauty," Poe said. "But it's uncultivated, or he'd know that to clothe misfortune with compassion is to see it as poignancy." He paused. "But the boy is lying, of course, not so much in what he has said, but in what he has not said. Think about it. It's totally outside of his character to volunteer information to the police. Then why should he do it? He's protecting someone, perhaps under compulsion, or perhaps for reward. Who? The murderer, most probably. So, he leaves the murderer out of his story. Does that make sense to you, Sergeant?"

"It's possible."

"Yes, *possible*. It's quickly formulated. I've thought of it almost as I've said it. Sergeant, go back and get the Gimp and bring him to me. I think we can get to the bottom of this almost immediately."

"How, Mr. Poe?"

"I have a method for getting at the truth which few can resist."

"I'll get the ugly little beggar," said Mullins, and went off after the Gimp.

"If you can get the truth out of that hardcase, Mr. Poe," I said, "you're a better man than I am."

"It's clear that you're too humane a person to attempt to employ force upon a child, though not all your colleagues, I'm certain, would be so scrupulous. I, however, have no need of force. My only bludgeon will be the gentle tick-tock of the pocket watch that hangs by your waistband chain. Let me see it, if you will."

I gave him my watch, which he took by the chain and swung above his glass. The watch caught the dancing candle-light and glittered as it swung.

"There is just the right amount of light," he said.

"The right amount of light for what, sir? Look here, you're not going to try to bribe him to the truth with my gold watch, are you? Because it was a gift from my late father—"

"No, no, Sergeant. "I wouldn't offer another man's watch away, nor my own in a bribe. Have you heard of mesmerism?"

"I can't say that I have, sir." Indeed, it was the first that I had heard of the hypnotic science, or art, but have read much about it since. At the time I thought: now we shall see what special powers this man has above those of an average intelligent man like myself. At that moment, I realized that my vanity secretly hoped that Poe would fail in his purpose, while my better nature was of course wishing for his success. I was ashamed to realize that I was not quite single-minded. I hadn't yet decided how I felt about Edgar Allen Poe. His work, of which I had read a good deal, had my highest admiration. My judgment of the man hung fire.

Mullins returned without the Gimp. "Funny-foot's nowhere to be found," he said.

"Damn!" whispered Poe.

Just then a street urchin stepped up to our table, smoking a cigar—a cherub of a boy, about ten, with a heart-shaped, pug-nosed face, and a wild mass of dirty golden curls. "My name's Danny" said he. "What's the reward for my story?"

## Chapter 8

## HYPNOTIZED TO TIME

Poe looked at me with eyebrows a third of the way up his enormous forehead. He said: "Sit down, boy, and take that cigar out of your mouth." He pushed a chair toward the child. To me he said: "Either he knows something or he doesn't. In any case, we shall soon see."

He held my watch by the chain and began swinging it in a slow arc near the candle, so that a small breeze caused a slight fluttering of the flame.

"This watch, Danny—it *was* Danny, wasn't it?"

"Yes, sir. My name's Danny Devlin."

"This watch, Danny, is very valuable. It's made of gold—do you see?"

"Yes, sir—"

"Beautiful, isn't it, Danny?"

"Worth somewhat, sir—"

"Watch it swing, Danny. Look how it glitters when it swings. It makes you sleepy, Danny, doesn't it?"

With a few passes he had the boy in his power.

He led with a few general questions, such as would the boy be truthful, to which the boy replied that he would, and did the boy know anything of what had happened on the night of the murder, to which the boy replied that he did.

Poe glanced at me. "He was there, and he'll tell us the truth as he knows it."

"It's like the Devil has come above," said Mullins, who seemed as entranced by Poe as the boy did.

"It's not black magic," said Poe. "It's merely science in action. Now," he said to the boy, "tell us about Monday night."

"Me . . . and the Gimp," the boy began, slowly, "and a few others was guardin' the laundry. Then we started a game of dice. We had the game by the east gate, so we was takin' turns—one at a time—goin' to watch at the west gate. With the laundry up you can't see nothin' through the fence—somebody got to be over there. It was the Gimp's turn to stand guard on the west side. He went over there. Some of us shootin' craps had our backs to the east gate, but I was lookin' that way. It was about dark, and I saw that gent, the one they arrested, coming kind of wobberly toward the Square. He was pretty close to us, and then we heard a horrible scream. It was a woman's voice. The man began to run towards the park, towards the gate. He ran in and when we looked he was holdin' the girl. She was dead, bloody—"

"Danny," said Poe, "you say that you heard the scream before the man entered the park?"

"Yeah. When he heard the scream he began to run."

"He heard the scream," said Poe, "and ran *into* the park?"

"Yes, sir."

Poe looked at me. That was it. VanBrunt had not misplaced his confidence in Poe.

"You said, Sergeant, that you only needed a contradiction to the Gimp's testimony to justify VanBrunt's release. Here you have it. The girl was attacked before VanBrunt entered the Square. It's not conclusive. The boy might be mistaken as to the sequence of events. But so might the Gimp, though I think his version is a lie by omission. The girl might have screamed for some other reason, a minor attack previous to VanBrunt's, it could be argued. But, in light of his avowed intention to propose marriage, witnessed by, among others, our friend Mullins here, that's unlikely. I think you now have what you need to justify VanBrunt's immediate release."

"Mr. Poe," I said, "can you make this boy repeat his story at any time you desire to hear it."

"I can. And furthermore, if we can find the Gimp, I can get the truth out of him. He would know the name of—or, at least, be able to describe—the murderer, for I have come to think that no one else but the murderer would have reason to have him lie."

"It's the Devil's work, Mr. Poe, that you be about."

"Not at all, Mr. Mullins. It's a scientific principle at work, one rediscovered in the latter times by Anton Mesmer, a person of doubtful morality but acute observation. Would you like me to mesmerize you?"

"Ye gads, *no!*" cried Mullins. Poe laughed, and turned his attention to the boy.

"Danny?"

"Yes, sir?"

"I am going to count to three and snap my fingers, and when I do you'll feel perfectly normal."

"Yes, sir."

"*One*. Mr. Mullins, would you please go up to the bar and get us a round of drinks. This concentration, combined with my somewhat weakened condition, has given me a head-ache. *Two*."

Mullins left the table looking backward over his shoulder as if at a coven of witches.

"Danny," Poe said, "we shall want to see you again. I want you to come every morning to watch the laundry—say at about ten o'clock—do you understand?"

"Yes, sir."

"*Three*." Poe snapped his fingers. The boy looked at him, shook his head slightly, and said: "It wasn't a man, you see, sir, it was an ape that done it. Do you want me to tell you how it happened?"

"No, boy," said Poe. "But the sergeant here has a penny for you."

I gave the boy a penny and watched him as he left. He was quite confused.

When Mullins returned with our drinks, I saluted the writer in the name of VanBrunt.

Chapter 9

A REPRIEVE

At Red Kate's table, Poe was flanked by Mullins and Max Fisch. The latter was well known to me. I had had occasion to arrest little Max, a screwsman, a burglar who uses skeleton keys or lockpicks. He was a pathetic fellow who suffered from a type of nervous disorder which caused a constant trembling, sometimes shaking, of his long-nailed claw-like hands. This affliction must have caused him much trouble on the job. Max was a notorious coward, of the cornered-rat variety.

Mullins, Fisch, and Poe were drinking rum. I gave Poe a keen look. He seemed in command of himself, though there was a bit of the glass in his eye.

VanBrunt and I sat down.

"Eddie," said VanBrunt, "I knew if anyone could do it, you could, but I never imagined you could do it this quickly, and that I should be free tonight."

"They say Eddie's a genius," said Kate.

"He's Nicky," said Mullins.

Poe looked at me.

23

"The Devil," I translated.

Poe smiled. "You must thank Sergeant Goode for your release, Peter. I was merely able to put things in balance."

"Sir, I'm an ordinary patrolman. I work according to the principles I know, but what you were able to do—"

"Not at all. Despite your numerous disclaimers, you're an excellent policeman, and a highly intelligent one. Furthermore, I should like to report that I am neither the Devil nor C. Auguste Dupin, my fictional detective, but merely a writer, to be rated by others, with a certain, as it were, storehouse of quaint and curious lore, some bit of which, here or there, may prove useful. But let me remind everyone that, though we have obtained Peter's freedom, we have not entirely cleared him of a charge of murder, which hoped-for end can only be attained, in my view, by the discovery of the true murderer."

"He can cast a spell on people," said Mullins, "and make them say anything he wants. How do we know what they say is the truth?"

"That's a fair question," said Poe. "But not to the point. First, get what might be the truth, any way you can, then confirm it. Half the battle is in the knowing. I'm certain that Sergeant Goode can find a method of having the truth speak for itself—which is to say, of having Danny Devlin repeat his story out of my influence."

"How do you do it, Eddie?" asked Kate.

"It's mesmerism, isn't it?" asked VanBrunt. "Sergeant Goode told me what you did. How long have you been practicing it, Eddie?"

"Animal magnetism, more lately called mesmerism, has been an interest of mine for some years. My goal is to employ it as a means of strengthening the will in the dying, so that they are able to hold back the encroachment of death beyond the capacity of the body—which is to say, ultimately, to cause the dead to remain quick."

"Black magic!" cried Mullins.

Poe laughed. "No, no—I said that for your benefit, Mr. Mullins. What interests me in mesmerism has nothing to do with the black arts. It's science—and science, indeed put to the service of humanity. I myself can eliminate pain in some circumstances. But there are few today in the medical profession who will listen when you speak of mesmerism—due to the charlatanism of some of its early practitioners. And, I might add—especially for your benefit, Mr. Mullins—due as well to the superstitions of earlier times. Yet no words are so true as 'This too will pass.' I conceive the day when teeth will be extracted painlessly from the jaws of mesmerized subjects; and when police officers, such as yourself, Sergeant, will use this science as a tool for getting at the truth, as you've seen demonstrated today—as I'll demonstrate now, if one of you will consent to be my subject."

"None of that witchcraft with me!" cried Mullins. He had a manifest awe, even fear, of Poe.

"It has been my observation that the untutored are filled with baseless fears, which allow for their manipulation by the unscrupulous," I directed at Poe.

"L'Imagination fait tout," Poe said; "le magnétisme nul."

"Fishy, you be the subject," said Kate.

"Not me," said Max Fisch, waving away the idea. "I don't like nothin' I don't understand."

"You'll do it," said Kate, "or I'll have both your Jack Cove ears in that bottle behind the bar."

"You'd not have my ears, Kate!" Fisch sank low in his chair, his hands repeatedly clapping his reddening ears.

"I've had better men's, and spit them from these red lips."

"Do what Kate says," ordered Mullins.

"I assure you," said Poe, "I'll do you no harm. Your watch, Sergeant. Now, quiet, please!"

Within moments Poe had the timorous man in his power.

"How does it work now?" asked Kate.

"Give me a question to ask of him."

"Ask him," said Kate, "if he's a fool."

"Are you a fool?" asked Poe.

"No, sir," said Max Fisch.

"But he is!" cried Kate.

"But he doesn't think he is," said Poe.

"Then the more fool he," said Kate.

"The more fool all of us," said Poe, and gave me a charming wink.

"Ask him," said VanBrunt, "if he knew Mary Hart."

"Ah," sighed Poe, and repeated the question to Max Fisch.

"I knowed her. A bleak mort."

"A pretty girl," I translated.

"Ask him," said VanBrunt, "if he loved her."

"My friend," said Poe, "you're pursuing a morbid line of questioning."

"No," said VanBrunt, "you mistake me. I merely wish you to know that all who knew her came to love her, as I've told you."

"In that case," said Poe, and asked the question.

"Yes, sir," answered Max Fisch. "I loved her. She were beautiful."

"Would you kill for her?" asked VanBrunt.

"Answer," said Poe, his face disturbed.

"I would if I was made to."

I didn't like the cast of things, and said so.

"You're quite right, Sergeant," said Poe, and snapped his fingers to awaken Max Fisch.

"What happened," said Fisch.

"Nothing," said Kate, frowning.

"Will you consent to be my subject?" Poe asked Kate.

"What, me?"

"Are you afraid?" asked Fisch. "It don't hurt none. It's

like it didn't even happen. It did happen, didn't it?"

"It did," said VanBrunt.

"I'll not have anyone in control of me," said Kate. "That's out!"

"She don't got to," seconded Mullins.

Poe rose from his chair. "I'm going to retire," he said, and placing a hand on VanBrunt's thin shoulder, he added, "I can rest now that I know my dear friend is at liberty." He then turned his gaze to Kate and said, "Do you mind if I take this bottle with me?"

"Take it," she said. "You're my guest for as long as you wish."

Her interest shifted to VanBrunt. She put an arm over his shoulder and kissed him on the forehead. "Me foolish old buck," she said, "welcome home."

I bid them good night, and followed Poe to our rooms on the second floor. Outside his door, he turned to me and said:

"Has it occurred to you that Red Kate might have killed Mary Hart?"

"Not until now," I said.

"Tell me," he said. "You know her. Is she capable of murder?"

"Indeed," said I. "She's probably dispatched a few."

"Jealousy is a powerful motive, Sergeant."

"Yes, sir—it is."

Poe opened his door.

"Sergeant."

"Yes, sir?"

"I should be careful of burglars. Many must have observed your gold watch."

"When I stay in a place like this, Mr. Poe, I make a man-sized mound of my belongings and the bed-clothes and such and put it under the blanket. Then I stretch out under the bed, my pistol at the ready."

"A tactic worthy of emulation. I have no pistol, but I have my bottle of rum."

"These clapboard buildings are tinderboxes, Mr. Poe. I should be careful not to drink so much that I might sleep through a fire alarm. Just in case, sir, there's a door to an outside stairway at the end of the hall."

"I see it, Sergeant. But don't worry. I'm a light sleeper."

"Goodnight, Mr. Poe."

Chapter 10

POE IS MURDERED

Twinges of conscience had troubled me from the onset of this investigation. First, I knew myself to be a dupe, chosen for my inexperience, for nothing else could explain my sudden rise in rank, from an ordinary leatherhead to a detective, and I felt keenly the dishonor underlying the situation, though I did not understand its nature, the what and why of it. Then I had clutched at a straw, when VanBrunt suggested bringing Edgar Poe in. This was hope for myself as well as VanBrunt, and I had pursued the idea and the poet with vigor. His reputation at what he had called "ratiocination" was great. Many eminent people had thought he had hit upon the solution to the Mary Rogers murder case, a real New York crime, in his tale "The Mystery of Marie Roget," set in Paris, France. He wrote brilliantly of crime and detection—who better to have on our side? But now, as I set up my false sleeping body on top of the small sunken bed and spread the moth-eaten blanket over it, I thought of the true nature of the situation.

Poe was a fine writer, perhaps a great one, given time, but he was not an actual detective, and the fear overcame me that I might have placed such a man in a dangerous situation. What would the world think of me if I were, even inadvertently responsible for his death? I slid under the bed and held my pistol at the ready. Now that I thought back on the day, I realized that it was Poe who had kept us here at Red Kate's. Why? Did he like the atmosphere, or did he have something else in mind? I had observed from time to time during the course of the day, a certain bulldog tenacity in the set of jaw and a kind of zealotry in his large, burning eyes. He was definitely not a timid man. The thought occurred to me that he was greatly interested in the situation. Perhaps he thought of Mary Hart's murder as potential material for his writing. It occurred to me for the first time that I might turn up as a character in one of his tales. He seemed to like me well enough, but what he really thought—well. I even had the temerity to dream that I might someday write a memoir about him and this—my first—case. I had dozed off. Had Poe come into the room, or had I dreamed it? Had someone shot him? I was shaken, and got out from under the bed and stood in the dark room, wondering what was real and what I had dreamed.

I stepped into the hall, pistol in hand. Poe was standing at his door, holding a pistol, his usually pale face ashen.

"What happened?" I asked.

"Someone," he said calmly, "has murdered me."

"Are you shot?" I asked excitedly. I looked him over but could see no blood.

"My other self," he said, pointing into the room. He had made a mound of his coat, pillow, and bedclothes, as I had. "If you will look closely," he said, "you'll see that I have been shot through the heart."

Red Kate and Mullins had arrived at the top of the stairs. We could look from the balcony down into the *Ballum-rancum* below, as the mob who were the celebrants of the ball could look up at us. Morning, noon, or night, the party was never over at the Emerald Isle. One could read on the faces in the mob the annoyance felt at the interruption of the festivities. The general question appeared to be: Should they dive for cover or carry on?

Kate stopped in her flight and called down to them that everything was under control, to go on about their business. She and Mullins came up to us.

"What happened?" she asked.

"Somebody tried to kill Mr. Poe," I told her.

"With this," said Poe, hefting the pistol like a man who knew weapons. "I was sleeping, the shot rang out, the door was slammed. Fortunately, I was sleeping under the bed and not in it."

"Under the bed?" said Kate. "What kind of place do you think I operate here?"

"But, madam," said Poe, "you compel me to embarrass myself in order to avoid any insult to you or to your establishment. I was sleeping under the bed," he whispered, "because that was where the consumption of your marvelous rum had driven me. But the pile of my clothes on the bed must have seemed the shape of a man—they do look so, do they not?—to the rogue who shot at them. It was a thief, no doubt. It happens in the best of places. I think I must have groaned or made a noise—perhaps I kicked in my sleep—and startled him, and in a reflex action he shot?"

"Why do you say that?" I asked. "Perhaps he—or *she*," I added pointedly—*intended* to kill you."

"I should think not," said Poe, "for the reason that an assassin who has calculated his assassination does not drop his weapon in departure. I stubbed my toe on this at the door. See, it smells of the shot."

"Look," said Kate. "The initials carved on the wooden handles, both sides—*M.F.* That's Max Fisch's pistol. I should know, as he's hocked it with me these many times. Nobody burgles in my place. I'll kill him!"

"He must have thought that gold watch belonged to you, Mr. Poe," said Mullins. "You seed how his hands shake. The gun must have popped right out of his grip."

I wondered aloud that Max Fisch should try his business

with Poe; for he, like Mullins, viewed Poe as being almost supernatural. "Greed would not overcome such fear," I said.

"Perhaps not," said Poe thoughtfully. "But enough fear can make a man act the shadow of a hero. I should like to ask Fisch about all this."

"He's gone," said Mullins. "Him and Mr. VanBrunt left together."

"Left?" Poe looked upset, a condition which VanBrunt's absence caused me to share with him. Poe tilted his head, and it was as though you could see his mind working. "What time is it, Sergeant?"

I consulted my watch. "Five in the morning, sir."

"Where did Mr. VanBrunt intend to go?" Poe asked. "Do you have any idea?"

"Yes, sir," said Mullins. "Him and Max Fisch was talking, and he—he was pretty drunk—he said that he wanted to talk to that Gimp boy who spoke against him. Max Fisch said he'd show him where to find the boy. Max Fisch was drunk, too, sir. I expect they are wandering around in the streets."

"Why didn't you stop him?" I asked. "Or stay with him?"

"I have me own work to do for Miss Kate. I got to control that mob down there, that they don't break nothing or each other—it's me job. I ain't no wet-nurse."

"I think we had better find VanBrunt," Poe said.

"Yes, before he gets his throat cut," said Kate. "You go with them, No-Nose. See that everybody's safe."

"Do you think he'll be at the Old Brewery?" I asked.

"That's where the Gimp probably is," said Poe. "It's the logical place to look."

"We dressed and made our way through the Five Points. Mullins' giant form and frightening face assured us of safe conduct, though the denizens of the hellish place were on the prowl about us. It took only a few minutes to get from Kate's to the Old Brewery.

Upon entering the room in which I had first found Poe, we found VanBrunt apparently in a drunken sleep at the same table. I shook him, but he could not be immediately awakened. Poe went over to the Gimp, and in a moment called me over.

"He's been strangled," Poe said. "The miserable end of a miserable life."

"The poor wretch!" I said. "Did VanBrunt do it? Have we been wrong?"

"Let's not leap to conclusions. Where's Max Fisch?"

"I don't know," I said, "but I think we'd better get these two out of here first. We can do nothing here anyway. If I bring in the Municipals, we'll have a riot on our hands. The department's not strong enough to deal with that. Mullins," I ordered, "take the boy's body, wrap it in the blanket, and bring it. Mr. Poe, let's you and I get VanBrunt out of here." We hauled his inert body to its feet, threw its limp arms over our shoulders, and proceeded apace.

"Mr. Poe . . . Eddie . . . I am worried about you," I confided. "Nay, sir, I am frightened for your life. I shouldn't have heeded VanBrunt and brought you into this horror."

Poe laughed. "You may have forgotten, Sergeant, but horror is my business. There is a movement of larger shadows behind the puppets we observe. Someone who has been physically close to us is responsible for the shooting in my room, someone in the immediate grouping of puppets before us, but it little relevancy bears. I am concerned with the puppeteers, the string-pullers who hide backstage. We shall find them out, Sergeant, have no fear."

We encountered no one on our way out; but, had we, I doubt that it would have mattered. To the denizens of the Old Brewery, it would not have signified to see two men carrying between them a comatose third, nor the body of a boy in the arms of an ivory-nosed brute.

Chapter 11

## NOISE OF NIAGARA

Over toward the east a whisper of light could almost be heard, like lace curtains slowly drawn back. Soon the skyline with its sails and masts, punctuated by church spires, would stand in ever more defined silhouette. "Mullins," I called to the striding giant, "when we get VanBrunt and the Gimp's body to the hospital, I want you to come back and find Max Fisch. Bring him to Red Kate's. Lock him in a room if you must."

"Yes, sir," Mullins said, and vanished into the smoky dark ahead of us.

"Note," said Poe, "how he can carry the body of the boy under one arm and still out stride a racehorse."

Near Paradise Square we heard the clomping of a cab horse coming in our direction and hailed it. Apparently the driver was reluctant to stop in the dark middle of the slum. He whipped the horses on. I let Poe take VanBrunt's full weight, and seized the nearer horse by its bridle, letting him feel my weight. When I had slowed its progress, I flashed my copper star up at the driver. We got VanBrunt and ourselves aboard and ordered the driver to take us to the City Hospital, "On the gallop!"

"As far as we know," I said to Poe, "Max Fisch was the last person to be in the company of Mr. VanBrunt—excepting, perhaps, the Gimp—and I'm anxious to hear what he has to say. More, there's the attempt on you. We must bring him to book for that, in any case."

"I doubt very much if Max Fisch had anything to do with the shot fired at me," said Poe.

"Do you suppose Mullins will turn up at the hospital?"

"He'll probably beat us there. His legs are longer and probably more powerful than the legs of these old drays." Poe looked worried. "There's something more wrong with our friend here than mere inebriation," he said. "His sleep is too deep. I fear that the alcohol has affected his brain. He's comatose."

"Perhaps he's hurt himself otherwise," I said.

"I see no abrasions."

"The hospital isn't far. Just up on Broadway."

"I hope that you haven't lost faith in the innocence of our friend here," said Poe.

"I have not, sir. Oh, there was the shadow of a doubt back there. Just for a moment. But when I undertook to release him, I put myself at risk, and, if I let him remain at liberty in these circumstances, I'll look a fool."

"Does that mean that you intend to place him under arrest again?"

"I'll consider him in my custody for now. As, indeed, he still is, in any case."

"Do you share my feeling," said Poe, "that the other boy, Devlin, may be in danger? If the Gimp was killed because his testimony was false, and the truth might have come out had he lived, Devlin may also be in danger because his testimony is true, and would tend to clear VanBrunt. The Gimp's murder was an attempt to make VanBrunt look guilty—that is, the murder of the main witness against him. But, if that's the case, it follows that the main witness in his favor could also be in jeopardy."

"Yes," I said. "I see that. We'd better pick the boy up."

"And keep him with us," said Poe. "When I mesmerized him, I suggested that he go to Paradise Square every morning at ten o'clock. It's his habit to do so anyway. I had simply to reinforce it. I thought a time might be at hand when we'd want to get hold of him. I'm certain that we'll be able to find him at Paradise Square at ten. It would be so much more convenient, would it not, if these boys had homes?"

"Their wretched lives are our disgrace," I said.

"If we must wait until ten," said Poe, "to see the boy, why not put the intervening hours to good use?"

"What do you suggest?"

"I'd like to interview Mary Hart's mother."

When we reined in at the hospital, the doctor on duty was waiting at the door. "You must be the policeman with the injured man," he said. "A giant with an ivory nose came rushing in here minutes ago and dumped a body in my lap. I tried to hold him, but had little chance of success. He said you were right behind him."

We went inside and the doctor made a quick examination of VanBrunt. The Gimp's body lay on a nearby table.

"What is it?" Poe asked the doctor impatiently. "Is it the drink?"

"I think not," said the doctor. "Feel here, at the back of his head."

"What is it?" I asked, as Poe probed VanBrunt's head.

"A soft spot."

"A swelling," said the doctor. "The skin isn't broken, so I should say that this man is suffering from a concussion, brought about by being hit with a blackjack. We see it all the time here."

"What's to be done?" I asked. "Will he be all right?"

"Chances are good," said the doctor, "that he'll come out of it, but it could be hours, even days."

"You'll see to the boy?"

"Any family?"

"None known to us."

"We'll see to the body. Another pauper, poor kid."

Outside, on the stone steps of the hospital, facing Broadway, we paused for a breath of cold morning air. The daybreak traffic of heavily laden carts and wagons, along with innumerable omnibuses, passed before us.

"I'd like a cup of strong, hot coffee," Poe said.

"I know a good cheap restaurant—the Stage Door—

across the alley from the stage door of the Phoenix Theatre."

As we walked down Broadway, Poe said, in an uncharacteristically loud voice, speaking above the roar of iron wheels on granite that someone once likened to "the sound of Niagara heard from the Cataract Hotel"—"Just look at this, Sergeant." He waved a hand at the spectacle. "Here we are at the center of the wealth and commerce of the greatest state in these United States. When the carriage trade appears later today, Broadway will be filled with carriages conveying occupants whose rich haberdashery will display a contempt for money. Let's say, the VanBrunts. They'll step down from their carriages, aided by footmen, and visit some of the most elegant stores in the world. At Tiffany's they might purchase a bauble that would keep a family alive for a year. At J. & C. Berrien they might spend Fifteen Thousand Dollars for a roomful of furniture. And no Blind Tiger whiskey for such gentry. They'll buy champagne at John Duncan & Son. The books that I need and cannot afford, they'll think nothing of purchasing as gifts for their semi-literate brethren. And this very Sunday they'll congregate before yon Trinity Church with its spire aimed at heaven and its doors opened to Wall Street. This is the glory of progress. But what of poverty? Do they ever look at it? I'd like to go out into the middle of Broadway and wave their carriages but one minute's jostle down Anthony Street to the Five Points and Paradise Square so that they could have a look at the source of their happiness; the misery they feed upon."


Chapter 12


THE PHOENIX IN FLAME


Phoenix Alley was a long, curving, cobbled alley lined with small shops. We turned into it, and when we had walked about half its length, we became aware of a thin, dark fog.

"Fire ahead!" I cried.

Now we could see plumes of smoke.

"It's the theatre," I said. "We must sound the alarm!"

But immediately we heard the alarm bells.

There was a great deal of anguished pounding at the inside of the stage door. Poe and I tried to open it, but it was locked, or jammed. We gave up, and ran the few yards out of the alley to the front of the theatre, where we were greeted by the sight of a giant on a barrel fighting off other giants by making wide, ruthless swings with a seven-foot hickory staff that dangled a dead rabbit at its end.

"The hydrant is under the barrel," I told Poe. "The thug is saving it for his fire company. He's a Dead Rabbit. The others look like Bowery Boys."

"But there are people trapped in that theatre, and these fools are playing at who's first!"

I reached out to stop him, but he strode beyond my grasp. He went up behind the Dead Rabbit, caught the staff at its end in a back-swing, jerked it from the hands of the surprised volunteer fireman, whirled it above his own head, and fairly batted the Dead Rabbit from the barrel as if he were a ball in a game of rounders. Immediately, the opposing volunteer firemen, the Bowery Boys, sent up a great cheer, and fell to removing the barrel from the hydrant, the wooden fire-plug from the log-pipe, and hooking up their hose.

Poe ran to the glassed front doors of the theatre and smashed them with the staff.

Three coughing actors emerged in a puff of smoke.

"Kevin!" I cried.

One of the actors was an acquaintance of mine. Kevin O'Connell, the comic-actor, who lived down the hall from me at my boarding house in Greenwich Village.

Kevin threw his arms around me, gasping. I held him steady until he caught his breath. Then he cried, "That divil of a gangster would have let us die before he'd let the Dead

Rabbits be beaten to a fire by the Bowery Boys. I thank your friend heartily for saving my life."

Poe looked perplexed. "Gangster? I thought he was a mad fireman."

"These volunteer firemen are all members of gangs," I said.

"Well, not all," Kevin corrected. I remembered now that he had been one.

"Most," I modified.

Kevin said: "The divils fight each other with brickbats and guns when there's no fire to fight, and then they fight each other for the right to fight the fire!"

We retired to the Stage Door Restaurant to have coffee, and to watch through the window as the fire was fought.

"I knew you were working at the Phoenix, Kevin," I said, "but what were you doing there at this early hour?"

"Rehearsing a trick. We've been at it all night. I think one of us got tired and fell asleep with a cigar in his teeth. Oh, it's been an *awful* night! We were doing a business with a series of trap doors, and we couldn't get the damned things to work."

"I especially dislike a theatre burning," said Poe. "My parents were actors."

"Were they, now?"

"My mother has played that very theatre. You may have heard of her—Elizabeth Arnold Poe?"

"Poe? Are you, by chance, the writer, Poe?"

"He is," I said, feeling a certain pride in the fellowship of such a well-known figure.

"I've read your work, Mr. Poe," said Kevin.

"I hope you enjoyed it."

"Oh, indeed! Particularly 'The Raven.' Why, it must be the most famous poem in the world! I don't know how anyone can write like that."

It was strange to think that this shabby man who sat sipping black, steaming coffee at the table with me should be the author of, as Kevin had put it, "the most famous poem in the world."

"It's down to smoldering smoke," said Poe.

"Let's go and have a look," said Kevin.

The firemen had smashed in the stage door.

We made our way through the still steaming debris and walked out on the stage. Morning sun glared down on us through great, jagged holes in walls and ceiling. Blue sky and white clouds peppered with ashes, drifted, plain to be seen, above us.

Kevin showed us the traps upon which he had been working, a series of three, each a square yard, nine feet across the stage.

"You see," said he, "I run ahead of my pursuer, somebody pulls the traps just as I cross them, and down goes my enemy. Down there are straw mattresses to break the fall."

"A beam has dropped from the ceiling, through the traps," said Poe, "and ignited the mattresses. They're gone. You see?"

Indeed, there were no mattresses.

"'Twould be a breakneck fall without 'em," said Kevin.

"How do the traps work?" asked Poe.

"Over here, these levers."

Kevin moved the levers into position. The doors sprung.

"Now, you see? Look at that! Now I've got working traps and no theatre. Can you beat it! And they talk of the luck of the Irish!"


Chapter 13


SPEAK OF THE DEAD


The leatherhead who had arrested VanBrunt had supplied me with Mrs. Hart's address, a tenement on Ann Street.

He had instructed me to tap on the window, first floor front.

VanBrunt had never met Mrs. Hart, but Mary had told him that her mother was blind. Only yellowed whites showed in the slits of her shrunken eyes. Her hair was yellowed grey like her winkled, careworn face. She hugged a Bible to her bosom, and leaned on a cane. I explained our errand and she admitted us, leading us through a musty hall, into a sparsely furnished room, and made her way to a center table. She offered us each a chair and a cup of tea. The footboard of a bed peeked modestly from behind a screen. A larger Bible rested on a stand near the table. Though I had trouble adjusting my eyes to the dismal light, I saw that it was open to "The Revelations of Jesus Christ."

Mrs. Hart apologized at having no biscuits to offer us. "I have no income now. Mary was my sole support. The ladies of the mission have been taking care of me since her death. But I don't know how long they'll be willing to do so. They've spoken of an institution that takes care of such as myself, poor, blind and useless."

"Never useless, madam," said Poe. He sipped his steaming tea.

"How can I be of help?"

"You can tell us about Mary's friends," I said.

"Mary wasn't a girl for making friends. She kept to herself. She hated the life down here and tried to stay apart from it. But she did tell me about Mr. VanBrunt. Really, except when working, she saw no one at all—until him. But she was in love with him, and from what she told me about him, I believe he loved her. It was Mary's intention to accept him in marriage, if he proposed."

"Then you are not aware that she had any other friends?" I asked.

"Perhaps one of the other Hot Corn Girls, but I know of no one specifically. When she wasn't working she stayed home with me and cooked and cleaned and did chores about the house. She read a great deal. After working all night, she'd come home early in the morning and read to me from the big Bible there. On Sundays, the only day I venture out, she took me to services at the mission. Oh," she said, hugging the small Bible closer to her breast, "you must be wondering about this one. I mean, because of my blindness. I can't read it, of course, but I never have it out of reach. Holding it is like holding the past. My other daughter, Lucy, gave me it. But it hasn't been opened since Lucy's death. She made me promise that no one but herself would read to me from it. And no one has. But please forgive me for chattering on. When one is lonely one talks at the drop of a hat, about everything and anything."

Poe said: "Did you approve of Mr. VanBrunt?"

"Oh, yes—from what Mary told me."

"Then you doubt his guilt?"

"I *know* he didn't kill Mary."

"How do you know that?" I asked.

"Because I know who killed her."

"Who?" I asked.

"The Butcher's Gang."

Poe was still, studying the blind face.

"Boss Mead's boys? What makes you say that?" I asked.

"Because they did the same to my other daughter, Lucy."

"The Butcher's Gang," said Mrs. Hart, "is a gang that's part of the Plug Uglies, and—"

"Excuse me for a moment, madam," said Poe. "Sergeant, are you familiar with this gang?"

"Yes, sir," I said. "The Five Points is full of gangs—the Forty Thieves, the Roach Guards, the Dead Rabbits—like the one you batted from the barrel—the Chichesters, the Shirt Tails, and so on. Some of these gangs began as social clubs, and evolved into volunteer fire companies. Some have become political and criminal organizations. I think I told you that Boss Meade began as a butcher. I'm a greenhorn, as Red Kate said, so no expert, but years ago, from what I gather, Meade started a social club made up of butchers, which eventually joined ranks with the Plug Uglies, a very large gang, numbering into the hundreds. The Plug Uglies are a strong part of Meade's constituency. They are also the Red Dragons Hook & Ladder Company, of which Meade is chief."

"That's right, said Mrs. Hart. "The Butcher's Gang is part of the Plug Uglies, and my son-in-law, Lucy's husband, was a member."

"Pardon me, madam," said Poe, "but what was his name?"

"Joseph Brody. But he's dead. You see, my son-in-law was in on a criminal arrangement of some sort with the Butchers and tried to cheat them. Soon after, Lucy was found dead, killed the same way as Mary, with a cleaver."

"I see," said Poe. "A reprisal. What about your son-in-law?"

"He vanished, and later I heard that he had been killed as well."

"Where did you hear that?"

"Why, Mary told me. I'd wait for her until early in the morning when she returned from vending, and then we'd take tea together and she'd tell me all about what had happened that evening and night—the gossip on the streets, and the important news. Then we'd turn to the Bible. She had heard that Joe had been killed. The news of his death did not make either of us unhappy, God forgive us. He was a brutal, stupid man who often beat my Lucy, and a criminal, and even a cheat among his criminal friends, which brought about Lucy's death, and now the death of my sweet Mary."

"The same weapon in both cases," I said.

"Yes," said Poe, "but how long ago was your daughter Lucy murdered, madam?"

"It's been five years. Lucy was twenty-one."

"How old was Mary?"

"Twenty-one."

"Then Mary was sixteen when Lucy was murdered?"

"Yes."

"Why should the gang strike at Mary?" asked Poe. "And why should they have waited so long? And why should they do so after Joe Brody's death? What benefit would there be to them in killing Mary?"

"There's something wrong there," I said.

"But who else would want to kill Mary?" asked Mrs. Hart. "And who else but the Butchers would use such a weapon?"

"That, my dear lady," said Poe, "is the question."

"But it couldn't have been Mr. VanBrunt," said Mrs. Hart. "Mary told me that she intended to marry him. My Mary was an honest girl and a good judge of decency in people. She told me many times what a fine man Mr. VanBrunt was, that he came from a respected family, and that he would deal honestly with her. We had hopes that he would find a life for me, as well. It was our dream that Mary should find a man like him. Certainly he would have no reason, no reason at all, to want to do such a thing to her. He could simply say that he was done with courting her, and Mary's pride would put an end to things."

"We agree with you," said Poe, "that Mr. VanBrunt is innocent, and I can say that he held your Mary in the highest esteem. If it's any consolation to you, it's a fact that he intended to propose marriage to Mary on the day of her death."

"Ma'am," I said, "what happened immediately after the death of your daughter, Lucy? I mean, before you heard of Joe Brody's death?"

"What happened? Let me see. Well, Joe quit the gang, that's what he told Mary. Mary told me that Joe quit in order to redeem himself, although it seemed out of character to me."

"Can you describe your son-in-law—physically?" asked Poe.

"My sight's been gone for many years, young man. I never saw him. He was described to me, of course. Tall, nice looking. But I didn't like his voice. There was cruelty, stupidity in it. I'm sorry I can't be of too much help."

"It's too soon to say that you haven't been," said Poe.

"On the contrary," said I. "I think you've been of great help, Mrs. Hart. This gang business puts a new cast to things."

"Did Mary dislike Joe Brody as much as you did?" asked Poe, getting to his feet.

"She loathed him. I think he was attracted to Mary, though she was just a child then. I suspected as much from certain conversations I overheard between Lucy and Mary."

"Was Lucy jealous of Mary?" I asked.

"No, no. Not over Joe."

"How, then? In some other way?"

"There was a bit of rivalry between the girls over me, I think. Before Joe came into the picture the girls and I had been very close. Lucy, being the eldest, I depended upon. But when she left to marry Joe, Mary took her place as my strong right arm. As I said, Mary would read to me from the Bible every morning. One day Lucy came over and gave me *this* Bible, that I hold in my hand. It was inscribed to me, she said, and it was never to be read by Mary, or anyone else, except herself, when *she* was reading it to me. Jealousy? Not exactly. As I say, it was a sort of rivalry over me that this Bible business showed. That's an example. But I kept my word to Lucy. I never let Mary read from Lucy's Bible. And I never let it out of my hands, as I promised her I wouldn't.

"No, no. Lucy did not blame Mary for the behavior of her husband. She warned Mary not to be alone with Joe. Mary, as I said, was only just growing into womanhood. Lucy and Joe had been married for several years, and Joe had been around to see Mary grow up. Both Lucy and I were afraid of

Joe, and afraid for Mary with regard to him. He was capable of anything."

I looked at Poe, who nodded.

"We thank you very much, Mrs. Hart, for the tea, and for your help," I said, rising.

"After Lucy's death," said Mrs. Hart, "or, actually, after Mary told me that Joe had been killed, I made her swear on this Bible that she would never mention him to me again, never use his name in my presence, and this is the first time in nearly five years that I've used his name. The very mention of it used to make me sick. That should make clear to you gentlemen how determined I am to be of help."

"Again," said Poe, "we thank you, madam."


Chapter 14


BAITS AND TRAPS


Outside, the November day was growing unseasonably warm and sunny. Had I been in Greenwich Village, or, even more so, in my country haunts, I should have appreciated the warmth; but when heat struck the slums surrounding the Five Points, the manure in the streets and the night-soil in the alleys ripened with energy. In summer the stench could prove unbearable. Here and now it remained at an acceptable level. Flies would be abounding if the heat continued. What we needed was snow, but, alas, that would bring more smoke. Poe sniffed the air with nervous nostrils.

"What have you got in mind?" he asked.

I apprised Poe of a few facts regarding Boodle Coign. "He's a member of the Plug Uglies," I said, "and a pigeon, an informer. Perhaps he can shed some light on the relationship of the gang to the murder of Lucy Hart Brody, to the possible murder of Joe Brody—we can't be entirely certain of that—

and to the murder of Mary Hart. There *must* be a connecting link!"

"Let's hope he can," said Poe, his face grey in the drench of sunlight. "To know the exact nature of that link would be, perhaps, to resolve the matter."

"It's bull-baiting day at Bunker Hill, and Boodle Coign is an owner, and dedicated to the filthy entertainment. Have you ever seen it?"

"Not *seen*—but heard of it, of course. How's it done?"

"A bull is chained to a swivel ring and dogs torment him. The sport is to wager on the number of dogs the bull will gore. Boodle will be there, it's certain, and I think it would be wise to go there and have a few words with him."

"Did I hear you say Bunker Hill?"

"Yes, sir. *Our* Bunker Hill is up near Greenwich Village. A fort was built there during the Revolution, and defended against General Howe. Later, a Fly Market butcher named Winship built an arena inside the fort for bull-baiting."

"Oh, yes, I have heard of it," said Poe. "I've spent a good deal of time, off and on, in the city, but I've never been to the old fort."

"It was my thought, sir, that you might take Danny Devlin with you back to Red Kate's and keep an eye on him while I went on to Bunker Hill and spoke to Boodle Coign."

"If I am to be of any assistance in this matter, I must hear for myself what is said."

"In that case, sir, I think we must deposit little Devlin in good hands somewhere, because it would be wrong to take him into the midst of such a crowd."

"Nor," said Poe, "dare we leave him at Red Kate's. Red Kate herself may be our killer, and that would be like presenting the lamb to the wolf."

"You suspect her to such a degree?"

"It's a matter of motive," said Poe. "If VanBrunt did not kill Mary Hart in a drunken rage, because she rejected him—

and we know from Mrs. Hart that Mary intended to accept his proposal, if proffered—*then*, who else had reason to kill her? The Butcher's Gang? Would they persist in revenge five years later?"

"It's possible."

"Anything is possible. But we must deal in *probabilities*, not mere *possibilities*, which place us all-at-sea. Until we know more we must work with what we have. I cannot believe that Mary Hart's death was random—a robbery or some such—not when the weapon used was a replica of one used to murder her sister five years earlier. That, though *possibly* coincidental, is not *probably* coincidental. It appears to be symbolic. After all—a butcher's cleaver—in both cases! Therefore I look for motive and come up with Red Kate's jealousy. It is to be hoped that jealousy is not our last word on the subject—but it *is* all we have for a motive. After all, who had such a girl offended?"

"I agree that Red Kate might be capable of murdering a rival, in business or in love, but do you believe her capable of murdering a crippled boy, however unpleasant, like the Gimp?"

Poe sighed. "It's too much to doubt that the murder of the Gimp is not connected with Mary Hart's murder, for there in the middle of both murders our friend VanBrunt is to be found. Clearly, he's a central part of the condition. Clearly, too, he did not knock himself out."

"But consider, Mr. Poe, VanBrunt was drunk when he went to Paradise Square to propose. Suppose Mary did reject him because he was drinking?"

"Are you acting the Devil's advocate?" asked Poe, smiling.

"Shouldn't one of us?"

"But, Sergeant, how can a man kill a woman and *then* run toward her scream?"

## Chapter 15

## THE STREET URCHIN

Walking through the Bloody Ould Sixth Ward at ten o'clock of a midweek morning was like walking through rip-roaring hell. Dance-houses, diving bells, and other dens of iniquity were booming. Near them the smell of alcohol overwhelmed the stench of miasma. Banjos banged, drums beat, horns blasted. Swarms of rag-footed, little tatterdemalions were underfoot. Pigs rolled in mud, oinking, or followed at your heels, begging a handout, like the innumerable thin mangy dogs of the area. Rats foraged, insouciantly. A dead horse was beaten by a cabman while several butchers gathered at the scene, cleavers in hand, and, behind them, hungry enough to be bold, a mob of the poor of both sexes, several races, and all ages collected like vultures for what remained when the butchers were satisfied.

In the center of the Five Points the women had arrived at Paradise Square with their wet rags. It was a good day for laundry. Clouds, like bunches of silken balloons, scudded across the blue, bird-peppered sky. Some of the laundry still steamed on the palings. The plutocrats among the poor handed out cornbread to the stave- or brickbat-bearing boys who would stand guard for them. Thus the lucky were assured of one small meal that day.

"There's Devlin," I said.

The ragged, dirty little boy stood before the laundry-festooned fence, smoking a cigar.

"It's youse again," he greeted us. "Youse'll get nothin' out o' me."

He was about four and a half feet tall and so light that he lifted off his feet when I collared him.

"You are going to visit some very nice people who would not approve of your cigar." I flung the rolled tobacco

into the street, where a mob of mop-headed urchins materialized to fight over it.

"Now see what ya done!"

"Come along," I said, "you little wolf's whelp! Do you
have anyone to stay with? Where you'll be safe?"

"I'm a orphan."

"We'll take him to the mission," I said. "They'll keep an
eye on him there."

"Oh, naw!" cried Devlin. "I hate them psalm-singers."

I knelt down before the boy and shook him by the shoulders. "Listen, my little man, there is somebody who may try
to do you in. Do you understand?"

"What? Me?"

"You know something important about the murder of
the Hot Corn Girl."

"I don't know nothin'."

"You know that the man who is accused of it probably
didn't do it."

"How do *you* know?"

"We have our methods." I winked at Poe, who was looking sadly down at the boy.

"You know," I went on, "that the girl screamed, and was
probably attacked, before the accused man had entered the
park. You know that, don't you? Admit it!"

"So what?"

"So *what*, is that the murderer may know you know it,
and may therefore want to do you in. Understand?"

"Jeese!" He stopped struggling and seemed inclined to
cooperate.

"You know I'm the law. See, here's my star."

"What you want I should do?"

"Just behave yourself and come along. And don't say
*Jeese*. They won't like it at the mission."

One group or other of social reformers always had an
outpost in the Five Points. The latest was the A.I.C.P., or, the

Association for Improving the Condition of the Poor. Many of the members were influential women whose male friends and relatives were wealthy. They were determined to see change in the Five Points. One specific and oft-stated goal was to tear down the Old Brewery, which they considered the source of the depravity that infected the area, and to build on its site a grand new mission house. At this time, however, they were located in a small, clapboard building on Little Water Street, off the Five Points.


Chapter 16


I FIND MY LOVE


Inside, several pretty Hot Corn Girls were engaged in finance with a man of about forty years of age who sat at a table counting stacks of coins. I stepped doubtfully up to the table, Devlin in tow, and asked of the man, "Is this the Association for Improving the Condition of the Poor?"

"He looked up from his business with a benign smile. "It is, sir, or rather it is one small outpost of our organization. Thadeus Thorndyke, at your service. What can I do for you?"

I told him my purpose, adding the question: "Are you a concessionaire?"

"I am a lay minister, sir—*and*, in the name of charity, a concessionaire." He addressed himself momentarily to the young ladies. "That's fine now. Until later, my dears. Report at the usual time this afternoon. Have faith in our Lord, who can make you money and keep you honest at once." The young women retreated.

"Now, sir. I see you are taken aback. Let me explain. We operate a hot corn concession for a two-fold purpose, first, to give the girls honest work and earnings, thus keeping them free from temptation and fostering their inherent honesty, and, second, to add to the coffers of the mission, to enhance its work."

"I see. I'd like to question the girls about Mary Hart."

"Oh, terrible thing, that! A lovely and innocent child, devil take her murderer, though God forgive him!" He looked down and back up. "The girls will be back at five o'clock to pick up their wares. It's getting near the end of our season."

"Are you one of the directors of this mission?"

"No, sir. I am but a helper. But you're in luck. Dr. Whitney, the Director of this outpost, is in back. I'll get her."

I looked at Poe, who pursed his lips. "Interesting," he said.

I could not know it, but one of the great moments of my life was about to flicker and pass into memory, the moment I laid entranced eyes upon the woman who would become my wife. She stepped out before Mr. Thorndyke from the back room, a woman in her early thirties, tall, well-formed, face tanned and radiant with physical health, eyes clear and blue and confident, hair upswept and piled in an amorphous light-brown crown.

"What can I do for you, sir?" she asked.

I was struck dumb. Poe intervened.

"Madam," he said, stepping in, "we've come to you for assistance with regard to the temporary safe-keeping of this boy." He took Devlin's cap from his head. "But allow me to present myself and my friends. I am Edgar Poe, this is Sergeant Jonathan Goode of the Municipal Police, and our young friend here is Master Daniel Devlin."

"Edgar Poe," said Dr. Whitney. "Would you happen to be Mr. Edgar *Allan* Poe, the author and poet, the editor of *Graham's Magazine*?"

"Yes, madam, I am that Mr. Poe, but that *former* editor."

"But, Mr. Poe, I am Eleanor Whitney."

Poe looked puzzled.

"Eleanor *Vance* Whitney. You once accepted several of my poems for *Graham's*."

"Of *course*," said Poe, his eyes lighting with recognition. "You're the author of that very powerful poem about the Old Brewery, 'Heathen House'."

"It is my intention to use all means at my command to rid the world of that horror," said my lovely, vehemently. A determined and talented woman.

"As I said, madam—a *powerful* poem. It enlisted my interest in your cause—and, indeed," Poe went on, "to such an extent that I have lately made a tour of your 'Heathen House' to see the conditions you described at first hand, as did my friend, Mr. Dickens—and about which he wrote in his 'American Notes.'" He glanced at me, furtively. "I also consider your poem about the late and much-to-be-lamented *Mr*. Whitney to be of great worth. It touched me more deeply, as I have recently myself suffered a grievous loss."

"I am sorry to hear that, Mr. Poe."

"My young wife, madam. An angel who trod on earth."

"We grieve together, then," said Eleanor Whitney. "But it has been, alas, some time since my husband passed on."

"The immediacy of your poem gave me to think that you were only recently bereaved."

"These things do not pass so readily, Mr. Poe. But I need not tell you. Forgive me."

"Not at all, madam. And how charming it is in these circumstances to meet with a fellow poet."

"But I am humbled before you, Mr. Poe. You are one of the great lyric voices of our age. However, I must admit to you something. Please don't be offended. It's just that I find your tales and stories to be—to be—"

"Morbid?"

She sighed. "Just so."

"You're not alone, madam. I write out of the German tradition of the Tales of A.T.E. Hoffmann, and I do so perhaps provoked by a world that contains an Old Brewery—or bull-baiting."

"I do not quite follow—"

"Excuse me," I said. "But we must explain our purpose. We are on an errand."

"Please, do explain!"

"We understand from Mrs. Hart, Mary's mother—Mary Hart who was killed in Paradise Square, and who worked for your association—"

"Yes, yes, I understand."

"—that you have been looking in on her, tending her in her need."

"Yes. We're trying to find a home for her."

"This boy was a witness to the murder, and we have reason to believe that he might be in danger. I was wondering if you could keep an eye on him while Mr. Poe and I go to investigate a matter pertaining to the case?"

"Certainly, Sergeant. I shall be happy to do so."

For the first time she looked at me full in the face, and my heart fell in my chest to see that there was no unusual sign of interest in her candid eyes.

Chapter 17

BULL-BAITING

The swivel-tied bull was scrawny, hollow of flank and knobby of joint. The dogs were at him snarling, tearing. A great devil of a dog tore a strip of muscle from the bull's flank. Blood gushed there, a red stripe. But immediately the enraged bull caught the dog with its horns and tossed it broken and squealing into the air. Poe slowly turned a stony-faced, contemptuous head, looking at the faces in the crowd. "What manner of beasts are these?" he said at last.

"Follow me to the owners," I said, "and see for yourself.

53

But have a great care. We are on dangerous ground."

We made our way through the crowd to the owners' stalls, where more bellowing bulls, more barking dogs, and more cackling human types, awaited their turns. I spotted Boodle Coign among a group of owners.

"I must call him out," I told Poe, "and it will be risky. It must seem that I'm accusing him of something so that the others won't suspect him of informing. But if I press him too hard, the others might come down on us like wolves, to protect him. A delicate balance. Stand clear until I get him alone."

I pinned my star to my coat and plunged into the group. "Coign, I want to have a word with you about some missing jewels."

The group closed on me. I'm a burly man, but these Plug Uglies were famous for their size and ferocity. I took Boodle by the arm, as if to lead him away, and found myself completely encircled by plug-hatted thugs. Boodle came to my rescue, as I'd hoped he would.

"It's okay, lads," he said. "This Friday-faced booly dog's got nothin' on me. I'll talk to him."

A space was made just large enough for us to walk through. I led Boodle over to Poe.

"Make it quick," said the Butcher under his breath.

"I'm collecting a debt, Boodle."

He shrugged. "Let's have it."

I told him, quickly.

"About Mary Hart's murder," he said, "I only know what I read in the papers. I do know something about Lucy Hart's murder, though. She was married to a Plug Ugly."

I nodded.

"Anyhow," he said, looking nervously about, "the cove's name was Joe Brody—"

"We've got that."

"Well, Joe Brody got the bright idea to threaten Boss

Meade by going to this journalist, Russell McNeil, and giving him some inside information, see?"

"Go on."

"But Boss Meade don't scare. Instead he tells the Butchers what Brody is trying to pull. They hack Brody's evil," he looked Poe over—"his wife, see—and they cut his conk."

"His conk?" said Poe.

Boodle tapped his nose with a long-nailed index.

"No-Nose," I said.

"But why didn't they kill Joe Brody?" asked Poe.

"No pain in that," said Boodle. "They hack up his wife and leave him to walk around without a nose, remembering. From what I hear, this Joe Brody was a ben—"

"A what?" asked Poe.

"A fool. Crafty, see, but a stupid cove. He had to be, to try a trick like that on Boss Meade."

"Do you know anything at all about Mary Hart?" I asked him.

"No; I told you."

"She was Joe Brody's sister-in-law," said Poe.

"She was? I don't know nothin' about it. Now you better let me go. They're watching us." I turned him loose. "Crushers don't get nothin' from me but a fibbing fist," he called out so his cohorts could hear, and marched off.

"What do you think?" I asked Poe.

"We have to have a long talk with No-Nose Mullins. But before we do, I'd like to have another look at the arena. I may want to pen some story with such a setting."

I had in my possession a Cuban cigar, which I drew from my vest and lit. I had been touched by Poe calling me friend. There was much in him that was different, unlike others, unique; it was the poet in him; and there was much in him too that was clear and understandable and admirable to a plain man like myself; viz., his courage, his honesty, his sense of honor, his courtesy, his kindness, particularly in evidence toward those whose minds were in relation to his as those of an order so much lower as to be different in kind. What went on in that complex mind? Perhaps it was not the thing in itself that he was looking at, the bull-baiting, but some ghostly meaning behind, beyond it. Much of the time there was something other-worldly about him, and sometimes I felt the need to draw him back, almost as if in fear that he should be permanently lost. I smoked my cigar for a quarter of an hour while Poe's eyes went from the ring to the crowd and back in a constant oscillation. Finally, he said: "How many are here, do you suppose?"

"Fourteen, fifteen hundred of the most vicious and dangerous coves and molls in the Frog and Toe, as they would call the City of New York. Come, Mr. Poe. We must be on to see Mr. McNeil of *The Broadway Star*."

Chapter 18

PLUG-UGLIES

We stepped out of the fortification and had gone a few steps across the muddy sod, when we were accosted by two plug-hatted giants, who were clearly up to no good.

"Back off!" I said, and took my pistol from my pocket. But one of the brutes outpaced me, slapping the pistol from my hand with the flat of a cleaver, which he immediately drew back and struck me with flatly across the hairline.

I awoke in a dimly-lit chamber which I could identify as a room in the fortification by the mossy stones of its narrow walls. The dim light came from whale-oil lamps, and the reek of the burning whale-oil was sickening in such close quarters. I shut my eyes and opened them again, and saw opposite me a bloodied figure chained to a wall. For a moment I thought I was having visions of our Savior, for my mind was dazed and my head pounded in tempo to an urgent tom-tom. I heard rough voices. Then I understood my situation. I was sprawled in a chair. The chair was in the middle of the room. The man on the wall was Boodle Coign, one of his ears cut off, blood streaming to the floor. Poe was nowhere to be seen.

Great fingers snaked into my hair and yanked my head back.

"He's awake." It was the man who had hit me.

He smeared his hand down my face, and I could smell blood, *my* blood. Consciousness deserted me, but returned immediately.

I pulled my feet under me and struggled forward, only to be pushed back. I shook my head and rubbed my eyes and looked at my hands, which were wet and sticky and red.

"What's that for?" I asked, indicating the man on the wall with a painful nod.

"He's a pigeon, as if I had to tell *you*. We suspicioned him for quite some time."

The other brute loomed before me. "You'll get the same, if you don't sing sweet, copper."

"Didn't you get it from *him*?"

"He told us you was interested in Joe Brody, his wife, and about that Hot Corn Girl what was kilt."

"Well?"

"Well, this: What's it all about? What you want to know about something that happened five years ago? What about the Hot Corn Girl?"

"You better talk, copper, or off with your ears." He menaced me with a cleaver, slashing down the left side of my head and then down the right within centimeters of my ears.

"It's the cleaver," I said, hoping to give them something to think about while *I* was thinking about how I could make my escape.

"The cleaver?"

"You boys carry cleavers. The Hot Corn Girl was murdered with a cleaver."

"Half of the blokes out in the arena is butchers. Dey all got cleavers. What's dat come to?"

"Boodle told us—" I thought of Poe. "Where's my friend?"

"Sleeping out on da sod."

"Did you . . . Was he hurt?"

"I snitchelled his gig," said the second brute, meaning he smashed his nose.

"We went over him," said the first brute, still waving the cleaver. "He ain't no copper—no star. Who is he?"

"A writer. A friend."

"A scribbler? I told you he wasn't worth draggin' in."

The first brute said:

"I ast you, what's it come to dat a mort was butchered?"

"She was Joe Brody's wife's sister," I told him.

They looked puzzled.

After a pause, the first brute said:

"Boodle went out before he told us dat."

He looked at the other, wrinkling his low brow into a washboard. He turned on me:

"You are saying—do I understand right? You are saying dat who kilt da mort, dis was de same as who kilt Joe Brody's wife?"

"Could be," I said. "We know the Butchers are an inside group in the Plug Uglies. They deal with politics—double voting, stuffing ballot boxes, or losing them. They're Boss Meade's personal strong arm boys. They carry cleavers hung by leather thongs from their belts—like you boys. We know that the Butcher's Gang killed Lucy Hart Brody and committed mayhem on Joe Brody."

I could think of nothing to talk about but the case. I had run it through my mind so many times I could recite my thoughts about it and think about a mode of escape at the same time. I reasoned that I wasn't telling them anything they didn't know, if they were guilty; and that, if they were not involved in Mary Hart's death, I might stir them to say something useful. Meantime, I considered the possibilities. Should I brace myself and make a headlong charge for the door? Should I feign unconsciousness and catch them off-guard?

"And we find it difficult to believe," I rambled on, "that Lucy and Mary Hart could be murdered by the same weapon, even if five years apart, and there not be a connection." I cried out, as if in pain, and slumped in my chair, closing my eyes.

"Rats!" came the voice of the first brute, "I must have hit him harder dan I taught. Get some water, Legs."

"Rather, gentlemen, disarm yourselves—and *quickly!*"

Poe stood in the doorway, pistol in hand. Blood oozed from his nose.

"Are you all right?" I wheezed, kicking an assortment of weapons toward the door.

"I shall have no need of an ivory conk," he said. "Would you be good enough to check on Coign, Sergeant?"

I felt Coign's chest. "He's alive," I said. Coign's arms were merely looped over the chains and I had no difficulty extricating him, so that his great beaten bulk fell heavily across my shoulders.

"Wait, Sergeant. We came here for information. You Butchers wanted to find out what Boodle told us. He told us that the Butcher's Gang killed Joe Brody's wife, Lucy. How about a fair exchange?"

"Why not?" said the brute called Legs. "You ain't gettin' out of here."

"We shall see," said Poe. "What do you know about Lucy Brody's death?"

"Sure. It was me and Butt, here, went up there that morning to get Joe Brody. We found him sitting over his wife's body. He done it."

"Why did Joe Brody kill his wife?"

"A bunch of the boys got drunk that Friday night," said Legs. "I was there, and so was Butt. They started teasing him about his wife and Meade. He left angry, and dead drunk. We never figured he'd kill her. But when we went there Sunday morning, she was dead. He must have done it that Friday night, judging from the state of her body."

"Fair enough," said Poe. "Let's go, Sergeant."

"We won't let you leave here with Coign, you know," said Butt.

I stepped out into the dark passageway, stubbing my toes on cleavers, pistols, brass knuckles, and black jacks. Poe backed out after me, pulling the heavy door shut.

"The fittings are here for a padlock," he said, groping at the door, "but I can't find one. Sergeant, have you got handcuffs?"

I balanced Coign's weight on my shoulders and reached an arm behind me, found my cuffs, and handed them to Poe, who looped a cuff into the padlock fitting.

"That should hold them," he said. "Lead on, Sergeant!"

I chose a direction, not knowing in the dim light any better way out than Poe would have known.

Chapter 19

LIGHT AT THE END OF THE TUNNEL

Before we had gone twenty paces the Butchers set up a noisy protest at our backs. They called for help, banged at the door, and heaved something heavy at it. The sounds of their angry, determined efforts reverberated down the stony passageways after us, echoing even ahead of us, so that, like bats in the dark, we could feel the walls before us.

"If someone hears," I said, panting, "they'll have an army upon us."

"Where is the way out, Sergeant?" cried Poe.

"Sir, I do not know! I only know that the other way goes into it."

But ahead there was light—faint light.

"What's that?"

"Take a turn, sir," I cried.

We came upon a glorious sight—a window, outside of which the day was bright with sun. But closer, and we saw that it was grated inside and barred outside.

"There is no way out here," said Poe.

Now we could hear the clattering of feet behind us, at some distance. "The place is a maze in the dark," said Poe.

"Let's hope that they've taken a wrong turn," I said.

"If so," said Poe, "the only way to undo our error is to continue in it beyond its power to confound us."

"Sir?"

"William Blake said that if a fool persists in his folly he will become wise."

"Sir?" I was exasperated, and about to say so. "Good heavens, Poe!—"

"We must go *through* the window," said Poe, who had begun to pry at the grating with the pistol. "This is an old fortification, and the weather of years has weakened its fixtures." The grate snapped, and Poe lifted it out. "Rust," he mumbled, "the Conqueror Worm of iron."

Voices sounded like an off-key choir.

"They're getting closer, sir!"

"I hear," said Poe, working at the window. He shattered pane after pane of glass with the pistol, then knocked out the woodwork. "Everything is old here," he said, "and rotted, and the country is but barely sixty."

"Sir?"

"A thought, Sergeant. I can see the masonry. It's quite weak. It was made for pressure from the outside, not inside. Ugh. I haven't the strength, Sergeant. Put Coign down and lend a shoulder here."

I joined Poe in pushing against the bars. We had, in a moment, established a rhythm, heave-ho, as it were, and felt a give, another, and a release of the bars, all in a grill, with a clang and a soft thump as they fell to the ground outside. We turned back to see a wavering light.

"I'll climb through," said Poe. "You hand Coign out."

I retrieved Coign's inert body and plunged it, helter-skelter through the window. I could hear Poe's efforts below.

Suddenly the hall brightened at my back, torch light merging with that from the window.

"There!" came a cry as I leaped. A ball whizzed above my dropping head.

I gathered up Coign.

"This way," cried Poe. "There's a carriage."

Poe ran ahead and opened the carriage door. I heaved Coign's bulk inside and climbed in after. Poe jumped into the open door, but hung outward, and cried to the driver, "Off with you! Go!

Go!"

A shot was fired from the window.

"Not me," said the driver. "Get away from my carriage!" A horse whip snapped down across Poe's back. He raised the pistol.

"Go, sir, or damn me, I'll blow your head off."

The carriage lurched, began to roll, gained speed, and plummeted ahead, Poe still hanging on. It was only when the carriage approached a more civilized section of the city, and Poe was certain that we had lost any pursuers, that he called for a halt. "I can shoot you off your seat through the carriage roof as well as from out here, sir," he said to the driver, and joined me inside.

"What now?"

"They've beaten Coign almost to death," I said.

Poe leaned out the window and cried:

"To the hospital!"

Now the carriage moved forward at a clip.

"How did you find me?" I said.

Poe wiped blood from his nose with his handkerchief. He was ashen, bloodless but for the red ooze at his upper lip, and soaking wet, though a mild November breeze rushed in the carriage windows. Outside, some of the pleasanter parts of the city could be seen.

"I knew they couldn't have taken you far. Why should they? They were among fifteen hundred of their own. If they took you, they must have done so to question you. That, they would not do in a crowd—therefore, one of the cells in the fortification."

"Where did you get the pistol?"

"It's yours. When I was struck I threw myself upon it. The devil of it was keeping it under me when I was searched."

"But why didn't you use the pistol when they were taking me away?"

"I hoped that there was something to be learned. I didn't intend to allow enough time to go by for you to be further injured. But you were quite unconscious. They should have to revive you first."

"You are a handy man to have around, Mr. Poe."

"But, bethink yourself, sir—had I used the weapon earlier, I should have been faced with a serious situation. Two toughs with raised hands, and an unconscious policeman, too heavy for me to lift, surrounded by enemies. No, sir, it was better that I did as I did."

"You mistake me, Poe," I said. "There was no irony in what I said. You are, indeed, a handy man!"

Mr. Poe did not take a compliment well, I saw, for now his face held a tinge of color.


Chapter 20


PHYSICIAN, HEAL THYSELF

At the City Hospital we turned Boodle Coign over to the

attention of physicians, and were ourselves treated for various abrasions. The blood was staunched in its flow from Poe's nose by the infusion of some unpleasant stuff, or so he told me. My head and hand were bandaged.

We went to have a look at VanBrunt, who remained unconscious.

"Is it all right?" I asked the doctor. "He has been thus for several hours now."

"With a concussion it's difficult to say. He could stay this way for a day—or forever."

"Physician, heal thyself!" said Poe bitterly.

"Sir?" The doctor looked at him.

"You speak in pathetic clichés," said Poe. "In your field, as in most, men of genius are few, and such are the only ones who can do humanity any good. My young wife is dead at the hands of physicians, whose ministrations, though no medico myself, I have been able, by virtue only of a mind that reasons, to see for the barbarisms that they were. Indeed, living on this earth is like living with stupid demons."

"Sir!" The doctor stood amazed at Poe's outburst, as I myself was.

He turned on his heel and strode out through the door.

"I apologize for my friend," I said to the doctor. "He has undergone great difficulties and is not quite himself. Is there a place where he and I might wash ourselves and comb our hair?"

"Down the hall," said the doctor woodenly.

We had told our carriage driver to wait, but we found him gone.

"Poe," I said, "why don't you go back to Red Kate's and get some rest. You were awakened by being shot at early this morning and you'd had little rest before that. Since then, we've been through all manner of difficulties and stresses, and, sir, you don't look at all well. Let's walk until we find a hack. I'll put you aboard, you go to our rooms, have something to eat, and get some sleep. What do you say?"

"I say, sir, that *The Broadway Star* is just around the corner."

Chapter 21

THE NEWS HOUND

The *Broadway Star* was in Newspaper Row between James Gordon Bennett's *Herald* and Horace Greeley's *Tribune*, a mouse between two elephants. We were told McNeil's office was on the second floor. There we found a short, burly, intense man with walrus mustaches, smoking a thick green cigar. He stared at us through owlish, silver-rimmed spectacles. I showed him my star and introduced myself and Poe.

"Poe?" he said. Interest formed where none had been. "Edgar Allan Poe?"

"I am he," said Poe.

"The poet, Poe?"

"The same."

"Well, sir," said McNeil, "a fellow writer. How interesting!"

"First, sir, a poet, then a writer, then a journalist," said Poe, slowly. "But, yes—a writer. I am an old hand in Printing House Square. I worked in the publication office of the *New York Mirror*, on Ann and Nassau Streets."

"I see," said McNeil, with a puzzled look on his face.

"There *are* distinctions," said Poe.

I suspected, as I believed McNeil was beginning to suspect, that Poe had insulted him. Poe was not helping our cause by offending McNeil. I broke in:

"We would like to have a word with you."

"I was just going out to eat," said McNeil coolly, as he gathered his things to leave.

"May we join you?" I asked.

He pursed his lips, grimaced, eyed Poe, and relaxed suddenly.

"Come ahead then," he said. "I am an admirer of Mr. Poe. I'd like to discuss his writing over an ale."

He took us to Fraunces Tavern at Broad and Pearl Streets. The place was crowded, festive almost, with its steamy, pungent smell of good food and drink. We took a corner table and ate with intermittent small talk. McNeil and I had good roast beef. Poe would have none of it, he said, after witnessing a bull-baiting. He ate minimally from a seafood platter, and drank amply of heavy dark ale.

"Bull-baiting," said McNeil, pushing back an empty plate. "It's a brute's sport, if sport it is to set a pack of hounds to torment a dying bull. It's something I'm going to write a series of articles about. I'll break the thing up, if I can."

"You are a genuine reformer, then, sir?" I said.

"I mean business," shot McNeil. "What did you imagine?"

"Well, sir," said Poe, "we journalists know the merit of a lurid tale."

"Circulation? Well, my stories make money, yes, if that's a crime; but I mean business, sir. I mean to have them out!"

"Who?" I asked.

"The corruptors. The politicians who use the gangs like swords hanging fire. I mean business, sir. I mean to have them out!"

"Highly commendable," said Poe.

"Well—" puffed McNeil. I thanked God that Poe had decided on tact.

I told McNeil what Boodle Coign knew about Joe Brody.

"Yes, Brody came to see me, but it wasn't much. He informed me that there was a connection between the gangs and the politicians, one in particular—Boss Meade."

"And—"

"And nothing. I told him that any fool knew that the Plug Uglies were connected to Meade. Meade's a respectable character now, if a political boss in the Five Points can be called such, but he came out of their ranks—first a butcher, many years ago, later a gang member, and now a politician, well known at City Hall. I told Brody that what I needed of a man such as himself—to be frank, a cutthroat—I needed evidence, proof positive."

"What did he say?"

"He seemed rather surprised at my reaction. I think he actually thought that it was news that Boss Meade and the Plug Uglies were tied up. He struck me as a stupid fellow. An improviser, but not a very astute one. So then, as if he were throwing me a carrot, he told me that Meade had lived for some time with a mort who had claim of being his common law wife. When Meade began to rise in politics, he bought her off by giving her the wherewithal to go into business as a saloon keeper. He didn't give me her name. It was implied that that was one gift he might offer me. It would have been useful, but not very."

I felt Poe's boot nudge under the table, hesitated, then said something other than I had intended to say.

"Joe Brody's wife was murdered," I said.

"Yes," said McNeil, "Lucy. Axed, wasn't she?"

"Cleavered," I said.

"Because of his visit to me, do you suppose?"

"Directly."

"Really!" McNeil pursed his lips, blew. "But he hadn't told me anything. Look, I'll be forthcoming with you, but I want the same. As a matter of fact, Brody said that he had his wife's diary, incriminating to Meade."

"What did he ask for?"

"Wanted the paper to give him some money for the story."

"How much?"

"He was—indefinite. It was rather vague, really, what he wanted."

"He wanted nothing," said Poe.

"Nothing? I don't quite—"

"He wanted nothing," Poe repeated.

I said: "He wasn't selling a story. Don't you see? He was going to put the screws to Boss Meade. Blackmail. You were his threat."

"I say—he *was* an addle-cove, wasn't he? I mean, to take on a bad bloke like Meade!"

"Meade came down on him like a hammer. He had Joe Brody's wife brutally murdered, and Brody's nose—amputated."

"I thought Brody was dead," said McNeil.

"He is," said Poe, "in a sense. He now wears an ivory—*conk*, and is known as No-Nose Mullins."

"He's one I don't know," said McNeil. "I mean, I *knew* Brody, but never heard of this No-Nose character."

"I read your piece on the murder of Mary Hart," said Poe. "Mary Hart is—was—Lucy Brody's sister."

"The cleaver again," said McNeil.

"The cleaver again," said Poe.

"When I wrote that piece, I had spoken only to the leatherhead who arrested VanBrunt. It seemed an open and shut case. A crime of passion. VanBrunt, mad with drink, could not accept rejection, and killed the girl. I was bothered by the weapon, but there was even a witness, a crippled kid, wasn't there?"

"He's dead—strangled," I said.

"Do you see a connection there? After all, life is very, very cheap in the Five Points."

"There is a connection," said Poe. "How could there not be, when Mary Hart's presumed murderer, Peter VanBrunt, was found comatose at the scene of the crippled boy's murder?"

"My God!" cried McNeil. "What's going on here?"

"That's the question," said Poe.

McNeil sat in thought for a moment, then said:

"You know, I wrote to the VanBrunt family—a gesture, you see—"

"To what effect?" asked Poe.

"I told them that he was in trouble. I sent them a copy of the newspaper piece on the murder. I thought the poor devil should have at least benefit of counsel. I understand that he's penniless."

"Did they respond?" I asked.

"They sent back that they would have nothing whatsoever to do with him."

"Loyalty," said Poe—"rhymes with royalty. The VanBrunts may be aristocrats but they are something less than royalty at its best, from which one expects noblesse oblige, at least."

"Speak not to me of royalty," said McNeil heatedly. "I'm an Irishman."

"So am I," said Poe. "But a Southerner."

"So am I," said McNeil. "But a Yankee."

Each glared at the other. Then laughed.

<br>

Chapter 22

<br>

## AN INVITATION

We found Dr. Whitney, the sleeves of her dress rolled up, filling oaken buckets with hot, roasted corn. "Ah, Sergeant Goode, Mr. Poe." She stopped work and drew us aside.

"That poor little Devlin! He told me about himself. What a sad tale! He remembers a cottage in Ireland—a voyage aboard a crowded ship—then very little—then being in care of one or another foster parent—and finally living on his own, hand to mouth. He thinks his parents are dead. He's been living in a box. Actually living in a wooden crate! He's an intelligent little fellow. What can we do to help him? There *is* an orphanage . . . . Oh, it disturbs me!"

She threw up her hands, then said: "Despite our best efforts, between twenty and sixty thousand children in this city are not in school. In fact, there has been a conspicuous increase in the numbers of vagrant children, boys and girls without schools, jobs, or like Danny, homes of any sort. It's estimated that there are at least three thousand vagrant children in lower Manhattan, most here in the Five Points. Poor tads, they support themselves by selling fruits, nuts, petty merchandise, or just plain scavenging. Even—dare I say it— prostitution. They live on the leavings of this great city. Almost every week there is the gloomy knell of an execution, generally a young man, once one of the street boys.

"And I believe the case for the girls is even worse. Often they are driven to harlotry out of desperation and are murdered or die an early death as a result of disease. How can this happen in Eighteen Forty-seven? It's a disgrace!" She paused, sighing. "You must pardon my vehemence, but I work for the A.I.C.P., and have the statistics at my fingertips."

"Where *is* Danny?" I asked.

"Out back, in our little yard. He's chopping wood. I've had to roast the corn for the girls. Mr. Thorndyke is late. It's after five." She put long, delicate fingers to wide, delicate lips, and flashed large blue eyes at the ceiling. "I usually have more help. The other ladies of the mission would be here, but we have several ill, and several otherwise engaged. We're quite politically active, as you may know. And that reminds me. I'd like to invite you both to attend a Democratic convention tomorrow at three at the Broadway Tabernacle. Afterwards perhaps you'll come to my home. I'm giving a dinner party for a few politicians and friends. We should all be

honored, Mr. Poe, if perhaps you would recite a poem or two
for us. Of course, you've made a sensation with your 'Raven.'"

"I'd be honored, madam."


Chapter 23


SPEAK OF THE DEVIL


Upon our arrival, several Hot Corn Girls had been waiting to receive their wares. Now and again during our conversation others had entered, prepared for work.

Danny Devlin came from the back room carrying a great
pile of wood, and heaved it down by the fireplace. He was
puffing on a two-inch green butt of cigar.

"*Danny*!" cried Dr. Whitney. "Where did you get that
disgusting—*thing*? Take that out of your mouth this instant!"

"Aw, *Jeese*!" cried the boy, removing the soggy cigar.

"Into the fire with it!"

He raised wide thick sandy brows and eyed the morsel
wistfully with wide blue eyes.

"I don't know where he gets them," said Dr. Whitney.
"This is the third one I've taken from him since you left."

"Have you searched him?" I asked.

"Indeed I have."

We looked back at the boy to discover that he was gone.

"Did he dispose of it?" asked Dr. Whitney.

"We shook our heads, not knowing.

"Girls?"

The Hot Corn Girls looked at us and shrugged.

"And," Dr. Whitney went on, "though I know he does
not realize what he is doing, he constantly takes the name of
the Lord in vain." She paused, frowning, then smiled largely,
and added: "But he *is* adorable, isn't he?"

"You have no children, ma'am?" I asked.

"Unfortunately not. I love children. But I've been an extremely busy woman. College. Post-graduate work in France and Germany. I served my apprenticeship with Dr. Harriet Hunt, of whom you may have heard, in Boston, and have every right to the title 'Doctor,' of which I am extremely proud. Though others may heap scorn and ridicule upon women physicians, our day will come."

Poe stood quite erect, his face pale as paper. I knew he was growing impatient.

"Dr. Whitney," I said, emphasizing the title, "I'd like to question the young ladies."

"Please proceed, then, sir. For as soon as Mr. Thorndyke arrives, he'll have them off on their rounds."

I asked the girls, as a group, if they, any of them, had known Mary Hart at all well. I was told that she had kept to herself. But then one girl stepped forward to say that she had been unusually friendly with the dead girl.

"Your name, please?"

"Sybil O'Shaughnessy, sir."

I asked her to wait after the others had gone.

"But my work, sir."

"I'll pay for the corn out-of-pocket, Miss O'Shaughnessy, and you can take it home early to your family. How's that?"

"Oh, wonderful, sir!"

"This is the end of the season for us," said Dr. Whitney. "You have given Miss O'Shaughnessy a gift of time, Sergeant. I'm sure she thanks you for it."

"Oh, I do, sir! I thank you. And I'll be glad to you tell you anything I know that will be of help."

"Then I thank *you*, Miss O'Shaughnessy," I said. "But first, I'd like to ask *you* a few questions, Dr. Whitney."

"Dr. Whitney," a girl interrupted, "where is Mr. Thorndyke?"

"I don't know, dear," Dr. Whitney said, "but don't

bother me just now. I must answer this gentleman's questions. Proceed, sir!"

"Am I correct in assuming that you knew Mary Hart?"

"I don't know if I should say *knew*. I knew her as I know these girls, but, you see, Mr. Thorndyke has direct dealings with the girls generally. I am usually occupied with other missionary matters. Today is quite extraordinary."

"Can you describe her?"

"But you must know what she looked like."

"I don't refer to a physical description. Did you—do you know anything of her personal life?"

"I don't quite see what you're getting at, Sergeant. Of course I know her mother. The ladies of the mission are attempting to relocate Mrs. Hart, to find a home for her. It's difficult to place a blind woman, as you can imagine. We hope, in a few years, to have an institution of some kind—a home for children, the old, and the handicapped—but, at present—"

I interrupted.

"Dr. Whitney, what I am about to ask may seem to you to be—odd. Please, simply answer my next question straightforwardly."

"Of course. Proceed!"

"Do you remember any contact between Mary Hart and a large man who—who—has no nose . . . eh, wears an artificial nose—?"

"My heavens, no!" She looked askance. "One *does* see so many odd things—and persons—in the Five Points—but no, I should have remembered such a person, I'm confident. But, as I say, I really don't generally deal directly with the girls." She shook her head negatively, pursed her lips, then smiled brilliantly. "I'm afraid not!"

Poe said: "We've discovered, through Mary's mother, that Mary had a brother-in-law named Joe Brody. This Brody was a member of a gang called the Butcher's Gang. You must have seen members of this gang around the Five Points. They're generally quite large men, and accentuate their height by wearing tall plug, or top, hats, which they stuff with soft material and use as helmets. They wear long duster-type coats, and spiked brogans. They're also called Plug Uglies."

"Yes, I've seen them."

"Well, as I say, this Joe Brody, Mary's brother-in-law, was a gang member. Through another member of the gang, we were able to discover that Joe Brody is now known as No-Nose Mullins, the use of the first appellation being self-explanatory."

"In other words," said Dr. Whitney, "you want to learn whether Mary's brother-in-law had been in contact with her."

"Exactly," I said.

"I can't help you there," she said. "I asked Mrs. Hart if she had any relatives and she told me that she did not. I wonder why she told me that."

"Because," said Poe, "she believes Joe Brody is dead."

"I see. But, if Mary had been seeing Joe Brody, wouldn't she have told her mother that he was alive?"

"If Mary had crossed his path," I said, "she would probably think it just as well to let her mother go on believing he was dead. You see, Mary's sister was murdered by the gang five years ago, and Joe Brody disappeared at that time. Mrs. Hart believed him dead, murdered as well."

"How horrible!"

"But Mrs. Hart hated her son-in-law," said Poe. "Mary would not upset her mother by bringing him up—or back from the grave, as it were. As the girls say, Mary was one to keep her own counsel."

"Why was Mary's sister murdered?" asked Dr. Whitney. "And the son-in-law—?"

"Our informer has explained that to us," I said. "It seems that Joe Brody, alias No-Nose Mullins, was threatening to expose a political personage, namely, one Boss Meade—"

"*Mead*!" cried Dr. Whitney.

"You are acquainted with Mr. Meade?" asked Poe.

"More than acquainted. Boss Meade is a member of my party. A Tammany Democrat, but a Democrat, nevertheless. He is to host the convention tomorrow. It's our intention to reform our party, to clean it up, as the gentlemen say. And Boss Meade is our prime target. He is corruption itself!"

"I should be careful, Dr. Whitney," warned Poe, "in any contest with such a man. A Mr. McNeil, a journalist—"

"But, of course," said Dr. Whitney. "I know Russell McNeil. He'll report the convention tomorrow, and will be a guest at my home for dinner. Our reform movement heartily approves the things he has been writing about the Five Points. He's the sort of man we want on our side. How good that you should know him!"

"What is important to understand," I said, "is that Boss Meade was once a butcher, was once a member of the Plug Uglies, and is now *the* butcher of *the* Butcher's Gang. It was this knowledge, I believe, and other, even more incriminating information, that caused the death of Mary's sister, Lucy. Joe Brody threatened to expose Meade. But Meade, not a man to be threatened, retaliated."

"That such a—*brute*—should control the Sixth Ward—*this* ward—or have any political influence at all—or not be in prison—is—horrifying!"

Chapter 24

## THADEUS THORNDYKE IS LATE

"But where is Mr. Thorndyke? It's getting quite late. Sybil," Dr. Whitney called, "would you be a dear, and run next door to see what's keeping Mr. Thorndyke. He should have been here an hour ago." She turned back to us. "He lives next door on the second floor. Poor man, he's attempting, somehow or other, to become a minister. I suppose it's all part of Andrew Jackson's anti-professionalism. He has no formal training. He's been a concessionaire most of his life, and now his re-birth unto our Savior, I fear, has brought him to poverty through charitable work."

Sybil O'Shaughnessy opened the door and screamed.


## Chapter 25


## THE LATE THADEUS THORNDYKE


Thadeus Thorndyke swayed in the doorway, the windy street behind him, a white patch on his chest, and a cleaver wedged in his skull. He looked about the room imploringly, and pitched forward on his face.

The girls screamed and huddled together. I tried to turn Dr. Whitney away from such horror, but she stood firm. Poe went to the body, gently pushing the frozen Sybil O'Shaughnessy aside.  Dr. Whitney took a stride, and went down on one knee beside Thorndyke. She lifted his shoulder and felt his heart. She extracted her hand and felt the neck artery. She looked up at me.

"Dead."

Poe bent over the dead man, pulled a sheet of paper from his chest, and read it. He handed it to me. I read:

*WARNING REFORMERS!!!*
*MARY HART WAS #1*
*THORNDYKE #2*
*DR. WHITNEY BEWARE!!!*

I pocketed it before Dr. Whitney noticed.

"There's a trail of blood out here," said Poe, from the doorway.

"One of you girls," I said, "run and fetch a leatherhead. Dr. Whitney, do you have the names and addresses of these girls?"

She nodded yes.

"Out you go, then, girls, be off with you. There'll be no work tonight."

Dr. Whitney and I dragged the body into the room to make way at the door for the girls to exit.

She said: "Sergeant, in the backroom you'll find a stack of blankets. Bring one to cover him."

A leatherhead appeared at the door. "What's this?" he said.

"I am Eleanor Whitney, physician. I believe it's obvious what's happened, officer."

"Yes sir—er, uh, *ma'am*."

I threw a blanket across the body. My nerves, which are usually quite steady, had been jangled a bit by the sight of the walking dead man with the cleaver in his head. I was annoyed with myself, especially in the sight of the commanding Dr. Whitney.

Poe had vanished from the door. I stepped out and saw a trail of blood, but no Poe. I called back to the patrolman:

"Where is the girl who fetched you?"

"She went on, sir."

"Terrified, no doubt." It would be difficult to get anything more out of Sybil O'Shaughnessy now. I cursed myself for not having questioned her first.

I followed the bloody trail the few steps to the next door, which was open, and into that house. Dr. Whitney followed me. The blood was on the stairs. I went up, found a door open, and Poe inside. He looked at us, said:

"He was struck at least an hour ago. There's a great deal of blood—some, here, where he must have sprawled, is quite warm—some, over there"—he waved a hand—"quite cold. I should say the blow rendered him unconscious, that after a time he awoke, a living ghost in a nightmare, and found his way to the mission door, probably quite automatically."

"I agree," Dr. Whitney said. "The cleaver prevented him

from bleeding to death, staunching the flow."

"Look how the outer ring of blood has not only become cold," said Poe, "—there is a draft here—but it's congealed and darkened." He looked at me. "This might have happened when we were with McNeil, having our lunch," he said.

Downstairs, Dr. Whitney gave the policeman a key to the mission. I left him in charge.

Poe looked ill. Again I suggested that he return to Red Kate's for some much needed sleep. This time he agreed.


Chapter 26


NO COWARD SOUL IS MINE


Dr. Whitney, Danny Devlin and I rode into the night. Our destination was Dr. Whitney's home in Washington Square. She had kindly offered to keep the boy with her until a place could be found for him.

I let some time pass before telling her the contents of the note. I felt that she had to know, and indeed had every right to know, that she was under such a threat. I was not very surprised to see that the news did not discompose her. I had remarked her courage at the mission, in face of a horror that should have caused most women of her sensitive breeding to faint.

"No coward soul is mine," she replied, apparently quoting someone, when I commented on this. "I have faith, sir, that most women are quite as brave, if not braver, than most men. I have borne a dead child and can bear no other. What more can happen? I have lost a husband who, though considerably older than myself, was to me an object of affection. What more, I pray, sir, can happen? I am in the worldly sense wealthy, but I should be poor in spirit if I allowed the beast who committed such an atrocity upon poor simple Mr. Thorndyke to intimidate me. No, sir. I shall proceed openly tomorrow to my condemnation of that Asmodeus, Boss Meade. I am a worker in the path of righteousness, sir, and I would gladly be a martyr to the cause of good."

"I do not doubt you, ma'am," I said. "But do you give time to other thoughts, at all?"

"What thoughts, Sergeant?"

"Beg pardon, ma'am. Your single-mindedness rather overwhelms me."

"To what, exactly, do you refer, Sergeant? I have a life in society, as well. My dinner party tomorrow, for instance—a reading by Mr. Poe—"

"You no longer wear black?"

"As you see, I do not. My husband, excellent man that he was, has been gone for well over a year. And, as I've said, he was quite my senior."

"You—*loved* him—*greatly*?"

"Loved? In a sense, surely. Sergeant, as you may have noticed, I speak my mind directly. You are not in the company of a lily. Are you asking if we might become friends?" I cleared my throat, for this was my moment. It was my *destiny*, though I did not know it. "Yes, ma'am. I should like very much to become your friend."

"Then, proceed, Sergeant—proceed, by all means!"

I deposited Dr. Whitney and Danny at the door of her great white house.

"I shall have the house watched," I told her.

"That will be a comfort, Sergeant. I shall look forward to seeing you at the convention. You and Mr. Poe. Is he very ill?"

"Exhausted, I should think. We've had a hectic day."

A butler had opened the door, to my regret. At my back I could hear the stirs of nature in Washington Square Common. The early evening moon beamed down, and a chaos of stars kaleidoscoped overhead. My love wore the faint moon's light like a gossamer wedding gown.

"Eleanor," I said, and took her hand, and kissed it with trembling lips.

Chapter 27

ABOUT THE BOSS

Poe and Kate sat at Kate's favored table, where we had sat the night before, when VanBrunt had enjoyed his brief freedom and reunion. They were sipping rum and talking quietly. It wasn't until I took a seat that they became aware of me.

"I've just been telling Kate about what happened at the mission today," said Poe, "and about VanBrunt and the Gimp."

"Thank God Peter's alive!" said Kate. "I'll go to the hospital as soon as possible."

I asked Poe—

"Have you broached the subject yet?"

"I thought I'd wait until you arrived."

"What subject?" asked Kate.

"Your relationship to Boss Meade," I said.

Poe said: "I've noticed that Meade's picture is up in nearly every drinking house in Five Points, along with those of George Washington and Queen Victoria—quite an odd combination, I might remark in passing—but Meade is not to be seen here."

"I'd use it for a dart board," said Kate. "Well, it's no secret, at least as far as I'm concerned. I don't suppose Meade would like me jawing it about, though. Yeah, I knew him— *well*—and *when*. My name is—"

"Katherine Mary Ross," I said.

"From County Kerry," she said proudly. "Meade's real name is Ruark—Patrick Ruark, also from County Kerry. He was a butcher, and a handsome devil. Devil be his name!

There was nothing in Ireland for the likes of me and nothing for me here when I came, a snip of a girl, but harlotry. Paddy Ruark—he hadn't changed his name yet—had ambitions. I met him drunk in my bed of business—a brutal, handsome giant. When he learned that I was from Kerry, he offered me an opportunity. *I'll set you up in a green grocery*, he said. *Run me a business.* A green grocery! I was green myself, and didn't know what he meant. But I learned that the green groceries of Paradise Square have got little to do with the few rotting vegetables that sit and stink up the air out front, and all to do with the cheap, poisonous whiskey they sell in back.

"It was in my—or *his*—green grocery that Paddy Ruark formed a gang. The gang was to be his power base and his stepping stone to greater power—of a political sort. Power was all he thought or cared about. He changed his name to one that sounded less Irish, for the really important politics of the city—business, banking, etc.—was firmly in the grasp of the Dutch, English, and Germans. He became Robert Meade, and eventually—you can imagine how—*Boss* Meade."

She reached over and took a sip from Poe's glass. His piercing eyes were fixed upon her. "Wirra!" she cried. "But when he went legit, he tossed me aside, calling me nothing but a cat, a whore. A cat I was, perhaps, but not a cheap puss. I bought into a tavern with the money I had made selling bad whiskey, and began to sell good whiskey on the grounds that honesty is the best policy. Now I have this place—tavern and lodging house. Next I'm moving out of Five Points, up to the Bowery, where respectable people go. Maybe Meade wants to become the mayor of New York himself. There's no end to him. But I'll eventually settle for a fancy saloon on Fifth Avenue and the society of bankers." She snorted.

"I wanted to marry him once. But if his gang's done this in an effort to frighten the reformers and to make Peter look responsible, I'm going to see McNeil myself, and fill his ears with what I know about Meade. *Boss!* Paddy Ruark, the pig!

Chapter 28

## MULLINS BOUNCES

Mullins stepped up to our table.

"Did you find Max Fisch?" I asked him.

"No. I searched the Old Brewery. All over Paradise Square. I couldn't find him."

"Sit down, Mullins," Poe said. "We have some questions to ask you."

Mullins pulled out a chair and sat down. His eyes seemed to be full of fear and hatred of Poe. Was he jealous because Red Kate appeared to like the poet?

"We have discovered," I said, "that you are—or were—Mary Hart's brother-in-law."

I detected a slight widening of his dull, stupid eyes. Yes, I could imagine him strutting along the infested, swine-ridden streets of the Five Points, a good-looking giant in a leather-stuffed top hat, kicking at the pigs with his hob-nail boots, a cleaver dangling from his belt.

Slowly, he said:

"I was . . ."

"Was what?" I said.

"Was Mary Hart's brother-in-law."

"Why didn't you tell us this before?"

"Because I don't want nothing to do with it. I haven't seen her in five years. She was just a kid, then. The last time I saw Mary, she was but sixteen. I knew her when she was ten. But I haven't laid my eyes on her for five years, I swear! It didn't have nothing to do with me."

"Tell us about Lucy," said Poe. "Tell us how it was that she was murdered with the same type of weapon that was used on Mary."

"I don't know . . ." Like a boy trying to fix his thoughts, Mullins shrugged huge shoulders.

"Tell them," ordered Kate. "And tell me. I like to know who is working for me. Mr. Poe tells me that your real name is Joe Brody. Is that true?"

"My name *is* Joe Brody."

"And you worked for Meade?"

"It was after you and Meade split up, after he opened the American Saloon," he said to Kate. "I heard about you, knew who you were. I was in the Plug Uglies. Lucy took up with Meade behind my back. It must have been going on for about a year before I found out. But it was just then that he was going to ditch her—like he done with you. But Lucy was real smart, smarter than me, and she never let on to Meade that she was smart. He didn't worry about her at all. She had been with him when he was making deals—"

"What kind of deals?" I asked.

"Deals like using city money to buy land for himself. Lucy was real smart. She had written everything down in a diary."

"Did you see this diary?" asked Poe.

Mullins shook his head. "I never saw it. Look, it was like this. I was drinking with the boys, and they let on about Lucy and Meade. I went home that night and asked her. She was brazen. I never could tell her what to do, on account of she was smarter than me, and I knew it. She could read and write. Then she tells me how Meade's going to do her dirt."

"You weren't angry to find out that your wife was cheating?" I asked.

Again, he shrugged. "We was going our own ways, by then. I wasn't so much angry at her as I was at Meade, making me look—"

"Cuckolding you," said Poe. "Shaming you."

"Anyhow, Lucy says there's a way we both can get even with Meade. I have everything in a diary, she says, names, dates—you go to that reformer, McNeil, and see what he says. So I go and feel McNeil out. He wants evidence."

Poe said: "That's when someone in McNeil's office apparently went to Meade with news of your visit. Meade would have tipsters everywhere."

"Then I go home and tell Lucy. We think what to do, how to handle it. We could get a lot of money from Meade, Lucy says, but we have to be careful how we do it. She has the diary stashed away someplace safe, she says. I don't even get to see it until we work things out. Then, on a Sunday morning, we were sitting and thinking what to do, and in breaks a couple of the Butchers. I was pretty drunk from drinking all night. Meade is a bad one, and he's got a hundred like me. So they catch me like that, drunk, and I can't handle them. They search the house, tear everything apart. They ask Lucy about the diary. She says there ain't no diary, that she made it up. But she *could* write one. One cove takes a cleaver to her, and she is down at my feet dead, her head split open. They take me away with them to the backroom of the American Saloon. Meade's waiting there. He asks me where the diary is. I tell him I never saw it. I tell him I don't think there ever was one. I tell him I think Lucy made the whole thing up to calm me down. And because she's angry with him, too. Who knows how a woman's mind works? They beat me a few times, and I say the same things over and over, because it's the truth, I *don't* know.

"Finally, Meade says he believes me. He says Lucy is too dumb to do anything like that, and that I'm even dumber. He tells them to take me out and make me remember not to ever cross him. He tells me never to show my nose in the Five Points again and he fixes it so I don't. I was in the hospital a few days, then I went to work on an oyster sloop, down to Virginia. Stayed down there about a year. When I came back, I didn't look the same. I grew a beard and let my hair grow long. I wanted to stay out of trouble with Meade. I remembered Red Kate. I figured she wasn't no friend of Meade and neither was I, so I came here and asked for work. She give me it."

"Regarding Mary," Poe said, "who do you think killed her?"

Mullins surveyed the table. "I know you're all on his side, but I figures VanBrunt done it. He said here at the bar that he was going to ask her to marry him. I figures he asks her, and she says no, and, him being drunk, he takes a cleaver to her."

"Where would he get a cleaver?" asked Poe.

"I don't know. Anywhere."

"Why would he take a cleaver with him? He was going to propose marriage."

"Maybe he had it to protect himself on the streets."

"Possibly," said Poe, "but not probably."

"Well," said Mullins, "maybe there *was* a diary, and maybe Mary found it, and maybe Mary and VanBrunt was going to use it to blackmail Meade. . . ."

"An ingenious theory," said Poe, startled by Mullins' capacity for invention, not heretofore observed.

"Yeah," said Mullins, "maybe Mary found it. Maybe Mary and VanBrunt was going to use it the same way Lucy threatened to. But I always figured VanBrunt killed Mary because she wouldn't marry him. I dunno."

Poe said: "Mary's mother said that Mary was prepared to accept VanBrunt's proposal of marriage. You knew he was going to ask her."

"But he was drunk that night. Besides, I didn't know that she would accept him. That's news to me. How could I? I haven't seen her for five years."

"Have you heard of a Mr. Thorndyke?" I asked.

"No."

"You know about the mission? The Association for Improving the Conditions of the Poor?"

"I've heard of it—the reformers?"

"The reformers," said Poe.

"What about the mission? And who's Thorndyke?"

"Thorndyke worked for the mission," said Poe. "He ran the hot corn concession. He was Mary's boss."

"Oh? So what?"

"He was murdered with a cleaver this afternoon," I said.

Mullins shook his head, his ivory beak slowly cutting the green smoke of his cigar. "I don't understand," he said. "What does it mean? What's the connection?" His consternation seemed genuine.

I slapped the warning note on the table and read it to him. "*Mary Hart was number one*," I read aloud, "*Thorndyke number two. Dr. Whitney, beware!*"

"Who's Dr. Whitney?" he asked.

"One of the ladies of the mission," said Poe.

"A lady doctor?" Mullins looked incredulous. "Well, then," he said, "that explains everything. Maybe it wasn't VanBrunt. No, it wasn't VanBrunt at all. Mary Hart was killed by the gang to scare the reformers."

"You think so?" said Poe. "You certainly leap about in your conclusions, don't you?"

"Well, it's what *you* think, ain't it?"

"I haven't thought things through to any conclusion yet," said Poe. "Have you, Sergeant Goode?"

"No, sir, I haven't," I said. "Mullins, that's all for now."

"Go ahead," said Kate to Mullins. "We'll settle accounts later." She looked at Mullins as he stood, tilting her head toward the bar. "Bring up another case of the good stuff," she said, "we're swamped tonight."

"Yes, ma'am," he said, and ambled off, into the crowd.

The Emerald Isle was packed. A contingent of Portuguese sailors, in that afternoon, added a boisterous festiveness to the din.

Chapter 29

## MIDNIGHT CONFIDENCES

"What do you intend to do about Mullins?" Poe asked Red Kate.

"He came to me because I'm against Meade," she said. "Why should I turn him out?"

"Indeed," said Poe, noncommittally.

I looked at Poe's haggard face and said, "Let's turn in."

He nodded agreement.

"Goodnight, Kate," I said, rising.

"Goodnight, gentlemen." We left her sitting in deep thought.

When we came to Poe's room, he drew me in, closed the door, and offered me the one chair in the room. He sat on the bed.

"Well, Sergeant, what do you think?"

"There's really only one thing I feel sure of, that is that everything we've learned today points away from Mr. Van-Brunt."

"I agree. You have observed the contradictions, of course. If we are to take at face value the note left by Thorn-dyke's murderer—then how account for the strangulation of the Gimp?"

"I wonder," I said, "if there really was—is—a diary?"

"If there is such a diary, it would have to be in the pos-session of Mary Hart's mother. That little family would seem to have had no friends."

"But surely she would have turned the diary over to the police—or to someone who could make use of it."

"Perhaps not. Consider—the diary was probably mor-ally, maybe legally, incriminating to Lucy. If such a diary ex-isted, it would be, after all, a record of Lucy's moral turpi-tude—a diary of adultery, debauchery and projected blackmail. The impoverished old lady remains a highly moral woman. She would not want the diary made public. Then, too, consider that she's blind. It could be that the diary is somewhere about and she knows nothing of it."

"It must have occurred to you," I said, "that Mullins, knowing the value of such an item, would have searched for it. He must have had opportunity."

"And we should certainly have seen the results. Had Mullins laid hands on the diary, it would have become apparent—to wit, he would not now be working for Kate, but would either be rich, relatively, or dead. No, Mullins doesn't have it."

Poe furrowed his high, wide brow. "But did Mullins have the opportunity? Did anyone, without causing notice? Had Mrs. Hart been broken in upon, she would have said. Her place is too small to have been burgled while she was there, and her not know, and she claims never to leave it."

"Except for church services—at the mission, on Sunday morning."

"All right," said Poe, "suppose someone—Meade, say, or his agents—broke in on a Sunday morning and got the diary—"

Poe got up wearily from the bed and pulled out a bottle of rum from the dresser drawer. He sat down again and poured two glasses. He handed me one and raised his to me. *Santé!*"

"Cheerio!" I replied, and drank. "No use trying to use Mullins's word against Meade. Mullins is not a good witness. His character is bad, and five years have elapsed. It's quite frustrating for a policeman. I should have arrested those thugs back at the fortification, but I couldn't. If we had marched them out at gunpoint, we'd have been mobbed. Had I sent a detachment of police back in, there'd have been a riot. I hope someday to see an adequate police force in this city."

"Have you read Vidocq?"

"No, sir—I haven't. Who is he?"

"Please call me Eddie, Sergeant, as all my friends do."

"Then let me be Jon to you—Eddie."

"Well done. Vidocq was a French police spy, whose memoirs ran in serial form in a journal—oh, sometime ago. I found them fascinating. Indeed, they suggested certain aspects of my story, 'Murders in the Rue Morgue.' I should think that you would enjoy reading them."

"I shall seek them out," I said.

Poe refilled our glasses.

"Why did you become a policeman—*Jon*?"

"I was reared on rectitude—*Eddie*. My father was owner-master of a ninety-ton schooner. He brought oysters up from the sea islands of the coast of North Carolina and carried back miscellaneous freights to Southern ports. As a boy, I made many trips with him, and so learned something about sea life.

"In Eighteen-Forty, his schooner sank in a storm off Long Island. All aboard were drowned, including my mother, who had sailed for pleasure. I was not aboard because of a mild but disabling illness, and was recuperating with an aunt. I was left penniless. I am still waiting for an insurance settlement.

"In Forty-five, I went on the revenue steamer 'Morgan' and remained with her for several months. I remember the great fire in New York of that year, at which the crew of the 'Morgan' and a contingent of United States Marines from the Brooklyn Navy Yard assisted as guardians of property. That was my first experience as a keeper of the peace.

"I grew weary of life at sea, left the 'Morgan,' took up residence in Greenwich Village, and went into business, selling products brought to Washington Market by the river craft. In spring, summer, and fall I was kept busy, but during the winter months I had nothing to do. I had never thought of police work until my cousin asked me if I'd like to take his place. As you can see, I am three-quarters of me bulk—"

"Burly muscle, Jon!"

"In any case, made for action."

"Hence, the police." Poe seemed to be thinking back. "I was not always as you see me today," he said. "As a young man, I was an athlete. I still hold the broadjump record for the University of Virginia."

"Yes, Mr. VanBrunt told me that—and that you were a soldier—an enlisted man."

"Yes—before I went to West Point. Back in May of Eighteen Twenty-seven—about twenty years ago now—I enlisted in the army under the name of Edgar A. Perry. I rose to the rank of Sergeant Major in nine months—something of a record, I believe. I was in for two years . . ."

"I became a police sergeant in about the same length of time."

"The two good Sergeants," said Poe, toasting us with raised glass.

"To the two good Sergeants!" I said.

We drank, and fell into an embarrassed silence, which I finally broke by saying:

"You comported yourself like a soldier today, Eddie."

"Ah, physical courage is nothing, particularly to one in my melancholy state of mind. But I don't know if I have emotional courage enough. The thought of my lost young wife fairly kills me, Jon."

"You may have saved my life."

Poe shrugged. "A worthy life. You are a bachelor?"

"I've never had time for women. But now that I've been promoted, I'd like to marry and have children. I am studying law, thinking of the future. I've been living meagerly, saving my money."

"Money," said Poe, "or the lack of it, has been the curse of my life. Had I the money to pay for good medical treatment—had I the money to buy decent food—had I the money for *blankets*—my darling might still grace the world."

"Was there no way?"

"I *worked*—harder than ten men. And not only in journalism and literature. I have laid bricks. I have clerked. I have done menial labor. Money will simply have nothing to do with me. Oh, I am the wrong man for this commercial world!"

"Perhaps too good for it, Eddie."

He placed his gray eyes upon me.

"You've made me feel better, Jon. Not in that last comment—I am none too good for this world, I assure you. But, you see, since my wife died, I have been . . . well . . . as you found me. Spiritually ill. Oh, rot! I've been drinking, and I have no tolerance for the stuff. I even dislike the taste of it, so I throw it down in a gulp. I want the result—forgetfulness. But seeing Peter has reminded me of my youth, when all was new and shining. And Peter, too, is the victim of circumstances. I have felt myself to be a victim of circumstances. But, no, the fault is not in our stars, but in ourselves. By allowing me to work with you, you have given me purpose. It gives me life again—instead of the gaping abyss between myself and my darling Virginia. It gives me an opportunity to return the gift of friendship which I owe Peter—and you as well, Jon. It gives me a problem to solve. I can forget myself in this pursuit as I can only do otherwise in the nothingness of total comatose inebriation."

The sky was beginning to lighten when we drained the bottle. Poe finally appeared calm.

"Jon," he said, "perhaps we should get some sleep."


Chapter 30


APPETITES


I arose at nine, fetched Poe, and had him packed aboard

a carriage before he was fully awake.

"I'm concerned about your health, Eddie," I said. "I'm taking you to my boarding house in Greenwich Village. There's no better breakfast to be had in Manhattan Island."

It was true. My landlady took great pride in being able to set before her boarders excellent and bountiful meals. Her boarders came from all over Europe—there was a Russian cap-maker, a German cabinet-maker, a shoemaker from Denmark, a clothier from Poland, a lamp-maker from England, and, from Ireland, an actor—Kevin O'Connell.

I said: "Afterward we'll get a change of clothes for you. Remember Kevin, at the fire? I think he's just about your size, don't you? I know he'll help us with the haberdashery. We must look good for Dr. Whitney at the convention this afternoon."

"Ah, yes," said Poe, at last waking up. "Today we attend the convention. I don't care too much for politics, but it should prove interesting. Besides, I believe Meade will be speaking. I'd like to get a look at him."

"Have you any appetite, Eddie?"

"I believe I have. Yes, by Gad, I am famished!"

"You've eaten like a bird since we met. A good meal will give you strength—and health. I myself have an enormous appetite—at all times."

Chapter 31

A GHOST ON GREENWICH STREET

We pulled to the curb in front of 130 Greenwich Street. Poe got out, and then it was as if he had been struck by an arctic wind, and frozen in his tracks.

"What is it?" I asked.

"This house. A grim coincidence. I stayed here once. It was the spring of Forty-four. I'd decided to come back to New

York after living for a time in Philadelphia, where things had gone bad again. I brought Virginia with me. We had to leave my mother-in-law, Mrs. Clemm, behind in Philadelphia, until we had money to send for her and our cat, Caterina. We were directed to this house, as being reasonable, warm, and serving good food. I had about four dollars and fifty cents in my pocket. We ate an enormous, delicious breakfast. One of the best meals I've ever had. I wrote my 'Balloon Hoax' while we were here, to make some quick money. We were so happy then, though we were awfully poor. But Virginia wasn't coughing. She'd improved so much. We thought—we hoped—"

"Come," I said, "let's get in."

Poe followed me upstairs. I knocked at Kevin O'Connell's door.

"Ah, good morning, Sergeant, and Mr. Poe," said the actor, smiling. "What a pleasant surprise!"

"'Morning, Kevin," I said. "Do you suppose you could provide Mr. Poe with a change of clothes?"

"I live out at Fordham," said Poe, "and we've been invited to attend a Democratic convention today and a dinner party this evening. I need some refurbishing."

"Certainly, certainly, Mr. Poe. Come in. We'll see what I have. The shirt off me back is none too much for the man who saved me miserable life to ask of me."

No sooner had Poe stepped over the threshold than he sighed, "Oh, Jon this is the very room!"

He looked so shaken that I said: "Kevin, we'll go on to my room, if you don't mind. Would you be so good as to bring over whatever you think appropriate. And please bring some of your actors' makeup. I'm going to remove these bandages. My bruised hide will have to do. We'll be in your debt. I think Eddie needs to rest a bit and have something to eat. He's a little under the weather."

"Of course, Jon. Pleasure to do so."

By now Poe had eased into the room. He looked about, trance-like. "Oh. . ." he moaned—"Oh, Virginia, Sissy, what are you doing here?" He turned to us. "Gentlemen, this is my wife, Virginia. I call her Sissy because she is like a sweet sister to me. Have you ever seen anyone so beautiful? I bid you look upon her fawn-like eyes and into the mystery of life. O dark, dark eyes. I assure you, gentlemen, that she is the gentlest of creatures. But don't look, don't look at the blood on her blouse. She was singing and the blood erupted. It has spoiled her blouse. How have you come to be here, Virginia? Were you waiting for me, your Eddie? Oh my darling, my darling!"

"He's hallucinating," said Kevin. "I've seen a lot of it. We'll pour a drink down his throat. That's what he needs." Kevin got a bottle of Irish whiskey and almost force-fed Poe a drink, holding his head with one hand and the glass with the other. "Come along now, old fellow. Drink this. You'll be all right."

Poe shuddered, and said, "Yes. Yes, that's better. Where did she go?"

"Into heaven, dear fellow. Your bride went into heaven, no doubt of it."

"Yes, yes," said Poe. "Thank you. Thank you. I saw her though, as plain as day, I tell you. But of course—that's impossible, isn't it?" He looked at the half-empty glass and drained it. "It must have been the effect of the laudanum," he said. "But it was so real."


Chapter 32


WEAK AND WEARY


In dark melancholy, Poe sat in my great armchair, gazing out the window onto the street below. Ten or fifteen minutes passed while I filled the wash basin and cleaned myself up and shaved. I removed the bandages and covered my abrasions with Kevin's stage makeup.

"You know, Jon," he said, "this has been a shock to me. As I told you last night, working with you has distracted me from my troubles. But just when I begin to think that I might pass one day without being reminded that Virginia is gone to me forever, something brings it all back and I feel . . . *struck* again."

"I know it must be very hard for you, Eddie. You must have been very happy with such a companion."

"She gave me the one bit of light I've found in this dismal place, Jon." It was clear that he meant the world.

I was combing my hair when Kevin knocked at the door and handed me a dark, clean suit and linen. "I think these will do," he said. "If you need anything, just let me know."

Poe washed and dressed and we went down to breakfast. Most of the tenants had already eaten and gone. We had the dining room to ourselves.

Breakfast was hot, strong coffee, veal cutlets, ham and fresh eggs, delicious bread and butter, and a bowl of fruit.

"It is all the same as it was that morning," said Poe, "only now it is all different."

"Will you eat, Eddie?" I said, passing him a platter of cutlets.

"Only coffee," he said, "and maybe an apple."

Chapter 33


KATE'S WRATH


Visiting hours at the City Hospital were between ten and noon. We expected to find Red Kate among the visitors. Mullins was with her. They had just come from seeing VanBrunt.

"He hasn't regained consciousness," Kate told us. "The doctor says he could be hemorrhaging inside of his head.

They might have to operate. You know, he hasn't been in good health, drinking and all. He might *die!*"

She fell into Poe's arms.

"I'll kill whoever did this to him," she said. "I'll have their ears!"

"You've been a good friend to Peter," said Poe, "and I count you as my friend as well, so I feel that I can say this without incurring your wrath, Kate. But, terrible as you would like to sound, you do not take ears—your heart is too soft under your bluster."

"What?" said Kate, tears streaming down her cheeks, making rivulets in her paint. "What do you mean, Eddie?"

"I mean that you have a jar filled with wax ears behind your bar. You are more bark than *bite*, my dear."

"Oh—Eddie—"

Poe patted her gently on the back, until her tears subsided.

"I heard tell of Max Fisch," said Mullins, Kate's vademecum.

"Where? How?"

"Some cove told me he saw Max in a diving bell in the Five Points."

"When?" I asked.

"When did he see him or when did he tell me, you mean?"

"Blast it man! When did he see him?"

"Last night. Told me this morning. I went over to the place, but nobody there remembers him."

"Is your informant reliable?"

"If he says he saw Max Fisch, he saw Max Fisch."

Kate said: "We saw Boodle Coign before."

"How is he?" I asked.

"He was on his way out," said Mullins. "I don't know him, but Kate does."

"He used to come in my place once in a while," said

Kate. "I never liked him. I don't like having Plug Uglies with their top hats knocking at my candles and their spiked brogans digging up my floor. They remind me of Meade when he was young, and they all work for him one way or another." She was standing alone now, wiping her eyes. "Looks like his friends took an ear from Coign," she added, "and not a wax one, judging by the blood on the bandage."

"I think he'll be leaving town," said Mullins, "the way I did five years ago. When they do this to you"—he touched his ivory nose—"or this"—he touched an ear—"it means that you better leave town for a while."

"If Meade is behind what has happened to Peter," said Kate, "I'm going to McNeil and tell him everything I know about Meade's past. It might not ruin him down in Five Points, but it'll hurt him with his rich uptown connections."

"Meade must be behind it," said Mullins.

"At least some of it," I said. I turned to Poe, but he was gone. "Where did Poe go?" I asked.

"Down the hall," said Mullins.

"I'm going to McNeil in any case," said Kate. "I've owed Meade ever since he threw me over like I was a sack of chew. I've made up my mind, I'm going to McNeil."

Kate strode out with Mullins behind her. I went looking for Poe.


Chapter 34


LAUDANUM


Down the hall were several doors. I looked in each and went on, coming finally upon one marked *Laboratory*. Poe was inside, sitting among vials and test tubes, sipping some kind of concoction.

"What have you there?" I asked.

"Forgive me, Jon," he said.

"What is it?"

"Laudanum," he said. "Everywhere I turn, I am haunted by Virginia's spirit. I would not be able to go on with you, without this, the only balm in Gilead."

I went with Poe to a nearby tavern, where he had several drinks while I smoked a cigar. He told me of the hemorrhages his Virginia had suffered:

"Each time it was as if she had died, and then each time she would grow stronger, so that there was hope—hope only to be dashed again."

At last I was able to get him into a hack, and we were on our way. It was nearly three.

Chapter 35

J'ACCUSE!

At Anthony Street and Broadway, a crowd flowed into the Broadway Tabernacle. This great, domed Congregationalist Church was often used for public meetings. Inside, a banner proclaimed a convention of Manhattan Democrats, hosted by Alderman Meade of the Sixth Ward.

I saw Dr. Whitney up front, by the rostrum. She was with the reform mayoral candidate, Fleetwood O'Brien, and several other ladies and gentlemen. I saw Wilson, the patrolman I had appointed to protect her.

"Dear lady," I said in greeting.

"Sergeant Goode, Mr. Poe. How fine you both look!"

"I do not *feel* fine, madam," said Poe. He was a bit glassy-eyed.

"I am sorry to hear it, sir."

"Mr. Poe has had a shock," I said. "An unhappy coincidence. He'll be all right. I'm happy to find you safe and sound—"

"Call me *Eleanor* . . . Jon."

"Eleanor."

"Have you met Mr. O'Brien?"

"I have not had the pleasure, but I've seen his campaign posters. Sir," I said, shaking his hand, "it is my intention to vote for you."

"Well done, Sergeant," said Fleetwood O'Brien, a wide-eyed, open-faced, middle-sized man with black hair parted down the center and black mustaches that separated when he smiled. "Mr. Poe, I am an admirer of your work. Your 'Raven' has become the talk of the town."

"Mr. O'Brien," said Poe, taking the politician's hand, "I wrote a story called 'The Gold Bug' that won me a prize and my first notice, but the bird has beaten the bug all hollow. Would you mind explaining the political situation to me?"

"Certainly," said the handsome reform candidate. "The Democratic Party in Manhattan is divided into several factions, only two of which are of real importance. They are Tammany and the Reform Democrats. Dr. Whitney and I are fighting for reform, to wrest control of the party from Tammany Hall, the sachems of which have used their power for their own benefit, for self-aggrandizement and personal gain. They are corruption itself. Through demagoguery they win the votes of the poor, and then keep their power by keeping the poor down, to make use of, to begin the whole process again. I only wish Dr. Whitney were able to run for mayor. She is, as it were, the better man."

"I'm sorry, sir," said Poe, "but we Southerners are unused to women in politics. Or in medicine. But Dr. Whitney has inspired the germ of a story in me."

"Dear Mr. Poe," Eleanor broke in, "I'm afraid that women in politics is a fact that you must become accustomed to. It won't be long before women have the vote, I can assure you. I am in contact with some very forceful ladies at this moment—Lucretia Mott and Elizabeth Cady Stanton, to name a couple—and we shall be convening in Seneca Falls,

New York, next year with several hundred women of like mind to consider the most expeditious ways to accomplish that goal. There'll be no stopping us!"

"I commend you, madam—*Doctor*," said Poe, bowing slightly and smiling.

How I admired my Eleanor!

"*Quiet!*" cried a ward-heeler. "Quiet, please! It's now my happy duty to introduce the man who has made the Sixth Ward what it is today—a defender of the poor and down-trodden, a defender of our great red, white, and blue against all who would attempt to lower it, especially the English—a man of the people, a self-made man, a man who has pulled himself up by his own bootstraps, a man who seen his opportunities and took 'em—former State Senator, Assemblyman, High Sachem of Tammany, Sixth Ward Chief of the Volunteer Red Dragon Hook & Ladder, Police Magistrate, County Supervisor, and our Alderman—Boss Meade!"

None in our company applauded.

"Another Goliath," said Poe in my ear.

Indeed, physically, Meade was a giant, one of the breed of Mullins and Boodle Coign, one of the type of the Plug Ugly. But the "ugly" in Plug Ugly referred to disposition rather than, necessarily, looks. Meade was a dark, handsome man, of the type called black Irish. He looked to be in his forties.

He said:

"There are those who would take our beloved Sixth Ward—our beloved Paradise Square—our beloved Five Points—and turn it into a playground for the rich! And how would they do this? Would they make rich the poor and downtrodden of Five Points? No! They would throw them into the streets, out of the only homes they know. They would throw them into the streets, I say, and let them freeze. They would let them freeze, but not in Five Points, not where they would instate the rich, personages with names like Whitney,

Astor and Grinnell. Such people would not have the likes of *us* underfoot. We are trash to be swept up by the broom of wealth.

"When the reformers say that they want to clean up Five Points, what do they mean? Throw the poor out of the only homes they have?

"Look at the Old Brewery. Now, I'll give you that it's a hell hole. But it's the only place those poor folks have to live in. Where would they go, if they were turned out? Could they set up camp on the lawns of the rich reformers of the 15th Ward, across the street from Washington Square—or in Washington Square itself? *No!* Then let the rich nativist English and Dutch reformers of *Washington* Square leave hands off the poor of *Paradise* Square. In the 15th Ward a population almost exactly as large as that of the 6th Ward lives on three times as much space, and they own the poor tenements of the Five Points, to boot. Reform? Let the rich and greedy landowners reform themselves—"

Eleanor shouted: "You don't want the Five Points changed because it's your power base. Make the 6th Ward *clean*, and who would you find there to support you?"

Fleetwood O'Brien shouted: "Meade, you demagogue! You know perfectly well that it is our intention to construct new, inexpensive housing for those poor unfortunates! And my name is not Astor, but O'Brien."

"You've probably changed it!" cried Meade.

"You *have* changed yours!" cried O'Brien.

"Back off," said Meade, "or I'll not be responsible for the patriotic wrath of the crowd."

Several black top-hats came floating across the heads around us.

"We will not succumb to your terror tactics!" cried Eleanor.

"Terrorist, am I?" said Meade. "What terror?"

"The murder of the Hot Corn Girl!"

"You had better speak to your lawyer, Dr. Whitney," said Meade, "before you repeat such a black lie as that."

"Mr. O'Brien *is* my lawyer. And what about the murder of Mr. Thadeus Thorndyke?"

"Now who, in the name of sweet Jesus, is Mr. Thorndyke?"

"You know perfectly well who he was. You had him killed—along with Mary Hart—to frighten us, the reformers, who will unseat you and your whole corrupt pack of wolves if it's the last thing we do. You are a disgrace to the Democratic Party, which my husband helped to found in Eighteen Twenty-three, before you came to our beloved country, probably. You are, indeed, a disgrace to America, and a disgrace to Ireland as well!"

"I'll not be responsible for the just wrath of this crowd," cried Meade, and the top hats floated above the heads of the audience, towards us, with new speed.

"Back out!" I said, taking Eleanor's arm.

"I'll stand my ground," she cried.

"Not here and now," I said, and pulled her back through the crowd, toward the door.

"Unhand me, sir," she said.

"I would do anything for you, Eleanor, my dear, but that," I replied, and fairly dragged her back toward the door. Suddenly a Plug Ugly loomed before me. I drew my pistol.

"Back now," I said, and he slowed his advance. I looked for Poe, Fleetwood O'Brien, my policeman, and the others. They were retreating apace. Wilson held his pistol at the ready.

We boarded carriages on Broadway and hastily departed the environs of the Broadway Tabernacle.

"You have disgraced me," said Eleanor to me.

"On the contrary," said Poe. "He's behaved wisely, gallantly."

"Indeed, Eleanor," said Fleetwood O'Brien. "I'm very

glad that the Sergeant was present."

"Let's call it a tactical withdrawal," I said.

She was a bit mollified, but still angry. I sought to change the subject. "Have you ladies of the mission found a place for Mrs. Hart, yet?"

"Indeed, we have. With the help of several of our ladies, she's been packing. She'll be leaving tomorrow to take up residence at the Fifth Avenue Home for the Aged."

"You say she's packed?" asked Poe.

"Well, what few things she has . . . a suitcase, a few boxes, a steamer trunk."

"Would you mind taking us to Mrs. Hart's?"

"What? Now?"

Poe looked at me. "Let's have a look at her possessions, Sergeant."

I nodded in agreement. "We'll see you tonight, at eight. Mr. O'Brien, you and patrolman Wilson please keep a sharp eye on Dr. Whitney, won't you?"

As Poe and I exited the carriage before Mrs. Hart's tenement, Eleanor said: "I wish I could go in with you, but I have so much to do before this evening, and I need some time to compose myself. The convention was a fiasco."

"Wilson," I called up, "keep close watch till I arrive at Dr. Whitney's."

I turned to Poe. "The diary?" I said.

"The diary," Poe repeated, rapping gently upon Mrs. Hart's window.


## Chapter 36


### NONE SO BLIND


The unseasonably warm weather had vanished and now the November dusk brought the threat of snow. Scudding dark clouds overhead: evening coming on.

"We had better not tell Mrs. Hart that Joe Brody is alive," Poe said. "We would only have to explain the rest to her, and add to her miseries. But, if we get a resolution to this business, and, with it, justice—"

Mrs. Hart opened the door. "Who is it?" she said.

"Sergeant Goode," I said, "and Mr. Poe. May we come in?"

"Oh, yes, Sergeant. I recognize your lovely deep voice."

"May I suggest," said Poe, "with the kindliest intentions, madam, that you enquire as to who is outside your door before opening it?"

"And that soft Southern accent, Mr. Poe—I would recognize your voice anywhere, as well. But I have no fear. What should I be afraid of? I am ill, old, blind, and alone in the world. If I were killed, what matter? But who would bother to harm me? I only wish I could trade my life for the lives of my daughters, but death would have the valuable and leave the worthless."

"There is no trading in immortal souls," said Poe. "Each is all, madam. Death is random and, in the aspect of eternity, fair. Only by human standards does death appear stupid."

"Come in, please, Mr. Poe—Sergeant. I would offer you tea, but, as you can see, all my things are packed. I am being sent off to an institution."

"It's about your things that we have come," I said.

"To pick them up?"

"No, ma'am. We'd like to have a look through them, if we might."

"But they are all packed. The ladies of the mission packed them—"

"Yes, ma'am."

"But I don't understand. What can you want to look through my things for?" She stepped backward against a chair and sat down, clutching her Bible, her knuckles white.

"We believe that there could be something among your

things of which you are unaware," said Poe.

"How can that be? I have so little. I touched most of the things as they were being packed—to see if I wanted to keep them."

"But something could have eluded you," I said. "May we look for ourselves?"

"Will it help in finding out who killed Mary?"

"We think so," I said.

"Then, go ahead. But you will repack them as you go, won't you?"

"Indeed," I said.

There were two valises, one leather and one of cloth, several boxes, tied with string, and a steamer trunk.

Poe already had one of the boxes open and was going through its contents, unwrapping and rewrapping as he went. I fell to with him.

We ignored anything too small to contain our conception of a diary-shaped object, but looked into larger pots, folders, and other such that might contain it.

"What is it exactly that you are looking for?" asked Mrs. Hart.

"Papers, letters, a book," I said, working.

"But how would I have come by anything that would interest you?"

"One of your daughters could have placed it among your things," I said. "Most probably Lucy."

"Lucy? Then it would have been put here over five years ago."

"Most probably," I said. "If at all."

"What would it be about?"

Poe and I exchanged glances. I said:

"We're uncertain."

"Uncertain? But—"

"This trunk is padlocked," said Poe.

"I haven't opened it in years," said Mrs. Hart. "It contains only a few precious things from my girlhood."

"You haven't examined those things for some time, then," said Poe. "Have you the key?"

"Yes, but . . . must you?"

"Did Lucy or Mary have access to the key?" asked Poe.

"Yes. I keep it here, pressed in my Bible. But those things are only memories of a happier youth."

"If we do not look, we shall not have done what must be done," said Poe, "in order to find whoever is responsible for Mary's death."

"Very well, then." Mrs. Hart resolutely fingered the pages of her Bible and extended the key into space. I took it and opened the trunk.

"Ah!" sighed Poe, at the sight of some dusty crushed flowers. He pushed them onto a piece of paper and placed them gently on the floor beside the trunk. "We shall be *very* careful, *very* delicate," he said.

I looked at the silent old lady, whose blind, shrunken eyes were welling with tears. Not much luck for some, I thought.

"Look," said Poe. "Wait. What's this?"

"A Bible," I said.

"A Bible?" said Mrs. Hart. "But—"

"Don't you see?" said Poe. "Look at the inscription."

It was inscribed by Lucy Brody, to her mother. I couldn't understand why Poe was so excited. It was just an old, coverless Bible.

Poe turned to Mrs. Hart. "The same size. May I see your Bible, Mrs. Hart?"

"My Bible?"

"I believe I've found your Bible—the *true* holy writ."

"But I have it here."

"No, madam, I believe you have something else there, with the cover of your Bible concealing it."

Mrs. Hart confusedly handed Poe her Bible, which he flipped open under my eyes.

"What is it?" asked Mrs. Hart, deeply agitated.

"Your daughter's diary," I said. "You've been carrying it with you for five years, thinking it your Bible. The diary itself has been filled in with blank pages to bring it to the proper size, then glued into the Bible cover."

"Lucy did it," said Poe, "probably just before she was murdered. She knew that it would never be out of your hands, that you would let no one but herself read it to you, as you promised."

"But how," said Mrs. Hart. "When?"

"When she was compelled to," said Poe, looking at me. "I should think quite soon after she fell out with Meade, or sensed such a falling out in the wind."

"Who's Meade?" asked Mrs. Hart. "The political person?"

"No, no. Not that Meade. This one is a figure of minor importance to the case," said Poe, hastily. "He's of no concern to you, dear madam, I assure you." He paused. "When did you see Lucy last?"

"The Friday of the week-end she was killed. It's so vivid. Strange, I can't remember what happened last week, but I remember the last time I was with Lucy as if it were a moment ago."

Poe looked grim. He said: "I can understand that."

Mrs. Hart went on: "She spent the whole day with me reading . . ."

"That's it!" said Poe, excitedly. "I should surmise that while she was here that day she must have transferred the diary to the Bible cover. Did you perhaps take a nap, that day?"

"Why, yes, I slept for an hour or so and was surprised to find Lucy still here when I awoke. I thought how sweet and thoughtful it was of her to have stayed."

Poe pointed toward the screen with the bed behind it.

"You were asleep behind the screen," he put the flat of his hand on the table, "and Lucy sat *here* and did her work with glue. The key to the chest was in the Bible. She took your Bible and put it in the chest and put the key back in her newly bound diary. She didn't remove the Bible from the room because it meant too much to both of you. She put it with your treasurers. She knew that the diary would never leave your hands, nor that you would allow anyone else to read from it, including Mary. It is as it was in my story, 'The Purloined Letter.' Mrs. Hart has been waving the diary under our very noses. Indeed, under her own, without knowing it."

Mrs. Hart said: "But something else comes to mind. I remember now that I discovered that the lock was broken the week after Lucy's death. I remember because I had to replace it. If she had the key and opened it with the key, why did she break the lock?"

"Joe Brody broke the lock," said Poe. "Searching for the diary."

"Then he must have seen the Bible in the trunk," I said.

"Yes," Poe said, "but it didn't mean anything to him. Why should it? He probably didn't even know that Lucy had ever given her mother a Bible. While on the other hand it was precisely what we were looking for."

"But when you first showed it to me," I said, "it didn't mean anything to me either."

"It would have, in only a second, Jon."

Poe hastily repacked the trunk, and locked it, giving the key to Mrs. Hart. He worked abstractedly while I read an entry from the diary.

"It's a gold mine," I said.

"What does she say?" ask Mrs. Hart. "Oh, I'm so confused!"

"Forgive me, ma'am," I said, "but I cannot disclose the contents."

"But, Sergeant . . . Does she mention me?"

"You see," said Poe, "Lucy had some important information pertaining to criminal activity, to which she had been witness. It was her intention to help the police."

"And that was why she was killed? But what about my Mary?"

"We don't know yet," I said. Indeed, my mind was racing like a mill-wheel at spring thaw. I saw part—and parts—a vague pattern with great gaps. I wondered if Poe's imagination could fill them in, and, as if on cue, Poe said:

"I think I can imagine what happened here."

"Would you care to clarify?"

"I cannot until the whole crystallizes."

"Well," I said, "I must get this diary to my superiors."

We completed the task of repacking Mrs. Hart's possessions, and stood before her, neither of us wishing to leave the old blind woman in such an agitated state.

"We'll take both books," Poe said, "with your permission, madam, and have your Bible rebound for you. I'll see to it myself, and return it to you by my own hand."

"Can we do anything more for you—*now*?" I said.

The old lady shook her head, then bethought herself.

"The big Bible on the stand. Mary used to read to me from it; but I told you that, didn't I? Would you bring it here to me, by my side, where I can touch it?"

I moved the Bible and stand from among her possessions, to her side.

"You will bring my dear Lucy's Bible back quickly, Mr. Poe? I feel lost without it."

"I promise you, madam."

"We'll stop at the mission," I said, "and ask if one of the ladies can come over to pay you a visit."

"I'll locate you through Dr. Whitney," said Poe.

"Yes. Very well, then. I thank you both. You've been very kind."

Outside, I told Poe: "I feel like a swine."

"What were we to do?" he asked gloomily. "We had to find the diary, if it existed, and we certainly couldn't tell her the nature of it. She's suffered enough. Should we have told her that her daughter was married to one vicious criminal and consorting with another?"

"Her faith is her strength," I said.

"Yes—or do we delude ourselves?" said Poe bitterly.

Chapter 37

HEADQUARTERS

En route to Headquarters we read the diary. It recorded the events of a year. It was highly selective, detailed, and deeply incriminating of Boss Meade. Captain Henchard and others at Anthony Street were implicated.

"If any of this can be confirmed," I said, "it'll rock Meade from power. Indeed, it'll put him behind bars."

"That will be a service," said Poe. "But I feel that we have taken a wrong turn at a fork in the road."

Police Headquarters for the City of New York was located in the basement of City Hall. There I learned that Meade had put pressure on Chief Matsell to have me taken off the case, or perhaps even off the force, as some had it. But he had had no success because others in high places wanted me to continue the investigation. I worked for some time analyzing the diary with several inspectors and City Hall politicos, while Poe, who knew about such things, went to a local bookbinder to have the Bible rebound. He rejoined me an hour later, smelling a bit of rum, and we went on to Washington Square.

Chapter 38

## A GALA NIGHT

Our cab reined in behind a magnificent carriage with red wheels and tongue and green body. The black coachman's livery was blue and silver, and the harness of the white horses was mounted with gold. Several richly dressed ladies and gentlemen alighted from the vehicle. We followed them up the steps. Eleanor greeted us at the door. Behind her the official greeter, the butler, stood in annoyed dignity.

The ladies ahead of us were resplendent in silk, lace, diamonds, and furs. But Eleanor, who was simply clad in a deep-blue velvet gown, a strand of lustrous pears about her neck, out shown them all.

"Gentlemen," she said. "I'm so glad to have you both back. Almost everyone has arrived. Come in, there are a few people I especially want you to meet and a few you already know."

Poe stepped forward and took her hand. He held it for a moment and then passed on into the house.

She gave me her arm and we joined the other guests.

"Poe and I have some exciting news. I'll tell you about it when we have a moment."

"Jonathan, I don't know what I'd do without you. Fleetwood has been telling me that I behaved a bit rashly this afternoon. But I cannot keep silent in the face of such a scoundrel as Meade. And this gathering is not entirely to my liking, either. Most of the guests are associates of my late husband and they've done nothing to earn their wealth but sit on urban land, and watch the rapid appreciation of land values that comes with increased population. It's *my* intention to continue to part them from enough of their money to tear down the slums of the Five Points, especially the Old Brewery, and build a new, great mission on its site. Do you understand my position?"

I wasn't sure that I did, but I liked her enthusiasm. It was my studied opinion that Eleanor could accomplish anything she set out to do. I regret to say that I had no such confidence in myself. With regard to the Hart case, I felt that I had been blundering about like a bull in a china shop.

Chapter 39

GLITTERING GUESTS

The drawing room was softly lit, the flickering light reflected here and there on pastel taffetas, shining brocades, and the jewels of the women. There were perhaps thirty people present.

On the far side of the room was a piano. Poe stood by it, engaged in conversation with a striking woman in black. He told me later that she had been discussing a two thousand dollar cashmere scarf she had bought that afternoon at A.T. Stewart's "on a lark." She was wearing a ring-diamond big enough to support a Five Points family for an indefinite period in comparative luxury. I thought of Mrs. Hart.

"Ah, Sergeant, how are you?" asked Russel McNeil. "I missed speaking with you today at the convention. But I did hear Dr. Whitney's denunciation! If we had more politicians with a tongue quick as hers, I think we'd be better off, don't you?"

Eleanor said: "You give me too much credit. It's simply my nature. I'll leave you two for a moment. But oh," she said, turning back, "first let me introduce you to Mr. and Mrs. John Wendel." She caught the couple's attention and said: "Oh, John, Elizabeth—I'd like you to meet two friends of mine: Detective Sergeant Jonathan Goode, and Russell McNeil of *The Broadway Star*."

112

"How do you do, gentlemen," said Mrs. Wendel.

"Mrs. Wendel, you're J.J. Astor's sister, aren't you?"

"That I am, Mr. McNeil. And my brother has told me all about you, I'm afraid," she said, smiling.

McNeil flushed.

"In fact, Mr. McNeil, since that editorial in *The Broadway Star* last month, we've been forbidden to mention your name in my brother's presence." She laughed indulgently.

"Elizabeth," said her husband, "it wasn't as bad as that."

"Well," she explained to McNeil and myself, "ever since that unnamable other newspaper called John a 'self-invented money-making machine' he's not been able to decide whether he was flattered or insulted. It's his uncertainty that makes him angry."

"Sergeant," said John Wendel, attempting to change the subject, "you're not here to watch the jewels, are you?"

"Oh, no, sir," I replied, "it's purely social. Dr. Whitney and I recently met through some common business in the Five Points."

"Eleanor and her social work," said Elizabeth Wendel. "I don't know where you find the time, Eleanor. If Eleanor were more subdued," she said to me, "we could call her an angel of mercy, but as it is . . ."

"I find her efforts most commendable, don't you, Mr. McNeil?" said John Wendel. "I think the ladies are jealous."

"John, you and Elizabeth know," said Eleanor, "that Mr. Whitney left his fortune in my care. I've always felt it my duty to use it for a good purpose. But enough of this unseemly talk. I must take the Sergeant and Mr. McNeil away for a moment. I want them to meet the Schermerhorns."

As soon as we were out of earshot of the Wendels, she said: "Russell, I know you want a moment with Jon alone. I'll leave you and see to the arrangements." Casting a sunshine smile she went west into the clouds of cigar smoke.

"Sergeant," said McNeil, "after the rally I returned to my office and began to write up some of the notes I'd made. Our copy boy told me that I'd had a couple of visitors while I was out. It was Katherine Mary Ross—Red Kate—and the ivory-nosed brute, Mullins. He thoroughly disconcerted the boy. Anyway, Red Kate returned alone, after I'd gotten back. She told me a great deal about Meade's unsavory past. I must say, his moral life leaves much to be desired in a public official. But, of course, that's nothing new."

"I believe I've heard that story, too, McNeil. And I quite agree with you."

"I intend to write an exposé on Meade's origins and his crooked climb in politics. I intend to use every weapon I have to unseat that gangster. We must have him out!"

"I'd like you to know, McNeil, strictly between the two of us, that I may have some interesting material for you shortly. I'm not at liberty to discuss it now, but it does concern direct malfeasance by Meade and I'll confide in you as soon as I have the approval of my superiors. As you know, there is division over Meade in high places, and those who support him are now in the minority."

He glinted his spectacles in a nod. "Fair enough."

"Am I free to believe that you will likewise pass along to me any information you unearth in this matter?"

"Of course."

We turned back to the other guests. I heard Eleanor's voice. "I believe we're all here, now," she said. "Shall we go in to dinner?"

"Jonathan . . ." she said, and gave me her arm.


Chapter 40


A SUMPTUOUS REPAST

Two servants opened the great oak sliding doors and we

stepped into the dining room. China, crystal, and silver glittered under a crystal chandelier. On a mahogany sideboard stood two large candelabra, surrounded by silver serving dishes. We passed over a Wilton rug and under portieres of satin. Where it was not hung with valuable pictures and tapestries, dark paneling gleamed.

Eleanor sat at the head of the table. Poe was placed on her right, I on her left. Fleetwood O'Brien sat at the foot, making him Eleanor's rival for table mastery. With Poe at her right, I felt third in importance to her, and a little hurt by it.

"Eleanor," said Poe, as the guests were seating themselves, "how is our little friend, Danny?"

"I think he's been content here with me. At least, he's made no attempt to run away. I think he rather likes me, though I'm constantly correcting and chastising him. I simply adore the little tad. I'm thinking of the possibility of adopting him."

"He's an intelligent boy, isn't he?" I remarked.

"He is," said Eleanor. "As a matter of fact, he's asked me if I could teach him to read. Poor, *poor* little fellow. When I think of the many like him who've been subjected to such unhappy, *miserable* . . ." Her voice trailed off. "He had his dinner about an hour ago and is off to bed now. I'll check in on him later."

The wave of conversation receded as the guests relished their food.

The meal began with a cold, silvery consommé, and cold squab. Then little crabs were served; then hot jellied chicken with asparagus; then pressed duck with chestnut croquettes; then rack of lamb, mint jelly, and an assortment of creamed vegetables. For desert, there was something called meringue a la creme, embedded with fruit. We finished with black coffee. I had never had such belly timber.

"I know the great power Meade has, of course I do," said Fleetwood O'Brien to Wendel, his voice rising, "but we of the Reform Party do not aim to give up. If we don't get rid of him this election, then it'll be the next. It's only a matter of time."

"Jonathan," said Eleanor, "how was Mrs. Hart?"

"She's ready to move," I answered. "We found something among her possessions which may turn out to be a great help to us on this case."

"Oh," she said, "I'm glad to hear it. Have you discovered anything about Mr. Thorndyke's. . . demise?  Have you anything to go on, outside of that contemptible note?"

"We may have," I answered.

Poe turned to her: "This is a sumptuous meal. And the claret, I might add, superb." His great, grey, hypnotic eyes stared into hers. I watched him there across the candlelit table and wondered just how he did it. He was speaking of food, and yet his gaze seemed to mean so much more. There's something just too blasted romantic about Eddie, I thought. And immediately I was ashamed of myself.

"Ladies and gentlemen," said Eleanor, getting their attention, "I don't know if you realize it, but Mr. Poe and Sergeant Goode are working together on a murder case, or rather several murders, which involve some of us at the mission. If some of you don't know, the name VanBrunt is involved. I'm sure you all know that name. The accused party is Mr. Peter VanBrunt." The guests murmured.

Someone said, "She means the ne'er do-well VanBrunt, the artist."

"Oh, of course," someone said.

"You might be interested to know," said McNeil, adjusting his spectacles, "that I wrote to the VanBrunt family upon his incarceration, and they responded by saying they had no such relative. *They are all Whigs!*"

"He needs legal counsel," said Eleanor. "Fleetwood," she said, "can't you do something to help the man? I wish you'd go on my behalf and see him. I understand he's being held at the police station on Anthony Street.”

“He’s been released,” I interrupted, “but has suffered an injury. He’s at City Hospital, at the moment. Unconscious, in a coma. It may be necessary to operate.”

“That’s my province,” said Eleanor, “as a physician. What was the cause of his condition?”

“The attending doctor says he has a concussion.”

“Ah, then there’s nothing to be done, really. But, Fleetwood, as soon as it’s feasible, I want you to see the man. He’s entitled to legal counsel. And if his family won’t furnish it, I will!”

“You are most gracious,” said Poe.

“Mr. Poe,” said McNeil, “if you’re helping the Sergeant, perhaps you’ll tell us something about the difference between solving a real murder and creating one for your fictional detective, C. Auguste Dupin.”

“The difference is quite simple. A mystery story is written backwards, its author knowing its solution. Suspense is built because the reader has confidence in the author as to the goal, but is made to share the doubts of the fictional detective. In a real investigation, we begin with a mystery, and must arrive at a solution. But I do think we’re on to something. I don’t want to speak prematurely, though.”

“Oooooh,” said the attractive woman in black with the big diamond, “murder . . . it’s too horrible. But I must confess, I love mysterious stories.”

“I think Mr. Poe underrates himself as a detective,” I said. “He’s helped me a great deal. His advice has been . . . invaluable.” I was a bit conscious-stricken to realize that I’d been piqued by jealousy just a moment before.

The table was being cleared.

“Ordinarily, we ladies would leave you gentlemen here to your cigars and brandy,” said Eleanor, “but tonight I have something different in mind. We’re fortunate to have two distinguished public figures with us. This afternoon we—most of us—heard Mr. O'Brien, whom we believe will soon be the honest Mayor of our great city. And this evening we are fortunate to have one of America's most famous poets with us. If Mr. Poe will consent, we shall hear one of his poems."

Fleetwood O'Brien said: "I think I'm speaking for all present when I ask Mr. Poe to read 'The Raven,' a poem that nearly everyone in the English-speaking world knows."

"Oh, at last," said McNeil, "I can hear it from the author's mouth. 'The Raven,' Poe! Give us 'The Raven'!"

"I shall be honored to do so," said Poe.

The guests fell silent, waiting.


Chapter 41


THE RAVEN


"Do you mind, Eleanor?" Poe asked, as he deftly snuffed the flames on the sideboard. He stood by his place at the table with the light of the chandelier dramatically illuminating his face, and began, slowly:

*Once upon a midnight dreary, while I pondered, weak and weary, over many a quaint and curious volume of forgotten lore—*

When Eddie recited "The Raven" every syllable was accentuated with such delicacy, and sustained with such sweetness, as I have never heard equaled by other lips. I had read the poem to myself many times, but my ineptitude had given it a sing-song effect. Now I was struck by the grander and more subtle organ tones of the vowels. The guests were still as mannequins, breathless. There seemed no life in the room but Eddie's. I felt under the thrall of a magician until the final words . . . *And my soul from out that shadow. . . shall be lifted*—nevermore!

For a full minute, Poe and his audience studied each other in silence; then, breaking the mood, he bowed and applause filled the room. The guests crowded around him, complimenting him on his reading, asking about the origins of the poem.


Chapter 42


TAKE THIS KISS


I went out on Eleanor's front porch, lit a cigar, and looked over the moonlit expanse of Washington Square.

The square had been a potter's field, and the bones of many a poor soul were beneath it. I fancied the dead looked up with blind sockets, through the sod, to the moon and the stars that were dulled to bronze this night by the black pall of wood smoke that hung over the city. This was the morbid and melancholy state in which Poe's reading had put me.

Bah! I was jealous. Poe was an artist—a poet-performer—doing his work, pushing his fame and fortune, just as I was a policeman, doing my job. I had come to think of him as one with me in my purpose, so helpful had he been. But perhaps that too was part of the alien resentment I felt at the moment. For he was better at my job than I was. His mind worked with speed and efficiency that, in truth, amazed me. He was a genius, and I was merely an ordinary unexceptional man. People put up with his antics, his sometimes arrogance, because of that extraordinary mind, that strange, compelling personality. For once, I felt sunken in my big frame, almost ashamed to be so healthy.

Washington Square by moonlight! I am no poet, but things poetic were leaping about in me. I blew a smoke ring that broke five inches away and blew back into my eyes. I was wiping them, when I thought I saw something out on the field. It looked like a running scarecrow. Poe was giving me dark visions.

Washington Square was now a park, and was sometimes

used as a parade field. Somewhere out there in the darkness the old hanging tree still lived, grown old with many rings. In the previous century a young black girl had been hanged from it. She had been charged with taking part in an arson plot. Again, an old scaffold had stood out there for decades. Once, for General Lafayette's benefit, twenty highwaymen were hanged together. It is said that people came by the thousands to enjoy the show.

"What are you doing out here by yourself, Jon?"

"Eleanor . . ."

"It's cold and damp out here. It looks like a night for cold rain."

"But the moon is out. You know, I thought I saw a running scarecrow."

"Eddie has given us all the spooks."

"You shouldn't be out here," I said. "You'll catch cold."

"I have a warm shawl. I wanted to see what you were doing. It was a brilliant reading, wasn't it? Eddie is a genius, but he must suffer so, poor man."

"Poor he is. I have had to finance him."

Dear God, I was ashamed to have blurted that out! I added hastily: "Of course, he'll repay me, I have no doubt."

"Why do you do it?"

"What? Help him out? Oh, it's been well worth it. He's been a tremendous help to me."

"I have no doubt that such a man can be a tremendous help and an equally tremendous hindrance. Sometimes he's not altogether his own man, is he?"

"He's suffering from the loss of his young wife," I said. "He's an honorable fellow."

"And gallant."

"Yes, very."

"Courageous."

"Yes, very."

"You like him, don't you?"

"Yes," I said.

"Kiss me, Jon."

I kissed her.

"It *was* a good reading, wasn't it?" she said.

"Excellent!" I said, suddenly giddy. "Eddie is filled with talent."

It was true. Eddie was an excellent man, and I was proud to say that he was my friend.

## Chapter 43

### THE CRASHER

Inside, I stepped up to Poe, who stood in a circle composed of Fleetwood O'Brien, the beautiful woman in black with the big diamond, the Wendels, McNeil of *The Broadway Star*, a Dr. Sloper, his widowed sister, Mrs. Lavinia Penniman, who was "simply thrilled" at Poe's performance, and his daughter Catherine, a plain, healthy-looking young lady who did not appear to be the heiress of a considerable fortune that she was reputed to be, and several others. The Slopers lived just down Washington Square North from the Whitney house, but were invited as more than close neighbors of Mrs. Whitney, for Dr. Sloper contributed a small amount of his valuable time to improving medical conditions in the Five Points. With the Slopers and yet somehow apart from them was a dandified young man named Morris Townsend.

"Sir," he said, "I've read 'The Raven' many times since its publication. I shall never forget my first reading of it—spellbinding—but I should never have fully appreciated the power of its repetitions, especially in the refrain 'Nevermore,' had I not heard you read it. Being without any gifts, your gift strikes me with awe."

"Thank you, sir," said Poe, "but my gift, as you call it, is hard work."

Dr. Sloper made a satisfied snort.

Thus dismissing the obsequious Townsend, Poe turned to me. "Where is Eleanor? What did she think?"

"She thought you were marvelous. She's gone up to look in on the Devlin boy. She's become very attached to him. But what I wanted to say—"

A broken series of screams bounded down the wide stairway, breath-catching, thick-voiced screams, the repeated word "help" attenuated by fear.

There was a jam at the foot of the stairs, where several men collided, myself in the middle. I bulled my way free, took the stairs two at a time, and was first onto the upstairs landing. A long wide hall extended in either direction. Gas lights cast confusing shadows, but toward the end of the hall that led to the front of the house, I spotted a plug-hatted giant, who, as I watched, caught in my own confusion, turned about and dove through the huge stained glass window that overlooked the front of the house and Washington Square beyond. A chaos of glittering, colored shards of sharp glass followed him out.

Later that night, one of the cabmen who waited in front of the house said that the figure bursting through the window with splinters of glass in a multi-colored aura about him looked like "the prince of darkness himself in flight." Our man did not fly, however, but fell, and landed with such crushing weight on the stone steps of the house that his spiked shoes chipped out chunks of brownstone from the smooth surface. The cabman said that he hit with a deep knee bend, but immediately rose, in huge proportions, and took the ten steps up in one leap down, hitting the sidewalk running.

Ahead of me and to the side, I could hear weeping. It was Danny Devlin. Then I heard Eleanor consoling him. I found the door and stepped in. Eleanor ran into my arms. "Oh, thank God, Jon!" she cried. "I opened the door. It was dark. I didn't bring a lamp because we have the hall lighting. I came over to the bed to find a lamp. Then I saw silhouetted in the moonlight from the window a giant with a top hat *smothering* Danny with a pillow! Before I could scream, he hit me across the chin with something. I don't remember anything else."

"Could you identify him?"

"No. Just that he was huge, and that top hat . . ."

Danny said: "He was wearing a scarf tied over his face! When he let the pillow go, I started yelling me head off. He ran out the door."

For a tender moment the three of us stood and held each other like a little family. Then I said, "You're safe now. I must try to catch him." I let them go and stepped into the hall.

"Poe!" I exclaimed. He was kicking the glass from the window sill. In an instant he had climbed out the window. He hung there another instant, dropped, crossed the street, and disappeared into Washington Square Park.

At the window, I was hit by a fine, cold rain. The sky lightened with a jagged strike, and I spotted the giant, who now took on the aspect of a running scarecrow. He was off, among the trees, his long scarf flying behind him, toward Washington Square South, probably trying to make it to Thompson Street. I went back down through a house full of alarmed guests and out into the street, where the carriage horses were pushing the carriages backward and jerking them forward, and giving their drivers great difficulty in controlling them. A few of the horses and a few of the men were bleeding from the flying glass. I entered the park at a nearby gate and was immediately flung headlong over something soft and moaning.

"Poe?" I questioned, getting up.

"It's me, Wilson. Go on, Sarge, I'm all right. He just sapped me."

There was a shot. I ran deeper into the park. There was another shot. The sky lightened, and I saw Poe about fifty yards ahead of me, to the east. The rain was coming harder now, wind-blown in waves. There was another shot. Three shots, then a fourth.

"The beggar's got a pepperbox," I told the rain. "He's got two left."

I saw the fifth, like a firefly, flare a hundred yards ahead. I lunged into Poe. "Hang back, Jon, he said. "He must have one left. It's no good at anything beyond twenty yards, but I don't know where he is."

"He's way off ahead there," I said. "I saw the last shot."

"Then we've lost him," said Poe.

In the face of the dark, and the now needling rain, I had to concede the point.


Chapter 44


LEFTOVERS


About faced, Washington Square North, with its lighted windows, presented a picture of plutocratic safety. I was now struck by the enormity of what had occurred. The rich of the Fifteenth Ward, who were, in their daily rounds, scarcely aware of the existence of the denizens of the Sixth Ward, which is to say the Five Points and environs, had actually been invaded by an archetype of the Sixth. The indifferently smug social order had been breeched. The Frog and Toe had visited the Progressive City.

"How's Eleanor?" Poe asked, as we trudged back to the house.

"She caught a glancing blow from a blackjack. But no serious damage."

"And the boy?"

"Tough little mugger. Nothing wrong with him."

"What actually happened? How did he get in? Do you know?"

"The Oulde Sixth Ward has finally had the temerity to attack the Fifteenth," I told him, echoing my own thoughts.

"There was a policeman's leather helmet by the bed, and a huge cape in the hall. Since he was wearing his plug hat, it would seem he carried it in under his cape. When he got close to the house he changed and walked in like a working copper, I presume."

"Strange," said Poe, "when Eleanor entered the room she must have been in full view, the hall light behind her. Unmistakable, I should think."

"What are you getting at?"

"The rogue had a repeating pistol, a pepperbox. Why didn't he shoot her? That was the gist of the threat on the note—Dr. Whitney beware!"

"Didn't want us coming up . A shot would have brought us."

"No faster than a scream, and he had to let the boy loose in order to hit Eleanor. And consider, why was he after the boy? What do the Plug Uglies have to do with the Devlin boy? He can only help to show that VanBrunt did not kill Mary Hart. But the fact is, the Plug-Ugly was trying to kill the boy. Another fact is, that he did not try to kill Eleanor."

"It is odd, isn't it?"

"And out here in the dark, and a considerable distance ahead, he'd have been better off not shooting and showing his location," Poe ruminated. "Then why did he do it?"

"To kill you?"

"That's an unpleasant thought, Jon."

I ventured, "It could have been Mullins."

Poe said, "It could have been Boss Meade himself, or— how many Plug-Uglies are there, Jon? The gang is famous for giantism, and they deliberately add to the illusion of their great height by wearing those plug hats. It could have been any of them—perhaps a lonely emissary sent by Meade himself."

I had to concede the point. Wilson waited at the open door, holding a palm to the back of his head. Shards of stained glass lay everywhere underfoot. I hated to think of the replacement cost of that huge stained-glass window. It had portrayed one of the late Mr. Whitney's sources of wealth, a full-rigged cargo ship. Eleanor had apparently directed that a quilt be hung at the empty window frame. It portrayed a much humbler vision of flowers. They were being watered by the miniature squall now underway. Wilson said, "I'm sorry, Sarge. It was all so sudden."

"Are you all right?"

He nodded. "You gotta mean business if you wanna kill a man with a sap."

"Did somebody mean business when he hit VanBrunt," asked Poe, "or was it just an abundance of malice that overcame better judgment?"

"You think it was the same person?"

"There are plenty of blackjacks around," Poe said, "and too many cleavers."


## Chapter 45


## RAIN ON THE PARADE


Eleanor was incensed. "Even in my own house—and with a policeman outside, a police sergeant and a candidate for mayor inside. Meade knows no limits."

The guests milled about in the hallway, some fetching their hats and coats, all in great anxiety. Eleanor said hurried good-nights as they filed out.

Poe took me aside. "I've got an idea," he said. "But let's wait until everyone's gone."

I advised the stragglers to depart, and in a few moments only Eleanor, the servants, Danny, McNeil, and Fleetwood O'Brien remained.

"I suggest," said Poe, "that Danny be moved for safe-keeping. In fact, I think he might be best off out of the city."

"Out of the city?" Eleanor did not like the idea.

"I have a home—a cottage, merely—at Fordham," Poe said. "We could take him by carriage, Mr. Wilson riding lookout to see that we are not followed. It's now clear that, as I had feared, this boy's life is in danger. If the Plug Uglies are behind this, I wouldn't put it past them to storm the house, and neither would I put it beyond them to discover where we had the boy hidden, if he remained in the city."

"That's right," I said, "we know they had a spy at *The Broadway Star*."

"If there are spies in *The Broadway Star*," cried McNeil, outraged, "I shall discover them—and have them out!"

"There must be spies in the ranks of the police, as well," said Poe. "No, the boy must be gotten out of this city. Our enemies have reached a point of arrogance hitherto unknown."

"If so," said Eleanor, "I'm going with him. And we shall use my carriage."

"We'll all go," I said. I called Wilson and asked him if he could handle a team. He said that he could, and I told him to prepare Eleanor's carriage for a long ride.

"It'll be Eddie, Eleanor, Danny, myself, with Wilson driving."

"Must we travel by night?" asked Eleanor.

"It's better so," said Poe. "If we're followed, we can lose our pursuers. There's no way to tell what can happen next here in the city—or, indeed, in this house."

## Chapter 46

### ESCAPE

Hail tapped with skeleton digits on the carriage top. Wind whistled between gapped, icy teeth. I stuck my head out into the cruel weather to see and dismiss many plug-hatted pursuers, giant white figures striped with shadows, running even alongside the carriage on enormously long legs, their eyes burning in the night like red coals with hatred.

Finally cobblestones gave out, and we were on a raw, rutted country road, our wheels turning up mud that flew like trout climbing falls, and closed on our flanks by dark legions of sometimes swaying, sometimes whipping trees. The glow of the city receded behind us, the black vacuum of the woods engulfed us, and all we had for light were the short, shaking casts of our carriage lamps.

"No fear of highwaymen tonight," I said, trying to comfort Eleanor. "Bandits do not need to work in rough weather, as do honest men, like poor Wilson, atop, and cold and drenched by now, I should think. I wouldn't want to be a coachman, though withal, I don't suppose it's much different from being a sailor, exposed to weather, as I have been." I seemed to sound a heartier note than I felt. I didn't know the degree of Henchard's corruption, and it had occurred to me that he might have set the police against me, against all of us who were attempting to escape the Frog and Toe. It was difficult to assess how much trouble we were in, and it is at such times that the imagination steps in with its gift of exaggeration. There were moments when I felt that we in the carriage were the last of a hunted breed.

Danny Devlin had burrowed into Eleanor's side, under her protective arm, as well as several blankets, and had fallen asleep. My lady Eleanor's head bent over him, as if to kiss the tyke. Strength of mind and gentleness of heart combined in her to bring forth the highest regard of others—she was the very portrait of a lady. Look, as we bounced most miserably, only she did not groan and grimace, as Poe and I did, but looked up occasionally with a half smile of contentment, while her blue eyes shown with an eagerness for the rough and dangerous adventure. Even the slight bruise on her chin, where she had been hit, lent to her firm but feminine features the dash of pugnacity, of daring. A rich woman, or any woman, but even more so a woman who might have lived an easy and uncomplicated life, it must have taken much courage for such a woman to have apprenticed herself to medicine in our age of brutes, uneducated and educated alike. My admiration knew no bounds.

"Does Wilson know the way to Fordham?" I asked Poe.

"I gave him instructions," he said. "I usually commute by boat, or by the Harlem Railroad, so I am no expert at the roads, but I think Wilson will get us safely there within three more hours, despite the weather, and then, my friends, you will meet my mother-in-law, Mrs. Clemm, who is dearer to me than anyone now on this earth, and our cat, Caterina, who has a soul. I call my mother-in-law 'Muddy,' for that was what my Virginia called her before she could pronounce the word mother. Muddy is all that I have left of Virginia now—or of anything."

Poe took a long draft from a bottle of rum. He seemed distant, ruminative.

"You shouldn't drink so much, Eddie," said Eleanor, "for your health's sake alone, which is enough, but also because we are all depending on you to help us get out of our difficulties."

"Of course you are right," said Poe. "I'm sorry, I quite forgot myself. But would anyone else like a drink, to warm themselves?"

"One to warm up on," I said, and took a draft from the bottle.

"Three hours to the Domain of Arnheim," said Poe. "It can be done in half the time by boat, up the Hudson, by the palisades, through the narrows to where the gorge opens on all beauty."

"Are you quite all right, Eddie?" asked Eleanor, with a note of alarm, for he looked very strange and excited.

"I am agitated at the thought of meeting Annie once again."

"Who is Annie?" I asked.

"Annie! Annabelle Lee! *Helen*—"

"Eddie! Eddie!" Eleanor reached out and touched his forehead. "He's burning with fever."

There was a long snarl from the sky and for an instant daylight abounded inside the carriage. In the flash I had seen Poe's face. The grey of his great eyes seemed to have turned black in the white-ringed, dark-circled sockets.

"In spring, the turf is green and delicious. Virginia and I go for walks, like children, in bare feet. There are jasmine, and sweet honeysuckle, and a grape vine, and a dead pear tree clothed from head to foot in gorgeous begonia blossoms—locusts, catalpas, elm, oak, and tulip trees, a sort of magnolia—all under and over and around us—Virginia and I. That is Arnheim where Landor's cottage can be found."

Great trees along the roadside bowed over us, rustling with ice now. As the miles passed, Poe fell into a fitful sleep. He groaned and shifted about. Eleanor took his pulse. She said:

"His pulse beats only ten regular beats, then it suspends or becomes intermittent. I don't think it can be simply the fever."

"What do you mean?"

"He may have a heart condition."

"My God! I didn't know."

"I can't be sure, Jon. It's just—"

"What can we do?"

"For the present—nothing. Just get him to bed as soon as possible."

"Snowing!" called down Wilson, faint in the wind.

Yes, the tapping of rain, sleet, and hail had stopped. There was a soft swirling of the air now.

"It's early for snow," I said, troubled all around. "We

could find ourselves snowbound without adequate provisions."

Poe lurched forward, wide-eyed.

"Jon," he cried excitedly, "where's your razor?"

"What do you want a razor for, Eddie?"

"To shave off my mustache."

"What do you want to do that for, Eddie?" I asked, pushing him back in his seat and covering him with a blanket.

"So that they won't recognize me."

"Who?"

"The killers who are after me."

I looked at Eleanor.

"He's hallucinating," she said.

"This happened earlier today, but I thought he was over it. I don't know," I said, "if this whole trip isn't a mistake. Eddie presented the idea to me so quickly, right after the attack on Danny and you, and with such assurance, that I fell in with it. He has a way of taking charge of things. Something of the Sergeant-Major remains with him. But I wonder now if it wasn't just the homing instinct of a sick man."

"No," said Eleanor, "Eddie's right. If a gangster can invade a home on Washington Square, anything can happen. The only safe place for Danny is out of the city, and why not at Eddie's?"

"But why did you come along, Eleanor? There was no need. I could have driven Poe and the boy up here, and Wilson could have stayed in town and watched over your safety."

"I didn't want to be separated from Danny so soon. I wanted to see him into safety. Look at him, sound asleep. I have good reason to fear Meade myself. Nor did I want to be separated from you, Jon." She reached out and took my hand. Thus the dark miles passed.

## Chapter 47

## HOME IS THE HUNTER

At two in the morning we arrived at the cottage. As we reined in, I could see little in the checkered light but a low white slope of roof. A door opened, golden in the darkness, casting a carpet of light toward the carriage. A large, lamp-bearing woman tossed more light about as she made her way unsteadily down a cloudlike carpet of snow toward us.

Poe emerged from the carriage like a drunken man.

"Oh! Eddie! Eddie!" cried Mrs. Clemm. "Eddie, come here, my dear boy! Let me put you to bed!"

"He isn't drunk," I said. "He's sick."

"He has a fever," said Eleanor. I'm Dr. Whitney, Eddie's friend. I'm a physician. I'm going to take care of him."

"What'll I do with the horses, Sarge?" Wilson asked.

"There's a shed off toward the hill," said Mrs. Clemm, pointing to the back of the cottage. We appeared to be in a very isolated spot. Values of both safety and danger ran through my mind. Supporting Poe, we crunched our way through the new-fallen snow and into the cottage.

"Where are we?" asked Poe.

"Why, you're home, Eddie," said Mrs. Clemm, "home with Muddy. I've been worried about you."

"Don't worry, Muddy, everything's going to be all right."

"Of course it is, Eddie. Of course it is."

She led us to a settee beside a cold dead fireplace. Indeed, the cottage was very cold. "Put him here," she said. "I'll start a fire. Eddie filled the shed with wood before he left. I've been saving it for when he came home."

"Where is the wood?" I asked.

"Through the kitchen, down the steps—the woodshed's attached to the cottage."

"Good, we'll soon have a fire in every room," I said, turning to fetch the wood.

When I returned, Eleanor said: "Jon, help us get Eddie out of his wet clothes."

"But these aren't his clothes," said Mrs. Clemm.

"They are borrowed, ma'am," I said.

Doctor and mother-in-law and I stripped our charge and redressed him, at my insistence, in street clothes. I wanted Eddie prepared in case of an invasion. I was surprised to see in what apparently good condition he was, trim, and quite muscular, unlike one who does sedentary work. I commented on this.

"Oh, he exercises. He does chin-ups on the trees and goes off running through the woods. He goes occasionally to a gymnasium in the city," said Mrs. Clemm. "He has always taken pride in his physique."

"He may have overtaxed himself," said Eleanor. "Does he ever complain of shortness of breath or of chest pains?"

"He's not a complainer, though the world has treated him most unfairly."

"Does he eat well?"

Mrs. Clemm shook her head. "We don't often have much," she said. "He'll eat a pretzel and coffee, and maybe a bit of fruit, or buttermilk and curds, for breakfast. We often only have dandelion greens for supper. I gather them from the fields and boil them. But now that winter's here . . . ." She shook her head. "His friends are always willing to give Eddie a drink, but not a meal."

"What is that scar he has across his shoulder?" I asked. "It looks to have been a serious wound."

"He will only say that it is connected to an affair of honor and that it happened while he was in the military. He served three years in the army, you know," she added proudly, "and rose to the rank of Sergeant-Major."

"Yes, I did know," I said.

Mrs. Clemm showed me about the cottage. It was simply furnished. There was an ingrain carpet on the floor of the main room. At the windows were white muslin curtains. In the two small upstairs rooms there were merely beds and a chair and table. The main room boasted a rocking-chair, the settee upon which Poe was now sleeping, two hanging book-cases, and a writing desk.

I set the fires going, and we reconvened in the kitchen, where Wilson stood, shaking the snow from himself. We sat down over hot coffee.

## Chapter 48

### EUREKA

Mrs. Clemm was a large woman, almost mannish in aspect. Her widow's cap gave her the look of one in mourn-ing, which indeed she was, for her daughter had died less than a year ago, in January, or the appearance of some kind of sec-ular nun. There was a stoicism about her, but no trace of martyrdom.

We explained to her in some detail who we were and how we came to be there. When she understood, she said: "Of course. I'm sure Eddie knows best. Whatever he's planned, it will be perfectly satisfactory to me. You're all quite wel-come."

"I've been worried about Eddie's health for days," I said. "I've tried to get him to eat, and take better care of him-self —"

"Oh, I know how ill he is, sir," she said. "He's often like this now, since Virginia's death. He's my nephew, you un-derstand, as well as my son-in-law. He and Virginia were first cousins. The Poes are a high-strung family. They came out of County Cowan, Ireland, and have certain of the Celtic tenden-cies—as well as the Celtic gifts. But I love Eddie as if he were my own son. It galls me that, despite his fame, we remain so poor. And it's not that he doesn't work. He works like a Trojan, but, somehow . . ." She brightened. "Even now he's composing his greatest work."

"What is the subject, if I may ask?"

"It's the solution to the riddle of the universe. He calls it *Eureka*. Eddie cannot stand to be alone, so, when he writes, I sit nearby, and sew or do some small domestic chore, and occasionally he rises and asks me to walk about with him outside. He needs the air to refresh him. Then he tells me what he's writing. I don't understand much of it, so he asks me what it is that I don't understand, and I tell him, and he explains it again, and sometimes I can understand it, then. The universe, everything, he says, was only one particle in space that exploded, and became all that we know. He has a way of explaining it. He often reads and recites to me and I enjoy it more than anything in the world. But listen to me going on when you must be exhausted. Look at this boy—did you say his name's Danny?—he's asleep in his chair. Shouldn't we get him to bed?"

"Jeese!" cried Danny, his eyes popping open, "I don't wanna go to bed. I'm not sleepy. I slept in the carriage. I'm wide awake."

"And in five minutes," said Eleanor, "you're going to be narrow asleep, or my name isn't Eleanor Vance Whitney."


## Chapter 49


### NIGHTWATCH


That night, Eleanor and Mrs. Clemm shared one of the upstairs rooms; Danny was put to bed in the other. Wilson and I were to take turns in the small downstairs room, the one, I was to learn, in which Virginia had died, wrapped in Poe's old army coat, and with Caterina upon her chest for warmth.

Wilson and I felt that one of us should stand watch in case we had been followed. I took the first watch, sitting at the kitchen table, with a cigar, coffee, and a book of Poe's poems, and Caterina in my lap for company.

I sat for nearly an hour, reading, listening to the wind shivering the trees, and thinking over the day's events. I got up to poke the fire and had my back to the room, when I was startled by a sound behind me. I turned to see Poe edging his way down on a chair at the table. He gave me a hard look, and said, with sudden delight:

"Ah, VanBrunt! I'm glad you're here. I knew you'd take me up on my invitation. Spring is the most beautiful time to visit us here in the country. You're going to stay for a week. Virginia and Muddy will be delighted. Tomorrow we'll go hiking. Look out the window," he cried, with a sudden burst of energy, pointing, "the cherry trees are in blossom. Their petals are falling like snow. You and Virginia and I will walk over to St. John's University. I have a dear friend there—a priest and professor. You can always count on good conversation. In fact, he even seems to understand *Eureka*—though of course he disagrees. But I tell him there is nothing to disagree about; it is merely a different way of saying the same thing. 'Let there be light,' and there was one particle of light, and that light blossomed into everything." He thumped the table with a fist. "I don't know why everyone should find it complicated, do you?"

"Eddie," I said. I put my hands on his shoulders, looked into his troubled, confused eyes. "Eddie, it's me, Jonathan. VanBrunt isn't here!"

He returned my gaze, questioningly, and suddenly slumped down in his seat, put his arms on the table, and dropped his head onto them, as though completely exhausted, spent.

"I don't know how Muddy puts up with me sometimes," he said in a muffled voice to the tabletop. With great effort, he raised his head, took my arms, drew me close, and whispered, conspiratorially: "Blow my brains out, Jon. Put an end to it, this fever called living."

"Eddie," I said, putting an arm over his shoulders, "come, lie down. You're sick and overwrought."

I helped him back to the settee, where he stretched out, and covered him with a blanket.

I had intended to deliver Danny into safe hands and to return to the city as soon as possible. I had not foreseen Poe's illness, though perhaps I should have, had my mind not been preoccupied with the case. But Poe had fallen ill in my service, as it were, and I felt it my duty to see him through.

Just before dawn, I put down *Tamerlane and Other Poems*, and rubbed my tired eyes. A dismal light shown at the windows. I got up from the table, stretching, and looked out. The long night was nearly over.


Chapter 50


WHO GOES THERE?


Because of the angle, I could not see much to the west. In the east a few stars paled in the lightening sky.

A few yards from the house, beneath the trees, something moved in the thick, shadowy underbrush. I strained to see what it was. Had my tired eyes been playing a trick? No, the underbrush was being disturbed, bending and tossing. Perhaps it was a deer, perhaps a bear . . . or perhaps an Indian. Then came a darker thought, in the form of a question. Had we been followed, after all?

My hair stood on end as I heard a scream of agony. Grabbing my pistol from the table, I fairly threw my bulk from the kitchen into the main room from where the scream had seemed to come. But now I saw that it was Poe who had cried out, from the depths of a nightmare. He was still muttering, tossing about. I did what I could to calm him, shaking him, speaking words of reassurance. When he was quiet, I hurried back to the kitchen, and peered out the window. All was still.

I wondered if I should wake Wilson and tell him what had happened. But what *had* happened? I'm not given to nervousness, but I felt decidedly edgy. The sensation embarrassed me. I decided to keep my fears to myself until something definite happened. I took up my post at the window, nervously thumbing back the hammer of my pistol and releasing it, cocking and uncocking the weapon. I became aware of what I was doing and placed the pistol on the window sill. Now I checked my watch—just past five in the morning. I stared into the surrounding woods, trying to see into, around, beyond, *through* the shadow-clad trees. I don't know how long I stood thus, transfixed, how often I left the window to go to the stove for coffee; but at last, as the morning brightened, and I could look into the clear image of nature, I found myself holding an empty cup. I went to fill it and returned to the window, sipping the stale, steaming brew, to discover a musket-bearing man dismounting in the clearing beyond the woodshed.

I dropped my cup, spilling the hot liquid down my thigh, and grabbed up my pistol and cocked it. But then I saw the unconcern of the man. There was nothing stealthy about his approach, nothing threatening. Indeed, his plain, open face looked as if it were preparing a greeting for the morning. As my eyes dropped to the musket at his side, they passed a glinting something. I looked back to see a star. He was a policeman of some sort.

I opened the door.

"Good morning," I called.

"Morning. I'm Crenshaw, constable of Fordham Village. Thought I'd get out early this morning and check on the neighbors. See everything's all right. Some times there are accidents, you know, especially when folks aren't prepared for such an early storm."

"Thank you, Constable. We're all fine," I said. "I'm Sergeant Goode of the Municipal Police, New York City, here on business." I showed him my star. "Tell me, did you see anyone about while you were making your rounds?"

"Around here?"

"Yes. Any strangers?"

"No. Only yourself. Why?"

"I thought I saw someone out there in the trees awhile ago."

"*I* was by here about an hour ago, on my way out to the Valentine mansion. Perhaps you saw me."

"About an hour ago? It must have been you. It's a relief. I thought we were being stalked by an Indian."

"Only a few friendly Indians around here. I saw the light when I passed earlier and thought I'd stop on my way back to the village and make sure Mrs. Clemm was all right. I know Mr. Poe keeps odd hours. Sometimes the lights are on all night. But I'd heard he was in the city, and thought maybe she was alone and might be sick or something."

"She's fine," I said, "but Mr. Poe is ill."

"Oh, sorry to hear that. Is it serious?"

"Nothing fatal, I think. There's a doctor here and he's in good care. Would you like to come in for a cup of very bad coffee, Constable?"

"Well, sir, there's nothing I'd like better. But perhaps another time. If everything's under control, I should be getting back to the village. Much to do there, after such weather. Need every Jack Cove they can get." He mounted his horse. "Nice to meet you. Look for me in the village if you need anything. Let me know how Mr. Poe's getting on."

He spurred his horse away. Before he entered the woods, he turned, gave the cottage a last look, and saluted me with a wave of his hand.

I felt reassured by his proximity. But for the time being there was no need to tell him any more of our business. That he did not ask more than he needed to know, gave me a good opinion of Crenshaw. The Constable was a man of judgment and discretion.

## Chapter 51

## A DREAM WITHIN A DREAM

On the third day, Poe's fever broke, and I encouraged Eleanor to get out of the cottage, for her own health's sake—for she had attended him at all hours and with the greatest care—as, indeed, she had us all. Leaving Wilson on watch, and Muddy in charge of medical and domestic matters, Eleanor and I set St. John's University as the goal of our outing.

All traces of snow had vanished. The wet leaves clung to our feet as we walked beneath the near-naked trees, exchanging early experiences and our desires and aims for the future. Although I found my affection for Eleanor to be increasing with the minutes, I felt that a certain reserve was proper in the circumstances. I did not wish to take advantage of the enforced intimacy of the situation. As we crossed a purling little brook, she took my hand, quite naturally, and, when we were secure on the opposite bank, did not release it. Compelled against reserve, I did not release hers. What followed, as she stepped ahead of me, holding my hand, and blocking my path, was like a wondrous, slow, and precise dance. I found her in my arms, her lips pressed with startling passion against mine. I was breathless with surprise. The isolation, the craggy landscape, the coagulating, flying clouds against the dark blue afternoon sky, the sun against it in strands, like gold beaten to airy thinness, the startled flapping, the wild dark break-away through the trees of a flock of crows—these were part of the moment. I pushed her from me and held her at arm's length. Her mouth was open, loose, her eyes half shut. I drew her back to my chest, half-consciously, effortlessly.

Afterwards, we went on. I said nothing for a time, because I desired to say the right thing when I spoke. I was in love, but deeply troubled. It was she who broke the silence.

"Jonathan, I love you."

"Can you mean that, Eleanor?"

"I try to say what I mean, Jon."

After a time, I was able to overcome my embarrassment, and broached the subject that troubled me.

"We are too far apart," I said. "I was struck dumb by love when I met you. Poe had to speak for me, remember? But that was love at first sight—in other words, powerful attraction. Now that I know you, I can't imagine a life without you. Now that you return my love—something that I couldn't have imagined—now that the situation is real, is serious, even possible, it takes on new and different meaning. I'm a bit of a snob, I fear. I'm just a poor policeman. You're rich."

"I'm rich, I guess, but through my husband, as you well know. What you don't know is that Eleanor Vance was a nurse, hired by an aging man who married her and sent her through medical training because that was the price she put upon the marriage. Nevertheless, I come from the same stock as yourself, good honest Yankee merchants." She laughed, mockingly. "Oh, Jon! Shall I give Mr. Whitney's money away? Then will you have me?"

"I must make my own fortune." Oh, but I sounded pompous!

"What! As a policeman? It would take ten lifetimes. My husband was very rich. Better simply do as I do, and try to ignore my wealth. Then I shall marry you and adopt little Danny. We'll scandalize New York society. What do you say?"

She laughed gently, then hummed a little tune the rest of the way.

Chapter 52

MY FAULT

That evening, as I sat beside Danny, who was listening to one of Muddy's stories, I put an arm over his shoulders in camaraderie. He looked up at me and blurted, "Jeese, I wish you wus me dad," and, breaking loose, ran from the room. I looked for relief to Eleanor, who looked back enigmatically, in such a way as to give no relief, no hint of compassion, and I felt that, somehow, in some way that eluded me, everything wrong with the world was my fault.

Chapter 53

BREAKING CAMP

Once his fever had broken, Poe improved rapidly. Eleanor remarked on his resilience. "I must have been wrong about his heart," she told me. "He is essentially healthy. I have never seen anyone come back so quickly from such a fever. His constitution is good. His problems stem from the way he lives. But it's very difficult to tell a genius what to do."

One evening, as Eleanor and I played chess, Poe sat up and offered suggestions about our game, being charmingly annoying. Then, enlarging on the subject, he insisted that whist was a much more difficult game than chess, and that it required more intelligence, as chess, in his opinion, required more intelligence than did mathematics. The latter he described as "a simple logical progression without the complicating factor of human nature."

Poe's poverty outraged Eleanor. "That a man of his fame, talent, and industry should be so reduced is a disgrace—not to him, but to us. Mrs. Clemm has no money at all. She's sometimes compelled to take a basket to her neighbors and actually beg for food. A woman of her dignity! She's very brave. Do you know," she went on, "that they pay only a hundred dollars a year for the cottage? A man named Valentine owns it. And yet it's difficult for them. But look at his work! He's constantly in print. Does no one pay him properly? Scoundrels! They pirate his work."

Now that Poe was on the mend, I thought it time for Wilson and I to get back to the city. "We've got to get back on the case. I'm going to be handicapped without Poe, but I can't stay here any longer."

I was certain now that we had not been followed. I felt that Muddy, Poe, and Danny would be safe enough. Then, too, there was Constable Crenshaw's ever-watchful eye. I'd spoken with him several times since the first morning and knew him to be dependable. But Eleanor decided that she would stay at Fordham, help Mrs. Clemm with Poe and Danny, and give her some support in general. "I'll stay for a week perhaps, or until you're able to settle things with Meade, and come back."

"Then we'll leave you the carriage," I said. "We can hire someone in the village to take us to the train. But how will you get back if you should want to leave sooner—I mean, before I can get back, or have someone come up to drive the carriage for you?"

"I can hire a man in the village to drive me back, if necessary, but it won't be. And I'll have you know that I can handle the carriage myself, if I have to."

"Well," I said, "I know that Muddy will be pleased at your staying. She'll need all the help she can get. You have a good heart, my dear."

"So do you, my Jon—that's why I love you."

"Only that?"

"I won't make you vain, Jon. But I'll keep you proud."

## Chapter 54

## THE WARRANT

On Thursday, the 23rd, Poe, Wilson and I returned to New York on the Harlem Railroad. We had been out of town for the best part of five days, during which Poe had recovered; nevertheless, it was against Eleanor's advice that he returned to the case. But he was intractable.

"I must finish what I undertake to do," he told Eleanor. "It is a matter of conscience with me." If truth be told, he did not look too badly, the enforced rest having afforded his recuperative powers the opportunity they needed.

Poe left me at Police Headquarters at City Hall, and went to fetch Mrs. Hart's Bible. I had discovered in him a man of duty, punctilious even in small matters, and honor-bound where his word was concerned. Ten minutes later I was back on the street, in company with Wilson and two burly leatherheads. I saw Poe approaching at a quick pace, wearing a long black cape.

"Was it ready?" I asked him.

In answer he lifted away the left side of the cape, displaying a large, heart-level inside pocket, and the top of the re-bound Bible.

"The cape is a loan from the bookbinder," he said. "He's an old friend. He did a fine job on the Bible. Too bad Mrs. Hart can't see it, but her hands, at least, will be able to approve it."

I handed him the warrant.

"What's this?"

"Read it."

"Too much glare," he said, handing it back. "Tell me."

"It's a warrant for the arrest of Boss Meade on several counts of malfeasance, including bribery, extortion, misappropriation of city funds, etc. My superiors have been able to substantiate several of the allegations made in Lucy Brody's diary. In fact, they've been holding the warrant for a couple of days for me to serve, as a reward for my work on the case. You've made a name for me in the department, Eddie."

"I'm sure Meade has enemies who have been waiting to leap upon him," said Poe.

"Yes," I said. "They've made me an acting captain. Apparently they don't want me outranked by Captain Henchard, who is also under suspicion. Indeed, I've been ordered to arrest him, if he interferes. It's been suggested that the Mayor's against Meade, because Meade has usurped some of the graft floating around, and has put pressure on Chief Matsell to act against him. These are very serious charges. Meade might cut and run. But, if he doesn't, he might blow Matsell out of office in revenge. Meade's attempts to get me off the case have backfired. I think we have him."

"But not for murder."

"That will come."

"Perhaps."

I lit a cigar. It annoyed me that Eddie did not seem to share in my enthusiasm. But then, Eddie could be a very irritating, as well as charming, fellow. When you were looking here, he was looking there. He kept one off balance.

"All right, men," I said to the others, "let's go."


## Chapter 55


## DANGEROUS FACTIONS AT ODDS


As we turned into Anthony Street I noticed an unusual number of Sixth Ward patrolmen with their copper stars pinned to their chests and surly expressions on their faces. A crowd of them had gathered in front of the Anthony Street Station. As we walked by, one of them said to me, "Don't try it." It was clear that Meade knew we were coming, had been tipped off.

"This has the shapings of a riot—a police riot," I said to Poe.

One of the Headquarters cops said, "We should have brought pistols."

We continued down the street. I said to Poe: "Meade cannot plan to resist arrest. What good would it do? Headquarters would only send reinforcements—and the army, if necessary."

Poe said: "If he does resist, he will have another purpose in mind."

"Pray tell, what would that be?"

"To create havoc, during which to make his escape. One of us should watch the American Saloon closely, to see to it that he doesn't escape, while another man goes back to Headquarters for reinforcements adequate to the situation."

"It's too late. I cannot alter the situation now," I said. "I'm under orders. But why do you suppose he hasn't fled already?"

"Clearly," said Poe, "he's just been notified of his impending arrest by some Headquarters spy who has run ahead of us. He probably wants time to gather what stolen loot he can to take with him."

As we approached the American Saloon I said to Wilson: "I want you to come with Poe and me. We'll go through the saloon. You other two go into the alley and come in the back. Meade's office is right by the back door.

"Now listen, you two Headquarters boys—and Wilson, too—some of these Sixth Ward policemen may try to stop us. Badge or no badge, treat any officer who gets in your way as an outlaw."

Chapter 56

NOT WELCOME

We stepped into the American Saloon. It was a veritable museum of patriotism. Amid the red, white, and blue of the place were hung old campaign posters. The heroes of Tammany looked solemnly down on us from a portrait gallery as we made our way breathlessly to the rear, amid Plug Uglies and Sixth Ward leatherheads. The bar ran the length of the left side of the room. On the right, scattered tables. The policemen leaned against the bar displaying their stars, some menacingly twirling their billy clubs. The Plug Uglies sprawled at the tables, some displaying the spikes of their brogans on table tops. A few Plug Uglies slapped the flats of their cleavers on the palms of their hands, or patted them where they dangled from leather thongs from their belts. As we passed a Sixth Ward copper with whom I'd been friendly, he whispered under his breath, "Better back off!"

A glint of brass knuckles caught my eye. Every policeman in the saloon owed his job to Boss Meade, and they were there to protect their interest. Faces I knew, faces full of rancor and jealousy, angry eyes everywhere.

A Plug Ugly stood in front of Meade's office door, his arms folded across his chest. I told him to stand aside. He merely smiled, hideously displaying teeth that had been filed to vicious points. He was a foot taller than I, but weighed no more. I heaved my bulk into him, pushing him aside, and pulled open the door.

Meade and Captain Henchard stood behind a big desk, flanked by two policemen wearing badges. Seated at a table were Legs and Butt, the two butchers who had fixed Boodle Coign's wagon.

Poe, Wilson, and I were outnumbered several to one. I hoped that the two Headquarters boys would enter by the back door, evening the odds.

"Alderman Meade, I've come to execute this warrant for your arrest. It comes from Chief Matsell and the Mayor of the City of New York, under the auspices of the Governor of the State of New York. I must advise you that it is your duty as a citizen to quietly submit to arrest."

"I will not submit!" Meade shouted. "Give me that, you turncoat traitor!" He snatched the warrant and tore it to pieces.

"I shall have to take you by force," I said.

Legs and Butt began to laugh, then the two policemen joined in. Then Captain Henchard. At last Meade broke into soft, menacing smile. Suddenly he frowned. I was looking now, not at the politician, but at the Plug Ugly of years before, a gray old cruel giant, made even more dangerous by the cleverness time lends even to young brutes.

"At 'em, boys!" he cried.

Chapter 57


WE GET THE OLD HEAVE HO!


Of the next twenty or thirty seconds, I can give no clear description. I can only say that we were plummeted from the office into the barroom where the flats of cleavers and bouncing billy clubs assailed us from every direction. By the time we were propelled from the front door we were a mass of bruises and bloody abrasions. When we regained our senses and looked about us, like drunken men, we saw the two Headquarters boys lying in the gutter, empulped, perhaps dying. They had been treated with special cruelty.

There was a gaping cut on Wilson's forehead that wanted some cat gut.

"I'll take Wilson and get some help," I said. "You stay here, Eddie. Keep a sharp eye. I don't want that bird flying.

I'll bring an ambulance for the Headquarters boys. Looks like you were right. We're going to need lots of help."

I left Poe on his own to do what he could to protect the fallen Headquarters boys and to keep an eye on Meade's back door, and led Wilson away. He was bleeding profusely.

I asked him if he could make it.

"I'm O.K., Sarge," he said, and promptly fainted.

I lifted him on my shoulders. Perhaps because both Wilson and I were Anthony Street boys ourselves, the coppers we passed refrained from any further attack, though we were jeered as we made our way in the direction of City Hall. Near Broadway I found a hack.

I reported to Chief Matsell, who had gathered a detachment of twenty policemen. I warned him that we were at the onset of a police riot, and that we might need the intervention of the army. "The Five Points is about to blow up," I told him.

He said he would contact the military. "But I do not like the idea of the Municipal Police being saved by the United States Army," he complained, though it was nothing new.


Chapter 58


RIOT


I marched to Anthony Street, twenty policemen behind me, amid hoots and catcalls from Plug Uglies and Anthony Street Leatherheads alike.

The ambulance had arrived ahead of us. The hospital attendants were unaccosted as they removed the two Headquarters boys. Poe was nowhere to be seen.

We stormed the American Saloon, only to find it all but empty. A few bar flies lingered. "Where's everyone gone?" I shouted.

"Off to Paradise Square," I was told, "to hear Boss Meade make a speech." We left the American Saloon, and marched down Anthony Street toward the Square.

There we found about a thousand heavily armed gangsters, with their no less ferocious molls, and a good sprinkling of Anthony Street leatherheads, cheering the all but inaudible words of Boss Meade, who stood upon a box on a wagon amid them. He saw us, pointed at us, and shouted obscenities. The crowd turned upon us.

A disciplined detachment of police officers armed with heavy clubs, and knowing how to use them, can wreak havoc, however outnumbered. My purpose was to disperse the crowd and make my way to Meade. I told the boys to form a wedge, and, raising my club on high, cried, "Advance!"

I kept my eye on Meade as well as I could while smashing heads, left and right. It was bloody pandemonium.

Then I looked up and saw that Meade was gone. In his place was No-Nose Mullins, staring over the fray, obviously seeking out a special face in the crowd. He leaped from the wagon, ivory nose catching the sun, long hair, and scarf, flying, and made his way to the east through an animal convulsion of mob violence. Vaguely, I wondered what he was up to. I felt a shadow at my side and raised my club. Poe stopped my arm.

"Take your pistol," he cried.

I took the weapon and shoved it into my belt. "Cover your head, Poe," I shouted, "or someone, friend or foe, will bash it in!" His calm amazed me.

But things were going badly. I had at least ten Headquarters boys down. The mob, which had at first backed off, was closing in on us now. I didn't look at the faces of the men and women, I looked at their hands. Cleavers, brass knuckles, barrel staves, axes, hatchets, pitchforks, a few muskets passed under my scan.

A bugle blew the charge, and into Paradise Square from the five streets of the Five Points, the United States cavalry converged, sabres flying. The hooves of their horses trampled the fallen dead and wounded. In fifteen minutes the back of the mob was broken, and the gangsters had scattered into every rat hole and refuge of the Five Points.

Chapter 59

BAT AND RAT ALLEY

I gathered about me the remaining five able-bodied Headquarters boys. I had seen Meade take off in the direction of the Old Brewery. I knew the rabbit warren of tunnels that lay under it, and guessed that he would try to make his escape through one of them. I had heard rumor of one tunnel that led all the way to the South Street pier. I knew that Meade kept a boat there.

A raid on the Old Brewery had never succeeded, had rarely been attempted, but things were different today. Its most vicious thugs were in the streets, fighting the cavalry. I thought: "I will be the first to bring it off!"

But not quite. For as my Headquarters boys and I entered the portals of the Old Brewery, we found Poe awaiting us. Waving for me to follow, he cried, "Down below! Follow me!" and vanished in a doorway. We followed him down to the second cellar. Again he had vanished, but his echoing voice gave us direction. We clanged over damp stone, knocking things and people aside, swinging our clubs in the dark. Ahead, a flame arced. Poe had found a torch. He stood illumined in a small doorway. The door had been torn off and lay at his feet. Above his torch was a board with the inscription *BAT AN' RAT TUNNEL* carved on it.

"He's gone in here," cried Poe. "Follow me." The stones beneath our feet were slimy with what seemed clay, or was it the screaming rats we were trampling underfoot? Frightened bats softly clubbed our heads and shoulders in their flight. So close were the quarters that we could smell their smoking wings as Poe singed them with his torch. We clamored through this subterranean hell for perhaps a city block, following the torch, when Poe dropped it, and it snuffed. From the clattering ahead I knew that he had slipped. The Headquarters boys single-filed close behind me. I came upon Poe, and helped him regain his footing in the dark. But not quite dark, now; for there was a vague light ahead, at a distance of perhaps twenty yards, and the sound of scuffling. Then came a flash. Poe's back was propelled into my chest like a cannonball, and each man behind me took the same blow. We went down like dominoes.

*Oh, God!* I thought. *Eddie's been hit!*

Then a second shot rang out.


Chapter 60


THE HUNTERS STALKED


My wonder at Poe knew no bounds. He was a shaman, a magician. I had felt the bullet that hit him myself, as had the men behind me, and yet he leaped to his feet and continued apace down Bat and Rat Alley. Was he made of steel? Awestruck, I picked up the chase.

There was light at the end of the tunnel where Eddie stood looking down at the body of Boss Meade, neatly plugged through the brain. The evil giant lay dead, his doppelgänger, as Eddie would say, his double, or his ghost, exited into the upper regions, known as South Street pier.

"Poe," I cried, "let me look at you." I pulled him about and looked him up and down. "How?"

"Never mind that now. Meade was ambushed by our killer. Quick! Up into the street."

I told the leatherheads to remove Meade's body to the morgue and followed Poe up into the street. Confusion of light and traffic on the street above at first made it impossible for me to gather my thoughts. I was still trying to understand how Poe took a ball in the heart to no effect. "Our killer?" Had my thoughts been at all organized, they would have amounted to *who, what, where, why*? Maybe there would have been a big HOW for exclamation point. I blurted, "Wasn't Boss Meade behind everything?"

"No!"

"Then it was the man who ambushed him?"

"Yes."

"But he can't be found. Look at this street."

"Quite a crowd, isn't it?" said Poe. "But we don't have to find him. We're as magnets to him. If we draw away, he will be compelled to follow." Poe hailed a coach. "Quick, aboard!" he said to me; and to the coachman, "The Phoenix Theatre, at your leisure."

"Sir, the Phoenix Theatre was just burnt to the ground. There'll be no theatricals there for a while."

"I beg to differ, my good man. I am expecting to see something between a tragedy and a farce. *On*, as I say!"

Chapter 61

POE SPRINGS THE TRAP

As the coachman left us, in front of the Phoenix Theatre, I distinctly heard him say, "Rid of another madman. How many more tonight?"

About twenty-five yards into Phoenix Alley, I heard footsteps behind us. My hackles rose as we clanged over the cobbles. "Poe," I said.

"Yes, there he is now, right on time for his final perfor- mance," said Poe, who looked intense and sounded gleeful. "Be on the ready. Judging by his performance in the park, I don't think he's a very good shot."

"But he hit *you*—didn't he?"

"He was aiming at Meade. It took him two shots and he was close upon his target. Keep about twenty feet distance from him and you have little to fear."

As if proving Poe's point, a ball ricocheted with several twangs against the close-set buildings that walled the alley.

"We have him now," cried Poe.

"Have *him!* He has *us!*" I turned and discharged my pistol only to be answered with another shot.

"Damn those repeating pistols!" I cried.

"Run," said Poe, needlessly, for I was running. "We'll catch him when he comes out."

"Who, for God's sake!"

"Why, Mullins, of course. Quickly, now!"

Mullins fired again. "We won't make it to the end of the alley," I cried. "Find the door! Find the door!"

"Here, here," cried Poe.

I ran by him. He reached out and pulled me in. We threw our weight against the fire-weakened door. It gave easily.

We found ourselves in a dark passage. There were stairs. We climbed them and groped toward a patch of light that showed the beautiful wide stage.

"We're on stage. The sundown is our limelight," said Poe. But he vanished in the dark.

"Poe!" I called.

"Here," came a voice.

I turned.

Mullins advanced toward me in the dim light, a top-hatted, ivory-nosed giant lifting a gleaming cleaver above me. I fell backward. The cleaver was poised to strike. *I was a dead man!*

There was a swoosh, a cry, and then there was nothing but the jagged light and dark of the burnt-out hollow of the theatre. Death had vanished before my eyes.

I jumped when Poe touched my shoulder.

"Where did he go?" I asked, bewildered.

"Through the trap door," said Poe. "I gave him the hook, so to speak. Now let's go down and pick that bad actor up, shall we?"

Chapter 62

THE HERO

We had crowded into Red Kate's bedroom to welcome VanBrunt home from the hospital. His head was still bandaged, but the bandage looked like a turban, and his aspect was that of a lugubrious sheik. He was pillowed-up in Red Kate's baldaquined bed, wearing the silver silk, gold-initialed dressing gown, which Kate had given him as a coming home present, and across his lap sat a silver bedtray with a silver coffee pot and toast holder, and a beautiful China cup and saucer. Red Kate was sparing no expense in his honor. He held up *The Broadway Star* before us. The headlines read:

VANBRUNT CLEARED, BOSS MEADE DEAD

"Well done," cried VanBrunt. He beamed upon the gathering. "Listen," he said, and began reading, "Horrible discoveries were made in the aftermath of the raid on the Old Brewery. The bodies of over fifty men, women, and children, many mere skeletons, others in various states of decomposition, and some showing signs of recent death, were discovered by the Army medical team that entered after the riot. Many of the bodies were found superficially buried in the walls and floors of the building. At least half showed signs of violent death."

He crumpled the newspaper and let it fall by the bed. "Kiss me, Kate," he said in a quick burst of exuberance, and she accommodated him with a buss on the lips. He was her man, it seemed, poor flawed fellow that he was.

"Wretched business," I said. "Perhaps we'll get the Old Brewery cleaned out at last."

VanBrunt was completely sober for the first time since

I'd known him. Sobriety made him twitch. When he twitched, Red Kate, who sat on a chair beside the bed, patted his arm maternally. He turned his red, white, and blue eyes from Kate to Poe and myself, who stood on the other side of the bed from Kate.

"Peter must stay in bed for two weeks," said Kate, patting his arm, "but he's going to be fine. I'll be opening my new hotel next month, and everything is going to be different. It's on the Bowery, very fashionable right now, up near Washington Square, quite respectable. Peter is going to be my manager, and I'm going to bask in the straight life. It's what I've yearned for these . . .well . . .many years. It'll be good to have a real gentleman as my manager. It'll be a big step for all of us."

"My dear friend," said Poe to VanBrunt, "you have been nothing but a worry to me." He smiled. "I'm so glad to see you . . . almost on your feet."

"My family had forsaken me," said VanBrunt, "and really I thought I had no friend in the world, but now I feel as if surrounded by a friendly family. Dear Kate, Sergeant Goode, and you, Eddie."

"I am something of a black sheep myself," said Poe. "But do not think, because thou has taken to virtue, there shall be no more cakes and ale. By which I mean—when you are managing Kate's respectable hotel—give entry to, and suffer, a wanton poet, should he appear at your door."

"Oh, always, Eddie!" said Red Kate.

"And Mr. O'Brien," said VanBrunt, "by Dr. Whitney's kind offices, has now taken me up—so there are two more friends."

"What does Mr. O'Brien say?" I asked.

"Well, when I came to in the hospital, he was right there, with a private doctor—all taken care of by Dr. Whitney—and they brought me here, as I asked. O'Brien had gotten a writ of habeas corpus, based on lack of evidence, and here I am.

He says that I will never see the inside of a cell again. He says that I shouldn't have been arrested at all."

"Did you know that Eddie was shot?" I asked.

"*Eddie!*" cried Kate.

"I wasn't hurt," said Poe. "I was carrying a Bible in a large pocket inside my cape. The ball was stopped by it, only penetrating about halfway in. It knocked the wind out of me, however."

"And the rest of us behind you," I said.

"What were you doing with a Bible?" asked VanBrunt.

"I had picked it up from a bookbinder's on our return from Fordham. I had it rebound for a friend, and now I am afraid that I shall have to have it rebound again, or replaced. The ball is still in it, having come to rest at 'Jesus wept'!"

I knew that Eddie was being dramatic—what an assertion!

"It would be quite a memento," said VanBrunt. "Offer it back to your friend as it is and see what he thinks."

"*She*," said Poe. "It's the property of a lady. Perhaps I should do so, with the story attached, as I can't afford any more bindings."

"When we returned from Fordham," I told VanBrunt, "my first thought was of you, to see how you fared, and also to ask you what happened at the Old Brewery. But when I reported to Headquarters, they were holding a warrant for the arrest of Meade. I found Eddie just back from the bookbinder's, and we went right on to Meade's American Saloon. Tell me now, what *did* happen at the Old Brewery that night?"

Chapter 63


THE KILLER'S CONK


VanBrunt shifted his position to think. "I don't remember very clearly. Let me see. I was talking to Max Fisch, and he told me he knew where the Gimp could be found, and he'd take me there, if I wanted to confront the boy, and ask him why he was accusing me. I know, of course, that I should not have gone. But I was drunk. Max Fisch took me to the Old Brewery. We went to a small room on the ground floor—"

"Not the room where you and the Gimp were found?" I asked.

"No, no. It was a tiny room, no bigger than a pantry, not in the basement, where they say we were found, but on the ground floor."

"How can you be sure?" asked Poe.

"Some things I remember, others I don't. But why is it important?"

"Because Max Fisch wasn't strong enough to have carried you to the basement. He can't weigh more than a hundred pounds. Of course, he could have gotten some Old Brewery cutthroats to carry you down. Do you remember being hit?"

"No."

"Do you see," said Poe, "the question is, did Max Fisch take you there to rob you, or for some other reason, involving someone else? But go on."

"Well, there were a table and two old chairs. Fisch took the one facing the door, across from me, and I sat with my back to the door. Then he brought out a bottle of rum and poured us each a drink. I asked him where the boy was. He said that the boy would come in good time. We talked—about Mary Hart. The murder. Then we sang some songs. But that's all I remember. Nothing more until I woke up in the hospital four days ago. When I first woke up, I just thought I had a hangover, my head was pounding so."

"Either you were already unconscious from the drink and struck anyway, or you were in such a fog that you didn't know you were struck," said Poe. "In any case, you were moved, and someone was there with Max Fisch."

"Our ivory-conked friend," I said. As Eddie put it to

me—he has a great sense of humor, you know—in order to find our killer, all we had to do was follow his nose."

Chapter 64

I BECOME FAMOUS

Poe vanished before the trial, having told me that he wanted no part of it. He had insisted that I take full credit for the capture of Brody-Mullins, who, by the way, had broken a leg when he fell through the trap door. Poe had also put Russell McNeil on his honor not to mention his name in the newspaper reports of the case McNeil was publishing in *The Broadway Star*. Therefore, when McNeil later published his book, *The Butcher*, composed from the newspaper pieces, I was its hero. In light of such publicity, my temporary, and highly political, appointment as captain was made permanent. And so it was that I became a famous detective.

Chapter 65

I INHERIT

During Brody's trial, in which I played so prominent a role, an element, as it were, out of the blue, added to my public notice. At long last, I was awarded a large sum by the Maritime Insurance Company, which held the policy on my father's schooner. The sum was adequate to insure my independence, and I decided to propose to Eleanor Whitney, who, by the grace of God, accepted; as, I might add, did the society set. Indeed, circumstances had so altered my standing, that, rather than our engagement causing a scandal, it was looked upon as a romantic *cause célèbre*. My inheritance alone would not have achieved this; it was merely the element required to validate my public standing. It was a season in which several New York heiresses had run off with their coachmen, and I suppose I looked good by comparison.

Chapter 66

P. T. BARNUM

For two weeks after the trial and before the execution, Gothamites flocked to the tombs to get a look at the multiple murderer. Among those to visit Brody was one Phineas T. Barnum, the great showman. Barnum asked for a conference with Brody, which Chief Matsell granted. He then informed Brody that he wished for certain of his possessions, including, most specially, his ivory nose, which was to be placed on a wax figure of Brody, cleaver raised on high, in the act of killing a Hot Corn girl. The figure was to be on permanent display in Barnum's American Museum on Broadway. In return for his concessions, the impresario promised Brody good food and cigars unlimited until the time set for his execution, a new suit, including an expensive plug hat, to wear at that event, and the most lavish funeral yet given to a Gotham gangster. Brody accepted.

Chapter 67

SKULLDUGGERY

At exactly eleven thirty, on Friday, June 16, 1848, Brody stepped on the death platform. After he exchanged handshakes with Mr. Barnum, Chief Matsell, myself, and others, the rope was cut and Brody's great body dropped through a trap that broke his neck rather than his leg. He was interred in Calvary Cemetery, at Barnum's expense, and a marble headstone was erected with the inscription:
*JOSEPH BRODY - 1812-1848*

The words were prophetic, for, within a week, Brody's body was sold to medical students by grave robbers. An intern at the City Hospital recognized the famous noseless cadaver, the ghouls were tracked down and arrested, and the body was re-buried, this time in potter's field, Barnum rejecting any further expense. The headstone remains over the empty grave.


Chapter 68


OUR ENGAGEMENT DINNER


On July 7th, 1848, Eleanor and I gave a dinner party at her house on Washington Square, its purpose being to formalize our engagement and to see again those friends who had played such a part in the affair which had brought us together. Poe arrived at my boarding house on Greenwich Street on the 5th, two days before, and just after the July 4th celebration. He was a bit worse for wear, and needed some tending and rest before the appointed evening.

After the celebratory dinner and several toasts "to the happy couple," we sat at the table and listened as Russell McNeil finished reading aloud from his popular account of Joe Brody's life and death, *The Butcher*.

"It's a good piece," said Fleetwood O'Brien. "I read it when it was first published in *The Broadway Star*."

"I'm amazed," said McNeil, "that neither you, Captain Goode, nor Dr. Whitney—nor you, Mr. Poe—have read it."

"I was still too shaken by those events," said Eleanor. "I did not wish to remind myself that that butcher had invaded my very home."

"I was in Philadelphia," said Poe.

I shrugged and lit a cigar. "I was there."

Eleanor excused herself and went upstairs. She returned in a few minutes, saying: "Danny's sleeping peacefully, little tad. Did you know that we are going to adopt him, Eddie, as soon as Jon and I are married?"

"Jon told me, yes. Congratulations on that as well. You are all—Jon, yourself, and the boy—quite fortunate. Of course, Jon is the most fortunate."

"Thank you, Eddie," said Eleanor. "You know, I still don't really grasp it all. I thought Meade was behind the whole thing. I suppose it was my own self-righteousness that deluded me."

"Meade had nothing directly to do with any of it," I said. "But McNeil here has written the story. Let him explain it."

"But it is from you," said McNeil, "that much of it comes. *You* explain it."

I said: "*You* interviewed Brody."

McNeil said: "But there are still details to be cleared up. Eddie told me several things that Brody confirmed. But—"

"Why not let Eddie explain it?" I said. "He's our great story-teller, and actually did most of the imaginative work on the case. Ratiocination—do ye call it, Eddie?"

## Chapter 69

## LUCY HART AND THE DIARY

"Reasoning, or the process of exact thinking; also, a piece of reasoning. Notice that I would differentiate between ratiocination and logic, which is a bound system and fails in that it is exclusive of human nature. From the beginning, then:

"Joe Brody had been a criminal since his childhood. The same might have been Danny's fate, had you two not inter-vened. Joe Brody's profession was that of petty gangster. He had probably murdered before the first case of which I am aware—murder was nothing to him, a condition of survival, that was all—and he probably would have murdered—perhaps many times again, had not Jon brought his career to an end. He was ignorant but cunning, and being the brute this world had made him, was merely trying to protect himself. He did not realize that the murder of Mary Hart and the accusation against VanBrunt would be of such interest to the world outside Paradise Square, where murder often went like the orphan of interest.

"The first murder that he committed of which I am aware was the murder of his wife, Lucy. But, as I say, he undoubtedly murdered before, so none of these subsequent misdeeds, dire as they were, can, I think, through his eyes, be seen in as monstrous a light as they are through ours.

"It was through the description of what occurred on the Sunday morning that they picked Brody up, given us by the Butchers at the fortification, that I first came to sense what had happened to Lucy Hart. The Butchers, so far as I could see, had no reason to lie, particularly as they had no intention of letting us escape, and they said that they found Brody sitting on a chair at the kitchen table next to his wife's body, which lay on the floor. They said that the room was quite cold but that the body was putrid. In a cold apartment, it would take some time to have reached such a state. Yet we know that Lucy was alive on the Friday night previous, for it was then that Joe Brody was taunted with her infidelity with Meade and went home to confront her. I had assumed for some time that he killed her that night, giving two days, more or less, until Sunday, when the Butchers found her in the condition described. This McNeil has had confirmed by Brody himself.

"It went like this: Brody and Lucy had a fight. Brody was drunk, hurt, angry, and felt like a fool for allowing himself to be misused by both his wife and his boss, Meade. Lucy, who usually could command his respect, for he thought of her as superior to himself in that she had had some education, could read and write, as he once put it, was afraid of him now. She *had* been keeping a record of her encounters with Meade—probably as an insurance policy should Meade toss her aside as he was wont to do with his women. The story of Meade's treatment of Red Kate was well known in the Five Points. Now Lucy decided to distract her husband's slow mind with news of this record, her diary, and to bring him into collusion with her against Meade; for the worst had happened, from her viewpoint, and Meade had announced that he was through with her only a few days before.

"She told Brody that she had such a diary, but she did not let him see it. In fact, it was already hidden, thought to be a Bible, and held in her blind mother's hands. She had hidden it earlier that day.

"But Brody was implacable, furious. He killed her with one blow of his cleaver.

"Then he got an idea. If Lucy had kept a diary, and he could find it, he could use it against Meade, not merely out of revenge, but for profit as well. He proceeded to search for the diary. But not finding it, he doubted its existence, thinking now that Lucy was only pretending to have such a document in order to distract him. Then he was inspired. He decided to pretend that the diary existed and to threaten Meade with it, to see what he could get. He was drinking heavily, and probably slept for several hours at some point here.

"Lucy, during her harangue, mentioned our friend, here, Mr. McNeil, the reformer journalist, who would like to get something on Meade. On Saturday afternoon, leaving Lucy's body where it had fallen, he went to you, McNeil, to test the water, as it were. He told you his business, said that he had some evidence, and, as an appetizer, told about that part of Meade's background involving Red Kate. This was interesting, but you wanted solid evidence. Brody told you about the diary. Was that solid enough? This exchange was overheard by someone in your office, a spy for Meade. This is why

Meade did not doubt Brody when Brody told him that he had been to *The Broadway Star*.

"Upon leaving you, and after stopping for a few additional drinks, Brody presented himself to Meade. He told Meade what he knew about Meade and Lucy, and about Lucy's diary, wherein she told all about Meade's crooked deals, to which she had been privy because Meade thought of her as being as harmless and brainless as a doll.

"Meade, uncertain what to believe, but having the confirmation of his own spy that Brody had been to *The Broadway Star*, played along for a time, asking what Brody wanted for the diary. Brody said that he wanted one hundred dollars, not having any idea what to ask for because he had no idea what such a diary, if indeed it existed, would be worth.

"Meade must have thought the sum a ridiculous one for so valuable a piece of evidence. He told Brody that he would pay him the money when the diary was produced, and gave him a day to produce it.

"It was Saturday night. Brody stopped to have a few more drinks, and then went home to ransack the place a second time, to no avail. He then sat down next to his wife's body and drank himself into oblivion.

"Waking Sunday morning, he was again inspired. Maybe Lucy had given the diary to Mrs. Hart, or maybe she had hidden it in Mrs. Hart's room. He knew, for Mrs. Hart was strict in this observance, that Mary Hart, his teenage sister-in-law, for whom he felt the most unbrotherly feelings, took her blind mother to church at the mission at eleven o'clock every Sunday morning.

"He waited until he saw Mary take her mother off to church, and then broke in and ransacked their rooms, breaking into the chest, but taking no note of the coverless Bible therein. He could not know that the blind woman was actually carrying the diary, in its Bible cover, with her as she passed out of his sight. *She* did not even know it. Of course, he found nothing and returned to his own rooms, where he was discovered by the gangsters—whom we met, Jon—Legs and Butt.

"They saw that he had killed his wife. This did not overly surprise them, as they had been among those who had taunted him with his wife's infidelity. They searched for the diary themselves, found nothing, and returned with him to Boss Meade, who now believed that Brody had attempted to hoax him. That Lucy Hart Brody was dead meant nothing to Meade, but that he was ultimately rid of her. But Brody's threat must be punished. The Butchers cut off his nose.

Chapter 70

## JOE BRODY A.K.A NO-NOSE MULLINS

"Brody spent a couple of days in the hospital, left wearing a bandage, vanished, and returned a year later, now wearing that ivory nose, long hair and a beard, and looking altogether unlike his former self, except, of course, for size.

"He knew of Red Kate's hatred of Meade, so, without much effort, he became her major domo. She was unaware of his background.

"Mary Hart was a year older now. She had become a Hot Corn Girl and was becoming a very lovely young lady. Her charms were widely noticed by men. No-Nose Mullins noticed her, as he had earlier. He made advances and was rejected, for Mary recognized and hated him. Her hatred served to increase, inflame, his passion for her.

"He would go to the mission and wait to see her. Several times she was compelled to talk to him, so as not to cause trouble. Nor did she want her mother to know that he was alive. He himself had been surprised to discover, upon his return to the city, that it was generally believed that the Butcher's Gang had killed Lucy Hart Brody and that he, in his former incarnation as Joe Brody, was also thought to be dead, another victim of the Butcher's Gang.

"His pursuit of Mary Hart went on sporadically for nearly four years. This brings in Thorndyke, as I will explain in a few moments. Finally, in part because it was true and in part to be rid of Mullins, Mary Hart told him that she would marry Peter VanBrunt, if he proposed. She described Van Brunt to Mullins, not aware that Mullins already knew him.

"That night at Red Kate's bar, when VanBrunt told Mullins and others of his intention to meet with Mary Hart in Paradise Square, by prearrangement, and to propose to her, Mullins, driven by violent jealousy, took cleaver in hand and followed VanBrunt. But VanBrunt stopped at several diving bells on his way to the park.

"Mullins went ahead, unknown by VanBrunt, to confront Mary Hart. Their confrontation resulted in her death. Whether he left the cleaver by the body with some vague design to place the blame at the door of the Butcher's Gang, is not quite clear. He seems to have had that in mind.

"But, as he left the park, he ran into the Gimp, and the Gimp knew what had occurred. Mary Hart's scream had brought people. It was dark. Mullins seized the Gimp, warning him to be quiet. It was just then that VanBrunt entered the park at the opposite gate, and kneeled down by Mary, taking her up in his arms. As he knelt, not seeing anything but his dead angel, he felt the cleaver at his knee and took it in hand.

"Mullins told the frightened Gimp to say only that what he now saw—VanBrunt, the body, and the cleaver—was all he knew of the crime, on threat of horrible death if he didn't and a reward of money if he did. So much for the Gimp's strange willingness to talk. Mullins mingled in the crowd. But one other person knew that VanBrunt probably did not commit the murder—that was Danny Devlin, who heard Mary Hart scream and *then* saw VanBrunt hasten toward that scream."

"Then we came into the picture," I said. "Red Kate sent

Mullins with us. He must have been afraid, for he knew we meant to question the Gimp, and the Gimp might give him away, but he also *wished* to go with us, to be on the spot, as it were, and to know what progress we were making."

"You, Jon," Poe continued, "observed, as you commented upon, the strange looks the Gimp and Mullins exchanged, but we attributed that exchange to their ignorance and to the fact that both were deformed, the foot and the face, and thought little of it. What we were seeing, however, was the shock of recognition.

"We adjourned to the diving bell, as you will remember. I was in a weakened condition and in need of fortification. We sent Mullins back to the park, if you can call it that, to get the Gimp. Instead of getting the Gimp, he warned him away.

"But my offer of reward for information to be brought to me at the diving bell had the result of bringing Danny Devlin to us.

"When Mullins observed my skill with mesmerism, my ability to make the boy tell the truth, for Danny would not have done so otherwise, he became very frightened of me, and his hatred of me began there, as it often does, in fear. I had succeeded in showing you that VanBrunt was very likely innocent of the charge against him. Mullins decided that he had work to do. He must get rid of me at the first opportunity, for sooner or later, he feared, I would get at the truth.

"That night VanBrunt was free. We retired. Thank God that I took your advice and example, when you told me that you always sleep under the bed rather than on it when you were in a dangerous place."


Chapter 71


MAX FISCH AND THE GIMP

"Mullins, alone with Max Fisch, the perfect person to

blame my intended death upon, improvised. He told Max Fisch to tell VanBrunt where the Gimp could be found and to encourage our, by then, drunken friend, to confront his accuser and to get the truth from him. VanBrunt went along.

"He and Max Fisch went to the Old Brewery. Fisch took him to a room suggested by Mullins, who had lived in the Old Brewery when young and knew it well, and got VanBrunt to sit with his back to the door—an easy task for Fisch, all of this, really, as VanBrunt was quite drunk. Fisch had been told that he would be rewarded. Perhaps he thought that Mullins meant to rob VanBrunt. He knew nothing about the inter-relationships involved.

"Mullins blackjacked VanBrunt from behind, his purpose being only to knock him out for a short time so that Van-Brunt would seem to have killed the Gimp and then to have passed out drunk. Then Mullins had Fisch help him with Van-Brunt. They took him downstairs to the room in which you found me on that Wednesday morning, Jon, where the Gimp lay sleeping and put VanBrunt at the table. Mullins then strangled the Gimp. Then he strangled Fisch, took Fisch's initialed and well-known pistol from him, and carried little Max off to another room, dropping him in a barrel. He only desired that Max not be found for a day or two—long enough so that he could still be blamed for attempting to rob me, and for my murder.

Chapter 72


## ATTEMPTED MURDER


"Mullins returned to Kate's, came up the back hall stairs to my door, opened it, and, he thought, shot me. He threw the initialed pistol on the floor and went to the back fire stairs, out, down, around to the front, and came up with Red Kate to find me alive. It must have been a shock to him. He probably had himself convinced by now that I had supernatural powers.

My survival was only one of the things that he didn't, could not foresee. And he did not get another good chance to kill me until he followed us into a trap, and ultimately, to his own doom."

"Why did he murder poor Mr. Thorndyke?" asked Eleanor. "Surely he was no threat to . . . anyone."

"He killed Thorndyke because Thorndyke could associate him with Mary Hart. He had visited Thorndyke on the pretense of receiving spiritual ministrations, but actually in order to contact the Hot Corn Girl who was his passion. But here his ever-inspired mind played him badly false."

Chapter 73

THADEUS THORNDYKE AND DANNY DEVLIN

Poe seemed lost in thought for a moment. He stood by his place at the table, looking at each of us. "After murdering Thorndyke he lurked about," he said, "waiting to see where we would go next. He knew Danny was at the mission and he didn't want to let the boy out of his sight. His limited brain was by this time heavily overtaxed. His very first impulse had been to attempt to place blame on the Butcher's Gang, whom he hated, because they had both disgraced and disfigured him, for Mary Hart's murder, as he had managed to place public blame on them for Lucy's death. Then the opportunity presented itself to blame Mary's death on VanBrunt. He seized it. But he couldn't blame Thorndyke's death on VanBrunt, because VanBrunt was in the hospital unconscious, due to his own, Mullins's, over-zealous blow to VanBrunt's head.

"He knew that we had begun to suspect the Butcher Boss Meade and his gang, so he reverted to that, leaving that semi-literate note on Thorndyke's chest, claiming for the Butcher's Gang even the murder of Mary Hart.

"Nevertheless, confused, afraid, he wasn't certain that Danny Devlin might not be a danger to him, being able, as he was, to show that VanBrunt was probably *not* the murderer.

"He must cover everything, for he could no longer follow the thread of evidence himself. So he followed you to this very house. He saw you, Eleanor, light up Danny's room and put him to bed. He watched from Washington Square, across the street. But he would not make an attempt on Danny then, for he wanted to blame the Plug Uglies once again, if he should be seen, and he needed his costume, plus a scarf to hide his nose. Brody reasoned a Plug Ugly might be identified as a Plug Ugly, not as an individual. After all, there are hundreds of Plug Uglies. Further, he knew that I was probably back at Red Kate's, and he wanted to hurry back because he knew that his absence would be noticed and you would soon be looking for him there as well.

"He told us that he had spent his time away looking for Max Fisch. Later, he told us that little Max had been seen. This was pure obscuration.

"The night of the dinner party was the perfect time for him to strike at Danny, tucked away in bed, all the adults downstairs, and everybody, including the servants, busy, preoccupied."

"What about Meade's demise?" asked Eleanor.

"Mullins saw an opportunity to kill the man who had had him mutilated, and took it. He had no intention of helping us. It was mere chance that his action should save us. I imagine that, if he had known Meade had us dead in his sights, he'd have let Meade shoot us first, then would have killed him." Poe shrugged. "You know the rest."

"Ably recounted," said McNeil. "I suppose you intend to write a version of it yourself, to compete with my official version."

"No," said Poe, ever the contrarian. "It's not my kind of story."

"But, dear friends," I said, "it certainly is *my* kind of story."

Capt. Jonathan Goode
New York Municipal Police, 1851

# POUR LES OISEAUX

## *A Parroty of the Hard-Boiled School*

Fabliau, France, 1929, the year of the Phoenix—a gleaming white city rising like plumes on a cocked hat, in a semi-circle from the sea. Its port-section slums are famous for vice, crime, and an exotic mixture of birds—my kind of town! I'm a private dickybird. I flew here from the States seeking an exotic English chick, name of Song Sparrow. She knows where the eggs are hidden, and I'm going to find out. She's been smuggling guano in from South America. I'm pretty sure that it goes through Fabliau to the Italian Mafia— what they do with it, hey, don't ask me. Ever since the Crash, people have been pulling some pretty crazy deals. Guano is fungible. These days it can buy just about anything, including the goose who laid the golden egg. I know it'll buy me an Old Crow in any of these wormy waterfront nests. The bar-keep's a big ugly-looking condor, one of the last of his breed. Is he a displaced Californian, I ask myself in pidgin. But I say it in his beak in plain American, that Peruvian parakeets and Hartz Mountain canaries can understand. The ugly old condor is as laconic as he looks and comes back at me with an owlish "oui" that's packed with innuendo and sarcasm. I slug down my Old Crow, swizzle-worm and all, and order another, take off my feathered Alpine hat, that I picked up on the wing, and place it on the bar, a kind of challenge. He can take it or leave it. He leaves it. He probably figures I got a quiver full of new-fletched arrows under my feathered boa. He's no dumb dodo. I'm looking for an English bird name of Song Sparrow, I tell him. He holds his long dirty wings out like what's it to me and I get a whiff of his wingpits. Fold 'em up, Pollution Pits, I tell him, as I take a gander at the rest of the roost.  A couple of old ducks sitting down at the end of the bar, quacking on about the Crash, a middle-aged bird in a tux who looks like a penguin, soft but there's something cold in his eyes; a Brooklyn bird name of Robin, with big, red breasts, a couple o' gay birds up the other end doing some kind of mating dance.  But no sign of the real Song Sparrow. Now I got a little red light inside, tells me when there's danger, and on it goes.  How do I put it?  There's something reminds me of reptiles—no, dinosaurs.  Yeah, that's it!  These birds look too innocent, like they're hiding something—their real nature, which is definitely saurian.  There are winged dragons afoot, and why didn't the canary sing, as Sherlock might not have put it.  Then I'm pecked from all sides.  It happens so fast I can't tell the pecking order.  All I know is I'm getting the bird.  It was at that moment, as I saw my life flap by me, that it first occurred to me what a worm I really was.  Bob White, this is your life, I said to myself in disgust. Then I heard a distinctly English bird call,  a sort of Oxonian chirp, and I found myself in a large cage.  Sing, cooed the beautiful, copper-eyed Song Sparrow, who had emerged from her condor costume.  I want you to turn canary, she told me, and sing your heart out, like the Hartz Mountain whistleblowers.  I said, Sure, why not?  I should die for twenty-five pounds of guano a day—and expenses?  I'm no sapsucker. We know that the passenger pigeons are bringing the stuff in, I sang, but we don't know how you're getting it out.  We fly it out, she tweeted, in stork sheets.  She eyed me sideways, giving me the once-over, and then hopped forward and planted one on my beak.  That was when I decided to quit being a Hawkshaw.  I'm folding my wings, I told her.  Let's you and me take off. She dipped her head in agreement.  Then we picked up a couple of pieces of straw from the floor and went looking for a good old Anglo-American tree to build our nest in, leaving Fabliau and all its smuggled guano behind us.

Cage closed!

# THE MURDER OF GARCIA LORCA

*No es sueño la vida.*
*¡Alerta! ¡Alerta! ¡Alerta!*

I tug the strings of my fear, my bad puppet, Diablo, and tap him about this space, my first and last stage, last props, last lights, behind and in front of my painted screen. See, I pull up a leg and he hops, hops, hops! Who are you, Diablo? Herr Hitler, con permiso. Then hop, Hitler, hop! Garcia will be dead when I do this jig under the Arc de Triomphe. Not amusing, Diablo. Be something else. I want light and color! Then look at my gypsy dress, all layered, laced, ribboned, and brocaded—scarlet, gold, and green. Feel the wide wind of my rich fan. Hear my diamonded castanets! When did you put that on? An instant ago, behind the screen, when you were talking. But now I'll be Franco and rise against the Republic. Another ugly joke! But in an instant, true! Just let me don this uniform. I love good fun, but this is wicked. Night must fall, Federico, even if it frightens you. Diablo, I command you, take off that uniform, with its golden shoulder-mops and scrambled eggs and salads. I wish I could drop the reins of your dark horse. Who am I now? Wait, I recognize you. You're a man from my hometown, a *granadino*. Your name is. . . *Diablo!* Yes, and I am jealous of your genius. I call you out! I name you Red! *Red, red, red!* I am a poet. I hate politics. Nevertheless, I charge you, Federico Garcia Lorca, with crimes against the state—of my ego. And what now? Bang, bang, you're dead! Am I dead, Diablo? In an unmarked grave! Is it dark, Federico? No darker than this dark century, Diablo.

# A MAN OF CONSCIENCE

*The night can sweat with terror as before*
*We pieced our thoughts into philosophy,*
*And planned to bring the world under a rule,*
*Who are but weasels fighting in a hole.*
                                    *—W.B. Yeats*


This happened in London, although it could have happened in Dublin or New York or any major city of the world.  It could have happened in some backwater as well, but it happened in London, not far from Piccadilly Circus.  But where it happened is of no real importance—when is more relevant, but that will become clear in the telling of it.  The story derives from a Scotland Yard confession, to which the author was privy before his retirement.

It was early evening of a cold December day just before Christmas, 1947.  The pavements glistened under falling heavy mist and traffic sounds were muted.  Two men were walking down a street.  The man following came up behind the man ahead.  The man ahead felt the barrel of a pistol in his back.  He was told to keep walking and was ordered into a dark doorway.

"This was a trick," he said in a hushed voice, back over his shoulder.  "I was told this was a meet for the cause."

"Get down those stairs."

The man ahead did as he was told and at the bottom was pushed through a door.  Inside, the room was dark but the man behind switched on a light.  It was a dank basement room of ancient drooling bricks, criss-crossing pipes, dust and cob-webs, deep below the street.  There was a table.  A few chairs.  An old desk.  Little else except looming shadows.  The man ahead saw a rat stand up and look at him in a far corner when the light went on.  Then he was struck a stunning blow to the back of his head.  He couldn't think.  He fell to the cement floor and as he fell his Mauser Schnellfeuer, the ugly machine pistol he kept in an inside pocket of his trenchcoat, was ripped away.  Minutes of heavy breathing passed.  Then consciousness returned.

"Awake?" said the man with the guns.  He held the Mauser in his left hand and a long-barrelled Webley in his right.

"Yes."  The man on the floor looked around.  As he took in this filthy empty room he was filled with fear and at the same time outrage.

"Where am I?"  Then he realized that he was bound hand and foot with heavy cord, could not move.  "Where am I?  Who are you?  What's this?  Who are you?  What *is* this?"  His head was clearing.  "Obviously, you are not the man I was supposed to meet."

"I am the man you were supposed to meet—inevitably.  I'm your punisher.  No, your redeemer.  We are Napoleon and Wellington at Waterloo."

"Punisher?  My what?  Is that what you said?"  Then he felt outrage become rage and raw anger.  "Who in hell are you?  Some kind of maniac?"

"Of course, we are both maniacs, living in a mad insane-simian world.  I told you, I'm your punisher."

"My punisher . . ." he muttered to himself, "my punisher."  Then, he looked up intently and saw, for the first time, a tall thin man with a salt-and-pepper mustache, a sharp pointed aquiline nose and eyes pale as ice-water.  The man's demeanor portrayed no emotion, only purpose.  Now the bound man felt a thrill of uncontrollable fear as he looked at the neat gray overcoat and the gray fedora downward slanted over the cold pale eyes.

"My punisher?  For what?  And who in hell are you to punish me?  Some kind of damn fascist cop?  Where is this place? How did I get here? Oh, yeah, I remember. You stuck a gun in my back. Why did you have to hit me so hard? My brain's scrambled."

"Better now?"

"I can see straight, but you've given me a thudding head-ache. What's this all about? I can see your intention isn't robbery, so what is it?"

"As to where you are, this is Purgatory. You are on your way to hell."

"What then, are you some damn loony representative of the Church? An agent for the Vatican or something? I don't have to tell you, do I, that I don't believe in hell?"

The tall thin man spoke slowly, with supreme confidence, "Oh, oh, I assure you, you're going to hell, whether you believe in it or not."

"You know it, then?"

"It? What?"

"Hell."

"I'm a veteran of several wars as are you. I've had your file for some time. You've sunk from soldier to terrorist."

"Hell—ha! Now look you, enough of these crazy meta-physics. Who are you and—"

"I'm not being metaphysical. Quite the contrary."

"What are you talking about?"

"I mean that I've been thinking about you for a long time. And I guess there's a hell. If you exist, there must be a hell to swallow you up. Maybe not in the earth, but on the surface of it. And that's where you're going."

The bound man thought that perhaps he was dealing with a true lunatic. This was no ordinary stick-up or assault or kidnapping that one in his business might expect. He thought he'd better go easy here. He felt that he was dealing with a fanatic. "Now look," he said, "just explain to me why you have me tied up in this room? Tell me who you are. Ex-plain!"

Dreamlike, the tall thin man said: "Who you are. Who I am . . ."

"Damn maniac!"

"Yes. I used to think you were the maniac. Maybe you are. But it won't change anything. I'm—" he searched for the right word— "implacable. But I know who you are. You, in particular. But I know who you all are."

The bound man struggled in the cord and tried to sit up straight. "All right. I think I've got it now. Oh, damn, I've got a headache. Damn, my head aches! You must be some kind of agent . . . CIA, FBI, MI5—something. This is an interrogation. Want information? Is that it?"

"No."

"No? Look, maybe I can help you. Give you some information. I know plenty. What is it you want?"

"At first I thought I wanted you dead. But as I thought about it I realized that would be no punishment for you. It would only set you free."

The bound man felt apprehensive. He couldn't figure this guy out. "Revenge?"

"I suppose so. But the more I thought about that the less important it seemed. Anyway, revenge must be taken in hot blood. There's satisfaction in that. There's no satisfaction in what I'm going to do. Indeed, I've condemned myself to a life of guilt. You've brought me to this."

"Not revenge? Not revenge! What then? What are you going on about? What do you mean, condemn yourself to a life of guilt? Why?"

"I'm a man of conscience."

"Conscience?" The bound man thought as fast as he could and said, "Look, are you some kind of madman, or what? Is there any water here? Got any aspirin? I feel nauseated. How long was I out?"

"Ah. I wonder."

"Now what's that supposed to mean?"

"I've been thinking about you for a long time. About this day. Suppose we say . . . suppose we say that I'm the husband of a secretary whose hands were blown off, opening one of your letter bombs."

"Are you?"

The tall thin man put his revolver on the table, fished in the desk drawer and brought out a bottle of brandy, a tin of aspirin, two glasses. "No," he said, as he stepped back and leaned down to the bound man. "Open your mouth. And yes." He took out a few aspirin and put two on the bound man's tongue, then poured brandy to wash them down.

"Now what's that supposed to mean?" the bound man said, swallowing.

"It means that it might be the case, but it's no longer the major reason. It means, as I said before, vengeance must be taken in hot blood. I am not your punisher. I am your redeemer." He became more excited as he spoke, his voice trembled and rose in heat and volume. The single overhead light made the creases in his face seem to jump and rearrange themselves as he paced back and forth in front of the bound man.

"It means that right after your plastique blew my old father to pieces in Dublin I wanted to kill you. In hot blood! I wanted revenge. Vengeance! Who wouldn't? But I cooled off. It means that after my friend Izsak, the great Olympic runner, had his legs severed by a blast of machine gun fire in an airport. . . . It means that I wanted revenge for Izsak! It means that I wanted to kill you. In hot blood! But I cooled off. It means that after my daughters ranging in age from nine to ninety were blown up in a hotel ballroom in Paris—I wanted to kill you! In hot blood! It means that after holiday travellers were blown apart at airports, I wanted to kill you. But I cooled off. I cooled off."

"I don't know what you're talking about. I had nothing to do with any of that—you're completely mad!"

"Am I?  Have I become mad?  Might be."  The self-called Redeemer shook his head as his voice lowered.  "Ask any psychiatrist, madness is contagious.  If I'm mad it's because you're mad.  If I'm sane, you're sane, too.  If we're both sane then there must be evil.  If there is evil, there must be good.  I've thought of all this.  Finally, I don't know what to make of it, but that neither one of us is a civilized human being.  And if human beings can be civilized, how does one account for endless wars?  Isn't the human race a bunch of monkeys fighting over bananas and nuts?  And I'm not a philosopher, I'm a . . . "

"Go on, what?  What are you?"

"Can't make any difference, really.  I've been a soldier."

"Ahhh.  Now we're getting somewhere."

"Oh, well, we're not really getting to anything in the sense that you mean.  Who hasn't been a soldier?  A political killer?  In a world where *you* exist, everyone's a soldier."

"What do you mean, *my* world?"

"As I said before, I'm a man of conscience."

"Couldn't you loosen this?" he asked, holding up his bound wrists.  "I haven't got any circulation.  My legs are asleep.  You're not a torturer are you?  You seem civilized."

"Seem civilized.  *You* seem civilized—whatever that can mean.  But it's a good question.  I think the answer is that I'm about to become a deep torturer."

"Then why did you give me the aspirin and the drink?  That's not the sort of thing a torturer does.  That's the act of a humanist."

"Oh. . . I wanted your full attention.  You can't pay any attention to me when you're suffering."

The bound man shook his head.  "I don't understand you, I admit it.  Deep torturer.  What does that mean?"

"It means redeemer.  It means I'm not out to punish your body."

"Then loosen these ropes.  They're cutting into  me."

"Perhaps. Even at this moment, I'm not certain which of us is mad."

"What do you mean, deep torturer?

"Redeemer. Redeemer! It means that I've thought and thought about it. I mean . . . look at the weapons you choose. The weapons of a terrorist, bombs and sprayed bullets. You are a terrorist. You are my terrorist and I am going to redeem you." He picked up the bound man's machine pistol from where he had put it on the table and waved it back and forth with contempt.

"My Mauser?"

"Yes. Look at it. Sprays venom. Now look at this." He takes his long barreled Webley revolver from the table, aims at the terrorist's head. "One shot." He cocks the revolver. "I am accurate. If I kill someone, it is my intention. I am not careless about murder."

"You don't mean to kill me, or you would have done it by now."

"I could hit you between the eyes at the distance of a city block."

"Meaning?"

"Meaning that I don't spray venom like a spitting reptile." He spat on the Terrorist's machine pistol and threw it into the dark corner where the rat had stood at attention.

"Meaning that I'm selective. I choose my victim."

"You sonofabitch!"

"Pointing my pistol at you was a wanton act. It was almost an act of torture. You see, I can tell the difference. I've still got enough humanity to possess a conscience. I know that what I just did was wrong, pointing my pistol at your head, cocking it. Oh, I've thought about it for a long time. No, I'm just a simple soldier. At first it was vengeance. But I cooled off. I thought about it. I asked myself what kind of human being . . . no, sub-human . . . could send letter bombs through the mail to blow off the hands of secretaries. I have

access to files.  I know your ilk.  I know you, particularly.
You're . . . your family's quite wealthy.  You, dear boy, are a
spoiled brat!"

"I have a cause!"

"You have a vanity!" the self-called Redeemer shouted.
"You have an arrogance.  You have a will to be constrained
by no political system, nor any conscience.  A terrorist kills
to feel infantile power.  If you got what you want, it would
pall immediately.  Immediately you'd want something else.
Then and there.  What you want is . . . is . . . obedience!  Power
over people.  You are a great ape in a jungle, a silverback.
You are what civilization was meant to conquer."

"I want to help in the struggle against fascism!"

"But, my boy, you *are* a fascist.  Your life is telling other
people what to do.  It's a disease in an adult, a mental illness.
You see, every baby is born a fascist. Every baby wants what
it wants when it wants it.  And this is as it should be.  And
every baby will use every means at its disposal to get what it
wants.  And what parent, late at night, has not been the victim
of a torturing baby, who uses its shrill cry to make you move
and move quick.  Babies are fascists—one in the same.  And
you, my boy, have simply never grown up.  You see, you're
that thing most to be feared . . . a willful child with a machine
gun or bomb."  He walked over to the dark corner and picked
up the machine pistol, came back and held it under the terrorist's nose, pushed it into his face.

You see?"  He went back to the table and dropped it
there, picked up his Webley and said, "A man's weapon.  The
weapon of a skillful, selective, mature human being."

"You're as crazy as they come."

"Admittedly.  As I told you, I'm not a philosopher.  I'm
a soldier."

"Not a torturer, or so you say.  Loosen these ropes."

"Why not?  The Redeemer took out a switchblade,
snapped it open and cut the Terrorist free.

"Oh, God, I'm like putty," the Terrorist said, rubbing his arms and legs to get the circulation going. He tried to stand but his knees would not cooperate.

"Oh, you're a helpless victim. How does it feel?"

"Not so helpless in a few minutes. Let me get my blood flowing."

"The thing is, you're like an infant. During the course of growing up, you never acquired a conscience. No, you've been deprived. When you commit an act of terrorism, apparently it doesn't trouble you that you've made handless or legless or sightless, or lifeless, another human being."

"What about you? You're a bloody soldier. You've wounded people. Killed them."

"Yes. Troublesome, isn't it? I've thought about it. As I was preparing for this I thought a good deal about it. The only thing I can come up with is the fact of randomness."

"What about your bloody bombs? What about Dresden? Hiroshima? Nagasaki? Bunch of sonofabitching soldiers doing that, wasn't it? There were innocents in those cities, weren't there?"

"Oh, God!"

"Don't call Him in on it now."

"Yes. That's a terrible question."

"Nothing selective there, eh?"

"Yes, it amounts to the question—don't you think—of whether we're all mad or sane, and, therefore, evil, and that, then, there must be good, too. Doesn't it amount to that?"

"Look, you bastard, I'm no bloody philosopher, either."

The Redeemer saw that fear had receded from his victim's eyes. "Crawl back, over there," he said, indicating direction away from himself. The Terrorist saw resignation in the pale eyes of his captor, some kind of loss, and sadness.

"Stay on the floor. Back! Maybe the answer is that evil is who initiates . . . who starts the thing."

"To hear you talk, babies start it."

"It's that we're wild animals, not yet fully human.  No, I've got to stay with my point.  My only sanity is my point."

"Which is?"

"That people have to suffer for the crimes they commit . . . for the evil they do.  That they can't suffer unless they have a conscience, and they can't develop a conscience without suffering.  That that's what I mean by deep torture.  I think the difference between you and me is that I have a conscience. It does seem different to me—that if a man tries to kill me, in defending myself, I kill him—than if I were the one who decided to do the killing first.  That does seem different to me. The secretary didn't try to kill you."

"I didn't try to kill her, either.  I didn't know she existed."  The Terrorist was exasperated.  With the impetus his freed limbs gave him he grabbed one of the chairs and sat, while the Redeemer followed his movements with his gun.

"You didn't care," said the Redeemer.  "You haven't got the imagination, the empathy required.  No, you see, there's the point.  You just meant to inflict pain, death, upon someone, anyone. That's your power. Yes. Yes. That's the point. You were the initiator.  It's all about power. . . like an animal."

"So I'm the bloke without a conscience, is that it?"

"That's it."

"Your point!  Your point!  Oh, I get your point, all right. It doesn't make a hellova lot of sense.  *My* point is that we're in a war here so—the war of the apes."

"But you are permanently out of the war.  You may get your circulation back, but you are not going back into circulation.  No, not you."

"You mean you're going to hold me prisoner?  You said before that you didn't intend to kill me."

"I don't.  That's why I'm going to have to be very careful."

"You do intend to torture me then?"

"I'm going to have to inflict pain. But I would do what I intend to do without inflicting pain if I could, but there's no other way."

"Damn you! What is it you intend to do?" The Terrorist thought he could lunge for this lunatic. He waited for the right moment.

"When you leave here," said the man of conscience, "and you will leave, you will be a changed man. You will begin a lifelong process of learning remorse. I'm going to make you grow up, laddie buck. You're going to learn what it is really like to share this planet with other members of your species. In your mind, which will gradually develop a heart, a conscience, you will be deeply tortured for the rest of your life. Because you have never understood what it is to see yourself in another being—sympathy—empathy. You've been locked in a cell all your life, laddie. But I'm going to lock you in so tight and for so long that you'll scream night and day for the word of another human being. For the sight of a face. For the grace to move with another in a dance. Even now, I can hear your *cri de coeur*. It is sweet to my ears."

"What in hell are you going to do?"

"I'm going to lock you in your body. All by yourself."

"What? What? What?"

"I'm going to cut your tongue out, so that you'll never be able but to vomit sound. I'm going to hold this pistol next to your eardrums and fire it, so that you'll never hear the sound of a voice again. I'm going to use my thumbs on your eyes. I'm going to castrate you. And I'm going to break your elbows and knees, and I'm going to see to it that you live. And for the rest of your days your punishment will be . . . isolation."

"And you, you bastard, you call yourself a man of conscience?"

"Oh, I know, I know. I've thought about it a great deal. I've thought it all out for a long, long time."

"You can't do it!  You haven't got it in you, to do a thing like that.  You're just trying to frighten me."

"Yes.  I can do it because I hate your kind beyond reason.  But, at first, I thought I couldn't do it unless—"

"Unless?"

"Unless, after I'd done it, I killed myself."

"My God, you mean to do it, don't you?"  The terrorist was dizzy with this talk.  One minute he thought his captor a garden variety nut case whom he could overtake and the next, some horrible philosophical maniac whose black whirling nonsense was seeping into his own reasoning.

"Yes, I mean it.  But then I thought. . . then I thought that would be cheating."

"Cheating what?  God?"

"No.  Myself.  My conscience.  You see, if I want you to suffer remorse, then I have no right to escape it.  That's what I meant when I said earlier that in condemning you, in . . . acting as your therapist, in awarding you the gift of a conscience . . . well, how could I run out on my own?"

The Terrorist realized then that only one chance for him existed.  He lunged at the Redeemer in desperation.

In a reflex action the Redeemer jerked the trigger of his cocked Webley and a red hole appeared between the Terrorist's unbelieving eyes.

"Oh no—Oh God!" the Redeemer cried, as the Terrorist fell to the floor.  "O no, O *God*!"

Later, out of that place, back among Christmas bells, in the icy splash of mist, still shaken, he walked the streets without purpose or direction, among average people who were just trying to live.

# MURDER IN THE FAMILY

*He that hath wife and children*
*hath given hostages to fortune . . .*
*—Francis Bacon, Essays*

I

Biology, loneliness, and love have always been busy on Fortune Island; even now, no doubt, in the year 2000, when the island is almost completely deserted, when all that is left at least of the human aspect of things is the administrative building housing the few officials who tend to its history, natural and human. To the best of my knowledge, the island was named for a plundered and derelict Spanish galleon, the *Buena Fortuna*, that, according to one history, "scuttled on the treacherous Outer Banks of North Carolina" in the Sixteenth Century. It's said that the gathering dunes eventually buried all but the prow of the ship, leaving only half of the name in plain sight, and so newcomers to the island looked upon the name of the ship as the name of the island and Fortune Island it became.

By the Eighteenth Century Fortune Island was a considerable port-of-call, with a fluctuating population of around eight hundred people. These included fishers, shrimpers, lobstermen, and tradesmen of all sorts involved with water traffic, and, of course, in many cases, their families. But then the great disasters occurred, one upon another. A hurricane in the mid-Nineteenth Century shut the main inlet while opening another miles up the Banks. People left in droves for the new port. The "fixed" population dropped to about a hundred, and continued to drop with the coming of Union troops during the Civil War. When the troops withdrew at war's end, Fortune

Island was virtually depopulated, a deserted island.

As you may remember, David, it is a whale-shaped island, its head to the north and out to sea, its finlike tail pointing southwest to the mainland.  Most of the northern end, or head, is covered with enormous dunes, as if the sea view had been walled away.  The roots of the dunes are entangled with the roots of mummified trees which once stood tall in the sea wind but now are buried and grip the depths of the dunes like anchors.  The tail of the whale, the low narrow leeward end, was, in my time, where most of the population, a few fishermen and shrimpers mainly, had little houses along little streets of a village in miniature.  A small white church with a steeple that one could see from the heights of Whalehead, near where my grandparents had constructed their own house, was the spiritual center of the island.  Out behind it were two cemeteries, one for black folk, one for white, each with a white picket fence not meant to keep people out but apparently to keep our ancestral ghosts in.

I grew up on Fortune Island at a time when the outside world with its school authorities did not seek me out, there far across Pamlico Sound, as other truants on the mainland were sought.  It was long before computers, remember.  I was, to all intents and purposes, unknown to the mainland world of Beaufort, Moorehead City, and Wilmington, where once and once only the man I then believed to be my father, the Sad Traveller himself—presumably sad with the grief and guilt of the world on his hunched shoulders, but probably what we would call today a manic-depressive, or a bi-polar type—the Reverend Jason P. Cogburn, had taken me on his preaching circuit.

Garcie, the black midwife who had brought me into this world and who continued to watch over me, had taken the mail boat up to Ocracoke Island to be with her dying brother, and so couldn't keep an eye on me that day, and the Reverend Cogburn, whom I always just called the "Traveller," was most reluctantly compelled to take his six-year-old charge with him, where in one church he leaned over me and shouted, "Do you believe?"

How could I believe anything coming from his twisted lips and smoke-blackened crooked teeth?  Skinny, in his tight black suit, with his hunched shoulders, he seemed like a hooded snake leaping into the air on its tail, and I shouted, "No!" *No, no, no*, I did not believe what he said, anything he might say, because I knew what no one else there knew, that he had none of the love in him which he preached about so readily, that he had terrified me since my mother's suicide in the sea, and then he slapped me, slapped me, slapped me with his long hard fingers until, crying and half screaming, I lied in his embarrassed, angry,  sweating face, shouting, Yes, yes, *yes*, that I did believe, but I did not and could not ever believe whatever it was he wanted me to believe, had never believed, whatever it was, coming from him.

I looked for help, protection, among the congregation; but nobody interfered with the Traveller, for he was the authority on discipline.  He set his believers an object lesson on how to deal with their own recalcitrant children, and most especially with a blasphemer, in this case a six-year-old who had dared to say no to belief.  Shouts of approval pierced my ears.  After all, I couldn't know that this was what they were paying for, what they would fill the collection box with their coins and even their bills for.  I had become, before their eyes, an example of the reformed and, finally, apparently, forgiven.  But I was never reformed and remain unforgiven and unforgiving till this day.

After the Traveller's sermon (a shouting match with the devil, or, more likely, a colloquy between the devil and himself) I learned that we had been at a church on the banks of the Cape Fear River.  I waited outside and could see across to the big city of Wilmington  and I remember seeing what a sympathetic church lady told me were Liberty Ships, hundreds of them, it seemed, a mothballed fleet, a long line of gray masts against lines of gray cypress trees, ghostly reminders of the recent war, and that is how I date this event. "No need to cry," the lady said, wiping my eyes with her lacy pink handkerchief. "Praise God, we have defeated the foe."

II

Congratulations, Ruthie, on graduating from Smith, like your mother and your Aunt Jessie, and now that I'm the proud father of a college graduate and a young woman of great promise, of a daughter who will someday—a day, I hope, far in the future—upon my demise go through my papers—no doubt consigning most of them to the shredder—I want you to be able to make a wise decision about the disposition of your Aunt Jessie's unfinished memoir, excerpted above. She claimed that that part of the memoir represented the earliest memory of her childhood, other than running about on the dunes and getting her toes wet in the sea, so I put it first. I have stuck with what appears to be the correct chronology throughout. It is a personal document, more like an elaborated letter, written to me for the purpose of deepening my understanding of our background. Upon my death, it will pass to you, and you may do with it as you see fit—write a biography (you *are* an English major), or a novel, maybe, or throw it in the fire.

Since your mother's death, there remain on earth but two people this memoir can effect, for good or ill, and they are you and me, and when it passes to you, only you. But you're a woman now, and I feel that you should know what is contained in these pages. With your upbringing, some of it may prove shocking to your sensibilities, but I hope that I am not mistaken in believing that your humanity will manifest itself in understanding and compassion. Your aunt was a great woman. When I think of what she accomplished, against such odds, I am amazed. Of course, your grand-

191

mother, my mother after whom you are named, deserves much credit for what Jessie accomplished. But as you will see, your grandfather also deserves kudos for one of the most unselfish acts known to me. Alas, my dear, they are all dead and gone, and finally have nothing to fear.

I felt that the manuscript, incomplete, confused as a house of cards shaken to the table, needed a few words of interpretation and here I try to supply those words, so it is really a double memoir, one to me from Jessie, one from me to you. In love, faith, and trust, I am your father, David Perle, speaking to you from the present, which is, I hope, your distant past.

Jessie Judas, winner of the International Lamarck Prize in Science, the Kyoto Prize for Basic Sciences, and many other awards, died last month, at five o'clock in the morning of March 20, 2003, a cold rain battering the window next to her hospital bed near Chapel Hill, North Carolina.

A nurse told me that her last words were, "It's Hazel." In her delirium, the last throes of the cancer that had eaten much of her flesh away, she was about a half century off the mark, for Hurricane Hazel had struck, killing her beloved Garcie, in 1954, but what she said indicated her recent preoccupation with the past. In the deep subjectivity of the coma that came and went, and under the influence of many drugs, that past must have seemed like a dream, part fairy tale, part nightmare. And so at the end, she would laugh, frown, cry, and whimper, her dying mind still alive with it all.

She was cremated, according to her wishes, and her ashes were scattered from a high dune on Fortune Island to fly over sand, sea, and shoal, into Pamlico Sound west and into the Atlantic east in a maelstrom of salt air. A few of her former colleagues at the University and Duke, and even a couple who had come all the way down from the Woods Hole Oceanographic Institution, and one from the Scripps Institution in California—and I—attended. Adding to the general sadness of the occasion was the fact that you were unable to attend.  (Ruthie, will you ever learn to stop taking chances? You are just like your grandmother Ruth—a daredevil. Please, for my sake, keep off those skis!)  Of course Judas wasn't Jessie's real name; it was the name our father had assumed, apparently penitentially, a man who was too hard on himself, as I now see it.  Tom Judas' real name was Thomas McQueen.  Why Jessie had changed her name to Judas, I had not been able to understand until I read her memoir.  It has been hard for me to decide what to think about this confessional piece, written, *in extremis*, when she had nothing to fear, least of all the truth.  But I have added a few thoughts at the end of the manuscript with which you might agree.

About six months ago I heard that Jessie was ill, perhaps dying, and I broke off a sliver of time from my work at the State Department, work which had kept me at great distances from Jessie for many years, and went to visit her at her house in Chapel Hill. She was just sixty then—and at her death— and I found her radically changed from the tall, vibrant red-haired woman I had seen only a few years before.  Then she had been the eminent scholar of a (to me) obscure branch of science, the author of several scholarly works and one book of personal essays on the academic life. But on this last visit I was shocked to find a frail, disheveled ghost of herself, her thick red hair become thin and ashen.

We spent a few hours together, reminiscing about our life together as kids in Boston.  That was the only life I had known with Jessie, growing up at that Brookline estate my grandparents had built, and which was sold before you were born.

When I was a child, I assumed Jesse was my sister. Later my mother explained to me that she was my half-sister—though, at that time, I could not see any meaning in that minor distinction—still later, the mystery of Jesse Judas deepened for me because she didn't share our name.  But what

I chose to ignore or took for granted as a child, I felt compelled to ask about on this last visit, time being as short as Jessie's wispy, colorless hair.

"Why Judas?"

"I think our father took the name Judas," Jessie said, "out of guilt for a failure of character—and only once in his life did his character fail him, as far as I know, and for which he paid a high price, not in what others exacted from him for it, but in the price he exacted from himself—he assumed the name Judas, and I for much the same reason, I guess, decided to carry it on."

"Why?  What did he do?  What did you do?  I wish I knew more about the past, Jessie."

"You will."

"But there's no one left but you to tell me."

"And I'll soon be gone. But you'll know all about it."

"How?"

"You'll see.  And when you know the whole story, I hope you'll have . . . well, strength and forgiveness."

"Whom shall I need to forgive?"

"All of us—your mother, your father, and me—and me especially." She coughed, waved the subject away.

She looked both imperious and weak.  I decided not to tax her with my insistence, and changed the subject.

"Do you remember the time we went to Fortune Island?"

"Do you?  You were only about seven.  By then there was no one there but the people from the National Park Service—a few public historical buildings—but Ruth and I knew where all the real people and places were.  We went to the house where I was born, which really wasn't there, you understand, but was a ghost house, and we walked through it with all its good and evil memories"—she seemed not to be talking to me anymore but simply remembering out loud—"and we went to the cottage where Ruth once lived, and we walked through the rooms where she wrote one of her books and where she began to teach me and possibly where you were conceived.  Mind you, nothing on the dunes but thin air."

"An insubstantial pageant faded."

"Yes.  Ghosts.  I hope to join them soon."

And too soon I had to be on my way, sorry to leave Jessie in such a condition and fairly certain that I would never see her again.  Well, we had never seen much of each other. By the time I had entered high school she was already a graduate student.  We were fond of each other, but she seemed always mysterious to me, a pleasantly bound but mostly closed book, and anyway more like an aunt than a half-sister, being fifteen or so years older.  When I think about it now, Ruthie, I realize that I knew very little about her.  But before leaving her on that last visit, she pushed a manuscript upon me, saying, "It's a piece of the story of my life. And yours. You might find it of interest."

And now I know why she and my mother always seemed in league against me when I showed them that I had a certain curiosity about aspects of the past, particularly about my father. Mother and Jessie would glance at each other conspiratorially and change the subject.  Their unforthcoming behavior only served to make me more curious, but they were adamant, and I remained curious to no end.  There was a secret between them, and I finally decided (for I loved and trusted them both, despite their odd behavior, because, after all, they lavished their love on me) that they would tell me the whole story in due time.  I guess that's why I became a diplomat. My talent is patience.


III

Dear David, over the years I've kept journals, diaries, scraps, and they've helped to keep my memory fresh. The following is for you:

195

I was born in a ramshackle house on Fortune Island, North Carolina in 1942 with the help of a black midwife named Garcie Cannon and very little else. That area of the Atlantic just off shore from the Banks was then known as "Torpedo Junction." German U-boats—submarines to the unhistorical modern—were sinking hundreds of merchant ships out there on that "stormy moat," as the poet Robinson Jeffers called it. I have been told that the fires of these sinking ships at night lighted the sky for miles. I have been told that I was born by that strange sinister firelight. Perhaps even as I was being born, our father's ship, just a few miles offshore, was torpedoed. He was about nineteen years old then, and had joined the Merchant Marines. Garcie told me that when he woke in the hospital in Raleigh, his hair had turned gray. This phenomenon of shock is called alopecia areata. It must have seemed strange to see such a thick head of gray hair on a man with such a youthful face. Our father, Tom McQueen, had inherited the house from his father and mother, a fisherman and a former schoolmarm, both dead before I could know them. How they came to live on that remote island I do not know, but I've always imagined that there must have been a great love story in it. Who else but lovers would suffer such a life, with no electricity, an outbuilding for cooking, so that the kerosene fumes wouldn't sicken them, and sand so deep and shifting that no car could maneuver it very far without getting stuck up to its running boards? Yes, David, in those days cars still had running boards.

As I say, I was born in that clapboard house with a production of Götterdämmerung going on outside at sea, where our father was being torpedoed into alopecia areata, or so I have come to think of the situation—which, in itself, sounds unpromising enough, but later Garcie elaborated it for me:

"You were a long, skinny baby with a lot of red hair and I had to fight to get you untangled from your own cord. Your mamma wasn't strong, and a weakness in her chest caused her to cough and spit up blood." That was Garcie when I was ten or so. And from before that, the Traveller preaching over my mother, her on her knees before him:

"You whored your way down from the mountains and across the Piedmont to the cities of sin on the coast—to Wilmington and the shipyards and the only man that would marry you, carrying his misbegotten child, that armed robber who's serving  his sentence in Central Prison in Raleigh for trying to rob the payroll of the company that makes Liberty Ships to help fight our enemies. What do you say for yourself? Speak! Can't you speak? Never mind. You have nothing to say. Only pray, pray, pray," and I have an infant's image, whether real or imagined, of my poor mother, her pale skin flushed, coughing and spitting, and asking, begging, imploring, "When will you forgive me, when will you ever forgive me?" And him, drunk: "Never! Only God can forgive you!"

Do I remember this or have I made it up out of Garcie's palaver? I could only have been two or three years old. And one day my mother must have walked into the sea, because she was gone for several days, vanished, and finally her body washed up on the shore, her frail feet and curled toes tangled in green weeds, I have been told, her red hair in dark strands against her iron gray face, like a beached mermaid. Then I had only the Traveller and Garcie, only Garcie really, and she needed a lot of help from me by that time, because her eyes were failing fast, her diabetes winning against the light.

They took my mother's body to the hard sand near the shore, and there was trouble with the mail boat, causing a delay, so she waited for two days in the back of an old station wagon, waited to be taken somewhere for medical examination before being brought back to the island for burial. I went there to be near her and squatted next to the station wagon. I talked to her through the window. The owner of the station wagon came and opened the door and there was a terrible stench from inside and he threw some liquid into the back seat, for the smell, and shut and locked the doors. I waved goodbye when they took her body out in the skiff to the mail boat, even though I knew by then that she couldn't see that I was waving, or maybe I thought that she could see me from some other place. Because of the Traveller, I do not believe in other places any more.

Of course I knew by then that the Sad Traveller, the Reverend Jason Cogburn, wasn't my father—he had made that very clear to me—that my father was an evil criminal named McQueen who was in a prison everyone called "The Wall." I hated my real father as much as I hated the Traveller; sometimes more, because he had deserted me by committing a crime and going behind the Wall and leaving me with the Traveller for a father. I didn't know which one I hated most. I suppose I prayed to God to give me someone beside poor blind Garcie. Because of the Traveller, I don't think I believe in God anymore.

Jessie McQueen. I didn't want that last name. I was ashamed of it. And I was certainly determined never to call myself Cogburn, although the Traveller never asked me to. I was nobody. I belonged to nobody. I lived in the house where I was born, which now seemed to belong to the Traveller, and, when I was lucky, I was treated by him as a step-daughter, and, when not so lucky, he treated me as he had treated my mother. He drank heavily whenever he came home and I was afraid when he did and I would go over to Garcie's to stay with her, unless he demanded that I stay with him, which he sometimes did, when he had grown tired of talking to himself and felt the need of someone to torment.

One day I climbed the stairs to the small attic that was crowded with old damp boxes to see if I could find any of my mother's, or even of my grandmother's, clothes—the Travel-ler would occasionally bring me something back from his trips—but I was barefoot and in rags most of the time. It didn't make much difference on the island anyway, I guess;

but I did need some things badly, and there among the boxes I discovered my father's books. The Traveller had taught me to read the Bible, and there was a dictionary among the books, and so I found a secret life for myself, a life away from the Traveller, away from the world. In the real world I was sinking deeper into my own isolation, but in the world of imagination, I began to expand. I called these books my secret treasure trove, and, handling them, touching them I could touch my father, who had smeared and dogeared almost every page. His mother, my grandmother, the schoolmarm, must have been my father's teacher, must have directed him in his reading. I could feel her hand on the books too. I put my fingers on her fingerprints. I could feel them in the attic with me, my father and even my grandmother. I could imagine him as a boy of my own age, curled up and reading *Tales from Shakespeare* by Charles Lamb, reading the *Essays* of Francis Bacon, especially the mystery of *The New Atlantis,* which was the mystery of an island like the one I was on. I discovered that Francis Bacon wrote that knowledge was power, and I, being powerless, took that to mean that my only way out of my life of subservience (though of course I didn't know such a word at that time) was through learning, and I set out to educate myself and have never hesitated in my quest for knowledge since.

It occurred to me that day up in the attic, thumbing through those books, that my father must have absorbed some of the things that I was reading helter-skelter and only partially understanding, like Bacon, that in his mind up there in Central Prison at Raleigh behind the Wall he must still possess chunks of Shakespeare, particles at least of Thomas Wolfe—because there was a dogeared copy of *Look Homeward, Angel* and another of *You Can't Go Home Again.* He had underlined passages, and I tried to glean what he had read and to put it into my own mind. There were books of poetry, mildewed but readable, books by Poe, Sidney Lanier, and

Walt Whitman. There was one that I read as best I could, and re-read for several years—*Of The Imitation of Christ* by Thomas à Kempis. "To achieve this," my father had written in the flyleaf in a round young hand, "is to achieve perfection." Then how could he have done what he did? How could he have become a criminal? How could he have left me alone? How could he have left me at the mercy of the Traveller? "He that has wife and children hath given hostages to fortune." To Fortune Island!

I found a copy of *Under the Sea Wind*, by someone named Rachel Carson at the bottom of one box. A woman. I didn't know then that women wrote books. It was a very exciting discovery. I was going to read it right away. I carried it out to the dunes with me and discovered that it was all about the dunes, about the little animals that I watched, about the wind and sea. Biology. About my own biology. I went over to ask Garcie about my biology.

"How did my mother and father meet, Garcie?"

"They met in Wilmington, how most men and women meet."

"How?"

"I told you, baby, your daddy was a soft-hearted boy and I guess he done seen a poor gal down on her luck and decided to help her out. Next thing they married and back here and she pregnant with you and he off for the Merchant Marines and he sunk and in the hospital and you born and he back here and off again to do that awful payroll robbery and in prison and the Traveller come tell your momma she need him and don't need your daddy and here we are, you sitting there eatin' grits and me talking up a storm. Now stop asking questions and let old blind Garcie get some shuteye, like I need to shut 'em for the dark, ha, ha."

"But why did my mother give up on my dad? Why did she divorce him?"

"She was a poor, sad, weak creature, more to be pitied,

who couldn't do for herself much less anyone else. Without a man she was like a dog with nobody to walk her. She was sick most of her life, child, sick and ignorant and frightened and always needing a man to guide her, to give her direction and protection. Weren't her fault. God just make some of us like that so that the rest who is stronger have some way of using their strength. Some is needy, some is good, and some is greedy. That's the way it works. Your father was strong most of the time with moments of weakness in him—one big moment, you might say. A little of the devil would get into him once in a while, like it gets into you when you go into one of your conniption fits, but he weren't no bad person like you being told by that Traveller. When he got out of that hospital with his hair all gray he was onliest just a youngan hisself, and he got talked into doing something he shouldn't ought to done, thinking it was the only way he had to help you and your mother. He was always the most guilt-suffering boy you ever did see, and I can bet you anything that he is suffering right now."

"What's it like where he is, Garcie?"

"They calls it the Wall, and he behind it. It's a big dark tower, like one of those castles in that Frankenstein movie, but I don't suppose you ever saw that. Don't suppose you ever saw a movie in your life, did you, baby?"

"No ma'am. You know I ain't never been off this island long enough to see anything, 'cepting I remember those Liberty boats I told you about."

"And you never stop talking about them, do you?"

"No ma'am. What if I went to school, Garcie?"

"Just give Garcie another job in minding you. The Traveller is schooling you, according to his way, and nobody argues so far. He don't want you to know some things."

"What things?"

"Don't ask me, he just don't, and he does the payin' around here."

"What things am I not supposed to know?  I already know things he doesn't know that I know."

"Like what, pray tell?"

"Like knowledge is power."

"That's a big mouthful for a little skinny blue egg just been cracked open.  Go on, now; let me get my nap."

I went walking in the shoal at low tide and looking at the little whelklings in their tubes.  I picked one from the clear water and held it in my palmed hands and I remember, I prayed to it: Please, give me someone.  I dropped it back with a tiny splash and stopped, listening, waiting.  No voice from the blue but the laughter of the black-capped gulls, laughter half drowned in the sea-smelling, soft, salt roar of the wind, and the susurrus of the shifting dunes.

Beaufort Inlet
Drum Inlet
Ocracoke Inlet
Hatteras Inlet
Oregon Inlet

—the ways in and the ways out.  Why do they call them Inlets?  They are Outlets.  Like my mother, who came down from the mountains and across the Piedmont and finally out to sea—those waters, my mother.

If I had understood the word, I'd have known that the Traveller was a sadist.  He made me cry whenever he could.

"Look what I've brought back for you from Wilmington," he said one day after his return from his preaching circuit.  His black coat hung on a hook inside the front door.  He went to it and found something and tossed it on the table, across from his bottle of bourbon. A magazine: "True Crimes."  I was about twelve.  He sat leering at me as I tried to understand the meaning of the odd gift.

"Go ahead," he said, "look through it."  I was sipping coffee.  I put down my cup and thumbed through the magazine.  "Find an article called 'The Case of the Disgraceful

Vets,' he said. "There's a picture of your daddy there, and three others who were involved in that botched robbery." He put a square flat index finger on the page. "That one—Tom McQueen—that's your father. How do you like him in his prison uniform? That's the man your mother loved. That man—not me. No matter what she said, she couldn't make me believe she loved me as she had that man. Damned and evildoers, both of them. And you had better watch yourself or you'll end up a wicked painted woman and a suicide, or like your daddy, a criminal behind bars. I'm watching you, but I can't always be here, so you better watch yourself. It's their blood that's in you. Where do you think you're going, young lady?" He tried, but he was too drunk to get up. "Hey, where do you think you're going?"

I took the magazine and grabbed my book and a blanket and went out on to the dunes on the sound side, found a comfortable place, and read about how my father and his friends had found the police waiting for them when they arrived at the shipyard. It seemed that the wife of one of the robbers had informed on them. The War was still on then and they were called disgraces to the uniform of the United States military and naval services and sentenced to ten years each.

I studied the blurry photographs on the pulp paper of the magazine pages. All I could tell from the pictures was that they seemed young, except for my father who seemed old with his pale hair. But I knew that he was as young as the others. I remembered a photograph of him from the boxes in the attic. In that picture he must have been about my own age, twelve or thirteen, and his hair was raveny dark, the way I always thought of him. I understood that he was a criminal and in jail. But I couldn't believe he was really a bad man. I wondered how he'd forgotten what he'd read in *The Imitation of Christ.* Does it just slip away sometimes when you aren't looking? I lost my temper sometimes, so sudden it was scary. I'd yell mean things at Garcie. Once I even pushed her, and

I was so sorry afterwards I cried and cried, and finally I cried myself to sleep.

When night comes to Fortune Island, it is like a big hand reaching out from the mainland, its fingers making dark shadows among the dunes, but for a time before that happens, there can be an horizonless silver of sound-water and sky until it darkens and to the northeast the soft steady recurring blink of the lighthouse appears in the dark like a star that you can almost reach out and touch, a star you can make a wish upon. I often empathized with the oyster, that, as it shuts its mother-of-pearl-lined shell, creates its own night, but its stars dim and die while ours spangle the sky.

More and more often, as I grew up, and the Traveller returned from his circuit, I would sleep out on the dunes and stare up, before, like the oyster's, the shell of my mind closed with my eyelids on the pictures they seemed to make. I had tried the attic for escape but I didn't like the feeling of being trapped up there. What if he were to climb up behind me? There was a little cave, not much bigger than a rabbit hole, which I had dug out, under the back wall of the house, and when it was raining or cold or both I would pile on my clothes and take my blanket and go there to sleep, but most of the time I would sleep with the other small creatures in the sand that walked with the wind. But some of the creatures on the dunes didn't sleep at night—the mosquitoes and sand fleas, "all those danged bloodsuckers," as Garcie called them—and I suppose it was a tiny crab that had crawled into my blanket that night that woke me, caused me to jump up and shake out the blanket. I heard a woman's voice behind me scream and then begin to laugh.

"Oh my God! You scared the bejesus out of me. I thought this place was deserted."

"Don't be scared. I'm just a little girl."

"Not so little, stretch."

"I'm tall for my age."

204

"Which is?"

"Twelve going on thirteen."

"What are you doing out here so late?"

"I was sleeping."

"Sleeping in the sand? Don't you have a bed at home? It must be three in the morning."

"I didn't want to be in the house with my stepfather. He's drunk."

"Oh you poor kid! Is he mean to you?"

"He's mean as a snake."

The woman frowned. "Does he hit you?"

"He tries, but I can dodge him most of the time."

"What does your mother say?"

"She's dead."

"Oh, I'm sorry to hear that. Well, don't you have somewhere you can go? A friend's house?"

"I can go to Garcie, but he looks for me there. I don't want to bring her any trouble."

"Garcie is your friend? An older woman?"

"She looks after me. She born me into the world."

"Not your mother—"

"Garcie's black. She's too old for any excitement. She was the midwife that helped to bring me in."

"I see. Well, my name is Ruth Perle." She gave me her hand to shake. It was warm and soft, but strong. And that was the way Ruth always seemed to me: warm and soft and strong and firm and brave.

"I never heard anyone talk like you." I said. "You're not from around here, are you?"

"I'm from Boston. Up north. I'm doing some work down here—on the Banks."

"What work is there to do down here—if you're not a fisherman or a boat-builder or—" What else was there?

"Never mind about that now. Why don't you come on home with me and spend the night? Are you hungry? I can fix you something."

"That'd be mighty nice of you.  I didn't eat any dinner or supper."

"Well, come on then."  Ruth had not let go of my hand, and now she led me off across the dunes, stumbling and sliding and laughing—together!  The words of our meeting may not be exact, blown away, as they were, by the night wind, but that was the gist of it.  What I couldn't know then was that I had found my someone, the someone I had so long prayed to the sky and the sand and sea to find, prayed to the whelklings, the someone whose voice I had often heard murmuring inside the seashell, the friend from another world.

"Are you married?" I asked her.

"I was.  My husband was killed in Korea."

"Mr. Perle?"

"No, no, I never used my husband's name.  I was a writer when I met him and I'm a writer now."

"You mean like Rachel Carson? Look, I've got a book by her," and I waved *Under the Sea Wind* under Ruth's nose.

"No, not like Rachel Carson.  I'm a folklorist."

"Oh," I said, vaguely disappointed, and wondering what that meant, but also still thrilled at the idea of meeting a real woman writer.  "Do many women write books? I never heard of any before Rachel Carson."

"You never heard of Margaret Mitchell?"

"No ma'am."

"Who wrote *Gone With the Wind*?"

"No ma'am."

"Unbelievable!" Ruth exclaimed.

I was vaguely hurt.  "I ain't never been off this island, excepting once when I saw the Liberty ships near Wilmington."

"Well, hell's bells, I found myself a Caspar Hauser."

"What's a Caspar Hauser?"

"A little boy who was kept away from the world."

"That's me, then—Caspar Hauser. But I'm Jessie McQueen—at least that's what they tell me, and they've been calling me that forever—well, as far back as I go."

I recognized the cottage we were heading toward. It had belonged, up until a few months before, to an elderly couple who had kept to themselves—almost hermits. There was a light inside, a golden glow at the window.

"What happened to the old people who lived here?"

"The wife died. The husband was taken off to a nursing home in Beaufort." She tugged and pushed at the door against drifted sand until she got it open. "Come on in—what did you say your name was again?"

"Jessie McQueen. The wife died and the husband is in a nursing home because he is so old," I said. "That's biology too."

Ruth looked at me as if I had said something very peculiar. "I suppose it is," she said, "in the larger sense."

"Oh, yes, ma'am, that's biology too. All animals die."

"I'm afraid I know that only too well, young lady."

"Yes, I suppose you do, ma'am. I didn't mean nothing by it. Just things come into my head sometimes and I out and say them."

Later, Ruth told me how I had startled her. She said, "I think I knew then and there that there was something very special about you." Every so often over the years she would remind me of what I had said that night and of its effect on her.

"Come on in, Jessie McQueen," she said, in her hearty way, as I remember it, all those years back, those time-eaten years, and I couldn't know then that I was stepping through golden gates into my future, into a life I could never have imagined. As the deck has been dealt, approximately a year to a card, I look back on that moment as the first card dealt, an ace of hearts. I also look back on the vision before me in that little house, with each passing year, more and more, as a kind of Cinderella vision of the magic possible in a world I could not then have believed existed.

Ruth had the place lighted with several soft-gleaming oil lamps—remember, there was no electricity on Fortune Island then—that just kept awake the drowsy colors of hundreds of book jackets, and there were paintings—"prints," Ruth called them—on the walls done in styles that then were as alien to me as would have been a dinosaur or a spaceman; I had never seen anything like them.  I had no idea, of course, but I was looking at prints of modern art: Van Gogh, Matisse, Picasso, Braque, all of whom and many more that I have come to consider familiar friends but who then seemed to me to be something from another universe.

"Oh, that's you!" I cried, seeing a black framed photograph dangling crookedly from a nail among the prints.

"That's me and my husband and my daughter.  It was taken about ten years ago.  Before you ask, my daughter is dead too. She died of polio when she was three.  She would have been nearly your age by now."

"I'm sorry," I said meekly.  I felt meek before such tragedy, but Ruth just smiled at me and shook her head.

"That shouldn't be hanging there."  She snatched the picture from its place and put it face down on a table. "People should be forward-looking. The future is our obstacle course with a pot of gold at the end."

Ruth was a tough-minded woman.  If she hadn't been, David, she would never have been able to make the decision, on the spot, as it were, to surrender your father for my future's sake, as you will soon see that she did.  But my eyes were still wandering in wonder. A Remington typewriter caught my interest, as a bright bauble catches the eye of a magpie.  It was black and chrome and bulky with black keys with white letters on them.  It seemed awesome, such efficiency, such power to make words on paper—and there was a half-typed page sticking out of it at the top.  I couldn't take my eyes from it, now, even as I heard a cranking noise and music filled the room.  I turned on my heel and there stood Ruth, smiling at me and tapping her foot to the music.    "What is that?"

"I thought you could use a little cheering up," she said. "That's Glenn Miller, 'String of Pearls.'  Well, what do you think of my humble abode?"

"If you mean this place—well, it's just wonderful!  I've never seen anything like it.  Our place is just bare boards, straight chairs, a table, and mattresses on the floor.  The Traveller—that's what I call my step-father—he don't care about having anything around."

"Why do you call him the traveller?"

"He's a circuit preacher—on the road most of the time—which I'm glad for because I hate it when he's home. He comes home and drinks for a few days and goes off again and that's about all I see of him and I'm glad of it."  I looked around. "Could you tell me what that is—that picture?"

"That's a Picasso print."

"What does print mean?"

"Well, it's not a real painting; it's a sort of photograph of the painting.  And the painter's name is Picasso.  The actual picture was painted back in Nineteen-five."

"So long ago. . . But what is it?  It looks like it's full of boxes."

"Do you like it?"

"I guess—sort of."

"That style of painting is called cubism.  It does look like a pile of boxes, doesn't it?"

"All different colors—tan, and yellow, and brown. . . But there's a fiddle sticking out of it—part of a fiddle, any-way. And there's a newspaper in some foreign language— what does that mean?"

"It's a French headline.  It says—"

"But why is it like that?"

"Because Picasso thought it would be interesting to look at."

"It is—but, you know what? Your whole house is like that—what did you call it?"

"You mean cubism?"

"Uh-huh. All the books and everything—it's like cubism."

Ruth glanced about the room and laughed. "I suppose it is."

"I don't mean no insult. I just mean the books look like they're going to fall over—the stacks of them."

"I'm not the neatest person, young miss. Now how would you like something to eat? How about scrambled eggs and bacon? I'll go out back and rustle us up something. You go ahead and look around at anything that interest you. I won't be long."

The way we cooked on the Island then was in sheds back of the houses. We called them summer kitchens. We used them because the kerosene heat made the houses unbearably hot in summer. The stoves weren't good in those days and fumes could catch up with you, make you sick or even kill you. Ruth took a lamp and went out the back door. I was overwhelmed at seeing so many books in one place. I couldn't get over it. I would have said then that I'd gone dreamy. Oh, I couldn't believe what I was seeing; it was a book with Ruth's picture on the back—*Appalachian Tales*, by Ruth Perle. She did write books! And she was so beautiful too, with her huge almond eyes and her long dark hair, so smart and so beautiful and she was out back cooking me bacon and eggs. I had gone dreamy all right, no doubt about it. The smell of bacon came in first, then coffee, then Ruth with her fresh air smell. We were both hungry, eating fast and not talking much but a "Pass the salt, please," but Ruth finished first, wiping the last of the yolk from her plate with a last bit of bread. She lighted a cigarette—I hadn't seen a woman smoking before—and blew the smoke out with a contented sigh.

"Now tell me about yourself," she said.  That's how I remember it—early morning, with the sky lightening outside, Ruth smoking and studying me with those big almond eyes— a word I learned later: chatoyant, her eyes—that looked like they could read your mind, and me, pent up with the story of my life on the verge of exploding from my lips, and a million questions waiting just behind it. Ruth let me ramble on for a long time before she finally stopped me with a question.  She was lighting another cigarette and spoke around it.

"Are you really reading that Rachel Carson book?"

"Oh yes.  I have a dictionary for the words I don't understand, though I can't find them all.  But a lot of it is written like the Bible.  You know, nice and simple.  It's very beautiful."

"So you're interested in that sort of thing.  I mean, the life of animals, sea life, biology?"

"It's funny: all my life I've lived right here and seen these little creatures running up the beach but I never really thought about them—they were just there.  Then I found this book, and began reading about them, and, because of the pictures in the book, the drawings, I began to recognize them, and now I go looking for them.  I want them to show me how they live.  I've been pretty lonesome out here on this danged old island. No kids. No friends.  Now it's like I have all these strange little friends. Fiddler crabs, and whelks, and the other day I met a huge ghost crab you could see right through— almost.  I talked to him for about an hour.  Then he went off about his business."

"What did he have to say?"

"That I'd be better off if I were invisible like him.  But in a way I am almost invisible.  No one knows I'm here."

"I can see you," Ruth said.  "I know you're here.  Come over here near the light and let me see your arms."

I stuck out my skinny, freckled arms for her to examine.

"Oh, you've been eaten alive," Ruth said. "I can't tell the freckles from the bites."

"The freckles are brown, the bites are red. I'm always like this except in the winter."

"You poor kid. I'll give you some citronella. Look at my arms." She held out shapely womanly arms with a tinge of dark hair on the forearms for me to observe. "I use citronella. It keeps the bugs away."

I was awestruck. This young woman from Boston knew more about living on Fortune Island than I did. I couldn't begin to imagine what else she might know, but I was to find out in the coming months.

"Miss Perle, I've been wondering, what were you doing out on the dunes so late at night?"

"My time is my own, sweetie—and call me Ruth. In fact, tomorrow I'm going up to Manteo."

"Where's that?"

"Right here on the Banks. Don't you know it? I'm going to see *The Lost Colony*."

"What's *The Lost Colony*?"

"A play by Paul Green—it's about Virginia Dare, the first English child born in America. Jessie, haven't you ever been off this island?"

"What I said, the Traveller took me on his circuit when Garcie was sick or busy or something and I remember seeing Wilmington—that's a very big city—from the other side of the Cape Fear River. I remember hundreds and hundreds of big ships."

"Listen, I have a wonderful idea. How would you like to go with me?"

I was so excited that it choked me. I nodded my head for fear that my voice would crack or come out in a squeal or a screech like an old owl.

"But you'll have to get your step-father's permission."

"Yes," I said, my pipes opening. "Oh yes!"

"Good. Now let's get a couple of hours sleep and then you can run home and ask if you can go. I'll open up that folding cot for you."

I lay in the dark but I couldn't sleep because I couldn't wait; but what if the Traveller wouldn't let me go? I would lie. That's all there was to it—I would lie my red head off. I would do anything to be able to go on this trip with Ruth Perle. I would not let anything stand in my way. I had to get off this island and see the world. *See the world!* The room was filled with light. Had I dreamed it all? No, it was true; for there was the astonishing Ruth, a reality, preparing for the trip.

In close to half a century, I don't think I've ever been so happy again as I was on that June morning in 1954, not even many years later when I received notice that I was awarded the Lamarck Prize. The joy I felt was like another being inside me trying to burst through my skin. I remember vividly the kinetic sense that my arms moved too fast, my skinny legs seemed to dance to the table for coffee, my head swiveled, not turned, but swiveled, and my heart pounded like a little drum in my chest. I ran across the hot sand of the dunes and for the first time in my life did not notice the heat. I might as well have been a skater on ice, I went so fast, the inner reaches of my mind my only hoveringly physical part, my dream come true. And there was no mean amount of fear. Why should I believe, hope, what would lead me to believe or hope that the Traveller would let me go? But I would lie. I would change my story and lie. I burst into the house and found that my worst fears were unwarranted. The Traveller was gone, off on his circuit once again. There was an envelope on the table—FOR GARCIE. Her money. I grabbed it and ran all the way to Garcie's shack. She had me count the money and read her the note. *Gone for about a week. Enough to keep her fed.*

"Later you take me to Walkup's to get some groceries, hear?" said Garcie.

"I'm going fishing, be back later."

"You watch yourself, now, child, hear?"

When I got back to Ruth's she had a tin tub filled with steaming water. She was naked but for a towel around her hair. I had never seen a woman completely naked before. Biology again! I lurched toward embarrassment but Ruth's matter-of-factness caught me back.

"Strip and get in there," she said, and I followed her orders unquestioningly but full of questions. "Well," she said when I had stripped, "you're not even a tabula rasa, you're a bas relief of bites, abrasions, and bruises. Let me look in your mouth," and she poked a forefinger around inside my gaping mouth with an intermittent hum as if she were looking for pearls and finding sand; but no, she pulled her finger from my mouth and said, "It's amazing. Your teeth are in pretty good condition. I don't suppose you get much candy, sweets, do you?"

"I don't eat much of anything most of the time."

Ruth said, "I'm going to take a picture of you, so we can check on your progress." And she stood before me with the camera up to her face and the dark V of hair at the bottom of her belly, her breasts crushed together by her arms as she looked for range—and of course I have often seen what she was seeing that morning (I still have that treasured, faded photograph): a gawky, gangly stringbean of a girl topped with a mass of dark reddish hair that looked as though it had never come in contact with a comb. "Pop!" went the flashbulb and, momentarily blinded, I must have jumped a foot off the ground. Ruth, laughed, put down the camera and picked up a lighted cigarette, stuck it between her teeth—and I was laughing now—and said, "Into the water with you, young lady. I hope you don't mind bathing in the same water that I just got out of, but we don't have time for another tubful. Now I'm

going to wash your hair and then I'm going to find you something to wear.  I've got a pair of bluejeans that should fit you.
We'll have to roll the cuffs down, but otherwise . . ."

When we were dressed, Ruth took another photograph
of me.  In that picture, my hair is combed, and I'm wearing
an old sweatshirt with cut-off sleeves that has SMITH COL-
LEGE written across the front—the shirt is red and the letter-
ing is gold—the jeans, a pair of Ruth's sandals, just a bit
short, for my toes curl over the soles, and I'm proudly holding
my first pocketbook, a small brown leather purse with a long
thin strap to put over my shoulder.  The strange thing is, I was
twelve and except for my height I look younger in the first
picture; in the second, I look like a young lady.  It was the
first time it had ever occurred to me that I might be—well, if
not pretty, at least presentable in the way that young women
ought to be, or ought to have been in the Fifties.

"Now here's our itinerary," said Ruth.  I must have
looked blank. "This is what we're going to do." And she told
me as we trudged across the sand dunes with her logistical
haversacks on our backs and cameras dangling from our
shoulders.  Ruth had explained that she had a tape recorder in
a trunk in her "vehicle," which meant car, I guessed.  We were
heading to Sheriff Walkup's General Store, and working up
quite a sweat getting there.

Walkup's General Store was the only store on Fortune
Island, and was a good hike from Ruth's place.  Walkup was
a retired county sheriff then somewhere in his late sixties or
early seventies, who had come to the island about twenty
years before and opened the General Store, a two-story building the lower floor of which was the store and the upper floor
the living quarters.  He sold bait and tackle, canned goods,
cereal grains, quite a variety of oddments, and was also the
Postmaster.  His wife was the wooden Indian figure at the
cash register.  On several occasions I had tried to make friends

with her, but she had no interest in children.  The most she ever showed me was cold tolerance.

We had to take Sheriff Walkup's skiff out to the mail boat, a pretty white little steamer about fifty feet long with green trim and a red, white, and black smokestack emitting dark, immediately dissipating little puffs against blue sky and white cloud, and followed by a great wing of happily screeching gulls.  We climbed into the skiff and Sheriff Walkup began pulling at the oars, puffing and pulling, then stopped about thirty feet from the steamer to wipe his wet forehead with a damp handkerchief.

"I'm getting too old for this," he said; then, brightening, "Lookee yonder, ladies!  You see that there feller waiting to get off?  That's my new strong back standing there.  Don't look like it, does he, in that there seersucker suit and straw Stetson, but I'm gonna have him in dirty work clothes before this skiff has to go out again," and he began painfully pulling at the oars once more while Ruth and I got a closer and closer look at the man on the steamer's deck.

"Look," I said, "he's got a guitar looks like."

"Good God," Ruth said, "he looks good enough to eat."

"He's beautiful," I whispered.

"Watch out, ladies," said Walkup.  "He's mine."

We climbed a rope ladder and got aboard the mail boat as the stranger tipped his Stetson in greeting, helped us up with our paraphernalia, and handed down the mail bag, his guitar case, and a battered old suitcase to Walkup.  Up close, he looked just as good but surprisingly pale, as if maybe he had spent too much time in juke joints playing that old guitar. We hated to see him climb down into the skiff and row off with Sheriff Walkup.  I wished he could come on our trip with us.  All duded up like he was, it'd been fun to show him off, like something you'd won at a shooting gallery.

Everyone on board took this adventure for granted, or appeared to, but I thrilled at everything I could touch, smell, or see—the rust on the iron rails, the wake coming from the bow and scudding outward in white foam, the spindrift that dampened my hair, the sudden distance between us and Fortune Island, my home, that seemed so much less important to me now than the invisible place where we were to land, the wild gulls flying in our wake, and the wilder clouds racing across the blue sky.  I had probably never felt so alive in all my long captivity.  The lighthouse I often saw from Fortune Island, the one that seemed a low, twinkling star to me when I was younger, that always seemed disembodied, was soon looming before me, tall, conical and stark white.  But before that, I looked back and saw a Stetson wave goodbye.

On Ocracoke, we squeezed into a pickup truck and were driven to the village, where Ruth unveiled yet another miracle.  Behind a building, I think it was a restaurant, Ruth removed a tarpaulin with a "Voila!" to display an old Army jeep.  I had never seen one before in my life.  It was—exotic! It was dirty and rusty and tough looking as a flat-faced dog, and Ruth had it barking in no time—and bouncing, and bouncing—for I soon discovered that jeeps could go anywhere but they could not go anywhere without bouncing, and I had to hold on for dear life for fear of being tossed ten feet in the air and left on a beach somewhere, forgotten by Ruth, who seemed intent on nothing else but mastering this wild machine.  We bounced, jumped, leaped on for fifteen miles, sometimes on the beach, sometimes on the road, sometimes, it seemed, we stayed in the air for miles on end.  My first lovely hairdo was in wild disarray by the time we reached the Frazier Peele ferry landing at Hatteras Inlet, where they told us we had to drive our jeep up the planks and on to the ferry first because it was too heavy to lift—the ferry only held three cars: two were put side by side,  then the men would lift the third so it would be behind the other two, crosswise.  As we made the crossing to Hatteras, Ruth, apparently unfazed, spent some time reshaping my hair. "I don't want you look-ing feral," she said. Again she could see I was blank.

"Like a wild girl," she said.

"Do I look like a wild girl, Ruth?"

"Not now," she said, smoothing back my hair, pushing here and there. "Now you look like you're ready for Atlantic City."

I pretended to know what she meant, but I couldn't help wondering if we were going to Atlantic City, too, wherever that was.

And then we were bouncing along again and Ruth didn't even slow down when we came to the Cape Hatteras light-house, which I was to learn was one of the most famous in the world. "That's the Cape Hatteras lighthouse," she called, dan-gerously taking her right hand from the jumping steering wheel of the jeep to point at what I thought was one of the greatest wonders that I had ever seen—in fact was one of the greatest wonders that I had ever seen, or almost seen, it re-ceded so fast from view, like a lonely giant peppermint stick. I had to turn my head almost all the way around to face front. Everything was like that with Ruth—whizzbang!

"We're heading up Hatteras to Oregon Inlet," she yelled. I must have agreed. I had noticed by now that disa-greeing with Ruth was useless. "Yes," I suppose I said, but then I yelled, "when are we going to stop to eat?"

"When we get there," Ruth yelled back over the growls of the jeep and the roar of the surf.

"Get where?" I yelled.

"Nag's Head," she yelled back. "I have friends there."

It hadn't occurred to me before that Ruth had friends on the Banks—I thought of her as all alone and from far away Boston. The realization that she had friends nearby raised another question in my mind. "But if you have friends, Ruth, why do you live so far away from them? Why do you live on

Fortune Island, where there isn't hardly anybody but me and Garcie and just a few others?"

"Because it's the perfect place to write, my Honeylamb. I do my collecting up and down the Banks—like this—and then I bring it back to Fortune Island where there isn't anybody to bother me and I can concentrate and write."

I thought about that for a moment and then I said, "Ruth, am I going to bother you?"

She gave me a quick, disturbed look. "Not you, Honey, never you. Don't you ever worry about that." Then she gave me the warmest smile—at the same time maneuvering on the beach without looking forward. Ruth could do it all.

We crossed Oregon Inlet on a much bigger ferry. In fewer than twenty miles of paved road we came to a populated area. What chance of the flarings and dimmings of the lights of memory brings us back the past and what chance encloses it in darkness forever, I do not know. It seems to me now that we pulled into a big yard in front of a big, gabled house; it seems to me now that the yard was full of children, some younger than I and some older, boys and girls, young men and young women, and that the king and queen of the place, told by graying hair and other signs of advancing age, were in front of the children, or at the middle of the group, or did they appear at the sides of the jeep to help us out? I remember the steamer trunk in the back seat of the jeep being opened and a tape recorder being taken into the house. Greetings, lunch, and hours of taping the voice of our host, as I remember a burly man who told many strange stories of the folklore of the Banks, stories of storms and pirates, and Blackbeard. I especially remember songs, stories and songs all afternoon, Ruth changing reels of tape, taking notes, urging the man on to talk and sing more: and I remember my embarrassment at having to eat with the other children, which was the embarrassment of a stranger who had been isolated for so long at having to socialize with an advanced race of people her own age, fully civilized, knowledgeable young people, whose education had not been neglected to the point of mental infirmity as my own had been. No one actually said, "Are you a dunce?" but I heard it over and over in my mind and I thought I saw it in the eyes around me, but probably not, for everyone was extremely kind, I remember, and one girl who appeared to be about my own age helped me with a personal matter, a biological matter, that had just begun to be a serious consideration in my life.

Then Ruth and I left their house to go to the play, which was long and involved Sir Walter Raleigh, Queen Elizabeth, Indians, and the first English baby born in the new world, Virginia Dare. The image that time has left me is the image of the top of the ship's sail, a rough rectangle of white against the actual night sky, moving away behind the tops of the wooden stakes of the fort, sailing away and to England to get supplies and leaving the remaining colonists on their own— and of course they waited for the ship to return but it never did to their knowledge and they wandered into the woods and were never seen again. I broke down at that image of the sail against the night sky and Ruth took me in her arms and comforted me. I was tired. Emotionally exhausted. So when Ruth asked me If I would prefer to drive back home that night or to go back and stay with that nameless family, I told her that I wanted to go home. I wasn't used to people and the strain of making small talk, and smiling and trying to grasp what was expected of me was too much. I wanted to be alone with Ruth, racing with the moon at the edge of the sea. I fell asleep—even in that bucking bronco of a jeep.

And here I go blank. I only remember that the next morning, or was it the morning after, I woke and found myself back in Ruth's cottage, stretching my skinny self awake on her folding cot, smelling coffee. I lay there and thought about that sail, that tiptop of the sail, bellying the ship away, and the poor people who were left behind and lost forever. I could understand them.  When the doctors recently informed me of my condition—terminal—the image of that sail flashed back as if I were there again, watching the play, and wanting to snuggle into Ruth's warm arms, Ruth.  Ruth—my friend, my mentor, my mother, my sister, my benefactor, my everything but one.

"I told"—and Ruth named the patriarch of the family we had visited— "that you were interested in biology, and he gave me a copy of *The Science of Life,* by H.G. Wells.  She held up a thick tome.  "I ought to know more about biology myself, so do you know what we are going to do?  We are going to read this book together, and anything you don't understand I will try to explain.  If I can't, I'll get us some help."

It took us something like two months to get through that book, with its enormous divisions of geological time making me feel smaller and smaller, like Tiny Alice, finally like an invisible dot, a fractal, and yet, as Ruth made me see, somehow, potentially anyway, more than I had imagined I could be.  I began to see the life around me now as moving toward, if not perfection, adaptation, which, I saw, was a kind of temporary perfection, as near as dynamic Mother Nature lets us get to perfection.  For things either get better or worse, depending on how you look at them, of course, what vantage point you take, but there is no stasis, no stopping of change; and of course things are ever so maladjusted, because forever trying to adapt themselves to ever-changing circumstances— yes, I saw that too.  Not unlike myself.  I saw myself as a little unimportant thing trying to adapt myself to my circumstances.  I had not seen myself this way before.  Before— what had I seen or understood?  Nothing, or a blue blank.  I had been a container of emotions carried about by the sea wind.  I began to sense purpose.  If not God's, my own.  And my purpose should be partly of my choosing.  I came to see that, or I was drawn out to see it, I suppose, by Ruth.

When the Traveller was away, Ruth took me on "field trips." Once we went to Wilmington, where Ruth bought me some clothes at Efird's Department Store, the fanciest store in town. I asked her to take me to the docks to see the Liberty Ships and was heartbroken to see that they were gone. How could I know now that I had ever seen them as my memory told me I had, hundreds of them in a row, and the gray cypresses behind them? Once we went to see the wild ponies on Shackleford Island. They are both of biological and folklorish interest. Once Ruth hired a motor launch to take us to Beaufort, a town not so big as Wilmington but much more beautiful, truly Old South, as Ruth might have said. There they gave a party for Ruth, the famous folklorist, "who has done so much to make the beauty and virtues of the Old North State known to the world through its voice in song and story," as the Mayor said in a speech that seemed to go on for hours. Now I realized that Ruth was not a stranger anywhere she went, but was widely known, unlike my unimportant self, of whom no one seemed aware. This realization didn't spur jealousy—I could never have been jealous of Ruth—but perhaps the first faint glimmers of ambition, the desire to do something important in the world, as Ruth had done: like her, but myself.

I had to introduce Ruth to Garcie. I had seen enough of Ruth in action to know that she would like and appreciate Garcie, and I was sure that Garcie would find Ruth an interesting subject of contemplation. They hit it right off. Garcie told Ruth some wonderful tales for her book.

A point of continuing interest between them was the Sad Traveller himself. I, in my "angel infancy," as Ruth called it, had not realized that Garcie did not like the Traveller. "I takes his money, yes I do, but I would always watch over my little Jessie even without his money. He a religious man? Maybe some, but in a crazy sort of way, too full of hate for me who believe in a loving God."

"Has he ever," Ruth said, turning to me, "has he ever—mistreated you?"

"You mean slapped me around?"

"Well—yes—but—anything else, either?"

"Sometimes.  The last time he was home—he was drunk, he always gets drunk when he comes home; he says he needs to relax—I was wearing shorts and he walked behind me and touched me on my backside, but then he acted like it was an accident.  I jumped away, and I was burning with shame—"

"And shock."

"Shock—yes, ma'am."

"Has he done that before?"

"No, that was the first time he ever did that, but he's slapped me around a lot of times."

Ruth looked worried.  Garcie said, "These things happen to young girls.  Can't say how many uncles I had growing up would pat my fanny."

"But it's not right," Ruth said.

"Lots of things not right, young lady."

Ruth conceded the point with a nod. But I could see that she was thinking of doing something and I was sorry that I had spoken out.  I didn't want Ruth and the Traveller to get into a fight over me.  I was afraid he might stop me from seeing her.  I had tried to play down my friendship with Ruth. Garcie said you always come to a fork in the road of life, and then another and another, and on till the end.  I didn't want to come to the next fork in the road of my life—I loved where I was, despite the Traveller and anything else that might spoil a moment of it here and now. Ruth told us about a folk singer and guitarist who met the devil at the crossroads and became great and died young.  She said he had traded most of his life for a moment of glory, and that that was a mistake.  I didn't know what to think about that, but it did make me think, and I guess that was the point. Ruth told us how she became a folklorist. She told us that growing up during the Depression had probably led her into Folklore. She was born in Twenty-nine and, thanks to her older brothers, had heard songs by Woody Guthrie and Leadbelly and others who could be described as folksingers from her earliest days, and, upon entering college, had started as an English major, but, with an ever-increasing interest in folklore, had decided had to change over to anthropology, and, eventually, to the relatively new field of social anthropology—which amounted to becoming a folklorist.

"You mean you had to do all that anthro-business just to listen to people?" Garcie shook her head in consternation. "Well I must be one those anthro-people myself, cuz I have been listening to folks all my days. Finds, in fact, it's hard to get a word in edgewise, most folks telling about themselves until it's running out of my ears. Goodness sake!"

Ruth burst into laughter and couldn't stop until I thought she was going to have a heart attack. But finally she pulled herself together and said, "I'd love to have you make a speech to the anthropology department at Smith, Garcie, it would sure give them a shock." This time Garcie laughed.

By October, Ruth and Garcie and I had become a cozy threesome. We spent hours on end at Garcie's shack, cooking and eating together and Ruth and I listening to Garcie's legends of the Banks, of which she had an endless supply. Garcie did not like to be recorded, but Ruth kept her tales for posterity by making notes on yellow pads. Ruth later told me that listening to Garcie reminded her of blind Homer, and how the Greeks must have sat around the bards, for Ruth said that there were many Homers, and listened to their tales to the accompaniment of plinking lyres. "Garcie may be nearly blind," I said to Ruth, "but you, you're the Homer."

Ruth winked at me and said, "O.K., smarty pants, you got me there."

Garcie knew the inside of her small shack as a clam knows its shell.  She knew her life and rolled breathlessly about in it without hesitation, telling one tale after another.  She opened up to Ruth as she had never done with me, and so I heard much that I had never heard before.  Ruth had a way of prompting people to talk, a subtle way of making them want to tell her things, and she was a good listener, as I had had occasion to observe, focusing her full attention on a speaker, letting him or her know with a word or two that she understood the import of what was being said.  Her patience with a speaker was inexhaustible.  Her eyes never drifted.  It was an art, she said, that she had learned from acting in amateur productions when she was in college.  "Don't be an actor, be a reactor," she often said.

I didn't know whether I wanted to be Ruth or just to have her to love.  And Garcie could tell that I had found someone who almost replaced what I'd lost in a mother.

"You just crazy about that young woman, ain't you, baby?  Well, she mighty nice indeed—mighty nice."

So we had a three-month interlude of pure happiness, or at least I did.  But we were flying toward Garcie's fork in the road, or, more properly, it was flying toward us, like a great big black seventy-eight record with an album of booming cacophonous music on it.  At its center it was turning at a hundred and fifty miles an hour, like a tornado, and coming at us at fifty at the rim.  We had weathered storms before—twice only recently—but nothing like this, nothing like Hazel.

Late in the evening of Thursday, October 14th, 1954, Sheriff Walkup pounded on Garcie's door. "Bad storm coming," he said, stepping just inside, his yellow slicker glistening. "Better get prepared."  His general store was powered by a generator, and he had a radio, which made him the unofficial town crier.

"Maybe you all should think about going to the mainland.  There's a cutter down by the village picking up now.

225

It'll be there for a few hours.  Tom—that's my new man—he can take you out to it.  It's up to you."

"We'll ride it out," Garcie said, "like we rode the last two out.  But thank you for thinking about us."

"I hope you know what you're doing, Miss Perle," he said.

"We'll be fine," said Ruth, undaunted.

"Step out here and look at those clouds," said Walkup.

"You know I'm blind," said Garcie, but Ruth and I stepped out into a light, windy rain to look.  Where had they come from, those dark, iridescent clouds, like malignant brains?  They hadn't been there a few hours before, when we arrived at Garcie's.

"It'll be a good night for storytelling," said Ruth. Walkup shrugged and climbed back over the dunes like a goldfish out of water.  He knew that the madly-rolling eye of the storm was looking at us, but he had given fair warning.  I caught his voice—perhaps words of farewell—on the wind as he disappeared over the top of a dune.

Garcie said, "Ain't nothing but just another storm."

You must remember, David, things were very different a half century ago.  Beach cottages didn't have radios, television sets, and newspapers were scarce—no front pages inked in red, green, and white hurricane winds swirling around a blank blue eye—so we sat on talking through Thursday night even as we could hear the wind about us dodging and ramming, missing and hitting, sputtering, cracking, and shockingly booming.  We naively thought of it as good atmospherics for Garcie's tales of sunken ships and the ghosts of skull-and-crossbone pirates.  Then she told us about the sunken church, inspired by the wind, I guess.  It was cursed because its congregation was evil, and it would rise out at sea during evil times, as when a hurricane was on the way, and *that,* said Garcie, was the sound of banshee singing that forecast the storm.  "At first," she said, "the storm is outside of you, and then you are inside of it, like old Jonah in the belly of the whale. But we've ridden out a few of them storms before and we do it again, my bet."

It was too noisy for us to sleep, so we sat on until dawn. Then a window broke and water gushed in. When the first wave receded, Ruth and I looked out and saw that everything from Whalehead down was under black or foaming white water, whirling, swirling all sorts of objects in its wake, then the windows shattered and the front door fell in and the debris laden tide filled the room. Except for one shriek, Garcie sat like stone in prayer, water already up to her hips, her body pummeled by broken objects. Ruth and I waded to the door and tried to stand it up, a hopeless task. Then Ruth grabbed me by the shoulder and pointed.

"Oh my God!" she cried. A shrimp boat, about forty feet long, was coming straight at us. The great dark hulk had been beached down by the village for repairs and had been lifted by the tide and now was drifting, without a mind to guide it, toward Whalehead. It was coming right at us when something, a twist of the wind, or a roof beam, something out there in the half-light, caught it and spun it like a top. Then it set off in another direction, its whole huge dark side passing in front of us like a wall that we ourselves were passing, but not quite passing: its bulk slammed into a corner of Garcie's shack and we found ourselves outside, the three of us, boards from the shack spinning around us, careening into us like little battering rams; and now we were up to our chests in whirling water, a maelstrom, and Ruth trying her best to keep Garcie from drowning. She swam and knocked away debris with one hand and pulled Garcie with the other, all the time screaming to me, "Are you all right? Are you all right?"

I went under and came up with a mouth full of salt water. I couldn't answer. I kept drifting away from the sound of her voice. Then I went under for what I thought was good, but a hand pulled me up by my hair and suddenly I was being pulled aboard a bouncing, bucking skiff. The hand laid me in the bottom like a caught fish, face down and vomiting brackish water. When I could look up, I saw Garcie's legs and Ruth's. I tried to get up on a cross bench and was nearly thrown out again, but pulled again by the hand and pressed down until I was sitting in the bottom of the skiff, my back against a man, his knees locking me in place. I had to see who he was and twisted my head to catch a glimpse of my savior—a glimpse of dark hair and pale face and I knew who it was.

Ahead, the dark and chopping Atlantic had seized everything but the second story of the General Store. We were headed for it. It was a good thing Sheriff Walkup wasn't pulling at the oars or we would never have made it, but, as Walkup had said, the new man had a new strong back. He was also a good sailor, for he found back-tows in the whirling water that helped him get us to the store. We climbed through a second story window and I fell to the floor.

I fell asleep and must have slept for several hours. I woke to dismal daylight and rain drumming on the tin roof. Mrs. Walkup, Ruth, and the new man were there, drinking coffee. Where was Garcie? "*Garcie!*" I screamed. "Where is Garcie?" They looked at me, then at Garcie. She lay over in a corner on the floor. "Garcie!" I threw myself on her, shaking her bulk, pulling at the rags that had been her dress. "Garcie, please! Wake up, oh, please! Don't leave me, Garcie—please!"

"Her heart failed," said Ruth, lifting me away and holding me. "I'm so sorry, baby."

I looked around blankly, incomprehendingly. I stared out the window where we had come in. "Where's the water?" I said, as though distracting myself from "where's Garcie?"

"It was a storm surge," Ruth said. "It's all gone back to the sea."

"It was a hellion named Hazel," Mrs. Walkup said. Then she shook her head, "And she stole my husband, little darling" she said to me, and she seemed as uncomprehending as I was, or she never would have called me that. I felt so sorry for her that I took her in my arms and, for a moment, we seemed to do a slow dance together. I wanted to cry for her, and I wanted to cry for Garcie, but I couldn't, I felt like my spirit had left me and all I could do was to wait for it to return. And that was it—the others were in varying degrees in the same condition. I could see that now as my own shock subsided.

Ruth handed me a cup of hot coffee and told me to go over and thank the new man, Tom Judas, for saving my life. "He saved all of us, except for poor Garcie," she said. "He came out in that little skiff just to find us and bring us to safety."

I looked at him. What an odd name, I thought. Judas betrayed Christ. It must be awful to have a name like that. I went over to him and said, "Thank you for saving my life, thank you for saving Ruth, and thank you for trying to save Garcie. It was wonderful what you did."

"The surge brought me right to your door," he said. He was sitting on the floor, still drenched. He didn't look the same. Of course he was exhausted, but what I mean is, that when we first saw him on the mail boat, he looked like he didn't belong; but now he was in work clothes and wet and disheveled as the rest of us and seemed to belong with us, seemed to belong to Fortune Island.

"You're a . . . hero," I said. "Ruth, isn't Mr. Judas a hero?"

"More than a hero, I'd say. A savior."

"Yes—Mr. Judas, you're a savior."

His face, not so pale as it had been when I first saw him, showed a pink tinge of embarrassment, as if, for a second, he'd grown younger, almost boyish. "I was just trying to help," he said, the color fading as fast as it had come, the soberness reasserting itself. "I'm very sorry about your friend. You must have loved her very much."

"Yes, I did. I didn't know how much till now." I looked over at poor Garcie. She looked like a big wet pile of laundry—my Garcie—but Ruth was making her vanish beneath a blanket. "You get used to people, sometimes, Mr. Judas, and you forget how much they mean to you."

He stood and reached out as if to wipe a tear from my eye, hesitated, and dropped his hand. "You're a wise young lady—*Jessie*." I remember just how he said that, with that little break and then my name. Now I understand it, but then, of course, it puzzled me, as everything did, it now seems, in those days.

They found Sheriff Walkup's body crushed beneath the shrimp boat, which had nosed itself into the dunes of Whalehead and stuck. After sending the bodies of Garcie and Sheriff Walkup to the mainland for embalming they were brought back to Fortune Island for burial, Garcie in the black cemetery and Sheriff Walkup in the white, as was done in those days. There had been no time to make repairs, no time and no equipment to pull the shrimp boat out of the dunes, no time to clean up the cemeteries. The picket fences were gone. The stones of the older graves had sat underwater like lagan, keeping their places, naming their dead; but the newer graves had lost their flat markers. No worry, though, the few inhabitants of Fortune Island knew where their dead were buried.

The new graves waiting for their coffins held no puzzle but that of death. First we stood by Garcie's grave, then by Sheriff Walkup's, then I went and said a few words to my mother. I knew where she lay, even if the world did not. What could I say to the ground? Hold her tight? The ground would do that without understanding what it did. I wondered if the Traveller ever came here. I doubted it. And where was he now? He had left the island before the hurricane. He was probably somewhere at this very moment, shouting at people that they should believe, that they were evil and that that was why this awful storm had come.  And that horrible man was all that I had left in this world.  No, not all.  Ruth and Tom Judas had come to join me at my mother's grave, Ruth, my benefactor, Tom, my savior.  They just stood by, and that was enough.  Then Ruth put her arm around my shoulders, and she never let go, at least not until I was a grown woman and could take care of myself.

IV

With Garcie gone, the Traveller had to make new arrangements for me.  I suggested Ruth.

"That painted heathen you're spending so much time with?"

"She's my friend," I said, "and she's already looking after me."

"Ain't she some kind of Yankee?  Ain't she a Jew?"

"She's from Boston.  She's real nice.  She's rich and she's almost famous.  She was the guest of honor at a party in Beaufort.  The mayor was there and made a speech about her."

"Fancy that!"  He didn't really care who watched out for me, he just had to get his shot glass full of meanness into it.  So we trudged over to Ruth's house, him sweating and puffing with a hangover, and me not skipping but wanting to.  It turned out just the way I wanted.  He offered Ruth money to keep an eye on me when he was away, which was most of the time—he only came home to get drunk out of sight of anyone who might know him for a preacher—and Ruth did exactly what I knew she would do; she rejected his offer of money but told him that it would be a joy to her to keep an eye on me, that he need have no fear that I wasn't being looked after properly and that he could go about his business without hindrance.

231

Later he said, "Who's that uppity little skirt think she's talking to?" But he was happy enough to have unburdened himself of me on her, and so didn't question the situation any further, except to ask me how much money I thought she had. I told him I had no idea, which was true because I had no idea about money at all at the time. And, as Garcie would've said, that was another fork in the road.

Ruth had already begun educating me. She said I had an excellent brain—truly excellent. She said, "You're like a sponge. I've never seen anything like it. You appear to have a photographic memory and almost total recall." The fact that my brain was what she called excellent was more exciting to Ruth than it was to me. By the end of our first year together, she had me up to geometry and algebra and we were heading toward what she called "trig." Ruth said that it was good for her to go over a lot of this material because she had forgotten it.

"You don't use it," she said, "and it tends to fade away." She unwrapped the textbook she had bought in Wilmington. There it was—Trigonometry! And she had me reading Shakespeare. We acted the plays together. I found that I could remember whole passages without trying. Ruth said that I was 'scary.' I loved *Romeo and Juliet.* "How am I ever going to meet a boy on this island?"

"Plenty of time for that," Ruth said.

Ruth had taught me all about sex, but I couldn't understand where the force of love came from, though I could feel it. I could feel my love for Ruth. Ruth said that biology connected the two. That was my favorite subject, biology. How mussels mated! Those little whelks in their tube—was love involved somehow? If so, I couldn't tell how. It was clear to me that Romeo and Juliet wanted more than sex from each other, but what more did they want? I was learning so much so fast, sometimes it fell into a jumble, triangles and rectangles and arthropods and whelks and Romeo and Juliet and men and women in a heap on the dunes at night.

The times I hated most were the times when the Traveller was home and Ruth had to go to New York or to Boston to see her publisher or editor or on some other business. I would sneak out when the Traveller had drunk himself into a stupor and go to Ruth's—I had a key to her cottage now—and sit among her things where I was happy and could feel her near. But once, when the Traveller was away, and she had to go to New York, she took me with her, and oh heavens was that exciting! And I had thought that New York was so far away but on the airplane it only took a few hours. Ruth let me sit near the window so that I could see the geometry below, and it was just like in the textbooks, everything so different from down there, squared away and clean—the green field, a square house. And we went to the Museum of Modern Art in New York and there were the pictures that Ruth had on her walls at home—the cubists, the impressionists, VanGogh and Gauguin and my favorites the Renoirs with the beautiful ladies who looked like angels. Why did Picasso make ladies so ugly? Why did one lady have two faces? And we went to Radio City Music Hall and saw the Rockettes—the kicking, all in a row. I had never thought of such a thing. I had begun to realize that there was so much in the world that I had never thought of on my lonely island. But now I began to realize how lonely I had been growing up on that desolate dune. How could I have not known? But New York was overwhelming, and I got sick, and I was sick all the way back to Fortune Island, and I didn't feel better until Ruth and I had tea together in her cottage, which felt like home to me.

Tom Judas had worked hard after the storm, saving what could be saved of the remaining dwellings on the Island. He continued to work for Mrs. Walkup and anyone else on the island who needed help. The church had been lifted off its footings, turned over, and sailed off into the sea like an empty ark, so a few of the fishermen along with Tom rebuilt it. He was much in demand. Carpenter, framer, plumber of wells, Tom could do it all. But most of that work was over. Now he was working on Ruth's cottage, fixing it up and adding a room. I thought of the new room as my own, but nobody said so: I just assumed. I spent a lot of time watching Tom work when I should have been studying. With his shirt off he looked very muscular. I liked to watch as his muscles stretched and contracted. He had become tan and even sunburned down his back. It seemed that he was always bending over something, hammering, sawing, or lifting. He glistened with sweat. I wanted him to talk to me.

"I have an excellent brain, you know," I said to him one day.

I couldn't understand why he burst out laughing.

"Do you think I'm funny?"

"No ma'am, I take you very seriously." But he kept on hammering at a plank. I couldn't help myself, but he made me think of biology. He could do so many things with those wonderful hands of his. He could play the guitar like nobody I ever heard before. Blues, he said; he said he played blues guitar, and sang songs that he wrote himself.

> *You send them out into this lonely life*
> *They get a lonely woman for a wife*
> *And then between them make*
> *A hostage to fortune for the future's sake.*

And you should have heard how he sang that one. He hit his guitar like a drum and then twanged it so a cat's fur would stand on end.

I learned he was an expert shot, too. Sometimes when the sea was quiet, when the surf was long and low, we could hear him out on the dunes popping Coke bottles. One day I went out there to join him and he showed me how to do it, how to load the clip in the pistol, pull the slide to get one in the chamber, how to aim and fire. I asked him if the gun was dangerous and he said No, not very, that it was just a little target pistol but don't go and point it at anyone because Yes, it could kill you if you were close up and got hit in the head by it. Always keep it pointed up, he said, away from people. I got pretty good at popping those bottles and he seemed to like having my company. Life had become exciting because I was learning so much about so many things; I, who had been alone with the whelklings for so long. Tom finally finished the work on Ruth's cottage. And it turned out that the extra room *was* for me. Ruth had it all gussied up with girl stuff, fluffy gingham curtains at the window, a bed with a thick patchwork quilt, some drawings I had made tacked up on the walls. I felt like a little rich girl, a princess.

And one day I heard Tom out there on the dunes popping those bottles and I went out to find him. He was leaning against a rock, his shirt off, a cigarette dangling from his mouth, taking pot shots at the bottles. He had told me that target shooting was his form of meditation, that he actually didn't think about the shooting but thought about other things when he practiced. "It's just something to do while I do my thinking," he had said. I often wondered what he was thinking about, but there was something about the way he told me that that indicated privacy, so I didn't ask. I thought that he did a lot of thinking though.

This time I went ahead and asked him.

"About the past, mostly," he said. "Sometimes about the future. Sometimes I think about you."

"Me? What do you think about me?"

"What a wonderful young girl you are."

That's what I was always thinking about him—I mean, what a wonderful man he was. I had to do something. I had to do something to show him how I felt. I was wearing a tissue-thin blouse Ruth had bought me in Wilmington. I knew if I got it wet, it would show that I wasn't a little girl anymore. I ran into the sea and came back to him and stood there, heaving my chest. He could see now that I was a woman, no doubt about it. But instead of reacting as I had hoped, he put his shirt over my shoulders and closed it in front and said, "I want you to come back to my shack with me. I have something to show you."

I didn't know what he had in mind, and, at first, it kind of scared me. But I could see sadness in his eyes, and I somehow realized that he was safe to be with. What had made me forget that for a moment? Myself, I guess. What I had been thinking about had caused me to worry, not anything he was doing. Anyway, when he led off, I followed and caught up and walked along beside him to the shack. It was a good long hot walk and we didn't talk. I had never been in his shack before. It was small, cramped, dark, full of stuff, a real mess, the kind men make when they don't care, when there are no women about.

He put the pistol in a drawer, saying he would clean it later. "But this is what I wanted to show you." He handed me a gold-framed photograph, one of those tinted pictures, of a woman and a  little girl of about two or three.

"Is this your wife, Tom?"

"Yes, that's my wife. My ex-wife. She married someone else, but she's dead now."

"And the little girl is. . . the little girl . . ." I looked and looked and then I realized what I was looking at. The woman's hair was bunched in a snood, but I could see now that it was red hair, and the little girl had red hair too. I knew who it was before he said it.

"The baby is you, Jessie."

"And that's my mother. But how— Then you're—"

I stood there staring at him. I couldn't believe it.

"I'm your . . . dad, Jess. I thought . . . it was time for me to tell you."

"But my daddy has gray hair, everybody knows that. You can't be him!"

"I dyed it. I didn't want anyone here to recognize me. After all, I've been away a long long time." He sat at the table, not taking his eyes off me.

I threw my arms around his neck. "I knew it was you! Oh, I knew it was you!" A throb came up from my chest and I began to cry. Tom put his arms around me and patted my back. "Easy. Easy." he whispered.

"I knew it was you all the time," I said, sitting down across from him, "but I was afraid I might be wrong so I never said. I was too scared to think it. But there was something— do you know how I mean, I mean—"

"I understand."

"But it's all coming true. It's coming true. Ruth—and now you!"

"Give me your hand, and let me explain," he said, reaching across the table, and I saw that he had tears in his blue eyes too. Tears for me? The tin roof of the shack began to drum with rain, as if in sympathy with us, and it became like a hollow, but steady rhythm above the noise of pounding water, almost echoing in the small enclosure, and I felt dizzy as I listened to him.

"I was young and foolish and believed I had to do something so that you and your mother wouldn't be dirt poor, and I committed a desperate and foolish act, an act that I have suffered for and have never stopped regretting, that I regret most perhaps at this very moment, when I have to tell you about it. Jessie, I'm ashamed and I want you to know that. And that stupid, youthful misdeed has kept me away from you all these years. It did the exact opposite of what I had hoped it would do. But I want you to know that I have never forgiven myself for it, for doing something that caused you to be without me during all those years when you needed me most." The rain came in bullets aimed at the roof. I was afraid the tin would puncture and we would die just at this moment, when I knew him, had him, could reach out and touch him.

"Your mother came to see me behind the Wall. She said that she had met someone who would take care of her. She wanted me to give her a divorce and sign the house over to her. I felt that it was the least that I could do. I thought you both needed that."

The roar of the rain made his voice seem far away, as if he were speaking to me on the telephone. "Later, I heard that your mom had died. All I could do then was to hope that your step-father, a man of God, I'd heard, would be good to you, love you as I did. I promised myself that as soon as I was freed, I'd come back here and see for myself how you were doing. If you were doing well, I would leave you alone, not interfere with your life, in any way. That's why I didn't want you to know who I was. I didn't want to be known. I just wanted to see. I had to see."

The drumming on the roof was beginning to soften, a cat's purr.

"I want to live with you," I said. My ears heard my creaky voice.

"I can't just take you away from Cogburn. Not just now. There are legal problems."

"Don't you want me?"

"I want nothing more in the world than that we be together, girl. I love you with all my heart."

A thought jumped in at me, sudden as the rain had been. "I've got to tell Ruth. She'll be so . . . so *astounded!*"

"Ruth already knows, Jessie."

"She already knows?"

"I've told her the whole story."

"You told Ruth before you told me?"

"I wanted to know what she thought. Ruth and I have become pretty close, you know."

"Close? What does that mean? Close? Are you in love with her?"

"At this point, let's just say that we're friends."

"I know you're friends, but what kind of friends?"

I had green eyes—*green*. I couldn't help myself. Something had happened. The water was dropping outside. The shower was passing over. "I have to go and see Ruth," I said.

"But wait now—"

"No, I have to go and see Ruth." I'll come back, I said to myself, I'll come back.

"Wait, Jessie, I'll go with you."

"No! I want to see Ruth alone. I'll come back after I talk to Ruth. Wait for me. Don't come over. Don't go away. Stay right here."

"I'll clean the gun," he said, lighting a cigarette. The match flared up, etching his troubled face, his eyes dark hollows under the glinting strips of his corrugated brow. He was exercising a tortuous calculation, but plainly could come to no conclusion.

"Hurry back," he called after me.

"Yes, I'll come back," I said, plunging out the door. Most days it was water but today tiny diamonds dropped from the sky, glittering at every facet. How could the rain be mere water on a day like today? How could anything be what it tried to be? The wet sand jumped under my feet. It was alive! I made it dance but I hurt it too. The atoms in my body were flying apart and crashing together. Something was going to heal, or break. It is just when everything is perfect that it explodes, for nature cannot bear perfection. Only an acceptable adaptation. If today was the happiest day of my life, I was also aware of the sun sinking out at sea. Ecstasy and terror. I punched the air and grabbed it as I ran toward Ruth's cottage. He had told Ruth before he had told me. Something was wrong with that. I wanted them both, I wanted them together, but I didn't want them without me. He should have explained everything to the two of us at once, for the three of us to share. But I knew what it was. I knew how they thought that they knew better. I had begun to see the treachery in grown-up thought, the kindly lies that only confused.

Ruth was working at the typewriter when I burst in. She stood up, seeing my confusion, my tear-stained eyes. For Ruth, I held no mystery. She read me as if what I thought ran across my forehead like the sign in Times Square.

"He's told you, hasn't he?"

"Yes. But he told you first. Why?"

"He wasn't sure how you'd take it. I told him that I thought you'd be fine. Was I wrong?"

"Oh Ruth!" I threw myself against her and she pulled me over to the couch where we sat together while I cried. It was all too much for me.

After a time, she said: "Were you angry because he told me first?"

"A little, I guess. Just a little hurt."

"I know, baby," she said. "It's an awful lot to take in, isn't it? All of a sudden you have a real father. But you suspected, didn't you?"

"I did. I don't know how but I did."

"I think you knew because you could tell that he loved you. You got it a little mixed up, though, maybe, didn't you?"

"I guess." I snuggled in her arms.

"Well, I have some more news for you, too," she said at last. "This is also pretty exciting. I got your high school GED test and your Sanford Binet back. I've brought you well beyond high school level and it looks like you're smarter than I am by a good twenty points. You're a gifted girl, Jessie. And you're going to have to go to school."

I jumped up from the couch. "What do you mean? Away?"

"I can send you to a very fine private school."

"But Tom—my *Dad*—I've just got him.  He's here.  I don't want to go away now."

"He thinks that if I'm willing to pay for your schooling, you should go.  We've talked about it a good bit."

Now this scared me.  "What school? Where?" I began to cry again, and Ruth pulled me back into her arms.

"I don't want to leave you, Ruth.  I don't want to leave him."

I believed Ruth could do anything she wanted to.  Hadn't she been able to get those academic tests that she told me were rarely allowed outside of institutional grounds?  Now I was afraid she wanted to send me away.  I reached down into my desperation and came up with a counter argument.  I sat up straight, facing her.

"You can't make me go anywhere, you're not my mother.  Are you and Tom—*my* dad—trying to get rid of me?"

"Sweetheart, why would we do that?  We love you."

"So you can be alone together?  Are you in love?  Do you want to get rid of me?  Am I in the way?"

I looked at her through my tears and saw that I had hurt her.  I threw my arms around her neck.  "Oh, I love you so much, Ruth.  Please don't send me away."

"Let's just take our time, baby, and see what happens," she said.  And that was it.  A few days passed, then a few weeks, and there was no more talk of sending me away.  I spent the mornings studying while Ruth worked on her book.  Tom had taken over Sheriff Walkup's duties at the general store and usually joined us at dinnertime.

Ruth and Tom planned to take me into Wilmington the day before my fifteenth birthday, to celebrate.  We had two rooms at the best hotel in town, the Cape Fear.  The plan was for Ruth to take me shopping, and to outfit me like a young lady.

"Like a debutante," Ruth said. She was so wealthy she made me feel like an heiress, just being with her. When she told Tom we were going shopping, he decided to tag along.

"I'd like to bear witness to the transformation," he said. And we set out in a gay mood. Being with Tom and Ruth was such fun, I had decided to forgive their occasional hand-holding, the looks that passed between them, which I could never quite understand. That day, at least, they were both focused on me. I had them both in my power, the power of my green eyes and red hair, even the power of my light tan freckles, which I urged to dazzle.

Those silly freckles have all faded away over the years, or have become an occasional brown mole here and there. Years of work in the sun have turned my fair, usually sunburnt skin brown and creased, all the red has fallen out of my hair, and, as a result of chemo-therapy, much of my hair has been lost. But that day I shined, or so everyone said. The saleslady at Efird's said that I was beautiful.

"Those green eyes. . . she has got to wear mint-green. Let's try this," and she took down a floaty voile dress of mint-green, and, holding it up to my shoulders, said, "and I think white shoes and a white purse." Ruth told me to go into the dressing room and try it on.

I think that was the first time I had ever seen myself from all sides and all the way around in back. Down to my underwear, I studied myself in the mirrors. Tall and thin I was, but I had nice long curves, more of a rump than I had realized, and in profile my breasts looked positively brazen in a new bra. My nose turned up more than I thought it did, but it was kind of cute, I thought, too. The saleslady handed me in a pair of white, open-toed pumps with heels at least two inches high. Of course I'd never owned a pair of high-heeled shoes before. I had to hobble, but I made my entrance. The first eyes I caught were Tom's. A father's eyes say, Look at my little girl. My emotions were turning in my stomach, this way and that, like snakes. I was happy and grateful and hurt all at once. Ruth said, "Oh, my dear, you look spellbinding." That was what she said, "spellbinding." The saleslady said, "She's fit for a grand party." Then I had a vanity attack, but with deep breathing, trying not to show what I was doing, my breasts heaving like that, I got myself back down to the almost right place, to where, I hoped, nothing was showing. "Not too bad, do you think?" I said, my ankles wobbling.

"Now all you need is a bouquet of flowers," said Tom. "I'll get you one before the day is over."

"It must be a special occasion," said the saleslady.

"Her birthday," said Ruth. "Tomorrow she'll be fifteen."

"Fifteen," Tom repeated in a wondering way.

"Fifteen, is it?" said the saleslady. "My compliments," she said to Ruth, "you look too impossibly young to have a fifteen year old. But looking at the two of you, I can see where she gets her looks. But where did the red hair come from?"

"Oh, she's not my daughter," Ruth said.

"Oh, I see," said the saleslady, taken aback. I noticed her curiosity. I suppose we did seem an odd threesome, but, momentarily at least, we were a very happy threesome.

Outside, Ruth told Tom that she was taking me to have a manicure and a pedicure and a permanent wave, so he might as well busy himself elsewhere. He said he would go and get the flowers and a few other things and meet us back at the hotel. I was so excited that I thought I actually saw some of my freckles jump off my arms. Well, I was seeing spots before my eyes, but my wobbling ankles really hurt. It was a hot day and I think they were beginning to swell. Or had my new nylons bunched? I felt so tall, wobbling along beside Ruth in my new heels. She was five six or seven and I swear I was looking down at her.

The Cape Fear Hotel had one of the best restaurants in Wilmington, or so Ruth said.  I was proud of my newly-shaped and pink painted fingernails and kept holding them in view of the youngish waiter to see if I could detect a reaction, but I guess he had seen a lot of nails on a lot of girls because he was all polite business.  He switched from a soft cultured southern accent to French—especially when he spoke directly to Ruth, who answered him in French, some of which I could understand—if only they had slowed down—coq au vin— and back to "Will the gentleman approve the wine?"  Tom knew what to do, which surprised me.  He took a sip and said, "Fine" and the waiter poured.  Tom had given me flowers to wear and for a birthday present a silver necklace with a locket containing a picture of himself and a picture of Ruth.

"Oh, I just love it," I told him, thinking right away that I might replace Ruth's picture with my own.  That made me feel so guilty, I felt like crying.  I took Ruth's hand and said, "I love you, Ruth."  Her big dark eyes grew glassy and she turned quickly to say something to Tom.  He looked kind of soppy too.  Gosh, we were all just looking so sad, I had to do something.  "I love all my gifts," I said.  "Thank you.  Thank you both so much."

"But tomorrow's the real party," Tom said, brightening.

"We're going to show you the town," Ruth said. "There's a fair on the outskirts.  Would you like to go to the fair?"

"We'll have a picture taken of the three of us," Tom said, "to mark the occasion."  I was so happy that night.  I never wanted to leave them, but I couldn't help feeling that somehow Ruth was stealing my dad from me, or was it that Tom was stealing Ruth from me?

Ruth and I had a room to ourselves and Tom had a room down the hall.  In 1957, and especially in a good hotel in the south, hanky-panky was frowned on, at least openly.  Certainly there were hotels where things went on, but not in the

244

Cape Fear.  The unnoticed and all-seeing bellhops kept the nightclerks posted.  In such a hotel, house detectives were not uncommon.  If progress is movement in a desirable direction, I am dumb to say where we have got to in the year 2000.  If I outlast this cancer by a few more years, I'll be content, but I have little desire to see what's coming much ahead.  Biology has been my field and my life, but I'm concerned as to where it is going.

Nevertheless, you must have agriculture before you can have high culture and you must have biology before you can have love, so I reach for faith out of thin air, like Shakespeare's poet, or like his madman.  But that night Ruth and I climbed into the softest bed I had ever—ever what?  It was beyond my dreams.  It was a cloud in the heaven I even then doubted, yet that bed made me believe in it.  At first, I was like the girl with visions of sugar plums dancing in her head; but I awoke from a sweet, forgotten dream of warmth to find the warmth and then the source of the warmth missing.

"Ruth?"  I got up and went to look in the bathroom.  No Ruth.  I felt a bit frightened.  Something must be wrong.  I checked the clock, thinking that I'd overslept, but it was just one o'clock in the morning.  She must have gone to Tom's room. But what for? What had happened?  I put my raincoat over my pajamas and stepped out into the carpeted, ornate hall.  One could see through the transoms, light or no light in the rooms.  A few were lighted.  There was a long dark wall table with a vase of flowers and a straight chair at each end, backs to the wall.  Soft night lights—everything white and gold. The thick gold carpet tickled my feet.  I came to Tom's door, a few doors down from ours, and I heard voices over the transom, which glowed with soft light.  I listened but could not make out what was being said.  All I could hear was groans, or maybe moans.  Was Tom hurt?  I started to knock, but something warned me not to, an instinct, a primitive sense, warning of privacy, secrecy.  If they had needed me, they would have awakened me, I reasoned. But what was it? I tried to see through the keyhole, but the key must have been in the lock and I could see nothing but shadow and a blurry wire of light, indicating somehow taboo, privacy, secrecy, saying that what was happening inside was not for me to know. But the moans and groans were growing in intensity, and I was afraid.

I went back down the hall and got one of the straight chairs and brought it back to the door and stood up on it and could just see over the top of the door, through the open transom. Ruth and Tom were naked on the bed, Ruth straddling him and rocking and him heaving, and I felt faint. Woozy. But above all, I didn't want them to know I was there. I got down and took the chair and put it back in its place and went to my room, trying to catch my breath. I threw up my dinner in the toilet, flushed it, closed the lid, and sat there, trying to get things in order. They are lovers! Or was it just biology? Did they have to do this on my birthday? My beloved ones were like animals! I had dreamed of love, but not like that, not like what I'd seen. My heart was not right, and the snakes in my stomach uncoiled and came up through my windpipe and I screamed. I whirled around the bathroom, smashing things. Oh, had anybody heard? I listened. Nothing. I felt trapped. I had to get out into the street, into the cool night air. I dressed myself in my new clothes, heels and all. I smeared lipstick on, and pushed my new permanent wave into place, took the key, and found the elevator. The doors slid open.

"Down?" said the bellhop, holding the handcrank, and down and out I went, one thought in my mind: "I hate them! I hate them!"

Their naked image was all I could see. I felt like a green-eyed monster. Not wanted, shut out! I wanted to kill them. No, I didn't! I loved them. I hobbled along in my high heels and my Sunday dress feeling like a freak of some kind. What was I doing? Where was I going? Where could I go?

Well, the answer to that one came quickly enough. I hadn't gone a block before a car pulled up alongside me. There were two sailors in it. "Where you going, baby?"

"Where are you two going?"

"Just cruising. Want to cruise?"

I got in the back seat. The sailor who was driving said, "Back at base, they call me Devil and him Angel. What do we call you?"

"It's my birthday," I said. I don't know why I said it, it just popped out.

"Okay, we'll call you birthday girl, okay?" Devil had done all the talking so far. Angel sat on the passenger side and looked, I thought, kind of forlorn.

"Here," said Devil, "take a snort of this," and he handed me back a bottle of whiskey in a brown paper bag. "It's a happy birthday drink."

"You don't look old enough to drink," said Angel.

"She looks plenty old to me," said Devil.

Devil seemed older than Angel, who seemed closer to my age. If people really did call them Devil and Angel I could see why. Devil was dark and tough-looking and sounded like a yankee, and Angel was blond and had a sweet face, really angelic, as I could see when he turned to talk. "Don't drink so much of that," Angel said.

The whiskey was like fire and my first impulse was to spit it out, but I gripped myself and swallowed, feeling it boil down into my guts.

"Good, eh?" said Devil. "Happy birthday to you!"

"Oh," I said, pulling the bottle away, "it's like fire."

"Oh, that stuff ain't nothin'," said Devil. "I'm going to drive us out to a place I know where they got a still and a place to drink white lightning—and you can dance there too. Like to dance, Birthday Girl?"

"Listen," said Angel, "how old are you?"

"Eighteen," I lied.

"Are you sure, because you don't look eighteen.  I got an eighteen year old sister and she looks a lot older 'an you."

"What you talking about?" said Devil. "You saw how tall she is!"

"But look at her face."

"Looks pretty good to me."

Something like that—because I couldn't tell for certain what they were saying.  I didn't realize it, but I was getting drunk, another entirely new experience for me.

"Go ahead," Devil would say, "have another drink," and I heeded his encouragement, ultimately getting down at least half a pint of whiskey.  And oh, the warmth, the sweet ease of it!  For the time-being the ugly image of Tom and Ruth faded from view, the beautiful, sweet face of Angel turned to me and kept on turning.  Then I saw that we were out in the woods and I began to get scared.  "You better let me out," I said.

"Let her out," Angel said.  "Let us both out.  I don't want to go to any still, I don't even drink."

"Aw, come on," said Devil.

"No, let us out!"

"Well, shee-it!"  Devil slowed the car and pulled over. "Go ahead, but you're gonna miss one hell of a time."  We got out—Angel had to steady me—and Devil roared off honking his horn.

There we stood, out on this narrow country road with a partial roof of rainy-sounding leaves coming from both sides and almost meeting above us in the middle, soft moonlight floating down through the clouds.  The soft hoot of an owl made it spooky.

"How far are we from town?" I asked.

"Not far," said Angel, "if we don't get lost."

"Do you know the way?"

"I think so. Come on."

My ankles hurt. I slipped off my shoes and walked in my stockinged feet. To make conversation, I asked about Devil. "Is your friend really bad?"

"Oh, you mean that Devil stuff. His name is Devlin, so they started calling him Devil. He tries to be a tough guy, because he's from Boston."

"I know somebody from Boston. She's my best friend in fact."

"Devlin's going to get himself in trouble with his drinking, though. That's something we all should be careful of, that drinking. I've known it to bring ruin on people, members of my own family, even. I don't drink none at all. Don't smoke, neither."

"Is that why they call you Angel?"

"My name's Johnny Engels—that's where that comes from. What's yours—your name?"

"Jessie McQueen."

"That's a nice name. What's got you so ripped up tonight, miss? You look like you been to a party—did you have a fight with somebody or did somebody walk out on you or did you walk out on somebody else? We saw you come storming out of the Cape Fear Hotel. Shucks, I couldn't afford to check in there even for one night. Heck, a half a night! And you in that beautiful dress—what happened?"

The trees seemed to be moving backwards, with all their shadows and moon-patches, receding behind us. I felt drunk, but clearing up a bit, holding my own, I thought. What makes that night so vivid is that it was the last night, the tail end of my happiness, which already seemed like a long-ago dream.

"Something happened that made me hate the two people that I loved best in the world, that's what happened. Let's stop for a minute, my ankles hurt." I sat down by the side of the road, and leaned against a tree. "Look at them, they're all swollen."

"Sure looks like."

"How old are you, Angel?"

"Eighteen."

"Angel, would you do me a favor?"

"Sure.  What?"

"Kiss me."

He made a little tight smile, squinted his eyes, and tilted his head.  It was a questioning, good-humored look.  "What?  Just like that?"

"Like this," I said, and, grabbing his ears in my hands, I kissed him hard on the mouth and held on until he shook me off.  "What's the matter?"

I thought any boy would respond with passion, but not Angel.

"Now that's what I mean about the alcohol," he said.  "We're going to get ourselves into all kinds of trouble."

"I'm a virgin," I said.  "Don't you want me?"

"Oh my, yes, course I do.  But you don't really want to do this out here like this.  It's because you've been drinking.  And let me tell you something.  There's nothing wrong with being a virgin.  Why, every man wants his bride to be a virgin, and he should be a virgin too, so that they know no other forever always until death do them part."

"Angel, you're a virgin, too, is that it?"

"Keeping myself for the future Mrs. Engels, miss.  And I got me sisters and I hope they are keeping themselves too.  Expect they are."

"Come on," I said, "walk me back to the hotel."

"But now which way do we go?" Angel said to himself.  "See up yonder—there's a fork there."

"There's more glow over left," I said.

"That's probably the town."

Do I imagine all this?  Did this interlude develop in my imagination over the near half century since whatever happened on that road that night happened?  I remember it almost word for word as if it had happened yesterday, but did I pose the words, did I develop the events? I can't help myself. This is what I remember, and this: that I wanted him so badly that my body ached; that I tried to think of a way to get him to come to my room; that I tried this: "If I'm left alone, I might kill myself. I mean it. I have nothing to live for anymore. I have been . . . betrayed."

"Don't say that, miss." The poor boy looked worried. "Now look, miss Jessie, I can't get into that hotel. There's a desk clerk, for sure, watches everbody comes and goes."

"I could go in first, and you come in and rent a room and then come to my room and sit with me."

"A room in a place like that would cost me my pay, and I don't have much of that left anyway."

"I have money." I pushed twenty-five dollars on him, money which Ruth had given me for anything I wanted—well, I wanted Angel.

"No, miss, I can't take your money."

"Not even to save my life?"

He puzzled.

"Suppose you read in the papers tomorrow that a young girl jumped from the window of the Cape Fear Hotel, then you'll be sorry that you didn't take the money and save her, won't you?"

"Well—I suppose—"

I won; he took the money.

Tangled laundry, my emotions, wet and steamy, and I couldn't pull a shirt from a towel. Tom and Ruth had behaved like animals, and I hated them for it, but I wanted to do the same thing with Angel, in part to get even with Tom and Ruth, in part because Angel was just about the first boy I had ever been with in any old way at all. He was the first boy I had ever kissed. That must seem impossible to some, but I am the only Jessie, wild girl of Fortune Island, and I know it to be true. I wanted to be under that boy and over Tom and Ruth, I wanted to outdo them at their own dirty game and I wanted to know how it felt to be made love to—what biology felt like—and maybe, for a brief instant, I was really in love.

I passed the door of Tom's room, where Ruth and Tom must lay now in an exhausted doze, and went to my room and set what I thought would be the perfect trap.  I stripped down to my skin and waited for Angel.

Soon enough came a quiet knock.  I opened the door, staying behind it, and let him in. Then, as he stood trying to adjust to the one endtable light I had left on, I slammed the door and slid a chair under the knob.  When Angel turned and saw me naked, he stepped back like he'd been  shot.  He even reached for his heart, as if to be certain that it was there and beating, or maybe to stop it from beating so wildly, to hold it still.  I threw myself at him and he fell backwards onto the rumpled bed.

"Oh my Lord," he said, "miss, what are you doing?"  I didn't know exactly—several things at once, I'd say now. But before anything could be sorted out, Ruth was at the door, trying to get in, shaking the knob, inching the door open. Angel found his way out from under me and ran to the door, as if for help.

Then I heard Ruth, "Jessie! Why is this door jammed?" And Angel, "I'll get it open, ma'am."  And Ruth again, "Who is that?  Open this door!  Jessie!"  And Angel, "I didn't do anything, honest, as God is my witness."  And me, "You jerk!"

Then Tom's voice, "Open this door, dammit!"

"Yes, sir.  But the harder you push the harder it is for me to open it."

"Who in hell are you?"

"Nobody, sir—just a sailor."

"What are you doing in there?"  That was Ruth.

The door flew open.  Tom stepped in, saw me, and backed out. Ruth replaced him.  "Get your clothes on, young lady."

"That girl is under age," Tom shouted from the hall. "If you've laid a hand on her—"

"God in heaven may strike me dead, sir, if I ever—"

"Or I'll strike you dead," said Tom.

Ruth pushed Angel out into the hall. "Tom, take this boy down to your room and talk to him."

Tom grabbed the young sailor by the arm. "Come on, boy."

"Did he lay a hand on you?"

"He didn't have a chance. But I wanted him to."

"You what?"

"Like you and Tom."

"Tom and I?  I just went down the hall to see—"

"I saw you—through the transom."

"Oh, honey, no!"

"You're going to send me away to school so you can have him for yourself!"

"Here, put something on. You don't understand."

"All I need to know, you bitch!"

And Ruth knocked me across the bed with a roundhouse right. "Oh, my God," she said—"I'm sorry, baby."

"I hate you!  I hate Tom!  I don't know which one of you I hate the most.  I hate you both!"

After due explanation, I suppose, Angel was set free to pursue his quest for a virginal bride. I finally fell into a troubled sleep, awakening several times to find Ruth, pillow-propped, holding me in her arms. Finally I went into a deeper sleep that lasted until noon.  When I woke, I realized that I was truly fifteen.  Today was my birthday.  Of course the big day we, or Tom and Ruth, had planned was not to be.  They had been busy arranging for a different kind of day while I slept. Ruth had hired a fisherman who owned a cabin cruiser, really not much more than a motor launch, to take us back to Fortune Island.  She'd found Mr. Masefield on the Wilmington docks, advised by others that he was a man who liked the isolation of the island and was always pleased to have an excuse to cross Pamlico and put up on the island for a day or two of fishing.

Tom and Ruth looked sad, maybe ashamed, and I felt horrible, ugly and mean. Ruth had bought me a birthday cake and she held it in her lap in the launch like a precious artifact. She stared at its box, not looking up for the whole time it took to get to the tail-end of the island.

Tom talked to Mr. Masefield and smoked cigarette after cigarette. I had never seen him chain-smoke before. Now I can only imagine what he was thinking; then I couldn't imagine at all. Whatever I thought he was thinking was unquestionably wrong, for I was seeing all this through the eyes of someone deliberately misled, albeit for my own good, as others understood that good.

Later, when Ruth thought I was mature enough to understand, she tried to explain to me that Tom, already so guilty, now felt worse than ever, felt that he had let me down in the worse way possible. This was the man to whom I owed my very life.

He had saved me from drowning during the hurricane; had come out to the most isolated area of the island at the height of the surge in that little skiff to save all of us, Ruth, Garcie, and myself, and then had actually pulled me from the flood; had appeared, like a guardian angel, out of nowhere. I owed him my life. Why couldn't I simply accept the fact that he and Ruth were in love, that they saw us as a family, that neither of them would have excluded me for any imaginable reason—that they loved me, Tom in his way and Ruth in hers. But I sat there, with one isolation inside another like a Chinese box of isolations, with sullen pride immingled with fear and watched the waves from the wakes of boats out of sight follow one another, this way and that, apparently pointlessly, and finally the darkness in me spread to the sky and it began to rain and Pamlico Sound roughened and frothed.

Ruth tried again at her cottage.  She made coffee and put candles on the cake and lit them and brought it to the table singing "Happy Birthday," but I would have none of it.

"Betrayers!" I cried, melodramatically. "You both want to get rid of me so that you can have each other without being bothered with me."  It was the first time I had spoken since Wilmington and I could see that my words came as a great disappointment.  Tom shook his head.

"If you only knew," he said.

"You two want to send me away.  That's what it is."

"No, no, no, no," Tom said, shaking his head.

"What Tom is trying to say is—"

"You just want to be through with me and have him to yourself."

"Baby, Tom and I love each other."

"Then why did you stop me with Angel?  Don't you want me to ever be in love?"

"Because you're too young," said Tom.

"You could ruin your life," said Ruth. "You have a brighter future than you can imagine, I promise you."

"Where were either one of you when I was alone on this damned island?  You have no right to try to run my life now."

"Come on," said Ruth, "blow out your candles.  Let's try to have a little party together."

"Here's how I'll blow them out," I said, opening the door to the wind and rain. They flickered, and blew out. Ruth said there was no use in my behaving like a brat.  She said she was tired and had to get some rest.  She tried to kiss me but I moved aside.  I went in my room and played possum. Pretty soon I heard Ruth and Tom go in Ruth's bedroom and close the door.  I couldn't control my emotions; I felt strange, as if I were watching myself from somewhere up in the night sky.

I ran all the way to what should have been my house but which was now the Traveller's.  I was still wearing my mint-green Sunday dress—but it was wet and wrinkled now—and my hair was all in wet ringlets. I had forgotten to wipe the lipstick from my mouth. I burst in the door.

The Traveller sat with bottle at elbow. He looked up from his Bible and said, "Painted woman! I've been back since yesterday. I suppose you were out somewhere with that Jew bitch. Do you know that she paid me two-thousand dollars for you?"

I sat down across from him, panting, trying to catch my breath. "What do you mean?"

"She bought my signature. I signed you away to her in case of my death. Guardianship, it's called."

"Ruth paid you two-thousand dollars for me?"

"What I said."

"She must love me," I said, "at least two-thousand dollars worth."

"Same as buying a slave, ain't it? Nobody loves a slave."

"She'd never think of me as a slave, I know that."

He took a long drink. "Well, what do you think, think I don't love you?"

"You! You don't love anything or anyone."

"I love God."

"You love being God."

"Well—" he lurched up. "Look at you," he said. "Like a grownup woman, with that paint on your face and that dress—where'd you get that? Never mind, I know. You look just like your red-headed mother, the whore of Wilmington."

He leaned with both hands on the table and moved hand over hand around it toward me. I jumped up and moved away.

"Come here," he said. "Don't run away. Give me a kiss. A father has a right to kiss his daughter, doesn't he?"

"You're not my father! I have a real father!"

"No, I'm not and yes, you do, and he's a criminal in the Central Prison in Raleigh. Or maybe he's dead. I don't keep up with such people.  Or maybe he's done out.  Maybe he's been out."

"My father's right here on Fortune Island."

"Sure he is—me—I'm here!"

I was afraid he was going to grab at me, as he had often done of late.  I kept moving away from him but then I saw that he had me trapped.  He was between me and the door.

"Now you just leave me alone," I said.  But he got a drunken leer on his face and moved toward me.  I was being backed to the attic door.  There was no place to go but up.  I ran up the stairs and looked for something in the dark to hit him with if he came up after me.  But he was there already, on the top step.  I kicked at him, to keep him from coming up, but he fended off my kicks and kept on coming toward me, looming in the light from below.  Then he swung out to grab me or to hit me and I caught the blow on my cheek and fell to the floor and he was on top of me, pulling at my dress.  One arm was pinned beneath me and with the other I flailed his face, neck, shoulders over and over and over and over and oh—oh God!

Finally, he left me there, broken open, used up.  I heard him half fall down the stairs to the main room, heard the bottle crash.  In a little while I heard the door slam, then slam again and again, wind-caught.  I lay there in the dark and listened to the door slam for what seemed hours.  He had ripped my beautiful Sunday dress up the front.  It didn't matter.  It was just a rag now.  Blood has a metallic taste.  Biology was not always beautiful, a miracle.

Where was love?  Why hadn't it been Angel?  I lay there in the dark and reached out on the floor around me, looking for something.  What was I looking for?  My locket! I felt for my locket and it was there.  Oh Ruth.  Tom.  This was my birthday. I was grown now, wasn't I?  The Traveller had his own little skiff and I wondered if he had gone off to the mainland in it, had just decided to leave me here in the attic by myself with nothing but damp books, musty boxes. I reached out and felt around for my father's books that had started me reading so long ago. I just lay there, feeling how worthless I was, and for the first time I could guess at my mother's life with the Traveller, how he must have made her feel, weak sinner that she was. No wonder she threw herself into the sea. I should go down to the shore and throw myself in, for I'm nothing now, less than nothing. I can't offer myself to anyone ever again. There will never be love of that kind in me for anyone after this. In and out I went, sleeping, thinking, sleeping, the door downstairs banging, until a candle-glow of light began to shape and frame the small window at the back end of the attic, a patch of tarnished silver.

Somebody got up and left me there. I had been split in two. I stayed where I was, looking up at the dark insides of the attic, and the other went to the landing. Which was I? The one at the landing left the other on the floor in the attic and descended, going where? Out! Away! But not to Ruth's, not to Tom's. They must never see me again. I was leaving Jessie McQueen in the attic with her books, her father's books, her grandmother's books. I was someone else, a new and different creature.

Him! He lay at the bottom of the stairs, his right leg twisted up under him, as in a wild dance step. I saw that the door was banging still, taken by the wind. He hadn't left; he had been here all night, sleeping off his alcohol, dreaming God knew what horrible dreams, because it wasn't in him to have sweet ones. His must have been full of demons, for he never saw a good thing; everything was sad and bad for the Traveller. I couldn't get out without stepping on him. I was barefoot and doubted if he would feel it. I jumped over him, stepping once lightly on his back, but he caught me by an ankle and kept me there.

"I fell down the stairs," he mumbled. "Help me to the cot. You pull and I'll push with my good leg."

"So you're awake."

"Off and on all night. I'm in terrible pain. I think I broke my ankle."

"Don't you remember what you did last night?" I shouted, kicking him.

"All I've ever done to you is to take good care of you after your mother died. I remember there was a tramp came in here last night that looked like your mother, a painted whore from Wilmington, picked up and assaulted by some sailors, no doubt. I am the man who married Magdalene."

"God, you're still drunk."

"Can't be. Hurts too much. Get me to the cot."

If he had let go of me once I would have fled, but he managed to keep a grip on me somewhere, my arm, my wrist, my ankles, as I dragged him and he kicked with his good leg over to the cot and pulled himself up on it.

"That's better," he said, settling. "Put something under that foot."

I pushed a chair over to him and lifted his bad leg up on it. I felt cold as ice. He pulled up his trouser leg and we saw that the leg was badly swollen and red.

"Get me a bottle of whiskey from the cupboard. I've got to kill the pain." I got it.

"Why should I help you? You . . ." I stomped to the door and made it stop slamming.

"Because I'm your father and you gotta honor me."

"After last night? And since when have you been any kind of father to me? I've hated you since before I knew what hate was."

"You keep talking about last night. Nothing happened last night but I fell down the stairs."

"Why are your pants open and half way down, old man? What do you think you were doing up in the attic?"

He took a long chug from his bottle. "I was looking for you. You're never here when I come home. I want you to be here. I demand that you be here, do you hear me?"

"I never know when you're coming home. How am I supposed to know? But you, damn you, you're not going to get away with what you did this time. Look at me, I'm bruises from head to foot. You raped me . . . you monster. . . monster!"

"Don't you ever say a thing like that again, girly, or you'll find yourself in big trouble. I'm a preacher of God, do you hear?"

"Ruth says you're a drunken con-man, a crook who takes advantage of poor stupid people. Why hasn't the church in the village ever asked you to preach there? Why do you have to go and find these crazy little churches in the back woods? That's what Ruth says. And Garcie said the same thing." I was breathless.

"Garcie! An ignorant nigger and a Jew bitch!"

"You talked my mother into divorcing my father when he was in trouble. That's how you got this house. And now you've sold me to Ruth like a slave being sold at market."

"It's for your own good. Suppose I had died falling down those stairs—well, there'd be somebody to look after you."

"But you made her pay you."

"Why shouldn't I get some of the money back that it cost me to raise you up? There's been a lot of expenses. Now I'm in pain." He winced. "The whiskey helps but it's not going to stop it. You got to go to the village and get somebody out here to help me, maybe get me over to Beaufort to a doctor."

"You can't walk out on me this time, can you? You're trapped here."

"You can see that; now get going!"

"I'll take my own sweet time," I said, using a phrase of Ruth's. "The longer you hurt the better."

"A curse on you, girl, a curse on you."

Of course there was a curse on me, and I couldn't have been more keenly aware of it. The girl in the attic reached out to touch what was left of her childhood. The girl down here reached out for a weapon. Possession? Derangement? Dislocation? Someone else was changing my clothes out in back of the house in the rain. Someone else took my lovely mint-green dress that was nothing now but a rag and stuffed it in the cave at the back of the house, the cave I could no longer squeeze into, the little cave half flooded with rain, the wet blanket, and now my beautiful birthday dress in tatters down that rabbit hole. I must have been the size of a rabbit to have ever fitted into that hole, to have hidden there as I so often did. Someone else put on jeans and a shirt and raincoat and hat and trudged off in the lightening rain toward the village.

Jesse McQueen was dead.

Who—whom had I become? Someone else looked out of my eyes. Someone else heard the gulls cry. Another face felt the rain. Someone else returned Mrs. Walkup's wave and someone else saw the General Store, and someone else turned beside it and went on to the shack behind it. The new person knew that Tom would still be with Ruth. The new person knew that the pistol would be in the place, in the dresser drawer, Tom's target pistol, which he had taught Jessie McQueen to shoot. This new person, I, I knew that, if I looked, I would find the pistol, and I did.

How small am I, this new person? Smaller than a snail. Smaller than a bug, to be stepped on. Everyone is gone from my sight. I have no one, no other. They are all gone. Yesterday is gone. Everything is gone but the one thing, the monster. The monster has always been there and the monster will always be there, no matter which tyne of the fork you take. I am an unclean and worthless creature. I know that now. I am removed.  I am someone other than who I once was walking with the pistol in my pocket as the rain pauses, stops, and the sun comes out.  I am close now.  I am near the door.

I pull the door open and step in and shut the door.

"There you are!  Did you get some help?"

"I'm here to help," I said.  "Just like when I was a little girl and you fell down."

"What's the matter with you?  You don't look right."

"No. I don't feel like myself. Myself must have died."

"What are you jawing about, girl.  Get me some help."

He raised the bottle to his lips in such a familiar gesture—I had an album of pictures of that gesture, some dating back to my earliest memories.  I saw the Liberty ships in Wilmington, the cypress trees behind them.  I could still feel the sting on my cheeks from his wet-handed slaps across my face.  I could still see the lady, sympathetic, making a motion for me to wipe my tears.  I took out the pistol, aimed, and shot.

"You raped me," I whispered, with a deep, stranger's voice.

He sat there with a stunned expression on his face, but not what I expected.  I saw that there was blood near his left shoulder.

"Why you crazy little bitch, you shot me."  He set the bottle in his lap and felt his shoulder.  "Damnation," he said, "that smarts something fierce.  What is that thing?  A twenty-two?  Where'd you get it?"

I shot him again.  It hit him in the side of the stomach, by the liver.

"Oh my God!" he cried, leaning forward.

I felt faint, dots dancing before my eyes.  I went to the table and sat down at his place, where he always sat, where I could look straight at him.

"You better think what you're doing, girl," he said.  I could see now that he was feeling a lot of pain.  I held the butt of the pistol on the table to steady it, and shot him again.  The bottle in his lap shattered.  He screamed.  His scream just sounded like something he did at his sermons. He was always screaming at people.  I pulled the trigger again, and waited. He was quiet this time, his eyes closed.  There was a lot of blood all over him.  I sat there waiting for something to happen. Then he moaned. I pulled the trigger—pop, pop, pop.

She was almost sure that he was dead, whoever she was. Minutes passed.

Someone was knocking.  I had to find myself.  I had to answer.  Then I heard Ruth: "Is anyone there?  Jessie?"

"Hello," called Tom, knocking harder at the door.

"I'm here," I called, suddenly afraid they would leave me alone with the Traveller, "I'm here.  Wait.  I'll open the door."  I felt as if the body I had left in the attic had rejoined me.  I was inside of myself again, terrified, horrified, alone.

I left the gun on the table and scrambled to the door. Ruth and Tom stood waiting.  I spread my arms to collect their reality.  Now all of that icy calm I had felt had gone out of me.  They told me later that I was hysterical, that I spoke incoherently, that I was sobbing and choking and that my knees went out from under me as I tried to tell them what happened.  Ruth told me that Tom caught me up and carried me into the room.  If this happened as I have been told, I have no memory of it.  Ruth found another bottle of whiskey and made me drink some of it.  I remember how I couldn't get my breath, how I was afraid that I might die there and then for lack of air, like a fish out of a tank.  Then I heard what Ruth and Tom were saying.

"Is he alive?" I heard Ruth say.  "I'll go get help."

Tom said that the Traveller was dead.  I distinctly heard him say, "He's dead."  Dead, dead, dead.  But that's not what I heard him say a few minutes later.  I still don't know for certain what to believe about that, because I was sure I heard him say, "He's dead."  I am almost sure I heard him say that. I think that's what he said. Between choking and sobbing and gulping air I said, "He . . . raped me.  Bruises—look at my arms."

They looked at me with faces filled with horror.

"Oh, no, baby," Ruth said in a whisper, sitting down beside me, hugging me, "oh, no, baby."

"This is all my fault," said Tom.  "I've done it again—bringing that stupid pistol to this island.  I'm a damned felon. I shouldn't have had the damned thing anyway!"

Ruth's face had changed from the knitted brow of horror to wide-eyed amazement.  "Your fault?  How can it be your fault?"

"I should have got her out of here, Ruth, somehow.  This is my fault.  All of it is my fault.  My poor wife's suicide, the life Jessie must have had with this brute, all of this is my fault, mine, and I'm not going to let her take the blame for what I've done, for my failure—for my mistakes.  The blame for this is mine!"

"But Tom—" Ruth started.

"No buts.  Please, Ruth, no buts!"  He waved his hands wildly in a desperate attempt to explain himself.  "Jessie didn't do this.  *I* did it.  As sure as if I'd pulled the trigger. You hear?"

He went to the table and picked up the gun.  "Hear him moaning?  He's alive."

Out of some tunnel, I heard my echoing voice: "You said he was dead."

"He's not dead!" Tom yelled, startling the room with his vehemence.

"Then we can get him to the mainland," Ruth said, "to the hospital."

"He'd never make it.  Turn away.  Both of you.  I want to see if he's got a pulse."

"What are you going to do?" Ruth said.

"Turn away," Tom shouted.  "Jessie, turn away."  We did as we were told.

There was a shot. Ruth was holding me and I could feel her shudder. Then we looked. At first I couldn't see anything different, but then I saw a small black hole in the Traveller's forehead. Tom stepped in front of the body and when he stepped away there was a trickle of blood from the hole. How did it get there?

"See," Tom said, "he was alive. You see the blood? I killed him."

Ruth said, "Are you sure, Tom—I mean, you want to do this, this way? It'll be the end of us."

"Us? What about *her*? The least she'd get is reform school. This wasn't self-defense. They'll call it premeditated. I don't want to spoil her life. Haven't I done enough to spoil it already? I came back here to watch over her and I've messed that up, but this time I'm going to make things come out right."

"Of course—you're right. Whatever you say."

"I'll probably get second degree. I could be out—well, I won't be in forever. I must have a solemn oath from both of you. You must promise on whatever you hold sacred that you don't know anything about this."

He spoke quickly and softly now, almost whispering. "It was something between him and me and I'll be sitting here holding the gun when they come. If I admit to it, nobody'll look any further. That's the story. You must promise me never to tell another. Do you promise? Do you promise? Do you *swear*?"

"If you want it to be this way," said Ruth, "Jessie and I promise you. Ruth shook me gently. "Your dad's right. Do you hear, Jessie? Do you promise?"

"I promise," I said, Ruth squeezing it out of me.

"We promise," Ruth said.

"There's more," said Tom. "Ruth, I want you to take Jessie and get to Boston as soon as you can. Get Masefield to take you back to Wilmington. He won't be far off. You can find him.  He might be asleep on his boat.  Get him and get to Wilmington and get to Boston.  And don't contact me. Not a word.  Do you understand?  Not a word!"

"Oh God, Tom," said Ruth, "No!"

"I don't want you to contact me in any way.  Do you swear?"

Ruth shook her head slowly from side to side and her big dark eyes were so full of sorrow that I had to look away. She said, in a broken voice, "I—I swear."

"Look," Tom said, "It's not the end.  We'll be together again.  All of us.  Just a matter of time."  He got up and took Ruth in his arms and kissed her, then me.  He gave me a long look.

"Now take her and go.  I want you in Boston by tomorrow.  That's the best thing you can do for me.  For all of us."

"I'll do it," said Ruth.  "You know you can depend on me."

He gave Ruth a rueful smile.  "When I feel you're safely gone, I'll go and get someone and tell them—how I hated the son-of-a-bitch, how I shot him, and that's all I am going to say to anyone, ever.  Even if they wanted to prove differently, which they won't, because I'll make their case for them, even if they wanted to prove differently, they couldn't."

And, David, that promise cost you your father.  Of course, he didn't know about you then, none of us did.  But this is why I ask your forgiveness, and why I insisted on bearing the name Judas, because I allowed him to sacrifice himself, and, in doing so, betrayed you even before you were born. But Ruth and I did exactly what your father—and my father—ordered us to do.  Ruth gave me pills to take, and she kept me sedated enough to follow her like a zombie, or be dragged by her, until we got off the airplane in Boston.  Between the sedatives that Ruth kept giving me and the dream-like swiftness of the next few days, I was already beginning to wonder if what had happened on Fortune Island had actually happened. When I asked Ruth about it, on those first days at the Brookline estate, all she would say is, "You've had a terrible nightmare, but you're coming out of it." Those words were comforting to hear, even if I didn't quite believe them, and they helped me to remove myself from what I knew to be true. "But Tom—"

"Tom is doing what he believes is right. If I didn't believe he was right, I wouldn't let him do it. I love Tom *because* he wants to do this, because he's the kind of man who would do this. This is his desire, his will, his wish—we have to respect him in this; our respect for what he's chosen to do is our love in action. Now go back to sleep and try to have a sweet dream. Believe me, there is no girl in the world loved more than you."

September on Fortune Island was not an autumnal month, but September in Boston can be nearly winter. The shock of the climatic change marked a change of life. Brookline is a suburb of Boston, so close, so integrated with the city that it might as well be Boston, and that September passed in a flash of adjustment from the tropical to the northern world, and the first snow filled the streets late in November. If sand dunes were white, it would look like that. Down and down the snow came with a raw wind. About a month after our arrival in Boston, Ruth discovered that she was pregnant with you, David. Had our dad known that you were on the way, would he have done what he did? Ruth made no attempt to tell him. The knowledge that you existed would probably have caused him to feel that his hope for redemption had been negated, that he had left stranded yet another hostage to fortune.

The Carolina newspapers gave us the bare outline of what he had done after we had left. He had brought Mrs. Walkup to the house and showed her the body. She had made contact with the authorities. He had told them that he had shot the Traveller for his own reasons, reasons that were none of their business. He had refused to cooperate with the court-appointed attorney, indeed, had refused to say anything except that he had shot the Traveller, had rejected a jury in favor of a judge, had pleaded guilty and was sentenced to fifteen years in prison, back behind the Wall through the gates of which he had so shortly before emerged.

It appeared that he had placed the last brick in that wall without regret. Ruth's letters were returned unopened. But about six months later we received a letter from a priest who had apparently befriended him—a priest, and Tom was certainly not a Catholic. Ruth said that he had probably chosen to talk to a priest because anything that slipped from him should not slip from the priest. Ruth believed that he'd needed someone to talk to, but even so wanted to keep his privacy. The priest wrote that he had written down the return address on the letters his friend Tom had rejected, feeling that he might need to tell someone someday of Tom's fate. It was a bad fate. There had been a riot in the prison, and Tom died, beaten to death, trying to protect a guard.

"He was a Christ-like man," the priest had written, and I remembered *The Imitation of Christ*, which I still thumbed through although I didn't consider myself a Christian any-more than Ruth considered herself a Jew. We had lost what-ever it took. Tom Judas was no more. You, Ruth and I were what was left of him, and so we had a duty to him to do our best as he had done his best, mistaken as it might seem to others.

Biology became my subject and I tried to find in it, from the lowliest one-celled creatures to humans, how love pro-gressed. I have been unsuccessful. But that it did progress into power, that it progressed to the point that it defied even the instinct of self-preservation, I have ample evidence. I *am* evidence. I have ample evidence in our dad, David, Tom

Judas, that strange mysterious man who sought nothing for himself in life but that rarity, redemption.

V

The dying woman could not go on reliving those last, horrifying events and the manuscript ends with her final attempt to rationalize them. In other words, Ruthie, Jessie gave up. Judging from a few extraneous scraps tucked in among the pages of the memoir, Jessie had plans to go further and round it out. In her stead, I'm going to try to do that.

My first thought is that the fact that she assumed and kept the name Judas until the end, indicates to me that she could never come to terms with the morality of the situation. I think she was plagued by guilt all her days, probably more so as she grew older and was able to gain perspective on the situation left behind at Fortune Island.

For some people, good people, guilt can be a poison in their bloodstreams, and I can't help but think that bearing such guilt all her days must have shortened them, perhaps harmed her immune system and left her open to the cancer that consumed her. But I'm not a doctor or a scientist, and this is only a fancy of mine, I suppose. And yet my instinct tells me that it is possible.

I buck at the thought that a person, even a young person, should go scot-free after killing someone, even if that person deserved killing. What will the new age think, the age of your future? Will it hold a more liberal view? I wish I could come back some day and ask you what you've made of this story. Were they right in doing what they did? Perhaps, Ruthie, you can come to terms with it in the pragmatic morality of some future time. I am left disturbed but sympathetic.

The alternative scenario would have left me with a father—but that's a selfish point of view. And what would have happened to Jessie? Perhaps, with the right lawyer, some claim could have been made for self-defense; but since she left the house, went some distance, found a pistol, and brought it back apparently for the purpose of killing the Traveller—well, that looks pretty premeditated. Of course she may have been in the disassociative state that she describes and perhaps could have been found not guilty for reasons of temporary insanity. There is certainly ample evidence that she wasn't in her right mind. But neither my father nor my mother were willing to risk it. It was my dad's desire above all things to protect Jessie, and he both failed and succeeded. He certainly failed in that he put the pistol within her reach, but how could he ever have dreamed that she would use it as she did. It wasn't even that kind of pistol, scarcely more than a target practice pop-gun. Deadly enough, however. Both he and my mother failed in not getting Jessie away from the Traveller in time. They should have seen trouble coming. Perhaps they had become too involved with each other, too distracted. Perhaps it was the guilt over their involvement that led them to such a desperate act.

They did, however, ultimately succeed in giving her a life undarkened by public censure, but they lost each other in doing it, and my father lost me. Would he have done it, had he and mother been aware of my existence? Perhaps not, as Jessie suggested. But the more I think about the situation, the more the questions ramify. You'll have to answer them in your own way as they did in theirs and as I must seek to do in mine. But, Ruthie, I can't find it in my heart to disapprove of them in the final analysis. They were living the situation, as soldiers live war, and we are placed in the luxurious position of historians. We are given time to think, they had none. They had to act.

Of course I always knew what an extraordinary woman my sister was, but it took this little memoir of hers to make me realize just how extraordinary, and indeed, how extraordinary my mother was.

But Jessie, a lonely little girl on a nearly deserted island, growing without benefit of grade or high school, without even a friend to talk to, visited constantly by a monster, and yet becoming what she became, that *is* extraordinary!

I realize now that when we look at someone standing at a podium, receiving an award, an honor of some kind, or we see a picture of them in the paper holding a trophy, we rarely wonder what went into that life, what's behind the public view. Rarely, however, could there be rape and murder behind that face, rarely in those eyes such terrible knowledge.

But Jessie was too polite not to smile on the night of her last triumph, and still her eyes, I see now, shuffling through the old photographs of the event, as I couldn't see then, were haunted, as indeed were my mother's, and, I remember, for an instant, she and Jessie looked out over the audience, at me, perhaps, looked for Tom, I am certain, or saw him in me as they chose to, and exchanged a look of the sort that had become a language between them, a language I had never learned to speak.

After the ceremony—I remember this vividly—my mother grabbed Jessie's arm, kissed her, and the two women walked off the stage, half-supporting each other. Jessie was wrong about one thing, though. She needn't have hoped for forgiveness from me—none was required. I know that they all did their best back in a time and in a place and in circumstances of which they were so kind as to keep me blissfully unaware.

A PRACTICAL NURSE

In a picture perfect neighborhood of a large southern city, a shiny red closed convertible pulled to the curb in front of a beautiful bungalow.  A young woman in white got out carrying a small overnight bag and approached the front door. After a couple light, tentative taps, she opened the door and stepped inside.  Another small, matching overnight bag sat just inside the door.  Next to it was a neat stack of personal effects that looked as if they belonged in it.  The young woman sat the bag she was carrying next to it, opened it, and dumped its contents on the rug.

"Hello!" she called.  "I'm Lorna Chandler.  Your son, Mr. Harry Freemantle, sent me."

From within, a voice answered.  "The nurse?  Did you lock the door behind you?  I didn't like waiting here with the door unlocked.  There's a bad element, you know.  I don't know why that son of mine has to do things in such an . . . unorthodox manner."

"I locked the door," Lorna Chandler said, stepping into Cora Freemantle's bedroom.  She thought the woman propped up in bed would be older, or at least look older.  She was beautifully coifed, her silver hair upswept.  She wore a pink silk peignoir, and, around a neck gone a bit floppy, a diamond-inset platinum multiple-necklace.  Her ears, hands, and wrists, were bejeweled.

"Yes," Cora Freemantle said.  "Yes.  Good.  What did you say your . . ."

"Lorna Chandler."

"Yes.  Lorna.  Do you mind?"

"No, I don't mind.  May I call you Cora?"

"Well . . . yes, of course.  You are a registered nurse?"

"A practical nurse."

"Isn't that . . . I mean—you don't have a degree or any-thing?"

"I have passed all the necessary examinations."

"But you are quite young. I should think you would be in a good nursing school—something to advance yourself."

"Money."

"Ah, yes, I see. Money. Well, perhaps in future . . . In any case, did my son explain my difficulties?"

"He said you had high blood pressure, several minor and one serious heart failure."

"No, no. That's true, but I can get around ordinarily. But I got dizzy with the high blood-pressure and I fell. Or perhaps I twisted my ankle. But I fell. But the fall wasn't it. The ankle was it. I mean—I can't get about. I can't put any weight at all on the ankle. The pain is excruciating."

"What did the doctor . . ."

"Sprained ankle. Stay off it. See the support?" She pulled the covers back to display her bandaged leg. "Ordi-narily, bad heart and all, I can get around. I walk my dog, Suzy Wong. By the way, where is Suzy? I didn't hear her bark when you came in. She always barks. You didn't let her out when you came in, did you?"

"She barked. I guess you were dozing. She's fine, now. Sleeping."

"With her paws under her coochic-coo chinny-chin? Yes, I must have been dozing. You're sure you locked the door?"

"I locked it. You have a lovely home."

"Yes, I think so. Now, you understand that you are to stay with me for the weekend, prepare and serve my meals, help me to the bathroom—well, you understand what I re-quire? My son Harry told you, did he not?"

"Yes, he told me."

"Sit down, won't you? You make me nervous just standing there."

"I'm sorry."  Lorna Chandler sat down in a chair near the bed.

"You have things?  A suitcase?"

"I left them in the living room."

"Well, there's a guest room  upstairs.  The maid uses it. She's black.  You don't mind that do you?"

"Of course not."

"Well, not necessarily of course not, but good; you take that.  This is not a very big house."

"But very nice.  I wish I owned it."

"Yes, I think so.  I don't need a big house—though I can certainly afford all the house I want—but I won't waste money."

"No."

"My second husband left me this house.  When he died."

"Yes."

"Do you want some coffee or something?"

"No."

"Where's your coat?"

"Outside, on my suitcase."

"Well, why don't you see to your things.  Take them up to your room.  Get settled.  Then come back down and make some coffee.  I'd like some."

"You'd like some?"

"Yes, I would.  After just waking up.  What time is it, anyway?"

They checked their watches.

"Nearly noon, Friday."

"Yes. My son was here this morning.  I dozed, and here you are—Lorna.  Chandler—that name rings a bell.  That's an old family."

"Yes, an old family."

"Yes, I recall.  Substance.  Are you a cousin?  Oh, forgive me, dear.  I didn't mean—"

"Distant.  Yes, a distant cousin."

"No offense.  An old lady gets used to speaking her mind.  We get tactless, I'm afraid.  Compensates for losing our other faculties.  Can't see too well—can't walk, etc.—but at least you can say what you think."

"Yes, that's good.  Say what you think."

"Yes.  Well, why don't you go on and put your things away."

"Yes.  Up in the black maid's room."

"Yes, at the head of the stairs."

"Yes.  And then you want some coffee."

"I'd like coffee—yes."

"Very well."

"Very well?  You sound like an English butler in an old movie."

"I'm sorry.  I'll go now."  Lorna Chandler rose and left the room.

Cora picked up her bedside phone and dialed.

"Oh, I'm so glad I caught you, Iris.  It's about this nurse your husband has sent over here to take care of me—what? What do you mean, you have to run, Mother Freemantle?  I'm talking to you.  And why do you, after fifteen years of marriage to my son, insist on calling me 'Mother Freemantle'? My name is Cora.  What?  Wait a minute, I want to speak to you.  I don't care about the children—"

Cora looked up to see Lorna standing in the doorway.

"Oh, never mind, Iris.  Iris?  IRIS?"  She hung up.  "My own daughter-in-law hung up on me.  Rude!  Rude!  Rude!" She banged down the receiver.

"What is it, Lorna?  Where's my coffee?"

"Would you like anything with your coffee?"

"What?"

"Perhaps a little wine?"

"Wine?  What *are* you talking about?  Coffee, that's all. Just coffee.  I don't drink."

"Oh. Because there's wine in the kitchen. Several bottles of wine."

"It must be the maid's."

"Oh. She has very good taste. Very expensive. You must pay her well."

"What business is that of yours? I pay her what maids get."

"Black maids? Black domestics?"

"Yes. I don't know where she gets the wine. Oh, bother, of course it's my wine. I have a right to have wine if I want it, don't I? This is my house, isn't it? What am I sparring with you about?"

"I'm your nurse, Mrs. Freemantle. You have high blood pressure. You should not drink wine. You were drinking wine when you became faint, and that led to your sprained ankle. I'm merely trying to do my job."

"Of course. But I will have my wine if I wish it, doctors, nurses or no."

"A glass with your coffee?"

"No coffee. A glass of wine."

"As you wish."

"There you go again—Lorna—sounding like an English butler. Are you deliberately trying to make me uncomfortable in my own house?"

"No, Mrs. Freemantle."

"Cora! Cora! My name is Cora!"

"Yes—Cora. You mustn't excite yourself. It could lead to a seizure."

"You are trying to make me see that I should not have the wine, is that it?"

"I'll get it."

"Don't ignore me!"

"No." Lorna Chandler waited.

"Bother! Go on, then!"

Cora fidgeted in irritation while Lorna went to kitchen and returned almost immediately with two glasses of red wine on a silver tray.

"What is that? Are you having a glass of wine, too? Aren't you on duty, or something?"

"I didn't think you'd like to drink alone."

"That was thoughtful of you," Cora said, sarcastically, "I must say." She sipped her wine. "Is Suzy Wong still sleeping?"

"Yes. Quite peacefully."

She's a Pekinese, you know. No mixed blood. Highly nervous. That's why I was surprised that I didn't hear her barking when you came in. You must get on with dogs."

"I don't care for them."

"How can you say that? Everyone likes dogs."

"Not everyone. When I was a little girl, I was walking with my mother and father—walking ahead of them and somewhat behind a stray dog who, for no reason that I have ever been able to discover, turned around suddenly and mauled me. He bit my hand—there, you can still see the teeth marks. The little ones bark and the big ones bite—like people."

"It's very unfair of you to base your opinion of dogs on an isolated incident."

"It wasn't isolated to me. I was five and it was my hand."

"That doesn't make sense."

"It does to me."

"It's a perverse attitude."

"I guess we are all perverse, each in his own way. The word means nothing."

"I know what perverse means. I was a school teacher."

"That must have been many years ago, in better times. Were there better times?"

"Yes, I think so. I think those were better times in some ways. But these are my better times."

"You mean because you have money now."

"Yes. Money and security. But you weren't alive during the Depression. You wouldn't know."

"Then why do you say they were better times?"

"Not the Depression. I meant the times before, the Twenties. When I was young and starting out. They were better times—for the world. But these are my better times."

"You married wealthy men."

"I assume that you don't intend to insult me. Yes. During the Depression, when I saw what could be, I decided to marry well, if I could."

"And you could, because you were good-looking and you knew it."

"Yes, I think so. Yes. And I did. I married well, and–"

"And now you are a wealthy woman. You have a black domestic and a practical nurse and, if you wanted, you could have more. Much more."

"I don't like to waste money. I don't need more than I have."

"You could give some away—to your family, say—and make their lives easier. You have it just as you want it."

"Yes, I think so." Cora felt uneasy; it made her heart pound hollowly.

"But you don't care for your children."

"Of course I do, in my own way. What made you think that?"

"Because you didn't marry for love. You married for money."

"I didn't say that I didn't marry for love."

"But you suggested it."

"Give me a cigarette."

Lorna Chandler gave Cora Freemantle a cigarette and lit it. "You shouldn't smoke. It raises your blood pressure."

Cora puffed. "Good! Now that you've said that, I hope you'll allow me to enjoy this in peace."

"Of course."

Cora thought for a few moments. "No, I don't care much for my children. You have insight, I'll say that for you."

"And less for your grandchildren."

"I can't stand the little demons."

"I could tell by the way you referred to them when you were talking to your daughter-in-law. I didn't mean to overhear—"

"But you did. In fact, I was trying to get hold of my son to ask him about you."

"Oh. Why?"

"Because you seemed—I don't know—I wanted to know something about you."

"But he wouldn't know anything about me. I come from an agency. You'd have to call them."

"What agency?"

"Guess."

"Guess? What are you talking about?"

"No, I mean you'd never guess."

"I'm not in the habit of playing guessing games, young lady."

"The Nightingale Nursing Service."

"Oh."

"Yes, isn't it cute? Do you want to call them?"

"Of course not. I was just curious. Old women are curious, you know."

"Yes, I know."

"You know, Lorna, there's something in the way you speak—I can't put my finger on it—"

"I'm sorry. I'm doing my best to make conversation, to keep you company."

"No, no. I'm sorry, dear. Just an old woman's frustration at not being able to do for herself. Will you get me another glass of wine, dear?"

"You shouldn't have another, should you?"

"I suppose not, but—"

"But you want one anyway."

"Yes."

"You want what you want when you want it."

"Don't be impertinent. But yes, I want what I want when I want it—and I pay a good deal to have it that way."

"You know, Mrs. Freemantle—Cora—you remind me of my mother."

"I suppose that's a compliment."

"Well, in a way. I envy people who can just shut everything else out but what they want, themselves. It's godlike."

"I'm not sure I understand."

"Let me get your wine." Lorna went and returned with more wine. It was as if she took no time at all to do anything—so smooth.

"What did you mean by—"

"Oh, I don't know what I'm talking about, I admit it. Most people don't admit it, but I do. Tell me about your first husband, girl to girl."

Cora shrugged. "There's not much to tell."

"But you had children by him."

"Yes, that's true. Two. A boy—my son, Harry—and a daughter, Carol."

"Where's your daughter?"

"She lives in California. I've cut her out for leaving me—old and ill. Harry is the only one I can count on. Besides, Carol has twins."

"You don't care for them?"

"The truth is, I don't care for children. In vino veritas." Cora giggled.

"They have to be tended, watched over, looked after, and loved."

"They're a nuisance."

"They steal your thunder."

"I don't know what that means."

"Children must come first."

"That's a strange attitude for a young woman."

"No, not at all. Yours is strange."

"There's nothing strange about it. What do you know about children? I've had them, and grandchildren."

"I almost had one."

"Almost?"

"When I was sixteen. My mother made me have an abortion. I wasn't married. The boy was gone. Not at all an unusual story."

"Your mother did the right thing."

"Why do you think that? She never loved me. She loved herself. Now I would have had a child to love and be loved by."

"You would have been alone in the world with a child to support. You're young, now, and free. You can have another child when you wish."

"How can you say that? Another child! As if children were interchangeable, like pet dogs, to be replaced!"

"Oh, but you can't replace a dog. Dogs are—almost human."

"Humans are human!"

"Now, now. I understand how you feel, but—"

"But you obviously don't understand how I feel, anymore than my mother did."

"Well, now, calm yourself. I'm the patient here. You should be taking care of me."

"You! You! How can you think of nothing else but yourself? You're a selfish old woman, don't you know that? Don't you realize what you are?"

Cora's face turned red. She struggled to rise, but Lorna pushed her back against the mound of pillows. "Don't try to get up. You'll fall, and it'll be my fault for letting you. You wouldn't take the blame yourself, would you?"

"Are you crazy, young woman? What are trying to do?"

"Take care of you and your hateful little peke."

"Suzy? Where is Suzy? What have you done with Suzy?"

"I'll get her for you. You'd like to have her in bed with you, wouldn't you?"

"Yes. Please get me Suzy." Cora Freemantle began to whimper. "Please bring me my little Suzy Wong."

Lorna Chandler left the room and returned, Suzy Wong hanging from her leash. She swung the dog onto the bed, where it lay, silent. Cora Freemantle screamed.

"She must have got tangled in the leash," said Lorna Chandler, "poor dear. But you can keep her in bed with you, if you wish."

Cora Freemantle could not breathe. "Help. . . I can't. . . She fell back onto the pillows, where she lay, silent as Suzy Wong.

"There's plenty of time," Lorna Chandler said, dialing the phone. "Hello. Can you come over now and pick up Suzy Wong? Yes, Iris, everything is fine. Before I call the hospital, I want this damned little dead beast in your care, where I hope it won't take you very long to discover that it's had such a coochie-coo sad accident. Tell Harry everything went as planned. And, I warn you, don't either of you forget for one minute that this house is *mine!*"

## HAYDN'S HEAD:  A PASTICHE

*for Jack O'Brian, columnist, New York Journal-American,*
*who tipped me off*

We are aboard the Orange Blossom Special, returning to New York from Florida, and I am hopeful that Tweedledum and Tweedledee, as Johnny calls them, a couple of bad eggs in plaid suits, are not.

"Odds are we've left them shaking their fists on the station platform, Pug," Johnny says, mopping his brown brow with a white silk handkerchief.  He gears his seat back, loosens his tie, tips his Panama over his eyes, and acts like he hasn't got a worry in the world.  I act like I am watching the midnight Miami lights recede, but what I am really doing is watching the window for reflections.  I expect to see Sam the Elephant's bonebreakers appear at any second.

Most all gamblers have a specialty—cards, craps, horses—but Johnny Belmont will bet on anything.  I have first heard of him a year ago, when he places a spectacular bet on the presidential election and loses to all concerned.  He is in deep trouble until his rich family steps in.  But they are very much put out, because he has bet on Stevenson and they are an Eisenhower family.  So they warn Johnny that they will not rescue him again.  At least this is the version I have heard outside of Lindy's restaurant, in that vague area of the environment around Broadway and Fiftieth Street which Damon Runyon has dubbed Jacobs' Beach in honor of his ticket speculating pal, Mike Jacobs.  On Jacobs' Beach you meet the sporting crowd—scalpers, bookies, touts, mobsters, and journalists such as Walter Winchell and, until he passes on in '46, Runyon himself.

But it is at Hialeah that Johnny and I have become pals. The Florida sharks do not know that Johnny is a black sheep without a red cent; so, with his good looks, his classy manners, and his family name, he has been able to borrow large amounts of hay from Sam the Elephant, who is called such because he does not forget so easy. But Johnny has been having the world's worst losing streak, and has tried to get on the good side of Lady Luck by placing some bets for me. Unfortunately, Sam the Elephant has heard of said bets; and, because he does not care from which individual he collects, has decided to hold me partners with Johnny when he calls in the bets.

We are tap city when we step off the Special at Penn Station—unless you count Johnny's lucky two-bit piece, which he never spends. But Johnny thinks we can get a stake at the Hotel Bon Chance, a gamblers' haven in the West Forties. I figure he means to check us in and flip his quarter into wealth. But I am worried that some of Sam the Elephant's boys might be keeping their eyes out for us there. Johnny laughs kind of grimly and says that we will have to gamble on that because the Bon Chance is the only place he can think of where he can raise a stake.

It looks like we are going to have to hoof it through a cold November rain, which is pouring out of buckets. It does not matter much to me, because I am not a dude, but it matters to Johnny, who is a clotheshorse. We have had to leave all our clothes in Florida, and he only has this one tropical suit left, which is on his back. So he shakes his head, and says: "Pug, I'm not going to let this suit get soaked."

I follow him through the crowd and up to the Lost and Found, which is open all night in those days, and it is now about midnight, as our trip takes us about twenty-four hours, and he tells the busy clerk behind the counter that he has lost his black umbrella. The clerk hustles off and is back in no time with three such. "That's it," cries Johnny, and takes the one that happens to be the best of the lot.

As we are walking away, Johnny says, "You know, Pug, one could get anything that way." He stops and looks at me with his green eyes bright like two Go signs. "Think of something, I'll bet you a belated C-note that they have it—that the clerk will hand it across to you."

There is nothing like a wager to cheer me up, and I need cheering. "You're on," I say. "We'll make it for the first C-note one of us gets."

"O.K.," says Johnny. "But I choose the item. It can't be anything with an I.D., and it can't be anything too unusual—like a zither. Fair enough?"

"Fair enough," I say, wondering what a zither is.

"Say a plain square box—a cardboard carton or package wrapped in plain brown paper and tied with twine—O.K.?"

"You're on."

"You ask for it. I got the umbrella. The clerk might remember me." On the 5-yard line from the Lost and Found desk, Johnny says: "I'll wait here." In two minutes I am back, carton in hand.

"I owe you a C-note," I say, dangling the package from a finger by the twine. "The bet's good," I add, and say that I will now return the package.

"Wait a minute, Pug," says Johnny. "How about another C-note on what's in it? Let's say on whether it's animal, vegetable, or mineral."

I say, "It's bigger than a breadbox, that's for sure."

"Takers?" says Johnny.

I shrug. "Takers," I say. "So where do we open it?"

"Not here," says Johnny. "I'll tell you what, Pug. We'll take it with us to the Bon Chance, and open it there. Then I'll have a boy re-wrap it and bring it back here to the Lost and Found. What do you say?"

"I suppose you want I should carry it?"

"And I'll keep us dry with the umbrella. Come on."

The Bon Chance is a few blocks uptown from Penn Station. Cats and Dogs of rain are bouncing knee-high as we turn off the avenue. On the next corner is a Yellow Cab stand, or used to be in those days. I duck to look into the first cab in the line and there as usual is Sleeping Bill, who could make a claim to being the worst hack in New York, as he never takes a fare. Actually, it is his own car, done up to look like a Yellow Cab, and he is no hack at all, but a bookie. I tap his windshield, but he is asleep at the wheel. I think he has been so since I left for Florida. Anyway, he's in the same position he was in when I left.

In a block or two on this numbered cross-street the pedestrian traffic has thinned down to Johnny and me. Ahead, through the watery dark I see *BON CHANCE* come and go in nervous green neon winks. I am looking at this sign, and thinking about a hot bath, when a dark, shiny limo sprays up beside us. The back window on our side is rolled down and there is the head of a white-faced, dark-hatted woman in it. She has thin red lips and big white teeth through which she hisses something at us, which I cannot make out due to the fact that the rain is doing drum rolls. A big boy in a chauffeur's uniform comes around from the other side. He is waving a revolver which has a silencer on it like a rolled-up racing form. He believes that action speaks louder than words, because instead of explaining himself he hooks a couple of thick fingers into the twine on the box I am conveying and tugs. I tug back. He then swings at me and misses, but corrects himself by bashing the big silencer down on my knuckles. Only now does he decide to make himself clear.

"Let go, you fat swine!" he cries, adding insult to injury. But before I can be offended, Johnny has collapsed the umbrella and batted it down on the pistol, which splashes into a jumping lake at the rear end of the limo.

"En garde!" cries Johnny, stabbing the guy several short ones.  The big guy lets go of the twine, and slips in the rain just as I step in with a right cross.  He falls against the limo and keeps on going down toward where the pistol has submerged, slapping at street water, grabs up the pistol, aims, and pulls the trigger.

Because of the silencer and the noise of the rain, I don't know if I have been shot or not, but then I realize by the look on the big guy's face that the pistola is waterlogged.

Johnny and I have jumped away when he has had the pistola pointed at us, so he has a head start when he ducks around the limo.  The door slams and the limo speeds off, making a wake like the Titanic.

"What the hell . . ." says Johnny, looking after the limo.

"It is this dumb package," I say.

"Did you see the plates?" says Johnny.  "They were diplomatic.  Let's get to a room and see what we've got here."

There is a new night clerk at the Bon Chance, a straw-haired, freckled kid with a Southern accent.  This is a break, as the old clerk would have sold out his mother to Sam the Elephant or any other shark for the price of a warm beer.  It won't help much if Sam the Elephant's boys are looking hard for us, but it is anyway worth the ink to register under a couple of phony names, so we do.  A kid who looks like the younger brother of the yokel behind the desk shows us up, carrying the package by the twine, like a suitcase.

In our room, Johnny offers to flip the kid double or nothing for the tip, neglecting to state the amount involved, and the kid eagerly takes the bet.  Johnny then offers to let the kid owe him "the ten spot."  But before the kid has about-faced, Johnny has flipped him into serious debt, which he immediately cancels, on the condition that we get top service, to which the kid gratefully agrees.

Johnny orders sandwiches, coffee, cigarettes, cigars, razors, etc.  He also needs a bottle of good Scotch.  He sends the kid away with our wet clothes. In those days, you can get a good steam press all night, even in a cheap hotel.

"Well, now, Pug," says Johnny, ripping open the package, "let's have a look at this."

I go over to the table on which the kid has placed the box and look into it. Johnny is pulling out a lot of excelsior. There is something round and gray down in the middle of the box. Johnny pulls more excelsior out, reaches in, and jerks back like he's been stung. I see it now and let out a whistle. It is a human skull.

As soon as it sinks in what we have here, we do a thorough search of the box for identification of some kind— "Provenance," Johnny calls it—even checking inside the skull, but discover zero. We pack the bony head away; and then, while we bathe and shave, we discuss the nature of things as they stand.

We ask ourselves: Who are the foreign couple in the limo? Why do they want this old skull? Should we call the police?

Johnny says, combing his dark hair down over his forehead and cutting a part in it, "Do the chauffeur and his lady know that the package contains a skull, rather than something else more valuable? Surely an ordinary human skull can't be worth much. Surely not enough to induce armed robbery."

Comes a rapping at our chamber door.

"Who is it?" Johnny calls.

"Bellboy. I got your clothes and a wagon full of food and drinks."

When the bellboy goes, Johnny says, "Get dressed, Pug," and pulls on his pants.

I am tying my tie in the cloudy mirror over the dresser when there is a second knock at the door.

"What now?" Johnny calls over the transom. He thinks it is the bellboy again.

"Please," comes a reply. "I am Professor-Doctor Albrecht Schmitt with my daughter, Agnes. We have rooms down the hall. I must speak with you."

"It don't sound like anybody Sam the Elephant would know," I say.

"Nor like the chauffeur from the limo," says Johnny. He opens the door a crack and peers out. Then he steps back and opens it wide.

This gent has a couple of inches on me and I have a couple of pounds on him, making us two barrels, but his weight is then as old as mine is now, and he has never been a lightweight boxer as I have before I lose my last match in the late 40's and begin consoling myself with pumpkin pies.

He has a gray, yellow-streaked walrus mustache, and thick, silver-rimmed specs. His daughter is taller and a hundred pounds lighter, a honey-blonde in powder blue who looks like a wicked witch has chased her out of a fairy tale. She eyes Johnny like he is Prince Charming.

The gent extends a thin manicured hand. "I'm Professor-Doctor Schmitt," he repeats. Gray moths flutter behind his specs. "I see you have opened our package. We were on our way up from Washington with that skull when we suspected we were being followed. You see, it is a valuable specimen, and there are those who would stop at nothing to possess it. Research is highly competitive. You Americans have a phrase—*it's a jungle*." He gives out with a nervous cackle.

Johnny lights a Fatima. He says, "It hasn't got a name or a number on it. How do we know it's yours?"

The Doc looks stumped. The gray moths look like they are trying to break out from behind their glass cages.

Johnny purses his lips, lifting his little black mustache, and blows out some Turkish smoke, giving Agnes the once-over twice. She looks at him with big sad blue eyes. He cracks a smile. "Maybe if you can tell me how you lost it?"

"Oh, no," the Doc almost stutters, "it wasn't lost. Just as we were leaving the train, we became *certain* that we were being followed. But we hoped we had lost our pursuers in the crowd when we came upon a row of lockers. Unfortunately, neither of us had an appropriate coin—"

"We had to work fast," Agnes breaks in. "In a moment's inspiration, my father saw the Lost and Found, and we deposited it there."

"Then," the Doc picks up, "we waited nearby to make certain that our pursuers had not seen us turn in the package."

"You can imagine," says Agnes, "our surprise when we saw—you, Mr.—"

"Morris," I say. "Pug Morris."

"—Mr. Morris, pick up the package."

"You were not at all what we were looking for in our pursuers," says the Doc.

"Sorry," I say, as I am pulling the ring from a Prince Albert.

"No, no," says the Doc, kind of flustered. "I did not mean—"

"Frankly," pipes Agnes, "we thought you might be some sort of confidence tricksters who preyed on Lost and Found patrons."

"If that should prove to be the case," says the Doc, kind of shrugging, "I'm sure that we can come to terms—"

This time I break in. "We picked up the package on a lark," I say, around my stogie, which I am busy lighting.

"We're gamblers," Johnny says. He explains the bet.

"I see," says the Doc, when Johnny has finished. "We followed when you left the station, and saw the assault on you. We should certainly have helped, for those who attempted to steal the package from you were assuredly those who pursued us from Washington, but I'm getting old, and the rain was beating down, and we had fallen too far behind to be of any assistance."

"They must have found us," says Agnes, "and then seen you ahead of us with the package, passed us by, and attacked—"

"We saw you turn in here," says the Doc.

"We told the clerk we were friends of yours and wanted rooms on your floor," says Agnes. "We've been drying off and making ourselves presentable."

"Now," says the Doc, "if you'd please be so kind as to give us our package . . ."

Johnny grins, and says: "We still don't know that the package is yours. Maybe it belongs to the pair who jumped us."

"Yeah," I say, "and maybe everything you've told us is a load of—"

"Pug!" says Johnny.

"—baloney," I say.

Schmitt's face falls. He thinks for a moment, and says, in a much more businesslike manner, "We haven't much time, gentlemen," reaches into a breast pocket, pulls out a fat wallet, and takes a couple of bills from it. "Will a hundred— er, two hundred—one each—be satisfactory?"

"Mister," I say, "we lose more than that before breakfast."

But Johnny takes the two bills, stuffs one in his pocket, and, handing me the other, says, "Here, Pug, cash this and call the cops."

I start for the phone, but the Doc cries, "Stop!" When I turn back, he is holding a .30 Mauser, with its little black eye looking right at me. "Put your hands up and hand me that box," he orders.

"Which is it, Professor?" says Johnny in his usual cheerful way, his hands half up, talking through the smoke from his dangling Fatima.

"Agnes," says Schmitt, "get the head."

Now we are all startled. Someone is at our door again.

"We are very popular tonight, Johnny," I say.

"Infamously, Pug," says Johnny.

Neck on neck, Johnny knocks the Mauser to the floor and I catch the Doc on the chin with a light fast uppercut.

Schmitt has gone down across the coffee wagon, taking a few items with him. In short, he has made a good deal of noise. Plus which, Agnes has screamed.

"It could be the Elephant's boys," I say.

Johnny grabs up the Doc's Mauser, looks sharp at Agnes, finger to lips, and steps to the wall by the door so he will be behind it when it opens. He nods at me.

I stay put and call, "Come in!"

It is the chauffeur and the pale-faced lady from the limo. The chauffeur is holding the revolver with the big silencer on it. The gat looks dry and newly oiled.

I back up some toward the table with the package on it, drawing them in. They bite, and step in, eyeing Agnes and the Doc's unconscious bulk.

"Where's the other—?"

But the chauffeur has got curious too late. Johnny jams the Doc's Mauser into his back.

"Well," says Johnny, "if it isn't my fencing partner! Drop it."

The chauffeur drops the big revolver with a thud. Johnny kicks the door shut behind him, steps around in front, and kicks the gat to the side.

"Who are you two?" he asks, pleasantly.

The chauffeur clicks his heels. "Colonel Ivan Lensky," he says, "Soviet State Security. This is my associate, Frau Yeva Von Heller of Austria."

"KGB," says Johnny. "How interesting. My uncle is Wild Bill Belmont."

"OSS," says Lensky. "I have met him. A double-dyed conservative McCarthyite reactionary."

"That's Uncle Bill," says Johnny, smiling.

"Who are you talking about?" I say.

"Spies!" says Johnny.

"We already know Doctor Schmitt and his daughter," says Lensky. "Who are you?"

"Not-so-innocent bystanders," says Johnny. "Gamblers who made a bet on a live lark and wound up with a dead head."

"That head is important to Frau Von Heller and myself—to the governments we represent. We are prepared to offer you two thousand dollars. I have on my person an instrument for that amount. Payment cannot be stopped."

"Two *grand*," I say. "That might keep the Elephant from our door, Johnny."

"Elephant?" The Colonel looks intrigued.

"An Americanism," says Johnny. He looks at Agnes, who frowns, and at the Doc, who groans, and at me, who shrugs. "Make it five thousand," he says.

"Ah," sighs Lensky. "It so happens—"

"That you have another instrument for five thousand," says Johnny.

Frau Von Heller says: "We represent the rightful owners."

The Colonel waves a hammy hand at Agnes and the Doc. "These two are frauds."

"No," cries the Doc, looking up from the floor, "don't give it to them! You would be betraying your country. It doesn't belong to them and you cannot put a money value on it. It's priceless!"

Now come more knocks. It is like a convention.

"House detective," comes a voice. "Open up!"

"No deal," says Johnny to Lensky and Von Heller, who have closed ranks. Lensky whispers something in Von Heller's ear.

"Shut up, you two," I say. "And behave."

"Open up!" says the dick outside the door.

"Get your father up," Johnny says to Agnes.

A key is inserted in the lock.

"He's got a key, Johnny," I say. "It's the house dick, all right."

Johnny shoves the Mauser in his belt at the small of his back and drops his coat tail over it. He pulls open the door, a ring of keys jangling on the other side of the lock.

"What the hell—" says the house dick. He is long and thin in a worn blue suit and looks at us from a long thin yellow face, sour as kraut. "Why didn't you open up?" he asks, scowling.

"There's been an accident," says Johnny. "We were busy."

"What's going on in here?" says the dick. "Folks down the hall say they heard noise and screaming. You realize it's two in the morning?" He gives me a hard look. "Hey, wait a minute. Ain't you Pug Morris?"

"You got me," I say.

"You ain't registered, Morris. Who's he?" he asks, spotting the Doc.

"He's my father," says Agnes, rising from the floor where she's been trying to get the Doc up. "He fainted and knocked over the tray and the lamp and I cried out. He's been suffering this condition for some time, but I'm still terribly upset and was caught off guard when it happened. I'm sorry we disturbed the other patrons."

I notice now that Frau Von Heller has her big black hat off. The house dick has stepped in close to get a good look at the Doc, and Von Heller and Lensky are edging toward the door.

"You're not leaving?" says Johnny, like a disappointed host.

"Duty calls," says Lensky. "I hope you and Mr. Morris will reconsider our offer."

"Ah!" cries Von Heller. She has dropped her hat. It is pretty obvious to everybody but the house dick, who has his back to her, that she has scooped up the big revolver with the hat.

"Keep your powder dry," I say.

She touches her pale cheek with a red nail, says, "Yes, it's still raining," turns on Lensky's arm, and the pair step out of the room; and, I hope, out of my life, but I doubt it.

"Everything here all right then?" asks the dick. "Want me to get a doctor for your father, miss?"

"No," says Agnes. "It isn't serious. And my father's a doctor."

Schmitt sits up and shakes his head. "I'm getting too old for this work," he says.

"I'd better help Father to his room," says Agnes.

"I'll help you with him," says Johnny.

"Wait a minute," says the dick. "Don't I know you, too? Ain't you Johnny Belmont?"

"Clarence Feathergale," says Johnny. "It's on the register."

"Feathergale! Well, Feathergale, *I'll* help the young lady and her father. The Bon Chance don't want no lawsuit on its hands."

"I'll be back when Father is comfortable," says Agnes, "to explain."

Johnny pushes the door after them, leaving it ajar.

"That dick has us pegged," I say. "He'll tip the Elephant's boys for sure."

"Maybe not," says Johnny. "Maybe he doesn't want any trouble here on his carpeted beat. In any case, we'll have to gamble that he doesn't. We can't walk out on a situation like this, Pug. That young lady needs help, and maybe our country needs help—and maybe there's enough money somewhere in this situation to pay off Sam the Elephant and to get us a new stake."

"So what makes an old skull so valuable?" I say.

Johnny snaps his fingers. "Pug," he says, "maybe it's not *what*, but *who*."

This gives us something to think about while we straighten up the room. We set the wagon up, put what is unbroken back on top, and I fix us a couple of drinks. I call down for the boy to clean up the mess on the rug and bring us some fresh sandwiches. When he has gone we finally put some food aboard. I am several meals behind.

As I'm swallowing the last corner of the last sandwich, Agnes taps and steps in.

"How's your father?" says Johnny.

"All right," she says. "He's resting. But he really shouldn't be doing this."

"Doing what, exactly?" says Johnny.

"This kind of work—for the government."

"It's on the level, then?" I say. "Listen, Miss Schmitt, I am really sorry that I have to deck him, see, but I want to make sure that he comes loose from that Mauser."

"He understands," she says. "He shouldn't have drawn the gun. It was an act of desperation. Oh, why on earth did you pick up that package! How did you *know* about it?"

"We didn't know," I say. "It was just a wild bet."

"Then, you really *are* gamblers?"

"You do not know the half of it, lady," I say. "We are even now being chased by loan sharks who will bite off our legs if we do not paddle."

"You're not criminals?"

"My name, Miss Schmitt," says Johnny, "is Belmont. I come from a long line of generals and statesmen. A good third of my family is in government—the other two-thirds are in money."

"Then you're patriots?"

"Black sheep, but true blue," says Johnny, with plenty of pride, "and with wounds to prove it."

"Johnny made a hero of himself fighting Hitler," I say. "That's how come he ain't in Korea. War wounds. And he has the medals to prove it."

"Well," says Agnes, impressed. "Perhaps you'll fix me a drink. I'm a little unsteady."

I fix the three of us some Scotch and soda and we settle down to hear what she has to say.

"Do you know anything about Austria?" she begins.

"Nope," I say.

Johnny just sips his Scotch.

"It's divided," she says, "Into American, British, French, and Russian zones. Vienna is in the Russian zone, but the Inner City is administered by each power in turn for a month, and patrolled day and night by groups of four soldiers drawn from the Four Powers."

"Sounds complicated," I say.

"It is," she says. "There are hopes for reunification, even plans ongoing. But things *can* go wrong."

"Well, what has this got to do with the head?" I say.

"My father and I are agents for the forces in and out of Austria who oppose Communism. That skull may become important—even more important—if reunification fails. You see, it is the skull of one of the greatest composers who ever lived—an Austrian named Franz Josef Haydn."

"What did I tell you, Pug," chirps Johnny, beaming. "It's *who*." He leaps up and digs the skull out, palms it, and says, like an actor: "Alas, poor Haydn! I love his music!"

He sits down with the skull in his lap.

"Then you may know," Agnes goes on, "that Haydn died in Eighteen-nine. Austria was at war with France then. A battle was advancing into Vienna. Haydn was buried in the middle of that battle. The local prison chief, a man named Peter, was an amateur phrenologist—"

"What is that?" I say.

"One who studies the conformation of the skull to divine mental faculties," says Johnny.

I guess he can see that I have missed him.

"They study the bumps on your head to see what you're like," he explains.

"They would think that I am pretty complicated," I say, "what with all my bumps."

"Extremely complicated," says Johnny.

"And so," Agnes picks up, "in the middle of all the confusion of the battle, the prison chief, Peter, had the body exhumed, and the head cut off.  He stripped the head of all flesh, studied the skull, and finally pronounced that Haydn had the bumps of music fully developed."

"And what if he hadn't?" asks Johnny, smiling.  "Would this Peter have cancelled his season ticket?"

"I don't know," says Agnes, laughing.  "Anyway, he had planned to return the skull, but had taken too long in his study of it, and now felt that returning it was too dangerous.  Instead, he had an ebony, glass-windowed box made, which he had decorated with a golden lyre.  The skull was placed in this box, on a white silk cushion trimmed with black.

"But Peter lived in fear of being caught with it, and later passed it on to a man named Rosenbaum, who was secretary to Haydn's patron, Prince Esterhazy.  Prince Esterhazy was, of course, unaware of all this, until he decided to give Haydn a more dignified burial than the one he had during the war; and, in course, had the coffin brought to him at Eisenstadt, the capital of Burgenland, in East Austria, where Haydn had lived under his patronage, and opened.  The Prince was horrified to discover that there was only a wig where the head should have been.  He investigated, and traced the decapitation to the prison chief, Peter.  He was furious, and sent the police to Peter, who confessed his deed, and that Rosenbaum now had the skull.  The Prince demanded that the head be returned. Rosenbaum returned a skull.  The Prince had it examined and identified as the skull of a twenty year old man. Haydn died at seventy-seven. Now the Prince had a search made of Rosenbaum's house, but it did not yield any result, as Rosenbaum's wife, the singer Therese Gassmann, had hidden the skull in her straw mattress and lay on her bed during the search.

"It was Frau Rosenbaum who was behind Rosenbaum's refusal to return the skull. The glass and ebony display case containing that gruesome relic you're holding had become the highlight of her famous musical evenings.

"Then the Prince tried bribery. His emissaries promised Rosenbaum a huge sum if he would deliver the skull. Whereupon the besieged Rosenbaum bought the skull of an old man from a Vienna mortuary. This skull was much closer in phrenological detail to Haydn's, and was accepted as the original and interred with Haydn's body.

"On his deathbed, Rosenbaum bequeathed the real skull back to prison chief Peter, who in turn bequeathed it to the Society of Friends of Music in Vienna, who owned a great number of Haydn relics. But Peter's wife gave it to her doctor instead, who presented it to the Austrian Institute of Pathology and Anatomy in Eighteen Thirty-two. They supposedly passed it on to the Society of Friends of Music, to whom it was originally willed by Peter.

"In Nineteen Thirty-two, Prince Paul Esterhazy—direct descendant of Haydn's patron—promised to build a magnificent tomb for Haydn, if the head were restored to the body. But, while the authorities were still discussing the matter, the Second World War erupted. As a result of new political divisions after the war, Haydn's skeleton lay in the Soviet Zone while his skull rested in the International Zone. All of this is public knowledge; but of how the skull was stolen and taken to the Soviet Zone, then retrieved by agents of the Western democracies, nothing has been made public. The world in general still believes the real skull to be in the possession of the Society of Friends of Music, in Vienna.  Both the democracies and the forces of Communism would like to claim the genius for their own, but neither can, until skull and skeleton are reunited.  No price can be put upon the propaganda value of such a coup.”

“And this is the real head?” I say.

“Yes,” says Agnes, “and the Communists know it.  If they get it, they will have Haydn.”

“How did it get to the States?” says Johnny.

“That remains a classified secret,” says Agnes.  “But it’s my father’s job to get it back to Vienna.”

“Why didn’t they send it on a battleship?” I say.

“Classified,” says Agnes.  “But let me say this much.  It’s not generally realized that the skull in Vienna is a fake, as I’ve said.  So everything has to be done—unobtrusively.”  She studies us for a moment, then says: “The head is priceless because you can’t put a price on propaganda value, but there *is* financial value attached to it.  The authorities are offering twenty-five thousand dollars to anyone who is of assistance in recovering the head.  So, if you’ll help us, you wouldn’t be doing it for nothing.”

I look at Johnny.  His green eyes are very bright.

“I can explain a little further,” says Agnes.  “There are two other skulls being pursued right now—bogus skulls—one in Europe and one in Asia.  They are meant to confuse the Communists.”

“Two phonies,” I say, “and we have the real one.  Just like three card monte, eh, Johnny?”

“What do you want us to do?” says Johnny.

“There’s a freighter leaving at four this morning from Pier Ten.  We want to be on it and at sea before Von Heller and Lensky or anyone else knows.  If you and Mr. Morris could get us safely to it . . .”

“Why not a plane?” I say.

"The Captain is our associate. The few other passengers will have been closely screened and will present us with no problems. It's all been arranged, you see. We were supposed to go directly to the ship from Penn Station. Your intervention—"

"Threw your plans off," says Johnny. "Of course we'll help. Pug, would you wrap up Maestro Haydn's head, please. Here, let's have one more drink for the road, then we'll go down the hall and collect your father and see how we can get safely to Pier Ten."

In a few minutes we are standing in front of Doc Schmitt's door. Agnes raps on it lightly, calling:

"Father! Father!"

When no answer comes, Agnes opens the door.

The Doc is stretched out on the carpet. He faces the ceiling, open-eyed.

Agnes runs over and shakes him. "Father! Father!" she cries. She looks back at Johnny, her face twisting with grief. Johnny goes to her, bends down, feels the Doc's pulse, listens for his heart, but it's all automatic, as the old man's eyes keep staring up, like he's looking through the ceiling at the stars. Johnny takes a shoulder and turns him over.

"He's been stabbed," he says.

"Not shot?" I say.

"There's a slit in the back of his coat, not a hole."

"Stabbed in the back," I say. "The dirty cowards."

"But why not shot?" says Johnny, like he's talking to himself.

"Noise," I say.

Johnny gives me an impatient look.

Agnes falls across the Doc's body in a dead faint. It must be delayed reaction. Johnny carries her to an easy chair, gets a damp towel from the bathroom, and pats her cheeks and forehead. Pretty soon she opens her eyes, which look bigger and bluer and sadder than ever. Johnny perches on the arm of her chair and puts an arm around her shoulders, which are shaking. She buries her face in his chest and in ten seconds his suit is wetter than it got in the rain. Finally she pulls back and says: "I shouldn't have left him alone . . ."

"Shouldn't we call the cops?" I say.

"No," says Johnny. "They'll tie us up and we've got to make that ship." He thinks for a minute, then says: "We've got to leave things as they are—for the time being. It's what your father would have wanted, Agnes."

"Yes," says Agnes, wiping her eyes. "He would want me to carry on with the mission. I must pull myself together—for him. What time is it?"

"Nearly three," I tell her.

She says: "And the ship weighs anchor at four o'clock this morning."

"Won't it wait for you?" I say.

"No," she says, shaking her head. "It's to leave without us. The Captain is to assume that we've failed."

"And if you fail," I say, "it will be our fault. Maybe this will cure you of making these wild bets, Johnny," I add, feeling pretty bad about the whole thing. "Now maybe we have even hurt Uncle Sam."

Johnny says: "This must have happened a few minutes ago, when Agnes was in our room. That means that Lensky and Von Heller aren't very far away. Pug," he says, "take Agnes back to our room. Give her a drink. I'll be right along."

"What are you going to do?" I say.

"Place a bet," says he.

"A bet!" I am disgusted—almost.

"Go along now," he says, and I can see that he means business. "But leave the head here."

I have almost forgotten that all this time I am holding the box. I shrug, put the box on the bed, help Agnes to her feet, and take her out. She is pretty shaky, poor kid.

In the hall, she says: "I can trust Johnny, can't I?"

"You can trust us both," I tell her. But I cannot figure out what Johnny is up to.

In our room, I fix two drinks and hand one to Agnes.

"I guess he's right," she says. "The main thing is to get the head to the ship." She threw down her drink like she needed it. "We can call the authorities about—about my father once that's done."

"Sure," I say, pouring her another drink. She is beginning to get back some color. I jaw with her for nearly twenty minutes, and I am beginning to worry about Johnny, when in he comes, carrying the box.

"Now, listen, Pug," he says, "we've got to be careful–"

I interrupt him with: "What have you been up to?"

"Calling us a cab," he says. "I got the cab stand to tap Sleeping Bill. He'll be waiting out front."

"All that time!" I say. "And why didn't you call from here?"

"I didn't want that house dick—or anyone else—to know that anyone from this room was going any place. Now stop asking questions," he says, "and keep sharp." He looks at his watch. "We better get a move on, if we plan to make that ship."

What makes me edgy as we step out of the elevator is that the lobby is deserted. The yokel night clerk and his kid brother are nowhere in sight. But, as we are halfway to the front door, the house dick appears from a room behind the desk.

"Checking out?" he says. "Trying to skip on your bill?"

"We'll be coming back," says Johnny.

"Then," says the dick, "let's have your keys."

Johnny checks his watch. "We haven't much time," he says. "We better pay him."

We go back to the desk. I, for one, feeling kind of sheepish.

"What's the tab?" says Johnny, pulling Doc Schmitt's hundred dollar bill from his pocket.

"Ten G-s," says the dick. "You boys owe Sam the Elephant ten G's."

"Can't stop now," says Johnny, turning us about.

"Oh, yes you can," says the dick, pulling a gat. "Now, if you two and your lady friend will just step back into the office for a minute . . ."

Behind the desk, the dick does a quick frisk on me and Johnny. I guess he thinks he is too much of a gent to touch Agnes. He puts his own pistola away and holds Doc Schmitt's Mauser, taken from Johnny, pointed at us.

He orders us into the office with a jerk of his gun hand.

Who should be waiting for us there but Tweedledum and Tweedledee, our bonebreaking friends from Miami, the bad eggs in plaid suits.

The night clerk and his kid brother are sitting on a small couch, looking meek and mild.

The dick is behind us, blocking the door.

Tweedledum says: "We was just on our way up to see youse. Tanks for coming down."

Tweedledee says: "Mr. Elefanti wants his ten G's, Belmont. I hope for your sake that you have scored well during your brief stay here at the Bon Chance."

Johnny says: "I have, indeed, boys. As a matter of fact, we were off just now to collect a large sum. How about giving me an hour?"

"You must be nuts," says Tweedledum.

"Let's break his arms," says Tweedledee.

"Let's break his knees," says Tweedledum. "Then he can still deal from up his sleeves and make Mr. Elefanti's money back, but he can't run, see?"

"Pug," says Johnny, "we haven't got time for this right now" and I know what he means.

I grab Agnes by the arm and slam back with the box, knocking the Mauser from the dick's hand, as Johnny is making two stabs with his umbrella to the soft round bellies in plaid.

We jam through the door, I lose my grip on Agnes, and she falls. I pull her up, and we beat it out of the hotel to Sleeping Bill's phony Yellow Cab. But Sleeping Bill is not ready for our getaway. He is—sleeping.

Johnny pulls him out of the driver's seat, stuffs the C-note into his pocket, and we leave him standing there. I think he is still asleep as Johnny steers us out through the flood like we are in a motor launch. We head for the river, downtown.

At corners we are making huge wakes of water, which blur the night lights outside so they seem to run crazily down the windshield and windows. But through the back windows I can see headlights that are staying with us.

It is just like this when a shot smacks through the back window between Agnes and me and goes out the front by Johnny's ear, and Sleeping Bill's old car kind of faces one of these steel pylons, that are holding up the West Side Highway. Johnny is a smooth driver and pumps coolly on the brake, coaxing it, but Sleeping Bill's car has made up its mind. At the last second Johnny finds some traction and pulls the wheel sharp. The car leaps, avoiding a head-on, and slams into the pylon sidewise, on my side, back by the gas tank. Then we hear a puff.

"We're on fire!" cries Johnny. "Get out! Out!"

Now the three of us are running in deep water over slippery cobblestones.

I hear Sleeping Bill's phony old cab blow apart. Well, Johnny gave him a C-note, and the car was worth maybe only fifty bucks.

Up ahead of us is coming a police car, siren squawking. The cops in the car don't see us in the rain and the dark. They pass right by us.

I look over my shoulder and see that the Elephant's boys have negotiated a U-turn and are now heading off from whence they came.

Agnes says: "There's the ship! Follow me!"

Aboard, Agnes takes charge. "This way," she says, leading us through passageways. "Cabin A," she says. When we are at Cabin A, she opens the door and walks in ahead of us. We follow her into a good-sized stateroom, I guess you call it.

She crosses the room and turns around to us. Now she is not like Agnes at all. She is like some altogether different person. It is all in the look on her face. I get a cold chill up my back.

"Good morning, gentlemen," comes a voice from behind us.

I turn around and there are Von Heller and Lensky. He is holding his pistola with the silencer.

I am certainly confused. I look at Agnes. She is holding her daddy's Mauser.

"I'll take the package," says Agnes.

"What is going on here?" I say. I must admit I am by now feeling pretty stupid. I look at Johnny, and I am amazed to see that he is smiling. He sees that I am mentally in a bind and is good enough to answer my questions before I ask.

"We are rounding up secret agents, Pug," he says. "Uncle Wild Bill would be proud of us."

"What does he mean?" says Lensky to Agnes.

"I don't have the slightest idea," says Agnes.

"How did she come by the Mauser, Johnny?" I say.

"That falling act she did at the hotel. These two women—not to call them ladies—are aces at scooping up guns."

"But Agnes," I say, sadly depressed, "your father—"

"Doctor Schmitt wasn't her father," says Johnny.

The hatch now opens behind Von Heller and Lensky.

Two men with pistolas in their mitts step in.

"FBI," says one.

"CIA." says the other.

"You might as well hand over your weapons," says Johnny. "There's a Coast Guard cutter blocking your way out to sea."

The feds go around the room collecting from Von Heller, who has a nice little pearl-handled automatic of her own, and Lensky, and Agnes. When the FBI. agent is taking the Mauser from Agnes, Johnny says:

"Agnes, I've been meaning to tell you all night that you have beautiful legs. Would you mind lifting up your skirt so that I can get one good look at them before you go?"

Agnes gives Johnny a grim little smile, shrugs, and lifts her skirt. On her right thigh is a scabbard with a long knife in it.

"That's what killed Schmitt,' says Johnny. "Oh," he adds, "thank you, Agnes. I shall never forget them."

*　*　*

It is a week later and we are sitting in a couple of beach chairs by the pool of Sam the Elephant's Miami Beach hotel. It is a glorious day and there are beautiful ladies stepping all around us and the noise of the diving board and splashing and palm fronds waving over our heads.

Sam the Elephant is in his gold bathing trunks and has a gold towel over one hairy shoulder and is wearing dark shades over his eyes and smoking a huge Havana cigar and sipping occasionally on a straw which draws up something green inside it. Johnny has been telling him the story, as follows, which clears things up for me too:

It seems that Agnes planned to slip away from Schmitt, with the head, at Penn Station, and catch the limo in which are waiting Von Heller and Lensky. The three were then going to drive to the freighter. The freighter was a Communist

307

ship. Agnes, however, has been suspected of being a double agent. In Washington, she has been ordered to pose as Schmitt's daughter, but Schmitt has been warned not to trust her. Agnes, of course, does not know that Schmitt suspects her. Then Schmitt's inspiration about the Lost and Found, plus Johnny's bet with me, messes up her plans.

Later, she dumps Schmitt the hard way, with a knife, when the house dick leaves her alone with him, calls some contact with the freighter, and explains what has happened. She leaves word for Von Heller and Lensky to meet her at the freighter, and that she has a couple of suckers who will help her make the pier without interference.

Then she comes back to our room to tell us the story of Haydn's head, to make enough time elapse before we discover the body so that we will think Von Heller and Lensky have killed Schmitt. Also because the story will help convince us that she is in danger and needs help.

We go and find Schmitt, with me, at least, thinking what she wants us to think, that Von Heller and Lensky have paid Schmitt a visit. But Johnny doesn't think so. What troubles him is that Schmitt is stabbed in the back. Why should Lensky need to use a knife when he keeps waving around a revolver with a silencer on it? And why in the back?

That's when he thinks of Agnes. He sends me off with her to our room, but he keeps the head with him. He's afraid she will use the shiv on me, take the head, and scram.

(When I asked him how come he knows for sure that she has a knife, he says: "It was a logical deduction, Pug, from the circumstances—besides, I felt it on her thigh when I put her in the chair." He guffaws.

"What about me?" I say. "She wouldn't tackle you, Johnny, because you had the Mauser. But suppose she used that pig-sticker on me?" Johnny says: "Why would she? She wanted to keep us with her. Besides, I had the head." Then he laughs and says: "I just had to gamble that she wouldn't knife you, Pug old boy." I say: "Thanks a lot!")

Then Johnny puts in a call to uncle Wild Bill Belmont, in Washington (He says: "I took great pleasure in waking him up at three in the morning"), gets the dope on the situation, and sets the trap at the pier.

Sam the Elephant is delighted with the whole story. He is also delighted that he will get his ten G's when we get the reward, which is to be within a month, from what we are told. But it is our nerve, says Sam the Elephant, which delights him most, the way we have come down to Miami and walked right in on him with our tale. Also, he is a great patriot, he tells us, and appreciates what we have done for our country. He is going to stake us until our money comes, and we will have the best.

He is laughing as he heaves himself up and waddles off, laughing and shaking his head.

A waiter comes out and passes him, bringing a telephone. It is Wild Bill in Washington has something to say.

Johnny is all smiles at first, but then he frowns.

"Wait a minute," he says, "are you sure?"

But I have already heard a click.

Johnny hangs up, looks at me, and says:

"Pug, we've got a problem."

"What's that?" I say.

"The head was a fake. The real skull has been with the Society of Friends of Music in Vienna since Eighteen Ninety-five. The authenticity of the skull in their possession has been proven beyond doubt."

"A fake," I say. "Does that mean we do not get any reward?"

"I'm afraid not," he says. "It seems that Schmitt knew he was carrying a fake. He was under orders to do everything he could to convince Agnes that it was the real thing, and she believed it. And so did we."

"But, Johnny," I say, "now we owe Sam the Elephant the ten G's again—"

"Plus," says Johnny, "five hundred expense money."

"Not to mention," I add to the list of our woes, "our hotel bill."

"We better get packing, Pug," says Johnny.

"So it looks like we are on the run again," I say with a sigh.

I am not overly interested in history, as I have a tendency to think that it is all in the past; but, for what I guess are obvious reasons, I stay interested in the subject of Haydn and his head. I follow it in the newspapers.

They finally get his head and the rest of him together in Nineteen Fifty-four in Burgenland. In Nineteen Fifty-five there is such a thing as an Austrian State Treaty, which is signed by the Four Powers. So it seems that nobody takes over Haydn's country, which joins the U.N. in the same year. All this is very interesting to me, because I feel like, in a little way, I am a part of it. Also, when I think of it now, it brings back the days when Johnny and me were always on the run. Being on the run was a lot of fun if you ran with Johnny Belmont.

# CHARLIE . . . FOR THE LORD

1

Through sad morning eyes the Manager surveyed his dirty dozen, sighed, and  stuck a fat green cigar between his sooty teeth.  He was under orders from his doctor not to smoke, having suffered a minor heart attack earlier in the year, but cigars had come to be his greatest pleasure, though they, and coffee, sometimes made him bilious.  He was over-weight, and had high blood pressure, but he had worked very hard all his life and told himself that he needed food for energy—coffee too, caffeine and nicotine, to get himself going, and to keep himself going.  Thus he had at first tolerated, then made use of, what had become an institution at the Harlem branch of the American Home Supply Company—the pre-work coffee-klatch.  It gave him the chance to look his boys over, to see how they were doing.

Some of these boys would be going to Viet Nam soon. The Manager was a veteran of what he called "War Two." He had a Silver Star and a Purple Heart.

"But that was a long time ago," he told Fairmore, the newest of his boys.  "You weren't even born yet."

"I want to serve my country," said Fairmore.  His Adam's apple bobbed over the big Windsor knot in his stained pink tie, pink as his cheeks, as he swallowed coffee.

"But," said the Manager, "we were fighting for something good.  I don't know about this war."

"But I want to serve my country," Fairmore repeated doggedly.

"Well," said the Manager, "you're probably on the right track.  Where are you from?  You don't sound like a New Yorker."

Fairmore told the Manager that he was an orphan, had no home. He had started from a foster home in New Orleans and had wandered to California.

"That's the Golden Land," Fairmore told the Manager.

When the eighteen-year-old Fairmore mentioned California the middle-aged Manager felt his golden dream being touched, a dream of the past. The Manager had spent the best time of his life in San Diego, before being shipped out to the Pacific Theater. He had met and married his wife there, and she had become pregnant with their son there.

The Manager said: "How do you come to be here, in New York?"

"Oh, I worked for this moving outfit in L.A. Just one truck, the boss, me, and another guy. It wasn't even licensed. The boss got a haul to Chicago. In Chicago, he got a haul here. He was supposed to pay me here, but he disappeared. I only had fifty dollars left from California—then I saw your ad. I was sure lucky to see that ad, I can tell you. I was getting a little scared."

The Manager realized how innocent Fairmore was, despite his knockabout life. He talked about all the places he had been and all the things he had done in a way that showed that he hadn't understood many of his own experiences. The manager decided to keep an eye on him.

His own son would have been a bit older than Fairmore now, had he lived. The Manager might have counseled him not to go into the present war. He might have told his own son to go up to Canada and stay there. But maybe not. What would his wife have thought, had she lived? Why had he survived the accident, to go on alone like this? What had been the point of these ten years? Work! And later, his lady friend, Mavis. When he had had his heart attack, she had acted as if she hadn't known him for the past five years. And he had bought her so many nice things! A good time girl, that was

Mavis. What was it? A fair weather friend! What was the point?

That week the Harlem branch of the American Home Supply Company was pushing 18" x 23" imitation-gilt-framed portraits of Christ. The portraits were of a life-sized, Hollywood-handsome Christ, hair combed, and not too long, a wavy chestnut-brown; neatly trimmed goatee; shoulders covered with an azure mantle. But the great selling feature was the eyes. They were ingeniously made to follow you wherever you went. Step this way, step that, they were on you.

Fairmore had no car, of course, so every morning he strapped eight or ten of the pictures of Christ together and carted them off toward 125th Street, where he was told to go—"then pick a tenement, and start climbing stairs." It was a big hopeful load and it was a summer hot not only with racial friction, but with extreme August heat and humidity, so Fairmore did a lot of sweating as he lugged the pictures. And by mid-week, it came to the Manager's attention that Fairmore had been placing a record number of items in a record number of places, coming back to the store two or three times a day to get another and yet another stack of eight or ten pictures and going out again, an inspired look on his face.

The Manager prided himself on being a tough man; but there was something about Fairmore—his innocence, his eagerness—that touched him through his city armor, and it had occurred to him, as he chomped his green cigar, that Fairmore might not understand that his smile was only meant to be a mask. Vaguely, he grew concerned that Fairmore might be placing more pictures than could be covered by his commissions—even that he might be seeding his record number of placements with his own money. The Manager did not care, usually, who paid, so long as his salesmen did not place any items with junkies or drunks, where you couldn't count on getting them back. But he was worried about Fairmore.

On Thursday morning, while the crew was having coffee, he spoke to him.

"Remember, Fairmore," he said, "you're a salesman. Your job is to collect that dollar down. You're getting it, aren't you?" He stuck his cigar back between his teeth. He felt dyspeptic. Mavis wanted him to take her on a trip somewhere. He thought of California. San Diego. His wife and son. "Aren't you?" he prodded.

Fairmore looked sheepish. "But I'll get it back in commissions, won't I? I mean, it's only a dollar, but I still get four. I get five dollars on each one, isn't that right?"

The Manager held his stomach with one hand and took his cigar from his mouth with the other. "Only when it's collected, Fairmore—only when it's collected. You get the first five that's collected. But the dollar down you keep now. You want to have some money at the end of the week, don't you?"

"Yes, sir."

"Don't put in your own money. A good sale, a good placement, is a solid placement. Make them put up their money—to show good faith."

"Lots of them don't have any money. But I can see that they want the Lord. That's why I know they'll pay."

"No, they won't, and we'll have to repossess the damned things. Make them pay up." He became aware that he was being paged, but he continued to study Fairmore's face.

"Haven't you been peddling anything but those pictures?" he asked. "Just those Christ pictures? Let me see your order book." He was paged again, this time with greater urgency. A pain gripped his side. He said, "Never mind. Later."

2

On Friday evening Fairmore stepped into a tenement building, the last picture of the day, and of the week, under his arm. He was tired and hungry, but he wanted to place the picture before he quit.

The building had seven floors and an elevator, but the elevator stood open with an *OUT OF ORDER* sign on it; and, in it, curled in a profusion of dirty newspapers and greasy rags, which had apparently been used in a recent attempt to repair the broken machine, slept a black man with bristling gray hair and a puckered, sullen face, one large hand clenching the neck of a half full half-gallon of cheap, red wine.

Fairmore climbed the marble stairs, delighting in how they had been worn away by countless footsteps, and feeling, as his feet pressed through the thin soles of his shoes into the concave surfaces, a sense of community with the people whose feet had worn them away.

At the seventh floor he began to knock on doors.

He could hear voices behind the first door: a man and a woman talking, her voice high, even, his deep, and rumbling. They paid no attention to his knock.

He stepped to the next door. Here a large young black man, naked to the waist, poked his head and one shoulder out of the door.

"Good evening, sir," Fairmore said. "I represent the American Home Supply Company. I am going to various homes in the neighborhood . . ."

"No, man; can't use it! don't need it! don't want it," said the man, and pulled the door shut.

Undaunted, Fairmore stepped to the next door and knocked.

A young girl of about his own age answered, and he said, "Good evening, miss. I represent the American Home Supply Company . . ." and so on. But the girl seemed uncomprehending. Fairmore might have wondered at the tracks on her arms, but he could not see them in the poor light. It's doubtful, however, that he would have realized that she was high on heroin.   The range of his experience did not include hard drugs.

She stared at the picture that Fairmore was holding up and did not seem to see him behind  it.  He paused, then repeated, "I am going to homes in the neighborhood to show people this beautiful portrait of our Lord which my company is putting out for only a dollar down and a dollar a week for one year.  It's a hundred dollar value for only half the price; but, really, due to its religious nature, it's beyond price—"

"Is that the Lord, Charlie?" the girl said finally.

"Yes, miss," Fairmore said, and then in the half dark and shadows he saw that she had her blouse unbuttoned, just hanging open, with her young, swaying brown breasts just covered at the nipples.  Her eyes were fixed and strange and wide, and he could see that her body was still covered with a layer of baby fat, and that her breasts were swaying as she swayed, pushing her blouse aside first this way and then that.

"Why he stare at me?"

"His eyes move, miss."

"He watching us."  Her concentration, more even than her state of undress, held Fairmore wordless and waiting. Then she said:  "How much, Charlie?"

"Just fifty-two dollars, miss," Fairmore said, trying not to look at her breasts.  "One dollar down and one dollar a week."

"I want the Lord," she said flatly.

"One dollar—"

"Charlie."  She looked at him for what seemed the first time.  "Mister Charlie . . ."  She tilted her head for him to come in.  "For the Lord, Charlie . . ."

She took his hand and drew him into the apartment.


3

It worried the Manager that Fairmore did not return
to the store on Friday night. He asked several members

of the crew if they had seen him, and when they said that they hadn't, the Manager toughened himself, shrugged, and said, "He'll probably turn up tomorrow. He'll want what he's got coming, if he *has* anything coming."

"He's a jerk," said one of the boys.

"A dumb turkey," said another.

"Why?" demanded the Manager. "Because he's decent?" He stuck his cigar between his teeth and puffed angrily. He was counting out commissions. Fairmore *was* a dumb turkey, he told himself. *Go west, young man!* Now what made him think of that?

The Manager was more worried on Saturday. He thought of calling the police. But, in New York, that was a ridiculous idea. He sighed and went on with his work. Several of the crew were quitting and he was going to put another ad in the Sunday papers, actually to notify them to run last week's ad again. But he had forgotten and now it was too late. He blamed the missing Fairmore for distracting him.

After the crew were off and had left, he worked with a few of the regulars on inventory. What to order? More of those damned pictures of Christ. Fairmore had sold them out.

4

Through the plateglass windows of the Harlem branch of the American Home Supply Company the Manager saw a police car pull in to the curb outside. A couple of local cops, familiar to him, got out and came up to the locked front door. The Manager signaled, made his way through the plastic-covered furniture and lamps and opened the door for them.

"A boy named Fairmore work for you?" asked a cop.

The Manager realized now that he had known that something had happened to Fairmore. He had known it all day.

"Dead. Got his head bashed in."

317

5

The Manager tried to tell Mavis about it later that night. They had had several drinks before he brought it up. He didn't know quite how to explain how he felt about it.

"Sounds like just another dumb kid," she said.

The Manager was a little drunk. He searched for words. It would have something to do with his wife and son, those ghosts, and with the wars, the one in which he had served, as a Sergeant, so proudly, and this one, in which he would have advised Fairmore, and his own son, were they alive, not to serve.

"Don't serve, I would have told them."

"Why not?" asked Mavis.

"Because what we were doing was honorable. I don't feel that anything we do nowadays is honorable."

And it had something to do with Mavis, and this trip she wanted them to take, of which, he became aware, she was now speaking.

He broke in on her. "Let's go to California, Mavis. Let's dump everything and go out to San Diego and get a little apartment and start fresh."

"San Diego! Are you crazy? What's out there? Besides, I like things fine right here in the Big Apple. All I want's a vacation."

The Manager thought of how Mavis had acted when he had been ill, with his heart attack. He thought of her indifference, of her selfishness, of her callous attitude about Fairmore's death.

"Maybe I'll go without you," he said.


6

The Manager didn't go into the Harlem branch of the American Home Supply Company on Monday morning. Somebody else would have to open up. In fact, he was fairly certain that he would never open up again.

The formula of his life must change.  Yet he needed some final thing, an emotional stamp.  So instead of opening the Harlem branch of the American Home Supply Company that morning, he made his pilgrimage to see the black girl, the last puzzle-piece in the week-old saga of Fairmore.  She was in the Women's House of Detention in Greenwich Village.

His police friends had told him the facts of the case, so when he asked her about them it was not in the manner or for the purpose of finding them out, but to hear her tell it, to feel her before him as in his knowledge she had stood before Fairmore, and to try to understand what it had meant.

She spoke in the blurred voice of a junky of how her father had come in and hit Fairmore over the back of the head with a wine bottle.  He was drunk, she said, and didn't want her whoring, especially with no Mister Charlies.  She said that he was always a little crazy when he first woke up, and he had been sleeping somewhere in the building, else he would have seen nothing was happening—"that little white boy scared shitless," she concluded.

Yes, the police had told the Manager that the old man had told them much the same thing.  The girl had fallen silent. To keep her talking, the Manager said:

"But if your father didn't want you to do it—"

"I got a big habit, but I wouldn't of gone 'gainst my daddy if I wasn't so high and that that boy had sumptin I really wanted."

A pain twisted in the Manager's side.

"What?"

"The Lord," the girl said, with final banality or profundity.

The Manager summed it up this way: he had been the Manager of the Harlem branch of the American Home Supply Company, and Fairmore had worked for him, and this girl was one of their customers, and Fairmore would have gone broke giving his own money away, come out at the end of the week with nothing; and he, the Manager of the American Home Supply Company, would have taken this girl's money, had Fairmore got it, and Fairmore's money, and spent it on a vacation for Mavis, and the American Home Supply Company would have lost nothing. The American Home Supply Company never lost anything.

He studied the girl's pretty, dark face, at once alien and familiar, and realized, saw with simple, startling clarity, that Fairmore had had his head bashed in and half his blood spilled over the bed of a girl even younger and more lost than himself, one of the dollar-down, faceless ones, for him no longer faceless, no longer alien.

# MURDER ON THE ROAD

I noticed what beautiful teeth the young man had. Mine are missing or turned to coffee, red wine, and smoke. The hitchhiker had a seabag stencilled with my name. I have an unusual name and it could not have been sheer coincidence. I was going west—he said west was fine with him. The Mojave highway was empty for as far as I could see. I stopped the car. He tried to open the door, but I had them all locked. I shot him, then unlocked the doors and pushed his body out into the roadside sand. I got out and rolled him out of view, down a sand dune, and buried him, dust to dust. Well, I might as well have done so, even if I didn't. What I did to him was nearly as bad, maybe worse. I let him live and become me. So most of my life I have been living inside a much younger man. It was quite an adventure, being young. He ran a lot, ran long distances and very quickly short, marathons and dashes. He got embarrassing erections on buses, hanging on to the strap, and would have to face away in a twisted posture, but the rest of him, being loose, not stiff, he could contort and hide his secret lust. In middle age, he was big-voiced and positive, sure of everything, in a way I find impossible; I, who doubt all. I have many photographs of him. Lifting barbells. Boxing. He is always glad to pose. Myself, I hate having my picture taken. It is certain to come back to me as an old fart, grinning stupidly at the camera, as if to say, "I am still like him, like that hitchhiker." But I am not just like him, not at all like him, inside or out. I miss him but I don't want him back. I would rather crawl forward and under; for, now that I think about it, he never was so hot, never the number he thought he was.

# THE CODE OF THE BLUE COMMUNE

The Tribe woke that morning to the bright hard sun of the Arizona winter sky. That is—all but one of the Tribe woke to that sun. One slept on, and would sleep on through eternity.

The one who slept was known as Little Lamb. No one knew what his real name was. He had come from the East with some others who had gone on to the West. Little Lamb had stayed. He had stayed because he had fallen in love with Ketchup, the red-haired mystery girl. Some said that Ketchup had come from the East, where she had been a groupie, a camp-follower of rock musicians. Others said that she had come from the West, where she had lived on the bohemian beaches of Southern California.

Ketchup was a mystery girl, not because she said nothing about herself, but because she told so many stories, many of which were contradictory, that no one knew what to believe about her. It was of no great importance, however, to the Tribe, that both Little Lamb and Ketchup did nothing to clarify their histories. It was an unwritten code of the Tribe, or the Family, as it was variously known, not to ask questions.

It was left to Marshal Tom McCool to do the necessary questioning, and unfortunately one of the two persons who might be able to spread some light on the subject was dead.

"Poor Little Lamb," as Ketchup had put it.

"Poor Little Lamb" had been six and a half feet tall, dark-bronzed faced, blue-eyed, handsome as a star, and heavily be-wooled about the head and face. "Poor Little Lamb" had been an outsized "Christ-figure," according to some.

"He's a land-locked Billy Budd," as one of the Family put it.

"Why would anyone want to insert a ten-inch dagger in

his throat?" asked Marshal McCool. "I thought you people were anti-violence, all for love, like."

"We're just people, Marshal." Ketchup threw a pair of pretty, pink-palmed hands out. "We are trying to get away from your kind of violence, but we grew up in your world, and the violence of that world is in us just as it's in you. The difference is, that we're trying to get away from it, in our heads and in our life-style."

"My kind of violence! Look, Miss, I came here to your flower heaven to investigate a murder. Not the other way around, if you please. Now, you say you don't know Little Lamb's real name or where he came from, but people around here say that he was in love with you. I would imagine that you might know something about a man who was in love with you. Isn't there anything you can tell us?"

"Little Lamb broke the code, I can tell you that."

"The code?"

"Yes, the code. Little Lamb had no right to love me. I mean special like that. Here we all love each other the same way. We women are married to all the men, all the men are our husbands. Little Lamb wanted me all to himself. He broke the code. Otherwise there never would have been violence. He made the violence happen. I'm only surprised that it was him who was killed. I half expected him to kill somebody else. He had returned to the standards of your world."

"You didn't return his love?"

"I loved him as I love all my husbands. But he spoiled my love for him."

"Did he break the code right from the beginning? How long has he been here?"

"No. At first he was like all of us. He told me once that he loved our way of life. That was after he'd been here a month or so. He would have been here around six months, now, I guess."

"Now, look, Ketchup, I'm looking for a motive. Somebody put a shiv in Little Lamb's throat. Somebody had a reason for doing that. Money means nothing to you people, or so you say, and I'm sort of inclined to believe you, within certain limits. So why did little Lamb get it? Did one of your people go ape on acid and perform a human sacrifice?"

"We're not lunatics here."

"It can happen, can't it?"

"It can, yes. But that's a whole different thing. We don't go in for the spooky stuff. We're not like that."

"Well, you people have been around here for over a year, and I must admit I haven't heard of any of that type of thing taking place out here. But there's a first time for everything, isn't there?"

"No. Not here. These are gentle kids. Real love children."

"Okay. Let's say, for the sake of argument that nobody went ape on acid or satanism. Money's out—and that leaves love. Or, more accurately, love's angry side, jealousy. Do you agree?

"I don't like to, but I think it must be that. It could be one of the other wives who was in love with Little Lamb and jealous of his love for me."

"I think that it's more likely that it's one of the other husbands. Think about it, Ketchup. Who among the husbands, besides Little Lamb, seemed like he might be on the verge of breaking the code? In other words, was there anyone else who had a special love for you?"

"Well, maybe Mooncalf. Mooncalf seemed not to love Little Lamb as he should. And Mooncalf did come to me more than to the other wives. We held a council once, and he was—well, we all sort of talked to him about it. You know, we rapped it out and he seemed to dig. After that, he was more regular."

"When was that?"

"Oh, a month or so ago. I'd forgot all about it."

"Why wasn't Little Lamb talked to at a council?"

"He was. Twice. But it didn't do any good. He had been divorced by all the wives and ordered out of the Tribe."

"Why was he still here?"

"Well, he just wouldn't go. There wasn't anything much we could do about it. We couldn't use violence to make him go."

"Somebody finally did."

"That's not funny, Marshal."

"I didn't mean it to be."

"Well, we had to feed him. He was a human being. We couldn't just let him starve."

After the questioning of Ketchup—whose real name turned out to be Tania Brady—Marshal McCool called in the young man known as Mooncalf. McCool had seen Mooncalf in town a couple of times: a bearded, curly-haired, lanky kid of nineteen or twenty, with a look of perpetual pain on his face.

"Look, fuzz," said Mooncalf as he stepped inside the kitchen tent which McCool was using as a kind of operations room, "I had nothing to do with this thing. I don't know what that flaming witch of a Ketchup has been telling you, but if anybody knows who killed Little Lamb it's her. Maybe she did it herself."

"That's a serious charge," said McCool, an expression of mild surprise on his face. "Why do you make it?"

"Because Little Lamb was going to leave for the West Coast today, and he wasn't going to take her with him."

"You're saying that she was in love with Little Lamb?"

"Of course she was. Did she deny it?"

"Well, according to Ketchup, Little Lamb was in love with her. She said that he had been making a nuisance of himself and had been expelled from the commune."

"She's a liar! Little Lamb was the most Christ-like person I've ever known. He could never make a nuisance of himself in any way. He was going to leave the Tribe because she wouldn't let him alone. All the other wives and husbands were upset about it. Little Lamb belonged to everybody, but she started everybody fighting over him by trying to claim him all for herself. That's why he was leaving, to help us all find peace again. He was good. A real saint."

"And you think that Ketchup killed him because he was going away without her?"

"Yeah. She begged him not to leave her. She must have lost that temper of hers last night and stabbed him."

"She thinks you did it."

"Sure, she has to blame somebody. She never loved me as she should have, so I'm the goat."

"I'm afraid the goat has already been sacrificed."

"I dig," said Mooncalf, and sulked out, following the line of Marshall McCool's gesture.

The third person Marshal McCool questioned that morning was the Tribe's elected leader, a tall, burly man who was called Father Time.

"I've heard your people refer to your camp as the Blue Commune," McCool said. What does that signify?"

"That signifies under the sky, mountaintop. But what's that got to do with Little Lamb gettin' his throat opened?"

"Nothing," said McCool, "Except by irony. Nature, love, and a man named Little Lamb with a ten-inch dagger in his throat!"

"This don't happen around here every day, you know," said Father Time. He was decidedly defensive, thought McCool, but it did not necessarily read as an attitude of guilt. It appeared to McCool that Father Time was genuinely upset that ill-fame of any sort should come to the Blue Commune.

This followed, thought McCool.

In the past these people had stayed out of the way of the local people and had caused the authorities no trouble. McCool knew that there were drugs all over the place, but why stir up trouble? So long as the local people had no complaints, he would leave the Blue Commune alone.

But now things would have to be different, and Father Time knew it.

"Look, Father Time," said McCool, "I've never bothered you or your people, have I?"

"No, you been straight," replied Father Time, rather grudgingly.

"Well, it comes to this: I can't promise anything, but I'll do my best to see that this thing doesn't blow up too big, if you'll play it straight with me."

"What do you want me to do?"

"Tell me whatever you know about this, naturally. And make it straight."

"And what do we get back?"

"Anybody who isn't directly implicated can get a three-hour start toward the state line. That's all I can do, in a situation like this.

"Living the way you do, the D.A. might be able to lock up the whole lot of you as conspirators, accomplices and accessories before and/or after the fact. And by this afternoon two-thirds of the county are going to be screaming for just that. If you want to get the innocent among you away clean, you'll tell me what you know. Otherwise—there's always the junk, too."

"What makes you think that the whole bunch of us freaks didn't get together and sacrifice Little Lamb to the sun god in an acid ritual?"

"Because he's just lying there in his tent with a ten-inch blade jammed to the hilt through his neck. That means that at least five inches of that blade are in dirt. It might not have happened there, but that makes it look as if it did. And that isn't exactly the setting for a ritual murder. If you people were going to perform a ritual murder, you'd lay your victim out on a rock, wouldn't you?  Or hang him on a cross.  Something symbolic and comic-bookish, or don't I read your mentality correctly?"

"We're not idiots, McCool."

"You better hope that I keep on thinking you are.  Now let's have what you know. For starters, was Little Lamb ordered out of camp, or was he going to leave on his own hook?"

"Neither, exactly. We all agreed, him and us, that if the ideals of the commune were going to survive, it would be better if he went away for a while.  Say, McCool, if that blade is still in the ground, how'd you know it was ten inches long?"

"The scabbard matches the dagger.  By the way, who owns, or owned, that knife?"

"Everybody.  It belongs to the Tribe."

"That's what I figured.  Would you mind telling me what you people use a ten-inch dagger for?"

"It's a religious thing, but not the kind of thing—"

"I told you, I dismissed that theory early on.  But what did you do with that sword?"

"We cut grass with it."

"You mean pot?  Marijuana?"

"Yeah.  It grows wild all abouts here.  In the summer, when it's growing, we go out at midnight and cut the stuff. The dagger was our official family cutter.  Like a religious ritual.  Dig?"

"Dig.  Where was the knife kept?"

"We kept it right in the middle of the camp, tied to a cross.  Anybody could take it."

"What about Little Lamb? Do you know anything about him?  His real name?"

"No.  He came to us six months ago.  He came with friends.  They went on. He stayed. He was a saint."

"That's all?"

"That's all.  We don't ask questions."

"If he was ever fingerprinted, as seems likely, we'll know who he was by tonight or tomorrow morning."

"And what will you know then, McCool, a name? He'll still be Little Lamb."

"Did Little Lamb stay on here at the Blue Commune because he fell in love with Ketchup, Miss Brady, or for other reasons?

"Not for Miss Brady."

"I've heard from some of your people that Little Lamb was in love with Ketchup. She even said that he was."

"Woman's vanity."

"And the others?"

"You the one said they had comic book mentalities."

"You mean you people gossip about each other just like the people out in the big bad world?"

"We are human here, too."

"All too human, apparently. Father Time, I am becoming disillusioned with you flower people."

"We're only trying, McCool. That's more than the rest of you do."

"What's your real name, Father Time? Your mother didn't christen you that, did she?"

"My name is Father Time. Furthermore, I have never been arrested. Neither have I been in the army. There is no way of ever identifying me as anybody but who I am—Father Time. So you might as well give up on that right now, McCool."

"Okay, for now. But as soon as I decide to know, I'll find out."

"How? Nobody in this camp knows my name. What are you going to do? Are you going to beat me with a rubber hose? Come on, McCool, I don't think you're the type. Forget it, I'm Father Time, that's all."

"Watch it, you might be Father Time in the State Pen for withholding evidence. Don't say I didn't warn you. Now, what about the dame, Ketchup?  And what about this kid, Mooncalf?"

"Ask me."

"Was there anything between them?"

"Mooncalf dug her.  What can I say?"

"He was in love with her?"

"Yeah, I guess."

"Was it—how do you people say it?  A special thing, out of the code?"

"Maybe.  Yeah, I guess."

"How did she feel about him?"

"He was only a kid to her, nothing.  Just one of the husbands."

"He's turned on her now.  He seems to despise her.  He appears to have worshiped Little Lamb."

"That's natural, ain't it?  He'd come on like he dug Little Lamb so nobody'd think he did it, wouldn't he?"

"Sounds good.  Go on."

"Well, he comes on now like he hates Ketchup so's nobody thinks his loving her was a motive."

"He accused her of doing the job."

"He don't think anybody'll believe that."

"Why not?"

"'Cause no woman would have the strength to drive that knife through a big man's neck and five more inches into the dirt."

"Well, you're quite a detective, Father Time, as well as a male chauvinist pig."

"I told you, we aren't idiots."

"So your bet is that Mooncalf was in love with Ketchup, and was afraid that she'd go off with Little Lamb, and, maybe in a fit of jealousy, killed him."

"I ain't saying that."

"But you are, by implication.  But how do you account for the fact that Ketchup said that she was being annoyed by

Little Lamb?  If she loved him—"

"She's a smart girl.  She would say that now, so as to stay clear of the trouble."

"Disown the whole thing.  Is that it?"

"Makes sense, don't it?"

"Take a guess," said McCool suddenly, "how many people have you got in this camp?"

"You mean how big is our tribe?"

"That'll do."

"Don't know, exactly.  Maybe seventy-five."

"And in the summer you go out at midnight and harvest that pot?  All of you?"

"Yeah, so what?"

"That's quite a haul, isn't it?  Father Time, you ain't gonna sit there and tell me that you people smoke all that pot. You sell it, don't you? You deal? Give it to me straight. Now let's have it. Who deals?"

"Okay, so I do the dealing.  So what?"

"In other words, you lead that pack of comic-book people out to those fields in the moonlight and with your magic dagger start the harvest celebration, then the tribe goes to work and brings it in by the bushel. You do the diviying. The kids get a share to keep them happy and stupid and you store the rest away, for the benefit of the tribe, only not really for their benefit, but to sell."

"I sell it to buy us all groceries.  We've gotta eat like everybody else."

"Can it, Father Time.  You sell enough stuff to supply the Army, Navy and Marine Corps with food for a century.  I was told that you haven't been in camp for a few weeks. Where have you been?"

"All right. I've been in Mexico and then in New York. Why bother to ask if you know?"

"Just wanted to hear you say it.  You picked up heroin for pot money in Mexico and took the heroin to New York where you supplied dealers. Say yes."

"I ain't saying nothing else till I talk to my lawyer. You're a fink, McCool."

"And you're a Brady, Father Time. The New York police sent a copy of a certificate of marriage between a Miss Tania Armstrong and a Mr. Timothy Brady out here when you people first started the Blue Commune. The local citizenry wanted to know what kind of people were moving in among them. The report I made to the Chamber of Commerce dispelled a lot of fears. Just a married couple and a bunch of harmless hippie drop-outs.

"Now, Father Time, tell me what really happened? Did Little Lamb and Ketchup get too close while you were away making deals? Those people that Little Lamb came here with—New York dealers? West Coast dealers? Were Little Lamb and Ketchup going to split out with the profits? You plunged that knife into Little Lamb's neck, Brady, and you and that fire-topped wife of yours decided to put it onto the kid, Mooncalf."

"That's right, Marshal. Now just sit tight while Tim puts some rope around you." Tania Brady held a hard, cold object to the back of McCool's neck. Tim Brady's face broke into a large cheerful smile. He said: "Good girl."

"So," said McCool, "he runs a knife through your boyfriend's throat and the next morning you help him get away. You people of the Blue Commune have a strange code. Only the gutter-rats of the underworld know how it works."

"Shut up, McCool," said Tania; "you think I'm going to let you have Tim, because of what happened with Little Lamb! Yeah, I went for Little Lamb, in my fashion, but he's dead. I've been with Tim a long time; I ain't gonna cross him for the Establishment. Come on, Tim, tie him up."

"There are two other men from my office here. As soon as they see you take off they'll be after you," said McCool.

"Sorry, McCool. Their car has four flat tires, and we'll

take yours.  How are they going to follow us?  Run?"

"You've got a smart girl there, Brady.  Maybe too smart. Keep an eye on her, or you're liable to end up like Little Lamb."

Suddenly McCool heard a scream and the sounds of a struggle behind him.  Brady, who had been trying McCool's legs to the rungs of a chair, leaped to his feet, a horrified, stunned look on his face, and wavered uncertainly.

McCool dove, ramming a shoulder into Brady's midriff. Brady's chest came down on McCools's back.  McCool heard the breath heave from Brady with a woosh.  He sounded like a crushed bellows.

But McCool's left leg tangled in the loose ropes, and he was jerked to the floor like a roped steer.

Brady staggered backwards, clutching his stomach, his chest heaving.  His eyes darted wildly from the sprawled McCool to the struggle that was taking place behind the lawman.  McCool got to his feet, keeping his eyes fixed on Brady. Whatever was happening behind him had Brady plenty scared, and that was enough for McCool.  McCool desperately tried to kick free of the rope that entangled his boot. Brady was coming at him now.

McCool stepped sideways, dragging the chair with him. Then, just as his boot slipped free, Brady was on him.  The impact of Brady's short, cracking uppercut sent McCool sprawling.  For an instant, he lay stunned, panting.  He was able to lift his head in time to see Brady's heel vanish beyond the tent flap.  He rolled over on his stomach and saw Tania Brady being slowly and methodically choked from behind by Mooncalf, who held the cheaply bejewelled scabbard of the ritual knife across her milk-white, slightly freckled throat.

The girl was still conscious, her fierce blue eyes rolling wildly, her throat clicking for air.  Half of Mooncalf's face was buried in her fiery mane; the other half, the part that McCool saw, had gone mad, the tender boyish mouth torn down like a jagged scar, the eye a glinting coin.

McCool scooped up the pistol that Tania had dropped and, in a continuous motion, hooked the fingers of his free hand over the scabbard, and sent the pistol glancing off Mooncalf's temple.

McCool yanked at the scabbard, and Tania Brady dropped to the floor unconscious between himself and Mooncalf. With the speed of a cat, Mooncalf let go the scabbard. McCool reeled backwards. Mooncalf kicked out, knocking the pistol from McCool's hand. Both went for the pistol. Mooncalf got it, and ran from the tent. McCool was on his heels.

Fifty feet away, McCool's Chevy, with Brady driving, was pulling off, heading for the town road. Mooncalf stopped short, whirled about, and caught McCool running, clipping him across the side of the head with the pistol. McCool's momentum, plus the blow, sent him sliding belly down. He looked up, drunkenly. Mooncalf raised the pistol in a straight-arm aim. He fired six times.

The shots echoed, whining back from the hills that surrounded the Blue Commune. They drummed against the clear, cold sky.

By the third shot, McCool's eyes were on the car. With the practiced eye of an expert marksman, he picked up the uneven line of punctures. He had counted to the third when he saw the fourth appear, a black pock on the car's white side.

The first shot smashed through the rear fender; the next, higher, through the rear door; the third hit the window of that door, turning it milky; the fourth and fifth made a tight group at the top of the car.

The Chevy swerved and ran off the dirt road into a ditch. It sat rocking for a moment, then came a small puffing sound, and a long delicate whisp of flame rose from the hood. Suddenly the car vanished inside an angry red cloud.

The sound of the explosion rocked the Blue Commune.

Leading him back to the tent, McCool casually took the empty pistol from Mooncalf's limp hand.

The two troopers who had accompanied McCool, joined the denizens of the Blue Commune who were already gathering about the smoldering car. McCool didn't have to look. He knew. He had watched as the sixth bullet turned red on Father Time's right temple. Why did you do it?" the Marshal said, eyeing Mooncalf doubtfully.

The boy, his downy face gleaming in the midday sun, breathed heavily several times, then said, in a shaky, quavering voice: "Don't you see? I loved Little Lamb and love is the most important thing in the Blue Commune."

# SMOKE



*A Dialogue as if Performed by Bogie and Bacall*

She paused, gazing without expression at the moldering, unfiltered cigarette she held between her fingers, then said, "You know, the thing about love is . . . "

"Like your cigarette " he said.  "It has to be unfiltered and leave stains on your fingers."

"When you say the word love," she said, "smoke should come from your tongue."

"You mean that it's dangerous."

"I mean don't say it unless you mean it.  It's a sacred word."

"And who uses it should be willing to die for its subject."

"Die for me.  I'd die for you."

"You mean you'd die for love."

"Look at my beautiful fingers."

"Stained."

"Look at my beautiful eyes."

"Red."

"Here, take a deep drag," she said, and turned the wet end toward his wet mouth.

"It's hot and wet," he said.

"Like my best kiss."

"Your smokey kiss."

"Like a street in L.A., where you have to run inside at every corner to catch a breath of air-conditioned air, or your eyes will burn and tear until you can't see where you're going.  Take a long drag."

"It's dangerous."

"Yes."

"I can taste your chewing gum in in.  Juicy Fruit."

"And now I can taste your breakfast.  Coffee.  Coffee and more coffee."

"Our habits become identity."

"Love is more than I can bear," she said, snuffing the butt out in an ashtray full of similar, lipsticked butts, ashes on her crimson nails.  "Almost," she added, shaking another unfiltered cig from a pack.  "I'm a chain smoker," she said, then laughed.  "I'm also a chain-lover."

"You've got the habit," he said.  "Both habits.  Both bad."

"But I'm starting on a brand-new pack of Luckies," she said, lighting up.

# NEEDLENECK
*a noir novel*

<blockquote>

*The "Divine Pageant" of the Paradiso belongs
to the world of what I call the* high *dream, and
the modern world seems capable only of the*
low *dream.*

—*T.S. Eliot*

</blockquote>

## Chapter 1

### THE SAINTS AND SINNERS CLUB

Long ago, in a dark time, a young man, apparently
uncertain and possibly afraid, stepped into an unfamiliar bar.
He felt that he was losing himself, was out in search of that
self, desperate to save it. Seated, he looked beyond the window of the dismal barroom, into the bleak, wintry street, as if
hoping to find there the answer to a puzzling question, but
saw only an old newspaper flash by the steam-frosted window, like a mad, flapping wraith.

Feeling suddenly constricted, he got down from his
stool, drew it back from the sticky, initial-carved mahogany
bar, and bumped into a young woman who was passing behind him. She laughed, doing a quick sidestep, avoiding a
full collision.

"Excuse me," he said, as his stool tipped over. He
caught a rising chrome leg in his right hand while smiling an
extended apology back over his left shoulder. She was side-
stepping perilously over his big, black heels. He righted the
stool, then stood dusting his smooth, rust-stained hands. The

338

young woman waited patiently, a good-humored smile on her face.

"Really," he apologized again, his voice cracking slightly with embarrassment, "I am very sorry."

"Apology accepted," said the young woman, with a shrug and a soft laugh.

"No harm done. But I'm glad I'm wearing boots and not nylons." She grinned, winked, and passed down the bar, toward the rear, his haunted, dark eyes following her, and took a seat at the return by the window.

The place was empty but for himself, the young woman, and the bartender, a humorously wicked-looking, wall-eyed old man, who, after drawing the young man's beer, had shuffled off to his post by the cash register, where he stood dozing. The young man pushed back his left sleeve and studied his calendar wrist watch, much aware of the girl's presence at the front-end of the bar. It was just three in the afternoon. The watch was a month old, a Christmas gift from Father Ryan, under whom the young man served as curate at St. Saviour's, a small lower-middle-class parish in the Chelsea neighborhood of Manhattan. Enclosed with the watch was a note, written in Father Ryan's spidery script, that read: *My dear Father Din, I have noticed that of late you do not seem ever to know what time it is. Perhaps this will help. Yours with love in Christ, Father Liam Ryan.* The watch was a fine, sophisticated instrument, but it could supply no answers for the questions that vexed him. Father Din brushed the cuff of his charcoal-grey-tweed jacket back over its complicated face, took a sip of stale flat beer, and tried to think of other, more pleasant things. He wondered about the young woman. He could not remember having seen her come in. He thought that she must have been here, but in the back, when he entered. Surreptitiously, he glanced down the bar at her, caught her eye, and looked away.

He judged her to be about his own age, twenty five, perhaps younger. She was wearing a snug-fitting, burnt-orange turtle-neck sweater, a wide black belt, a long skirt of muted-green-tweed, and black boots, the block-heels of which added about three inches to what Father Din guessed to be a natural height of five-seven. She was perhaps too heavy-breasted to be a fashion model, but she had the general figure and looks of one. Her hair was light-caramel-colored, worn long, and flowing from beneath a Hunter-green, tasseled tam. Suddenly she crooned down the bar, in a rich, soft voice: "Pardon me . . . I was wondering if you'd shoot a game of pool with me? There's a table in the back." Only now did Father Din quite realize that his eyes had drifted back to her. He had been staring at her. He started to speak, but before he could find his words, she had added, sweetly imploring: "Oh, please do! I'd enjoy it so much."

"Well . . . sure. Why not?" Turning to rise, he knocked over his beer glass. He watched as beer ran wildly over the bartop. "Oh, this is awful," he said. He forced a laugh, adding: "You must think I've had too much."

"Now don't go getting paranoid, buddy," the bartender croaked. "After twenty years almost in this business I ought to be an expert on who's had too much and who ain't, and I say you ain't. Now, don't you worry about it; I'll have it cleaned up in a sec. You want a refill?" He had mopped up the bar while speaking.

"Beer isn't the right thing for pool, anyhow," said the young woman, coming up the bar. "It makes you too dopey. If you want to shoot good pool you've got to drink something that'll wake you up. Do you mind if I order for you?"

"Well—"

"Oh, please: let me," she insisted. "Give the gent a Scotch Rocker, Tiger . . . on me."

"Really, I don't think—"

"Now, not a word!"

"You want a fresh one, Toddy?"

"Yeah, Tiger, one for me too." She turned to Father Din. "I hope you don't mind my ordering for you. Sorry, if I'm being presumptuous. Tell yourself that I'm a lonely girl who's gone and let herself get a bit too high." She smiled, her eyes warm and gleaming. "My name's Toddy Muir," she went on, rather breathlessly. "Oh, and this is Tiger—Tiger Hartzmann." The bartender nodded, and placed their drinks before them. "He got that name—Tiger—when he was a wrestler. Right, Tige?"

"Yeah, I used to wrastle," said the bartender, a gleam of suppressed pride in his old-time celebrity surfacing for an instant on his watery wall-eye. "I was on TV nearly four hundred times. But that was a long time ago. Listen to Toddy, she'll have you thinking I still had the diamond belt."

"You *are* still champ," Toddy asserted.

"Listen to the kid!" He gave Father Din a wild, wall-eyed wink. "No, I'm just a tired-out old man. But I held the champeenship gold belt fourteen times. Lost it the last time to the Great Destroyer. Then I had to give up wrastling; it was too hard on my kidneys. I've got what they call a floating kidney. Have you heard of that?"

"Yes, I have," Father Din affirmed. "But I thought wrestling was . . . well, safe, like show business."

"Hell, show business ain't safe," said Tiger. "It wasn't wrastling that started my kidney floating around; it was show business. The first time it bothered me was right after I did a long fall through a skylight at Universal, when I was a stuntman. That was twenty years before I became a wrastler." He shook his great head at Father Din's ignorance. "You kids don't know nothing," he said. "It's the generation gap all over again, only this time it's the Xers versus the baboos."

"Baboos?"

"Babyboomers."

"You tell him, Tiger," said Toddy, nudging Father Din in the ribs with her elbow.

"Well, go ahead," said Tiger, mildly aggrieved, "take your drinks and go shoot pool, before my little girl here has a conniption." He limped back to the cash register, shaking his head, and instantly fell into a doze.

Father Din took the glasses from the bar and handed Toddy Muir her drink. "I'm sorry—" he began; but Toddy cut his sentence short by putting a long, transparent fingernail to her puckered lips. Then she took a sip of her drink, and smiled over the rim of her glass, saying: "You mustn't be so sorry all the time. Repeated apologies can be a sign of emotional insecurity." She studied his face, frowning beautifully. "You have a good face," she went on. "A square jaw—that's strength. And your nose isn't too small. A prominent nose is another indication of strength, and also of leadership. Take de Gaulle, for instance. Your eyes aren't large. But that could mean that you have depth. You know, it's odd; your face is small for such a big man. I'd like to feel your bumps."

"My bumps?"

"Yes. You know: phrenology."

"Oh. You mean read my character by interpreting the bumps on my head?"

"That's right. I used to be into all that sort of thing—Tarot cards, palmistry, pyramid-power, astrology, haruspicating. You know—New Age stuff."

"Do you believe in that sort of thing?"

"Oh, I don't know. Not really, I suppose. Of course, I was just joking about the bumps—it doesn't seem believable that doctors once took phrenology seriously. But it makes a more pleasant subject than the daily news, don't you think?"

"Well, I guess you've got a point there. As a matter of fact," said Father Din, inspired, "I do tend to believe in semeiotics—signs, you know. Signs and wonders. I came in here because of the name—The Saints and Sinners Club. Sometimes I feel that God sends us messages . . .”

“Any old how,” Toddy broke in, not caring for the direction of the conversation, “I think that you have a good face. That’s why I don’t like to hear you say you’re sorry so often. What have you got to be so sorry about?”

“No,” said Father Din, “I only meant to say that I should have introduced myself . . .”

Toddy waited, expectant, but Father Din could think of no name to give but his own. Toddy raised her eyebrows—two long, fine golden feathers—and smiled, blinking. “Have you forgotten it?” She laughed.

“Hop, Hopkins,” he blurted. “Sam. Sam Hopkins.”

“Pleased ta meetcha, Sam,” she said, grinning, and using the name in a way that had an element of teasing in it. She grabbed his hand and pumped it. “Shall we play now?”

The backroom was long, narrow and dark; it ended in a twin-doored wall, from which the only illumination, a pair of lighted glass signs reading, left, LADIES, right, GENTS, dimly shown. But Toddy, floating rapidly in the vague light—rather like an ascending angel, thought Father Din—with the certainty of familiarity, found the fine chain—Father Din could hear it clicking against the bulb—and in a moment they stood in a wide, bright circle of light.

“I hadn’t realized it was getting so late,” she said.

Father Din checked his watch again. “It’s after four.”

“It gets dark so early in winter,” Toddy said, wistfully. “I hate winter. I like to see the sun shining.”

“Oh, I don’t know,” said Father Din. “I rather like winter. It’s . . . private.”

“I think winter is a downer,” Toddy insisted, collecting the balls that were scattered on the table. “It’s so depressing. Sometimes I feel that I’ve lived in winter all my life.”

They chose cuesticks and racked up the balls for rotation, which Toddy said was her favorite because it was simple.  Toddy shot first, breaking the triangle and scattering the bright balls about the table.  The yellow threeball sank.  She sank three more lowballs and scratched, sinking the white cueball.

Father Din could handle a cuestick.  He often shot pool at St. Savior's Boys' Club.  He was no Minnesota Fats, but here, with Toddy Muir's warm, soft eyes fixed upon him, he bungled even simple shots.  But that was of no importance.  What was important was that he felt as if he were being caught up in something; as if he had lost control of the situation.  Fortunately, there was still time to turn back, from what, he wasn't quite sure.  He decided to leave as soon as the game was over.

"You're not from around here, are you?" Toddy asked.

"I'm looking for an apartment," he lied.  "What neck of the woods are we in, anyway?"

"Funny you should say that!  The locals call it Needle-neck, because of the junkies.  They've invaded the neighbor-hood."

"That doesn't sound good."

"No, but it is gentrifying around here, too.  In spots.  A lot of artists and gallery owners are moving here—where the rents were rock-bottom—but that's beginning to push the prices up a bit.  This is still a pretty dangerous area, though.  I don't mean to discourage you, but there's a lot of junkies down here, lots of muggings and robberies.  A lot of the new galleries are run by women, and the hypes go after them.  A couple have been raped.

"You see," she went on, taking aim, "I grew up here.  When I was a little girl, there were still flower children and hippies everywhere.  But, like they say, the more things change, the more they remain the same."

As Father Din watched Toddy Muir moving about the table, shooting easily and expertly, his thoughts began to shift, to focus with his dark eyes on her long, lithe arms, bending and reaching, capably and rhythmically, over the dazzling green of the felt. There came upon him a pervading sense of unreality, heightened by an undercurrent of nervous excitement. Perhaps it was the drink that had done it. His limit was an occasional glass of Irish whiskey, to keep Father Ryan company. Whatever it was, he had a sense of being out of time, island-isolated. Toddy was lighting a cigarette, long, sandy lashes delicately flicking smoke away. She placed her cigarette on an ash tray, aimed down a cuestick: shot.

## Chapter 2

## LIVING A LIE

How had Father Din come to this place, to the back room of a bohemian bar, wearing a civilian suit of grey tweed, the very color symbolic of his weakening ties to the Church, the pale and paling ghost of priestly black?

Father Michael Din was born to parents who were born in the middle of the Great Depression. Michael never knew his grandfather, the original "Din" which was an Ellis-Island-rendering of something with a long tail on it. All Michael knew of his grandfather was that he was a socialist and an atheist. He was rarely spoken of during Michael's childhood. Young Michael's own father was a flag-waving patriot, hard-headed and hard-hatted, proud to serve in Korea and, perhaps in reaction to his own father's lack of it, deeply religious. He joined the Jersey City police department after Korea and worked his way up to his Detective's shield. He died of heart failure while young Michael was still in seminary. Din's mother, Elizabeth, believed in staying home and taking care of her man. Her aspirations had matured in the decade that fell between the Second World War, when women manned war-time industry, and the Sixties, when women turned in droves to achieve that which was material and that which was individual.  She had been satisfied.

The great and simple secret of Michael Din's life was that he worshiped his father and since childhood had wanted nothing more than to please him and to be as much like him as possible.  He had become an altar boy in his local parish because, as his father had put it, "Nothing would make me happier."  This presented no problem to young Michael.  It pleased his father and he did not see how it could interfere with him becoming a cop, like his father.  But it did, for the politically powerful Bishop of his diocese selected him for the priesthood.  Detective Din was told and heartily approved.  Young Michael died inside, and yet he lived.  He would not utter a word against the plan—not spoil what seemed to be the fulfillment of his father's dreams.  At fifteen he entered Seton Hall, the prep school of priests, two years later a New Jersey seminary, and six years later a parish in the Chelsea section of Manhattan.  During these years, he felt like a sleepwalker, a sleepwalker who was dreaming of another life.  Women played a large part in his dreams, their mystery and beauty, and the secular life of the policeman played a part as well; for, in truth, he suspected himself of being his unbelieving grandfather's boy.  As a poet knows from his earliest days that he is a poet, Michael knew from his earliest days that he was not a true believer.  No, that wasn't exactly it.  To be exact, he believed in God, but doubted the relevancy of the priesthood.  For as long as he could remember, he felt that he had been living a lie.

Chapter 3


ODD MAN OUT


A hundred and twenty-five subway-roaring blocks uptown from the Saints and Sinners Club, in Harlem, a group of Black Muslim jazzmen had just finished a complex and protracted riff for a temple congregation that showed its approval with slight smiles and nods that seemed no more than a pigeon's involuntary head-thrust. The jazzmen, indeed, most of the congregation, wore what seemed a uniform of white shirts and dark ties and suits. The one jazzman who was out of uniform seemed to be in a sour mood as he shoved his saxophone into its case. He was clearly an outsider, and looked like one who intended to remain an outsider in any given situation—a man who did his own thing. As did the other jazzmen, he took a seat in the congregation, a sullen expression on his face.

Behind the podium was a huge blackboard, at one end of which was a chalk drawing of an American flag with a Christian cross superimposed on it, and at the other end was the half-crescent symbol of Islam. Under the American flag and the Christian cross was written: "Slavery, Suffering, and Death." Under the Islamic half-crescent was written: "Freedom, Justice, and Equality." "Which one will survive the war of Armageddon?" was at bottom-center. With this set behind him, the speaker took the podium, energetically crying, "Welcome to this special teaching!" He was tall, athletic, dynamic. "You are here to get some good news," he cried.

"MAKE IT PLAIN," chorused the congregation.

"Good news for us is bad news for them," he cried, waving at the outward world.

"PRAISE ALLAH!" the congregation shouted.

"What's good for the sheep is bad for the wolf!"

"MAKE IT PLAIN!"

"Freedom for the black sheep is destruction for the white wolf!"

"ALL PRAISE DUE TO ALLAH!"

"When I tell you that the white man is the wolf," cried the speaker, "I tell you the simple truth of history."

"MAKE IT PLAIN!"

"The white wolves are an endangered species. And we

must see to it that their conservationists do not put them back in the woods—do not replace the dying breed!"

"SAY IT OUT!"

"Death to the white wolf!"

"DEATH TO THE WHITE WOLF!"

All around the outsider, the sullen-faced jazzman, dark-suited men leaped to their feet to shout approval.  He sunk, sprawling in his chair.

"Our God is a live God!"

"YES!"

"Our God is a black God!"

"YES!"

The speaker looked directly down at the sprawling, sullen jazzman.  "You are deaf, dumb, and blind," he shouted. "You are lost in the North American woods.  You are alone with the wolf!  The new day is delayed because of you!"

"MAKE IT PLAIN!"

"Man, you must cleanse yourself, physically and morally.  You are a swilling body of hogmeat!  A floating broth of toxins!"

"MAKE IT PLAIN!"

"The hog is a filthy animal—and you eat it!  And when you eat it, you become it—a grunting hog!  Hogmeat makes addicts, thieves, and prostitutes!   The white devil has fed you on hogmeat until you have become hogmeat!  He has fed us his own immorality, until our people have been turned into prostitutes, thieves, and addicts.

"His Christianity has taught us to deal in dope, and you and I know this is true because when we were Christians we dealt in dope and prostitution.  Yes, we were liars and con-men and cheating bad women."

"We lied!"

"YES!"

"We stole!"

"YES!"

"But now we protect our women and children from the white, Christian wolf!"

"YES!"

"And from the Zionists!"

"YES!"

"All praise to Allah."

"YES, YES, YES!"

Again, the speaker looked directly at the sprawling jazz-man. "Is there one here who would give up the hog?" he asked, with which the sprawling jazzman gathered himself up, rose with a new dignity, and walked up the aisle and out to the street, where he lighted a cigarette and scanned the neighborhood, as if seeking a shock of recognition. "But nothing really changes," he muttered.

Chapter 4

FEAR AT FIVE

Toddy sank her last ball; now the eight ball; now she went around the table knocking the remaining balls (those Father Din had been unable to sink) into a corner pocket. "Well," she said, replacing her cuestick in the rack, "Will you have another drink with me?"

"I'm sorry, but I can't," said Father Din. I have to go now—"

"What? That would be cheating a poor girl out of her just rewards, don't you think?"

Father Din looked blank.

"Well, I won. That means that you have to buy me a drink. You men make the rules, and that's one of them, isn't it?"

"Well, I do owe you a drink," he conceded. "But I can only stay for one."

They sat down at the bar.

349

Toddy grinned at Tiger. "Two more Rockers, Tiger, if you please. I won, so Hopkins here has to pay."

"I should've warned you," said Tiger, smiling approval on Toddy but with his small, wet, wall-eye focused on Father Din. "She never loses a game. At least not at that table. She's been shooting back there since she was a kid. I taught her myself, but she can beat me now." He set up two drinks.

"Don't tell him that, Tige," Toddy objected, but full of triumph. "You'll scare him off. And just think: if he keeps on shooting, and I keep on winning, and he keeps on buying, you'll get rich, and I'll get drunk. And that's what we're here for, right?"

"Wrong!" Tiger shook his head. "I like to see you get high, just enough to feel good, Toddy, but not drunk," he said, ambling away.

"Don't worry about me being frightened off," said Father Din, "but, really, I can't play another game. I have to go to work."

"I thought you were down here apartment hunting."

"Well, I was, but I'm also a salesman."

"And you sell at night? It's almost dark."

"Oh—I have to meet a client at his home."

"I've been drinking and shooting pool all day, since this morning. Nobody to keep me company but Tiger, and he's been asleep most of the time. Some Chinaman came in about an hour before you and had three double shots in about thirty seconds and left. He didn't even speak English. He had to point to the bottle. Early this morning old Martha—she's a local character—she came in and sang "Those Were the Days" about a hundred times and had almost as many eye-openers, but she was still too drunk from last night to make much sense. So you might say that I've been alone all day— until you. When you're alone you don't realize how much you've had." She grew a bit pensive, dreaming into her drink.  Tiger lounged against the cash register, softly snoring.  "What time is it?" she asked.

"Nearly five."

Toddy took another sip from her drink and said, "You'd better go."  Father Din felt as if the lights had gone out.  He moved his glass in a circular motion, swirling the cubes in his drink, and then took a sip from it.  He looked at Toddy.  She was pale, soft.  He wanted to touch her cheek.  He fought back an impulse to do so.  A pang of loneliness overcame him.  "Is there anything wrong?" he asked.

She looked up and smiled.  "I'm all right."  Then, after a thoughtful pause: "You're a nice sort of guy . . . an attractive guy . . . but not very sure of yourself, are you?"

"I guess I'm a bit clumsy.  I had a fit of nerves."

"No, that isn't what I mean."

"It must be that I'm not used to the work yet.  I'm new at it."  He looked at her.  "Do you mind if I ask you a question?  You don't have to answer, of course."

"What is it?"

"Why is a young, beautiful girl like you sitting alone all day in a place like this?"

Toddy laughed.  "What's a girl like you doing in a place like this?  Isn't that what men always ask girls in cat-houses?"

"I only wondered if there was anything wrong."

"Wrong?  Why do you say that?"

"Well, you looked so—so sad, just then.  Or afraid.  Are you afraid of something?"

"Nothing I can't handle," she said.  She emptied her glass and called Tiger, ordering another round.  "You better go now.  I didn't realize how late it was getting."

Minutes ago, in an exuberant mood, she had wanted him to stay.  Now she wished he would leave.  It was perverse of her, to behave so: to make a man feel wanted, needed, when it was his desire to leave, and then to make him feel superfluous when he desired to stay.  He was contemplating her motives, when a bull of a man, bald, bullet-headed, well-dressed, came in the door, and she sat up, alert as a doe that has just caught wind of a hunter.

Chapter 5

THE HIGH PRIEST<br>OF THE CHURCH OF MORAL FREAKS

"'Lo, Priestess. Well, no greeting? Still in a snit, eh? Why didn't you leave then? You knew I was coming." Tiger placed a tumbler filled with Scotch and ice in front of the man and stepped back, his wall-eye glaring. The man drained the tumbler, returned it to the bar. "Again!" Now he turned his pale eyes on Father Din. "Who's this?"

"A friend," Toddy said.

"So, she can speak," said the man, turning back to her. "Well, if we're speaking again," he went on casually, "why not answer my question? Why did you stay here if you knew I was coming? You said on the phone you were going to leave. Could it be that you love me after all?" He laughed softly; then he downed his second tumblerful of Scotch and replaced the empty tumbler on the bar. "Again!" he repeated. Tiger snatched the tumbler and went up the bar. "Well?" asked the man. "Could that be it?"

"I despise you," Toddy said, staring into her drink.

The man laughed. "Another aspect of love," he said, lightly. Once more he turned his cold, pale gaze on Father Din. "Could your friend here be the glue that kept you stuck to that barstool? No offense to you, sir," the man added quickly, smiling. "Since Toddy won't introduce us, I'll have to introduce myself." He paused to drain his third tumbler of Scotch, waved a beringed finger at Tiger, indicating that he wanted still another, and turned, leaning against the bar, to fully face Father Din. "I'm called Monk," he said placing a

352

cigarette in a holder and lighting it. A veil of smoke rose back over his endless forehead like a thin peruke of fine grey hair. "Do you find that an odd name?" he asked, the veil rising  above his pale eyes, his dark, closing brows.

"No, not so odd," said Father Din.

"Perhaps," said the man, "I should explain. I had a little friend once who insisted upon associating me in his mind with a small, brachiating primate. I suppose it was the shortened form of the latter that produced the name Monk; but I prefer to think that the name has religious connotations. I am a kind of neighborhood priest, you see. I tell you these things because yours is a new face hereabouts. You aren't from around here, are you?"

"No."

"No, I didn't think you were. You see, I know almost everyone in this area—or know of them—who they are, what they do—it's my business." He drank half the Scotch from his tumbler, mouthed his cigarette-holder, puffed, drew it away quickly. "Yes—as I was saying—I'm a sort of neighborhood priest. When I make a new convert, he always asks me, 'Who are you? Who should I ask for?' and I say, 'Now that you are a member of my flock, just ask for Monk.' I tell them that if they have any trouble finding me all they have to do is ask a cop."

"I don't follow you. Why should they ask a cop?"

Monk ignored him. "So you see, the name has a sort of religious value, don't you think?" He aimed his cigarette at Father Din's forehead and took a long, slow drag. "I see you don't care too much for my humor," he said, smiling. "Yes, I am the high-priest of the Church of Moral Freaks," he added, chuckling softly. "And I guess that would make our taciturn friend here the high-priestess. That's my little joke. You noticed that I greeted her by calling her priestess?" He looked at Toddy. "He isn't a cop, is he, Priestess?" He looked back at Father Din. "You aren't a narc, are you, my friend? I can spot the traces of fuzz in a newborn baby. No, you're a dude. A runaway husband, perhaps? What's your name?"

Father Din decided that it was time to leave. He finished his drink. "Sam Hopkins," he said, putting money on the counter.

"Are you leaving, Mr. Hopkins?" Monk asked.

"I think I'd better."

"Oh. Did you find my description of the young lady offensive?"

"I think you've made several offensive remarks, Mr.— Monk."

Monk laughed. "Well, what would you expect? I'm a priest of evil. Malice is my middle name."

"That sounds more juvenile than amusing," said Father Din. "Otherwise, you sound halfway intelligent."

"I *am* an intelligent man. It's apparent that you are, too." He paused. Father Din was looking past Monk at Toddy. She sat crumpled over an empty glass as if trying to read something in its bottom. Again he changed his mind, deciding to stay a while longer. He called for Tiger to bring him another drink. Purposefully, he did not order one for Toddy. She ignored what she might have taken for a slight, and ordered herself another. She looked foggy, bedraggled, and fearful.

"Juvenile? Not at all," said Monk. "Think about it. Think about war, and of race-hatred; think about your own innermost secret desires," he went on, in a bland, considering voice, "and you'll see that—like those religious sects where every member of the sect is a minister—we are all priests of evil. All men convert to the Church of Moral Freaks at some point in their lives. I only claim my exalted title as the High Priest of Moral Freakishness by virtue of the life-long effort I've made to rid myself of hypocrisy. Others pretend—even succeed in convincing themselves—that they desire goodness and virtue. I make no such pretense. I like to think of myself as representing the raw malice of mankind, its deep, permanent, bestial nature."

"Not very admirable," said Father Din.

"Naturally not," said Monk. "But that's because men can't face themselves; they can't accept what they are—beasts in a jungle. If they could accept the fact that they were only beasts, they might learn to admire the beast's fang and how and for what purpose he uses it."

Father Din eyed the man. Monk clearly meant what he was saying.

"But things are getting better."

"How do you mean?"

"Psychiatry," said Monk carelessly, "is helping us to see that we are all weak and cruel or perhaps cruelly weak in our strength. Vicious, in other words. It's teaching us to be unashamedly what we are. Ultimately, man will lose all of his ideals. He will excuse himself until he goes back down on all-fours to snarl and bite with pride." He laughed, finished his drink, and called Tiger to bring him another. He put a new cigarette in his holder and lighted it. "There's an odd contradiction, however," he resumed, "psychiatry is telling man, in effect, without realizing it, that it's every beast for himself, and individually we like that; but each of us fears the unbridled beast in the other guy, you see, so we support all sorts of laws that prevent—or at least dissuade—us from freely biting others."

"You prefer anarchy?" asked Father Din.

"I prefer law—when I'm the only one breaking it," said Monk. "It keeps the other beasts at bay." He drank the first half of his fourth drink; replaced the tumbler on the bar, snuffed out his cigarette, and put the holder in his breast pocket. "It's been interesting talking to you, Mister—what was it?—Hopkins. I don't often get the chance to talk with an intelligent person. My business, you see. I deal with scum. It's always been that way with me. All my life I've dealt with scum in scummy businesses. Started out as a boxer; then I was a soldier; then I was a thief, and later a private eye. I'm writing an autobiography. You must read it when it's published. That won't be for a long time though— not until after I'm dead. I haven't finished it yet. I've lived a violent life. I like violence; it's in my blood. It turns me on. I'll die violently, I know. By the sword. But that's what I want." He laughed. "I frighten you, Mr. Hopkins?"

"You disturb me . . ."

"Well, that's just as well. Because it's time for you to be on your way. I want to be alone for a few minutes with my high priestess. Yes, I'm afraid the sun goes down, Mr. Hopkins. The sun goes down."

"It's been a cloudy day," said Father Din. "I won't miss it. I've decided to stay."

"Look, my friend. You're a stranger around here. I'm trying to do you a favor. I've enjoyed talking to you, but it's time for you to leave. Go! Now! Don't make a nuisance of yourself. Don't encourage me to hurt you. Because if I should be forced to do that—"

"No!" cried Toddy. She slammed her glass down on the bar. "Leave him alone! He has a right to be here. I want him to stay. It's you! You leave! Leave me alone!"

"Are you drunk?" said Monk, startled.

"Yes, I'm drunk. What does it matter? I'm still sober enough to know where you've been today and that you've got twenty years worth of junk on you."

"Keep your mouth shut," Monk fairly hissed.

"Why should I?" Toddy challenged, her eyes melting with drink and emotion. "I've had enough—enough," she said, bursting into tears.

Monk slipped off his stool, slapped her quickly across the mouth, and then tried to stifle her scream by cupping a hand over her mouth. She bit the hand and pulled free, mouth open, but she did not scream. Her eyes were wide. Monk cursed, holding his bitten hand.

"Get out of here," Toddy said, thickly. Then, in a higher pitch: "I tell you, I can't take much more." She pushed her hair back from her face, using both hands, and turned back to her empty glass. "I want another drink, Tiger." Tiger picked up her glass; looked at Monk: "You can't hit her and get away with it," he said, wall-eye fiery with impotent rage. "I'll take a baseball bat to you."

"I don't see anyone interfering," said Monk, looking from Tiger to Father Din. "How about you, Mr. Hopkins; anything aside from a gloomy look?"

"I'm glad I stayed," said Father Din. He got to his feet. "I think we've all had enough of you."

"Remember," said Tiger, raising a finger in warning, "Lieutenant Figlia's after you. You ain't gonna walk in and out of that station like it was a hotel no more. That's a tough flatfoot, and he don't take bribes."

Monk stuck his cigarette-holder between his teeth. He spoke around it, lighting a smoke. "Mind your manners, you cock-eyed old fool. This place could burn down—like that"—he snapped his fingers. He took the holder from his mouth and exhaled smoke. "O.K.," he said. "None of this is important. Toddy, you stay if you want to, and I'll go. I'm going to be up at your place at ten tonight. If you're sober I'll talk to you then. I'm going to make allowances for you be- cause you're drunk. But if you keep this up, I'm afraid your husband is going to be in for a bad time—a whole lot worse than usual. As for you, Hopkins, you'd better find a hole and crawl into it. And make it deep." He turned and stamped out into the evening dark.

Chapter 6

## A RUMOR OF CAVALRY

"I'm sorry I dragged you into this, Sam," Toddy said. "I should have left an hour ago. I don't know why I didn't. I've been thinking about having it out with him for weeks, but I didn't have the nerve to do it when I was sober. I had to get drunk to do it. I guess I'm a coward."

"You're no coward, honey," said Tiger. "There ain't many guys around here who would talk to him the way you did. Jeeze, why did you ever get mixed up with that bastard?"

"You know why," Toddy said, her eyes going hard and cold. "Get me another drink."

Tiger regarded her doubtfully. "Don't tell me I've had too much already, Tiger. I know better than anybody how much I've had, and it isn't anywhere near enough. Now get me another drink, if we're friends."

"You too, Sam?"

"You know, Tiger," said Father Din, "I'm not a drinking man, but somehow tonight I don't feel as if I've had enough either."

"Right on!" cried Toddy. She gave him a poke in the ribs.

"So I was right after all," said Father Din, after Tiger placed fresh drinks in front of them and went up the bar to serve a couple of customers who had just entered, "you are in some kind of trouble. Do you want to tell me about it?"

"Are you sure you want to hear a drunken broad tell her long sad tale of woe?"

"Who is Monk?"

"He's . . . let's say an old acquaintance." She fidgeted with a cigarette and match. "I smoke too much. But nobody I know is trying to quit—anything!" She lighted the cigarette and sighed out the smoke. Then she said, shrugging her shoulders: "Oh, what's the use! He's a mistake I can't undo." She looked hard at Father Din. "You know, there's something about you . . . you make me want to talk."

"Do I? I'm glad if I do."

"Well, Sam," she said, her mood lightening, "you really are something else. Here I thought you were interested in my legs and it turns out that it's the real me you're after."

"I only want to help, if possible."

"Oh, that's too bad. I was hoping for something more." She looked quickly away, took a sip from her drink, and looked up again, saying: "I admired you, the way you handled yourself with Monk. Most of the guys I know are terrified of him."

"You'd be wrong if you thought he didn't unsettle me. I find it hard to believe, though, that anybody could mean some of the things he said."

"Oh, he means what he says—somewhere, deep down. He likes to put people on, though. Like that priest of evil business. That's supposed to be a joke, but he means it, too. That's exactly what he is."

"He didn't mean that, about burning this place down, did he?"

"He's had other places fire-bombed. I know that for a fact."

"Then why isn't he behind bars?"

"Nobody'll testify against him. Hell, nobody knows just how many crooks are free because some witness was murdered. It happens all the time."

Tiger wiped the bar. "I see you got a lot to learn, son; Monk shmears the cops. He's like a little king around here. It ain't no secret that he peddles dope and pimps and is into a half a dozen other rackets—gambling, protection, pornography—you name it. That's why I don't mind telling you—everybody knows it. But try to get him on anything and see what happens. I'd have the fire inspectors in here closing me up; and two days later the place would burn down anyway."

"But Figlia's different," said Toddy. "Monk can't buy him off."

"Who's Figlia?" asked Father Din. The name sounded familiar to him. Then he remembered. It was the same name of a young girl whose funeral he had helped to direct.

"A nark. Narcotics. He's on special assignment in this precinct—he used to be in Harlem; and before that over in Chelsea. He had a daughter who O.D.'d on smack."

"That's motivation," Toddy put in. "That's why he can't be bought. And there can't be any question about it: he's here to get Monk."

"He's working in tandem with the local precinct," said Tiger; "the reason bein' that most of the robberies around here are committed by junkies."

"Hey, Tiger!" came a call, and Tiger, cursing under his breath, ambled, more like a shaggy old bear than a tiger, back up the bar.


Chapter 7


ODD MAN IN


The man who called Tiger was a very tall, skinny black man. He wore his hair in a plaster of waves and ringlets that dipped down the right side of his forehead, almost covering and no doubt at times stabbing into his right eye, in the manner of certain black jazz musicians of an earlier era. There was a somewhat feline handsomeness about him, but this was offset to a degree by the shabbiness of his clothes—he wore, following the custom of old-time jazzmen, a satin-collared tuxedo, worn shiny, and a sullen scowl. A battered black saxophone case dangled from one long thin hand; the other hand was waving about and stabbing the air with a long delicate index finger. "You and me, bro, are born pork-chop-sandwich and hot-sauce Baptists. You can change, but you're asking too much of me when you ask me to give up my heritage."

"What'll it be, Tory?"

"Double gin on some cubes."

"And you?"

The man with Tory was about the same age and bore a striking resemblance to him. He looked like Tory might have looked with a close-cropped haircut and a natty funeral director's dark suit—a clean-cut version of Tory.

"He'll have a plain tomato juice, Tiger. Or an Orange Crush. Or moo juice. Ask me how do I know?"

"How do you know, Tory?" asked Tiger, one eye eerily focused on Tory and one on the natty dresser.

"Cuz Mister Spit-shine here—he be my righteous Big Bubba. He only eat, drink and do pure things. Sometimes he so goody-two-shoes, he make me sick."

"It's all that gin and hog in you that makes you sick," said Tory's brother. "Gin, hog, and only Allah knows what-all. You are destroying your holy black self with white man's toxins." He looked at Tiger. "Do you have tomato juice? If so, please bring me one, with a twist of lemon." He looked at Tory. "I don't want to be seen standing at a bar. Let's take a table. I'm going to sit over there. Bring the refreshments." He went over and sat at a table in a dark corner, a tall neat figure, crisp and clean in the shadows.

Tory moved up beside Toddy. "Hey, baby, what's happenin?"

"Hi, Tory," she said.

"Do you know what is an evil thing, Toddy? It is, that everyone in this world is out recruiting somebody. Ain't nobody can be what they be without recruiting somebody to be just like they be. Only time anybody is happy is when everybody is just like them. Am I meeting a new recruit, or ain't ya gonna introduce me?"

"Sam Hopkins," said Toddy, "meet Torrance Amsterdam."

"Tory will do fine." He reached out across Toddy and pumped Father Din's hand. "You see that white shirt on Mister Slick over there—Mister Stiff-as-Starch—that's my brother, Morris Amsterdam, A.K.A. Mahmoud Zero—or is it X?—or some such, and he is after recruiting me into the Muslims. But I tell him what a man called Monk tells me: I have already been recruited into the Congregation of Moral Freaks." He began to spit laughter, then went into an aw, aw, aw, aw, aw, and only got ahold of himself when Tiger put a tray of drinks in front of him. "Later," he said to Toddy, flipping Tiger a bill and, without waiting for change, took the tray over to the corner to join his brother.

Torrence and Morris Amsterdam were born outside of Elkin, North Carolina. Their mother and father had picked cotton for wages. Their grandmother and grandfather had picked cotton to hold on to a shanty and a quarter-acre of land. Their great-grandparents had picked cotton for the Amsterdam family, as slaves. *Their* grandparents had been rich in Africa, owning cattle. And so it goes, back into the obscure antiquity of history, the twilight before it, and the darkness before that. Morrie and Tory were jazzmen. Morrie's elegant fingers could make magic on the piano. Tory could blow his soul through the balloons of his cheeks and the brass rigamarole of his saxophone and never run out of it. But Morrie wanted more than a piano player's cigarette; he wanted Justice; and so he became Mahmoud Zero, one of Allah's avengers. Tory, on the other hand, doubted if there was justice in all the universe, ever was, ever would be. But complaints abounded, plaints and complaints, to be screamed, hummed, eased, and jammed out of the big brass mouth of his sax.

Tory and Mahmoud were at the Saints and Sinners Club to meet a couple of Mahmoud's associates. Tory had suggested the spot as a good place for Mahmoud to meet his friends because he liked the place, liked Tiger, and because he was behind in his drinking, at least three gins back. He was always behind in his drinking. Today, he was behind because he had given his brother a hand at the mosque in Harlem, where a sideman had been arrested and a replacement was desperately needed. The Black Muslims have no liturgy. They do not sing in the temple; but they usually start their services with a protracted, sort of progressive jazz riff. Tory suspected that the combo could have gotten along without him. He suspected that Mahmoud had used the excuse of a missing member to bring Tory to the Muslim service, a chance to convert him. After the jazz riff, Tory and Mahmoud had seated themselves among the congregation and heard what Tory suspected Mahmoud thought would be his conversion sermon. At the end of the sermon converts were invited up front. Several former Baptists and Methodists, struck with guilt for having held to the white satan's religion, made their way up to pledge conversion. Tory was not among them. Mahmoud had been hectoring him all the way downtown. He was ashamed, disgraced in front of his brothers and sisters, that his blood brother could not see the Light.

Chapter 8

THE HORSEMAN OF THE APOCALYPSE

"How did you get involved with a man like Monk?" Father Din asked Toddy, realizing that every question was getting him more deeply involved with this strange and beautiful young woman and with the troubles that went with her.

She shrugged. "My husband, Jack, got me mixed up with Monk. Jack and I don't live together anymore. He lives in a loft across the street from my apartment. But we don't see much of each other these days: only sometimes when he comes over to pick up his stuff from Monk. He's a junkie, one of the members of Monk's congregation. He used to be an artist, a painter: he only used the loft for a studio in those days. And the last thing he painted was a portrait of a junkie. He knew this little seventeen-year-old Puerto Rican boy who had been using heroin for years. He got the boy to sit for him, and he worked on the painting for a few months, but it never satisfied him. He felt that he couldn't psyche the boy out. Then he told me that he was going to shoot up with the stuff so he could see what the boy got out of it. Now that really scared me; but he told me not to worry, that one or two shots of the stuff couldn't hook anybody. Well, I still didn't like it, but I didn't like to argue with him in those days. I respected him, you see, and I trusted him. And as far as the painting went, he was right, I guess; because it turned out to be a really wonderful portrait, the best Jack ever did. Not re-alistic, of course. The face smeared and blended with the background—a kind of dream image, or nightmare. He was offered two-thousand dollars for it at a show he gave a month or so after he finished it, and that was a great price. It was painted over all of these broken, bad-luck mirror pieces stuck on the canvass. It made for a really interesting ef-fect. Sometimes you could see bits of yourself looking back at you from the portrait. Jack said it reflected the society that made junkies, and then he said it showed that becoming a junkie could happen to anyone."

"There but for the grace of God," said Father Din.

"Yeah, that was it."

"What happened to the painting?"

"Jack wouldn't sell it. He still has it up there in the loft with him. He won't part with it. He hasn't had another show, either. That show was even reviewed by some newspa-pers. One reviewer said that the painting—Jack called it Horseman of the Apocalypse—"horse" is slang for heroin in case you didn't know—'was the biggest step forward in American painting since Jackson Pollock.' By then Jack was shooting the stuff three and four and even five times a day, and always complaining that the stuff wasn't any good and that he needed another shot to get the same high that one less gave him a week before." She looked up at Father Din.

"Monk was Jack's connection. Dedi Pavon, the model, introduced Jack to Monk, and pretty soon Jack was letting Monk use our apartment for his headquarters in the neighborhood.

"Jack's family has money. I guess they think of Jack as something of a black sheep. But they send him a check every month anyway. Which is their way of keeping a hold on him. But junk is very expensive. It was running Jack a hundred dollars a day the last I heard, and it may be several times that by now. I don't ask because I don't want to know." She paused. "But the thing is, Monk offered Jack a cut-rate for the use of the apartment, and Jack took him up on it. I tried to tell Jack that it wasn't the apartment Monk was after, it was power over *us*; but Jack wouldn't listen: he was beyond reason. That was then. But later, when Jack finally saw that what I had told him about Monk was true, he tried to face Monk down. But Monk only laughed in his face. And when Jack lost his temper and took a poke at Monk, Monk threw him out of the apartment. I tried to go with him, but Monk wouldn't let me. I thought then, though, that Jack was saved. I thought he'd go and get the police and have Monk arrested, no matter what it cost him to do it. But within fifteen minutes Jack was back outside the door, begging Monk for a fix. Man, that did something to me. I didn't see how Jack could let Monk throw him out of our apartment and then come back begging for more . . . it was shameless . . . and . . . disgusting. I couldn't help myself, I hated him for it. Well . . . I hated what he had become. It's awful to find yourself hating someone that you've loved. I wanted to hurt him, to shock him into sanity . . . I don't know what. Anyway, when I heard him crying outside the door like that, all I could feel for him was contempt. Something snapped, and it was all over. I didn't say a word to Monk on Jack's behalf. I just went into the bedroom and got in bed."

She snuffed out her cigarette viciously: looked up. Her eyes glittered and were opened wide as if to hold back tears. The muscles in her jaws were knotted; her mouth twisted. "Maybe it was all those months of watching Monk get more and more power over Jack, and watching Jack let him do it. You wouldn't believe it." She lowered her voice. "It was disgusting. Monk came into the bedroom that night stark naked—carrying his belt from his trousers. He handed me the belt, threw himself across the bed, and stuck his huge, powerful-looking butt into the air. He told me to whip him. I couldn't. Then he told me he'd break my arm, if I didn't. I couldn't. Then he said he'd kill Jack, if I didn't. Then finally I could. I whipped his ass till I raised welts and he loved it. I never had sex with him. Only that. He can't have sex in a normal way. I've been half out of my mind."

"A casebook sado-masochist," said Father Din.

"The weaker Jack got, the more he just seemed to fade away. Monk was in charge of everything. He just took over our lives. It was as if Jack was dying, or dead. And that meant that our marriage was dead, too. I mean, doesn't a marriage die with the death of one of the partners?"

"I don't think so," Father Din ventured in a quiet voice. He felt almost schizophrenic—one minute libidinous and aggressive—one minute counseling like a parish priest.

"Oh, but I do," Toddy shot back. The shock of her own attack upon Monk had temporarily sobered her, but now the drinks seemed to be catching up with her again. She burst into tears, and began fishing in her pocketbook for a handkerchief. She found it, and held it over her face while continuing

to sob. All those pent-up emotions of months were released. Finally she stopped shaking and wiped her eyes and
face, blew her nose, and smiled sheepishly at Father Din, who
had sat like a statue, one big hand on her long, shivering back,
while she cried.

Tiger, seeing Toddy crying, had come down the bar to
her and now stood, gnarled hands whitely gripping the bartop,
in mute empathy. He was visibly relieved when Toddy
looked up to smile at Father Din. "There now," he said. "Do
you feel better, honey. Are you O.K.?"

"Oooh, Tiger," Toddy sniffed, "you old dope. I'm
fine. Women like to cry once in a while; don't you know
anything?" She looked at herself in her compact mirror and
grimaced. "Oh, I'm a fright! Excuse me," she said to Father
Din, "I better go to the ladies room and put myself together
again."

"Is she all right?" asked Tiger when she was gone.

"For now," said Father Din. "But she's not all right."


## Chapter 9


### AT CROSS PURPOSES


Ansar Rashid was in America to serve Allah, or so
Mahmoud had been given to understand by Ansar's numerous Atlantic Avenue connections. In truth, these connections
had mistakenly thought that they were introducing a mem-
ber-in-good-standing of Viper-8, whose major effort in the
great Jihad was to write letters and make phonecalls claiming
credit for the deeds of others, to his American counterpart in
the Black Muslims. In fact, Viper-8 had evaporated with the
arrest of three of the eight of its total, forlorn membership;
and, though Mahmoud was a member in good standing of the
Black Muslims, he was no terrorist. Brooklyn's Muslim Atlantic Avenue grapevine, an exchange of tall tales and fantas-

tical gossip, much of it disinformation planted by F.B.I. operatives, had both ends of the story wrong, one end because Ansar was a great self-aggrandizer and the other end because they completely misunderstood the current mission of the American Black Muslims. Mahmoud assumed that he was to show Ansar the American ropes, how the Black American suffered at the hands of the Great Satan. He further assumed that Ansar would take his new-found understanding of the plight of the American Black back to the Middle East and spread the word. Ansar assumed that Mahmoud's purpose was to help him establish an American Jihad against the Great Satan. They had not known each other long enough to know that they were at cross purposes.

Ansar did not like meeting in a place that served alcohol. He was annoyed. "Why have you dragged me to this den of iniquity?" he asked of Mahmoud, throwing his Loden coat across the back of his chair. His every gesture reeked of agitated self-importance. Out of his coat, a cold-weather gift from his Brooklyn friends, Ansar proved to be pot-bellied, soft as a pillow.

"We were in Harlem," Tory answered for his brother, "you were in Brooklyn. This is half-way between."

"Please, Tory," said Mahmoud, "try to be quiet. Listen and learn. Please forgive my brother's intrusive behavior, Ansar. His wits have escaped with the vapor of alcohol. Still, this did seem a convenient place to meet. That is, geographically. My brother lied to me. He told me this was an eatery. I don't like it any more than you do. But—would you like something to drink? I mean fruit juice of some kind, or Co-Cola?" Ansar waved the suggestion aside. "And what about you, Miss Azziz?" Mahmoud asked of Ansar's companion. "A glass of white wine?" Camilla Azziz was a teenager. From Palestine, her family had gone to Kuwait, and then on to Chicago, where Camilla was born, an all-American girl. The face that went with her prime pulchritude did not suit it. It was worried in its frame of wild waves of curly black hair.

"Miss Azziz will have orange juice," said Ansar. He spoke a good, accent-lilted brand of English; but there was something irritating about it, as if there were either a demand, an order, or some kind of sarcasm, in every sentence.

"Let's make an itinerary," said Mahmoud.

"If we do, it may have to be adjusted," said Ansar. "I am here on serious business and could be interrupted at any time."

"Woah, woah," said Tory, standing up. "Serious has just hurt my sensitive ears. I'll go get us some drinks." He took the tray and went up to the bar. When he returned, the tray laden with four gin and tonics, Ansar was saying, "Are you sure this is a safe place? That bartender looks like an Israeli agent." Tory was putting the drinks on the table. "You mean Tiger?" he said.

"Tiger," quoted Ansar. "Could that be a code name?"

"Tiger's just a broken down old man," said Tory. "He used to be a wrestler. Years ago."

"I don't trust this place," said Ansar. "And I do not trust this man," he said, pointing at Tory. He looked at Mahmoud with gleaming eyes. "Why has he led us here, to meet in such a place? Could it not be a plot? Camilla, get your coat! We are leaving now. I will not stay in the stench of alcohol," he said, eyeing the four gin and tonics.

"Good," shot Tory, pulling the tray toward him.

"Are you coming?" Ansar asked of Mahmoud.

"Give me a moment," said Mahmoud. "I must speak with my brother."

"We will wait outside." Ansar fairly dragged Camilla to the door.

Tory sprawled at the table, gin in hand. "I think you been put in charge of a coo-coo bird, Mister Slick."

"I can't explain it to you now, my brother, but Ansar may have reasons to take extreme care."

"You mean even paranoids have real enemies—eh?"

"I don't like to leave you in this drunken condition, my brother, but at the moment I am called to higher service, in the name of Allah. But it is my ardent hope that you will re-think your life style. You have embarrassed me several times today, but I am your brother and I love you. Please go somewhere and get some sleep. I do not like to think of you wandering the streets in your present condition." Mahmoud leaned down and kissed his brother on the cheek. As Mahmoud pulled open the door to leave, Dedi Pavon brushed passed him, entering.

## Chapter 10

## TAPERING OFF

When Toddy returned from the ladies' room, she said, "I washed my face in cold water and fixed it up, and I feel positively sober again. I'm so sorry I burdened you with my long tale of woe, Sam. Whatever got into me, I just had to get it out."

"Remember what you told me about apologies: a sign of emotional insecurity, you said."

Toddy laughed. "Anyway, who said I was emotionally secure? That only went for repeated apologies, which I don't intend to make. What you must think of me, though. Now, at this moment, I can't imagine myself telling you all those things . . . I don't know what came over me. It's just that I haven't had anyone to talk to. It's been so long since I've really talked . . . And there's something about you . . . you make me feel like talking . . ." She covered Father Din's hand, which was resting on the bar, with her own. "I feel that I know you even though I don't. It's strange . . . you're such a good listener . . . so quiet and patient.  Not like a salesman at all."

Gently, Father Din removed his hand, and Toddy moved hers to the pack of cigarettes that lay on the bar, removed one, and brought her other hand to meet it with a flaming lighter.  "Smoking is like hoping," she said.  "I keep meaning to quit."

Chapter 11

THE LIVING IMAGE

Dedi Pavon paused just inside the door, high-fiving Tory at a distance.  Doing a little warming jig, he surveyed the room, his face showing the tell-tale lesions of Kaposi's sarcoma.  Father Din had seen many such faces in the last few years, the faces of AIDS victims.  The boy was shivering, hunching his narrow shoulders, rocking from foot to foot, rubbing his hands together: understandably, for he wore no overcoat, hat or gloves, only a thin mustard-hued suit, a luminous pink cha-cha shirt, and an old pair of blue plastic shoes.  Father Din thought the boy was a candidate for pneumonia, and, as if in keeping with this casual prophecy, the boy hacked, hacked again, and fell into an uncontrollable fit of coughing.  He tugged a sticky-looking handkerchief from his breast pocket and covered his mouth with it until the fit subsided.  He blew his dripping nose, stuffed the handkerchief back in his pocket, threw back his shoulders and, with a brand new grin that displayed a prominent black void of missing teeth, exclaimed, "Ave Maria!"  He stepped up to Father Din.  "If you spit out there it will freeze and break on the sidewalk like a ten-cent diamond.  Amigo, you got to have cold blood to live in this town, you know that?"  He laughed ingratiatingly.  Then, seeing Toddy, apparently for the first time, he slapped his scarred cheek in surprise.  "Ay!  I didn't

371

know it was you, with your nose buried in the glass. Is this your friend I have spoke to?"

Toddy looked him over. "Where's your coat, Dedi? Are you crazy?" Then to Father Din: "Sam, this is the boy I told you about, the model for Jack's painting—Dedi Pavon. Dedi, this is Sam Hopkins."

Father Din encompassed Dedi's frail, proffered hand and shook it as if he were rocking a small bird to sleep. "Hello," he said.

"Pleased to dig, mon." Father Din let the hand fly free. "I didn't see it was you, Toddy. I was going to put the con on your friend here, see if he wouldn't like to buy a nice watch, cheap. Hey," he exclaimed, new hope shining his eyes, "maybe you would like that anyhow, eh? I could give you some good bargain . . ."

"Sam doesn't want any hot watches."

"How you know what the mon wants?" Dedi challenged, with the look of an insulted salesman. "You shouldn't bust in when people's doing business. That ain't polite." Then, pathetically: "Besides, you know I'm a sick boy. How'm I gonna buy medicine with you telling people I'm selling hot merchandise?"

"I've already got a watch," Father Din intervened. "Got it just recently." He extended his left wrist. "See?"

"That's a beauty!" cried Dedi, raising his eyebrows. "Damn! Everybody got a watch! What a life! Oof!" He pinched his nostrils against the stink of the world. "I should go back to Puerto Rico. I need the sun to shine on me. I'm a sick boy." He fell silent for a moment, a doleful expression on his face: then, surprisingly, he assumed a bodybuilder's pose, flexing his biceps, and said with vehemence: "I could be Mr. Puerto Rico in six months." Toddy and Father Din laughed. "But who wants to be muscle-bound?" Dedi said, shrugging his shoulders. "I-yi-yi-yi," he cried, rolling his head despairingly, "I don't know what to do."

"Where's your overcoat?" asked Toddy.

"What do I need an overcoat for? I know how to make me warm." He winked. "But I got to get El Dinero, big green daddy, to get what I need. You know Monk. He don't take no watches, hot or cold. *!Ay, ese hombre no me gusta!* But he the mon. He got the smack, so—" He was suddenly overtaken with another coughing fit. When it was over, he went on: "See? I'm a sick boy. Ask my sister, she will tell you. I need medicine. *Caramba*, how'm I'm gonna get the bread?" He took his thin homely face in his hands and swayed it from side to side. There was such a look of despair on that hand-held face that Father Din was tempted to buy himself an extra watch, but the almost certain knowledge that what he paid for the watch would be spent on heroin, combined with the probability that the watch was stolen, militated against the gesture.

Suddenly Tiger came up and took Dedi by the arm, saying: "Not in here, Dedi. I've told ya before, I don't want ya to peddle none of your hot merchandise in my bar. I got enough troubles without that." He pulled the boy toward the door.

"O.K., O.K., mon," Dedi protested, "I only come in this dump to see if my sister was here. Hey, Toddy," he called back, "you seen Pilar?"

"You can see she ain't here," Tiger said. "Come on, now, I got customers to serve."

"I gotta come in to see, don't I?" He called back to Father Din: "You sure you don't need no watch, mon?" Then he was propelled out the door. Tiger stood waiting to see that he was gone. He then turned to clean the table where Tory sat, nursing the last of his gin.

"What's the matter?" said Tiger, wiping the table, "You look worried. Got troubles?"

"I'm worried about my bro. He's too innocent to live."

"Hey, one of your friends must have dropped this," said

Tiger, flopping a paperback on the table. "It was on the chair."

"Must have slithered out somebody's pocket," said Tory, thickly, reading its title: *Official Document In-House Circulation Only, Central Intelligence Agency #918593K, Ingredients and Preparation of Home-Made Bombs.*

"Oh, wow!" cried Tory, shaking his head.

Chapter 12

WARNINGS, WARNINGS, WARNINGS!

Tiger went up the outside of the bar and came back down behind it to Toddy and Father Din. "I feel sorry for Dedi," he said, picking up their empty glasses, "but what can I do? I can't afford to buy him no fixes. He spends more on dope in a week than I make, working my ass off." He shook his head. "Poor kid. Remember when I used to let him come in to shine shoes, Toddy? The money he made, he used to go to the five-and-dime and buy things for his sister. He used to come in and show me what he bought her. Fancy can-openers that you screwed on the wall, and sets of steak knives with bone handles: he liked to have a nice home, he said." He gave a sympathetic little laugh.

"Hell, he was only about eleven or twelve. You remember, Toddy? You wasn't so much older yourself. But then, you was always in back, shooting pool. We never had much business during the day, and she'd be out of sight back there."

"I was already sixteen or seventeen when Dedi first started coming in," Toddy said. "That was a couple of years after I lost my parents. My dad spent a lot of time here in the last year of his life. Tiger was his friend. At the end, I guess Tiger was the only friend he had; so I used to come in to talk to Tiger about my dad. I was only a little girl then, but in this neighborhood a girl's little girl stage goes fast."

"Your father was a fine man," Tiger said earnestly. "But Dedi and his sister, Pilar—uh, they only had a little room to live in, and no parents neither, none that I ever heard of. Pilar was older—let's see, she'd be, oh, twenty-five now, maybe. She was a pretty kid. Took good care of her little brother, too, for a long time. But she was uh, you know, in the life, a prostitute. I don't judge her for that. How else could a little girl raise a boy all by herself? She could have just given him away, you know. Some of these desperate people do that. They just give their kids to somebody and go off on their own. But not her. And I respect her for that. I don't know how she managed to dodge the authorities all those years. They probably never even knew she was there. But, too bad, somewhere along the line she got on junk. And then later Dedi got on it. "So," Tiger waved his palms, "that seemed to . . . end their lives." He turned away wearing a hopeless face and went up the bar to refill their glasses.

"He's a good guy," Toddy said. "But he's old. There isn't much he can do. I guess there isn't much any of us can do," she added, after a pause. "What time is it?"

"Seven-thirty. Do you have to be somewhere?"

"Monk will expect me to be at the apartment at ten. If I'm not there he'll make it tough on Jack. I don't want to be responsible for what he might do to Jack."

Tiger brought their drinks and went away again.

"But what will Monk do to you?" Father Din asked, after a pause. "I mean, he was in a pretty bad temper when he left."

"Oh, he won't hurt me. At least he never has. Maybe just slap me around a little. He's not simple. He likes to use one person to hurt another. It's all a kind of a game with him."

"And you're going up there tonight?"

"I told you, I have to. If I don't, he won't give Jack his stuff. Jack picks up from Monk once a week. He sells him a whole week's supply at a time. Can you imagine what it would mean to be cut off?"

"Then, if you'll let me," Father Din found himself saying, "I'd like to go with you."

"Oh, Sam, no! Monk would just love to see your face again tonight. Especially somewhere out of public view."

"But I don't want you to go alone."

"I can't let you come with me," Toddy said, shaking her head negatively. It appeared that this was her final decision. Father Din decided to let the subject drop for the moment. But he was stubborn, and he had decided that he would not let her go without him.

Strange, at three o'clock this afternoon he had entered this place with no clear idea of what his purpose was, rather like some hypnotized subject of a night club act, and in less than five hours he had become involved, absorbed, in someone else's life. Now, he thought, all he wanted to do was to protect a beautiful woman. Suddenly he felt a wave of nausea.

"What's wrong?" Toddy asked, looking at him with alarm.

"I don't know. I feel uncomfortable. My stomach..." In a moment he found his way to the men's room and was vomiting into the toilet. He ran some cold water into the dirty sink and dowsed his face with it. "Warnings, warnings, warnings," he muttered to himself: for in his mind warnings were being sounded through the medium of Father Ryan's voice. But Father Ryan was like a desperate parent with no argument at his command but that of an incommunicable experience, like the father who doubts the success of the project upon which his son has embarked, but, when asked what the basis of his doubt is, can only explain his feeling by saying that the project doesn't sound right.

"I think I know what is in the back of your mind," Father Ryan said, the last time they talked, "and let me assure you,

Michael, that the pursuit of any such course of action can only lead to great heartache and suffering, both for yourself and for others. You'll wind up a spoiled priest." Father Ryan meant women, but was afraid to say so in so many words, as if saying what he feared might make it real. He had seen it before—the disaster of the young priest and his Eve.

"But, Father Liam," lied Father Din, "my only intention is to try to make more outside contacts. I'm a parish priest, not a monk. Look at Father Corrigan—"

"Outside contacts! You have a parishful of outside contacts to make. What are you talking about? Outside contacts, indeed! What nonsense! Michael, I don't mean to say that you haven't done your duty—you have—until lately, anyhow. And as for Thom Corrigan, look at the trouble he's causing—the publicity! His books. His television appearances. Openly flaunting a mistress. Why, he talks like a communist. He's a disgrace to the Church."

"He's doing good works . . . ."

"That is highly questionable. But, leaving all that aside, you are not Thom Corrigan, you are Michael Din, and a different kind of man. Thom Corrigan is a sophisticate. No man more appreciates your particular talents than I—but, Michael, you are a very naive young man. My advice to you would be: hold back, wait, let time happen to you, graduate into the world."

"Warnings, warnings, warnings," muttered Father Din, dowsing his face with cold water. He looked at himself in the old mirror over the sink. The new fresh face of a collegiate. "Maybe he's right," he said. "But," he added, raising his eyebrows, "I swear, I look drunk." He laughed. "I wish I could lie down for a few minutes." He stumbled out of the men's room and rejoined Toddy at the bar.

"Are you all right?" she asked.

"Look," he answered, "didn't you say that you had to be up at your place at ten?"

"Yes."

"Well, it's only a bit after eight now. Would you let me go up to your place and lie down until, say, nine or nine-thirty?"

"You'd be taking an awful chance. Suppose Monk were to show up early?"

"I'll take the chance on feeling better before he arrives."

"Are you sure?" she said. She knew it wasn't the best thing to do, but she wanted to stay with him. "Only if you promise to leave by nine-thirty," she said, knitting her brows. "Remember, it's you I'm thinking of."

Chapter 13

## WAITING FOR TROUBLE

The vestibule was too small to hold them both, so Father Din waited on the sidewalk, holding the outer door open, while Toddy fumbled for her keys.

Looking back from her building, one of those tenements that materialized in long monotonous rows in every large eastern city around the turn of the last century, Father Din could see the multicolored glow of the signs of the rock clubs along the Strip, and beyond that, above an indefinite dark void, and casting a much greater, though less intense, glow high into the night, the uneven lights of the mid-town sky-scrapers. Overhead the sky lowered like a taut black sheet. Occasionally, suddenly, it tore, revealing jagged, twisting light. Long, low, slowly-building rumbles, as of some cosmic drummer, preceded each flash. A storm was coming; its harbinger, the wind, had arrived, beating Father Din's coat against the backs of his legs, flashing through his hair like grazing bullets of ice.

Directly across the street was the building that housed Jack Muir's loft. It was a large, characterless edifice. Probably before being converted for studio use it had been a factory or a warehouse. Now, on the second and sixth floors, long rows of windows were lighted, so that they looked like great toothy smiles across its face. "And," thought Father Din, feeling the forced suspension of conscience which he must maintain, else concede his own error, "did a mocking laughter really emanate from the dark gulf between them?"

He wondered from behind which row of windows Jack Muir might be watching; wondered, instantly, what kind of man Muir was. Would he like him, despite what he had been told about him? Muir had problems; but then, so did he. The deeper he had sunk into his own problems the more responsive was his charity for others. Again, he found himself trying to believe that he was not being a fool. Nevertheless, he followed Toddy into the dismal, oily-green halls and stairwell, up stairs of deeply grooved white marble, turned peppery, braced in stiff metal. The wooden handrail of the metal banister was carved with hearts and initials, doubtless by turn-of-the-century immigrants, and resembled, to him, the long sticks upon which medieval stewards kept records. A commingled odor of life, death, and decay assailed his nostrils. His stomach heaved again. The sudden heat caused him to break out with perspiration. His head pounded. When he reached the fourth landing, he had to sit down at the top of the steps for a moment, while Toddy went on to the front to unlock her door. She came back and pulled him to his feet. "Oh, Sam, I'm sorry you feel so rotten," she said, as she led him to her door.

"It's just that I drank too much," he said, stepping behind her into the apartment.

"The cold air made me feel much better," she said, taking Father Din's great black overcoat and hanging it on a clothestree inside the door. She hung up her own coat, and then excused herself, laughing, saying: "But my kidneys can't hold anything in this kind of weather. You make yourself at home. I'll be right back. Go into the livingroom and sit down."

While she was gone Father Din surveyed the apartment. The hall door gave into the kitchen, a medium-sized room with the standard equipment, plus a bathtub. The tub was sunk inside of a plywood cabinet that had been decorated with painted daisies. The enameled cover, similarly decorated, and looking rather like a legless tabletop, stood leaning against a wall. Some clothes were soaking in the tub. The livingroom adjoined the kitchen. The marks of demarcation between the two rooms were the indications of a wall, and a brass rail-groove over which, upon a time, rolling doors had glided. However, the livingroom was much narrower and somewhat longer than the kitchen. An oriental screen stood at an angle between the two rooms, blocking part of the front room from view. This room was furnished with two easy chairs, a couch and a coffee table. An imitation Tiffany lamp hung in the middle of the room. The walls were decorated with posters. Kurt Cobane & Nirvana. Generation X. Greenpeace. There was a large poster of Madonna, hair flying. Father Din walked to the windows and opened one a crack. Another set of teeth had been added to the face of the building across the street, lending it an even more grotesque appearance than it had had a few minutes before, when seen from the street.

To his right, a door stood ajar. He stepped over to it and looked in. It was the bedroom, a small oblong, hung from ceiling to floor with purple velveteen drapes. A canopy bed, baldaquined in a satiny rose-colored material, filled the room but for a space around it just large enough to permit of a pair of legs. He retreated back to the window, and was posed, looking out, when Toddy returned.

"I'm sorry I was gone so long," she said. "I stopped across the hall to borrow a bottle of Scotch from my neighbor. She always has one. But when she doesn't, I do, so we're neither of us ever stuck when we have company."

"But not for me, I hope," Father Din said. "I've had too much already."

"No, I'll make you a cup of tea. That's the best thing in the world for an upset stomach. You just lie down on the couch. I've been thinking it over. I can handle Monk. So, you've got to be on your way before nine-thirty at the latest. That gives you an hour."

"I need it. I feel awful. I've never drunk so much in my life as I have today." He sat on the couch and took off his shoes.

"Then why today? Is today something special? Did you have a fight with your wife?"

"I'm not married. But maybe today is something special, I'm not sure yet." Father Din closed his eyes.

Toddy stood looking at him for a moment, a big, youthful fellow, sprawled on her couch. There was the shadow of a clean, fine beard appearing at his chin and jaws. She reached down and touched his damp cheek with her finger. His mouth twitched. She wondered who he was, really. Surely he was no salesman. Or it was a strange salesman who was so ill-at-ease and clumsy with strangers. But what was he then? Who was he? He was lonely, she knew. And why should such a nice-looking young man be lonely? Had he fallen out with his girl? He was attracted to her, that was plain. All she possessed, it seemed, was trouble. Was it trouble, then, that he was after? She was re-arriving at that one remove from sobriety that is a gift if going and a penalty if coming.


Chapter 14


TWO SAD NOTES


*My dear—*

381

*What can I say—I cannot live—I love you, my
darling girl—but I cannot live—Aunt Sybil
will look after you, won't you Syb—Be lucky—
I'm sorry—I can't explain—*

*Daddy*


*Syb—*


*Please—*


*Toddy has a trust fund—check with Morgan
and Atley, 400 Madison Avenue. Not much
but will allay your burden and take care of
educational expenses. Call super &/or
police. Don't let Toddy come home. Further
info. among papers in my desk.*

*Thank you*


Toddy had read both of those notes hundreds of times—so
that she could recite them word for word—trying to penetrate
through to the state of mind of her father when he wrote them;
but she couldn't, not really, not so that she could finally understand—though she thought she understood his loneliness—and she ended, always, as she began, feeling deserted. People were such enigmas—you never really
knew. But she thought that he must never have loved her with
anything like the love he had for her mother, in spite of the
fact that she gave him every ounce of her love during those
terrible years when her mother was dying and he and she were
alone together, and she was growing up. She didn't count,
that was all . . . not enough to keep him alive . . . . And now
it was the same with Jack.

## Chapter 15

## RUSSIAN ROULETTE

Jack Muir paced back and forth behind the row of large casement windows that fronted his fifth floor loft.

His pale-blue eyes were set wide apart, and were slightly downcast at the outsides: and now, somewhat sunken, they gave him the appearance of a man engaged in hopeless prayer. He wore a pair of tie-dyed thermal long-johns, which bagged at the behind and knees and hung loose at the ankles and a baggy threadbare football sweatshirt, from which the name, number, and school had been removed, leaving only four gold letters—HIGH—to indicate its origins. His sandals flip-flapped as he made his stalking panther rounds inside the barless cage of his casement windows. Outside the wind was battering the loose panes of glass like an injured suppliant wanting in. One extraordinary thud brought a curse from Muir's petulant lips.

Suddenly he desisted from his pacing and maneuvered the fifty feet to the rear of the loft, overcoming an obstacle course of littered work tables, stacked canvases, and easled paintings. At the rear he bent over a small, paint-stained sink that was a mere afterthought affixed to the wall, and hastily brushed his teeth and rinsed his eyes with a damp wash-rag. He poured himself a glass of water, popped two big methadone tablets into his mouth and washed them down, gulping. He half filled a saucepan with water, threw a hand-ful of Bustello coffee into it, and placed the pan on an electric single-burner in a corner which was already giving off heat from its glowing orange ring. Now he stumbled toward the front of the loft and threw himself down on the bare mattress that rested there and lighted a cigarette. He smoked for sev-eral minutes, staring up at the cracked ceiling through the changing cloud-patterns of smoke above him; then, hearing the coffee boiling, he got up and went into the back and returned with a mug and stood drinking the steaming brew and smoking the butt-end of his cigarette while staring down at the two fourth floor windows of the building directly across the street.

He had often stood behind the windows at which he was now looking, in a similar attitude, contemplating these casement windows behind which he now stood—behind which waited his work, his unfinished paintings: almost, one might say, adding the appropriate state of mind to this proposition, his destiny as an artist. Now, for several months, things had been quite the reverse: of late he had been standing as he now stood, contemplating the windows of what was once his apartment, his home, and wondering as to his destiny, not as an artist, but as a man.

Monk was his Mephistopheles, to whom in his blindness he had sold his soul. For knowledge! What kind of knowledge? Was it truly, as he had at first thought, for the knowledge that is the experience of profound creation? The sensations of genius without genius—can they be had, bought? No! He saw now that he had been like a child who demands that which he cannot properly use.

But was it truly for that that he had sold his soul? Or was it out of fear of failure? Doubt, doubt, that was all he had known for years. But a year ago he had had everything for which a wise man should have been grateful. Most important, he had had Toddy, who loved him. He stopped and looked down at the two black squares, like blind, lonely eyes, across the street. His nose was running badly, but he had no cold: it was withdrawal. He itched. But it wasn't bad at all, getting straight, kicking, being clean: the methadone made it easy. But one had to be careful to use as little as possible, or be hooked on it as well. He sniffled, dug in his pockets for a handkerchief or a piece of tissue, found none, and blew his nose between his fingers, farmer-style. He pulled his shirt up and wiped his nose on it, all the time keeping his eyes on the windows across the street.

He put down his empty coffee mug, which had been hanging, all the while, like a monstrous-odd jade ring, from the little finger of his left hand, and pushed up the sleeve of his football shirt, exposing a thin pale arm with a riddle of red dots and blue bruises at the crook and tracks up to his shoulder and down to his wrist. He jerked the sleeve of his shirt down to his wrist and turned to face his work.

The easled canvases stood about the huge room like so many accusing ghosts in the twilight. The room was like a moonlit graveyard. Ghosts, or headstones, beneath which were buried the aspirations of a young painter who no longer lived.

Suddenly he strode across the room to a small bureau and removed from the top drawer a dully glinting object of gun-metal blue. In the still, dark night of the enormous room there was only the clickety-clackity-click of the cylinder being rolled: then, as the hammer fell on an empty chamber, a sharp metallic snap.

Muir crossed the room to the mattress and threw himself down, breathing heavily. In a few moments his breathing became more even, and he lighted a cigarette, blowing the smoke up into the dim opacity above him. The loneliest of all moments had been overcome, survived. Inside, he glittered with ecstasy. It was better than dope. He was convinced, now, that he could live. For fifteen minutes he lay in the now thoroughly darkened room and smoked and enjoyed this overwhelming sensation of euphoria. Then he snuffed out his cigarette and fell asleep.

Chapter 16

COLD TURKEY

Fifteen minutes later Jack was awakened by a call from

385

the street. He stood up, and something thudded to the floor at his feet. He took a step in the dark and kicked something. He heard the revolver slide weightily across the bare boards of the floor. He groped about by the mattress, found the flashlight, and then turned on a floor lamp that stood nearby. Muir went to the window and opened it, looking out. A cold blast snapped him awake. He looked down and saw Dedi Pavon's upward-tilted, wedge-shaped face atop a crazily foreshortened body, and, below the body, peeping out like little blue birds, two pointy, blue-tipped feet.

Dedi called up: "Hey, Jack, lemme in! She's freezing out here."

"Hold on," Muir called back. He searched for and found his trousers, and groped in them for his keyring. He found his keys and dropped them down to Dedi, hearing them hit, tinkling on the sidewalk below, and then pulled on the trousers. He looked across the street. Those enigmatic windows were still dark. He closed his own window and went into the rear to re-heat the coffee. In a moment, Dedi burst in the door, shivering and wiping his drizzling nose on his sleeve.

"Ay, it's cold as a dead fish out there!"

"Want some coffee?" Muir asked.

"Not that black mud you make, mon—no thanks. I got a weak stomach."

"It's P.R. coffee," said Muir, bringing two mugs despite Dedi's objection.

"I know it's P.R. coffee," said Dedi, who had received a mug into his hands and was now eyeing its contents suspiciously, "that's why I no want it—it's way too strong. I only drink that weak gringo slop. You know I'm a sick boy." Nevertheless, he drained off half the coffee from the mug. He settled down, taking a seat on the mattress, and lighting a cigarette. His small, pocked, lesioned face assumed a lugubrious expression. "Hey, Jack," he said, challengingly, "why you not been around to see us, eh? Pilar think you don't love her no more."

"I've been kicking," Muir said, "I wanted to be alone. Tell her I'm sorry." He sipped his coffee, nervously.

"Kicking! No shit? What you wanta do that for?"

"Lots of reasons."

"No shit? Well, what you on? Meth? Or you been shooting tranks?"

"Shooting nothing," Muir said; "I don't intend to go out shooting. Besides, you can get an abscess from shooting tranquilizers, if you miss the vein. Shit, I'm through with needles. I'm sick of the whole scene."

"You taking methadone, eh?"

"Taking methadone," Muir affirmed.

"What, you at a clinic?"

"No. I traded my smack for the meth."

"Good deal?"

"Even Steven."

"You serious, eh?"

"I'm serious. I mean to get straight."

"Oh," Dedi said, rubbing his cheek and looking away, "you start again. Everybody start again." He looked quickly back at Muir. "But, you know," he said, "like it's a good thing to get yourself clean out inside. I kicked lots of time. Pilar, she kicked. Everybody kicks. It's a good thing."

"It's not going to be that way with me," Muir said, his face assuming a determined expression, "I'll never start again. Anybody can kick if they've got the will. That's the body habit. The rest is in the mind."

"That's cool, mon," said Dedi, nodding his head up and down, "that's real cool. I know you mean that. But, you know, mon, that's pretty tough. Once you know what stuff is like, you always want to do it again. Hey, mon," Dedi exclaimed suddenly, "what's that? Is that real? What's you doing with that gat?" He pointed across the room to where the revolver lay.

"That's not what they call them anymore," said Muir. "You're out of touch, Dedi."

"Lissen, that's what Humphrey Bogart calls them in the old flicks, and if it's good enough for that cat it's good enough for me. What you want with that thing anyhow for?"

Muir went over and picked up the revolver and brought it back to the mattress, where he sat down. He hefted the pistol, looked it over, and then put it on the floor at his feet.

"What you gonna do?" asked Dedi. "You gonna kill somebody?"

"I use it in a game I've been playing," was Muir's enigmatic answer.

Dedi looked at him suspiciously. "I don't like to use no gat," he said, after a contemplative pause, "that way is too easy to kill somebody." He gave Muir a meaningful look. "That's big trouble, mon." He pulled from his belt a foot-long iron bar thickly wrapped in electrician's tape and hefted it admiringly. "Don't even break the skin if you use it right. But that—" he jerked his small, underslung knob of a chin at the revolver and grimaced.

"It was good enough for Bogart," Muir said.

"I dig, mon: but you ain't no classic. Look, Jack, what'sa matter with you? You make me worry about you, mon, and that ain't good, 'cause I'm a sick boy, see; I ain't supposed to worry."

"You know what's the matter with me," Muir said, lighting a cigarette, "I'm a crazy artist, you told me so yourself."

"No joke, mon! I know what you into again: you into that killing Monk shit. That's a bad scene, mon. Dig! Leave it alone. You gonna get your ass in a sling, then what's you gonna do? Monk'll get you—he's a bad cat. But if you get him, your ass still in a sling. It ain't no good either way."

"What am I supposed to do, let him keep my wife? Besides, I don't intend to kill anybody. I'm just going to go over there and break it up, that's all."

"Get broke up, that's what you gonna do.  And if you go over there with that gat, Monk'll kill you."  Dedi shook his head. "How come a real smart cat like you is so dumb?  Eh?  Lissen, mon, let them people alone.  If you wanna get straight, you do that, mon, just don't go back there no more.  Go see my sister; she in love with you.  You and me, we could be brothers.  Why you not marry my sister?  Hey, why don't we do that, bro, that sounds real good?"

"And let that bastard get away with what he did to me?"

"Oh, yeah, I dig," said Dedi scornfully; "you a real macho, big mon, look at me.  But that mon gonna eat you up.  That geek bite off you dumb head like you was a chicken."  Dedi stuck a thumb in his mouth and jerked it out, folding it into his fingers.  "Look, ma, no head."

"It didn't happen to you, you don't know how it feels."

"Look, you a real bright guy, but you been alone too much.  That makes things get into your head.  What you gotta do is get a real nice woman, bro, who like you, and then you go some place with her—  You know what a good place to go is?  Like Puerto Rico, see?  Your old mon is rich.  He would send you to Puerto Rico— "

"Lay off, Dedi," Muir said, getting to his feet, "you're pushing me, I can't think."

"Don't think, bro, that's the trouble with you.  Same thing with all you gringos, think, think, think, and never do."

Muir went to the rear of the loft and came back with two more mugs of coffee.  He handed one to Dedi.  He remained standing.

"I seen Toddy just now with some new guy," Dedi dropped casually.  He sipped his coffee, slurping.

"Where?  Who?"

"At the Saints and Sinners.  Some guy name Sam."

"Sam?"

"Si, Sam something.  I don't know.  A real dude type.  I almost sold him a watch.  Toddy and Tiger messed it up."

389

"What were they doing?"

"Just drinking. They was pretty high. You know this Sam guy?"

"I don't know anybody named Sam."

"Toddy said he was a friend of yours, I think."

Muir looked blank; then he said: "Were they— I mean, did they look . . . close?"

"Well, you know, bro, hard to say—they was high, like I said. Anyhow, what's you care? You got Pilar. She love you. What you going on about Toddy for? That bitch only make you unhappy, anyhow."

"Shut up, Dedi, you don't know what you're talking about."

"Hey, bro, don't get uptight. I'm only trying to help you."

"Don't try so hard. Drink your coffee and tell me what you want. I don't need a watch, if that's what's on your mind. Have you got a TV set under your shirt? By the way, where's your overcoat?"

"I fucked up, mon. My overcoat is at the scene of the crime. I busted a warehouse last night. Watchman almost got me. I had to split, pronto, dig? I got two boxes of watches that nobody will buy, and I lost a good overcoat that I really needed. What a life!"

"Can the coat be traced to you?"

"Come on, bro. It was just a coat."

"And you talk about me getting into trouble—"

"That ain't nothing. Nobody going to get excited about a couple of boxes of watches. Trouble is, see, I ain't got no way to fence nothing since they busted my guy. What I'm gonna do? I'm a sick boy! I gotta buy medicine tonight."

"Take some of my paintings down to the corner and peddle them. They ought to bring a couple of bucks for the canvas alone. Take that portrait I did of you—anybody'd pay a grand for it."

"Hey, you sure think you funny, Jack. Mon, you a real scream. I only wish—shit, if you had a TV I'd steal it from you."

"I was offered two grand for it at the show."

"Sure. At the show. That was a year ago, bro. Where is that cat who offered you the two Gs? You tell me where he is and I'll go take him the painting. If he still want it."

"So, you think I'm a has-been, eh?"

"You said it, bro." Dedi laughed. "Hey," he exclaimed, "how 'bout that gat? I could get some nice change for that, I bet."

"I told you, I need that for a game I play."

"I think you loco, bro, you know that?" Dedi got to his feet, kicking his trousers down at the cuffs of his pants. "I guess you ain't gonna give me no bread, eh?"

"I haven't got any to give. My check doesn't come till the first of the month. I'm flat. Tap City."

"How come you broke already?"

"I had to buy the revolver to play my game, didn't I?"

"And that's what you spend your bread on? Shit, you worse off than me. Well, that means I gotta pull a job."

"Don't go getting yourself into trouble, macho," Muir said.

"Well, I gotta have my medicine, don't I?"

Muir shrugged. "Where are you going to meet Monk? Over there?" He indicated Toddy's apartment with a jerk of his head.

"Yeah; he'll be there at ten."

"Maybe I'll be over," Muir said.

"Well, I tell you what, bro," Dedi said, pulling open the door, "you wait till you see me come out before you go in, O.K.? 'Cause I got a weak stomach, Ace."

Chapter 17

## HIS SISTER'S HONOR

Dedi worried about the fact that, for the first time since he had used heroin, Jack was trying to kick it, and he worried about the revolver.  He worried as he walked with the wind at his back toward the center of the Strip.  On the opposite side of the avenue Toddy Muir, one hand holding her tam in place, the other gripping the collar of her coat, and the man whom he had met a little while before under the name of Sam Hopkins, who slouched in a great black overcoat and heaved his long legs before him like a man climbing a steep hill, came fighting their way against the same wind that was pushing Dedi forward, a wind that would have negated by scattering into the void any cry of recognition he might make.  He saw them, and went on, virtually lifted and cast forward like a kite, or a small, outlandishly feathered bird, hapless in the wrong climate, tail to the wind.

He staggered on, jacket collar up, small frail hands sunk deep in pockets, probing thin, spasmodically contracting thighs for warmth, shivering, shaking, and thinking of Jack Muir, his friend, and of Pilar, his sister.

As Dedi reconstructed the past, Pilar was not more than eight at the time that he was born, and they had lived at some seaside shack in New Jersey.  When his father appeared with a knife with which to cut the cord and sink him for good where no one would ever look, and found what Pilar had done—how, desperate to save him, she had gnawed the cord through—the father began to rage.  She had picked up the infant and run from the house.  He came following her through beachfront streets and along the beach, stumbling and waving the knife, and calling drunkenly after her that he would kill them both, until she found sanctuary for them at the home, another beach-shack, of her mother's brother.  It was the uncle who drove their father away by firing at him with a rifle. Now Jack Muir was important to Dedi, and to his sister. And there was Monk. Even now, he, Dedi Pavon, was doing a dance macabre to Monk's music. Behind any dream of his triad happiness—he and Pilar and Muir all together and loving in a Screen Gem Classic movie-set existence—were other, more immediate thoughts, the former only as a false dawn, beautiful and insubstantial, when compared with these later ruminations, these actual fires of a sun which was necessary to existence.

Dedi had decided what he was going to do before he left Muir's loft. At the far-opposite end of the Strip from Jack Muir's loft and Toddy Muir's apartment—past the Saints and Sinners Club and the other dives that formed the thick, crusted, bright-colored patch, like the front-and-center zircons of a cheap costume choker, which was the center of it, and set apart from that gaudy center by a double row of dead buildings, blank dark warehouses and a scissors factory—there existed, like the mirage of a small oasis among the grey, night-desert tones surrounding it, a small hotel. Dedi Pavon had never been inside this hotel (which, thirty years before, some previous perhaps altruistic owner of it had dubbed the Saint Christopher, after the patron saint of travellers, but which was known along the Strip, as the Busy Nook, thus redubbed by some humorous errant sailor upon his return from it to the Saints and Sinners Club after an hour's hiatus) but his sister had heard of it, as he knew, having had the misfortune to have overheard her name mentioned in connection with it in his fourteenth year: and ever after he had felt the need to avenge himself upon it, perhaps by burning it to the ground (but this idea he relented of when it occurred to him that there might be other poor misused girls like his own sister in the hotel), or perhaps by some other means of destruction, or some injury which he could inflict upon it which would even the score: but never until now had two needs coincided so perfectly as did his need of money and his need of revenge to produce an action on his part which he could consider something of an artistic achievement, if it could be brought off . . . "Do or die," Dedi said.

Chapter 18

THE BUSY NOOK

When Felix Potter, camel-faced night-clerk of The Busy Nook, and Peeping Tom extraordinaire, saw the young, badly pocked "Spic" enter the small, dank lobby, he thought: "He wants some action, and I have nothing to do all night but let the working girls check themselves in and out. Maybe I can get the boy to sit back here with me."  But he said, in a stern voice, not, however, unmitigated by a kind of twilit, violet-flavored mouth-cologne: "Yea-ahs . . ?  And what might I do for you?" But the boy, somewhat disconcertingly, proceeded to walk up to the desk, lift its gate, and step boldly in beside the night-clerk.

"Well?  What do you want?" demanded Potter, alarm pretending to be anger.  And that was the last thing that Potter remembered about the incident when he related these truncated events to the police an hour later.

"He must have hit me," exclaimed the night-clerk, who seemed to find it hard to believe that anyone would have the temerity to commit such an act.

"Did you recognize him?" asked Lieutenant Figlia.

"I'm not certain."  Potter was holding an ice-cube wrapped in a washcloth to his temple.  "All those Spics look alike to me.  But there was something about him . . . maybe I've seen him in the neighborhood.  But I'm not sure . . . no, I'm not sure."

"Would you recognize him if you saw him again?"

"I believe so . . . But, as I say, I'm not sure. It all happened so fast. The thing was, he had no overcoat. It crossed my mind that he should be wearing an overcoat on a cold night like this."

"No overcoat?" Figlia made a note, commenting, "There was a small overcoat left behind in a warehouse burglary last night. Possibly the same man. Kid," he amended. "And you said he was small?"

"Quite," Potter affirmed. "And gay."

"What makes you say that?"

"AIDS! Written all over his face. Safe sex is the only way to go," he added, taking a package of condoms from his inside pocket and displaying it as if displaying his own virtue. "Or come." He laughed.

"How much did he get?"

"Oh, that's the awful part." Potter rolled his head and eyes in different directions. "Dreadful! I should have cleared the drawer an hour ago—ordinarily we clear it every two hours—but I happened to be busy doing something upstairs—an emergency, you know, a toilet backed up—and I hadn't got to it yet . . ."

"How much?"

"About three hundred and fifty dollars."

"Three and a half!" The young Detective Third Grade, Verdi, whose case it was, blew between his teeth, and winked at Figlia. "That's a big take for a little pimp-haven like this," he said. "The service must be terrific."

Potter looked away; then, looking back, said: "My boss'll kill me."

"You shouldn't spend so much time upstairs, Mr. Potter," said the young Detective, grinning. Everyone in the precinct knew of Potter's proclivities. The working girls brought stories in to the station house.

"I have my duties to perform," the night clerk countered, indignantly.

"I bet you do," rejoined the Detective. "I hear you have to keep an eye on your guests."

"I only check to see that nothing is going on that shouldn't be," Potter said, flushing.

"Well," said the Detective, chuckling, "tell that to your boss."

Figlia gave the Detective a sharp look that erased his grin.

"But what are you going to do about this?" Potter demanded to know.

"Whatever we can, naturally," said Figlia. "But if you're hoping to get any of that take back before your boss finds out, you might as well forget it. There must be five-hundred kids in any neighborhood who fit the description you've given us."

"It was probably some junkie . . ." said the Detective. "Or maybe one of those Bravos, the motorcycle gang. They own a building near here."

"Come to think of it," said Potter, "he did look kind of hopped up or something . . . his eyes were funny."

"Sure," said Verdi, "funny eyes. I'll put that in my report."

Chapter 19

CONNECTING THE DOTS

Lieutenant Figlia knew the streets of the East Village, but his forays had been random. Detective Verdi was local. These were his streets. He knew them club by club, alley by alley. As they maneuvered the late evening traffic, he acted as a tour guide for Figlia. The streets of the East Village were teeming with activity. "Rockers," Verdi said. Music thumped and machine-gunned from the doors of the clubs. "Painters, sculptors, performance artists," Verdi said;

and more music blared from the open gates of the galleries. "Junkies, dealers, rapists, celebrities of every sort—it's a freak show in a carnival." Verdi steered slowly through the traffic. "I thought we might go over and roust the Bravos."

"Tell me about them," said Figlia.

"They're two-tiered. Juniors and seniors. The juniors range in age from around twelve to sixteen, seventeen, the seniors go on from there, up to twenty-five or so. They're racially mixed. The juniors are just your ordinary juvenile delinquent street gang, the seniors are full-blown gangsters. They deal in drugs, extortion, prostitution, everything. The seniors are recruited from the juniors. They own a building over on Third, their headquarters. It's supposed to be a sort of club house, but God knows what goes on in there when we're not looking. Ownership of the building is listed as a corporation. One of the members of the corporation is listed as Martin Kent. We figure it's Monk Stolz. We figure he supplies the club house and they do errands for him. The seniors aren't as difficult to deal with as the juniors are. The juniors get hopped up every so often and go crazy. They rampage through the streets. The seniors stick pretty much to business."

"How many are there?"

"Oh, hell, all together—might be two hundred."

"What's the point of rousting them?" said Figlia.

"Let's them know we're here."

"I don't like wasting my time," said Figlia. "Let's go back to the station."

Verdi looked disappointed. He drove on in silence.

Figlia said, "So you think Monk Stolz owns the building?"

"Oh, yeah," said Verdi, "that building and half a dozen others around here."

"So he's a real estate tycoon, too," said Figlia.

"These dealers got to have something to do with their money."

"Was there a time when I never heard of that son-of-a-bitch?" Figlia asked, connecting the dots back to that day six months earlier when he pulled up in front of his daughter's building, summoned by Sergeant Purl of his old Chelsea precinct.

The Chelsea studio-apartment was alive with post-mortem activity. "I found the sheet in a drawer and put it over her," said Sergeant Purl. The middle-aged precinct detective held Lieutenant Figlia by the arm with one hand and lifted the sheet away with the other.

"Yes," Figlia said, "that's Rose. That's my daughter." He saw broken glass, and the powerful odor of Scotch rose from the bed.

"Sit down, Lieutenant." Purl swung him a straight-backed chair.

Figlia sat down.

"You don't know anything about this, then?"

Figlia shook his head. How would he, as a cop, want this story told? "Rose's mother died two years ago. Rose knew I had been seeing another woman—my present wife, Gena. When Gena and I got married, Rose resented it, and moved out of the house. That was a year ago. She came back here. I guess she wanted to be near her mother. I mean, where she grew up. She's only just eighteen." He leaned over, his hands on his knees. "Hell, I spent fifteen years in this precinct—at your job, in fact—before I transferred to narcotics. Chelsea was like a hometown to Rose. She was baptized here at St. Savior's. God, Purl," he said, "leave me alone."

"Sure, Lieutenant. You just sit tight for a minute."

## Chapter 20

## THE WOMEN IN FIGLIA'S LIFE

Figlia had married his first wife, Cynthia, a frozen saint, when they were both eighteen. When he returned from Viet Nam, a bemedalled hero with a battlefield commission, he became a policeman, and they began to part ways.

Several factors contributed to this parting of the ways. For one thing, Cynthia, who had been an undemanding fiancée, made a demanding, jealous, and possessive—if not sexual—wife. She had no family of her own of which to speak, and she was jealously hostile toward Figlia's, which at that time consisted of his mother and his two sisters. Cynthia tried to drive a wedge between himself and his family, and his resentment of this became a factor in their dissolution.

Still another problem was that Cynthia, and he as well, had desired children, and none were immediately forthcoming. Then when he joined the Police Department all of these factors conjoined; for Cynthia had opposed his becoming a police officer, her true anxiety in this matter resting in her neurotic belief that he would meet women who would tempt him, and that she would lose him to one of them. She knew that he was not deeply religious, as she herself was, at least in the formal sense, and would not hesitate to divorce her and marry another, one who could get on with his mother, and who could bear him a child.

Over the first few years of their marriage, Figlia became, in the course of doing police work, increasingly worldly, while during the same years his wife became an embittered, semi-mystical hermit. Then, the child came, the product of cold, but required sex, his daughter, "little Cynthia," or Rose, the lynch-pin of their marriage.

In spite of his wife's wilder imaginings, Figlia had always honored his marriage. Now, with the child, with his work, which he loved, he felt that his destiny was decided. Two out of three was, to a worldly, rather fatalistic man, not a bad score. He did his job (and was steadily raised in rank and importance) and took good care of his family (but regretted that his duties kept him so much from his daughter, who was growing up), and nearly twenty years later his wife, grown into a veritable harridan, dropped dead at her prayers.

Figlia was sorry about his wife. He felt a low-keyed remorse that they hadn't loved each other. Looking back over their years together, he had also to admire her for her prophetic skill; because, in the long run, she had been right. At forty-three, loneliness had won out over good intentions, and he had acquired a mistress. Indeed, it was a youngish widow whom he had met during an investigation of an apartment house burglary, at the old precinct, in Chelsea. Gena had had nothing to do with the case. It was the apartment next to hers which had been burglarized, and he had only questioned her as to whether she'd heard anything. They immediately liked each other; he saw her again, then frequently; and soon they were in love. He was thinking of divorce. Then, as if on cue, Cynthia died. He was shocked, giddy, happy, guilty; and three-months later he introduced Gena to Rose.

Perhaps it was too soon. Perhaps it would always be too soon. Rose had belonged to Cynthia. Rose had been Cynthia's consolation prize. When, several months later, he married Gena, Rose, now eighteen, moved out. On several occasions, seeing how this estrangement was hurting her husband, Gena went to see Rose, only to be rebuffed, or to be abused as a homewrecker. They had killed her mother and ruined her own life. She hated them. Gena advised her husband to wait, not to push. He waited. He didn't push.

Finally Figlia felt free to transfer out of the routine of precinct work, something he had wished to do for years, and into the Narcotics Division, which allowed him a free-roaming life. Occasionally, when near it on some business or other, he would drop up to Rose's apartment. If she were at home, she'd open the door a crack, look at him contemptuously, and shut it in his face. He had heard vague neighborhood rumors, most emanating from activities centered at St. Saviors, that she had acquired a boyfriend. Once, after having the door slammed in his face, he returned to his car and sat in it for a long while, remembering those past years when she would run for half a block to leap into his arms, and he almost cried with his arms hanging on the steering wheel and his face buried in them. But one thing became a greater certainty each day—that he had been right to marry Gena. This he could not doubt even in the face of his daughter's death.

Chapter 21

THE NIGHTMARE OF FOREVER

Figlia had been present at dozens of scenes of death, and this one was typical, except for the fact that the dead girl was his daughter. He wondered why he didn't feel more, why he didn't find himself rolling about on the floor and screaming. Delayed reaction. He'd seen it before, and now he knew how it felt: the numbness of it. But the pain would come. He had seen people break down hours, days, even months later. He hung on to being a cop.

"I tried to see her," he said to Purl, "but it was no go. I've never been in this apartment. Can you imagine? But I thought she'd get over it."

"She would have," Purl said. "I got a teenager myself. It's hard for them. A lot of stress, but most of them get by."

"How do you read it?" Figlia asked.

"No indication of a habit. No tracks. No other needle marks."

"Then she was murdered."

"Not necessarily. Could have been her first time out."

"I know," said Figlia. "But isn't it murder just the same?"

"I know what you mean," said Purl. "She shared the place with a boyfriend. Did you know that?"

Figlia shook his head.

"A junkie. Three months out of rehab. He claims to be clean. About eighteen. There's an outfit on the bed by the— by her. Needle mark's in the right arm. Was she left-handed?"

"Yes."

"She was? Well, see, I thought maybe the kid could have shot her up. Nothing's too clear yet. She wasn't suicidal, was she?"

"No. God, I don't think so. What's the kid say?"

"Says he went on an errand for another guy who waited here. When he got back he found her."

"And he called in?"

"Right."

"Where is he?"

"At the station. Couple of the boys are going through the files with him. He says this other guy's name is Kenton."

"There has to be an autopsy, doesn't there?"

"You want to know for sure, don't you? It could have been a simple O.D., or it could have been bad stuff—poisoned, or God knows what. And if there's bad stuff on the street, you'd want to know. Or it might have been an accident. Then a coverup."

"I want it done fast."

"Of course. It'll get priority." Sergeant Purl put a comforting hand on Figlia's narrow shoulder. "Let Homicide West handle this, Lieutenant."

Figlia flushed. "What in hell am I a cop for, if not for this? Besides, this is a narcotics case, isn't it? That's my beat.  I'm going over to the station and talk to the kid.  What's his name?"

"Billy Sawyer."

Figlia watched blankly as the Medical Examiner's people removed the sheet from Rose's body.  Later, he saw them zip her into a plastic bag.

Dusk settled on the hot city as Figlia walked the two blocks to his old precinct house.  He knew the detectives who were questioning Billy Sawyer behind a big one-way mirror.  He wiped sweat from his brow with a folded handkerchief held in a shaking hand, and studied the face of the skinny, frightened boy.  He tapped on the one-way mirror, and one of the interrogators stepped out.

"What have you got?"

"He says it's this bird."  He handed Figlia a thick manila folder.  "Says this one sent him up to Penn Station to pick up a package, and when he got back—"

"Stolz!"

"You know him?"

"I know of him.  A dealer.  I broke up a party of his.  He said he'd even the score.  Maybe he has."

"Yes, sir."

"Is the boy on anything?"

"No, sir.  He's clean."

"What was in the package?"

"A porno film.  8mm.  A good-looker, maybe black, kinda pale; a white dyke; and a black guy.  They're circling a bald headed, naked white side of beef with whips.  They really lay it on him," he added.

"That would be the illustrious Mr. Kenton—Stolz, himself," said Figlia.  "I've heard he's kinky.  Know any of the others?"

"No, sir."

"Does he?"  He pointed at the boy.

"No, sir."

“No drugs?”

“No drugs.”

“What’s it look like to you?”

The young detective looked nervous. “I think he’s telling the truth.”

Figlia crossed the room to his old desk, the one he had when he first got his gold detective shield. He draped his suitcoat and hat on the coat tree and sank into the swivel. It felt like the same chair. Everything seemed the same but for the computer that had replaced his old Remington. He shook off a sense of déjà vu, and phoned Billy Sawyer’s parole officer. Billy appeared to be drug-free. He was a religious boy, acting as a sort of acolyte at St. Savior’s. His association with Stolz was a parole violation; but, in the current climate, not likely to be acted on.

Figlia talked again to the questioning detectives, who told him that, after Billy Sawyer graduated rehab, his first contact with Monk Stolz was for the purpose of borrowing money. He was to pay off this debt and to receive fifty dollars extra for his trip to Penn Station. This angel would have to wait a while for his wings. Two hundred and fifty dollars is a good deal of money for an errand. Surely he should have suspected that what he was doing wasn’t kosher. Figlia saw the possibility of the kid spending some time in the slammer; but it wasn’t likely, if nothing else came up. He went in alone to talk to the boy. The boy rose, then sank back into his chair.

“Are you her father?”

“Rose was my daughter.”

“She talked about you. She said you were on the outs.”

“Did she?” Figlia eyed the boy coldly.

“But she was proud of you.”

“Was she proud of you?”

The boy stared at his knees, where his thin red hands rested.

“Where did you meet Rose?”

"At St. Savior's. The drug rehab center."

"Rose wasn't on drugs, was she?"

"Oh, no, she just went to Mass there."

"Since she was a little girl . . . How could you bring a pig like Stolz to my daughter's apartment? How could you? And then leave him alone with her!"

"I didn't know about him. Honest, I didn't know what he was like. I didn't even know his name was Stolz. I thought it was Kenton. I got H from him a couple of times when I was on it, and I did a couple of odd-jobs—just pick up and delivery—when I got out. He seemed all right. He loaned me money when I needed clothes, so I could look for a job. If I'd known he was that kind of creep . . ." Figlia reached out and pulled the boy to his feet, shaking him. The boy went limp in Figlia's hands and let his head bob. Tears flew from his face. Figlia let him sink into the chair.

"I loved her," the boy said. "Honest I did."

Back in the squad room, Figlia telephoned Gena, who was waiting at their Long Island home for a second, confirming call.

"Yes?"

"It's true."

"No . . . Al, are you all right?"

"I'm all right. I want the funeral as soon as possible. We'll have Father Ryan here at St. Savior's. He christened her. I'll go around and see if I can talk to him tonight. I need a drink. See you later." Now, six months later, the nightmare continued, and Figlia lived with it.


Chapter 22


SOMETHING LOST


A golden glow of light emanated from the front windows of the Mid-East Gardens Restaurant in Greenwich

Village. Inside, Camilla, Ansar, and Mahmoud were surrounded by a three-walled mural describing in elaborate Arabic calligraphy  outstanding events in the life of the Prophet Muhammad. The murals were in subdued, rich colors and gave the large diningroom filled with moving waiters and seated diners an atmosphere of coziness. They were led to a table, passed the extremely beautiful calligraphic description of Muhammad's Marriage to the Rich Widow, the Vision at Mt. Hira, and the Flight to Abyssinia.  Ansar stood behind his chair, in front of The Plot to Murder the Prophet, bouncing on the balls of his horny feet. Camilla and Mahmoud were seated, and looked up at Ansar from their places at the table. Mahmoud said, "Aren't you going to sit down, my friend?"

"I have no appetite. I have things I must do. You must instruct me how to find this address," he said, throwing a scrap of paper in front of Mahmoud.

"Horatio Street," read Mahmoud. "Just walk north three blocks. Uptown. You can't miss it."

Ansar grabbed up the paper. "I am welcomed any time, I am told. I must go. I will rejoin you here in not too long. Camilla, you eat! Mahmoud, my friend, keep her safe. Allah be praised!" Ansar was such an energy that he did not seem to leave them, but to vanish before their eyes, leaving a stir of particles in the air.

Mahmoud ordered couscous and lamb for Camilla and himself, and, among several sharable dishes, a bean pie. He turned to scrutinize the young woman while they were waiting. "Camilla—that's a pretty name."

"I'm a freeborn girl. That's what Camilla means in Latin. My mother chose the name. She told me never to tell my father what it really meant. He has absolutely no idea." She frowned. "Also—one in attendance at a sacrifice. Scary, uh?"

Mahmoud had sensed that all was not well with her. "Is

there anything wrong?" he said, after a moment's reflection.

"Everything's wrong," she said. "Mostly him."

"What do you mean?"

"Can't you tell? There's really something wrong with him. I've always known who he was, but until yesterday I'd never laid eyes on him. My family and his are tied together from way back. My folks gave me to understand that I was—well—sorta promised to him, in the old country style. Growing up, I had two ways of looking at it. One was, that someday this romantic figure out of the Middle-East, like Sinbad, was going to come and claim me for his own. I liked that one. The other one was, that the whole notion of a real Ansar was a figment of my family's imagination. That I would never really meet this guy, that the whole thing was fantastic, like the Arabian Nights, which I read in State Street High School in Toddling Chicago. The whole thing seemed crazy as hell to me. And I really couldn't believe that my Mom and Dad could possibly have meant it. Fundamentalists, strict, O.K., but my mom and dad, nonetheless. I've been thinking about taking off on my own for a year or so now. I couldn't take the atmosphere around the house anymore. But I didn't know anybody on the west coast—I'd thought about Hollywood—or on the east coast either. Then a couple of weeks ago it got to floating around the house that Ansar would be in New York—Brooklyn, Atlantic Avenue—so I took my chances that he'd turn out to be Sinbad. He ain't. More like Arafat."

"You have run away from home?" said Mahmoud, disapprovingly. "Young lady, what you have done is very, very wrong."

"Gimme a break," said Camilla, ruffling her hair with both hands. "That kind of stuff is the reason I ran away in the first place. Do you know what this jerk did when he first laid eyes on me? I went down to Brooklyn to meet him. He says, 'I claim you hereby in the name of Allah.' Here's this little beer barrel—that I never laid eyes on—and he claims me!  I said to myself, from the frying pan into the fire, but I figured what the heck, I'll see where it leads for a day or two.  After all, I don't know anybody else around here and I don't have much money."

"Do your parents have any idea where you are?"

"They might think that I came East to meet him."

"We must phone them sometime tonight and let them know that you are safe.  I can only imagine the anxiety you must be causing them."

"Is that other guy we met really your brother?  The hipster?"

"Tory?  Yes, he is my benighted brother."

"He seemed real cool to me."

"You are very young," and, he thought, "very attractive."  Mahmoud wondered if she might have some Ethiopian blood.  In any case, she was a jewel that must be kept safely hidden from thieves.

Camilla liked the bean pie.  "I've never had anything like it," she said, just as Ansar came up to the table.  He was carrying a shopping bag from Saks Fifth Avenue.  It bulged with clinking paraphernalia.  Emanating from it was the foul stink of rotten eggs.  He clanked it down beside his chair, and threw his coat over the back, where it hung like a dead baby camel.  He sat down.  "All has gone as planned.  I'm hungry now."

Mahmoud called the waiter.  He wondered if he should tell Ansar what Camilla had told him.  He decided for the moment on discretion.  He would wait and see.  Ansar had begun to disturb him as well.

They sat through Ansar's enormous meal sipping coffee and making small talk, Camilla and Mahmoud locked in a conspiracy of discretion, Ansar fingering food into his face as if there might soon be no more on the planet.  Suddenly Ansar was finished eating.  He rose without consultation.  "We must go. I have much work to do," he said. He looked at Mahmoud. "You will leave us. We will go to Brooklyn." He heaved on his Loden coat, patted its big pockets, and a look of sheer terror came over him.

"My book!" he exclaimed. "My book! Where's my book? I must have it. I cannot do my work without it." Now he was looking under the table, now like an Indian scout he followed the trail of the Persian rug out to the cash register, to the front door, then back to the table, desperation replacing terror.

"It probably dropped out at the Saints and Sinners Club," said Mahmoud. "You threw your coat over the back of the chair there, too."

"Of course!" said Ansar. "We must go back!"


Chapter 23


"MY NAME IS MICHAEL"


BILLIE HOLIDAY MEETS LAST CUE. Under the bold headline was a photo of the beautiful, black jazz singer; beside it, "She Died Game" heading three columns. The framed page of a "Daily News" article, a strange gift from Monk, who insisted that it be hung on the wall over the table, confronted Toddy as she entered the kitchen. She took two steps to the kitchen table and filled her glass with Scotch. Then she remembered that she had offered Sam Hopkins a cup of tea to soothe his whisky-corrupted stomach. It was quarter past nine. Soon time for Sam to be moving on. Maybe it was time for her to move on, too. Just pick up and walk out the door with the unknown Sam. Soon time for Monk . . . . She got out a battered tea-kettle, half filled it with water, and placed it over a flame. In a few minutes, the tea-kettle whistled. She put a tea bag in a cup and let it steep. She glanced at the clock. Soon, it said, soon. Sam must go soon. She banged her empty glass down on the counter-top, and went into the living room. Sam turned on his side in his sleep, away from her. She snuggled down close beside him, spoon-fashion, slipping her right arm around his chest. There was barely enough room. She closed her eyes and pressed herself to him, balancing on the edge, squeezing herself closer and closer to him, flattening her breasts against his back. She put her lips to the back of his neck, kissing lightly, searching around the base of his skull to his ear. She shoved her hips closer and lifted her right leg over his, her long mossy-green tweed skirt sliding upward, revealing black underwear and a strong firm rounded thigh. Her right hand with its tapered translucent little fingernails unbuttoned his shirt and slipped inside into the valley of his chest beneath the undershirt.

The wind outside gusted at the glass panes in their ancient sashes nearby and produced a muffled rumble. The sound seemed to come from far away, muted and dangerous, like that of a distant approaching army.

Toddy felt her heart beat on Sam's back like an accompaniment to the prickly nerves tingling from her calves up her spine and through her shoulders and arms. Her searching hand reached down to Sam's waist, moved along the belt to its buckle, undoing. She gently but firmly rubbed his crotch. He turned toward her with a groan, his left arm encircling her waist, pulling, his right arm lifting her onto him, her long legs astraddle. Toddy sat up, and, grasping her orange sweater, arms crossed, she pulled it up, up, revealing lacy black, creamy white, and then honey blonde hair, falling, falling, as she slung the garment to the floor.

Father Din was full awake. His sexual experience had been scant, and had left him bewildered and ashamed, longing for absolution in order that he might live the life that had been chosen for him. But this beautiful woman who sat astride him in the dim light exuded such a power, compelling, drawing him to her—closer, closer. She was real. And she wanted him.  Her tenderness, the sweetness of her being, were all powerful.  This was communion.  *This* was what he had dreamed of without knowing the meaning of the dream.  That part of himself which he had struggled to hide, which had hitherto been his mystery, had connected.  She leaned toward him a little, eyes closed.  He drew upward, toward her, reaching up, his hands molding her breasts, inching inside their black lace cover, freeing one pink nipple.  He looked at her closed eyes and whispered, not in confession, but in a soft declaration, "My name is Michael."  But Toddy heard only the couch creak as he raised them both slowly, to stand, shedding their clothes like leaves in winter.

With their arms entwined they stepped together crabwise, to the bedroom door and nearly stumbled onto the big bed.  Toddy spread over him in a relief of passion.  She pressed a liquid tongue between his lips, his teeth.  Little beads of sweat formed on her forehead.  "Oh, Sam, Ooooh," she crooned.  Like a baby being comforted, he heard her breathy lullaby.  Toddy reached under a pillow and withdrew a small packet, a condom.  She handed it to him and then wiggled herself onto him, feeling the heat from him thumping inside her.  She was alive! Oh, bloody hell, she was singing in her veins.  The long nights of misery and loss which had submerged her, left her bereft of spirit and companion and communion, pushed away as if pulled by the magnet moon.

Chapter 24

HARD COPY

Name:  STOLZ, KENNETH
Criminal Identification No.:  X112857
F.B.I. No.:  LL2456
Date of Birth:  4/18/60
Known Aliases:  Kenneth Stark, George Kenton, Harry

Kent, Thomas Paterson, Duane Lewis (last two names of former associates). Sometimes uses nickname: Monk.

History of Arrests:

First Arrest: Dec. 19, 1971

Charge: Pettit larceny.

Disposition: Charge dropped.

Second Arrest: April 21, 1974

Charge: Grand larceny (auto).

Disposition: Charge dropped, changed to Juvenile Delinquency (general detainment, due to age of subject). Subject released in custody of Juvenile Court, probation five-years.

Third Arrest: May 12, 1975

Charge: Robbery (mugging). Parole violation.

Disposition: Remanded to Boys' House of Detention until his sixteenth year.

Fourth Arrest: August 5, 1977

Charge: Aggravated assault.

Disposition: Charge dropped (insufficient evidence: victim withdrew complaint).

Fifth Arrest: Oct. 16, 1977

Charge: Homicide (suspicion of murder).

Disposition: Indicted, tried, found not guilty.

Remarks: The victim here was the same woman who brought the charge of aggravated assault against Stolz (see above). However, there was not enough evidence to bring a conviction.

"Vengeful bastard, ain't he?" said Captain Hubbard, who was reading Monk's file over Lieutenant Figlia's shoulder.

Figlia's straight black hair was thinning and through it his scalp gleamed. "So am I," he said. Hubbard took his hand from the back of Figlia's chair and came around the desk, seating himself on its front edge. He was a bulky black man in his early fifties with white hair, and tired, half-masted gray eyes. He was drinking coffee from a plastic container.

"The man is criminally insane," he said, his half-hidden gray eyes contemplating Figlia's large brown ones; "you could go on reading his file for a week. But that file is just the tip of the iceberg."

"He's an animal," Figlia said, pushing away the file on Kenneth Stolz with his free hand: his other hand was rubbing the back of his neck, massaging loose the cord-like muscles there, that had grown rigid as steel cables as he'd sat reading the printout of the man who was responsible for his daughter's death. "He has to be hunted down and . . ."

". . . brought in?" Hubbard finished Figlia's sentence.

Figlia's eyes grew hard. "What else?" he challenged.

"I don't know . . ."

"Look, Hub," Figlia snapped, "You think I haven't heard the stories that circulate about me? Of how I'm supposed to be on a vendetta? Obviously you believe they're true. I thought I could expect more from someone who's known me as long as you have. I thought I could expect—"

"Hold on, hold on," Hubbard said, breaking in, "take it easy now. It was you—only a moment ago—who said 'So am I' when I called Monk a vengeful bastard; isn't that so? That's the only reason I said anything."

Figlia stared at Hubbard for a moment, then wearifully dropped his head forward, inserting his chin into the open V of his collar, and closed his eyes.

"You're tired, strung out," Hubbard said. "Why don't you lie down in back for an hour?"

"When I finish this," Figlia said without opening his eyes.

"You've read it before."

"I want to read it again. I want to know how he does it. How he always gets away with it."

"He's a smart cookie and he's got plenty of money to play with. More than we'll ever see in a lifetime. But he doesn't always get away, as you can see."

Figlia opened his eyes. "But he gets away with the big things, the worst things," he said bitterly. "How come?"

"He either bribes or scares anybody who could talk against him—or else they disappear . . ."

"He bribes cops too," said Figlia.

Hubbard shrugged. "What can you do?"

"What can you do? Is that anything to say?"

"O.K. then," said Hubbard, ruffled, "what should I say?"

"Well, he's been around here for some time, Hub, from what I can gather. Why can't you get anything on him?"

"You want me to pick him up for jaywalking?"

Figlia closed his eyes and corrugated his forehead. He was only vaguely aware of Hubbard's short, sharp curse, of his getting to his feet, walking away. He looked up in time to see Hubbard's white head nodding, a door being pulled to, shutting it from view. He cupped his hands over his eyes and leaned back in his chair, staring into sudden pools of blue.

He swiveled into an upright position. Suddenly the room seemed to be filled with clatter. What time was it? Almost eight. He pushed aside several pages of the file until the came to one marked SECOND SHEET. He read:

Name:  STOLZ, KENNETH

Criminal Identification No. . . .

His eyes drifted down the page.

Height:  5'11"

Weight:  225 lbs.

Hair: Dark brown. Note: Subject shaves head.

Eyes:  Gray.

Nose:  Thickened at bridge; medium length; narrow at nostrils, sharp at tip.

Mouth:  Wide; thick lips.

Chin:  Round; prominent. Note: Subject sometimes wears beard or goatee.

Bone Structure:  Heavy.

Unusual Marks:  Tattoo, center of chest.  Hanging man with Latin word "Nullus" on forehead of figure.  Executed in green, red, and blue.  Pierced right earlobe.  Note:  Subject sometimes wears small earring.  Bullet wound scar on right side of chest near shoulder, upper pectoral.  Knife or razor-slash scar across left upper arm, at bicep.  Shrapnel wound scars scattered on outer right thigh, inner left thigh.

Note:  See SUPPLEMENTARY REMARKS.

Figlia pushed several more sheets aside and found SUP-PLEMENTARY REMARKS.  He read:

PSYCHIATRIC REPORT, BOYS' HOUSE OF DE-TENTION, PHILLIPSBURG, NEW YORK:  Kenneth Stolz is a boy of above average intelligence, but is wracked by inner conflicts stemming from a childhood spent under the domi-nance of an autocratic/authoritarian father and a neurotically submissive mother.  The result:  the sado-masochistic syn-drome is prominent.  The psyche is torn between . . . however, the id . . .

Figlia turned the page on this psycho-babble.

Stolz is possessed of a highly dangerous, vindictive . . .

Figlia turned the page.  He read:

HABITS/CHARACTERISTICS:  Kenneth Stolz is known to be a periodic alcoholic.  There is no evidence, how-ever, that he has ever taken hard drugs.  He is known to have dealt in drugs (spc. heroin, opium, morphine, cocaine, and crack cocaine) but it is believed that he holds users in con-tempt.  It is believed that he spent some time in Africa, em-ployed as a mercenary soldier (details are lacking).  His political affiliations, if any, are unknown.  According to ear-lier records he was baptized as a Catholic, but religious affil-iation is probably nominal.  He is of German stock and speaks the language.  His English has the perfection of a second lan-guage: he probably heard a good deal of German spoken at home as a child.  He is a good talker, and has been employed as a salesman.  He uses current slang.  It is believed that he

has some pretensions as a writer, and is fond of bohemian cir-
cles.  He is interested in the occult.  He is known to engage in
unusual sex practices.  Should be considered unpredictable,
highly dangerous . . ."

Figlia gathered up the pages scattered over his desk and
put them into a neat stack, and re-clipped them.  He picked
up a glass ball full of drifting snow, Santa Claus and rein-
deers, and placed it on top of the file.  Then he got up and
staggered into another room, rubbing his sore eyes.  Monk
equated with death.  The thought of death gave urgency to
life.  He needed Gena.  He found his topcoat and left for Long
Island, home and hearth.

Chapter 25

TRAPPED!

"What's that noise?  Toddy?"
"Mmm—what noise?"
"*That*.  That banging."
"Oh, my God!"
"Who is it?  Is it Monk?"
"Yes, probably."
They sat up, stung awake.
"What time is it?"
"Nine forty-five," Father Din said.
There came another round of rapid pounding at the door.
"Now you've done it," Toddy said.  "I warned you."
"I knew what I was doing," Father Din said.  "I wanted
to see you through this evening."
"You're crazy.  You don't know what you're getting
into."
"Don't tell me you didn't want me to stay.  Not after
what we've just done."

416

"Maybe I did. I did and I didn't. I wanted you to stay but I was afraid for you."

"We both wanted it this way. We'll face him down together. You'd better let him in before he breaks the door down. Hasn't he got a key?"

"I locked the door from the inside."

"Then he knows you're here . . . ."

Toddy nodded.

"What will he do?"

"I don't know—anything—nothing."

"Would it be better for you if I stayed out of sight until he's gone?"

"No. The apartment's too small, and once he comes in he won't leave for hours. It's no use; you have to meet him and get away as soon as possible. I'll try to head him off and explain before he sees you."

"Suppose you try to take him out with you?"

"He won't go. He's meeting people here."

"Then suppose you don't let him in at all?"

But as if in answer to this, the door gave a splintering gasp.

"No, no—nothing'll work now but making it up with him."

The door gave another gasp.

"Pull yourself together," Toddy called back as she ran into the kitchen, pulling on her sweater; and—"O.K., wait a minute; I'm coming."

Father Din stood up, and pulled on his clothes. He quickly ran a comb through his hair; then shrugged his shoulders, trying to re-shape his jacket. He heard Monk's voice sounding in the kitchen. "Where were you? I've been pounding on that damned door—"

"I fell asleep. Monk, listen . . ."

"—*Well?*"

"My friend is here—Sam Hopkins, the one you saw in Tiger's. He was drunk, Monk—he got sick. I brought him up here so he could lie down. He's been sleeping." She was breathless.

Father Din, following Toddy's lead, moved into the middle of the livingroom, clear of the Oriental screen, so that Monk could see him.

## Chapter 26

## THE BRAVOS

"What can I *do*?" cried Ansar, outside the Mid-East Gardens. His question, more of a plaint, was directed above to the unanswering sky. "Suppose I lost my book on the bus– " he posited, turning back, as Camilla and Mahmoud caught up with him.

"We'll wait for the same driver who brought us over to come round again," said Mahmoud, "but I think you probably lost it at the Saints and Sinners Club. I don't see how anything could drop out of those pockets when you were wearing the coat."

"I must be sure. We will wait here for the same driver to come around."

The three huddled at the bus stop, a treacherous cold corner, under a street lamp. The dull stars were being chased across the planetary night sky by an invisible force. Small, wicked eels of lightning wriggled down the sky. The street was quiet, but they could hear the traffic rumble from the broad avenue two blocks away. Finally a big rattling box of light came toward them, pulled to the gutter, snorted, and opened its doors. Ansar stepped up to the door, inspected the driver, and turned away, shaking his head. "Not this one," he said to Mahmoud. "This driver is a female." Then they heard a doggerel rhythm floating out of the dark toward them. And now they could distinguish a crowd of shadowy figures emerging into view. A gang of rappers, shouting: *If you can, then kill a cop, cut his belly, make him pop! A cop is full of ugly gas, rip his belly, save his ass!*

Camilla whispered, "Oh, my God!" She hid herself between Ansar and Mahmoud and hunched down in her coat as if trying to become invisible. In a moment, they were surrounded by chanting rappers who wore on their black plastic coats logos of knives stabbing through bleeding hearts. They continued their chant of *A cop is full of ugly gas, rip his belly, save his ass! The Bravos say it with a will, you got to learn to kill, kill, kill!*

Ansar looked nervously about him at the dancing, chanting figures who had formed a circle around himself, Mahmoud and Camilla. Mahmoud was worried. He thought they might be mugged. Camilla was terrified. Back in Chicago she knew which streets to avoid. Just then another brightly-lighted bus emerged from the darkness and pulled up at the curb. There was a human traffic jam at the door, with one of the Bravos up front by the driver arguing that he was paying for all. He paid for himself and at least twenty others followed him aboard, ignoring the driver. The driver ignored the fact that no one else paid. It was the right driver, the one who had brought Ansar, Mahmoud and Camilla over from the East Village. "We must get on," said Ansar. "I must find my book." He grabbed Camilla's hand and dragged her aboard. Mahmoud reluctantly followed.

The Bravo chorus had fallen apart while boarding. Now, seated, or hanging from straps, they gathered their syncopation up and began to chant in unison again—*If you can, then kill a cop! Cut his belly, make him pop!*

Mahmoud and Camilla sat down close to the driver and the front door, but Ansar wandered back through the bus and through the Bravos, looking under seats, asking the chanting gang members if they saw a book anywhere.

His crazy indifference to danger worked a small miracle. The gang members, used to causing fear, treated him with a degree of respect, breaking their chant to help him look. Mahmoud observed that a number of the gang were bandaged, bloodstains showing through gauze. He ventured to ask one sitting next to him what had happened.

"We-comin-from-St.-Vincent's- Hospital," chunked out the surly face. "We been wilding, man!" The sullen face turned to him. "Who is your friend look like Arafat?" he asked. "He's cool. He's chilled out. He's ice."

"That's Ansar the Great," said Mahmoud. "He can do magic. Watch out what you say to him. Be careful."

Mahmoud had turned to face his interlocutor. He was trying to hide as much of Camilla as possible. She shrunk behind him, shaking. The bus driver made no stops, but stared grimly ahead, foot down on the gas-pedal. Ansar wobbled back to them, saying, "My book is not here. That Zionist must have it." Mahmoud saw their stop ahead and called to the driver. The driver pulled to the curb, opened the doors, jumped out, and ran up the street.

The Bravos began to cheer his disappearing form. Mahmoud pulled Camilla behind him off the bus. Ansar followed. The Bravos followed Ansar, as they might follow a Messiah. Mahmoud, who rarely cursed, said, "Oh, shit," under his breath, and pulled Camilla toward the Saints and Sinners Club, which seemed at the moment an oasis of safety. Ansar came directly behind them, chanting something about his book, and the Bravos followed Ansar, chanting, *The Bravos say it with a will! You got to learn to kill, kill, kill!*

Even to the bohemian denizens of the East Village, this was a sight to see, and they stopped in their tracks to gape. Some took up step and followed along. Now the whole augmented mob burst into the Saints and Sinners Club. "I want my book," cried Ansar to the startled Tiger.

Tiger looked about him in dismay. His seated customers half-rose from the bar and the tables. He was afraid this gang would chase them out. "You mean the bomb book?" he said to Ansar. His face hardened. He was not a man to be easily intimidated. "What does anybody need a book on making bombs for?"

"If you have found it, you must return it," said Ansar. "The rest is none of your business."

"Bomb book," said one of the Bravos. The sullen faced Bravo from the bus said, "Ansar the Great is making some bombs. *To blow them up, he cannot wait! He's the man, Ansar the Great!*

Mahmoud pulled Camilla back through the crowd and into a corner.

*He's the man, Ansar the Great!*
*To blow them up, he cannot wait!*

Tiger went to the cash register, picked up the book which rested beside it, and threw it on the bar. "There's your damn book," he said, "now all of you get the hell out of my place."

"Hey," said one of the Bravos, "speak with respect to Ansar the Great!"

"He is a Zionist," cried Ansar. "He knows no respect!"

A local sculptor, a powerfully built man, got up from his table, where he was surrounded by drinking buddies. "Tiger told you guys to clear *out*. Now clear out!"

Mahmoud could not see what happened next. The crowd was too thick. But there was a scuffle, several female screams, and a thud.

Like a plasmodium, one of those multinucleate masses of protoplasm that can separate into many cells and then rejoin itself, the Bravos regained their gang form and flowed out the door. But once outside, they disintegrated again into separate entities and formed a half moon around the corner bar. Somebody heaved something heavy and metallic through one of the plateglass windows. Inside, Mahmoud and Camilla could not find Ansar. Outside, Ansar was stuffing his book into his Saks Fifth Avenue bag and stuffing the bag into a garbage can. The Bravos renewed their crack-induced chant, *Kill, Kill, Kill!* Now they were joined in their chant by some passersby, who had no idea what was going on, but loved the excitement. Several garbage cans were thrown about, cars rocked, random sounds of broken glass punctuated the long moans of the cold, windy night. A police car and a mobile television unit materialized out of nowhere. The police stayed in their car, looking nervously about; the television people plunged into the scene, their cameras rocking.

Chapter 27

R.S.V.P.

Monk's massive bald dome shone like a full yellow moon under the raw glare of the kitchen light, his tin-white eyes seemed aglitter with reckonings, and the smooth skin of his face was opalescent, ghostly and ghastly.

Father Din felt dishevelled and ridiculous, but summoned his dignity, and pulled himself up to his full six feet three inches. Monk studied him coldly.

Acting as if nothing could be more natural than the present situation, Toddy said: "You remember Sam, don't you, Monk?"

Monk turned on her scornfully. "Don't be a fool. Of course I know who he is." He returned his attention to Father Din. "Maybe you'd like to explain why you've chosen to ignore my warning?"

"I got sick in the bar and Toddy brought me up here to rest."

"And now I guess you think you're just going to be on your merry way, is that it? It wouldn't be very polite of you to come to my party and leave just when I arrive."

"You mean, if I wanted to go, you'd try to stop me?"

"Not try! What caused the trouble between us earlier, if you'll remember, was that I asked you to leave and you refused. Now I'm inviting you to stay. I know you're not going to refuse me twice in one day."

"Why do you want me to stay?"

"By now you know more about me than I do about you, and I don't like that."

"There isn't anything to know about me."

"There's always something to know. For instance, I'd like to know what you know about me."

"I don't know anything about you."

Monk gave Toddy a baleful look. "You remember what my priestess said in the bar." He looked back at Father Din. "You know that."

"What do you mean?"

"Come on, Mr. Hopkins, you know exactly what I mean. That's why I've got to know who you are. Let's set aside for the moment our earlier difference. That was an unfortunate situation provoked in part by this young lady, who has seen fit of late to turn herself into an irresponsible lush. But consider how your being here must look to me. When I saw you down in the bar I thought you were just some jerk trying to pick up a woman. I was and I still am certain that you heard and understood what Toddy said about me; but, assuming you were just what I took you to be, it seemed safe enough to just let it go. You were slumming. Drinking. Something like that would add vague color to your memories of the night before, if you succeeded in remembering anything at all. Then, too, I had a hunch that you were somehow in the wrong yourself, and not likely to cause trouble. With your wife maybe . . . or on your job . . . a runaway or an embezzler . . . perhaps you were wanted by the police . . . There was something in your attitude . . . guilt. And that gave me a certain sense of security. He's not likely to run to the police, I said to myself. But now, finding you here, makes me wonder if you aren't some kind of agent. You could be D.E.A. You must see how curious you've made me. I can't help thinking: either he's courting disaster or he has a good reason for being here . . ."

No one had moved. Monk stood in the middle of the small kitchen, between Father Din and the door. His stance was erect, military, but he seemed quite at ease, his powerful, heavy body resting in an absolute gravitational relationship with the floor under his feet. It seemed that he could stand that way for hours, tireless and dominant. Toddy stood aside, near the kitchen table, with arms folded under her breasts in the attitude of a woman suffering a winter chill. She looked from Monk to Father Din and back. Her torso seemed to sink into her hips, and her face was pale and pinched, like a tired housewife's. She shifted her weight from hip to hip and sank deeper.

Father Din remained in the livingroom, just clear of the Oriental screen, not ten paces from Monk. He also appeared to be, and felt he was, sinking. Again he pulled himself up. For the first time today, as a result of hearing Monk's reasoning, he realized the irrational nature of what he had done, was doing. It was as though he were some kind of wheeled machine with a jammed gear, heading at an accelerating speed toward a precipice.

Outwardly, however, he insisted on the case as Toddy had put it. "I tell you I simply got drunk. I'm not a drinker; I'm not used to drinking. I threw up in the men's room of the bar. Toddy mentioned that she lived only a few blocks away, and I asked her to let me come up and rest until I felt well enough to go on my way. She told me that I'd have to be gone by nine-thirty, but, the truth is, Toddy fell asleep herself and didn't wake me.  That's all there is to it.  Most of what you've said sounds like some kind of double-talk to me.  I don't know what it is that you keep saying Toddy said.  I don't know anything about the police or agents or the D.E.A., whatever that means . . ."

Monk thought for a moment; then, slowly, decisively, with narrowed eyes, he said: "You know that I'm a—dealer."  Quickly he flipped the pink palm of a thick hand up, stopping Father Din before he could refute the statement.  "Don't you see, Mr. Hopkins," he amplified, "that whether you picked up on it in the bar—which, I can see now from your lack of surprise, you did—or not, the only way I can know for certain is to force the knowledge upon you and then to decide how to deal with you.  I know that you know and that knowledge eliminates confusion and doubt.  Now it's your turn.  It's up to you to convince me that I can let you go."

"But how can he do that?" Toddy asked.

"I want to know who he is, why he came up here, what he wants.  Maybe you're just a damned fool who got himself drunk enough to walk in where angels fear to tread; still, I have to be sure that it's safe to let you walk out again . . ."

"I'm going to sit down," Father Din said.  He looked weak in the knees.

"Just a minute!" Monk commanded, before Father Din could seat himself.  He stepped up to Father Din and frisked him from shoulders to ankles so rapidly that Father Din did not understand what was being done.  For an instant he thought Monk was going to hit him.  Then Monk was standing back again, an unreadable expression on his face, three feet away.  "Go ahead, sit down," Monk said.

Father Din sank into a chair.  "You didn't actually think I had a gun?"

"Why not?  I have one."  Monk turned and threw off his black leather trench coat and hung it over Father Din's overcoat on the clothestree.  Then he sat down at the table, across from Father Din.  Seated, he looked like a squat, malevolent god.

"Suppose you decide that it isn't safe to let me walk out," Father Din said.  "What then?"

"Fix me a drink, Toddy," Monk ordered.

"Straight on ice?"

He looked at her.

"Sam, I'll fix you that tea I promised you."

"Make it coffee, would you?  What I want to know is," Father Din pursued, "what are you threatening me with?"

"I have a question for you, Mr. Hopkins," Monk countered.  "Were you two making it when I interrupted you?"

"No, Monk!" Toddy exclaimed.

"Sleeping," Father Din said definitively, and with a tone that was meant to erase suspicion from the air.

Chapter 28

TABLE TALK

Monk took out his cigarette holder, prepared a smoke, and lit up.  "But I'm inclined to believe you," he went on, exhaling a mixture of words and smoke.  "I don't think you'd have nerve enough to do it, either of you, knowing that I was going to show up."  He sat at the table across from Father Din.

Toddy placed a drink before Monk, and a cup of coffee before Father Din.  She sat down, holding her hands in her lap and her drink between them.  From somewhere in the house seeped the distant music of a Latin rhythmist.  In front, the windows rumbled softly with outer turbulence.

Monk said, "I've known the Priestess for a long time and I've never heard her mention you.  Where do you know each other from?"

426

"Just from the bar," Father Din said, before Toddy could entangle herself in another lie. "We only met this afternoon."

"So, my Priestess, then you don't know any more about our friend here than I do. Old friends . . . that's what you said in the bar, wasn't it? You've become a pathological liar. I'm proud of you."

"I'm a fool," Toddy said warmly.

"Yes, I know," Monk responded. "I haven't met anyone in a long time who wasn't . . . unless perhaps Mr. Hopkins is not what he seems to be." He checked his watch against the wall clock. "Where are the little lambs of my congregation? It's after ten. Hopkins, don't ever deal with junkies; they're the most undependable people on earth, even worse than drunks." He shot down the remainder of his drink.

"*Noch ein*, Toddy; fix me another. Not so much ice this time. Leave room for the Scotch." He lighted another cigarette. "Hopkins, this is the way it's going to be—you're going to spend the evening with us as my guest, and I'm going to decide what's to be done about you . . ."

"Does that mean that if you thought you could trust me you'd just . . . you'd let me leave?"

"Why not, in that case? There must be a hundred people around here who know who I am and what I do. Some of them wouldn't have anything to do with dope—using or peddling—but neither would they have anything to do with the cops. That's the kind of neighborhood it is: live and let die. Maybe you belong in Needleneck. I'll know before the party's over."

"Let him go now, Monk," Toddy urged, serving him a fresh drink; "he won't cause you any trouble."

"Let me remind you, Priestess, that if you had learned, like a good girl, when to keep your pretty lips puckered, Hopkins probably wouldn't be in this situation. However, you're right in saying that he won't cause me any trouble. I'll see to it that he doesn't." Another mirthless laugh pictured itself with a gust of smoke. "You see, Hopkins, you've been brought to this impasse by the ancient evils of alcohol . . . or, specifically, by a drunken, loose-mouthed woman . . ." He gave Toddy a mocking nod. "Now, that's one thing about dopers: they don't talk. Drunks talk: but dopers just keep nodding off. I'm talking about heroin users. Have you ever tried talking to one?"

"I don't know much about dopers."

"So—" Monk said lightly, "I've discovered nothing. You remain an enigma. You're either an innocent, or too clever to be taken in by so obvious a gambit. Which is it, I wonder?"

"You enjoy playing games, don't you?"

"Oh, very much," said Monk. He removed a Manila envelope from an inside pocket of his suit-jacket, caught a longish thumbnail in the corner of the flap, ripped it open, and dumped the contents, several small glassine bags, containing a whitish powder, on the table. He tapped a stubby index-finger from one to the other, pushing them about, making patterns. "This is heroin," he said. "It's not a sexy drug—like coke, like crack, or the designer drugs. Journalists don't go on about it. But three times as much of it is being used now than was twenty years ago. For a junkie, this is food, sleep, sex, love, heaven, and hell, all in one."

He looked at Toddy. "Have you told Hopkins about your husband?" he asked, and went on without waiting for her answer—"She's married, you know. Her husband is a member of my congregation. A moral freak, like herself. A weakling, a beggar, a whiner, and a groveler. He traded me the use of his wife and his home for the privilege, revocable at my amusement, to buy his stupor of dreams from me. I own his soul. I bought it with this stuff. But the funny part is, he paid. Do you understand the economics of heroin, Mr. Hopkins? Opium poppies, which are its ultimate source, are cheaper than daisies on site. The growers sell 'em for next to nothing. Why should the drug be worth millions on the streets? Because to bring it in you have to climb the Wall. The Wall is everything that tries to keep it out. The Wall is what makes it expensive on the streets. The Wall is supposed to stop it from coming in, but, because it makes it expensive, it encourages people to bring it in. To stop it from coming, you tear down the Wall."

"Legalize it, you mean."

"Of course. Take the incredible profit out of it, and who would bother to bring it in? The junkies would have to go cold turkey then. I've worked for and made deals with the C.I.A., the D.E.A., and state and local narcs. They're part of it—the Wall. The Wall is as much a part of the drug trade as the growers and the dealers. Everybody makes a buck, including high government officials, here and at the source. None of us want drugs legalized. Who would, when we're all doing so well?"

"Some would still come in. I mean, individuals would send their friends . . ."

"The dribble. Of course. But nothing like now. I'd have to go and find another gold mine."

A knock came at the door. Monk lifted an open hand in a gesture of "Don't move."

"Who is it?" he called.

A woman's voice answered indistinctly.

"It's Pilar," he said. "Let her in."


Chapter 29


FIRST COME, FIRST SERVED


Toddy opened the door and a young woman stepped into the kitchen. She was of middle height, with wide, high cheekbones, large ebony eyes, and full, beautiful lips which twisted scornfully down at the corners as she gave Toddy a cursory

429

nod of recognition. "Who this?" The young woman spat the words challengingly, eyeing Father Din from head to foot. Her face had a satanic cast to it, and her whole attitude was aggressive, pugnacious even; yet Father Din saw the dark hollows under the light-washed bones of her upper face, and the tension in her thin, erotic body, and felt an affinity for the young woman.

"Sam Hopkins," said Toddy, "he's a friend of mine."

"My name is Pilar. Are you a friend of Jack, too?"

"No, I'm not. I only met Toddy this afternoon."

Pilar's expression, which had become for a moment less severe, revealing a face that hinted of submerged generosity, resumed its harshness. "How you know he ain't a cop?" she shot at Monk.

"I *don't* know," Monk said, enjoying her state of upset.

"Then why you let him be here?"

"He's my special guest."

"I'm not a cop," said Father Din. "You don't have to be afraid of me."

"Ha!" Pilar exclaimed. "*Afraid*! You think I'm afraid of a cop!"

"*Silencio*!" Monk snapped. "This is none of your business. Now! Let's see your dinero, Pepperpot."

"I've got it. What you think, I come to ask you any favor?"

Monk winked at Father Din. "Now, that's a smart dame for you. You see, she understands me." Then, down to business: "Get it up, then. You're late as it is."

Pilar opened her pocketbook, whipped out a roll of bills, and handed it to Monk.

"Give me the stuff," she demanded.

"Why don't you fix here," said Monk, counting the bills with deliberate slowness. "I like to watch dames shoot up."

"I got to go. Give me my stuff!" Pilar reached out for

the several glassine packets of heroin which Monk had set aside.

"Easy," he said, pushing her hand away. "Can't wait to turn yourself into a zombie, can you?"

"For God's sake, Monk, give them to her," Toddy urged.

"Give me that!" Pilar cried, trying again to seize the packets.

Again Monk pushed her away, this time roughly.

"Damn you, gringo bastard!" Pilar cried.

"Give them to her, please," Toddy begged him.

"You stay out of this," Pilar shouted, "you *bitch*! I no need your help, you no-good *bitch*! What you done to my Jack! I take my Gem blade outta my cheek and I cut off your nose! You no look so good then, ha!" She was moving on Toddy now, and Toddy, sudden fear in her eyes, was backing up. "You think you *some*thing. You think you too good for spics. You even think you too good for Jack, and he better than you, way better . . . Everybody know what *you* do to him. You give him the *horns*. You give him the horns with this bad man. I fix you—" and with a click of her cheek she spat a glinting object into her right hand and raised it up, menacingly. Toddy screamed. Father Din caught Pilar's wrist and drew it down, wresting the object, which was indeed a single-edged Gem razor blade, from her hand.

"Please, don't do this," he said, gently. She fell into his shoulder, and buried her head there, and sobbed.

Toddy was ashen. She went over to a chair and sank into it, slowly shaking her head.

Monk let out a plangent horse whoop of laughter, the first instance of true hilarity of which Father Din had observed him to be capable. "Animals," he cried, with true if somewhat diabolic mirth, "beasts! Ho-ho, hoo-hoo." He appeared to be more than a little drunk. Almost immediately, however, his mad laughter went into diminuendo, ending in a last sharp nasty cackle, and ceased abruptly. "Here, get your junk and get the fuck out of here," he said.

"I'm sorry," Father Din whispered into Pilar's ear, "I didn't mean to hurt you . . ."

"I know," she whispered, "I got a bad temper . . . But that—"

"Shh! Hush." He patted her back gently. "Don't . . ."

"Si, I don't." She withdrew from Father Din's embrace, and stood apart, rubbing her eyes.

"Well?" Monk spat. "What are you waiting for? Get out!"

"He *such* a nice man," Pilar said contemptuously.

"Go on, split," Monk said, "before I break your little fingers."

Undaunted, Pilar ignored him. Addressing herself to Father Din, and not without a certain hauteur, she said: "These people are no good. They are bad people. I warn you." Her eyes darted to Toddy, who had regained some composure. "Has my brother been here?"

"No," said Toddy.

Pilar looked at Father Din. "You . . . thanks," she said.

Father Din nodded.

"Go!" Monk cried, and made as if to rise.

Pilar took a hurried step to the table, scooped the glassine bags into her pocketbook, and went to the door, pulling it open. There she paused, looking back, then said, her eyes molten, "You will please to do me one big favor, Mr. Monkey," gritting her teeth, "you will go to live your days in hell with the witches and burn forever," with which she disappeared behind the slamming door. They could hear the quick, nervous tapping of her high heels going down the hall.

"Stupid!" Monk said. "They don't think. She'll have to come back next week. I'd take it out in trade, but she probably has AIDS from screwing her brother. But she'll pay. Stupid people always pay."

"You're a miserable S.O.B.," Father Din said. "Did you

ever ask yourself why?"

Monk considered. "The weak always try to convince themselves that the strong are unhappy, Mr. Hopkins, because it makes them feel better to believe it. But go ahead, tell me, why do you think I'm miserable? Toddy, bring that bottle over here."

"Because you've stripped yourself of humanity—or you've tried to. There's nothing left of you but the beast."

"Ha, no, that's where you're wrong. I'm psychologist enough to know that that can't be done." He was quite drunk now. "No, Mr. Hopkins, I have to disappoint you—I am a happy man. But come to think of it, there is one thing that could add to my bliss . . . I'd like to see Toddy hooked, like Jack Muir is. That's one of my ambitions. I'd like to see her crawl and beg. If she makes me wait much longer, I'll shoot her up myself."

"He's only trying to frighten me," Toddy said to Father Din. "He says that every time he gets drunk."

"You don't think I'd do it?" shot Monk, lighting a cigarette.

"Oh, you'd do it. But you don't."

"And so I won't?"

"No. Because you don't want to."

"And why do you think I don't want to?"

"Because it would spoil your fun. If I were as sick as Jack, I wouldn't know when he was suffering."

"Very acute, Toddy. She has brains; that's why I like her. That's why she's my Priestess . . . my Priestess of the Church of Moral Freaks. And she understands the way my mind works. She's partly right, you know. But there's another reason too. I'll tell you what that is in a few minutes. I want you to know. But, do you know, Toddy, I might do it anyway. I might do it some night, and we'll see what you do about it, how you decide to avenge yourself upon me. A nano-second after that needle's in, you'll be in another world, and that's a world that it isn't easy to come back from. Ask Jack if he knows how to come back from it."

"But people *do* come back," said Father Din.

"Hopkins, I may just keep you here all night. In my business I don't get many opportunities to talk with an educated man—or at least with one who isn't nodding off with an imbecilic expression on his face, like some grunge rocker after a concert. I hope it never becomes your misfortune to deal with the kind of scum I'm often forced to deal with. Illiterates, many of them—clowns of a low order, even if some of them drive big black limousines. That's the reason I like to work in an area like this, where there are painters and writers—intellectuals. But, as to addicts being cured—yes, you're right, there are ways to come back; but those who go are seldom strong enough in the first place to be able to come back, otherwise they wouldn't have gone. That's one reason I won't force the Priestess into it—she's not ready yet. I couldn't stay with her to see to it that she got enough to get her hooked. That'd take several shots a day for a while. While I was gone, she'd come off. She's still too strong. She doesn't *want* to be hooked. But she has one weakness; she knows it—and that's her weakness for Jack Muir. Now, starting there, I begin a program of conditioning. The groundwork hasn't been laid yet—she isn't as yet perfectly predisposed to addiction, the way Muir was—but when I get through with her, she'll be perfect addict material. I'll turn her into Needle Woman."

"You'll never do that to me," Toddy said with resolution.

"Oh, yes I will, Priestess. Then you'll be just like your Jack of Hearts." He paused. "I threw Muir out of here myself. I told him that if he wanted any more smack from me, or from anybody, he'd have to go across the street to that loft of his and be a good boy and stay away from Toddy. I even gave him a boot in the ass on the way out the door. Then

I took the Priestess into the bedroom."

"Please stop, Monk—"

"But that's what happened, isn't it?"

"Yes yes yes!" Toddy wailed, clenching her fists.

"Now be careful," Monk persisted, heedless, "or I might decide I need you tonight." He winked at Father Din, who sat staring stonily at him. "I get these moods," he said.

"For God's sake, man," Father Din said, "isn't there any limit?"

"Limit? What limit? Does she know any limit of degradation? Do you?" He snorted. "Look at you—you sit there like a little tin god of self-righteousness, but still you sit—because I've ordered you to. I could make her do anything tonight. Do you know why? Because her Jack of Hearts would beg her to. What limit are you talking about? Isn't that true, Priestess? Tell the simple-hearted—not to say - minded—Mr. Hopkins—tell him!"

Toddy refused to speak or move, but sat with her arms folded on the table and her face buried in them.

"Leave her alone," Father Din commanded.

Monk, who had been slouching a bit over his drink, pulled himself up and raised his dark brows. "Oh," he said, "are we going to have trouble with you?"

"Leave her alone."

"If you and I are going to get along, you better wipe that self-righteous smirk off your face. And keep it off."

Chapter 30

HAUNTED

"Something has to be done," Father Din thought, looking at Monk. He recalled a scene as if he were reliving it— his mother and father playing their parts as they once had, himself standing outside the kitchen door, on the backporch

435

of their cop's second-mortgaged house in Jersey City, listening.  He must have been about seven years old.

*"Something had to be done," his father said.  His father had brought a bottle of whiskey home and was sitting at the kitchen table, taking drink after drink as if his intention was to drown something from his consciousness.  Young Michael had never seen his upright father in such a condition.  He leaned back against his suit jacket, which hung over the chair, exposing the compact snubnosed Police Special on his belt, his tie pulled loose, his hat on the floor next to his chair, and his dark hair in disarray.  His mother sat close beside his father at the round oak table.  She made no fuss, as she usually did at his homecoming, but sat quietly, fingering his shirtsleeve.  His father's partner was named Mike, after whom Father Din had been named.  "Mike," said his father, "Mike and I—we just couldn't help it.  Eventually, he would have killed her.  There just wasn't anybody on Earth to help her.  He'd nearly killed her twice before.  She was afraid to leave him.  He had her terrorized.  Hell, he had everybody terrorized.  We've taken him in a dozen times.  As fast as we bring him in the system lets him out.  He was evil, I tell you, evil!  I know I've sinned—Mike and I have sinned—but something had to be done."*

*Then Father Din's mother spoke those electrifying words:  "But couldn't you just frighten him?  Warn him?  Scare him off?  Did you have to kill him?"*

*"We didn't mean to.  Honest to God!  I swear!  It just went too far.  Don't be afraid, no one will ever know."*

*"We will," his mother had almost whispered.*

Ever since that evening Father Din had prayed to forget what he had heard, and, until this evening, he almost had.  But Monk had brought the terrible scene back, more vividly than ever.

Chapter 31

MAYHEM

Casually, Monk reached under his left arm and drew out a big Uzi automatic and placed it on the table. "What do you think this is," he said, "amateur hour?"

"Put that away," said Toddy, gripping the edge of the table.

"Don't worry," Father Din said, "he wouldn't fire that in here. The whole neighborhood would hear it."

"And what good would that do you?" said Monk. He laughed, a mad cackle. "But the truth is that you're right, I wouldn't let this off indoors. It might disturb the neighbors. It just isn't done, is it? I was only trying to shake you up. Tell the truth now, you were frightened, weren't you?"

"Only a fool would pretend that he isn't frightened when a man who's had too much to drink takes out a gun."

"You're a sensible man, Mr. Hopkins. You deserve a reward for being such a sensible man. Listen, have you ever seen this?" He made a V-for-Victory or Peace sign with the first and second fingers of his right hand. "Do you know what this means?"

"Peace?" essayed Father Din.

"No, no, no no no," said Monk. "Look, let me tell you in your ear; this is not for the ladies." He and Father Din were sitting cater-cornered from each other at one corner of the table, and were only about two feet apart. Monk leaned forward, looking at his V-ed fingers, leering, like a man with a dirty joke to tell, and put his thick, fin-like left arm over Father Din's shoulders, pulling them into a conspiratorial huddle. Father Din had no desire to listen, but the fraternal arm pulling him in was heavy and powerful and apparently benevolently determined, and he thought it wise to appease it, so he leaned forward into it, let it take him, his right ear to

Monk's mouth to hear, his eyes focused on the two thick V-ed fingers that hovered below them, waiting for the promised illumination, when suddenly it came.

The arm over his shoulders slid up to the back of his neck and suddenly evolved into a headlock. He tried to pull away, to stand, but Monk's weight and power held him in place, as if in a stock.

"What are you doing?" he cried through clenched jaws, as the arm about his neck became a tremendous weight, and he felt that his neck would snap. For a moment, light faded from his eyes. His ears roared. Then he could hear again, as the pressure slackened a little, and he heard Toddy's excited voice, Monk's calm, deliberate tone, but he could not make out what they were saying, and then light came back into his eyes like a vortex starting at a distant point and coming at him with great speed, and colors flashed, took shape: he saw Monk's bulky knees—apparently both he and Monk were still seated—and then he saw the thick V-ed fingers, like some disembodied incarnate fork, hovering, threatening— Monk whispered wetly into his ear: "This'll clear your head"—and the fingers rammed up and back into his nostrils till his whole face seemed about to split open. His head fell backwards, cradled on Monk's arm, so that he was like a man in a dentist's chair, his mouth gaping, gagging, the two-pronged fork searching out his brain.

Chapter 32

TRIAGE

Father Din saw a small pool of blood on the floor where his head had rested, before being gathered into Toddy's arms. Then he passed out again. When he woke the second time, he was lying on Toddy's bed, his nose, still flowing, like a double-tapped keg. He tried his jaw. It worked. Then he felt the back of his head. The hair was sticky and matted. Toddy came in with a basin filled with ice and damp towels.

"Don't try to get up," she ordered.

"I'm all right," he said.

"No you're not," Toddy said emphatically. "You should be in the emergency ward. Now lean back."

Father Din did as he was ordered. Toddy put cotton in his nostrils to stop the bleeding, and held ice-cubes to the bridge of his nose to retard the swelling. "What's the damage?" he asked. "Is my head bleeding in back?"

"No. You bumped it, but it's not cut. The blood is from your nose. You rolled in it. And there's a small cut under your chin—one of his rings made that. He punched you. It's your nose that's hurt, but I don't think it's much more serious than a bloody nose, really. It feels solid. He said he could have ripped it off. Oh, what a horrible thing to do! I've never seen anything so awful. My God, I tried to make him stop, but I couldn't budge him. He's made of iron."

"Where is he?"

"In the kitchen, finishing up my Scotch. He doesn't seem to think anything of it. He wants me to make him something to eat. Can you imagine it? He's hungry. Just as if a minute ago he hadn't sat—doing that."

"Wasn't somebody else here? For just a minute back there. . ."

"Dedi Pavon—Pilar's brother—the boy you met at the Saints and Sinners. He helped me bring you in here. Monk wouldn't lift a hand."

"I'm surprised that he let you help me. That man is insane, you know."

"Whatever he is, I hate him. Oh, Sam, I feel so terribly guilty. I feel responsible for dragging you into all this. I'm so sorry."

"Nonsense," said Father Din, touching her cheek, "I got

myself into this.  I insisted on coming up.  You warned me.  So, for that matter, did Monk.  But I wanted to come."

"But if I had watched the time, you'd have been gone now."

"I didn't really want to be gone.  No one's fault—except mine.  But I've got to get you away from him," he said, getting to his feet, his rigid muscles tearing over his long bones as they straightened them.  His head roared with the surf of an inner sea, and he stood holding the bedpost for a moment, waiting for his vertigo to pass.  Toddy watched him, shaken, trying to fathom his mind.  Then he staggered into the living-room, swaying like a drunken man, on rubbery legs.  Toddy followed him, wondering, frightened.

Monk and Dedi looked up from their business in the kitchen.

"Hey, mon," Dedi called, "you O.K.?  Need any help?"

"No . . . thank you," Father Din answered.  Toddy came up beside him and took his left upper arm in her own arms and helped him on.  Father Din hesitated at the threshold of the kitchen, and stood studying Monk, again the image of a squat, malevolent god coming to mind.


Chapter 33


THE DICTATOR


"Come in here and sit down," Monk ordered.  "If I haven't made this clear before, I'll make it clear now.  I'll kill anyone who tries to get between me and the Priestess, here.  If you've got any ideas about running off with her—remember this—" he tapped the table with two thick fingers— "I'll track you down and kill you."  Kaleidoscopically, his mood altered, and he said, not unpleasantly, "I want to tell you about my book.  I told you that I was writing a book, didn't I?  I'm going to call it Priest of Evil, and subtitle it The Autobiography of an Honest Man. Come on. Sit down. I won't hurt you." He had a waterglassful of Scotch in front of him, and was smoking a holderless cigarette.

On the table was an "outfit," an open tin pillbox containing a disposable plastic hypodermic, extra needles, cotton, and a pink birthday candle. Dedi, quick to observe Father Din's interest in the outfit, beamed proudly. He said, "That's my outfit. Nice, uh? It ain't chrome or silver or platinum, though, like I heard Keith Richards and them rich rockers got; but I sent away in the mail for this glass-type hypo, and when she comes I get me a new box, maybe a gold cigarette case— take it off some rich old lady in the street, wow, ha."

Father Din looked pity at the scarred boy. His head was clearing now, and he was able to stand, with reasonable steadiness, on his own two feet; and so gently pulled his arm free of Toddy's support, thinking it unwise for Toddy to stand too long holding his arm while Monk looked on.

"Monk," Toddy began to plead, "please let Sam go now. He ought to get to a hospital. You might have broken his nose. And besides, none of this has anything to do with him. He won't talk."

Neither Monk nor Father Din paid her any attention. Father Din sat down at the table, holding his head with his left hand, and began to stare at Monk from under it, like a man trying to see into the distance. He knew now that Monk was not an ordinary criminal, but a true sociopath, a soul-less unreachable creature.

"Here," Monk said, pushing his glass of Scotch across the table to Father Din, "you look like you need this more than I do."

"—and I'm gonna get me a needle made out of a diamond someday—" Dedi picked up, like a boy in a trance, "and I won't ever have to sharpen it, like with these—"

Father Din drained off a large shot from the glass, coughed, shuddered, and shook his head. Toddy came behind him with a washcloth and began washing the blood out of his matted hair. When she was finished with that, she placed a band-aid under his chin. "There," she said, "how do you feel?"

"Better," he said. "I'll be fine."

"You know," Dedi wandered on, heedless, "it's pretty weird, mon—sometimes you poke the needle in your arm and you see that needle push the vein away, you dig? 'Cause she's dull—you know? Maybe only ten, twelve times stay sharp, then you gotta start sharpening them. If you don't, you get black-and-blues—"

"Shut up, Dedi," Toddy snapped. "I don't want to hear about it."

Dedi looked up at her with big brown amazed eyes. "What'd I do?"

"Just be quiet," Toddy said, kindlier.

"Who are you talking to?" Monk said. "Can't you see that he just got off? He's not there."

"Only did half a bag," Dedi said dreamily.

"Would you believe it," Monk said, ignoring Dedi, "I really didn't mean to hurt you that badly, Mr. Hopkins. That trick looks more ferocious than it is, if you do it right. A good subduer. I learned it from a Dutch African mercenary, a regular Zouave, one of the best fighting men I've ever known. He's in prison now. Once you get your fingers in, if a man doesn't struggle he won't get hurt, but if he does, you can pull his nose off his face. You were struggling, that's why I popped you off the way I did. An uppercut under the chin to calm you down."

"I'm very grateful," said Father Din.

Monk chugged his drink. He re-filled it from the bottle, which was now two-thirds empty, and gulped down another drink.

"Go on," he said to Toddy, "sit down, nursey. I hate it when women fuss over a man like that. Get out of the way," he shouted. "I want to talk to Mr. Hopkins about my book." He looked drink-mad, frightening.

Dedi said: "Hey, mon, I bet your head don't feel so good, eh? You know what you need, mon? You need a fix. Hey, Monk, why you no give heem a fix?"

"Shut up," Monk said; then: "Have you ever seen anybody shoot up, Mr. Hopkins?"

"No, thank you."

"Well, you've got to see that." He refocused glassily on Dedi Pavon. "Dedi, get ready; I want you to fix for Mr. Hopkins."

"I don't want to see it."

"I don't care what you want," Monk said softly. "It's very difficult for me to make that clear to you, isn't it?"

"Hey, Monk, I ain't ready yet," Dedi said.

"Do as I say!" Monk said. "You only had half a bag," he added after a moment, "so this time use a whole bag."

"That's too much," Dedi protested, "and it's too quick for me. I'm a sick boy. I ain't got no strength. Lemme just shoot the other half of the bag—"

"No," Monk said, "a whole bag. You love it so much, then use it."

"I don't like to shoot with strangers watching me," Dedi said.

"Strangers?" Monk looked around. "Oh, do you mean Mr. Hopkins? Why, he's no stranger anymore; he's just one of us now. He's been baptized. Haven't you?"

"In blood," said Father Din.


## Chapter 34


## THE FIX


Dedi poured the contents of one of the glassine bags into a spoon, added water, stirred, and held the solution over the flame of the pink birthday candle (Monk said, "That's to liquify and purify the stuff"—); when he had "cooked" the heroin, Dedi rested the spoon containing the solution inside the open pillbox; then he took up his plastic hypo, and previously having sharpened the needle, attached that to it; next, pumping the plunger, he rinsed the hypo with water, squirting long, miniature garden hose streams on the floor. He placed the hypo on the table; and, tearing off a small piece of cotton, added that to the contents of the spoon. ("They draw the stuff up through the cotton," Monk commentaried, "to filter it.") Then he stood up and took off his jacket and rolled up his sleeve. His arm showed under the harsh kitchen light like that of a skinny boy's, but for the red rash and blue bruises at the inner elbow, the arm's crook, and the strange long jagged scars, or "tracks," where veins had collapsed along the forearm.

Monk, enthusiastic for this kind of sport, urged the boy to get to it: "Mr. Hopkins is waiting." The boy looked around him—at Monk, imploringly, then at Toddy and at Father Din. "I should wait . . ."

"Go on," Monk ordered.

Father Din sat in grim silence, feeling that it was hopeless to try to intercede. It was not for himself he feared, but for Toddy, even the boy. Monk was crazy drunk. The Uzi automatic lay on the table. He now believed Monk capable of anything. And everyone present knew more about the use of the drug than he did. Nonetheless he ventured: "Why not let him wait, if he wants to . . ."

"Because I say not," Monk cried. "He's shot two bags at a time before—it's not that that's bothering him. It's that he's shy. He doesn't want to give a performance. But I say now, Dedi—for the last time, I say *now*."

Dedi gave in; he shrugged his thin narrow shoulders, pulled the tie from his neck, drew a length of iron pipe (the same that Mr. Potter of The Busy Nook never saw, and which

Jack Muir had examined earlier, with its bands of black electrician's tape around it), and fashioned a tourniquet, which he held—he was standing—by locking it into position between his knees.

"See the veins pop out?" said Monk, his eyes obscene, as the big blue veins showed in bas-relief from the skinny arm like long balloons.

Dedi, with the efficiency of long practice, drew the pale fluid up into the hypo through the soggy cotton, and began roughly probing, apparently quite impervious to any pain, among the veins at the crook of his arm. "See!" Dedi cried, suddenly excited, "see how she pushing that vein over . . . dull—" and indeed it was quite ugly, Father Din thought, to see the living tender vein being pushed about beneath the almost transparent skin—Toddy had turned away from the sight—"There's one; I got a good one," Dedi cried—What was he doing?—

"That's what they call 'registering'," Monk said, as Dedi drew his blood up into the hypo, clear to be seen, through the plastic, sloshing about, mixing a little with the heroin solution—"uuuuuuuooohgg," Dedi moaned in something like pleasure: twisted in his Quasimodo-like position, and under the cruel glare of the kitchen light, the boy looked like an obscene monstrosity—but the needle was in, and his thumb was closing down on the plunger with a steady pressure, as Father Din watched in a kind of stupor of unbelief—"More!" Monk cried, his voice thick—"More," Dedi repeated; then, rhythmically, like a musician: "More, more, more, more, more, more, hey, more, hey, more, hey, hey, more . . . ah, ah, ah . . ."

"Boot it, boy, boot it," Monk cried, and suddenly Dedi drew back the plunger, filling the hypo to the top with his blood—"Washes the last drop of dope out of the hypo," Monk sang—"Boot it, boy—that's it"—and back down went the plunger, driving the blood before it into the veins, out of the plastic—and Dedi tugged the needle away from his arm—

"Hey, good!"

"Look at him!" Monk cried excitedly—"Look at him!"

"Hey, mon . . . I wanna go rest . . . Toddy . . . I'm gonna lay down, eh . . ."

"Go in my bedroom," Toddy said.

"Is he all right?" Father Din asked.

"He's O.K.," said Monk.  "Toddy, I want something to eat."

Chapter 35

A CONFESSION

"She ain't got no right to do this to me."

"Fuck you, Tory!"

Monk picked up the pistol from the table and stuck it in his belt, buttoning his jacket across to hide the weapon.  Then he stood up and walked across the room to the door and pulled it open.  Outside stood Tory Amsterdam and two women.

"She can do any damned thing she wants.  You don't own her, Tory."  This rebutting remark came from a short-haired, putty-faced woman of about forty.  The woman wore an elaborate, deadly looking ring on the second finger of either hand, and at this moment both hands were fists.

The apparent object of this altercation was a cherub-faced, gold-eyed beauty with an elaborate Egyptian hairdo of woven pigtails.  She wore a multi-skinned kaross that came to her upper thighs.  Black tights showed shapely legs down to her boots.  She smiled gleamingly at Toddy and sighed "Hi, baby;" then, seeing Father Din, who rose from his chair, she asked, "This the boy you was talking about?"

Toddy said: "Yes.  Sam, this is my friend, Opal Nearing.  Opal, this is Sam Hopkins . . ."

"Hi.  Oooh!  What happened to you?"

"He ran into an old friend," Monk said.  "What the hell do you care?  Shut up and get in here."  He slammed the door.

446

"Oh, you here, Monk?" said Opal casually. "Funny, I never seen you when I came in."

"Let me give you a piece of sound advice, Supi-yaw-lat:  start looking."

"Who?" asked Opal.

"Theebaw's queen.  That's Kipling."

"I don't know no Kipling.  He a dealer?  You think you're the only dealer in town?"

"The only one for you," said Monk, "and don't ever make the mistake of forgetting it."  He looked at Father Din.  "Here's a whole nest of hopheads for you, out of the woodwork . . ."

The two antagonists stood silently boiling, waiting.

"What's he doing?" Opal said, tossing her head, indicating Monk.  "On a toot?  Having a party?  Somebody die?"

"Shut up, you black slut!" Monk exclaimed, eyes bulging.

"Hey, man," put in Tory, "you don't supposed to talk to her like that."

"You be quiet, too, hornblower," ordered the putty-faced woman.  "Can't you see he's out of his skull?"

"What?" said Monk, not quite hearing this last.

"That still don't give him no call to talk to Opal like that."

"Be quiet, Tory," Opal said.  "I'll speak for myself."

"So what are you going to do about it?" goaded the woman.  "Go ahead, get your head split.  That'd be great.  What do I care, anyhow?  Go ahead, stupid, get busted up; see if I care!"

"Oh, you goddamn old ofay bulldyke!  You old white bull-cow!"

"Tory, don't you ever—"

"I said for the two of you to shut up, damn it!" Monk roared, and the room fell silent.  Monk paused; then said:  "Yeah, Supi-yaw-lat, I'm giving myself a party tonight. And do you know why? Because I'm being stalked. There's a hunter out in that jungle, and I'm his prey, and he's getting too close this time. This time he's only a few blocks from this room. This is the big one—the big moment of my life. This is the gunfight at the O.K. Corral. This is Armageddon."

"That nark?" asked Tory.

"Figlia," said Monk. "He's going to hide behind that gold shield of his and blow me away when I'm not looking."

"Well, what do you know?" said Opal. "The great man's scared."

"No, I'm not scared," Monk said. "I'm preparing for my greatest adventure. This thing with Figlia means a lot to me. He's what they call an honest cop. Well, I killed his little girl—did you know that?"

"Are you talking about Rose Figlia?" blurted Father Din. He realized now who Figlia was. Father Liam had handled Rose's funeral. He had helped.

"What do you know about Rose Figlia?"

"Just something I saw in the paper," said Father Din.

"Oh, fuck it," said Monk. "I have more important things to think about—anyway it can't be proved—let's see what his honesty amounts to." He thought for a minute. "On the contrary, this is one of my greatest opportunities . . ." He dropped his sentence and looked around, as if coming out of a reverie. "You, Tory, I've got a job for you. Come in the other room for a minute." He got to his feet and lumbered into the livingroom, swaying like a shot bull, with Tory following.


Chapter 36


TORY GETS HIS ORDERS


Tory's raised voice was audible in the kitchen: "I CAN'T!"

"You CAN and you WILL," came Monk's voice.

"Oh, man . . ." Tory groaned.

"Wonder what that's all about," said Opal; then, smiling at Father Din, "Say," she said, "Toddy told me she only met you this afternoon, but that she think you O.K. I think she kinda goes for you, you know?"

Father Din looked at Toddy, who was standing at the stove, cooking eggs for Monk. He looked at Opal: "Is that what she said?"

"Well, you know . . . sort'f. 'Course, she's married—you know that?"

"Yes."

"Good, then it's all square. See, I don't like nobody to get cheated. I tell them two fools"—she indicated the other woman and Tory with specific rolls of her eyes— "that I like 'em each—see I'm honest—for what I get from 'em—Elga, she buy my stuff for me; and Tory, he—well, never mind what he give me—ha!—but what I mean, I play square, you dig?"

Father Din nodded.

"What's happen to you?" she said. "You look all swollen."

"An accident."

"But, you know, Sam—O.K. if I call you Sam, ain't it?—Toddy been lonely. I told her before she should let that fool Jack of hers go and forget him; get her somebody new, and get out, you dig?"

Father Din nodded.

"'Cause this is no good no way. You understand?"

Father Din nodded.

"'Cause that man of hers ain't never going to be like he was, you know?"

Father Din nodded.

"'Cause Monk got him right under his evil thumb."

Father Din nodded.

"Now you come along, nice stud like she said you was—maybe she got herself a chance. She and me is old friends. Used to model together. That's how we met. That's where she met Jack. I used to pose for him, too. He done lots of pictures of me. Studies . . . I thought he was a pretty good artist, but I don't say I know much about that stuff. But now he ain't. Monk took his manhood away."

"Hey, bitch!" said Tory, coming into the kitchen behind Monk. "What're you up to? You trying to add somebody new to your list?"

"If I am," Opal turned on him, "it ain't none of your business, big mouth." She grinned at Father Din. "That big mouth of his is only good for blowin' out blue and cool on that sax, and kissin', but he can't talk with it and make no sense, that boy. Can you, big mouth?"

"You gonna push me too far someday, Opal," said the musician, solemnly shaking his head.

"I thought you were on break," Elga said to him. "Shouldn't you be getting back? You know, there aren't many people who like your kind of music anymore—you shouldn't keep them waiting."

"Don't worry about it, bull-cow!"

"She's right," Monk said. "You've got your stuff—you know what to do—so get out. Go blow your brains out. But, Tory, remember: I want that done, and done just as I told you to do it, or don't let me find you, do you get me?"

Tory nodded gravely.

"Hopkins, did I tell you that I produce my own movies? Produce, direct, and star in them. These three are my cast. Now go on, get out! I'm tired of listening to your stupid argument."

"Are you coming?" asked Elga of Opal.

"You go on across the hall, I'll be there in a minute."

"No you ain't," said Tory, "you ain't going back in that apartment with that old bull-cow. You going to come to the

Cuttlefish with me.  You going to sit right there where I can see you while I play."

Opal arched an eyebrow, defiant.  "I go just where I please to go, boy, and right now I'm staying here."

"Don't call me no boy.  I'll slap you up 'side your—"

"Try me *first*," said Elga, making fists of her hands and jutting her massive bosom against the skinny black man's stomach.

Monk got suddenly to his feet and, taking Elga and Tory each roughly by an arm, hurtled the argument into the hall.  Slamming the door after it, he came back to the table and sat down heavily.  In an instant, the musician's voice could be heard in a piercing scream, then a curse.  A door was slammed, and fast, angry footsteps diminished down the hall.


Chapter 37


!ALERTE!


"Opal," Monk suddenly commanded, "go get me another bottle of Scotch."

"I'll have to go to the store," Opal protested.  "It's cold out there, and maybe ain't none open.  It's late."

"I don't care where you get it, just get it.  Here."  He threw a hundred dollar bill on the table.

Opal picked it up, saying, "Be right back," and went reluctantly out the door.

"Where's my food?" Monk demanded.

Toddy swung around, holding her forehead with her right hand and a frying pan with her left.  "Here it is," she cried, "burnt on the stove!  I can't cook with all these people running in and out.  I can't stand much more of this!"  She threw the pan back on the stove with a clang and, holding her face in both hands, began to sob hysterically.

Monk looked at her, drunkenly amazed.

Father Din had started to his feet to comfort her when the door burst open and Opal re-entered, a quart of Scotch in hand.

"Hey, what's going on here?" she asked, seeing Toddy. "Why you cryin' like that, baby?"

She threw the bottle of Scotch, with a "Here," to Monk, who caught it, a surprised look on his face, and went and put her arms around Toddy.

"What!" she exclaimed, looking at Father Din. "You another one? Why ain't you up here holdin' this girl?"

"Shit!" said Monk, twisting the top off the new bottle.

Father Din stood up, reflexively.

"Don't pay any goddamn attention to that little whore," Monk said. "You, Opal! Where did you get this liquor? I know you didn't go to the store that fast. Who do you think you're putting one over on? Where's my change?" But this train of thought was interrupted when a loud moan came from the front of the apartment.

"What's that?" asked Opal, glad for the distraction.

"It sounds like Dedi," said Toddy.

Opal, surprised, still holding Toddy, said: "You mean little Dedi in there all this time?"

"He said he wanted to rest."

"He shot up?"

"Yes."

"He O.K.?"

"Of course he's O.K.," said Monk. "The little sewer-rat is dreaming about old time movie stars. You know what he's like."

"That little boy is very weak, you know," Opal said, a look of concern in her big-eyed, doll-like face.

Just then came another moan from the bedroom, as if to punctuate Opal's words.

"Is something wrong?" asked Father Din.

"Could be," said Opal. "That don't sound right to me."

"He's just dreaming," Monk said.

"Let's take a look," Opal said. Toddy nodded assent, and the two women went through the livingroom and disappeared into the bedroom.

"I wonder where Jack is?" Monk mused.

"Maybe he couldn't get the money," Father Din ventured.

"Maybe he's dead," Monk said. He looked at Father Din. "I suppose you think this is pretty small-time for a man like myself?"

"I don't know what you mean. I suppose there's a great deal of money in drugs."

"Oh, there is," Monk said. "But what I pick up here is only chickenfeed, a matter of a few grand. You don't think that a man like me would trouble himself for the price of a suit, do you? This suit I'm wearing cost more than what I pick up here. No, this is my—my hobby. This is my rest and relaxation."

In a few minutes Toddy came back from the bedroom, her face pale.

"There's something wrong with Dedi, Monk. His face is all twisted, and he's drenched in sweat."

"What?" said Monk, who had nodded off open-eyed for a moment. "What's that?"

"It's Dedi," said Toddy. "He's sick."

"So?" said Monk. "What am I supposed to do?"

"Well, you've got to do something. I think he O.D'ed"

"An overdose?"

"Yes, I think so. We ought to get him to the E.M."

"A doctor?" said Monk, suddenly alert. "That's out. No doctors, got it? Wait a minute, I'll take a look at him." He got up and went to the sink and washed his face with cold water.

Father Din went into the bedroom. In a moment, Monk and Toddy followed him.

Chapter 38

## O. D.

It was impossible for all of them to get into the small, bed-crowded room, so while Father Din slid in beside the bed, Toddy and Monk remained in the doorway, looking on. Opal sat on the bed, beside Dedi. The boy was having difficulty breathing, and his face was bubbling with sweat. There were great damp rings under the arms of his limp cha-cha shirt. His legs twitched about. His skin was a mottled blue.

"This boy has O.D.'ed," said Opal grimly. "It look bad to me. He oughta go to a hospital."

"That's out," said Monk. "Got any naline, Opal?"

"I ain't got nothin'," said Opal, looking at the boy, slowly shaking her head.

"Then get some ice cubes and rub on him. Open his collar. Do whatever you want, but he doesn't go out of here and nobody else comes in either. That's the way it's going to be."

"This little boy'll die, Monk," said Opal, wiping Dedi's forehead with a handkerchief. "You gotta let somebody get him some help."

"Then he'll just have to die," said Monk. "He's got AIDS anyway. He's not the first junky to O.D. Nobody cares. The cops don't even care. Around here the street-cleaners pick up their bodies like so much garbage. But listen, all of you: the first person who tries to go out that door will find out how serious I am." His grogginess of a few moments before was gone. He seemed again in firm control of himself. He turned and left the doorway, calling back from the next room: "Besides, the little freak irritated me."

"I'll go get some towels and ice," Toddy said, following Monk into the kitchen.

"You said he could die," said Father Din to Opal.

"Happen all the time."

"Isn't there anything we can do for him? Will the ice really do any good?"

"Do I look like a doctor?"

Father Din widened the boy's collar.

"If that man in there let us get him to the hospital maybe he be O.K."

"But he won't."

"Well, maybe that's up to you. You the only man here."

"He's got a gun."

"Yup."

"I know you think I should do something," Father Din said, uncertain whether to kneel and pray or ball his fists and fight. "He might shoot somebody . . . you . . . or Toddy."

"Or you?"

"Believe me, that's not what I'm worried about."

"Don't matter what I believe."

"You'll have to think what you like," Father Din said, unsure of his own stance. "Is he always like this?"

"When he get drunk he bad. But he in a real fit tonight. I think he kinda scared of that Lieutenant Figlia."

Father Din wondered aloud: "Wouldn't it be safer for him if he got the boy out of here?"

Opal nodded in the direction of the kitchen with mixed contempt and awe: "That devil know what he doin', drunk or sober. He got a plan already. He thinkin' all around our heads. I seen it before."

Toddy came back, squeezing in beside Father Din, bringing ice cubes wrapped in a towel. She brought a dry towel also, and with it she wiped the perspiration from Dedi's brow. "This isn't going to do any good," she said, only saying what they all knew.

Dedi moaned. He opened his eyes, but did not seem to see any of them. "Oh . . . *hey!* . . . Jack!"

Toddy winced at the sound of her husband's name.

The boy struggled to raise himself up on his elbows. "Jack! Pilar! Hey! I no feel so good, mon . . . Hey!"

"Try to rest, boy," Opal said. "Rest."

Chapter 39

LAST RITES

Dedi was ghastly bluish pale, mottled like marble. His
skinny, chickenboned hands tried to open, tried to shut. And
it seemed that the thick air could not be sucked down into his
lungs. As his little cage of a chest struggled to expand, his
back arched; then, as if exhausted with the effort, the whole
pathetic structure, a mockery of inspiration, would again col-
lapse. Each word came hissed on a small sigh: "Pilar . . ." he
uttered: then, with an effort terrible to see: "Bogie . . . he . . .
the . . . mon . . . Pilar!" He tossed for breath. "Pilar! . . . hey,
help . . . me . . . ."

The three near the dying boy looked helplessly at
him. Then, decisively, Father Din said: "Leave me alone
with him for a few minutes, would you?"

"What are you going to do?" Toddy asked.

"I have an idea. Maybe I can . . . save him. Let me try."

Opal climbed off the bed and took Toddy's arm. "Come
on, baby," she said, "we can't do no good. If the man thinks
he can do something, let's do what he say."

"But *what* . . .?"

"Come on, baby," said Opal, and led Toddy out of the
room.

Father Din sat on the edge of the bed and took one of
Dedi's small hands in his own.

"Can you hear me, Dedi Pavon?"

And somewhere in the deep reaches of his mind Dedi
understood he was receiving the Last Rites of the Church, as
they were sometimes given on the battlefield; that a prayer

was being spoken over his floating, swaying self. Oh, that Jack and Pilar could share with him the incredibly sweet, incredibly sad music of the words! And Dedi could see Jack, now, in the small, cataracted, half-blind eye of his mind, as through the opacity of a vague and meaningless light. Jack was holding Pilar's hand: everything was going to come out right! Oh, it was all coming true! It was radiant, now, with fine, clean truth! Oh, why must it be gone! Jack's smiling face was gone! Pilar, a Pilar who was truly happy, was gone! *"Donde esta mi hermana? . . . Alquien tragame mi hermana. Pilar?"*

Father Din prayed for his own forgiveness in hope of God's forgiveness of Dedi. Had he the right to give Last Rites, he wondered.

"Wait, my son . . . my brother . . . ."

Wait?

In a few minutes Father Din came into the kitchen. His face was gray and damp. His mouth hung open.

Monk and the two women looked at him.

"Well?" said Monk impatiently.

"He's dead."

Monk got up and started to pass Father Din on his way to the bedroom. Father Din grabbed his arm.

"Now that you've killed him," Father Din said, "what are you going to do with him?"

Monk looked at him, hard-eyed. "He killed himself," he fairly hissed. He jerked his arm free and went on into the bedroom. In a moment, Monk came back into the kitchen with the boy in his arms. Monk laid the boy's body on the floor and went through its pockets. He found several cheap rings. He then removed the boy's wrist watch. There was nothing else to take.

"Where's his suit jacket?" Monk asked. "He gave me a couple of hundred dollars; he must have got that someplace. I know he's got more on him."

Opal found the jacket down behind a chair, handed it to Monk, and stood by in silence. Monk went through the jacket, finding a wallet with a hundred and fifty dollars in it, and saying, "The kid must have knocked over a piggy bank this afternoon." He emptied the wallet of money and threw it on the table. Surreptitiously, Father Din took the wallet from the table and went through it. In a moment he found what he was looking for: Dedi's address, on a clinic card. He replaced the wallet on the table. Monk was then pulling a half a dozen watches from where they were pinned to the lining of Dedi's jacket. "I can pass these out to the Bravos like tips," he said, putting the jacket back on the corpse. "Punk," he said, eyeing the tape-wrapped pipe which the boy carried, now stuck in his belt. "Give me that wallet." He stuffed the wallet into Dedi's inside jacket pocket. He threw the boy's body over his shoulder, its limp arms and legs hanging like those of a ventriloquist's dummy.

"What are you going to do with him?" Father Din repeated.

"He's dead. Monk said. "I'm going to take him to the poor people's morgue. Open that door."

Opal pulled open the door and waited.

"Anyone coming?" Monk asked.

Opal stepped into the hall.

"No," she said.

"Where are you going?" asked Father Din. "What are you doing?"

"Get out of my way," Monk said.

"Not until you explain."

"All right," Monk said, "I'll explain. How's this for an explanation?" He reached into his belt and drew out the huge automatic pistol and set its cold muzzle to rest in the middle of Father Din's forehead. "Now get out of my way," he said, "and remember, nobody leaves this apartment. Anybody leaves, I'll track you down and kill you."

Father Din blinked, and stepped aside. But when Monk could be heard lumbering up the stairs to the fifth floor, Father Din followed after him. On the fifth floor, Father Din saw Monk climbing the stairs to the roof, and when he reached the roof, he saw Monk, silhouetted in the oddly gleaming moonlight, marching across the roof with Dedi Pavon's body draped over his hand as a shotputter holds a shot, and, in exactly the same way that a shotputter puts the shot, Father Din saw Monk put Dedi Pavon's body off the roof and into space, down which it fell six stories to be pulped in the alley below.

The icy wind whipped at Father Din's hair and face, but he could feel nothing save the weight of the blank sky upon his mind.


## Chapter 40


## FIGLIA IN LOVE

Outside, the seventy mile per hour gale from off the chopping, tumultuous Atlantic deracinated a delicate tall poplar which had grown for twenty years overlooking the headland, two-hundred yards from the bursting surf, and sent it, a whirling, root-feathered spear, crashing into a weekend-fisherman's deserted shack, which, upon impact, vanished, like a house of cards in a wind tunnel, its thin, weathery boards blown scattering wildly into the night. For the force of the gale the shrub-like conifers that dotted the cape lay in flat obeisance and the rocks of the promontory roared. Then the big wind began to push a dazzling whirl of fine white flakes before it, and from the land it seemed that a gossamer curtain had been lowered far out at sea. When it woke in the morning, Long Island would find that it had slept under a blanket of snow.

Inside, warm and snug on the cushiony couch in the

livingroom of his ranch-style house, far from the cape, but still on Long Island, in the town of Beachberry, which grew no berries and which was some distance from the nearest beach, Detective Lieutenant Albert Figlia watched a televised weather report . . .

". . . the possibility exists that the storm will change its course and be blown out to sea. However, at best it's certain that much of the metropolitan area will see some snow. At worst," the dapper-looking, striped-shirted weatherman said, smiling sheepishly, "I'm afraid we're in for a blizzard."

"And how in hell am I going to get back into the city in the morning if we have a blizzard?" Figlia demanded of the weatherman, who shrugged his shoulders, as if in reply, and said, "This is meteorologist Herb Kline reporting," and vanished.

"I'd better drive back in tonight," Figlia said, "just in case he has it right for once. I don't want to be stranded."

"You talking to yourself again?" asked Gena, his wife, who had stopped at the threshold of the livingroom on her way through to the kitchen. "When you start talking to yourself, I know you're tired. Why don't you go into bed, Al? I'll be right along."

Figlia, still in his rolled-up shirtsleeves and day-rumpled trousers, argyle-stocking-footed, looked quickly up at her from the silly mythology of an Old South Plantation House, a picture of emerald lawns and white fluted pillars, before which the florid face of Colonel Drummond of Deep Down Done Chicken fame, his white locks wafting in a gentler breeze than that which rumbled the windows of Long Island, his chicken-fat yellowy mustaches parting for the insertion of a gooey drumstick, floated like a redneck's conception of a fatherly god.

"I was just thinking aloud that I'd better drive into the city tonight," he said. "There's maybe a blizzard coming."

"Oh no!" Gena exclaimed, frowning. She was a tall,

slender woman, taller than her husband, and in her middle thirties, over a decade younger than he was. She stepped back into the livingroom, pulling the belt closed around her long satin dressing gown. "Well," she said, brightening, walking toward him and giving him a wink, "I'm glad you were able to visit the homefront and relieve me of these! She bent over, grabbed up from the carpet the lacy lingerie that Figlia had lovingly removed from her an hour before, and shook the lavender handful at him.

He stood up, facing her. They were almost eye-level and his sad, brown-eyed gaze invited her closer. Of late, whenever he left for the precinct, she saw that dark, Monk-thinking look, like a shadow. He knew she saw it; knew he could not keep it from his face. He averted his eyes and buried his head on her shoulder, kissing her neck. "Fair lady, we do have world enough and time," he whispered, and led her out of the room, across the hall, into the dim bedroom where a small bedside lamp shaped like a lily shone like a beacon.

They lay naked beneath a comforter. From the living-room came the faint dazzle and hum of unattended commercials and sitcoms. Nearby the tiny ticks of ice that shot through the wind tattooed upon a window pane. Figlia was certain that the mixed blessings of life had taught him some-thing, had taught him what love is. He had shaken in the hop-per of his mind the ingredients of life. He was a quietly con-templative man. He believed in God, but he thought that organized religions were human creations, anthropological stuff and nonsense, bred in the lonely, primitive heart. It was his opinion that God's will had been withdrawn from nature and humankind was on its own. He had come to believe this in war, and on the hard streets of his patrols, come to believe that the war of good and evil was between connectedness and dis-connectedness; or, on a lower plane, but symbolically the same, between social and anti-social behavior.

The ultimate in anti-social behavior was loveless sex, he thought, as in prostitution; the ultimate in social behavior was sexual love.  The sparks of the heart's warmth he felt with Gena were the stars of the universe.  He thanked the God that made the universe for having set him free from a loveless marriage, for giving him this chance to know what love was.  Gena could feel her husband's heart beat upon her chest.  He wiggled his torso down between her legs, and rested his head on her stomach, just below the rib cage.  He hugged her around her upper thighs, squeezing hard.  He inched his way back up, leaving a trail of warm kisses.

Afterward, the comforter at their feet, Gena lay in Figlia's arms.  "I guess I will have to make that coffee, now, won't I?" she whispered.

"Yes, and make it strong.  Then I'll go."  Neither of them moved.  There had been world enough, but now there was no more time.

"I hate to see you take that long drive back to-night.  Where will you sleep?  At the station house?"

"I'll take a hotel room."

"Good."

Figlia sat up, stretched, yawned, and began to grope about under the bed for his shoes.  Gena pulled her robe on and went to brew coffee.  When it was ready, she found Figlia seated on the couch in the livingroom, lacing his shoes.  "Turn it off," she said, meaning the TV, and placing a tray holding two cups of coffee on the table.  "It's so distracting."

"No wait," said Figlia leaning forward.  "What's that?"
SPECIAL REPORT
No picture came, only a voice, filled with newsman urgency: "We have as yet an incomplete report of a disturbance in Manhattan's lower East Side.  The disturbance could be of a racial nature, but nothing has as yet been confirmed.  More as information comes in.  We return you now—"

"What's that?" said Gena.

"Maybe a riot," said Figlia. "It's down where I am."

"And now here's Kathy Field downtown on the Lower East Side." Kathy Field stood, mike in hand, on the sidewalk in front of the Saints and Sinners Club.

"That's right on the Strip," Figlia commentaried, "only a few blocks from the station. I passed by there at least twice today."

"This is Kathy Field reporting from the East Village, where what police spokespersons have referred to as a serious disturbance, but what looks to us more like a riot, is under-way. There are crowds of East Villagers out here, some participating in the disturbance and others merely rubber-necking. From what I can discover, it all started here, in this grunge-rock bar that you see behind me—the Saints and Sinners Club—when a teen gang, called the Bravos, invaded the place, which is habituated by artists and musicians and other bohemians. The owner, a man called Tiger—and we think his last name is Hartzmann—an ex-wrestler, tried to evict the gang single-handedly. Others joined in to help him, it appears, and we believe there has been a stabbing, the seri-ousness of which we are not as yet certain. Oh, I believe this is Mr. Hartzmann. Step in, Mr. Hartzmann. Would you care to tell us your version of what happened?"

Tiger stepped before the camera. His breath steamed from the cold. His wall-eye was rolling.

"I think I remember him from wrestling matches on TV," said Figlia.

"Well, that's what happened," said Tiger, "just what you said. I don't want no big-mouthed trouble makers in my joint."

Kathy Field nodded, non-commitally, and pushed the mike forward, almost into Tiger's mouth. "Then you don't view this as a racial incident?"

"Naw," moaned Tiger, disgustedly. "Chrissake, I don't

see what all the excitement's about. I just trew out a few loud-mouths. Now everybody's running up and down, TV cameras . . . Christ! It's the media, that's what it is. It's you!"

"But a man was knifed, wasn't he?"

"Stabbed. Yeah. But it happens down here. Nothin' new." Tiger looked cold. He wore only a gray cardigan sweater over his starched white shirt, collar open. His hands were plunged in his trousers pockets. His teeth seemed to chatter.

"Mr. Hartzmann when you leave us, do you intend to close the Saints and Sinners Club for the night?"

"No. I don't close shop until four in the morning and unless the police ask me to close earlier, that's when I'll close. Why should I have to close my bar because a gang of bums start causing trouble?" Behind Tiger a teenaged girl stood staring dreamily into the camera, mittened hands over her ears. Behind her, floating in space, was a large placard. On it was written:

MINORITIES COALITION LIBERTY PARTY<br>MEANS FREEDOM!

Kathy Field dropped Tiger cold, and, with a wave of her hand toward the placard bearers, signaling her camera person, plunged into the crowd. The camera caught up with her, sticking her mike into the face of a pale, blue-eyed, good looking young man with a Fu-Manchu mustache, who held one end of the sign. "And what do you say happened here tonight?" she cried. The young man said, "A very basic thing has happened here tonight. We were denied our basic right of freedom of expression . . ."

"It doesn't look like much yet," Figlia said. "Looks like the media is trying to blow a mole-hill into a mountain. Must be a slow news night."

"Yes," said Gena, "but a man was stabbed, maybe killed."

"Honey," said Figlia, "it happens fifty times a night and

nobody shows up most of the time. Ms. Field there probably thinks she can get some racial divisiveness into it. Trouble is, she might succeed. Maybe it's a good thing I'm going in. Hubbard will need all the help he can get."

"It's not your job," Gena objected. "You go to a hotel and get a good night's sleep. Now, that's an order, Lieutenant."

"Yes, Ma'am," said Figlia. He drained the coffee from his cup, finished tying his shoes, and went looking for his suit jacket and overcoat.

"Wear your scarf," Gena called after him, "it's freezing out."

"That's why I don't think that business'll get very big," Figlia said, returning. He was dressed for the outdoors. "It's too damned cold for much outdoors mischief."

Within five minutes, Figlia was pulling onto the Long Island Expressway, beginning his third trip of the day along that drab, curving commuter run. He focused his thoughts with his eyes fixed upon the dark, forward, cloud-scumbled sky. Occasional auto-lights glared that from view. At the beginning of a long, sweeping curve, he passed a tree that stood on a hill in high tableau against a section of cloud-pale, electric sky. Its bare boughs were like skinny, gnarled fingers, clutching the clouds.

## Chapter 41

### FIGLIA IN CHARGE

Forty minutes later Figlia pulled up in front of the station house. He went directly to Hubbard's office and knocked. "Come in," called Hubbard. Hubbard's sleepy eyes opened happily. "Al!" he exclaimed, "I'm glad to see you back. I've got my hands full and I need some experienced help." For a quarter of a century Hubbard had been

465

losing more than his share of sleep—thus the eyes, perennially at half-mast—and tonight was no exception. "I just spoke with your wife. I think I woke the poor girl up. For nothing, as it turns out. She said you were on your way in." Hubbard leaned back in his swivel chair, lighted what must have been a cheap stogie, judging from the face he made, and spat dryly several times. The whites of his eyes were red and he did not look well. He said, "Gena told me you saw the trouble on TV. These racial entanglements can get messy. I guess I should know, being black. It's already all over the media."

"What happened out there?"

"I've heard all kinds of things," he said, coughing. He cleared his throat. "Look, I'm not feeling so hot. I think I'm running a temp." He coughed again, and spit up into his handkerchief. "I mean, I don't know exactly how the trouble got started. Anyhow, some sculptor is making it over at St. Vincent's. One of the Bravo punks shoved a shiv in his belly. There seemed to be a couple of other jerk-offs involved, but they don't seem to have anything directly to do with the violence. We're going to run them out of here. We need room for the real thing. The gang stays, though, until we can sort out which one of them did the knifing. Hell, you know it won't stick to charge the whole bunch of 'em. We know there's drugs going in and out of their place—you know they own a building just a couple of blocks from here?—their 'headquarters'—but the guys we've got in the tank are clean. How 'bout you taking this thing on, as a favor? Pull all the tangles out of this baby, O.K.?"

"Do you think I should shut the club down? There was a stabbing—"

"I tell you what, I wouldn't want to be the one to tell that cock-eyed old wrestler I'm shutting him down." He thought for a moment. "Why close him up? It's not that kind of situation. Nobody's dead. We know the stabber is one of the

Bravos. The guy who did the knifing was wearing a Bravo coat, you know, black plastic with a knife and a bleeding heart. We got him in the tank. We just have to sort them out. But do what you think best. Close him down, if you want to. But it wasn't his fault. As for me, I'm going home and go to bed. My night chief is out sick, or moonlighting. It's hard to tell the blue flu from the real flu except that I think I've got the real thing. I may not come back for a day or so. I'll put young Verdi in charge, officially. You keep an eye on him." He rose from his desk, grabbed his trenchcoat, and pulled open the door. "See you in a day or so. I'll keep in touch by phone."

When the door was shut behind Hubbard, Figlia called Gena. He promised he'd get some sleep. He hung up and sat for a long time, holding his head in his hands. Now, unofficially, he had a whole precinct to worry about.


Chapter 42


PROCRASTINATION


Jack Muir cupped his hands around a lighted match and dipped his cigarette into them. He puffed with numb-cold lips until smoke came, keeping his eyes on the windows of Toddy's apartment.

He was standing, hunched and shivering, in the doorway of his own building; across the street, slightly cater-cornered from him, was the doorway of Toddy's. No one had come or left by that door for the past half hour.

He was certain, however, that persons whom he knew, or of whose existence he was aware, had entered the building before he had taken up his windswept post; because perhaps a quarter of an hour earlier he had seen Monk's unmistakable bald dome and thick body pass in front of the window next to Toddy's bedroom; and he had seen Toddy, too; and he had seen another man—a big, dark fellow—probably the man whom Dedi mentioned having seen with Toddy earlier in the day, at the Saints and Sinners Club.

Another woman—he believed it was Opal—was up there, too.

Once, Monk passed in front of the window carrying something, but Jack had been unable to make out what it was: the other man had followed Monk, obscuring the view. Muir drew his head, turtlewise, down into the high collar of his khaki army-surplus overcoat. He wore a woolen-knit ski-band of bright yellow pulled down over the tips of his reddened ears, and a long scarf of the same color about his neck. Below the long, flared skirt of the army coat, a short length of grungy, torn jeans could be seen, disappearing into a pair of down-at-heels boots.

A large, bloodstone-and-pounded-copper brooch was pinned to the coat, over his heart. He avoided looking at the brooch. The gleaming copper, which he kept polished, made him feel even colder than he was, as did the touch of the icy pistol in his pocket.

How would he appear, he wondered, to a stranger who passed and saw him there. No one would guess that his parents were wealthy, and that he himself might have been, might still be. A passing stranger might take him for a half-starved hippie derelict—or for what he was, he thought bitterly, a dumb junkie—with his hollow, haunted face, and Dachau eyes.

Afraid? Yes, he was afraid. Afraid of what, though? Only a few hours earlier he had conquered his fear of death in a game of Russian roulette. But he knew that his wife was the distance of that building across the street from him, and that he wanted to go to her but was afraid to do so. Now the wind went by, a ghost rolling a garbage-can lid. The thing clanged down the middle of the street, passing in front of him, then veered off toward a parked car, crashed into a fender, and clattered into silence.  The racket scared out from under the car a pair of hair-on-end, courting cats, who scurried off into the alley next to Toddy's building, bushy-tailed.  A few moments later, from out of sight, Muir heard their screams of conflict or lust.  His teeth chattered.  He spit out the butt-end of his cigarette and stamped on it, as much to warm himself as to put it out.  The sparks scattered across the sidewalk to the gutter and spun off in miniature dying flares in the wind.  It was no good.  He couldn't bring himself to do it.  He stepped out of the doorway and into a wind that felt like a heavy hand on his chest, and started walking toward the Strip.  As he walked, he took the pistol from his pocket and put it inside his coat, in his belt.  It had become almost too cold to touch.

Earlier, he had heard the Martian wail of police sirens sounding from the Strip.  Now, as he approached its center, he was reminded of them.  Obviously, there had been trouble.  He counted five police cars, most of them double-parked, their beacons slowly turning.  A truck from one of the television networks was on the scene.  The remainder of what must have been a crowd wandered about, occasionally being shooed from here to there by police.  Some of these, upon being told to move on, or to "Break it up," went into the bars, which, along the Strip, on week-nights, were often open until four in the morning, their late-night customers being mostly mug-of-beer-drinking or white wine bohemian types, artists and would-be artists, long-drawn-out-talkers.  By day the whisky-drinking set held sway.

A cop strode toward him, and Muir knew that he was going to be told to move along, so he turned and started back toward his loft.  He had no deep interest in whatever was going on—or had gone on.  He also had an unauthorized pistol tucked in his belt, and many old needle-tracks on his arms.  He glanced back over his shoulder and saw the cop lose interest and turn away.

Then he ran into Tory, who came plunging out of one of the bars. Stoned on heroin, Tory was drunk as well, smelling potently of gin. The skinny black jazzman with the poodling locks grinned when he saw Muir. He was toting his battered tenor-sax case in his left hand. He flapped out his right hand flat for Muir to slap, saying:

"Hey, man, what's happenin'?" He didn't wait for an answer. "You missed a bad scene," he went on.

"You mean all this?" Muir said, throwing a look back at the police cars. "What happened?"

"Naw, man," Tory said thickly, "Up at your old lady's."

"What happened?" A sharp look came on Muir's face. "Is anything wrong?"

"Wrong?" Tory shrugged a skinny right shoulder; his left hung like part of a rope that was tied about his neck on one end and to the handle of his sax-case on the other.

"What's *wrong*? I never heard of *wrong*. It's just that bullet-headed, ofay—beg pardon—mother Monk."

"What's happened, Tory?" Muir urged. "Get to the point."

"Aw, nothin'—nothin' happened, man. You worried 'bout your old lady? Sheee-it!" He waved that aside. "No, man," he went on, "he just drunk. But you know how he get when he get like that—bad-assin' all over the place. It's me, man. He's drivin' me out. You know what he tried to tell me that I should *do*?"

"What?" Muir asked, momentarily relieved.

Tory widened his glazed eyes. "He told me he want me to burn old Tiger out. He told me I gotta pop a Molotov cocktail in on that old man. Now why I wanna do that?" he asked, tucking his chin in and raising his eyebrows. "Huh? You tell me."

"Are you going to do it?"

"Shit, no! He got the wrong man for that kinda gig. I'm strictly an artist. You know me, man. Huh-huh," he grunted, shaking his head in the emphatic negative, his dangle of curls flapping on his forehead, "not *me*."

"What's he got against Tiger?"

"How'm *I* s'pose to know?  What he got against everybody?"

"Toddy's all right, then?"

"She's all right."

"But he's drunk."

"Aw, Jack—*man*, you know she's been with him when he was drunk before . . . I mean, I don't wanna hurt your feelings, man—but what could you do about it, anyhow?  You'd best forget that scene."

Muir knew Tory meant well, but his remarks still stung.  He changed the subject, reverting to Tory's problem: "What are *you* going to do?"

Tory laughed pathetically.  "I dunno, man.  It's like this: I'm gonna hope that he's drunk enough so he don't remember telling me to do that thing."  He looked a question mark down his nose at Muir.  "Mmm?" he added.

"Suppose he does remember?"

"Then I'm gonna tell him that I thought he was too drunk, and that maybe I shouldn't do what he said till he was sober."

"That won't work," Muir said.

"I know," said Tory, shaking his head sadly.  "I don't know what to do, man . . ."  He threw his arms out, helplessly.  The heavy case held the one close to his side.  He set the case down, and repeated the gesture with tremendous emphasis.  "I just don't *know* . . . ."

"You better go hide," said Muir.

"Dig, man, I think that's what I'm gonna do.  See if my brother will put me up.  But first, I'm gonna find Opal and take her with me.  And if I get a chance before I split, I'm gonna break that bulldyke girlfriend of her's neck."

"What happened here?" Muir asked, indicating the situation on the Strip.

"Oh, man, everything. Looked like there was gonna be a riot. I ain't heard how it started." He rolled his eyes. "Say, man," he said suddenly, "I'm freezing. Think I'm gonna round me up my old lady, and Goodbye, Tory! Trouble is, I got another session to do tonight, but then I'm gone . . . up where they got soul-food and hot-sauce. Bury me not on the lone prairie . . ." He grinned a little sadly. "Dig you later, man," he said, and picked up his sax-case and started off, calling back: "I'll meet you right on this spot in one year, Jack— but don't wait!"

Muir stood for a moment, watching Tory reeling off as if pulled by the weight of his saxophone case. Then he entered the bar from which Tory had plunged. He needed a good, stiff drink. One—and then he was going up and take Toddy out of that apartment, away from that—what did Tory say?—mother, Monk.

Chapter 43

ESCAPE

Upon re-entering the apartment, Monk had demanded to know where Opal had gone. Toddy had shrugged for answer. "I knew she'd run," Monk had said. "But I don't have to worry about her. She won't say a word. *You* might talk, but she won't. On the other hand, you wouldn't run. I knew that when I went up to the roof. I knew Hopkins would follow me, and I knew that you wouldn't leave without him. You see, I know my congregation." Monk had taken his seat, grinning with self-satisfaction, and had poured himself a drink. After a pause, he'd said: "Nothing's a chance when you know what you're doing."

But now it seemed to Father Din that Monk had been

silent for a long time.  He was thinking this when he felt himself being nudged in the ribs.  Toddy indicated Monk with a
slight dip of her head.  Father Din looked at him.  He
sprawled in his chair, his small goatee pressed into his jutting
chest, his eyes half-masted.

"Is he . . ."

"Shhhhh!"  Toddy leaned toward Father Din, putting her
mouth to his ear and her hand over it, and whispered, "Opal
put veronal in his bottle."

"When?" asked Father Din.

"Before Dedi . . .  We've been waiting for it to hit him."

"I wish it had hit him before he did that to Dedi," Father
Din said.

"So do I," said Toddy.  She studied Monk's face.  "I
think he's out," she said.

"He might be faking."

"No, I don't think so, but there's only one way to find
out.  Come on, let's get out of here."

Toddy got carefully to her feet, and tiptoed to the
door.  She took her own coat from the clothestree, putting it
over her arm, and got Father Din's out from under Monk's,
and carefully opened the door.  She held Father Din's coat out
to him, saying, "Here.  Hurry."  Monk snorted, and Toddy
froze, stock-still.  In a moment Monk's mouth dropped open,
he nuzzled his goatee deeper into his chest, and began to
snore.  Toddy stepped into the hall, again holding Father
Din's coat out to him.  "Come!" she urged.

Father Din followed her into the hall.

He started to pull the door to, but Toddy stopped him,
saying, "Leave it.  It might wake him."  In a moment they had
their coats on and were in the street.

Toddy looked up at Jack Muir's loft.  "There's no light
up there," she said.  "Either Jack's asleep, or he's out.  It's so
quiet.  Think it could wake Monk if I called up for him?  I'm
so afraid he'll go up to my place, and with Monk—"

"Try," said Father Din. "You should try. Your kitchen is toward the rear. Monk won't hear you, not with this wind." They crossed the street, their coats blowing, and Toddy called up to the loft several times, but there was no response from the row of blank, black windows.

Father Din waited, the cold air having a beneficial effect on his mind and nerves. His head was clearing. But still, he felt weak. He had eaten nothing since that morning's breakfast. His nose was caked inside with dried blood, and ached. Occasionally, his stomach would seem to float upwards, uncomfortably, like a helium-filled balloon.

He pulled his collar up against the wind, and looked at the storm-ominous sky. He knew that it could not be more than a hundred yards from where he stood to where Dedi's body must be, cold and broken. The thought made him shudder. Toddy came up beside him and took his arm. "It's no use," she said. "Let's get out of here."

Chapter 44

MALADIES

An hour earlier, after turning a quick trick at the Busy Nook, Pilar had shot up, and now felt that she was basking on the golden shore of a great, warm sea.

Indeed, it would be so easy to drift into sleep in such womb-like, sun-warm comfort, that she must now draw herself up in the seat of the cab, and think hard of what she intended to do.

She and Dedi lived by night. This would be her night-time lunch—usually she'd go out again, after preparing and eating it—and Dedi's night-time supper. Pilar liked to believe that Dedi would stay home and go to bed. Now she tried to concentrate on the meal she would make, hoping, too, that Jack would share it with them. There would be . . . But the

474

thought slipped away.

She tried to remember what she'd bought, and found that she couldn't. She would like to have some fried plantains! She looked into the tops of the paper bags that sat next to her on the seat. A loaf of bread . . .

Suddenly she found herself coming out of a kind of drifting sleep. It had been a delicious, eternal moment, but she remembered that she must stay awake. If she slept, the driver would go right on by Jack's building. She'd given him her address, but had not told him that she meant to stop and pick someone up. The fact was, she didn't know Jack's address—she knew the building, of course—but not the address. The only address she knew was her own, and it had taken her some time to learn it—not that she was dumb; she just hated numbers. She rolled down the window and let the icy wind blow in upon her.

Dedi was a sick boy. This horrible disease! But he had never been strong. *Ay!* She remembered the terrible night of his birth, when she herself was no more than a child. If it had not been for her mother's brother, who shot at their father with a rifle, scaring him off, neither of them would be alive today.

He was so crazy-drunk that he would have cut them up with his knife, that father of theirs, that prick! She had saved Dedi, gnawed him free of their drunken Mama's body with her own sharp teeth; and he would always be hers because of that—he was hers! But many times since they had laughed at how close he had come to being dropped down the hole. "You little wet-fur rat," she would yell at him playfully, "I should have let you go into the shit, where you belong." And Dedi would say, "Thank you for picking me out of the shit." Then they would laugh and laugh. He was a good little prick, Dedi, and he respected her, else she'd take a strap to him. But she liked best to rub his little belly, and to kiss his big ears.

She remembered how, when Dedi had rickets, she fed him pigeon broth until he grew strong again. Then he gained weight; but still, he had asthma. Then she cured him of that with a brew of manatee fish bones, ground into powder and boiled in water. Her spiritist had told her that she had the gift of healing. But Dedi was a bad patient; he would lie to her and say that he took the elixirs she made for him. "You little liar!" she would yell. "You did not drink that." And he would cry, and, crying, say, "But you can stab my sister in the tit if I lie!" Then she would believe him. But nothing could heal him now from this new illness. Why did she not get the AIDS? It should have been her.

Dedi got everything—rickets, asthma, tapeworm, and as soon as he was old enough to stick his little thing into a woman, he got the white flower; but she cured him of that, too, with saluarron and bismuth. *Caramba!* that little dog would hump anything! He's a real *machisto! Mio tinayel!* . Well, that's the way a man should be. He never got the AIDS from putting it in the wrong place. It was the needles, sharing them on the street.

She was sorry that Dedi was a junkie. That had been her fault. You can't cover the sky with your hand. He was a junkie because of her doing it. That made her feel very sad, so she tried not to think about it. She stabbed her own arm for the first time when she was only twelve. She'd made her first money from her first man a year before that. Now she'd been in the life, a whore, for . . . but she didn't like numbers. Numbers can be used to cast spells.

"What number did you say, lady?" asked the driver.

"Go on. It's a lot more blocks."

"No, it's no use trying to cover the sky with your hand," thought Pilar, "you can't do it. What's true is true. I'm a whore. But I am also a witch. I can do sorcery. It cost me many dollars to learn that, but my spiritist told me it was true. And today I found a broken medal. That's a sure sign that she was right.  So nobody can treat me like a whore and get away with it.  Monk will find out very soon that I have cast a spell on him and that he is doomed.  When I talked to the dead, they heard me.  He will see.  I'll make his lungs fly out of his mouth and carry him away to hell.  That *atomico!*  That *chulo!*  That *bubarron!*  I don't let any big blubber lips like him treat me like that."

The cab leaped a bump in the road and Pilar had to save her groceries from falling to the floor.  She searched her pocketbook for cigarettes, found one, and lit up.  She pulled the cigarette from her violet lips and hissed the smoke out as if it were distasteful, acrid.  She threw the butt out the window, sparks flying backwards like little comets.  The Saints and Sinners Club rolled by like a gaudy package on wheels.  She had just missed seeing Toddy and Father Din enter.  She rolled the window up.

"Getting cold enough for you, lady?" asked the cabbie.

"You just drive," Pilar snapped back at him.

"No, lady," the cabbie tried to mitigate, "I only meant that it's starting to snow."

"I no care what it does," said Pilar, "you just drive."


Chapter 45


HOME FREE


Father Din pushed open the door of the Saints and Sinners Club and followed Toddy in.  They were greeted by Opal, who sat at the return of the bar, near the door.  "Oh, honey," Opal said to Toddy, "I'm glad to see you two got outta there.  I been scared!  I didn't know what I should *do*."

"He passed out—*finally*." Toddy said.  "What happened here?  I mean the broken window."

"Some kind of riot," Opal said.  "Nothing for us to worry about.  We got enough trouble of our own, and he back there at your place. Oh, *man*!" she exclaimed. "Honey, that was a *baahd* scene. That poor little boy!" She looked at Father Din. "What you think we should do? Did he throw that little boy's body off the roof? I figured him for doing that." She looked like she was going to cry.

"Into the alley," Father Din said.

"I knew he meant to do that. Then the police find him, and they say, 'Look, he fell. It don't matter, he's just another junkie.'"

"You don't think they'd investigate further?"

"'*Vestigate*! They don't care. 'Round Needleneck, they *always* finding junkies' bodies. In doorways. . .in alleys . . ."

"What about his sister," asked Father Din, "won't she go to the police?"

"Pilar?" Opal shook her head negatively. "She scared if she see a blue coat in a store window. 'Sides, one of us would have to talk. And I know you ain't gonna catch me doin' any talking. Tory want us to get lost up in Harlem—maybe stay with his brother at the Temple up there—and I think he's right. Till this all blow away. He said that Monk put a bad job on him that he don't want to do. So he got a reason for gettin' out of here, and now I got a reason too. Anyhow, you the main witness, Sam. What you gonna do?"

Father Din shook his head. "I don't know yet." He felt that he should go to the police, identify himself, and have Monk arrested. But then, tossing a corpse from a roof didn't sound like much of a charge. Monk would probably laugh himself free.

"Where's Tiger?" asked Toddy, growing impatient for a drink.

"He's in back," said Opal, "watching my two fools shooting pool."

"Tory and Elga?"

"Ah-ha. I had to get my coat outa my place, so I got Elga too. She was just sittin' in there by her lonesome, sulkin'. Tory come staggerin' in here a few minutes ago. He said he saw Jack before, on the street."

"Jack wasn't going up to my place, was he?" Toddy asked in alarm.

"Tory said he wasn't. But he's all shot up and stoned. He don't know from nothin'. He had to do another session tonight, at the Cuttlefish, but he never went back. He still after Elga's head. And now it's worse. Elga just beat him at pool. He raised such a noise, Tiger had to go back and keep a eye on him. Jealousy! He won't go till he beats her, and I want to get out of here. Before Tory come in, I was only waitin' to see would you come in." She shrugged. "Anyhow, what if Jack goes up there? I give Monk enough of that dope to keep him out all night. He can't hurt Jack if he asleep. And Jack wouldn't do nothin' to a man like that, not who was sleeping. Monk would do that to Jack, or to anybody he felt like it. But Jack just ain't that kind of guy."

"But you can't tell about Monk," Toddy said. "Nothing seems to stop him for long. He might already be awake. And suppose Jack should—"

"Listen, honey," Opal reassured her, "he bad, but he human. He ain't gonna wake up till morning, and then he gonna have some headache. Wait a minute, I'll get Tiger." She slid like a big, sleek cat off her stool, and went to the back.

"God, I pray he doesn't go up there," Toddy said.

"If Opal's right," Father Din said, "I don't think you need be overly concerned. Monk was certainly out cold when we left." He had his own doubts, though.

In a moment, Opal returned, followed by Tiger.

"I told him to come on out here and take care of us payin' customers," Opal said.

"Toddy," said Tiger, "I had a lot o' trouble in here tonight. Some maniac calling me a Zionist. I'm not even sure what that is, but he made it sound bad. Did you see all the cops?"

Father Din and Toddy shook their heads, blankly.

"You didn't?  They're all over the street."

"They got other things on their mind, Tiger," Opal said.

"I got a guy knifed in here tonight.  A regular.  A nice guy.  He was trying to help me.  Makes me feel lousy."

"In here?" Toddy said, unbelievingly.

"Right over there.  Look." He pointed.

Father Din and Toddy looked.  They saw the blood stains.

"God," Toddy exclaimed.  "What a night!"

"It must be the last night of the bad world," said Opal.

"What hit you?" said Tiger to Father Din.

"I got at cross purposes with Monk."

"He's at cross purposes with the whole world," said Tiger.

Chapter 46

READING THE SIGNS

"I think, Toddy," Father Din said, hesitatingly, "I think you should check into a hotel.  Is there one near here?"

"There's the St. Christopher," said Opal.  "That's only a few blocks from here, right up the Strip.  But it's a real dump.  The nightstalkers turn tricks there.  Everybody calls it The Busy Nook."

"What do you think?" Father Din asked Toddy.  "At least it's close.  Is it safe?" he asked Opal.

"What's safe?  Safe as any place.  They don't like trouble."

"I can't think," Toddy said.  "I'll do whatever you think is best.  But what about Dedi?  We can't leave him . . . like that."

"I don't know yet," said Father Din.  "There are other things involved.  If a connection is made right now between

480

Dedi and Monk, and Monk finds out about it, I don't know what the consequences will be for Jack, or . . ."

"Or for me," Toddy finished his sentence.

"Or me either," said Opal.

Father Din remembered Monk's vivid threat—I'll track you down and kill you!  He said, "I think it would be best if you checked in that hotel.  Then I'll go and get help—advice."

Tiger placed a cup of steaming black mud in front of Father Din, and drinks before Toddy and Opal.

"I put a good strong shot in the coffee," he said.

"I wish you hadn't done that," said Father Din.  His head was just beginning to clear.

"Look," Tiger said, "I been in this business a long time, and I know when a guy should take a drink and when he shouldn't.  You had a lot to drink when you was in here this afternoon, and if I ever saw a hangover, you got it.  Go on, drink it.  You need it.  Do like I say, like I was your old man, O.K.?"

It was the first time that Father Din had smiled in hours, and it hurt.  He took a sip of the laced coffee for Tiger's benefit.

"Attaboy!" Tiger exclaimed, pleased.  "I think I'll have one myself.  I need it after the day I've had."  He threw his hands out.  "Look at this place!  Empty!  Everybody's still scared to come in."

"Why don't you close up?" asked Father Din.  "It's two-thirty."

"This is my home," said Tiger.  "I live here."

He looked at Tiger, who had literally wrestled with life.  He thought of his own father, who had seized the day against evil.  Somehow he had entered the wrong tunnel when too young to have read the signs correctly.  It was a fine tunnel for those like Father Ryan who were meant to go in that direction, but it was wrong for him, and he for it.  For the right man it might have led to light, but it had brought him to this dark time and place. He was determined to back out of it and find the right entrance to the right way before it was too late.

Chapter 47

STALKING MONK

Instead of the one "good, stiff drink" he'd planned to have, Jack Muir had had three. First Opal and Elga, then Toddy and Father Din had passed by across the street from where he sat, but Muir had not been looking out, instead he'd been looking inwards, at himself, and not liking what he saw.

Now, determined, he climbed the first three flights of stairs leading to Toddy's apartment, taking the steps two at a time. But he took the last flight with less resolution and a great deal more caution. He edged along the hallway, his back to the wall that was on the door side, his revolver held out ahead of him, in his right hand. Halfway down the hall, he realized that the door to Toddy's apartment was open. The pool of light there was streaming from her kitchen. But there was no sound from the apartment. No one spoke. Nothing!

Perhaps, he thought, Monk had laid a trap for him, something humiliating, or perhaps deadly. Fear raced over his nerves as fingertips race over the strings of a harp. Still, he slid toward the open door, his back against the wall, tiny bubbles of cold sweat breaking on his forehead, heart pounding.

He stood next to the open door and waited for some sign from within. Then the thought came terrible upon him that he did not wish to hurt anyone, not even Monk. He breathed heavily, his heart fluttering. "I must be crazy," he thought. But now he was as much afraid to move away from the door as he was to enter it. Still, no sound. But this was it. If he did nothing now, he would damn himself forever. He

482

eased himself away from the wall, leaned forward, and looked in the door.

Monk lay sprawled back in a chair at the kitchen table, his head sunk down on his chest, asleep. Muir felt faint with relief. He dropped into a squatting position, his right hand hanging over his right knee, loosely holding the revolver, and his left hand to his forehead. He took several slow, deliberate deep breaths, trying to slow the pounding of his heart. When he resumed a standing position, the blood rushed to his head, and again he had to wait to get his equilibrium. Then, very cautiously, he stepped inside the apartment.

He went quietly into the livingroom, peeked into the bedroom, and returned to the kitchen. Two Scotch bottles, one empty, one nearly full, were ranged on the table. There was a bloody towel on the floor beside a chair. The broken wrapper of a band-aid lay beside that. Whatever had happened, Muir reasoned, it couldn't have been very serious, or a band-aid would not have sufficed to take care of it.

He leveled the long-barreled revolver on Monk's slowly lifting and falling chest with a shaking hand. He thumbed the hammer back. He leaned into a step toward Monk. But just then Monk gave a grunt out of his sleep and Muir's trigger-finger reacted, in a reflex, tensing, and the hammer fell with a dull metallic snap on an empty chamber. Muir's heart nearly failed him.


Chapter 48


"STAY WITH ME"


His scalp was still tight and his hair still standing on end five minutes later. He had plunged from the apartment. He was leaning against the front of Toddy's building, still trying to calm the erratic beating of his heart, when he saw Pilar Pavon's taxicab draw to a stop at the curb.

483

Once Jack was settled in the cab, and the cab was on its way, Pilar asked: "What you doing, Jack, hanging around in front of Toddy's place like that, eh? You was looking for trouble, no? Oh, Jack, you a fool!"

"I guess I am," Muir said mechanically. He had forgotten to load the revolver. It held only one bullet in its cylinder of six chambers. But being a fool had its compensations. If the pistol had been fully loaded, Monk would be dead and he, Jack Muir, would be a murderer.

"Have you seen Toddy?" he asked.

"Don't speak to me about her," Pilar said, moving away from his side.

But Muir demanded an answer.

"Yes, I saw her," Pilar snapped. "When I picked up my stuff, before midnight. Her new boyfriend was with her."

"Was she all right?"

"Sure, she was O.K." Pilar stared straight ahead, coldly.

"Monk must have been pretty drunk tonight."

"I think so. At first, he wouldn't give me my stuff."

"How does he get along with this . . . friend of Toddy's."

Pilar shrugged. "I don't know."

"Do you know anything about this guy?"

"No."

They fell silent for a few minutes; then Pilar said: "You ask so many questions, now you tell me if you have seen my brother?"

"He was up at my place earlier, at around eight. Haven't you seen him?"

"No. He wasn't with Monk yet, when I was there. I hope he is at home. I worry so much. He always coughing. And where have you been? I no see you in a long time. Why you not come to see me? You no love Pilar anymore? You only like women who shit from up high?"

"I've been doing something."

"What? You painting a picture?"

"No."

"Well, what you been doing?"

"Something I had to do alone."

"What?"

"I've been kicking."

"What?"

"I've kicked, Pilar. I'm through with junk. I'm clean. I'm only taking meth. I'm going to kick off completely."

Pilar looked at him, uncertain. If true, what would this mean to her, she wondered.

Did you tell Dedi?"

"Yes."

"Did you meet Monk tonight? No, I guess you didn't."

"No."

"Then he will know . . ."

"Know what? For all he knows, I could be dead."

"Shhh!" Pilar hissed. "You must never say such a thing! To speak of yourself as dead . . ."

"Crap!"

"No, it's true. But tomorrow I will fix it up with my spiritist. Don't worry. But Monk; he is the one you do not want to know about it. He will come against you now."

Muir remembered the snap of the empty revolver. "He won't bother me," he said. "He's got what he wanted."

"Then you no wish to go back to Toddy?"

"What does it matter what I wish," asked Muir, quietly.

"And what does it matter what I wish, either?" asked Pilar. "Nobody care what I wish."

"Maybe I better get out," said Muir, leaning forward to tap the driver.

"No, Jack," said Pilar, taking his arm, "please come home with me. I make you something good to eat. I no quarrel, I promise."

Muir sat back in the seat, feeling like a heel. His gaunt,

tired-eyed face betrayed a profound exhaustion.

"You look terrible," said Pilar, after a pause. "Stay with me tonight, Jack, eh? I have a surprise for you. It is something I will show you tonight. I will show you how much I love you. Ah, Jack, *que bontos ojos blue tienes*. What pretty blue eyes you have. Please stay with me all night, Jack."

Muir looked at the young woman. "Yes," he said wearily, "I'll stay with you."

Chapter 49

CHECK IN

Camel-faced Felix Potter, a large blue welt on his left temple, sat behind the imitation-onyx-topped desk of the St. Christopher Hotel, in an old-fashioned oak swivel chair, his bulging eyes at half mast, dreaming of keyholes. The bell banged him awake.

"Yes," he said, jumping to his feet. Dignity assumed him as a sheet assumes a ghost. "What might I do for you?" Not the type for the Busy Nook, he thought. *He* would never bring a young woman like *that* to a place like *this*. . . . "Do you wish a room?" He had decided upon cordiality.

"Yes," said the young woman.

Ah, it was *her* party. Of course, it would be. There was a dark, morning shadow on the man's jaws and chin. Big fellow, his face, across the bridge of his nose, seemed swollen. Barroom brawl? She, slumming, probably picked him up in one of the joints on the Strip. Been drinking all day, and now this: out-of-the-way, and what all. The man, who had been about to speak, fell back into silence. *She* had decided. Strange, too, for she would be easy to take.

"A double?" Potter persisted, amused.

"Yes." Again, *she* decided.

"Sign here," Potter said for the first time that day. He usually just handed a hooker a key and received it back a half hour later.

"That's a nasty looking bruise," she said.

"Yes," said Potter. "A most unusual thing occurred here this evening." His loquacity would get him in trouble one day. Why scare them off? They looked promising. But the Devil teased him on. "Most unusual indeed. We were robbed. First time since I've been in the hotel business. Twenty-five years. Some young hoodlum walked in here and knocked me unconscious. Could have killed me." He snapped his fingers. "Just like that."

"That's terrible," she said.

"Yes. Cleaned us out. A very unpleasant experience, I assure you."

"Oh, I should think so."

"'Twas. Terrible. Oh, well, that's the way of it nowadays. Here's your key. Room 22, second floor, to the left. You can walk up. I'm afraid the phones are out of order, something to do with the storm, but if you want anything—"

"That'll be all right," she said, snatching the key. She went up the stairs, the man following behind almost as if reluctant to go with her.

"Strange pair," thought Potter, popping a violet-flavored lozenge into his mouth, and sinking into his swivel chair.


Chapter 50


CONFESSION


In room 22, Toddy pulled off her coat and threw herself on the bed with a sigh of relief. She closed her eyes, shutting out a jagged crack in the ceiling plaster. "What a dump!"

Father Din looked about the room, more than a little bit disheartened at the thought of leaving her in such a fleabag. "If you'd rather go someplace else . . . ."

"Where could we go? You know we couldn't find a legitimate cab in this snow at this time of night. And no car service will pick up anyone from this place." She opened her eyes and smiled at Father Din. "Really, this'll be fine until tomorrow. Besides, I can't move. I wouldn't go anywhere else if you offered to carry me. I'll tell you one thing. I don't think Monk would ever think to look for me here. He'd think I had better taste." She paused, and said, "Sam, come over here and lie down with me."

"No, no, Toddy—I'm afraid I can't. I have somebody I must see. Somebody I think can help us. I've never felt myself to be such a fool as I do tonight. I should have done something!"

Toddy sat up, looking at him. "There was nothing you could have done. You did what you could," she emphasized.

"But it's much more than just that, Toddy," he said. "Much more."

"Are you married? Is that it?"

"No . . ."

"Then you're not married?"

"No. I'm a priest."

"A *priest!*" She sat up, stared at him, unbelieving. "You're a priest?"

"Yes. My real name is Michael Din . . . Father Michael Din."

"*Michael* . . . that's what you meant. I thought—when you said 'My name is Michael'—I thought you were quoting something . . ." An ironic little smile shaped Toddy's mouth. "Well, I'll be damned!" she cried, slapping her forehead. She sat up on the edge of the bed. "If I don't have the craziest luck."

She looked at him. "You know, I've only known you for about—what?—twelve hours, but we've been through so much together . . . I thought I knew you." She turned away and sat silently for a few moments. Then she turned back, looking at Father Din. "Now I understand so much," she said. "But what were you doing?"

"I'm not sure I know myself."

"All right," she said decisively, "never mind that. But if you could just tell me one thing . . ."

"What is it?"

"Do you like me? Do you care about me? Do you want me? I have a right to know, don't I? I'm frightened. If I only understood how you feel. You see, I'm ready to try something new. I don't want any more of what I've been having. Tonight was the end for me. I've had it."

"Doesn't my being a priest change any of that?"

"I'm afraid not," Toddy said. "Well, maybe," she added, "but I feel the same about you. I suppose I should feel badly about having been with a priest, but I don't. After all, I didn't know. And besides, I think the moral sense has gone numb in me. I need . . . love. Do you understand?" She threw up her hands. "Priest or not, I want you to keep on being Sam. Can you? For my sake?"

"Can you accept an honest answer, Toddy?"

"I think so."

"Then my answer is that I don't know yet. But I'm coming to a conclusion. Something's been building in me for . . . well, actually for years. It's the only answer I can give you now. But you asked me before if I liked you. I do like you. More than any woman I've ever known. That answers another question, too. Yes, I do care. But I won't be any good to you or anyone until I . . . find my way, I guess."

Toddy's eyes filled; but she said: "You said that you were going to see someone who could help us? Well, when you go, take this key with you, in your pocket. Touch it, think of me, and if you want to come back tonight, I'll be here."

"I'd better go now," he said.

"You're a man of principle, aren't you, Sam? Or

Michael," Toddy corrected. "Well, Michael, remember while you're gone that principles are cold things. A woman is warmer than a principle."

Chapter 51

THE SHOCK OF RECOGNITION

Toddy was not able to sleep. When Father Din left, she'd got undressed and into a bed that sank in the middle like a hammock. Now she lay on her side, watching as the blue-and-red neon sign outside the window blinked its monotonous signal.

ST. CHRIST PHER  (RED)

(———————————)

ST. CHRIST PHER (BLUE)

(———————————)

ST. CHRIST PHER (RED)

(———————————)

ST. CHRIST PHER (BLUE)

(———————————)

O.K., O.K.," she exclaimed irritably, "I believe you," and tossed over to face the semi-dark. But the sign appeared there as a shadow on the wall. Exasperated, she leaped out of bed, turned on the light, and lighted a cigarette. She began pacing up and down, barefooted, on a rug that felt like mouse-skin.

The room was warm, stuffy. Apparently, heat, needed by the naked, was the only convenience demanded at The Busy Nook. She relived each moment of the previous day and of this morning in her mind. She knew that she wanted Sam Hopkins, Michael, and it was so wild an idea that she became even more agitated. A priest! Sam Hopkins. No! Father Michael Din. Mike, she tried the new name in her mind. No, he would prefer to be called Michael.

490

How long can a woman go on loving a ghost?  It was as though Jack Muir had died long ago, and she had gone on, as if in mourning, like some wife of an ancient time, waiting for death, waiting to join him.  Why hadn't Monk buried her with Jack?

Oh, yes, she had loved Jack.  Patiently, she had waited for his return from his zombie-life.  He had refused to return to her.  Yet still she had waited.  But there must be an end.

She stopped pacing abruptly.  The hand holding her cigarette dropped to her side and her shoulders hunched to her neck.  She stood frozen.  Then the bulging eyes, the lugubrious camel-like face dropped away from the transom.  She heard fast footsteps going down the hall.  She didn't hear herself scream, but someone in the next room did.

"Knock it off in there!" came a cry.

Chapter 52

NIGHT LIFE

Now where are you tonight, Michael? Father Ryan wondered.  Oh, my boy, you have given this old man a very difficult day.  You have shown me how indispensable you have become to me, in practical affairs, and in the heart, too.  For Father Din had a full and loving heart, as anyone could see.

Father Ryan opened his wallet and removed a tattered and folded page, on which Father Din had typed a poem he had written some years earlier.  The poem had disturbed Father Ryan when he first read it, with its evidence of Father Din's early forays into the dark side, but he had come to see the compassionate disillusionment of the piece, its sadness for the sufferings of humankind.  It was called "Night Life."

*When I've gone out to walk at night,*

491

*to tour the streets, mean-dark, false-bright,*
*of this sick city that is no home*
*but for the Giant and the Gnome,*
*the Monsters of Despair, I've seen*
*pathetic sights and sights obscene:*
*The fat black man who has no eyes*
*but two great holes from which he cries*
*long hours, holding out his cup*
*for Times Square crowds to fill it up;*
*the woman with the bleeding leg*
*who climbs the subway stairs to beg;*
*the legless men who crabwise creep*
*on wooden gloves to morning sleep;*
*the varicosed, tumescent, sick,*
*already dead and yet still quick;*
*male hustlers, leaning in long rows,*
*posed in mock movie-hero pose;*
*porn shops with tainted men inside*
*some of whom have kissed a bride;*
*retarded vendors at their stands*
*masturbating, hiding hands*
*beneath big stacks of filthy mags;*
*and drunks on jags, and hags in rags,*
*asleep in doorways commandeered*
*from rats and stiffs; the other weird*
*displaying signs of coming doom*
*Hellfire and Brimstone in the tomb;*
*and faces stupefied by dope,*
*expressionless of love or hope—*
*these sights and worse are near Times Square*
*at night when I go walking there.*

Yes, anyone could see that Father Din was a deeply caring young man, but that alone did not prove a vocation for the priesthood, the discipline and sense of responsibility required. Other vocations require discipline and responsibility, but they may also require a deep subjective involvement or a highly objective distancing. The priest should position himself at a middle distance, and maintain his equilibrium there. Michael tended to extremes.

At first, Father Ryan's new young curate had been a blessing. Father Ryan was in his late sixties and had little energy to spare. Father Din relieved him of calls for Last Rites and funerals, attended Boys Club meetings, helped with the parish drug rehab program (of which Billy Sawyer, Rose Figlia's boyfriend, was a graduate), and acted as minister to the many AIDS victims of the Chelsea parish. But that was during the period of Michael's hyperactivity, a time when Father Ryan had begun to suspect that there might be something wrong with this piling on of labors. As when, for instance, in summer, when all else seemed to fail to distract the young curate, he'd plunge into the cold, blue rippling water of the Parish Athletic Club pool, and drive furiously from end to end like a trapped seal. Father Ryan thought that there was something desperate about this, because it did not appear to be an act of pleasure. And when the young priest assumed more and more things to do that simply need not be done, and did the things that did need to be done with such frenetic energy, things that by now seemed to be taxing his strength, perhaps even his emotional health, something, Father Ryan began to suspect, must be seriously amiss, and something must be done to find out what it was.

The confessional was no help. Father Din said nothing in the confessional that indicated a problem, and, outside the confessional, had ceased altogether to speak of personal things to the older priest, who now felt cut off from one for whom he felt no small affection.

Lately things had changed for the worse. Father Din began to drop duties and to go off by himself, neglecting his work to spend his time God knew where or how. And, if Father Ryan was not particularly adept at the finer points of scholastic philosophy, the years having robbed him of much learning, time and experience had given him a functional understanding of the major motives of humankind. He knew people and the signs of their discontent. Father Din had something on his mind. Father Ryan essayed that it was women. Yes, and Father Ryan knew women. How should he not, who had been raised amidst the caterwaul of seven sisters?

But where was Father Din now? Gone for long evenings, even overnight. He had sat up all night tonight, waiting to confront Father Din. He had read and drunk coffee and had had an occasional Irish whiskey and then more coffee. He was determined to stay awake until Father Din returned. He was reading Father Thom Corrigan's book, *Husbands of the Church*, and getting angrier and angrier.

Sipping from a large glass of Irish whiskey, he tried to think charitably, but found that he could not. He felt that it was wrong of him to think it, but think it he did—Thom Corrigan was a disgrace to the priesthood. He prayed the Lord to forgive him for his lack of charity; but it was a deep additional worry all that night, that he knew there to be some association between young Father Din and Thom Corrigan, the celebrity, the poet-priest and political activist, for they had been seen together several times and it had been mentioned to him, in the way of warning. Lord, it is Your way to try us constantly.

Father Ryan turned the lights low and sat smoking a lumpy green cigar. He would wait. He would wait. He would wait. The cigar ember died and went cold.


Chapter 53


SCENARIO FOR SCORSESE


Father Ryan was on a television talk show. He was with

Father Corrigan, who was defending situational ethics. The host agreed with Father Corrigan and was openly hostile to Father Ryan. The audience was hostile too, and booed him as he began to defend his position. "The only morality," Father Ryan shouted back at them, "is a shared morality. The only morality is a shared morality, the only morality is a shared morality, the—"

Father Din removed the dead cigar from Father Ryan's hand and shook his shoulder.

"Father! Father! You're having a nightmare," he said.

Father Ryan shook himself free of the horrible dream. "Michael . . . Where have you been? I've been worried."

"I'm sorry, Father."

"I'll turn on the table-light."

"I must talk to you, Father."

"Oh, my, what's happened to you? You look terrible." Father Ryan studied Father Din's appearance with deep shock. The young man was in blood-spattered civilian clothes, his nose and the front of his face near his nose were swollen and distorted. There was a dark, rather bluish tint under both of his eyes. "Have you been mugged?"

"Father, I've got to speak with you . . . about—I'm afraid I'm in trouble."

"Should we go to confession?

"No. I want to tell you things, but I must speak to you as a man."

Father Ryan went to his desk, sat down, and leaned back. Now he was tight-lipped, staring at his young curate. He felt that this was it. He was glad that the young priest wanted simply to talk, for now he might be able to get to the bottom of things, but he was also more than a little afraid of what he was going to hear.

"You're always offering me Irish whiskey, Father. I'd like one now."

Father Ryan said nothing, but rose, crossed the room, and returned with two tall glasses filled with whiskey. "In vino veritas," he said, clinking his glass against Michael's. "But I don't know if that applies to Irish whiskey. Sometimes I think that it causes much more blarney than truth. Go ahead, Michael. I've been expecting something like this for some time."

Father Din said, "I've got to begin somewhere. Let me begin with an only child who worshiped his father, who wanted more than anything in the world to be just like him, but that father wanted the child to be something else, something that he thought was superior—a priest.

"When those who led the Jersey City Archdiocese selected that little choir boy for the priesthood—robbing the cradle, as it were—they had no idea how they were distorting the dreams of a child. But when the child's father was proud, honored, what then could the child say? Could he go against the father that he loved? Anyway, everything seemed so distant and unreal then. It only seemed that the child had to go through this thing and somehow come out on the other end of it.

"At Seton Hall, I never doubted for a moment that all this would be over some day and that I would be what I'd always wanted to be, like my father, a cop. Yes, a cop! The rest of it didn't seem real. Then in seminary—all right, it was six lousy years of Latin—it was asking who should be saved, the woman or the child—but I was still going to be a chip off the old block. Once this was over, I would be me again, I would be like my Dad, somehow I would be a cop. But it didn't stop. I found myself here. What was I thinking? That, now, I couldn't disappoint my father's memory, that I must somehow remain a priest, that I must wear alien clothing and live an alien life? I am Michael Din. I am my father's son. He had no right to do this to me. Nor did the Church. And forgive me, Father—my dear Father Ryan—neither did you."

"You are in a crisis of doubt, Michael."

"Doubt!  Yes!  All doubt!"

"Why haven't I heard any of this in Confession?  How have you managed to keep it secret?"

"Let me recite my newest poem.  It's called "Scenario for Scorsese."

"Who is Scorsese?"

"A movie director, Father.  This poem is a form of confession.  It'll make things clear to you."

"Go ahead," said Father Ryan, chomping his cigar.

Father Din began to recite, his voice wavering:

> "There was a young priest
> who stalked the pornographic
> night of the X-rated
> movie houses and the
> prostituting streets
> outside them in what had
> become a sexual compulsion.
> Sometimes he felt that he had lost
> all control of himself and
> with that loss his very soul.
> But his soul was saved through
> the confession of his sins
> and their forgiveness
> by a fellow priest who
> was not his own publicly
> acknowledged confessor
> but a fellow sinner,
> an older priest who had had
> a twenty-year quasi-marriage
> and who would in turn ask
> the young priest for
> absolution after
> confessing to him.  When

the young priest made
confession to his acknowledged
confessor and spiritual guide
a little later, he had only
to confess to the evil
thoughts of the days since
he last stalked the streets,
thereby keeping his
spiritual guide in the dark.
He behaves as if in a
dream when he is in the grip
of this compulsion, as if
he himself has become a
character in the dirty
movie he is watching,
and in this state of
disassociation picks up
the first prostitute he sees,
and, with release, becomes
guilt-ridden and disgraced
until he must seek out
his secret-confessor.
He will find a telephone
within minutes of the event,
plug in the number, wait,
and say in a voice
thick with mixed emotions
of shame and anger,
"I must see you."
His secret confessor
never refuses,
no priest does,
but he will take
the confession with a
heavy heart, for

his friend and
for himself.  The
confession, it seems,
has become part of
the compulsion, as both
have come to suspect.
Advice is traded,
elements of which might
have proven helpful to
either priest, but none
has been acted on,
until . . .”

"Until what?" said Father Ryan.

"I don't know," said Father Din.

"Even your style has changed.  You write like a hippie now.  I presume the other priest is Thom Corrigan, and I presume the poetical influence is his as well.  I won't presume to judge the poetry, however, but the story it tells is an extremely hurtful one to me, personally.  It shows an ultimate distrust in me, an ultimate lack of faith in my ability to understand, and it shows a priestly dishonor in both you and Thom Corrigan.  Do you still believe in God?"

"Of course I do.  I am and always will be a good Catholic, like my father, but I was not made to be a priest.  I'm wrong for it.  Perhaps not good enough.  Definitely not good enough.

"Do you know, Father, that until no more than a few months ago I had never seen a woman naked?  I have been counseling people on their sexual problems when they know more than I do.  Old ladies know more than I do, or knew more.  I wasn't fit to talk to them.

"I know that you know what a priest-teaser is, Father, one of those women, or sometimes men, who try to titillate the priest in the confessional with lurid tales of sex, going into the most graphic detail.  I don't know that this boy of whom I am about to speak was like that, but he would come to me constantly, and tell me about his visits to pornographic movie houses.  He would describe in detail, though I would try to stop him, acts of which I could not even conceive.  When I asked myself what it was that I was doing, I would try to believe that I was trying to help him.  How could I help him if I did not understand—I would tell myself—what he was talking about?  I convinced myself that it was my duty—though certainly, instinctively, I knew I lied—to go and actually see some of these films.

"But there had to be more than what I saw.  The actual experience must be different.  I had to find out.  I picked up a prostitute one day, but the experience was so ugly—I'm sorry Father—so ugly that I could not believe that it represented what I hoped for—longed for.  Now I *had* to know.  I had to find a decent partner—I had to.  And again I lied to myself.  Somehow, I developed an interest in the most avant-garde art, and began frequenting the galleries in the East Village and SoHo and TriBeCa, the artistic haunts.  I would tell myself that I am going to look at art.  I am going to listen to music.  Lies!  Lies!  Lies!  I was looking for life, real life, not the phantasma of the church.  I was looking for a *woman*.

"Now, in retrospect, it all seems clear enough.  But I swear to you, Father, by Jesus Christ whom we both love, I did not really know what I was doing until tonight.  Tonight I made love to a real, live woman, a woman filled with tenderness, with passion, and now I know another part of life that that young choir boy in Jersey City has missed; a part of life, God forgive me, that has been stolen from him.  From *me*!"

"Are you in love with this woman?"

"I don't know.  Yes.  No.  I have no right to be.  But let me tell you the rest.  There's more.  I'm in trouble, the deepest trouble."

"Trouble?  What is it?  Something else?  Something more?"

"Father . . ."

"Connected with this woman, is it?"  Father Ryan's face was stony.

"Yes.  But there's so much more, I'm afraid."

"Speak plainly."

Chapter 54

EVERY SIN IN THE PROGRAM

Father Din recounted the events of his day, speaking slowly, in measured tones, trying, with great effort, to be perfectly truthful and factual.

Father Ryan listened, puffing a cigar, sipping whiskey, as the story was told.  "You mean then," he said, waving smoke from his face, "that this boy may still be lying in that alley?"

"I'm afraid that it's possible, Father."

"Oh, Michael," Father Ryan said, shaking his head sadly.  "Charity requires that I think of you as being in the grip of madness.  I'd have to sit down at my computer and reckon them up, but I do believe that you have committed every sin the program."

"I committed a mortal sin, Father, yes.  Toddy is married.  But my sin doesn't nullify my ministrations to Dedi Pavon.  The grace of Christ flows through my office as a priest and not through me."

"That is indeed correct; but the boy—"

"Father, under those circumstances, I did what I could.  Please try to see that my actions would influence the safety of others.  This man is possessed, Father, a killer."

"What you say, Michael, may be reasonable; it's the

501

logic of a soldier or a policeman, however, and not that of a priest."

"It's the way I think, Father. I'm *not* a priest. That's what I'm trying to tell you!"

"But I *am* a priest. I am no longer a man. 'I live now, not I, but Christ lives in me.' That is St. Paul speaking. *Tu es Sacerdos.* You're a priest!"

"Well, St. Paul was wrong! Christ can live in a man, and in a husband as well. This is a new age, Father."

"The Church thinks not. *Roma locuta est. Causa Finita est.* What is a new age in eternity? You've caught the contagion of the Father Corrigans, the worldly men. You *blaspheme!*"

"And what of using our own God-given minds?"

"*Pride!*"

"But Father, shouldn't we take pride in what God has given?"

"Michael, I need not instruct you in the knowledge of our Church; I know that you understand these things as well, and perhaps better, than I do. If you choose to be perverse in your polemic, what can I say to you? Again, you're using the argument of the public man, not of the priest, who reasons out of faith. You must give one thing up to receive the other. You, like a willful child, would have all that your eyes rest upon. I am tired, Michael. You're too clever for me; but, even now, you are not being honest with yourself, and you know it."

"Please, Father, be calm, for the sake of your health."

"I'm perfectly calm, Michael. Now then, let's start by asking ourselves what has to be done. What do you say?"

"I must leave the priesthood."

Father Ryan shook his head. "No, Michael, it isn't over yet. That would be the easy way, and later you'd never forgive yourself for having taken it. You are engaged in a battle, and it has to be won or lost. You can't simply back off from it.  You must win your way through to what you are going to become, whether it be a priest or something else.  But faith will come.  However, that wasn't what I was referring to.  I meant what do you think should be done now.  I want you to act."

"Call the police."

"Exactly.  We must have this man Monk arrested, and you must help to build the case against him."

"I've been told that he walks in and out of police headquarters as if it were a hotel.  And think, Father, if he were to get away with this, he would take reprisals against everyone involved."

"Are you afraid?"

"Not for myself, Father.  I'm thinking of Toddy Muir and of her husband and others.  I can't witness against this man without naming Toddy.  And if I name her, she'll have to testify.  I have no doubt at all that this man would be quite capable of killing both her and her husband."

"Then what we must do is see to it that this information gets into the right hands.  I know just the man to contact.  He's a narcotics detective, an able and honest man.  I'll make a few phone calls and find him.  I think I have his home number.  I'll call there first.  I don't think he'll mind if I wake him.  Not for something like this.  In fact, I think he'll be grateful."

"Why do you think that, Father?"

"Because his daughter died of drugs and he hates those who deal in it."

"You're referring to Lieutenant Figlia, aren't you?"

"That's right.  I forgot, you helped with Rose Figlia's funeral."

"Yes.  And now I understand so much more about the whole situation.  I understand life so much better, and I've seen everything in a new light."

"Faith, Michael.  Faith.  It will come.  In the meantime,

go and clean yourself up.  Shower, shave, and put on the garb of the priest that you are—now and forever.  It is my intention to have the Diocese send you away for rehabilitation.  There is a place that takes care of sick priests—drug addicts, alcoholics, priests who have fallen ill of soul.  Priests like you, Michael.  I only wish I could send Father Thom Corrigan there, too, but—"

"He's a celebrity, and I'm nobody."

"Go and clean yourself up—your outer self, at least!"

Chapter 55

CALLING IN A FAVOR

Lieutenant Figlia sat at a desk in the middle of the squadroom.  He had chosen a place here amidst computers and telephones, rather than in Hubbard's office, for a reason: he was having a great deal of difficulty staying awake—the noise out here helped. Figlia put a stubbly chin in the elbow-braced palm of his left hand and looked out on the scene around him.  He saw Monk Stolz wherever he looked.

The bluecoat at the desk in front of his was checking in an odd couple:  a tall, skinny black man, and a short, muscular white woman.  The man had several bandages about the head and face, the woman had a bandage over her right eye.  They were both drunk or drugged; and yet, Figlia thought, they had probably sat in the emergency ward of a hospital for hours.  They must have been in dandy condition when they were picked up.  He listened as they were checked in . . .

"O.K.," the bluecoat said, "I'm in a hurry.  You.  What's your name?"

"Torrance Amsterdam.

"Age?"

"Twenty-six."

"Address?"

He gave it.

"What's in that case?"

"A sax. I'm a musician."

"He only thinks he is," said the woman.

"An' you only *think* you're a man."

"All right, cut it," snapped the bluecoat. "Haven't you two had enough for one night? You, what's your name, lady?"

"Elga Hargo."

"Lady?" said Tory. "Ha!"

"I said cut it," the bluecoat warned. "You, Hargo, what's your age?"

"Forty-two."

"Address?"

She gave it.

"Occupation?"

"She's a dyke," said Tory.

Elga leaped, grabbed Tory by the collar, and pushed him down over the officer's desk. Figlia jumped up and helped the bluecoat separate the battlers. Elga was taken across the room and handcuffed to a bench. Tory found that very funny, until he was warned that if he didn't behave he'd be handcuffed to her free arm. He sat on the floor in front of the bluecoat's desk on his saxophone case and fell asleep.

"What's the story?" Figlia asked, mildly amused.

"Fight over a pool game."

"A pool game?"

"Well, that's what I get from them two. But there was a bimbo involved."

"Over a woman?"

"More likely. He took a poke at her, then she preceded to shove a billiard ball down his throat and try to wrap a cuestick around his head. One tough broad!"

"He's on junk, isn't he?"

"You should see his arms. He's got enough tracks to operate a trans-continental railroad."

"Did he have anything on him?"

"A few bags—not much. He's no dealer."

"A few bags. That's enough for a nice long vacation upstate. How about her?"

"No, she was clean." The bluecoat glanced at Elga, then looked at Figlia, smiling, "Well, you know what I mean."

"Yeah. Well, she's got a nice assault charge. She won't be seeing her bimbo for a while either. You better check with the medical people about the guy; he's going to need something before the night is over. We don't want him keeping everybody awake. And I want to speak to him later. Both of them. I think they might have starred in a porno-flick I saw recently. Tell me when they've sobered up."

"Yes, sir."

From across the room another officer called: "Lieutenant Figlia, there's a call for you. You want to take it at your desk?"

"Switch it here," Figlia called back. He put the receiver to his ear. "Yes? Figlia here."

"Lieutenant Figlia?"

"Yes?"

"This is Father Ryan."

"Well, Father! Good to hear from you."

"It's good to speak with you again, Albert. The Parish misses you."

"I know you're joking, Father."

"I have faith that you'll return to the fold, Albert."

"Perhaps so, Father. But what prompts this call? It's after four in the morning. It's hard to believe you'd wake in the middle of the night with a sudden urge to save me. How did you know where I was, anyhow? I'm only here on temporary assignment."

"I took the liberty of calling your home. I'm afraid I woke your lovely wife. But I simply had to talk with you. It's something of the utmost seriousness. Both a police matter and a matter involving the Church. In fact, it involves a priest, my assistant and curate, Father Michael Din."

"Well, what is it, Father?"

"Have you received a report on the body of a young boy—about sixteen years of age—being found? The body would have been found in an alley. The boy was small and dark-complected, a Puerto Rican."

"I haven't heard of anything tonight. Is this a certainty?"

"Yes."

"I'll check it out. But how does your priest fit in?"

Father Ryan told him. Now Figlia was wide awake. "The man called himself Monk?"

"Yes," said Father Ryan, "Monk. I suppose you'd like to speak with Father Din?"

"Absolutely. I'll have a patrol car pick him up. Have him wait there."

"He'll be ready and waiting. Albert, is Father Din in any trouble?"

"Not with us, Father—not if his story checks out. Sounds like he might be in a lot of trouble with you, though. And maybe with Monk Stolz."

"He's a good young man, Albert. You'll see to his interests, won't you? He's only confused."

"I'll look after him, Father. And, Father . . . Thanks. I mean for calling me personally. This is a big one. I think when I explain what's happened to Gena, she'll even forgive you for waking her up."

"Give her my blessings, Albert. And thank you."


Chapter 56


DEAD BIRD, LIVE FOX


Figlia issued the order for one of his patrol cars to cross

precinct boundaries and go into Chelsea to pick up Father Din. It was made clear that he was only a witness and was to be treated with the respect due a priest. Figlia had in mind the fact that Father Din might not be dressed as a priest. He also ordered that Father Din be kept in the patrol car, and not allowed to enter the station. Figlia would go out to the car. If there were spies in the station, Figlia had no intention of allowing them to discover anything. He checked his pistol. If Stolz so much as blinked an eye, Figlia would put a bullet through it.

He put on his overcoat, hat, scarf, and gloves. Then he went and stood inside the front door, waiting for the patrol car to pull up. Outside was a kaleidoscopic lace of snow on night, broken only by the faint red glow of the turning beacons of a few parked prowl cars.

Figlia felt positively gleeful. According to Father Ryan, Monk was drugged, and sitting up in an apartment with the door wide open, in a drug-induced sleep.

Figlia smoked, and eventually a patrol car came crunching up, hubcap-deep in snow, to the front of the station. There was a big, dark fellow in the back seat. Figlia pushed through the door and went, slipping, down the steps, and got into the car next to the back-seat passenger.

"You're Father Din?"

"Yes."

"I'm Al Figlia. What's the address?"

"I don't know. But if you drive straight ahead, I'll point out the house. It's a few blocks."

"All right, Father, we're not going to set any speed records in this snow, so you tell me all about it on the way. Officer . . ."

"Yes, sir?"

"No siren, no noise, everything very quiet—got it?"

"Yes, sir."

"Go ahead, Father."

"Well, it's just as Father Ryan told you . . ."

"I want it from you, Father."

Father Din told him, and Figlia listened.  "That's all of it, then?" Figlia asked.

"Yes.  Except for details.  My father was a cop," Father Din put in.  "A Jersey City detective."

"He was?

"Yes.  He always wanted me to be a priest, but I wanted to be a cop like him.  I was in attendance at your daughter's funeral, Lieutenant."

"You were?  You know then why I want this S.O.B."

"I understand," said Father Din.

"Douse the beacon," Figlia said to the driver.

"I have already, sir."

"There it is," said Father Din, "on the right there."

"Pull in here," Figlia ordered.  The driver pulled the car in to the curb, climbing crunchingly up on drifting snow.  They got out.

"You," Figlia said to the driver— "Stay at the door.  No one out.  You," he said to the driver's partner, "and you," to Father Din, "you come with me."  He led the way into the alley beside the building.

"I don't see anything," said the driver's partner.

"There was no report on it," said Figlia, "the body's got to be here."  The driver's partner waved a flashlight up and down the narrow, snow-filled alley.

"It was near the rear of the house," Father Din said.

"There it is," said Figlia quietly.  He pointed to a small mound in the snow, near the wall of the next building.  The driver's partner aimed the beam of the flashlight at the place.

They went to it.  Dedi's twisted, smashed, rigor-mortised little body lay under a two-inch blanket of snow.  It reminded Father Din of the corpse of a frozen bird—but no peacock, a dead sparrow.  He looked away.

"All right," Figlia said, "that's that.  Come on."  The

driver, the driver's partner, and Father Din, in that order, followed the fast-moving Figlia into the house and up the stairs. The alarmed, angry superintendent stood watching them ascend, his eyes crusted with sleep, shivering in his tattered robe.

Figlia took the stairs two at a time, gun in hand. At the fifth floor landing, he stopped and turned to the bluecoats behind him. Seeing that Father Din had followed, Figlia gestured for him to go back down the stairs. Then, too involved to give further thought to the priest, he turned and went on to Toddy's door. It was shut.

Father Din said he'd left the door wide open, Monk asleep. The shut door was a bad sign. Figlia tried it. It was locked. He cursed under his breath.

Figlia indicated that the driver's partner should kick the door in. The driver's partner was a big man, well over two-hundred pounds. One lunging kick over the doorknob and the lock snapped. The door swung open. There was no one in the kitchen. If Monk was in one of the other rooms, he'd be awake; he'd know. There was no point in being quiet.

"Stolz!" Figlia called out.

Silence.

"This is the police, Stolz," Figlia called. "Come out in the open. Let's see you." But even as he called, Figlia knew his man was gone. He edged into the kitchen, the two bluecoats following. Father Din waited at the door. He saw Figlia go into the livingroom, kick open the bedroom door, look, then with a very audible curse re-holster his revolver, and come back into the kitchen.

"You," Figlia said to the driver's partner, "go down and call the wagon. And the B.C.I. I want pictures of the body. Hold on. Notify the M.E. and the D.A.'s office. I want everything involved here on all the records. I'm going to play this strictly kosher, just in case it adds up to something later. And you," he said to the driver, "start searching this place, top to bottom."

"Don't you need a warrant?" asked Father Din.

"No," said Figlia, sniffing at the mouth of a Scotch bottle. He took a long draft from it, then went over to the driver and handed him the bottle. "Have a drink. Warm you up," he said. "It's on the house." Figlia looked at Father Din. "You told me he'd been drugged. That Scotch is clean."

"He had been," said Father Din. "The other bottle. But that was about three hours ago. He must have come out of it. He's very strong."

Figlia nodded thoughtfully. "And realized that he'd better get out," he said. "You realize, do you, that he probably intended to kill you?"

"Yes, I see that now."

"Only he had to play games about it. That's his weakness, and that's what saved you. If that girl Opal hadn't drugged him, he probably would've shot you up and tossed you off the roof, too. I hope you realize that you've behaved very recklessly, Father."

"Yes. I see that now."

"Where is Toddy Muir now, Father?"

From outside could be heard the faint whine of sirens.

"She's checked in at the St. Christopher Hotel."

Figlia shook his head disgustedly. "That whorehouse! All right," he said. "Shall I have you driven back to the Rectory?"

"I'd appreciate it," said Father Din.

"I'll want to speak with you tomorrow. I'll want a statement."

"I'll come in," said Father Din.

"Make it at three," said Figlia.

There was a clamor in the hall, and four officious policemen entered the apartment. Figlia told one of them to drive Father Din back to the Rectory. But as he was being driven along the Strip, through a blizzard of snow, Father Din remembered Toddy's last words: "I'm warmer than a principle."

He told the driver to let him out, and trudged the rest of the way through the storm to The Busy Nook, knowing that Father Ryan, and perhaps Figlia, would be furious with him. "To hell," he said, trudging on.

Chapter 57

## GETTING IT RIGHT

The transom was shut and a towel hung over the doorknob, blocking the keyhole from all eyes, yet Toddy could not feel at ease. It was silly of her, she felt, to be so shaken by a Peeping Tom, but shaken she was. Something like this might have been expected in such a place, and Peeping Toms, she had heard, were generally harmless and quite timid people. But the events of the day had left her emotionally vulnerable. She had lain across the bed and cried for nearly an hour, until the shock had subsided. She should have left the St. Christopher, had she known where to go at this hour of the night—or morning—but for the thought that Sam—Father Din, she corrected herself—might return. He would not be able to find her, and she did not know where to find him. No, she must get hold of herself; it was only that the spookiness of her nerves tormented her.

The grotesque, leering face in the transom had come into her vision like a negative reply to a prayer. As if God had said: "See what you are asking? Well, here's your answer." But she knew that this was her guilt whispering in her ear. And meanwhile, outside, over and over again—

ST. CHRIST PHER (RED)

(————————————-)

ST. CHRIST PHER (BLUE)

512

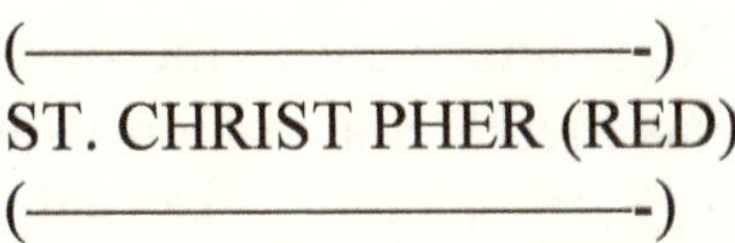

ST. CHRIST PHER (RED)

It was stupid, she knew: but somehow that sign seemed to drill at her a warning. It was Christ, Christ, Christ, Christ, over and over, and it was ominous, frightening, for she had long ago renounced that Christ.

And down the street, only a few doors away, stood the scissors factory, its terrifying pair of forty-foot high shears always poised to cut the sky in half. She was being superstitious, primitive. Like Father Din, she was seeing signs.

She did not, for the moment, remember her own fascination, and even belief in, astrology, and other occult pseudo-sciences. The sinner always hopes that the experience of sinning will be a more profound one than it is. The sin turns out to be merely unhealthy, and the sinner sickly. She had thought of these things. Now, she got up from the bed and went to the window. She hadn't noticed how hard it was snowing, nor how wild the wind was. She stood looking out into a night that was paling with the coming dawn. The street below was aflood with heaping, drifting flakes. A ghost of snow moved through it with a gentle, sweeping motion; then, caught in an upper wind, whirled away, dissolved, was gone, mingled in the thick white air.

She did not know her own heart. "Suppose," she thought, "that Sam—Father Din—comes along in the snow, coming to me? Should I let him in? Would it be wrong? Should I turn him away?" And what about Jack? "Where are you, Jack?"

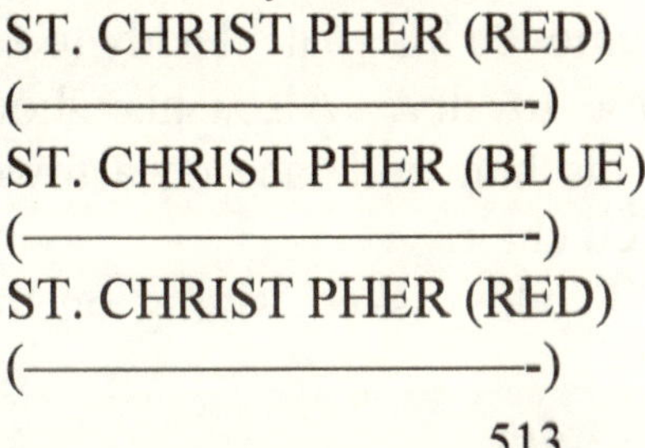

And so she turned with an idea, and went to the bureau and opened the top drawer. It was there! She couldn't save herself from a little, nervous laugh. "It's a plot," `she said aloud, taking the Gideon Bible from the drawer. "Everyone's trying to save me." She went to the bed, lay down, and began to read at random in the book. It was Job—whose story she read through. Then she shut the Bible and went back to the window. There were fresh foot-tracks in the snow in front of the hotel. And just then a soft knock came at the door. "Who is it?" she called, frightened and at the same time hopeful. "Who's there?"

"It's me—Michael."

Toddy gave a small, wild cry of relief, and ran to the door. She pulled it open and there stood a tall snowman.

"You're covered with it," Toddy said, backing into the room.

"I've been to see Father Ryan—my boss—and the police have been notified," he said. "They've picked up Dedi's body. Monk was gone . . ."

"Aren't you coming in?"

"No, I don't think so. I've been thinking things over –"

"But you must—at least for a minute. Please." Then, with inspiration—"Monk was gone. That means he could be anywhere. He might come here and find me. Please, Sam, you can't leave me here in this awful place alone."

Father Din looked at her. His eyes were red-rimmed, and had a tense, troubled look in them. Then, with a slight heave of his chest, he began slapping the wet snow from his coat. "All right," he said, "I'll stay with you till morning." He stepped in and removed his coat. Toddy took it and hung it near the radiator to dry. Also, his shoes, his socks. Father Din dried his hair and face on a towel. He slumped into an overstuffed chair.

"This Father Ryan," Toddy asked, sitting on the bed, "you say he's your boss?"

"Something like that," said Father Din. "I'm very fond of him, and I argued with him tonight. I think I hurt him very deeply."

"I'm sorry. I suppose it had something to do with me?"

"No, only with me."

"But he convinced you, didn't he?"

"What makes you think that?"

"It's obvious. You're in uniform. You're not the same man you were a couple of hours ago. It's funny; I thought that if you came back at all, you'd have decided to quit. I didn't expect you to come back having decided the other way. But you have, haven't you?"

Father Din studied the thin rug that was like mouse-skin. His wet foot prints walked up to him from the door. After a few seconds, he said: "Father Ryan made it seem so simple; even I could see it. I wouldn't agree with him—still being a stubborn, stupidly clever fool—but I understood. Ever since the beginning, when I was selected for the priesthood, everyone has been telling me that faith would come. All I had to do was to wait." He looked at her.

"Candidates are supposed to be selected because it's seen by someone who knows that such a person has a vocation. But in fact no one knows who has a vocation. The truth is, an overzealous, if well-meaning, Bishop can rob the cradle. It can happen for all sorts of reasons—political, personal—and then an unsuited guy like me ends up in a position where no matter what he does, he can't be right. Paul said that there are diversities of graces."

"You mean that you would be good in another circumstance?"

"I would hope so. And then there's that other thing. 'There are eunuchs who have made themselves eunuchs for the kingdom of heaven,' Christ said. I can't make myself a eunuch, though, God knows, I've tried."

"If you feel that way, why are you wearing your backwards collar?"

"I'm not sure. Some last concession to Father Ryan, a man for whom I hold a deep affection. And I also feel I've got to end this thing in the right way. I started it with a lie, maybe I can end it closer to the truth. I'm still a priest and I'm going to dress like one until I'm not one. No more false flags."

"But you only came to give me my key back."

"And to tell you what happened. I had to see you again, to say—"

"I know. You don't have to say it. In a way, I feel relieved. I was more than a little afraid of the idea, though I might have gone through with it. Do you understand?"

Father Din looked up at her and nodded. She was beautiful.

"You love Jack."

"I suppose I do; but it's hopeless."

"Don't let yourself believe that."

"Do you know," Toddy said, half serious, half amused, "I prayed for you to come back to me tonight. But I didn't expect that you'd come back to me as a priest. Maybe the Lord knows what I really need."

"I think so," Father Din said, his eyes dropping. She kissed him lightly on the forehead, then went to bed and fell into a troubled sleep.

## Chapter 58

## MAHMOUD SAVES CAMILLA FROM THE MADMAN

At three o'clock that morning, Ansar, Mahmoud and Camilla were not so much released as expelled from the station. There were no charges against them. But where could they go? Ansar insisted that they go back to the Saints and Sinners Club, which stayed open till four. He wanted to retrieve his paper bag full of paraphernalia from the garbage can outside Tiger's where he had stashed it during the excitement.

It wasn't a long walk from the precinct house to the Saints and Sinners Club, but it was a cold one. The three exchanged very little conversation. Ansar went immediately to the garbage can and retrieved his crumpled Saks shopping bag. Mahmoud and Camilla went inside.

Opal, whom Mahmoud knew as Tory's girl friend, sat at the bar. Mahmoud saw an opportunity to get Camilla clear of the crazy Ansar, at least for the night. He introduced Opal and Camilla and asked if Opal would let Camilla spend the night with her. She agreed, saying: "I'm not going back to my apartment tonight, but I'll find a place for us. I know lotsa people around here. I'm all by myself tonight anyhow. Tory and Elga are in jail."

"I know," said Mahmoud. "I just left Tory. You probably won't see him for a day or two. He's going to be charged, for sure. Drunk and disorderly, for Tory, assault and battery for Elga, from what I hear."

Just then Ansar walked up to them. "Now I must find a place to do my work," he said. He was carrying the paper bag. He pointed up the bar at Tiger. "Tell that Zionist he cannot win."

"Opal," said Mahmoud, ignoring Ansar, "Ansar and I need a place to stay. I don't know about him but I've got to get some sleep. Where can we go at this hour?"

"Only one place close—The Busy Nook—I mean, the St. Christopher Hotel—right on down the avenue."

Mahmoud explained to Ansar that Camilla would stay with Opal, "because that's no place for a nice young girl."

"Then she will meet us here tomorrow," said Ansar, "at five o'clock. You will bring her. I have very important business in the meantime. *You* may need to sleep," he said, looking at Mahmoud, "but Ansar must work."

"What are you doing, anyway?  What is this work?"
asked Mahmoud.  "Look, Ansar, I don't know you, and I try
to mind my own business, so I haven't asked what you're up
to, but if I'm going to spend the night with you—"

"I am preparing to make a statement.  Where and when
is not important—only the statement is important."

"But not tonight.  Not with me.  Right?"

"It is impossible tonight.  But if it were, then I would do
it tonight."


Chapter 59


THE DREAM IN ROOM 28


Ansar dreamed back from room 28 at The Busy Nook to
a lost childhood in Hebron, the poorest and least developed
of the West Bank's major towns.  His hometown was largely
agricultural, low in applied technology, a town that young
people left, looking for work.  They might try the Persian
Gulf, they might try Jordan, and yet, being children of the
country, hicks of a sort, they could hope for perhaps no more
than a hillbilly finds in the Marine Corps—at best a clean bar-
racks life.

The possibility was great for much less.  And Ansar had
never been particularly clever.  Indeed, his associates had often thought him a fool, a man capable of stepping backwards
off a balcony.  Without quite understanding what others saw
in him, but understanding that it was difficult for him to earn
the lasting respect of others, Ansar had developed, as a sort
of performance that had become second nature, his gruff,
pseudo-decisive manner, which earned him a short-term,
grudging respect, that fell away when he was better known.

But always, Ansar said, things would be different this
time, and he had been constantly driven to more and more
extreme behavior.  He was not really an ideologue, a word too

complicated to represent him, nor did he hold the tenets of the Muslim faith with a very strong grip; but these were what Ansar had to use.

    ST. CHRIST PHER (RED)
    (——————)
    ST. CHRIST PHER (BLUE)
    (——————)

Now he puzzled into the night over his bomb book. He tried to follow the diagrams, but things kept getting lost between his eye-on-the-book and his eye-on-the-materiel. The diagram of the bomb did not look like the stuff on the table beside it. Ansar shook his head and began to rearrange things. He had to get this right. It was the supreme test of his life. But he had still made no decision as to what he would blow up. Perhaps the Police Station. That would certainly earn him respect.

Chapter 60

**THE DREAM IN ROOM 29**

    ST. CHRIST PHER (RED)
    (——————-)
    ST. CHRIST PHER (BLUE)
    (——————-)

In room 29, Mahmoud had undressed and carefully folded and hung up his clothing and now lay back on the bed in his clean white underwear, his arms up behind his head, waiting for sleep. But he was overtired and must wait for his nervous system to relax and prepare the ease of his dreams.

He was comparing this Ansar and himself and some others of his acquaintance to his brother, Tory, who did not seem to have faith in any human enterprise but music. Tory would not join in any effort or cause. Even when it came to his beloved jazz, Tory was without discipline. He had never been

519

at his best in the cooperative effort of modern jazz but always preferred the long, almost lonely riffs of Dixieland. The more on-his-own he was the more brilliant he was, the more in unison, the flatter he became.

Mahmoud, who used to be Morris and sometimes Maurice, had been the leader of their early groups—there had been a dozen or more—but he could never contain Tory and they had fallen out many times.

Then Mahmoud had found the most important group of his life, the Muslims. Hope in a New Order. But Tory did not desire hope any more than he desired order. Tory was his own lonely song. And now he sat in the local tank awaiting charges. But what could ever happen to Tory, Mahmoud asked himself. He would be the same in jail or out. He would always be the same. Why, Mahmoud wondered, did he envy his brother?

Chapter 61

TATTOOS

"That little dog!" Pilar exclaimed, between spoonfuls of soup. "He promise me to come home at night. I twist his ears off when I get him!"

"Oh, Pilar," Jack Muir said wearily, "he stays out all the time."

"No he don't!" Pilar almost shouted. "I tell him and he do what I say."

Muir shrugged indifferently and lighted a cigarette.

"I should have let him go into the shit-bowl," Pilar said.

"He'll be all right," Jack said, his thoughts elsewhere.

"You love him, too, don't you, Jack?" Pilar said, her almond eyes warming a bit. Muir looked at her. He smiled.

"Sure I do," he said, reaching across the table to pat her hand. "Don't worry about him; he's tough, like Bogart."

520

"Oh, he love Bogie," Pilar said, enthusiastic. "He watch him all the time. He love video classics."

"I know," said Muir, slipping back into his thoughts.

Pilar finished her soup. She put the cup in the sink. A roach ran out of the sink and up her arm. She jumped back, squealing, and slapped the bug off. "I need a fix," she said.

"I've got meth . . ." Muir offered.

"No, I need a fix," said Pilar. She went to the sideboard and got her pocketbook.

"Do it in the bathroom," said Muir.

"O.K.," Pilar said, unoffended. She went into the tiny bathroom and shut the door. In a minute, Muir heard water running. In a few more minutes Pilar came out, her eyes already turned into opaque, well-oiled glass. "Come to bed, Jack: I got a surprise for you."

Indifferently, Muir followed her into the small bedroom the windows of which looked out on a narrow, ugly street. With her back to him, as he sat on the bed removing his shoes, Pilar took off all her clothes but her bra. She had a slim, muscular body. Her calves were wiry and thin, her thighs of hard, medium thickness, her buttocks were a gleaming gold, and deeply, darkly etched in the middle. Her waist was narrow, her torso, from the back, very V'd, and her shoulders broad. Out of her shoes, she looked much shorter, but at the same time much stronger, than with them on. For the first time in weeks, Muir felt the stirrings of sex. Pilar turned to him then, her eyes gleaming. Her small breasts, where they swelled up out of her bra, had the same dusky golden hue as her buttocks, and the same dark etching in the middle, between them. "Take off your bra," Muir said. He was undressed now, and under the covers.

"Wait," said Pilar. She turned on the bedside lamp, then turned off the overhead light. Then she got into bed.

She sat next to Muir, turning her breasts toward him. She reached behind her and undid her bra. "Look," she said. The bra fell away. At first, Muir saw nothing but the two round, golden, bouncing little breasts. Then he saw that his name had been tattooed over the brown, full nipples— JACK over the right nipple, and MUIR over the left.

"My God," he said, "what have you done?"

Pilar's face, which had been for a moment like that of a child's who had a surprise gift to give, showed sudden panic.

"You no like, Jack?"

Muir grabbed her into his arms. He pushed her dark head down on his shoulder, and sat rocking her.

"Don't you like what I did, Jack?" she asked again, in a few moments, her voice muffled against Muir's shoulder. "You see how I love you," she said. "You see how I love you? It hurt, Jack. See how I love you?"

"Yes, yes," Muir said softly, rocking her the while. He was appalled; but his feeling of pity for Pilar was even stronger than his revulsion. "Yes, I see how you love me," he said, but he said it so softly that Pilar couldn't hear.

"What?" she said, lifting her head from his shoulder. "You no like, Jack?"

"No," said Muir, "it's fine, it's fine."

"You like them?" Pilar brightened visibly.

"Yes," Muir lied.

Pilar put her head back down on his shoulder. She reached down and put her hand between his legs, edged it up to his crotch. Muir kept rocking her gently. "Oh," he moaned, not with sex but with a vague yet terrible guilt. Then Pilar's hand fell away from him. Her head became heavy on his shoulder. Gently, he stretched her out on the bed, covered them, and lay looking into her drugged, sleeping, Aztec face. He lay like that for half an hour, during which his pity left him, as his attention gradually shifted from thoughts of her soul to thoughts of her tawny, animal body. The girl had a beauty of her own, and his artist's eye began to discover it. One of Pilar's hands rested on the pillow, next to the black stream of her hair, and the fingernails of it were large and long and blood-red. The hand was like an exotic talon. Muir kissed its palm. He rocked her in his arms till they both fell asleep.

Muir woke with a start. He got out of bed, slipping his feet into his shoes, threw his army overcoat over his shoulders, and went to the window. Outside, a heavy layer of snow lay on the street, with still more of the intrepid stuff dancing down out of the faint dawn sky. He sat by the window for half an hour, watching and smoking. Then Pilar stirred in bed and called him to her. He went back and got in bed with the warm, naked girl.

"Jack?" she whispered, out of her sleep.

"Yes . . ."

Pilar took his shoulders in her hands, her long nails cutting into his flesh, and pulled him down upon her.

"Love me, Jack," she whispered.

Chapter 62

CHECKING OUT

A sleep-refreshed Felix Potter knocked on the door of room 22, waking Toddy and Father Din. Father Din pulled himself out of the overstuffed chair in which he'd slept, and went to the door. He opened it. "Yes?" he said.

"Oh, it's you," said Potter, surprised; indeed, shocked to see Father Din's priestly collar. He cleared his throat and became official. "It's noon," he said. "It's check-out time. You'll have to vacate."

"Noon?" said Father Din. "Yes, all right, we'll be out in a few minutes."

"Well, hurry, please; the maid will be here soon, you know, to change those sheets," said Potter, with hardly

523

concealed mischievous pleasure. Actually, the maid would only put the top sheet on the bottom and a clean sheet on top.

"All right," said Father Din, closing the door, "we'll hurry." But before he could shut it, the door was pushed open again by a uniformed policeman. "Who are you?" asked the bluecoat. He looked past Father Din and saw Toddy, who was sitting up in bed. "Mrs. Muir?" he called to her.

"Yes."

"Excuse me," said the bluecoat, "I thought you were alone in there."

"Is there something wrong, officer?" asked Potter, who stood to the side.

"No, I guess not," the bluecoat said. "You go along."

Potter gave him an imperious look, and went down the hall. The cop looked in.

"I was detailed down here last night—or I should say this morning—to keep an eye on your door. I was told that when you woke I was to bring you to the station for questioning. Nobody said you'd be . . . I thought you were alone." Father Din explained his presence.

"Well, looks like you didn't need me," said the cop. "I'll go down and see that there's a car waiting."

"I must be important," said Toddy, when Father Din closed the door.

"You are," he said. "And good morning." He ran fingers over his chin.

Toddy sat in the bed, smoking.

"I have to be at police headquarters at three," he said. "That's in three hours. Right now, I'm going to see Pilar Pavon—to see if I can help her in any way."

"Do you know where she lives?"

"She and Dedi lived together, didn't they? That was the impression you gave me."

"Yes, they do; but I don't know where she lives."

"Well, I know. I took a clinic card out of his wallet last

night, when Monk wasn't looking.  Pilar will be at that address, I hope."

"I guess so," said Toddy, rubbing her eyes.  "It's too early for me to think.  I don't wake up until dark.  If I wait for you at the police station, will you eat with me?"

"I'll be there at three," said Father Din, "but you'll have to wait for me while I make my statement.  Better have a little breakfast as soon as you can.  I'll see you then."

Father Din shut the door behind him.  The bluecoat, sitting tipped back on a chair in the hall, nodded, "I've got a car waiting outside," he said.  "She won't be long, will she?"  Father Din smiled, shrugged, and went on down to the lobby.

He paid the hotel bill, and then went into the snowy street.  He had walked a block, when a fareless taxi came grinding along on chains.  The snow was like a thick white fog through which one could barely see.  The driver made no attempt to pull his cab over to the curb, but stopped it in the middle of the street.  Father Din negotiated a mountainous snow-drift and slipped-slid to the door of the cab, and got in.

"Where to?" asked the cabbie.

Father Din gave him the address.

"Some storm, eh?"

"Yes, quite a storm," said Father Din.

"Supposed to turn to sleet later."

"Is it?"

"Yeah.  Then it'll freeze."

"Probably," said Father Din.  "Like hell freezing over, isn't it?"


## Chapter 63


## CHECKING IN


Curious and annoyed, Felix Potter slid on down the hall, knocking on doors and calling out, "It's noon.  Check out

Time.  Anyone wants to stay, they've got to pay."  Mahmoud opened the door to room 29.  He was dressed.  Potter pounded Ansar's door, but no answer came.

Mahmoud said, "Use your key.  He's probably asleep."

Potter shrugged, lifted his key-chained keys and un-locked the door, pushing it open.

Mahmoud stepped in front of him, blocking his view, and in.  He saw at a glance the situation was as he'd feared.  Ansar had fallen asleep at the room's one small table, paraphernalia scattered about it.

Mahmoud did not want Felix Potter to see inside.  He turned back to Potter, who stood trying to peer past him, and said, taking a roll of bills from his pocket, "Look, my friend and I will keep this room for the rest of the day.  He's ex-hausted.  Needs some sleep.  What do we owe you?"

Felix Potter felt that the world owed him an explanation, but he could see that he was not going to get one.  He looked at the roll of bills and said, "Fifty dollars for two."  Why not?  It was incredibly high for the Busy Nook.  Potter could pocket at least half of it.  The several bills warmed his palm, and the warmth scurried up his arm and into his heart.


Chapter 64


THE VISITORS


Two hours earlier, at ten, Pilar Pavon woke to find her-self alone.  Jack Muir was gone; apparently Dedi had never come home.  At first Pilar thought Jack must have gone to get something at the store, but when he did not return by noon she knew he wouldn't be back.  Men!

She got up, put on a pot of coffee (the weak percolated gringo coffee that Dedi liked), washed, brushed her teeth, poured herself (when the last perk sounded) a cup of coffee, and sat down (still wearing her warm winter housecoat) at the kitchen table to drink it. "And a good-looking *muchacha*," she said, extending a draped, curving calf, which was perhaps a little too thin, and studying it. "*Stupidos!*" she spit, tossing her tousled raveny hair out of her face, and taking a sip of hot coffee.

Suddenly she frowned, the cup poised at her lips, as if remembering something. "No, he would never do a thing like that," Pilar said aloud, and, surprised at the sound of her own voice, looked about the empty room.

Early that morning, before falling asleep for the second time, she had gone on a match hunt and found the revolver in Muir's army-coat pocket. She'd asked him what he was doing with it. He'd told her it had been given him and that he intended to sell it. At that point, her mind had been too hazed-over for her to put things together. Now it occurred to her that when she'd picked Muir up in front of Toddy's building, he'd had a gun, and she saw what that might mean. "Maybe he gonna kill Monk, or maybe Monk gonna kill him," she thought. "What I should do?" But she could think of nothing to do but wait for Dedi and Jack Muir to find her. She could not find them, especially in a blizzard. While she waited to hear something from them, she busied herself with house-keeping chores, stopping occasionally for more coffee, ciga-rettes, and pills. It was a little after noon when the doorbell rang. She breathed a deep sigh of relief, thinking it was Jack returning, or maybe Dedi, who always lost his keys. The buzzer to let people in no longer worked. She would have to go down three flights of musty, littered stairs to open the door.

But it was not Jack at the door. It was Opal and a strange girl. "What you want?" demanded Pilar, holding the collar of her housecoat against the swift, cold breeze that swept in through the open door.

"I thought somebody ought to come see you," said Opal. She stood, booted and bundled for winter, her back to the whirling, wind-driven snow.

"What you mean?" asked Pilar sharply. "What you want?"

"You mean nobody's told you yet?"

"I don't know what you are talking about. You tell me, or go away."

"I got to talk to you," said Opal. "I got to tell you somethin'. Can we come in?"

"Who is your friend?"

"Her name's Camilla."

"Hi," said Camilla.

She nodded at the girl. "Is it important?"

"Yes."

"O.K.," said Pilar, "but it better be important. Come on. I live upstairs."

As Father Din's cab pulled on to Pilar's street, Opal's cab could still be seen grinding in the snow a block ahead.

"This is it, Father."

"Will you wait for me?"

"How long will you be? It ain't so good to sit still in this weather. I'm thinkin' of the car."

"Maybe a half hour at most."

"O.K., Father, I'll tell you what"—he looked at his watch—"I'll be back in a half hour. You know you owe me a lot of money already, Father, but let's forget it. I don't like for a priest to pay. And you can depend on me—I'll be back."

"Here," said Father Din, handing the cabbie a bill, "get yourself some coffee."

The building was a sad and dreary replica of the ones to each side of it, only featured with uniqueness insofar as its scars were differently placed. There was a broken window on the first floor, backed against the cold with a jagged piece of cardboard. There was a crudely drawn swastika, done in red paint with a two-inch brush, near the entrance. There were hearts, names, and curses carved into the chipped, slimy-green-painted wood of the rickety outer doors, through which wind had driven snow, so that it was nearly as deep between that outer and the inner doors as it was in the street. None of the mailboxes had locks. Only a few had names on them. Pilar & Dedi Pavon. Father Din rang the bell under the mailbox and hoped it would work. After a moment, he rang again, and then heard someone descending the stairs.

Opal opened the door. She did not recognize Father Din as Sam Hopkins. Clean-shaven, his collar sticking stiffly up under his chin, he was a stranger, a priest. "What is it?" she asked.

"It's me, Opal—Sam."

Now she saw. "Sam! Why, you a priest. Why you dressed like that?"

"I *am* a priest, Opal."

She stood for a moment, blinking.

"Why if that don't beat all! Toddy know that?" She raised her eyebrows.

"Yes, she knows."

"Well, if that don't beat all! I just don't know what to think. What do I call you then?"

"My name is Michael Din. You can call me Father Din if you want to—or Michael, or Sam, Opal, I don't care."

"But what was you doing—?"

"That's a long story. Perhaps I'll be able to tell you about it sometime. But I've come to see Pilar—about Dedi."

"Me too," said Opal. "But when I come, I didn't think I'd have to *tell* her about it. I only come to help. 'Sides, I'm afraid to go back to that house, and last night Elga—you remember her—and Tory, they got into a fight and both of 'em is in jail, so I didn't know what else to do. Two places I know I'm not going near, that house or that jail."

"You mean to say nobody has notified her yet—I mean, before you?"

"Ah-ah! Nobody. I just told her." They were standing

in the hallway now, on the first floor.  Opal closed the door.

"My God!" Father Din exclaimed, slapping his fore-head, "they probably can't locate her, and it's my fault."

"Why is it your fault?"

"I took the only I.D. card Dedi had on him from his wallet last night.  That's how I knew the address here.  I never even thought of it until this morning.  I should have given it to the police last night."

"That could get you into some kind of trouble, couldn't it?"

"I suppose it could," said Father Din.  "When I saw that Dedi was dead, I stuffed the card in my pocket, I forgot about it until this morning.  And no one asked me about—"

"Well, you're a priest," interjected Opal.  "They won't do anything to you.  Will they?"

Father Din snorted without humor.  "How is Pilar taking it?" he asked, shifting from thoughts of Figlia's wrath.

She rolled her big, cherub-like eyes up toward the apartment.  "Oh, not so good.  She just keeps cryin' and cryin'.  Can't stop her.  Maybe shouldn't.  I'm doing what I know how, but what can I do?  What can any old body do?  She some musta loved that poor little boy.  Maybe you can help her."

Father Din followed Opal up the three flights of creaking, littered stairs and into the apartment.  Camilla sat across the table from Pilar, like a dark little lady-in-waiting.

"What you want?" Pilar snapped, as Father Din entered.  "I no call for a priest.  I got a spiritist."

"Do you remember me, Pilar?  My name is Michael Din.  We met for a moment last evening.  But perhaps you don't recognize me, dressed as I am?"

Pilar studied him for a moment with angry, tear-stained eyes.  Then she said: "I remember you.  You are the one who stop me from cutting Miss High-Class nose off, when I lose my temper.  You were nice to me.  How come you no dressed like a priest last night?"

"That's just what I asked him," said Opal.

"That's a long story, Pilar. I've come to—"

"I know. Don't tell me no more."

Father Din nodded and smiled strainedly. "I have your brother's card here," he said after a pause. "I've brought it to give you." He placed the card on the table in front of Pilar.

She looked at it, reached out and touched it with her fingers, but didn't pick it up. "Clinic card," she said. "He always sick. If he had took the medicines I fixed for him, he would be strong like a bull. But he would lie and not take them, and that is why he always sick. The clinic don't help. He had sores all over on him when he was born. Our father, he was drunk and he wanted to kill Dedi—maybe me too. Our mother was sick . . . they left us, then we only had each other . . ." Her face twisted grotesquely with mingled hatred and heartbreak, and she put it in her hand on the table. She let out a long groan that rose in timbre into a high, shrill wail. Opal went over to her and put a hand on her back.

Father Din stood in the middle of the small kitchen, again feeling as helpless as he had last night when her brother died. He tried to make himself say consoling words, but it was no use: it wasn't in him. He felt that such words would burn, rather than soothe, like salt in a wound. He was speechless now listening to Pilar's moans of mourning and anguish.

"*Stupido!*" she said in a weak voice, banging the table top with a small fist. "*Stupido!*"

Father Din had seen Dedi Pavon alive and dead, now he saw Dedi's sister in her grief. He stood in silence before this poverty-stricken, morally-stricken, grief-stricken woman whose every sound of grieving cut him to the quick, and waited.

"There, baby," Opal cooed over Pilar's shaking shoulders—"there, now, there—"

Finally, Pilar raised her head, wiped her eyes on the

sleeve of her housecoat, and asked Father Din: "You know what happened?"

"He was there," said Opal.

"I forget," said Pilar. She looked hard at Father Din. "Why you not *do* something, eh? You a priest? Why you not save him?"

Humbly, softly, Father Din answered that he didn't know how to.

"So," said Pilar, nodding. "Big good you are! I am *Catalicos Romanos*, too, see: but what good can it do for me? I cannot tell priests like you that I must sleep with men to make money to feed my little brother. What would you say, if I said that? You would put a curse on me."

Father Din did not speak.

"*He* knows," Pilar went on. "But *I* know who will help me. Jack will help me. He will go and kill Monk with that pistola that he has. He always say he will, but he don't. But now he is. He will do it for Dedi—for me. He will do for me and for my brother what he don't do for his wife. You will see."

"Jack Muir has a gun?" asked Father Din.

"*Si*. And I already put a spell on Monk yesterday that he would die before midnight tonight. And it is Jack who will kill him."

"Then you must help us stop him."

"Why? What you mean?"

"Because, if you care for him, you don't want to see him get into serious trouble, do you? He could be killed—or go to prison"

"Sam—I mean the Father is right," said Opal. "You don't want to see Jack get into no bad trouble, Pilar."

"Yes," said Pilar, "you are right."

"But," said Father Din, "you say he has a gun."

"Yes, *si*." Pilar looked thoughtful. "He has kicked," she said, after a moment.

"Kicked?"

"*Si,* he has kicked. He no use anymore heroin. Only meth."

"Wow!" exclaimed Opal. "That's why he didn't show up last night. When he kick it, baby?"

"A week. Maybe more. He has done this by himself. He has done this thing for his wife. He will go for her soon. I knew it this morning."

"I see," said Father Din. "Where is Muir now? Do you know?"

"He left before I woke up," said Pilar. "I do not know where he is. I would tell you. I speak the truth."

"I believe you," said Father Din. "Now won't you let me drive you down to police headquarters? I have a cab coming to pick me up in a few minutes and the police will want to talk with you."

"You should go with the Father, baby," said Opal. "You want to see Dedi once more, don't you?"

"You'll have to identify him," Father Din said softly, "and through my mistake the police don't know where to find you."

"Yes," said Pilar, "I go with you."

Chapter 65

THE MORGUE

When they got out at the police station, Opal said: "This is close enough for us." She waved her hand and walked away, pulling Camilla Azziz in the direction of the Saints and Sinners Club. Father Din took Pilar inside.

In the station, Father Din saw Toddy sitting alone in a far corner of the squad room. She started to rise and come over to him, but he signaled, not letting Pilar see, for Toddy to stay where she was. He led Pilar up to a bluecoat and asked to see Lieutenant Figlia.

In a moment, another bluecoat came and led the way to Captain Hubbard's office (Hubbard had called in sick that morning), inside of which, behind Hubbard's desk, sat Figlia eating chicken from a cardboard barrel. When he saw Pilar with Father Din, he got to his feet and came out from behind the desk. His clean-shaven face was gray. "Hello," he said to Father Din, and glanced at Pilar with a question in his eyes for which he also seemed to have the answer. "Relative of the boy?"

"Lieutenant," Father Din said, taking Pilar's elbow, "this is Pilar Pavon. She's Dedi Pavon's sister."

"Yes, yes," said Figlia, looking thoughtfully at Pilar. His eyes threw a question at Father Din. Father Din answered it: "She wants to see her brother's remains, Lieutenant."

"Can I see him?" Pilar asked.

"Yes," said Figlia. He went to his desk and pressed a button. With a reply, he said: "Send in a policewoman." He pulled a chair out for Pilar. "Please sit down, Miss Pavon," he said. Pilar sat down. Figlia looked at her, kindly. "You have my condolences, Miss Pavon."

"Thank you . . ."

"Are you Dedi's closest relative? I mean, don't you have parents?"

"No, sir. We got nobody, just us."

Figlia glanced at Father Din. "I had a hunch that you'd know where to find whoever the body belonged to, but we haven't been able to find you. I should have asked you last night, but I'm afraid I wasn't in top form. That's what happens when you get too involved; you're inclined to forget routine procedures."

"It was my fault, Lieutenant," said Father Din. "If you'll wait a moment, I'll tell you about it." He indicated a reluctance to speak before Pilar, who, in any case, showed no interest in what was being said.

"Your fault?" said Figlia.

A knock came at the opaque, beveled glass window in the door. A bulky shadow fidgeting. Figlia called for the shadow to enter, and a policewoman came in. "Sir?" she asked.

"Please take Miss Pavon here to identify a relative's remains. There's a tentative I.D. on it. She'll tell you who. Miss Pavon?" Pilar looked up, dreamily. She looked quite ugly now. "Will you go with this officer, please."

"*Si*," said Pilar listlessly. She got up, nodded at Father Din, and followed the policewoman out.

"Now what's this business about it being your fault?" asked Figlia with low heat. He sat down behind the desk, reached into the cardboard barrel, and drew out a drumstick. "I'm sorry, but I have to eat sometime. You don't mind, do you? Would you like a piece? It's very good. Colonel Drummond's Deep Down Done. I've become very fond of it."

"No, thank you," said Father Din. He hadn't eaten in so long that he'd lost his appetite, and the odor of chicken was nauseating. "I'm terribly sorry about this," he went on, "but I'm afraid I'm responsible for your not being able to locate Miss Pavon."

"So you said, but how comes it?"

Father Din told him about taking the card from Dedi's wallet.

"Well," Figlia said, "your intentions were good, Father. I don't suppose I have a right to be too angry about it; it's partly my fault for not asking. Neither of us were quite ourselves last night."

"Then they'll be no charges? I mean, for tampering with evidence or something?"

"No, Father; but if you keep trying . . ."

"I won't, I promise you," said Father Din.

"Here's another question I should have asked you last night—in a few minutes I'm going to have you make a detailed statement—but tell me, did the Pavon boy have any money on him, and, if so, how much you think? I'm assuming that Stolz took it."

"Yes, perhaps two-hundred dollars that Monk took from his wallet."

Figlia flipped the clean bone of the drumstick back in the barrel.

"He also had a tape-wrapped iron bar about ten inches long."

"Yes, I saw that."

"You see," Figlia said, "he fits the description of a robbery perp, kid who knocked over the St. Christopher Hotel early yesterday evening. Same type, the bar, a junkie—it all fits. Plus the money—just about the right amount. Well, that's not very important now, is it?"

"I suppose not," said Father Din, remembering Dedi and the "hot watches." "There's something else that you should know, Lieutenant. I think it is very important."

"What's that?"

"You've talked to Mrs. Muir?"

"Yes, and we have her statement."

"Well, this boy's sister, Miss Pavon, has been seeing Mrs. Muir's husband."

"Jack Muir, also on junk, according to his wife."

"Yes—that is, he was; but he isn't now. Miss Pavon told me that he said he'd kicked his habit."

"Yeah?"

"Well, he's got a gun."

"I see," said Figlia. "And you think that Muir is looking for Stolz?"

"It's possible."

"Yes, it is, isn't it?" said Figlia, his worried eyes darting with thought. "This is a very bad situation. I could almost wish that Stolz were gone—I don't want bodies all over the streets down here. But I want that man myself. I only hope he's crazy enough to have stayed. And he might be. I've been studying psych reports on him. He's a periodic alcoholic. He stays cool and sober for months at a time, but when he goes, he goes for two or three weeks. He usually tucks away in a hotel room or an apartment—some casual place he decides on—gets himself a lady, and maybe a gofor, and sits around making a dangerous nuisance of himself until he's ready to rejoin the world. It looks like he's on one now. At such times he can be especially dangerous. Booze doesn't square well with his kind of mind. He gets delusive. He's hurt people before during these toots. It's on the record. My feeling is, from what you and Mrs. Muir told me about the state of things last night, that he won't be able to let the situation drop. I have good reason to know that he believes in revenge."

"You mean, he'll look for her."

"I think he'll be looking for anyone who was there. But I doubt if he'll be on the street. He's too easy to spot, and he knows it, and he knows that we're looking. No, he won't show up on the street, and that'll severely limit his search. But I'm almost certain he'll sneak back up to Mrs. Muir's apartment to have a look—I'd bet on it—and that's why I've got it under twenty-four hour a day surveillance. And I've told Mrs. Muir that—although I'm not instructing her, or using any coercion whatsoever about it—I don't think she should go back there. Unless it's to get some clothes or something, and only for a few minutes—in and out quickly. You understand—that's only advice, not an order. As I say, the apartment is under surveillance. She'd be safe enough. But . . . ."

Father Din saw what Figlia was getting at.

"You really want to get that man, don't you?"

Figlia nodded slowly, seriously.

"Now you're on record advising her not to return to the apartment, but I can see that you half hope she does so that she can act as bait for Stolz."

"I've advised her not to. But, as I say, the apartment is being closely watched. She'd be safe if she did—but only for a short time. We've got an A.P.B. out on Stolz. If we can pick him up we might save ourselves some confusion."

Father Din felt a sudden dislike for Figlia. "You want my statement?"

But just then a bluecoat barged in. "We got him, Lieutenant!" The officer was flushed with excitement. "We got Stolz outside in the squad room!"

"How?" said Figlia, standing. "What happened? Tell me!"

"We just picked him up off the street. He was stumbling along the Strip, drugged to the gills. Drunk and drugged. A patrol car spotted him—they weren't sure it was Stolz—they pulled over, went up to him, and took him. According to the boys, he just stood there swaying. But he was clean—no drugs, no weapon. If he had any, he must have stashed them somewhere. But he looked sick, he was having trouble breathing, so they took him over to St. Vincent's emergency before bringing him here. Docs over there said he was O.D.'ed on some kind of barbiturate. They shot him with uppers of some kind. Then the boys brought him over here. We're feeding him coffee. He's in pretty good shape now. We got him cuffed to a bench out in the squad room. A mean looking S.O.B.!"

Figlia seemed to sway behind the desk. "At last!" he sighed.

At that moment, in the hollow coolness of the morgue, Pilar Pavon's knees gave out from under her, and she was only saved from falling to the floor by the buxom police-woman who caught her about the waist and shoulders in almost the way a man takes a woman into his arms to kiss her. In a moment, she was standing straight again, but leaning a little against the big policewoman's shoulder. The policewoman held her elbow. When the sheet was pulled aside, she looked into her dead brother's face, and then looked quickly away. She tried to scream but gagged on it. Choking, her eyes alone went back to Dedi's face. She did not see his body, and so could not know how his joints had had to be cut, twisted and snapped back into place so that he could fit on his bier, nor did she observe that the back of his head was missing.

Chapter 66

FREEDOM HOUSE

FREEDOM HOUSE shone on a brass plate affixed to the red brick facade of the four story house on Washington Square North. It was an historical site. But unlike many of the other buildings on Washington Square, it was not owned by New York University. It was owned by Father Thom Corrigan, the best-selling author. It had been in his family since the days when it was used as a staging area for the fugitive slaves of the Underground Railroad. Corrigan's ancestors had come to the New World as radical followers of the Unitarian Universalist, John Murray, but by the time of the great Irish immigration in the 1840s, one of them, possibly for political reasons, had made his conversion to Catholicism and the family had been Catholic, if of an exceedingly radical stripe, ever since. The Corrigans had prospered and by the time of the Civil War, possessed much valuable real estate. It was Thom Corrigan's great-great-grandparents, dedicated abolitionists, who set up Freedom House to aid fugitive slaves on their way to Canada.

Over the past few years Father Din had been a more and

539

more frequent visitor here. He had sat with Father Corrigan and his mistress and listened as Corrigan expounded a doctrine comprised of a mixture, in almost equal parts, of Marxist philosophy, Zen Buddhism, Unitarianism, and an almost unrecognizable form of Catholicism, anti-papal and pro-Communist, wherein Christ was shown to be the first true Marxist.

Corrigan was a Jesuit, of the teaching order, and to Father Din, almost magically free of the constraints of an ordinary parish priest. He seemed to do and say as he pleased and come and go as he willed. It was understood that he had been "corrected" many times, but he was very rich and famous and clearly more in agreement with the times than with the Pope. No man could be less like Father Ryan.

Father Corrigan had just returned from Central America and a group of his friends were throwing him a welcome home party. In attendance was a Hollywood star, a Harlem pimp, a famous radical lawyer, and a number of people from city, state, and national government. Corrigan had just finished singing a loose medley of Pete Seeger songs with his mistress when he was called to the telephone. He picked up the receiver in a high mood. "Corrigan, here," he said.

"Hello, Father Corrigan. This is Father Ryan over at Saint Savior's."

"Well . . . good to hear from you, Father."

"Father Michael Din is my curate."

"Yes, I know that, Father. I know who you are. Good to hear from you. Can I assist you in any way?"

"I was wondering," the voice hesitated. "I was wondering if you had heard from Father Michael. I understand that you see him occasionally."

"No, I haven't, Father. I've been out of the country—Central America. As a matter of fact, some of my friends are throwing me a homecoming party right now."

"Oh. Well, compliments on your new book."

"Thank you, Father.  Have you read it?"

"Yes.  Just last evening."

"What did you think?"

"I think we disagree on many things."

"Oh, I'm sorry to hear that, Father.  Perhaps we could get together and talk them over.  Your parish isn't far from my house."

"Yes.  We're very close, aren't we?"

"About Father Michael . . .?"

"I'm afraid that he is in very serious trouble."

"Of what sort, Father?

"Of all sorts.  I think he may be in trouble with the police.  I think he may be in danger.  He is certainly in trouble with our Church.  He may have to be sent away for rehabilitation."

"In order for him to remain a priest, you mean?  But Father, Father Michael and I have grown to be friends.  I think I know him quite well now.  All men are not suited to this calling, and shouldn't we set them free if they aren't?  Father Michael is a good person, but I think one not made for the priesthood."

"His deepest problem, Father, is one of faith.  And as you know, faith will come."

"Faith will come has been repeated ad nauseam to people like Michael.  It is not always true."

"We disagree on that, too" said Father Ryan.  "I have lived with the problem myself and I say that it finally comes. He has made so many mistakes.  I am afraid for what he might do next.  But you haven't heard from him, then?"

"No.  Is there somewhere else he could be?"

"The only other place I can think of—the only other possible contact I may have with him—is through a police Lieutenant named Figlia, a former parishioner here.  I just now hung on the phone until it went dead.  But I'll try again.  I want to help Father Michael.  I'm terribly worried about him.  Will you contact me if you hear from him?"

"Absolutely, Father."

"Christ is in Father Michael."

"Absolutely, Father."

"Goodbye, Father."

"Goodbye, Father."

Chapter 67

FALSE WITNESS

Toddy Muir cowered in a corner of the squad room.  She had seen Monk brought in and now sat many desks away from him, across computers with rattling printers, beeping Fax machines, and ringing telephones.  Fear and relief fought inside her as she watched Lieutenant Figlia and Father Din approach Monk.  Suddenly Monk bayed like a wolf that has spotted the moon, and the eerie sound ricocheted about the squad room.  Cops and suspects and witnesses alike seemed to duck and dodge.  Now he roared for all to hear, "You're a priest!  I knew there was something strange about you, you filthy hypocrite!"

"Is this the man?" Figlia said.

"This is the animal," Father Din said.

"And you, Figlia, you haven't got a damned thing," said Monk.  "Your daughter was a junkie who O.D.'ed.  What's new?  Just because I was there—that's no evidence of anything.  If the Sawyer kid wants to say I was there, so what?  So was he, and he's a junkie, I'm not."

"*You . . . killed . . . Dedi . . . Pavon,*" said Father Din, leaning forward, emphasizing each word, for he believed that, in a sense, Monk *had* killed the boy.

"You lie, you filthy priest!  He was dead and you know it.  I just gave him the toss.  You want to charge me with messing with dead bodies, go ahead.  It's laughable.  You

542

people haven't got a thing worth wasting my lawyer's time on and you know it. You might as well let me walk now."

Lieutenant Figlia and Father Din looked at each other grimly. They both knew that Monk was right. It was all a couple of handfuls of air. Monk was grinning at them as if at a pair of fools. He knew he would walk, now or later. One phone call and he would be free to destroy the lives of Jack and Toddy Muir. He would even the score with Opal. He would search out Tory. He lived for vengeance.

Father Din decided that, at whatever cost, this man, this monster could not be allowed to walk free. He remembered what his own father had done in a similar situation. No. He had decided. A black tension twisted his face. He said, "But Dedi Pavon was *alive* when you threw him off the roof. He begged you not to do it. I saw it. I heard him beg and I saw him struggle. It was deliberate murder!"

It seemed for a moment that Monk could not understand what Father Din was saying. He looked blank. Then he appeared to go into what looked like anaphylactic shock. "You *lie*!" he shouted. He glared at Figlia. "He's lying, I tell you!" He looked back at Father Din, furiously trying to free his cuffed wrist. "You can't do this—it's a *sin*! He's lying, I tell you!"

"A priest wouldn't lie," said Figlia. "And who do you think a jury will believe, you or a priest?" He turned to Father Din. "You will swear to this in court, on the Bible?"

Father Din nodded, staring straight at Monk with an almost supernatural look of loathing on his face. He did not blink, whatever was going on in his mind. "I will swear in court on the Holy Bible that I saw this man deliberately murder Dedi Pavon. I will swear that the boy begged for his life."

"You'll roast in hell for this, priest!" said Monk, his voice thick.

"You *are* hell," said Father Din. "You yourself are

hell. Where you go is hell," he paraphrased Satan in Paradise Lost.

Figlia looked gleeful. "Put him in a holding cell," he told Verdi. "Would you please come with me, Father. We have some work to do."

Chapter 68

VANISHED!

Furiously, Monk calculated with the abacus of his mind. He would not get bail on a capital crime. He had too much money and a long record. No judge would set him loose this time, not with a priest as prime witness to a murder. Monk believed himself to be innocent of Dedi's death, but he knew that nobody else would. He would never see the outside again if he remained in custody. There was only one thing to do. He had to get out now—right now, through the front door. Once out, it would be no trouble to find his way to South America, where he had friends and could live like a king. Extradition was improbable from Colombia. But this was his last chance at freedom. It was now or never.

Monk took a sip of coffee. He seemed to be stalling. Verdi didn't like that. "Come on," he said, "let's go," unlocking the cuff from the bench. The cuff fell loose. Verdi jiggled the key free. The cuff came up across his face, cutting open his cheek. Verdi reared back, blood flying.

Monk cannonballed toward the door, knocking two bluecoats aside like bowling pins. Verdi pulled his gun and charged out the door, holding his bleeding cheek with his free hand. Monk was halfway up the block, shooting steam in the cold. The cold hit Verdi hard. He wore no coat. He felt the presence of several patrolmen panting behind him. But he couldn't look back, afraid of losing sight of Monk. He would catch merry hell if he couldn't catch this bastard.

Verdi saw Monk swerve and slide at the corner of Third Street like an out-of-control van. He was actually kicking up a spray of snow and ice behind him. At the corner, Verdi cursed, seeing what was in store. Monk was heading toward the Bravos' club house.

"Shit," he cried, "the sonofabitch!" And up the steps and through the door that was never locked. And then Verdi was inside the door himself, and Monk was ahead of him on the stairs, banging at every door with the flying handcuffs, shouting, "RAID! RAID!"

In a New York minute, the hall was filled with Bravos. None of them laid a finger on Verdi, they just filled the halls and stairs and blocked him and began to chant—

*If you can, then kill a cop,*
*Cut his belly, make him pop!*

By the time Verdi got to the roof door, Monk was half a block down, making his way along the connected roofs, a moving silhouette against the tragic winter sky. Verdi hit the roof and his feet went out from under him in the snow. He slid and slipped to his feet and saw nothing, no one. Monk had vanished.

The late winter afternoon was darkening before Verdi's eyes, as was his hope of promotion. The wind knifed his coatless torso. It seemed to take a special aim at his heart. He felt his cheek. It was deeply gashed, but the blood had caked with the cold. "Damn! Damn! Damn!" he cursed. He walked in a circle, kicking out at air.

Back down on the street, two patrol cars had joined the chase. Verdi ran up the street to the vague point where Monk seemed to disappear. Bluecoats ran up and down the street in a disordered search.

At the station house, an officer burst in on Figlia and Father Din. He looked scared. He said, "Something's happened, Sir." He shook his head. "Stolz got out of the station.  But don't worry.  We think we know where he is.  We got everybody out there.  We'll get him."

"Dammit to Hell!" Figlia yelled.  "Let's go!"

Father Din followed Figlia out of Hubbard's office, but not out the front door.  Instead, he went to Toddy.  "Did you see what happened?" he asked her.

"I saw it all, everything," she said.  "Oh, my God, he's loose again!  What are we going to do?"

"I'm going to take you somewhere where you'll be safe."  He picked up a telephone from an empty desk and punched in a number.  "Hello," he said, "I want to speak with Father Corrigan."  He stood waiting for a minute, then said, "Father Corrigan?  I must see you."  He banged down the phone and followed Figlia back to Hubbard's office.  Just inside, Figlia said, "When you told me about the Pavon boy, earlier, you said he was dead from an O.D.  Now you say he was alive when he was thrown off the roof.  Which is it?"

"That boy begged for his life."

A look of deep doubt crossed Figlia's face.  Then he gave Father Din a sad little smile.  "But you won't change your story again, will you?"

"No.  Never!"

Figlia reached out and put his hand on Father Din's shoulder.  "Good," he said.  "Then we've got the son-of-a-bitch!"


Chapter 69


CRAZIER THAN SATAN


While Ansar slept, Mahmoud went out and bought several containers of black coffee.  Back in the hotel room, he drank coffee and read Ansar's "bomb book" through from cover to cover.  He was sitting up on the bed reading when

Ansar stirred.  Ansar looked up at him, a dazed expression on his bearded face.

"There's a container of coffee there," said Mahmoud, "sitting on the heat vent.  Probably still warm."

"I think I have made it so that it will work," said Ansar.

"I doubt it," said Mahmoud.  "I've been reading your instructions.  You haven't got the trigger mechanism hooked up right.  If I thought that thing would go off, I wouldn't be sitting here."

Ansar had retrieved the coffee and was sipping it.

"Now what in the name of the Unspeakable do you intend to do with that thing?"

"I told you, Ansar is going to make a statement."

"What kind of statement, you idiot?  What do you intend to blow up?"

"Do not call Ansar an idiot.  What does it matter what I blow up?  It is the statement that matters.  I can blow up the police station.  I can blow up the United Nations.  I wish I could blow up the whole world.  Send us all to Allah to be judged for the wicked creatures we are.

"Now you listen to me, Mahmoud.  I am no fool.  I did not hook up the trigger mechanism properly yet, so the bomb would be safe.  But now, look."

Before Mahmoud could rise, Ansar had turned a few wires.  "Stay back!  The bomb will go off now.  Now you listen to Ansar.  You think you are a Muslim?  Then you should not be afraid to die in the Jihad.  You will travel with Ansar over Al Sirat, the bridge over the infernal fire to paradise.  You will become a hero in paradise.  You will have died at the right hand of Ansar!"

"The Great?" said Mahmoud.  "This is just plain vanity and stupidity.  Islam is a faith of peace.  You're even crazier than Satan!"

Chapter 70

PENANCE

"It was almost physical.  I felt struck across my . . . soul," Father Din confessed to Father Corrigan, "as if by a giant mailed fist right out of a cloud.

"Not five minutes before, I had borne false witness against this man, believing myself justified because he was a monster.

"But it was like a sign from God, when he was able to escape from that crowded police station.  It was a sign and I knew it immediately.  It was *I* who had been the monster.  I had committed a mortal sin in a moment of anger and passion and God had let Monk escape.

"I'd broken two of the ten commandments; adultery and bearing false witness.  God was angry, repulsed by me, and showed me how He felt by letting Monk go.  I knew I had to confess as soon as possible.  Somehow—I don't quite know how—I've become a Judas priest.  I will *not* remain one, even if I leave the priesthood, which I think now is inevitable."

Father Corrigan said:  "The essential condition for receiving the sacrament of penance is having the right disposition.  "You know that.  If you are genuinely sorry for your sins and do not intend to repeat them, do not intend to repeat the offence against One Who is All Good, then God may return to dwell in your soul, from which, by your sins, you have expelled Him.

"And if you have a firm resolve to amend your life, you're not required to guarantee your future sinlessness.  Michael, we all fail, and ask forgiveness, and try again.

"I know the priestly life has been difficult for you.  It may even have contributed to your moral problems.  I mean, perhaps a more normal life would have found you a better man.  Your confessions of the past have made me aware of your difficulties. Michael, I know how long you have struggled with these matters. What has happened to you in the last couple of days is the direct result of an imperfect vocation. You have horrified yourself. Shall we call that your penance?

"You know, Michael, I have a vision of the future. I see you married, a husband and father. I see you living the life you were meant to live. I want you to refuse rehabilitation. I want you to leave the priesthood. I think that is what you want to do and I think that is what should be done. I can put you in touch with a halfway house for former priests, run by a friend of mine. A former bishop, believe it or not. Now say me the Act of Contrition."

Michael put his hands up in prayer. "O my God, I am heartily sorry for having offended Thee and I detest all my sins because I dread the loss of heaven and the pains of hell, but most of all because they offend Thee Who art all good and deserving of all my love. I firmly resolve, with the help of Thy grace to confess my sins, to do penance and to amend my life."

"To the degree that you and God share an understanding of your heart, you are free of sin. Go, and sin no more." Father Corrigan patted Father Din's shoulder.

"You and your friend are welcome to stay here as long as you wish. I have a few empty bedrooms. The young lady will be safe here, and you'll have time to think. You talk it over with her while I see to my guests. And—call Father Ryan. He's worried sick about you. I'll send the young lady in here so you can talk."

In a moment Toddy entered Father Corrigan's study. "Do you know who's out there?" she said. "There are celebrities of all sorts."

"Toddy, Father Corrigan has offered to put you up here for a few days. You'll be safe here. What do you think?"

"It would be wonderful to be somewhere where I didn't

have to be afraid. But look, I don't have anything with me. Nothing. I need my bank book. I need some clothes. I need—all kinds of things."

"I'm going to call the station and talk to Figlia, if he's there. It's possible that they've got Monk by now."

"Oh, God, that would be wonderful."

Father Din called the station and got an answer. In a moment he had Figlia on the phone. "Did you get him?" he asked.

"No," said Figlia. "The bastard eluded us somehow. He probably knows every rat hole in Needleneck. But we'll get him."

Father Din told Lieutenant Figlia that they would be staying with Father Corrigan, gave him the address and phone number. "Would it be safe for Mrs. Muir to get some things from her place?"

"The apartment's covered. Just get in and get out."


Chapter 71


GOOD NEWS AND BAD


As they headed cross town in a cab, Father Din said: "Toddy, I have some good and some bad news for you. Which do you want first?"

"The good news, I guess. I really need it."

"Pilar told me earlier today, before we went to the police station, that Jack has kicked, or is kicking the drugs."

"Oh," said Toddy, staring ahead. She seemed to be absorbing the information. Turning to him, she said, "Is it true? If it's true, it changes everything. Why didn't you tell me this earlier?"

"Because of the bad news that goes with it. I thought about telling you, but I really didn't want you to have any more to worry about than you already had."

"Oh, God, now I'm afraid to hear. What is it?"

"Well, he has a revolver on him and Pilar thinks he just might be out looking for Monk, to settle the score."

"Oh, my God," she said. "The fool! Monk'll kill him!"

"Now you see why I didn't tell you sooner," Father Din said.

"But Jack . . . he's really off the stuff?"

"Pilar says so."

"She wouldn't lie about that . . . I know. Oh, Lord! Just when he's off—finally! And then he goes looking for even worse trouble. And what if he's heard about Dedi, if he heard about how it happened? He loved that poor kid."

"Try to take the better view, Toddy. Tell me this, though, would you try again now—knowing that Jack's quit the drugs—if you had the chance?"

"You're a priest. Isn't it your duty to tell me to try?"

"Don't be difficult, Toddy. I asked you as a friend."

"I'm sorry." She paused. "Yes. Yes, I would try. If it were true."

The cab drew up to the curb in front of Toddy's building. Father Din told the driver to wait, that they would only be a few minutes. He took Toddy by the hand and stepped up to the two bluecoats sitting in the patrol car.

"This is Mrs. Muir. She's going up to the apartment to get a few things."

"Yes, Father. We got a call from Lieutenant Figlia. I'll go up with you and check out the halls and the apartment. There's no ground floor back door. We checked. It's in the super's apartment."

He told the other officer to keep an eye on the door and led the way up to Toddy's apartment. After checking the rooms and the hall, he returned to his partner in the patrol car. Toddy hurried about the apartment, gathering her things while Father Din waited.

Chapter 72

## SHOCK WAVES

Opal and Camilla waited for Ansar and Mahmoud at the Saints and Sinners Club, Opal lubricating herself with a gin and tonic, and Camilla  sipping some of Tiger's ever-brewed coffee.

Tiger held a cup of coffee too.  He listened as Opal told the pretty young Camilla all the reasons she should return to Chicago and her parents.  He nodded in agreement at each and every one.

"But I haven't got any money," Camilla objected.  "I'll have to find a job and make enough to pay my fare back, and, if I do that, why should I go?  If I have a job, I might as well stay here."

"You should go because that fellow you're with is going to get you into a lot of trouble," Tiger said.  "You should listen to Opal.  Young people can't see very far ahead, and that's how they get into trouble.  That boy is dangerous."

"I know he's a little weird, but—"

"Look," said Opal, "you're a very pretty little girl, and nobody can get themselves into more trouble than a very pretty little girl.  I should know.  I was a very pretty little girl once, wasn't I, Tiger?"

"Still are.  Look," said Tiger, "I've got an idea.  Why don't you let me lend you the money to get back to Chicago?  You can pay me back some day, no hurry."

"Tiger, that is the sweetest thing!" said Opal.

"Oh," said Camilla, "I couldn't do that."

"You can and you will, girl!" said Opal, slapping the bar.

Tiger left them for a few minutes and returned with an envelope.  "Opal, there's five hundred dollars in this.  I want you to take this young lady out to J.F.K. and stay with her until she's on a flight for the Toddling Town.  Buy her ticket, give her some spending money, and whatever's left is yours. Bring it back here and spend it."

"I don't know how to thank you," said Camilla, her eyes moist. She reached across the bar to pull her walleyed hero close for a kiss when the remaining plateglass window of the Saints and Sinners Club was blown out. Shards of glass sprayed the room like hail. Suddenly everyone was wearing little cuts. The room had actually rocked, as if in an earthquake. The boom engulfed them. Then there was a series of smaller explosions that seemed to go on and on, with short pauses here and there.

When it seemed that the worst was over, Tiger looked about. Nobody seemed to be seriously hurt. What was it? Had Monk kept his promise to lob a Molotov Cocktail in on him, to burn him out? But there was no fire. He climbed over the top of the bar and went to the door amid screams of fear. And now, outside, he saw that the Busy Nook was burning. Fire trucks were already gathering in front of the hotel. It looked as if several floors were gone. The fire raged up through the place where the roof should be, brightening the night sky like a giant torch. There was a bittersweet smell in the air.


Chapter 73


ARMAGEDDON


There was a pervading sense of unreality about Toddy's apartment, like an evil place remembered in a bad dream. But the bad dream was still alive. Had it only been the day before, since Dedi's death? Father Din would be glad if he never had to look at this place again.

He was startled out of his reverie by half a dozen rapidly fired shots. Or were they backfires? He raced to the front windows and pulled one up. For a moment, he saw nothing unusual. The police car. The building across the street. Jack Muir's loft. Snowbanks. The cab. Where was the cab? It was halfway up the block. Then the police car again. Then the bodies of two bluecoats, one hanging out of the car, one lying spreadeagled in the snow.

He stared down in horror. Monk! He must be here, in this building.

Out of the corner of his eye, somewhere up the Strip, near the Saints and Sinners Club, he saw a flame that looked like a red whale shoot across the sky. Toddy's building seemed to tremble. He whirled about and grabbed Toddy. For a moment they appeared to dance.

Then the door burst open. Monk, his face razor slashed and bleeding, pushed Jack Muir into the apartment in front of him.

"I've been waiting for you two to show up. I've been watching the cops watching for me. But I picked up a secret weapon at Pilar's, this bullet-proof shield," he said, jerking Muir's arms tighter. "The bitch tried to slice me up with a razor blade and now she's with her brother in hell. But the one I want most is you, you filthy, lying priest! I'm going to blow you into eternity where you can roast in hell forever. Then I'm going to take care of these two . . . lovers."

As Monk raved, Toddy screamed a scream that sounded endless until Father Din realized that the last part of it was the sound of a siren outside on the street.

"Hear that explosion?" cried Monk. "*I* did that. That was Tory doing my bidding. Tiger won't threaten a man like me again. I always even my scores." He stared wildly: unkempt, disheveled, confused, but plainly sober. He kicked the door shut behind him.

As he did so, Jack Muir lifted his arms and slid between Monk's to the floor. Father Din saw that Monk had a new weapon, perhaps a hastily acquired Saturday Night Special. Or was it Jack Muir's own pistol?

Monk kicked Jack Muir in the ribs, hard. There was a cracking sound and Jack screamed in pain. Toddy cried out and ran to Jack. She tried to pull him away from Monk, across the room. Father Din dove at Monk, gathering the arm that held the gun in both of his. He tried to drag Monk to the floor with his weight.

"Stolz!" Figlia called from beyond the door. "Let 'em go!" he shouted, plunging into the room.

Jack Muir kicked backward along the floor, Toddy dragging him by the shoulders. A bullet that was meant for Father Din broke a floorboard in half. Monk began beating at the back of Father Din's neck with his free hand, but Father Din twisted around, taking the blows on his shoulder, and then faced Monk, holding the revolver-wielding arm in both of his, as Monk tripped backwards.

Father Din landed on Monk's stomach, the gun arm between himself and Monk, and the explosion came muffled and smoky between them. For a moment, Father Din thought he'd been shot. Then Monk's head fell back, like a man putting his head down on a pillow after a hard day.

Two bluecoats helped Father Din to his feet. He looked about. Toddy and Jack Muir lay huddled, halfway into the livingroom.

Father Din looked at Monk. "Is he dead?"

"No," said a cop, bending over Monk, removing the revolver.

Father Din knelt down beside Monk. He took the hand that had held the revolver in his own.

"Help me," came the sound from Monk's twisted mouth. He gathered strength and said, "I've been . . . crucified . . ." He was hit with a seizure of coughing. ". . . by my own . .    congregation . . ." Then something incoherent. Figlia bent down close to his mouth to hear.

Father Din said, "What's he saying?  What is it?" Figlia looked at Father Din.  "The scum wants you to give him Last Rites."

"Yes," said Father Din, dazed.  "Yes." He fumbled through his pockets, found his small vial of Holy oil, and anointed Monk's forehead with trembling fingers.  "Through this Holy unction," he said mechanically, "may the Lord pardon thee whatever sins thou hast committed . . ."

He looked over at Toddy.  From across the room Toddy looked back at him, then buried her face in Jack Muir's hair.

# THE DEVIL'S TAVERN

*There are three kinds of lies:*
*lies, damned lies, and statistics.*
*—attributed by Mark Twain to Benjamin Disraeli*


Sam Stock is a man of his time, a hyperproductive computer programmer employed by the New York branch of the International Ministry of Wellness as a data analyst, a stat man, a Super Cruncher. He finds correlatives—hamburgers and high blood pressure, gum soles and flat feet, life and death (one-hundred percent). Everyone is at-risk. Life correlates to danger. But cyberchondria abounds. Sam thinks he might be contributing to the general unease. His work as a technocrat may have contributed to the fears of the public—their fear of walking, of breathing, of whispering (aspiration produces deadly micro-globules of sputum). This winter in New York people are lining up at the mobile Wellness Stations to get bat flu shots. Three cases had been reported in Miramar. The queues, Sam has noticed, are extraordinarily attenuated. People don't want to get near to one another. But of course, the bat flu shots are mandated. Those who do not get them are considered public enemies and are sought and found and sent on to mental health clinics. Just the other day, Sam saw that a group of senior citizens who protested the ban on donuts was rounded up and sent to the Senior Mental Health Center for examination. Sam Stock thought that, yes, they should have their heads examined. After all, carbs can be deadly, and some of those donuts pack icing—vanilla, strawberry, and chocolate; veritable gummy guns of destruction. But there was something troubling about declaring all those old people insane.

Sam tries to balance these thoughts as he maneuvers the lunch hour streets in search of a health food stand. It depresses him to think of the recent ban on mustard. He had to admit that mustard was the only thing that made much of the proffered food of the city palatable. But he himself was the first to find the correlation between mustard and misbehavior. It was bruited about that upscale gangs of rebellious youth in Brooklyn were now attacking public officials with gobs of grey poupon, and of course there was that incident in Atlanta where the mayor was assaulted with deep-fried hush-puppies after instituting a ban on them.

Sometimes Sam Stock thought that officialdom was going a bit too far. He understood the impulse, natural to people in power, to tell others who have no power what to do. But sometimes . . . ah, a stand full of Free-Toes—sugar-free, carb-free, fat-free, and food-free. And not even a dab of mustard to put on them! Sometimes Sam Stock thinks that life is becoming tasteless . . . munch, munch.

Twenty-twenty, the centennial of Prohibition, that was a big year for the Ministry of Wellness! The events of that year included a world-wide ban on smoking, the Bacon Act, and, perhaps the greatest coup the Ministry had ever effected, the institution of the Department of Mental Wellness, which allowed the authorities to take action against people who refused to care for themselves, people who puffed, tippled, or consumed food that was found by the experts on fat at the Ministry of Wellness to be unhealthy. These slackers were of course costing us all money under the Universal Wellness Program. They were to be considered insane and sent to an asylum until they mended their thought-processing ways. Sometimes Sam Stock thought the authorities took advantage of this law to declare insane anyone who in his or her life of quiet desperation heard the sound of a different and distant drummer. It was from the dark underbelly that rumblings could be heard.

There was the mysterious case of the physicist who smoked, the notorious case of the tippling mayor, the amazing case of the cake-eating songstress—these stories were heard of and retold, novelized on-line by rebel writers—*Smokey, The Mad Scientist*, *The Red Nosed Mayor of Castorbridge*, and *God Bless America: The Dreadful Story of Cake Smith*. Sam Stock reads these cautionary tales and tries to learn from them; but sometimes he yearns for romantic adventure. The idea of sharing a chocolate-covered donut with a beauty on a tiger-skin rug set his heart racing. His Free-Toe melts like icing in his mouth at the thought.

How could Sam Stock fail to notice Lorelei Rhinestein? She had been about the office for some time. But Sam is always intent on his production of correlatives. He sees another one—reading and suicide—and begins to run it. But he is distracted. Lorelei Rhinestein has lovely violet eyes. She reminds him of a flapper of eld. She has just come in from getting her bat flu shot and is flushed with . . . anxiety? The Ministry of Wellness does not want to tell the public about the many deaths correlating to bat flu shots. Sam Stock puts down "bat flu shots and death." He runs it—ummm! He looks at Lorelei Rhinestein. The flush is leaving her face. Not only will she live, he thinks, she will triumph. How not, with such eyes?

In the days following, he finds her name and her *modus vivendi*. She brings her own lunch. Fried chicken from home, long since banned from restaurants. She eats surreptitiously, suspicious even of associates. An atmosphere of danger clings to her drumstick. Sam Stock suspects her of transfats. He could see her in some ancient noir film, the banned-for-smoking "Casablanca" perhaps, still extant in cyberspace. Sam Stock blushes to think of it. Yes, he thought, she's like Ingrid Bergman—mysterious, beautiful, hat down over her violet eyes. But of course Ms. Rhinestein wears no hat. Though not yet banned, hats—with the one exception of protective helmets—had been deemed bad for the circulation. The more fashionable members of the ruling class wore them; but, Sam Stock noted, Authority says yes to itself and no to everyone else. He bet that in secret they even ate cake. They did as they pleased.

Sam Stock is increasingly restive, so when Lorelei Rhinestein asks him for a date—a date with a woman of danger—he decides to give adventure a chance and finds himself saying—

"Delighted. Where shall we go?" Men do not ask women for dates, nor do they decide where their time shall be spent; men cautiously wait to be invited, and even here could be entrapment. Can mystery and candor exist simultaneously in enchanting violet eyes? Fling it, he tells himself, I'm taking a chance on love!

Lorelei Rhinestein wants to go to New Jersey. She knows a place out beyond the Pine Barrens. She drives them. It's Saturday night at the Jersey Devil's Tavern. Where are we, he wants to know, what is this place? What does it remind him of, dark and forebody with the moon overhead? In the woods, isolated, oh, what did they call them, roadhouses, speakeasies? Something out of cyberspace on-line noir dramas.

"I don't like the looks of this," he tells Lorelei. His hackles rise, tickled, but really he does like the looks of the place. The place is like Lorelei herself, mysterious, beautiful in the moonlight, dangerous.

"I've been watching you, Sam Stock," says Lorelei. "I've been watching you and thinking maybe you need a real outing. If I'm wrong I think I can trust you to keep this to yourself, but if I'm right about you . . . well, we may be able to share something exciting. You don't look like a scaredy-cat. The last boy I brought here—a personnel director for the Nursing Corps—he ran away like a rabbit and got lost in the Pine Barrens for two days. First time he had missed a day's work in his life.  He threatened to report me to the Ministry of Wellness, but I threatened to tell them that *he* was the one who brought *me* here and he kept his mouth shut."

"I'm not afraid," Sam Stock blusters.  He is afraid but for some obscure reason it embarrasses him.  Contradictions abound in a nature taught from childhood to be afraid of everything and at the same time to swim with Bubbles, the friendly shark.  Sam Stock allows himself to be led into the Jersey Devil. People sit at candlelit tables, drinking adult beverages, smoking cigarettes and cigars, or dancing to the strains of "Smoke Gets in Your Eyes."  Seated, Lorelei orders the house cocktails, two Jersey Devils, looks over the flickering candle at Sam, and, in a low voice, sings—

> *They asked me how I knew*
> *My true love was true*
> *Oh, I of course replied*
> *Something here inside*
> *Cannot be denied . . .*

Sam tries to ignore her alluring, husky, melodious voice. "What kind of place is this?" he asks, looking through a haze of smoke, here and there set aglow by dim lights.

Lorelei observes how wide his innocent blue eyes are in the mesmerizing undulation of the candlelight. "Sam Stock," she says, "this is a den of iniquity, a speak-drink-and-smoke-easy, and I have lured you here in order to make a criminal of you."  She is saying this in such a manner that it sends a thrill of fear up Sam's spine, but then she laughs, and says, "Don't be afraid, Sammy," and Sam is so tense that he laughs too—a nervous hack—as the aromatic Jersey Devils arrive in tall, red, steaming glasses.

Three Jersey Devils later Sam finds himself smoking. At first he coughs but then he gets the hang of it and begins to like it.

"Inhale," urges Lorelei, and sings—

*Oh, so I smile and say*
*When a lovely flame dies*
*Smoke gets in your eyes . . .*

Six months later, at work, Sam is dying for a cigarette. After all, smokers are people who have one friend no worse than others, the sometimes of their pleasure and the ultimate difficulties, the big troubles, the being able to be quiet in the hurried world, the holding hands without a word, the sad truth of the matter as recognized by ashes, or ashes recognized, whatever is looking up from nothing, from the smoke-filled no-bottom of everything, the oh for just a moment, the please slow it down, the oh God I'm late, the don't forget, the oh forgotten, but smokers are people who have at least one friend. The relationship between smoking and disease is merely a correlative one, he tells himself and the greatest correlation of all is life and death (100%), but right now he needs a cigarette. Everyone who has a moment of contentment, he tells himself, dies; therefore, contentment kills.

Minutes after this moment of illumination, there was a raid. Sam is arrested by the dreaded Green (really olive drab) Shirts of the Ministry of Wellness, for smoking an illegal Gauloises in the men's room and taken away to the insane asylum for mental reprogramming. His psychiatric report confirms that he may ultimately prove to be a danger to the State. He has a definite proclivity toward disrespect of authority. Sam says, "Authority says yes to itself and no to everyone else! It says No!" Sam tells Doctor Forbrane, his counselor, to shove it.

"And all this rebellion started with a single cigarette," Doctor Forbrane tells his colleagues over cigars and port. "Good thing we wiped out marijuana," he continues, stabbing his Montecristo into space for emphasis, "or all of the little people would have become non-productive. But have no fear. I have implanted in his brain a continuously ticking taser in order to pacify him. He will represent no more challenge to Authority than a popinjay. He will, in fact, become a useful member of society. Wellness will be his way!"

One year later, Lorelei meets Sam upon his release. "Are you cured?" she asks as she drives him away from the asylum.

"I'm fine now, but they caught me just in time. Got a cigarette?"

"In the glove compartment," Lorelei says, hitting the gas, heading for the Jersey Devil's Tavern, which, despite all efforts of the Green Shirts of the Ministry of Wellness, exists forever just beyond the Pine Barrens.

E.M. Schorb is a prize-winning poet and novelist, a member of Mystery Writers of America, The Authors Guild, and the Academy of American Poets.  His novel, *Paradise Square,* received the Grand Prize for Fiction at the Frankfurt Book Fair.  Another novel, *A Portable Chaos,* was the First Prize Winner of the Eric Hoffer Award for Fiction.

His 2016 *Dates and Dreams: Short Fictions, Prose Poems, Cartoons* was awarded the Writer's Digest International Self-Published Award for Poetry.

Schorb's poetry collections include, *Murderer's Day,* winner of the Verna Emery Poetry Prize and published by Purdue University Press and *Time and Fevers*, recipient of the Writer's Digest International Award for Poetry and also an Eric Hoffer Award.

Schorb's latest novel, *R&R: a Sex Comedy,* won the Beverly Hills Book Award for Humor.